CONRAD'S OTHER EYE

Stuart Slade

LION BY LION
PUBLISHING

Dedication

This book is respectfully dedicated to the memory of Montgomery Curtis Nebinger. A cool gentleman and a fine friend,

Acknowledgements

Conrad's Other Eye could not have been written without the very generous help of a large number of people who contributed their time, input and efforts into confirming the technical details of the story. Some of these generous souls I know personally and we discussed the conduct and probable results of the attacks described in this novel in depth. Others I know only via the Internet as the collective membership of "The Board" yet their communal wisdom and vast store of knowledge, freely contributed, has been truly irreplaceable.

I must also express a particular debt of gratitude to my wife Josefa for without her kind forbearance, patient support and unstintingly generous assistance, this novel would have remained nothing more than a vague idea floating in the back of my mind.

Caveat

Conrad's Other Eye is a work of fiction set in The Big One alternate universe. All the characters appearing in this book are fictional and any resemblance to any person, living or dead is purely coincidental. Although some names of historical characters appear, they do not necessarily represent the same people we know in our reality.

Copyright Notice

Contents

EYE OF THE GAMBLER
New York City, New York, 1928

Conrad's Other Eye

CHAPTER ONE

THE GAME

Jimmy Meehan's Apartment, 161 W. 54th Street, Midtown, New York City, October 31, 1928

There is a point in a poker game when a gambler knows that he doesn't just face disaster; he is already deeply immersed in it and there is no way left open except to spiral deeper into the growing catastrophe. By 4:30 am, Arnold Rothstein knew he had reached that point. His losing streak started early in the evening and had only got worse as the game developed.

At 10.00 pm, he had started writing IOUs to cover his stakes in a desperate effort to win enough money to cover those he had issued earlier in the evening. Only he had continued losing and been forced to issue yet more notes to cover his debts. He couldn't continue playing, since his losses had virtually bankrupted him; yet he couldn't stop, because then he would have to face making good on the paper he had issued.

To make matters worse, he wasn't quite certain how much money he had lost. It was a paramount rule for gamblers. *You never count your money when you're sitting at the table. There'll be time enough for counting when the dealing's done.* The situation was complicated by the intricate series of side-bets that had been developing all night. Even Rothstein's legendary brain had lost track of exactly how much he had lost and to whom. He did know that it didn't really matter. His gambling losses were so high there was no way he could possibly pay them. In this company, with these people, that was a potentially fatal problem.

He looked at the five cards he had been dealt. His heart skipped. It wasn't technically a bad hand. The ace of spades, the ace of clubs, the eight of spades, the eight of clubs and the queen of clubs. Two pairs, aces and eights, with a queen on the side. A good start, and a good player could finesse it into a solid win. Unfortunately, it was the last hand Wild Bill Hickok had ever been dealt and was universally known as the dead man's hand.

Rothstein looked impassive as he discarded the queen. "One card."

Alvin Clarence Thomas, known to his friends, of whom there were few, as Titanic, due to the number of other players he had sunk, dealt the card requested. Rothstein took it and added it to his hand. It was the nine of diamonds. Not an improvement, but at least it broke up the ominous black.

Across the table, Peter Stuyvesant discarded two cards. "I'll take two."

Titanic Thomas dealt the two cards in question. Stuyvesant picked them up. Studying carefully, Rothstein detected a note of boredom from the man. He wasn't entirely certain what that meant in terms of Stuyvesant's hand, but he did guess it meant the game was ending.

Across the table, George "Hump" McManus threw down his hand in disgust. "I'm out."

"Just you and me, Pete." Rothstein used the contraction deliberately, knowing that Stuyvesant disliked the shortened name. He hoped the irritation would reveal something, but Stuyvesant's face was impassive. "I'll call you."

Stuyvesant nodded slowly and laid his cards down. "Full house; kings and queens."

Rothstein felt the cold fingers of the dead man's hand brushing the hair on his neck. He threw down his own cards. "Two pairs; aces and eights."

"Dead man's hand. How appropriate."

McManus shook his head. "I don't know about the rest of you guys but I'm all in here. Time to call it a night."

Thomas ran his eyes around the table. The players, except Rothstein, were nodding. Rothstein himself was staring at the last pair of hands with something very close to desperation on his face.

"Okay, we'll call it quits." Thomas gestured at the pile of paper and banknotes on the table. "I'll need some help figuring this all out. Lillith, could you give me a hand here?"

Across the room, at a small table by the door, Lillith started to rise from the table she'd been sitting at all evening. She would have wanted to sit down anyway, since her crippled feet made standing for long periods painful, but Igrat had insisted they take a seat away from the tables and not walk around the room. Several of the other women had behaved differently.

Igrat put a hand on her forearm, stopping Lillith's rise. "Stay seated until the men are ready for you over there. With a game this big, there are going to be a lot of accusations flying around."

The gunman near them didn't appear to be listening, and his words seemed directed at nobody in particular. "Good advice, that. You three staying put made our job a lot easier. If there is a spotter in this game, we know it ain't one of you."

The gunman lost his disinterested look and his eyes met Achillea's. A brief flash of mutual recognition passed between two stone-cold killers. Each gave the other a brief nod of respect; knowing that, if one day one had to kill the other, it would be nothing personal, purely professional. "Nobody wants to see another Barco situation."

"What was the Barco situation?" Lillith couldn't help asking the question, even though she suspected she probably would rather not know the answer.

"High-stakes game like this one. Only it was a set-up, and everybody there was in the rackets. This one's straight, by the way." It was Igrat who answered; her sleepy, heavy-lidded eyes scanned the room carefully.

"A couple, George and Julia Barco, were working a fix. He was playing; she just kept wandering around the room, getting drinks, and so on. Only she was seeing the other player's cards and tipping off her husband using a pre-arranged code. It was stupid; something that might have worked in an amateur game, but not in a roomful of professionals. They got spotted and George Barco got the crap beaten out of him. She got bent over a table and the men took turns with her. Afterwards, they each had a bottle of bootleg gin forced down their throats and were dumped in the ditch outside a hospital. She vomited up the booze and lived; he didn't."

Lillith shuddered. It was the kind of story that affected her deeply. Once, a long time ago, she'd been where Julia Barco had been that night. That was why she couldn't walk without pain.

Over at the table, Thomas waved to her. "We're ready for you, Lillith. Like to come over?"

Lillith glanced at Igrat, who nodded slightly. Although Igrat was Peter Stuyvesant's adopted daughter, she was actually here as Thomas's guest. She and Titanic had been having an affair that had already lasted for a little over a year.

Lillith was Stuyvesant's guest. She was also a gifted accountant and a lightening calculator who could analyze a balance sheet just by looking at it. It was rumored she was the only person who had ever received an apology from the Internal Revenue Service. Her talents made her uniquely suited to settling up after a game like this. Over the years, she had built a reputation for exactitude and impartiality that made her trusted by everybody.

She saw the pile of paper on the table and sighed.

"The game was fixed." The note of desperation in Rothstein's voice was becoming more apparent as the depth of the hole he was in became more apparent.

"I don't fix games. I don't have to," Thomas glanced over at Igrat. She shook her head. She'd been watching for a spotter in anticipation of exactly this situation. He reflected quickly on the first time he had met Stuyvesant after his affair with Igrat had started. He'd been ready to escape from the threat of a shotgun carried by an outraged father. Instead, Thomas discovered that Stuyvesant didn't care what his daughter got up to, as long as she was happy. He'd also learned that Igrat was an expensive luxury to have around. It was fortunate that his gambling brought in so much money; even he couldn't spend it all without her enthusiastic assistance.

The gunmen in the room, security provided by Jack Diamond in exchange for a substantial cut of the winnings, exchanged glances and shook their heads as well. They'd been watching as carefully as Igrat had, and for exactly the same reasons.

"Arnie, you got an accusation to make against somebody?"

Rothstein was now on the verge of panicking. He glanced around the room hurriedly and pointed at one woman. "Her, she was the spotter."

The girl was young, inexperienced and the accusation terrified her. She had heard of what had happened to Julia Barco. The knowledge started her crying, her body jerking in abject terror. "No, I didn't do anything! I didn't, honest! Tell them, George; I didn't do anything!"

"Don't worry, Kiki; nobody believes Arnie. And I won't let anybody hurt you." McManus turned to Rothstein and his voice was hard, dangerous. "Accuse my girl again like that, Arnie, and you're dead."

Lillith looked up from the table. "Jimmy, you broke even. George, you owe Arnie $51,000. That should eliminate any accusations of cheating right there."

Jimmy Meehan twisted his mouth slightly. Breaking even in a big game didn't put food on a professional gambler's table.

Rothstein looked slightly relieved, trying to persuade himself that perhaps the situation wasn't as bad as it seemed. When Lillith continued, those hopes were quickly dashed.

"Arnie, you owe Titanic $30,000, Nate Raymond $200,000 and Peter $319,000. A grand total of $549,000."

"I've got cash." McManus guessed that this was a good chance to establish himself as a serious player. "Titanic, why don't I pay you out of the money I owe Arnie? That'll let you pay Jack's cut right away. Peter, why don't you and

Nate divide the rest between you? That'll help Lillith here keep things straight."

"That's damned fair of you, George." Thomas spoke warmly and with genuine feeling. He respected nothing more than a good loser and he liked the way the man had jumped to the defense of his girl.

"Nate, you take the twenty-one grand cash George is offering. I'll carry all the money Arnie owes me as IOUs." Stuyvesant smiled at the younger man; he knew that Raymond's business was tight on cash, and his winnings tonight would solve the problems. There was another issue as well, but that was for the future.

Nate Raymond smiled his thanks. The twenty-one grand would make a world of difference to his business. Everybody else in the room noted Rothstein hadn't been consulted on the settlement. The king of New York was in process of being dethroned.

"Well, Arnie, that means you now owe $498,000; $319,000 to Peter and $179,000 to Nate. Speaking as Peter's accountant, may I ask when we can expect payment? Right now would be an acceptable answer." Lillith wasn't smiling.

"I haven't got the cash right now." Rothstein was wavering between aggression and despair. The instability in his voice was worrying. The gunmen providing security were already watching him closely, in case he tried to blast his way out. Killing his creditors had to be somewhere in his mind. "I've got bets on Hoover for president and Roosevelt for governor. They're certainties. They'll bring me in at least 550 grand. Give me until after the election so I can collect on them."

Lillith stared at him for a second. "Hoover is a rock-hard certainty. Roosevelt, not so much so. To win that amount of money, you've got to get both, right?"

Rothstein nodded but said nothing.

Lillith turned to Nate Raymond. "What business are you in, Nate?"

"Electrical supplies, switches, lights, cabling and so on. Not luxury stuff, but good-quality. I reckon every house on the West Coast is going to need electrical installation equipment over the next few years."

Lillith looked at Stuyvesant, who nodded in agreement. "Nate, you hold $179,000 of Arnie's debt. We'll buy it off you, plus a five percent share in your business, for a hundred thousand. We'll be silent partners; you won't even know we're there unless you need some investment money. Ask around; we pick good people with good ideas, back them up and let them run things their way."

Raymond couldn't believe his luck. An uncollectible debt had just turned into a major investment in his business from daffy-dills who had more money than sense. "Done!"

He stretched out his hand to shake on it, and then looked around in confusion. Raymond wasn't quite certain whose hand he should be shaking. Stuyvesant grinned at him and pointed at Lillith. Her handshake was smooth, cool and firm. "We'll have our lawyers meet tomorrow to draw up the paperwork?"

"That will do nicely." Lillith was about to say more, but she was interrupted by a disturbance.

Igrat brought Marion "Kiki" Roberts back in. The girl had ruined her make-up with the crying spasm and panic attack that had followed Rothstein's accusation and Igrat had helped her fix it. Now, Kiki was looking at Igrat with something close to hero worship. That was unusual; most women hated Igrat on sight.

George McManus put his arm around Kiki's waist and gave her a quick squeeze. His remark was directed towards Igrat. "Thank you for looking after her."

"Not a problem. But, George, she doesn't belong here." Igrat looked at Kiki, who had still to recover from the shock of the unfounded yet potentially lethal accusation that had been made against her. "Kiki, I mean it. I know it's fun to dance with the shadows now and then, but this kind of party can turn ugly really fast. I belong here; you don't. The truth is, there is nowhere else I do belong. You've got a good man and a good life. Be happy with that."

The couple left. Igrat watched them sadly, for she knew that Kiki was going to ignore her advice.

Nate Raymond and his girl, Ruth Keyes, were also leaving. He had a happy smile on his face; for him, it had been an unexpectedly successful evening. Ruth Keyes was less happy. She knew what had happened to Julia Barco, and had seen how something as bad, or worse, could have befallen Kiki Roberts. Igrat hadn't spoken to her, but Ruth had overheard the advice. She, at least, was going to take it to heart.

Igrat caught her eye and nodded slightly. Ruth tensed and drew slightly closer to Raymond. *Trying to keep me away from her man.* Igrat thought with secret amusement. That was when a thought struck her. *She looks a lot like Achillea.*

Back at the table, Lillith had finished writing up the balance. "By the time everything is done, Arnie, Peter holds a total of $498,000 of your paper. Once again, I have to ask, when can we expect payment?"

"I told you, once my bets come in, I'll pay you. Not before. I'm good for the notes. I just don't have the cash to hand."

"That's not our problem and I can't accept a delay in payment on your paper based on the uncertain outcome of a bet. You know the gambling rule Arnie. Pay up or we go to collection."

Lillith's voice was soft and quiet, but the threat there was explicit. Gambling debts were technically unenforceable in law, so collection actions tended to involve methods other than legal ones. Rothstein knew that he had rivals who would be all too pleased to take advantage of an excuse to cut him down.

Rothstein paused and breathed out, shakily. He knew Stuyvesant was a legitimate businessman, with no more than the usual contacts in the bootlegging and gambling industry that every wealthy man had. He also knew that, had the positions been reversed, Stuyvesant would have paid his debts on the spot.

With a flash of insight, Rothstein realized why Stuyvesant had made himself into a very wealthy man without getting involved in the rackets, while he, Rothstein, had been unable to do so. Stuyvesant would never have got himself into this position. Therein lay the difference between honest businessman and gangster.

"Alright, you win. Give me until noon tomorrow and I'll come up with as much cash as I can raise. We'll come to an arrangement on the balance. You'll get it all as soon as I can free it up." Rothstein shook himself. He would have to sell off some of his prime assets to pay this huge debt.

Idly, he wondered if Stuyvesant would be interested in taking a speakeasy as a part of Rothstein's debt settlement. That thought made him pause. *Stuyvesant is a wealthy man; very wealthy, indeed, with a strange selection of people as his inner circle. Such people have secrets to hide. Perhaps it may not be necessary to pay up after all.* With that comforting thought, Rothstein left.

Behind him, Lillith was packing the IOUs into her bag. "Time for us to leave, Peter?"

Stuyvesant nodded. "Thank you for hosting an interesting game, Jimmy. Gentlemen, thank you for your services and please take our regards to Jack Diamond." He slipped each of the security men a hundred dollar tip and started towards the door with Achillea and Lillith. As he was about to leave, he turned to Igrat. "You coming, honey?"

Igrat shook her head. "I'll see you tomorrow. I have a feeling I'm about to go down on the Titanic."

Conrad's Other Eye

Senatorial Suite 309, Park Central Hotel, Midtown, New York City, November 1, 1928

"These agreements seem perfectly satisfactory." Attorney Owen Kirschenman looked up from the legal documents he had been studying. "I must express some surprise that you were able to get them ready so quickly."

"I'll be honest, most of the content is boilerplate." Stuyvesant sipped at a glass of milk. His stomach still felt slightly soured by the excess of bootleg whiskey and the cigar smoke laden air of the big game at Jimmy Meehan's. "Apart from my shipyard, my business is investing in newly-formed companies that are opening in markets that have future growth potential. I'm not looking for short-term gains, but long-term profitability. So I have a lot of small shareholdings like this, in industries I believe will prove to be strategically critical. This agreement is a standard one for us. The only unusual part is buying up Arnold Rothstein's debt."

"That was a generous gesture." Kirschenman was genuinely appreciative of the consideration. In his eyes, the money in question might not be a lot for Stuyvesant, but it was for Nate Raymond.

Beside him, Raymond nodded vigorously. He was already planning to use the hundred grand as collateral for the purchase of new tooling for his business. That gave him a thought on how to elaborate the scheme he had in mind. "Mister Stuyvesant, do your interests include machine tool companies? I want to get wire-making and insulation coating equipment for my factory and it seems to me that I ought to buy it from one of your companies. If they have the appropriate tools."

Stuyvesant nodded and wrote a name on a piece of paper from a pad. "Here you are. Tell them I'm an investor in your company as well and they'll make sure you get quick delivery. By the way, we're partners now, so it's Peter and Nate, if that's all right with you?"

"How is Ruth feeling?" Lillith was writing out a check. She pulled it out of the checkbook and waved it in the air to make sure the ink was dry.

"Scared. The way Arnold was throwing accusations around, she thought she'd be next. She doesn't want to go back to a big game like that. Doesn't want me to go back either. Can't say I disagree with her. The way that game went gave me the shakes."

"You a gambling man?" Stuyvesant leaned back in his seat, then took the check from Lillith and signed it. He was watching Raymond closely.

"Been in my share of games. I got a strict rule, though. I decide how much I can lose, put that in my pocket in cash. When it's gone, I leave. Never sign an IOU, never borrow and never make bets I can't cover from cash. If I win, I put my original stake back in my pocket and play with other people's money. If it's gone before the game is over, leave with my original stake."

Stuyvesant laughed delightedly. "We do exactly the same thing. I think we'll get on well together, Nate."

"Mister Stuyvesant, I wonder if I might ask you a question. You laid great stress on investing strategically over the long term and I must confess your words are a relief to me." Kirschenman sounded guarded and cautious. "What is your opinion on the stock market? And investors in it?"

Stuyvesant looked at him sharply. "It's a gamble as well. It's like the game at Jimmy Meehan's. There's a huge amount of money in the pot, but most of it doesn't really exist. People have bought in on margin, using money they don't have. Not just individuals, but companies. They're assuming the current rate of increase is going to continue indefinitely. I've seen that kind of thing before and it never ends well for anybody left holding the pot.

"We're invested in the market, but only money we can afford to lose. If you're heavily into the market, I'd suggest you keep your running shoes on and bail at the first sign of problems. First out will get their money back; those that hang on, won't."

Kirschenman nodded. "That's my feeling as well. I wish my brother-in-law would listen. He's borrowed every penny he can raise and bought into the market on margin with the proceeds. If the market goes down, he will lose everything. And yet he tells me I'm the fool for not doing the same. You see a crash coming?"

"In a year or so, no more than that. There'll be a warning, but it'll be at the last moment and it will ignored, mostly. The ones who will spot it and run will be the ones who make money out of the crash."

"A year." Kirschenman was very thoughtful at that. "As little as that. No offense, sir, but you've sent chills down my spine."

As well I might. I'm a much greater expert in stock market crashes than you might think. One day, look up South Sea Bubble in an encyclopedia. Stuyvesant's face showed no sign of his thoughts. "Look, we've got all the paperwork done and Nate's got his check. Why don't we meet up for a celebratory dinner tonight? Nate, tell Ruth we'll leave the cards and gambling chips at home. Lindy's at 7:30 agreeable to everybody?"

There was a round of nodding while Kirschenman and Lillith packed away their respective copies of the agreements. Then Raymond and Kirschenman took their leave.

As soon as they'd gone, the atmosphere in the room changed. Lillith frowned as she thought over the agreement. "Boss, are you sure about this? We haven't even done a due diligence on Nate's company."

"I know we haven't." Stuyvesant's expression was very hard to read. "If we did a due diligence, we would find out that Nate Raymond is a fraud. His company doesn't exist and our investment is worthless. Well, that's not strictly true; we've still got nearly $200,000 worth of Arnold Rothstein's paper for half its face value, so we'll end up ahead. But, that's a secondary interest at the moment.

"If my guess is right, Nate Raymond is planning to order a whole clutch of machine tooling and pay for it with a bad check. By the time the check comes back, he'll have sold those machine tools and vanished with the cash. Only, it isn't quite going to work the way he thinks. The only thing I want to know before we take him down is whether Owen Kirschenman is involved in the planned scam or not. I have a hunch he may be as much a victim in all of this as we are supposed to be. If that's correct, we'll have to look out for him. He seems a nice guy."

Lillith nodded in agreement. "You're hoping that Rothstein will pay up. He didn't sound too keen on doing so at the game."

"He'll pay up. Eventually. Even if he doesn't, we can hold that paper over his head for years. One day, we might need something from him."

Stuyvesant picked up a newspaper and started to read the front-page story. President Gerardo Machado had won re-election in Cuba, although his opponents decried the conduct of the elections and alleged the results had been rigged. *They're probably right*, Stuyvesant thought. *Anybody who steals cows will steal an election. And vice versa.*

His train of thought was broken by the telephone ringing. Achillea picked it up, listened for a moment and then said simply, "That's fine, send him up."

She put the receiver down, and looked at Lillith. "Now, we should find out what's going to happen next. Arnold Rothstein is on his way up."

"Umph." Lillith got out the folder containing all of Rothstein's IOUs. "I analyzed his bets on the election, by the way. If Hoover and Roosevelt win, he'll be up by over $570,000; if both lose, he'll be down by around a million and a quarter. Hoover wins, Roosevelt loses, he'll clear $300,000. Hoover loses, Roosevelt wins, he'll be down by $900,000."

She was about to say something else when the door was opened by a bell-boy. Rothstein stalked in. He threw his hat and overcoat on to a seat and collapsed into a chair.

"Make yourself at home, Arnie." Achillea's voice was dry and not very amused by the display.

Lillith made a show of flipping through the pile of IOUs. "Just so there is no misunderstanding, Arnie, your total indebtedness is $498,000. You promised us a substantial cash payment today and offered to make an agreement on the balance."

"I can do better than that." Rothstein's voice had a vindictive, spiteful content to it that nobody in the room missed. "I'm going to pay you off right now."

"Excellent." Lillith didn't manage to hide the suspicion in her voice. Rothstein hadn't brought a briefcase or any other means of carrying money.

Close to the door, Achillea shifted her position slightly so that she could stop him leaving. One hand unobtrusively rested on her favorite M1903 Colt Hammerless, the other on her bowie knife. She didn't need either. She was perfectly capable of killing Rothstein with her bare hands before he could do anything to stop her.

"Here you are. Payment in full." Rothstein reached into a pocket and flipped a nickel on to the table.

Lillith raised an eyebrow. "That had better be an extremely valuable nickel. To be worth close to $500,000, I'd expect a bank roll of mint 1913 Liberty Head nickels, at the least."

"It's worth five cents. Just like any other. It's all you are getting."

"I take it that means you intend to renege upon your debts?" Lillith seemed unfazed by the display of aggression or the bad faith that went with it. Across the room, Stuyvesant actually seemed amused.

"I don't have to pay any so-called debts to you. That game was fixed. Anyway, you're in no position to demand money from me. I know all about you."

Despite his blustering, Arnold Rothstein was neither stupid nor insensitive. On a superficial level, nothing in the room had changed, but that was indeed superficial. Just below the calm was an icy stillness. Detecting it gave Rothstein the encouragement he needed. *These people really do have something to hide. Something big.*

The door to the suite opened, interrupting Rothstein's self-congratulation. Igrat entered, her eyes running around the room, absorbing the signs of tension. Her first words were directed to her father. "Let me guess; he's welshing on his debts."

"I am not a welsher." Rothstein was furious. "I don't have to pay any losses from a fixed game. And you people are in no position to demand that I do. One word from me in the right place and a lot of things you don't want revealed get made public."

"The game wasn't fixed Arnie." Igrat's low, husky voice was very calm. "Unlike most of the games you play, that one was clean. Titanic doesn't fix his games. He doesn't need to. You, on the other hand . . . Well, would you like a quick game of dollar poker? I play it by your rules."

There was a rustle and rattle as Igrat got a billfold out of her handbag. Of all the people in the room, only Achillea noted that the noise masked the schnick as Igrat opened the switchblade she carried in her purse. The four-inch blade was double-edged and honed to razor-sharpness.

"You're throwing a lot of threats around, Arnie." Stuyvesant's voice was still mild. "I wonder if you have anything to back them up?"

"How much I've got on you is for me to know. It's enough to get the whole lot of you lynched. After you women get the same treatment Julia Barco got first, of course."

The reaction to that confused Rothstein. He expected the threat to panic the women and infuriate Stuyvesant, but neither happened. The threat appeared to amuse them rather than anything else. He tried again. "When people find out who you are and what you've been doing, they'll tear you apart. I don't care how long you live, you'll be running for the rest of your lives."

"I doubt it." Stuyvesant's voice was still neutral. "This is 1928, after all. Arnie, you owe me close to half a million dollars. I'll charge you the same interest rate as you charge your debtors. Ten points weekly. I'll give you three days to pay up before that rate kicks in. Now, if you've nothing intelligent to say, please leave. You're beginning to annoy me."

"You're not getting a penny out of me. If you don't tear that paper up, you'll wish to God you had." Rothstein rose to his feet, put on his overcoat and hat and started to storm out, bumping into Igrat on the way. After the door slammed behind him, there was a definite exhalation of breath.

"So, does he know?" Lillith looked around. "If anybody could work it out, he can."

"Don't overrate him." Stuyvesant was thoughtful. "He's smart and tricky, but nowhere near as clever as he thinks. But he could have put things together the right way, and he's self-confident enough to believe the answer he comes up with. That's always been our greatest danger; somebody who is smart enough to work it out, confident enough to believe the answer and yet not smart enough to realize he's got more to gain by being our friend than our enemy. Rothstein fits that description perfectly."

"I'm surprised he didn't pull a gun on us." Lillith didn't sound as if she was worried by the prospect.

"He wouldn't have lived if he had tried." Achillea was very confident of that, and with good reason. She had been ready for Rothstein to try it. The only question in her mind was whether she should shoot him, stab him or break his neck. *Probably all of the above*, she thought. *One should be certain about such things.*

"He wouldn't have got very far." Igrat was grinning. She reached into her bag and pulled out a .38 Special with a snub, two-inch barrel. "He won't miss it until he gets down to the lobby, at least."

"What's dollar poker, Igrat?" Lillith was curious.

"Game Arnie likes to play. Each person pulls a note of a given denomination out of his billfold and everybody compares the serial number. Treats them like a poker hand. So, for example, a tenspot, serial number D7 981376 7H is three sevens. If somebody else has a tenspot, say R3 546184 8T, that's two pairs; fours and eights. Three of a kind beats two pairs. Winner gets all the bills. Of course, Arnie has gone through his billfold and only carries high-value hand notes."

"I'm surprised you're not in his bed." The remark could have sounded spiteful, but Achillea's voice was more a mixture of curiosity and affection.

Igrat's reply was deadly serious. "Let me tell you something about Arnie. He takes, never gives. Everything goes one way with him. Towards Arnold Rothstein. He demands instant payment of all debts owed to him, no matter how dubious, yet delays and prevaricates for weeks or months before paying his most legitimate debts. He has no friends, only associates. He'll dump anybody as soon as it benefits him to do so.

"Take a look through the people he's associated with. Every one of them found themselves taking the fall for him. I'm with Titanic because he looks after me. Rothstein wouldn't even consider the idea of doing so. Another thing, he describes himself as a gambler, but he isn't. He very rarely, if ever, gambles. Usually he gives the appearance of gambling, but has already loaded the odds massively in his favor. I think that's why he's convinced the game was crooked."

Igrat's comments made the room go quiet. Eventually, Stuyvesant's eyes met those of Achillea and she nodded slightly.

Service Elevator, Park Central Hotel, Midtown, New York City, 10:47 pm, November 4th, 1928

It had been an easy evening for Vince Kelly. He'd used the service elevator to take champagne dinners up to several rooms, and deliver a young lady of negotiable virtue to one of those rooms. As a result, he'd been tipped well for his efforts.

He'd exchanged a few friendly words with the girl on the way up, and she'd remarked that her client for the evening had a reputation for treating his girls with generosity and respect. She'd tipped him as well before she got off at her floor and Kelly had taken his elevator back down. Since then, he'd been reading the racing paper.

Footsteps on the service stairway made him put his paper down. A man was coming down the steps, walking slowly and painfully. His arms were clasped over his belly. Kelly wasn't sure whether he was sick or just drunk. "Sir, are you sick?"

"Just get me a taxi." The man held a dollar in one hand. "I've been shot."

Kelly called for help on the service phone. The man sank to his knees and was obviously in no position to go far. The house detective, Lawrence Fallon, arrived at a run. The last thing the hotel management wanted was a shooting scandal. Fallon took one look at the man, and the blood trickling down his stomach, and ordered Kelly to call for an ambulance. Then, he took a closer look at the badly wounded man.

"Oh my God. It's Arnold Rothstein!"

CHAPTER TWO

DEATH OF THE BRAIN

Stuyvesant Polyclinic Hospital, 137 2nd Avenue, in the East Village, New York City

"Thank you for coming, Father." Father Michael MacGregor was genuinely grateful for the chance meeting that had been thrown his way. "Florence Hay has been a parishioner of mine for many years and a true strength to our congregation. Any time anybody needed help, there she was. Not obtrusive or overwhelming, you understand, just a quiet reassurance that she would be willing to do anything needful. Now, she's in her final days and to have a member of the Society of Jesus come visit her and take her last confession has been such a comfort to her."

Conrad Lorenz smiled gently at the old priest beside him. The old lady hadn't had any sins to confess that merited more than a token act of contrition. Still, it had done no harm and, if his presence had brought her some comfort, then it needed no other justification. He was about to reassure Father MacGregor on that score when he heard voices in agitated conversation from around the corner.

"Rothstein's been shot. That means trouble from here on in. Now everything will come out. The chief wants this case wrapped up quickly before that happens."

"Who do we arrest?" The second voice was as agitated and panicked as the first.

"Who cares? We've got to get this thing contained before everything starts coming out of the woodwork. Tammany Hall is demanding action now. Rothstein lost a fortune in a card game a few days ago; that's what is behind this. George McManus was there, and he threatened Rothstein. He'll do."

"Are you insane? Do you know who his family are? They're our people, as department blue as they get. George's father was Detective Sergeant Charles McManus, one of Inspector Tom Byrnes forty immortals. George's brother Steve is still on the force, a detective. Tom McManus was in that room as well. He was a detective until '19. Nah, you'll have to pick somebody else to hang this one on."

The voices faded away as the speakers rounded an unseen corner. Conrad went white with shock, overhearing what was undoubtedly a cold-blooded plan to hang an innocent man for the murder of Arnold Rothstein. He knew now why his footsteps had been steered to this hospital, at this time.

"Get away from me, you disgusting drunk." The woman's voice echoed around the corridors in a way that the semi-whispered conversation preceding it had not. "You make me sick. Seeing a man of the cloth, stinking drunk from rotgut gin."

Conrad didn't quite break into a run, but he rounded the corner quickly. He saw woman shaking with a combination of rage and grief. One glance told him the man facing her, whatever else he was or might pretend to me, was not a priest. His nose confirmed that; the man indeed reeked of speakeasy gin. When Conrad spoke, his voice had all the authority of a Jesuit and an inquisitor behind it. "Do you know that this charade has put your immortal soul in danger? And that deceiving this poor woman in the extremity of her grief redoubles that danger? What makes you take path so beset with mortal sin."

"I am Father Considine, of Long Island City." The man's words were blurred and shot through with fear.

"And by so lying, you further expose your soul to damnation. Speak the truth if you wish to save yourself."

The man was white and sweating with fear, as if he could already smell the sulphur-laden fires of Hell waiting for him. "Forgive me, Father, but Walter Howey of the *Daily Mirror* gave me ten dollars to get a picture of Arnold Rothstein on his deathbed. Ten dollars is a lot of money for a man who has little."

"You would risk your soul for ten dollars." Conrad was genuinely amazed. "You would be well advised to go to the nearest church and make a full confession. And take care before you do so, because your soul stands in mortal danger of eternal damnation. If you were to pass away now, unshriven, I fear for your eternal future."

The man stumbled away, heading for the stairs leading to the street. Once he was gone, Conrad heard the woman speak to him, her voice much calmer, although the overwhelming grief was still there. "Father, I am Carolyn Rothstein. My husband is dying in there. He is Jewish, but I'm Catholic. Please, could you sit with me while I wait for the end?"

"Of course. There is truly no hope?"

"The doctors say that he may still live, and that his strength may carry him through. In my heart, though, I know the truth."

Arnold Rothstein was stretched out on his hospital bed, his eyes three-quarters closed and his skin a pallid white. Carolyn Rothstein hurried to him and sat down at the bed, holding one of his hands in both of hers. Conrad quietly sat beside her. A man was standing beside him, one whom Conrad instantly recognized as a detective by his cheap and ill-fitting suit.

"Who did it, Rothstein? Who shot you?"

"You do your job, copper, I'll do mine." Rothstein's voice was as weak as his appearance hinted.

"At least tell us, did they do you in your apartment or outside?"

Rothstein smiled weakly and lifted his finger to his lips in the classic silence gesture. "That would be telling."

The detective gave a frustrated glance upwards and took his seat beside Rothstein's bed. He paid only scant interest to Carolyn Rothstein, but much more to her companion. "He won't say anything, Father. It's odd. When he was . . . before he was shot, he always said he wouldn't hesitate to put the finger on anybody who tried to put him down. Yet now, when it really matters, he's sticking to the code and won't give us a thing."

"Perhaps he doesn't know." To Conrad, that was an obvious explanation.

The detective was eyeing him curiously, as if he recognized Conrad from somewhere. "Could be. The bullet wound was from one side, so he might have been shot from ambush. From a doorway, if he was outside. That would explain something odd. Rothstein is a tall man, yet the bullet track is downwards. Either the man who shot him was even taller, or he was standing on something. It was a precious good shot, though. Bullet cut right through his belly, wrecked his bladder and chopped up his guts. Dead on the center of mass, for a shot from above and to one side."

"Father, I know you. Weren't you involved in the . . . "

"I was, in a small way." Conrad spoke hastily, to cut off mention of the specific case. Carolyn's attention was fixed on her husband and she appeared not to be conscious of the other occupants of the room.

"The way I heard it, New Jersey would have sent an innocent man to the chair if it hadn't been for you."

"From what I have just heard, New York is about to do the same." The censorious note in Conrad's voice caused the detective to flush.

"Look, Father, there's a few things you should know before you pass judgment. There's a war going on in the police department right now. There's Tammany Hall, Mayor Walker and the corrupt department on one side, and a few honest cops on the other. The honest cops get pushed into backwaters and generally treated like dirt. If they get too close to finding out anything Tammany Hall wants kept secret, they get framed or shot down in a mysterious incident that never quite gets investigated.

"For all that, they try to do their best. And, do you know the worst thing? Everybody in this city treats the honest cops as if they were as bad, or worse, than the corrupt ones. Everybody wants honest cops, until they get pulled in for a traffic violation or getting drunk in public. Then they whine because an honest cop won't take a sawbuck to let it slide.

"I want to find out who shot Rothstein, who really shot him, but I know there's those who'll put this on the first person they can think of. Why? Because this is Rothstein. The Brain, The Big Bankroll, the man with his finger in everything. The more people look into this, the more dirt will come out. By the time this has finished, it could kill off Tammany Hall. Not before time, either."

The detective paused for breath, allowing Conrad to get a word in. "I'm sorry, Detective. I spoke without thinking and judged without first learning the facts. Thank you for taking the time to straighten me out. If I can be of any assistance to you . . . "

"I would be very grateful, Father. There's few men an honest cop can trust in this town. And fewer women, come to that. The name is Flood, Patrick Flood. This is an odd one, that's certain. The roots of it seem to be at a gambling game a few nights ago. Rothstein claimed it was fixed . . . "

"It was fixed." Rothstein's voice was weak and it was painfully obvious he was slowly slipping away. "I've fixed enough games in my life. I know when it's been done to me."

"If you say so, Rothstein." Flood was dismissive of the dying man. "Father, he lost a lot of money, half a million or more, and refused to pay up."

Conrad frowned. "If that's so, it is indeed unusual. Gamblers don't kill each other. They can't collect from a dead man. And a single bullet doesn't seem to fit either. If this was a professional hit, the gunman wouldn't stop there. Ammunition is cheap; they pump their victim full of bullets until he's a bloody mess and their gun is white hot. This is an odd one. What caliber was the bullet?"

"It was a .38 Special."

Flood didn't get any further. Another detective, a plump man with a well-fitting suit, pushed his way into the room, nearly stumbling over Carolyn Rothstein in the process. "Detective John Cordes. Who shot you, Rothstein?"

Arnold Rothstein's eyes were closed. The pallor of death was already beginning to bleach his face. Yet, he managed to open his eyes to look at the detective with disdain. "Your mother." He slipped into unconsciousness. Conrad, with all his experience of death, knew he would not return.

Carolyn Rothstein was still holding his hand. Tears were trickling down her face. "We were going to get divorced. All he ever cared about was gambling and his deals. He'd buy me things and, a week or so later, he'd take them and pawn them to get funds for another one of his schemes."

Conrad nodded. It was something he has seen all too often. He was about to say something, but Cordes cut across him, speaking to Carolyn without sympathy or tact. "I need to know who else was at the game."

"What game?" Her voice was flat and disinterested. Her attention was still fixed on her dying husband.

"The one where he lost a half a million." Conrad marveled slightly at Cordes. He seemed to be entirely bereft of any human feeling.

"He lost half a million?" Carolyn seemed unconcerned. "He never told me anything about his businesses. If I asked about them, he'd just pass it off with a joke."

Conrad caught Flood's eye. The detective winked at him. It was obvious there was information to be shared, but Cordes wasn't going to be one of those who benefitted from the sharing process. On the bed, Rothstein suddenly gave a gasp that was cut off halfway through. Conrad saw the white pallor of his face suddenly marked by the spreading yellow shadows of death. He knew Rothstein had gone.

Cordes gave a contemptuous snort and slammed out of the room. Carolyn seemed oblivious to the disturbance and just sat there with her eyes fixed on the body that had once been "The Great Brain"

Waiting Room, Stuyvesant Polyclinic Hospital, 137 2nd Avenue, in the East Village, New York City

"She's on her way back to her home. She's in shock, of course, but she'll be alright. One of her friends has come over to take her home and stay with her." Conrad paused. "What's going on here? Is it true Rothstein lost a half-million?"

"At least. It was one hell of a game by all accounts. Rothstein kept getting good hands, but not quite good enough. It's pretty obvious that the people there are prime suspects."

Conrad's Other Eye

"Do we know who was at the game?" Conrad agreed with Flood. A card game where one man had lost so much money was sure to provide the most likely suspects.

"I do." Flood gave a half–grin. "The game was organized by Titanic Thompson, with Jimmy Meehan as host. Most of the players were out-of-towners. Father, this wasn't a mob game. Nate Raymond was there, along with Red Martin Bowe and George McManus. They're shady characters, but everybody else was pretty respectable. Meyer and Sam Solomon, for example. Meyer's a well-known broker on Wall Street; about his only connection with the rackets is his booze supply. His brother Sam likes to gamble and isn't bad at it. Unlike his brother, he was a bit of a wild kid, but he grew out of it and there's never been any suggestion that they were anything but honest gamblers.

"An out-of-towner called Stuyvesant was there as well. Word is that's he's a pretty sharp businessman. A bit like an honest version of Rothstein, in a way. Just invests money in businesses he likes the look of and leaves them alone to make money. Unlike Rothstein, he doesn't loan-shark his investees. Word is, he was the big winner on this one. Most of the men there had their women with them; few of them their wives, of course."

Conrad thought quickly, trying to remember what first name Stuyvesant was using. "Wouldn't be Peter Stuyvesant, would it?"

"That's right. You know him?"

"We've met a couple of times in the past. He never struck me as being anything more than a businessman." Conrad was beginning to get a chilled feeling deep in his stomach. "You think he did it?"

"Nah, he seems a decent enough guy. He did buy up Rothstein's debts, but the version I got was that he did so because the other winners needed the money now and he could afford to wait. George McManus is the prime suspect."

"So I heard." Conrad injected a wry note into his voice to take any sting out of the implied criticism.

"I guessed that. Let me make another guess, you also heard that the police will cover up for him." Flood looked at Conrad and got a quick nod of agreement.

"Well, that's a problem. You see, McManus really is a very good suspect. He's got a reputation for violence and drunkenness, and he has taken a shot at people in the past. He's a mean drunk and he changes character real fast once likker gets inside him. He ended up owing money to Rothstein at the game, but he gave it to the people Rothstein owed. Good move on his part; gained him a lot of markers. Problem is, Rothstein liked collecting debts but hated paying out. I can see him trying to collect off McManus anyway, the fight getting violent and Rothstein getting shot."

"Have we got the gun?" Conrad was trying to get the pieces in order.

"We think so. Cabby found a .38 revolver in the street. Snub-barrelled and, guess what, registered to Rothstein himself. Only, the cabby picked it up and pawed in before handing it in. Any prints on it are long gone. Only thing we know is, it was found directly under the window of an apartment in the Park Central Hotel, Manhattan. The apartment rented by George, the Hump, McManus. As I said, Father, McManus is a very good suspect for this."

Room 349, Park Central Hotel, Midtown, New York City, November 5, 1928

"It's a bit late to get Rothstein a priest." The police officer waiting by the door of the apartment rented by George McManus had taken an astonished look at Conrad.

"It always was." Flood's rejoinder was grim, but Conrad knew there was an element of truth in it. Arnold Rothstein had always been destined for a bloody end. The only question had been when and where. His brains and daring had meant he'd survived longer than most in his world. But the cardinal rule in gambling was that, in the long run, the house always won.

Inside, the apartment was neat and tidy. If there had been a fight here, there was no sign of it now. The only thing out of place was a cushion on the floor in the middle of the room. Conrad looked around curiously. There was no blood on the floor; nothing to suggest a man had died here. Flood opened the doors off the room and looked around. The apartment was that in name only. It was two rooms, a living room and a bedroom, with a small service kitchenette and a bathroom barely large enough to contain a toilet, sink and shower.

The detective and the priest looked at each other. Conrad summarized what both were thinking. "If this is the crime scene, there's precious little sign of it."

"I told you the shot that killed him was expertly-placed. Rothstein bled out, but hardly any of the bleeding was outside. He bled into his abdomen. Even his clothes had hardly any blood on them. Whoever killed him knew exactly what they were doing."

"And that's an odd thing." Conrad reflected on what he had learned about George McManus. "I understand he was an amiable man when sober, but a nasty piece of work when drunk. Surely, such a man would not have committed murder when sober and would be incapable of placing a shot so accurately when drunk?"

"A good point, Father. But, there is something we do know. Somebody phoned Lindy's last night. A man in this room asked the receptionist to link him to Circle 3317. That's Lindy's, and it's also Rothstein's unofficial office. Or was, rather. Abe Scher, the manager at Lindy's took the message and passed it through to Rothstein. The message was 'tell A.R. I want to talk to him." Scher didn't recognize the voice. An hour or so later, Rothstein was shot. If that call wasn't him being set up, nothing was."

"And Rothstein came over? It seems unlikely he would have fallen for a obvious trap like that."

"We have an eye witness that says a man answering Rothstein's description, wearing a blue Chesterfield overcoat, entered this hotel and took the elevator up to this floor. So, we know he got here."

"Was he wearing his overcoat when he staggered down to the lobby?" Conrad was trying to get the timeline of the shooting sorted out, but there was a serious problem nagging away at the back of his mind. *Why was Rothstein's gun found in the street? And why was only one round fired?*

Flood looked at the notes he had on the case. "No, he wasn't."

Conrad thought for a second. Then he went over to the coat closet beside the entry door. There was a blue Chesterfield overcoat hanging there. "Well, I think he got here."

Flood nodded. Conrad looked at the overcoat a little closer and then frowned. "Detective, we have a problem here. There's a name tag inside this coat. It reads, George McManus. He was here. Was Rothstein?"

The detective looked very unhappy. "Up to a minute ago, I would have said he was. But now? The fact is we've got no real evidence that Rothstein was here at all. We know George McManus was. It's his apartment and his coat in the closet. But Rothstein? We have one shaky identification that could be McManus wearing this overcoat and that's all."

"Which leads us to another problem. Rothstein was shot, very badly hurt. Yet, he walked down the service stairway before collapsing. That's a long way for a badly-injured man. He had an apartment here himself. Why didn't he go there? In fact, how did he make it all the way down there himself? It would make more sense if he was shot somewhere near the service elevator, wouldn't it? If that was the case, the route he took would be the shortest way to get help."

"And, if he was shot here, wouldn't he have called for help? The fact he had only one bullet in him tells us whoever shot him wasn't around to stop him. Father, I really don't like this room as the crime scene. I think he was shot somewhere else. Ambushed, probably from a doorway, and staggered to the service area downstairs."

"Perhaps if we checked for his prints . . . " Conrad was stopped by Flood bursting out laughing.

"Father, in any other city, with the possible exception of Chicago, that would be worth trying. But, do you realize *Rothstein has never been fingerprinted?* After thirty years in the rackets, fixing the World Series, shooting two policemen and being involved in every questionable deal in the city, not to mention having a pistol permit, nobody has ever fingerprinted him. Even if we found unidentified prints here, we've got nothing to compare them to."

"Surely they'll be taken from the body."

Flood laughed bitterly. "You want to take a bet on that?"

Conrad was beginning to understand just how corrupt New York City was. Rothstein had been an ally of Tammany Hall. That meant he was untouchable, as far as the police were concerned, anyway. Obviously, somebody else felt differently. That brought an idea to his mind. "Detective, the call luring Rothstein was made from this room. Perhaps we could check the telephone, see if the prints on it will tell us who made that call?"

Before Flood could answer, the door burst open and Detective Cordes strode in. "I've got an eyewitness."

His voice bellowed around the small apartment as he made his self-important way across the room. He picked up the telephone and ordered the telephonist to connect him with the precinct house. Flood and Conrad sighed. This time, Flood voiced what they were both thinking. "Well, it would have done."

The remark went completely over Cordes' head. "Bridget Farry, the chambermaid, came up here to see if the room needed cleaning. Farry says nobody else visited the room before she was called away to service another apartment."

"I'd like to see the gun." Flood assumed that the gun that had been found in the street was being held in the evidence lockers back at the precinct station. Therefore, it was a considerable surprise to him when Cordes reached into an overcoat pocket and pulled out the revolver, wrapped in a paper bag. To an awed Conrad, watching the exchange, it seemed like a perfect example of how the police were methodically destroying all the evidence in the case.

Flood took the gun and examined it carefully. "The grips are broken, probably from when it fell into the street."

He then tried to open it. Flood struggled with the cylinder for a moment and then checked the chambers from the front. "It's jammed tight. Cylinder won't open or rotate, trigger is frozen, hammer can't be cocked either by trigger or thumb. This a useless piece of scrap. It is an ex-gun."

"So that's why Rothstein was only shot once." In Conrad's eyes, at least, one mystery was solved. "The gun jammed up and the killer couldn't get it to fire again. A friend of mine said that about revolvers. They might not jam often; but, when they do, it takes an armorer to repair them."

"Father, this is police business. I'll thank you not to interfere." Cordes spoke with rudeness only slightly tempered by the ingrained habits of an Irish catholic speaking to a priest.

"Johnnie, the father is a well-respected investigator who's helped out a lot of forces around the country. If we don't have him on our side now, the feds might decide to take an interest and bring him in to help them. We don't want the feds involved, do we?"

Cordes shook at the thought of telling the Tammany Hall bosses that he's been responsible for the feds nosing around in their business. It was the sort of thing that got a man sent to Staten Island. "Sorry, Father, I spoke in haste. I just didn't expect to have the Spanish Inquisition helping us."

"Nobody ever expects the Spanish Inquisition." Conrad replied gravely. The quip bought a burst of laughter from the two detectives. "Do you have a suspect other than George McManus?"

Cordes' mouth wrinkled up. "There's one; it's an outside runner, though. Woman called Julia Barco. She was involved in a gambling dispute with some gamblers. Her husband died, she got roughed up. It's rumored Rothstein was behind the game and she might have been looking for revenge. Pat, why don't you and the father here talk to her? She might be more amenable talking with a priest around."

Durkin's Speakeasy, 42nd Street, Hell's Kitchen, New York City

There was an air of disbelief at the bar of Durkin's Speakeasy. It was given form and substance by one of the patrons who looked at the pair who had just come in and shook his head. "A priest, a flatfoot and a wiseguy meet in a speakeasy. There's got to be the start of a joke there somewhere."

Conrad thought for a moment. "How about this. A priest, a policeman and a wiseguy meet in a speakeasy and start to discuss their respective businesses. Eventually, they get to the subject of collections and what they do with them. The policeman says 'well, I get all the money I collect on my beat, keep two dollars in every ten and have to send the rest up to my boss.' The wiseguy says 'we do it a bit differently. When I collect from my patch, I have to send a fixed amount every week up to my boss; anything above that amount I keep.' Then they both look at the priest, who says 'we do it differently as well. Every Sunday, after taking the collection from my congregation, I stand in the middle of my Church and throw it all up in the air. What my boss wants, he keeps. I get whatever he lets fall back down."

There was a howl of laughter along the bar. The atmosphere lightened. The wiseguy who had started the exchange wiped his eyes. "That's a good one, Father. Now, what are you two doing here?"

"I'm investigating the shooting of Arnold Rothstein." Flood took over from Conrad as lead in the interview. "We believe it may be connected with a high stakes poker game a few days ago. We understand that some associates of Jack Diamond might have been there. We just wanted some insight into what happened from people who weren't involved in the game itself."

The wiseguy glanced over to a table in the shadows where two men were sitting. One of them nodded slightly and the wiseguy relaxed.

"I'm one of the guys who was keeping an eye on the place. The host there gave us a cut to make sure everything was on the level and nobody stuck the place up. It's true, Rothstein lost a lot of money and claimed the game was fixed. But it wasn't. I won't say the others didn't gang up on him when he started losing, but that ain't cheating. You might be right; one of the winners might have got sore at Rothstein not paying up prompt, but it doesn't follow they did it. Lot of people getting tired with Rothstein. List of those who wanted to see him go was getting longer every day."

The man glanced over to the table. He got another slight nod.

"Look, Rothstein's changed over the last year or two. He used to spend all his time with society. Last couple of years, he's around us. Our bosses getting a feeling he might be thinking of muscling in on us. He used to be tight with my boss, but no more. Now, that game a few nights back. Mostly pretty straight people there. They weren't going to have Rothstein blown away over a debt. Those that couldn't afford to wait sold their debt to those that could. Those that could afford to wait knew they couldn't collect from a corpse."

"There was some rumor that Julia Barco might have gone after Rothstein. Revenge deal." Flood mentioned the idea lightly as if he didn't take it seriously.

Again, the wiseguy glanced at the table in the shadows. Another slight nod.

"Let me tell you something. What happened to Julia Barco wasn't right. She didn't deserve that and, if any of us had been there, it wouldn't have happened."

Looking at the man, Conrad knew that he had his own sense of ethics and that the fate of Julia Barco had strongly offended those beliefs. They might have been a different code from the rest of society, but that don't mean this wiseguy took them lightly. "Was Rothstein associated with that game?"

"Nah. That game wasn't authorized or protected. The Barcos should have had more sense. Look, if we'd been there, her man would have got a beating, sure. She'd have got a couple of good hard smacks in the kisser, but that's all. They'd have had their winnings and bankroll taken and given back to them they cheated. All the rest of it, that wasn't the way things are done around here. So, yeah, Julia Barco's got cause for revenge, but she ain't going anywhere to do it. Nah, you gotta look elsewhere for this."

Once they were outside, Flood relaxed a little. "Well, there we have it, straight from the top. There's something else going on here and we need to find out what."

"Straight from the top?" Conrad was curious. "That gangster was helpful, certainly, he didn't seem to be a top guy."

Flood smiled. "Notice how he checked everything he said with two guys in the corner? Well, one of them was Jack "Legs" Diamond, the other was his brother Eddie. Two of the most vicious crooks around, but neither of them will say a damned thing, especially to us, unless all the bosses have agreed on the party line. We got what we got straight from the top. Anyway, we'd better go see Julia Barco."

Conrad thought for a moment. "I'd like to drop in on Chesterfields before that. There's something I want to find out."

Chesterfield's Milliners and Haberdashers, Garment District, New York City.

"We have the finest selection of Chesterfield overcoats in New York . . . sir. That is how we acquired our name." The store manager had taken one look at Flood's suit and dismissed him as a potential client. Flood's identification had simply added resentment to contempt. In Conrad's eyes, that Flood remained purely professional was a tribute to his companion.

"Do you recognize this man?" Flood produced Rothstein's picture.

"Of course, that's Mister Rothstein. Such an excellent customer, of exquisite taste. Everybody here was shocked to hear of his death."

"That means he spent a lot of money here and paid his bills on time." Flood made the aside to Conrad in a voice that echoed around the genteel displays.

"Either that, or he hasn't paid his bills and the store have been left out on the hook." Conrad promised himself that he would include the caustic remark in his next confession. "I assume Mister Rothstein bought his overcoat here?"

"Indeed, Father. A dark blue Chesterfield, with a black velvet collar and slightly-sloped pockets with a small flap. Right hand pocket was extra-large and double-lined."

"That was for his .38." Flood explained, ignoring the manager's appalled protestations. "Do you recognize this man?"

"I do. A Mister McManus. He bought one of our overcoats as well. Strangely, it was exactly the same as Mister Rothstein's; the two coats came in together and were the only ones we had that were like that."

"Let's see." Conrad put the bits together. "Going by what we've been told, Rothstein went into the hotel wearing his overcoat. He went out not wearing it. McManus left wearing an overcoat; we can assume he arrived wearing one. The overcoat left in the apartment was McManus's. There are only two Chesterfields of that description. Therefore, we can assume that McManus left wearing Rothstein's overcoat; probably took it by mistake because he was drunk or in a panic. We've just placed Rothstein in that room. Despite the lack of blood, it does seem likely that was where he was shot."

Julia Barco's Apartment, Midtown, New York City

"I suppose it's all right for you to see Mrs. Barco." The woman who had answered the door was dressed as a nurse; her display of concern for her patient fitted the uniform. "It's one of her better days today. Not that there are many good days for her since it happened."

The nurse led them in to the apartment where a woman was sitting. For a moment, Conrad thought the figure was a store dummy. It had the same immobility, the same set pallor to its skin. Any move Julia Barco might have made when the nurse entered the tiny sitting room was imperceptible.

"Mrs. Barco, there are two gentlemen to see you; a detective and a priest."

The illusion of a store dummy was broken. The figure turned around and looked directly at them. The woman's face seemed to be that of a mannequin. It was dead white, the sort of white that comes from a fresh coat of whitewash on a concrete wall. Her features, the eyebrows and the lips, were painted on against the white and looked artificial. Conrad had an eerie feeling that Julia Barco's face was a mask she had created to hold up against the world.

"Mrs Barco, we're investigating a murder."

"George's murder?" The voice, when it came, was cracked, strained and hoarse. To Conrad, it was a cruel mockery of a woman's voice. "George is dead, you know. They killed him. They tried to kill me as well."

Flood's voice was calm and relaxed. "Did you know any of the people at the game?"

She didn't answer, but shook her head.

Flood got out some pictures of known professional gamblers. Rothstein and McManus were in there, mixed up with others who weren't connected with the case. "Mrs. Barco, if I showed you these pictures, would you recognize the men who killed George and did this to you?"

She shook her head. When she spoke, the phrases came out slowly, separated by long pauses. "When they caught us, they made George watch while they raped me. Over and over again. Then they made me watch while they beat him. They beat him down with clubs and kicked him. Then they dragged us out and dumped us by the roadside.

"They forced gin down our throats. A whole bottle of it. George was unconscious. He choked and died. When they left, I stuck my fingers in my throat and vomited it up. Not enough. Not soon enough. Bootleg gin with a lot of fusil oil in it. I can only just see now, Detective. Everything is blurred. The doctor says I will be blind soon. A few weeks; a couple of months at most. I will be completely blind."

Flood went through the motions of interviewing Mrs. Barco, but it was obvious she was quite incapable of being involved in the shooting of Rothstein. As they left, Flood looked at her, staring fixedly out of the window again. "There's a reason why they call that stuff rotgut, you know."

The nurse spoke very quietly. "She never leaves the room. Spends all her time staring out of the window, as if she was trying to gather memories. Or forget them. Wood alcohol is rotten stuff. Damn the people who made it illegal to sell decent booze. We get two or three people a month, going blind like her, and we're one of the smaller places. Even if she could see, she wouldn't go outside. After what they did to her, she's scared of everything that moves."

Getting back on the street was a blessed relief after the claustrophobia of Julia Barco's apartment. Conrad and Flood turned the collars of their overcoats up against the bitter chill and walked off down the street. Conrad didn't want to say anything that Flood might take exception to, but it was fairly obvious that Cordes had sent them here simply to get them out of the way. "Did you see the picture of Julia Barco before she was brutalized?"

Flood nodded. "Long black hair, olive complexion, brown eyes. Stocky build. The description could fit her as well as Ruth Keyes. But, Father, you saw her. She's all messed up inside and I don't just mean her eyes. There's no way she could have done Rothstein. And, Father, I'll tell you this right now. If she did gun down the man who did that to her, I wouldn't convict her."

CHAPTER THREE

CONSPIRACY

Senatorial Suite 309, Park Central Hotel, Midtown, New York City, November 6, 1928

"This is going to be interesting. Conrad is downstairs with a detective. They want to talk about the Rothstein killing." Achillea put the telephone down and looked at Stuyvesant with a raised eyebrow.

"Don't ask me. I don't know how he got himself involved." Stuyvesant wasn't particularly concerned. There was only one reasonable suspect for the Rothstein shooting. With George McManus hooked up with both the New York Police Department and Tammany's West Bronx Ward Chief, Jimmy Hines, there was hardly any chance of him being convicted. "The police are just going through the motions of checking up on everybody who was at the big game. Since we ended up holding most of Rothstein's paper, which is now worthless by the way, I'm surprised we haven't been visited before this. Although the simple fact that Rothstein's death cost us half a million dollars is enough of a defense for anybody, even if we needed it, which we don't."

"Conrad knows, remember, and he's very good at putting things together." Lillith was perturbed by how easily Stuyvesant wrote off a half-million dollar debt.

"I know, but he is one of us and he will not be mouthing off. He's obsessed with proving people innocent, not with finding out who really did it, so his mindset will figure strongly in all this. It looks very much as if McManus did it and Conrad won't be seriously involved, unless it suddenly becomes apparent that he didn't. At the moment, I'll bet Conrad thinks that McManus is the guilty party and he's concerned that his political connections will frame somebody else to protect him. Anyway, there they are. Action stations, people."

The knock on the door accompanied his last words. Igrat rose to let the visitors in. Leaving no sign, on either side, that Conrad and the occupants of Suite 309 had known each other for more years than Detective Flood could dream possible, was simply a matter of long practice.

"Mr Stuyvesant? I'm Detective Patrick Flood of the 8th Precinct. I was wondering if you could spare the time to answer a few questions concerning the death of Mr. Arnold Rothstein?"

Stuyvesant nodded, then looked at Conrad. "Is our conversation covered by the privilege of the confessional?"

"Mr. Stuyvesant, the Reverend Father is a skilled investigative consultant who has kindly volunteered to help us with our investigations. I understand that, by the end of a friendly card game, Mr. Rothstein ended up owing you a considerable sum of money?"

"That's correct; I bought the debts he owed to the other players. By the end of the evening, I was holding around half a million dollars worth of his paper."

"Why did you buy those debts? It sounds like a very chancy investment."

"Not really. Firstly, the other players needed the money urgently and I was able to get the paper at a substantial discount. Rothstein would have had to pay up eventually. He's primarily a professional gambler, and word that he's welshed on a debt that big would destroy him. He'd never get to lay a bet again. Also, to be honest, holding his paper was an investment. There could come a time when I need his connections. Finally, I'd rather he owed me money than I owed it to him."

Flood laughed. "Now that I can understand. But it must have worried you to know that Rothstein could even be thinking of reneging on half a million dollars worth of debts."

"His death has certainly put a nasty hole in my balance sheet, yes. Him getting killed was the one thing I hadn't allowed for. But I don't gamble money I can't afford to lose. Buying those debts was a gamble and I did it with money I could afford to lose. But, it still hurts."

"Did you see Mister Rothstein after the game?"

"He came here the next day to discuss a schedule for payment of his debts. He made an offer, we discussed some other things and I told him I would be back to him in three days to discuss his proposal. Then he left. I never saw him again."

"Even though you, Mister McManus and Mister Rothstein all have apartments in this hotel?"

"Excuse me, but that's not quite correct." Igrat spoke from one side of the room. "Rothstein didn't actually own an apartment here. His baby, Inez Norton, does. That's the deal, you see. Daddy buys his baby an apartment and gives her expensive gifts. Only Rothstein gave Inez her apartment, and then promptly mortgaged it for every penny of its equity. In name, it belongs to Inez; in reality, it belongs to the bank. The poor thing must be terrified she'll be thrown out on to the street."

"And you are, Miss . . . ?"

"Igrat Shafrid. Peter is my adopted father."

"I see. Thank you. So, you are saying that Inez Norton is also going to suffer severe losses from Rothstein's death."

"Unless she can find another daddy, quickly, yes. And, frankly, she's a bit over the hill for that. She's getting pudgy, and her face is hard. Rothstein was her last chance. With him gone, she's in real trouble."

"Thank you. Mister Stuyvesant, have you any idea who might have killed Mister Rothstein?"

Stuyvesant thought carefully and shook his head. "Nobody I know had anything to gain from his death. In fact, most of us have lost out from it. This seems to me like it must have come from the other side of the tracks. Perhaps some of his criminal friends owed him money, he pressured them to pay up so he could settle his debts and they killed him instead?"

"A very plausible theory. Thank you for your time, sir." Flood got up and left the apartment with Conrad.

As they did so, it occurred to Conrad that the description of the mysterious woman who had been seen entering McManus's apartment could also apply to Achillea.

Bull Pen, 9th Precinct Police Station, 345 West 47th Street, Hell's Kitchen, New York City

"I would say we have ruled out every likely suspect on our list other than George McManus." Detective Flood was gloomy. Going after a suspect closely linked to the New York Police Department's own was hardly likely to make him popular or enhance his career prospects. Unfortunately, the most obvious suspects all were either elsewhere, incapacitated or likely to suffer varying degrees of financial distress from Rothstein's passing.

"McManus was the only person who ended up owing Rothstein money. He gave it to the ones Rothstein owed so Meehan could pay off the expenses of the game. Gentlemanly gesture. But everything we've learned is that Rothstein hated paying his debts, but wanted those owed to him paid on the spot. Suppose, he went after McManus for his money, McManus pointed out he'd already paid some of Rothstein's debts with it, there was a struggle and Rothstein got shot with his own gun, possibly after he pulled it on McManus? That would explain the odd angle of the bullet and why the gun jammed up so badly." Conrad liked that theory; it fitted everything that had been discovered so far.

"If that's the case, and it sounds good to me, then McManus has nothing to worry about. Rothstein went to McManus's apartment to demand money to which he was not entitled. When McManus refused, Rothstein pulled a gun. McManus defended himself by grabbing it and Rothstein got shot in the struggle. That's self-defense, at worst, for McManus. A good lawyer could make a reasonable case for accidental death. It's a much neater package than Stuyvesant's theory."

"What theory?" Cordes had entered the room while Flood was talking.

"Businessman who was at the big game came up with a good idea for what might have happened. Stuyvesant, the one who ended up holding all of Rothstein's paper. His idea was that Rothstein tried to call in debts from gangsters and they killed him rather than pay up. We've talked to a few people on the street and it seems like a lot of the syndicate people wanted Rothstein dead. There's something else, as well; something in the background. Can't put a name on it, but Rothstein himself changed a lot over the last few years."

"Try dealing drugs." Cordes tossed the remark into the conversation. "You didn't hear this from me, but there's been a lot of whispers recently that Rothstein's been involved with importing narcotics. That put him on the outs with everybody. Even Tammany Hall don't want him around no more. Nobody minds bootlegging. Loan-sharking is something people will tolerate as long as it doesn't get too brutal. Gambling, and gamblers, is something everybody regards as a part of normal life. Acting as a go-between, again, nobody minds that. All of those things Rothstein did and nobody held it against him. Narcotics is different. It's dirty, and the people involved want it kept quiet. Tammany Hall knows that it depends on people voting for them and, if Tammany associates are in the narcotics business, that won't happen no matter how much money they slip the voters."

"And that opens up a whole new slew of suspects. It brings us back to McManus as well. His connections with Tammany Hall are almost as extensive as Rothstein's. If they wanted Rothstein dead, McManus could well have decided to set himself up as Rothstein's successor. He might have been smart enough to see the situation as a way of getting him with no come-backs." Flood was thoughtful. "One problem with Stuyvesant's theory. If this was a syndicate hit, we probably wouldn't have found the body. Rothstein would vanish and we'd assumed he'd gone on the lam to avoid paying his debts. For a syndicate killing, this was very sloppy. Although, that might point at McManus as well. I prefer the Father here's theory of the crime."

Flood explained to Cordes the concept Conrad had come up with and how it fitted in with all the evidence they had and the opinions they'd heard expressed. "And, after Rothstein went down, McManus panicked. Not realizing he'd never be convicted, he threw the gun out of the window, grabbed his coat and ran. Only, in his panic, he took the wrong overcoat."

"So, McManus did it, but he was defending himself against a man threatening him with a lethal weapon. You're right, he would never be convicted. I like it, Tammany Hall will like it, all the Police families will like it. You done well for us, Father; we owe you."

"We don't know it happened that way." Conrad honestly believed that he had the right answer to the riddle, but he felt it needed confirmation. Preferably from McManus himself.

"Father, it don't matter. Tammany Hall don't care who did it. Mayor Jimmy Walker don't care who did it. We want this case wrapped up fast and final, before any more of Rothstein's mess starts trickling out. Your theory fits everything we've found and means nobody gets found guilty of the killing. It couldn't be better. All we have to do now is get word to McManus that he's in the clear as long as he sticks to the self-defense line and everybody is happy."

Conrad sighed to himself and mentally shook his head. Like Tammany Hall, he didn't really care who had killed Rothstein. All he was interested in was making sure the wrong person wasn't convicted. For the time being, he was certain that George McManus wasn't being wrongly charged, and that no innocent person would be accused in his place. If he was acquitted, fairly or unfairly, by a corrupt court, that was none of his business.

At that point, the telephone rang. Flood answered it. After a few moments of conversation, he put the receiver down. "That was Burglary. Not that it matters much, since we've solved the case, but Rothstein's attorney, Maurice Cantor, has just reported that his office has been burgled."

Office of Maurice F. Cantor, 350 Broadway, Lower West Side, New York City

"When did you realize you'd been burgled, Mister Cantor?"

Assemblyman Maurice Cantor, Democratic representative for the 11th District of New York and attorney of record for Arnold Rothstein, looked confused. "I didn't, not for a long time. I must have been working here for hours and never suspected a thing. Everything looked so normal, you see. Nothing was thrown around; there were no papers on the floor or anything. I didn't realize somebody had been here until I looked at my medal of Saint Thomas More. The one my wife brought me from Canterbury, because he's the patron saint of lawyers. It was a bit of a joke, me being Jewish and all, but somehow having it with me did make me feel better.

"I always keep it with the face looking to my desk. Then, for some reason, I noticed it had been turned around. That made me look for a couple of other things. They had been moved slightly. If I hadn't noticed the medal was turned around, it might have been days or weeks before I realized somebody had been in here. It's like a ghost, a ghostly ghost, has been through the place."

"What is missing?" Flood had little patience with the lawyers who paid extravagant praise to thieves, although in his considered opinion there was little difference between the two professions.

Cantor hesitated. "When Arnold Rothstein did business with somebody, he wrote the details in a loose-leaf notebook. When the business was concluded, he would cross out the entry. Once all the entries on the page were crossed out, he would tear the page from the book and burn it. So, what was left of the books represented all his unfinished business. Those books have all gone."

"You mean Rothstein's black books really existed?" The incredulous tone in Flood's voice penetrated the air as if it had been electrically charged. He had been convinced that the rumored black books, containing all of Rothstein's secrets, were just a myth.

"They did, and they were kept here in a special safe, one that I never went to. Because the more I looked at it, the easier it would be to find; wear on things, and so on. I took them out the day Rothstein died, to make a quick assessment of the value of his estate, and put them back less than an hour later. I wouldn't have looked at them again for months; only I thought a thief this good may have found them. And he had. They were all gone, every one of them. What the Rothstein estate will do now, I don't know. With the records gone, there's no way to find out who owes the estate money or what debts there are to settle."

Cantor's grief was a little too florid for Flood's taste. He wished Conrad was with him; in his eyes, the priest's insight into human nature was his greatest strength. Flood had a feeling the disappearance of those books was more than a little convenient for too many people. Certainly, his family estate would suffer a serious loss from the disappearance of the records, but Flood knew, now that Rothstein was dead, there would be little or no regard for the welfare of his wife or girlfriend. That raised another question in Flood's mind. "Just how much does Rothstein's estate contain?"

"Without the debts registered in those books, it's currently standing at one million, seven hundred and fifty seven thousand five hundred dollars. From that has to be paid mortgage fees on properties he owns, totaling one hundred and fifteen thousand dollars, and bank debts of a hundred and forty thousand dollars. Then there's other outstanding mortgage debts of forty two thousand dollars, representing total secured debts of two hundred and ninety seven thousand dollars.

"We also have to pay the salaries of his staff, totaling one hundred and fifty two thousand dollars. This brings the total secured indebtedness of his estate to four hundred and forty nine thousand dollars. Then there are the unsecured debts levied against the estate. By the time everything is included, Arnold Rothstein's net worth was around two hundred and eighty six thousand dollars, without being able to collect on the contents of those books.

Flood was stunned. "But, this was The Big Bankroll, The Great Brain. Are you telling me he was broke?"

"That's exactly what I am telling you, detective. It's ironic; in an effort to pyramid his fortune and maximize the income from his affairs, he effectively ruined himself. He played everything close to the vest, circulating money between ventures and paying out money with one hand seconds after he had received it with the other. His fortune was an unstable house of cards that had to collapse sooner or later. His will was ridiculous; he left people huge sums of money that just did not exist.

"Detective Flood, I wrote him a new will while he was dying and guided his hand over it. For that, in the future, I have no doubt I will be accused of everything from fraud to knavery. But the will I wrote gives the people who really depended on him, his workers and a few others, at least something. There are trust funds now under the control of this firm that we can use to pay them a small stipend while they reorganize their lives. I am willing to answer for that to any power, here or higher, who think I did wrongly."

Bull Pen, 9th Precinct Police Station, 345 West 47th Street, Hell's Kitchen, New York City

"Conrad, I wish you'd been with me. The burglary was one of the most skilled I've ever seen. I'm waiting for the report of the crime scene examiner, but I doubt if he will find anything. Cantor said it looked like a ghost had been there and he was right. I've never seen anything like it."

"Does it link in with the Rothstein shooting?" Cordes really didn't want to know, if it would mess up his case. He had a perfect solution; it would keep Tammany Hall happy, while doing nothing that would involve anybody influential. He didn't want the happy outcome spoiled.

"His black books vanished. That is something we can play either way. Either it was people who owed him money destroying the evidence, or people he had on his payroll concealing the fact they were in business with him. At the moment, I would say it's not related to the shooting itself, but is a consequence of it. What do you think, Father?"

Conrad thought carefully about the situation. "I agree. The theft is a consequence, not a part, of the killing. There'll be a lot of people frantically covering their tracks right now. Even Mayor Walker is running scared. This could give LaGuardia just the excuse he needs to kick Tammany Hall out of power." *And then there will be a change in this city, the like of which it has never seen before. Almost a century of corruption and vice running unchecked and it will all come out. I wonder if George McManus knew what he started when he gunned Rothstein down?*

"We'll keep quiet and leave it to Robbery then." Flood sounded decisive, despite the fact he was the junior of the two detectives. "How's the hunt for McManus going?"

"It's going." Cordes sounded a little guarded.

And I know why, thought Conrad. *He's industriously looking in every place imaginable, except the ones where he might possibly find George McManus. For the self-defense claim to work, McManus has to walk in on his own two legs.*

Cordes lit a cigar while Conrad had been thinking over the situation. "We're sending a wire to all the other police forces, especially in Chicago, Detroit and Los Angeles."

Conrad mentally drew a map of the United States with circles around those three cities. It seemed to him that Florida was about as far from any of them as one could get. *That's probably where he is.*

The ringing telephone ended any further discussion. Flood picked it up and listened for a few minutes. "Well, that was the technician. They found no prints, no damage or any other evidence of an entry point for the break in. The safe was cracked open by an expert, who didn't even scratch the paint. No prints there either. It's just like Cantor said. For all the evidence we have, a ghost floated in through the walls, opened the safe, took the books and floated out again. He's never seen anything like it. Whoever the thief was, he's better than anybody I've ever heard of."

Conrad listened to that and made up his mind on a theory about the robbery that he had been carefully avoiding. *I've heard of a thief like that. In fact, I know her quite well. She's threatened to seduce me more than once.*

Senatorial Suite 309, Park Central Hotel, Midtown, New York City, November 6, 1928

"How's the case going, Conrad?" Lillith brought in a tray with a teapot, cups and a plate of British Chocolate Oliver biscuits and set it down on the casual table. She lifted the pot and delicately poured Conrad his tea.

"We're certain McManus did it. The police think that Rothstein attacked him when McManus told him his winnings had been paid to the other gamblers in partial settlement of his debts. Rothstein pulled a gun and got shot in the struggle. I've found nothing yet that would challenge that theory. This is one of those cases where everybody and nobody had a motive to kill Rothstein, and the most likely suspect is also the one who actually did it. The pulp magazines will hate it. Is the lodge tyled?"

Lillith frowned slightly and nodded. The question meant that the meeting was secure and that nobody outside the family group would be able to find out what was being said. Stuyvesant put his newspaper down and looked at Conrad curiously. Behind them, Achillea took up her guard position near the door.

"What's the problem, Conrad?"

"There's one thing in the case that doesn't fit. Maurice Cantor's office was burgled; very professionally, very professionally indeed." Conrad looked knowingly at Igrat. She fluttered her eyelashes innocently.

He sighed slightly to himself before continuing. "Rothstein's black books were stolen. Now, it's not surprising that somebody would want them, but the police here are bewildered by how good the thief was. Normally, the place would have been torn apart. The way it was done is your style, Igrat. Did you do it? And, if so, why?"

Igrat glanced at her father who nodded slightly. "It was me, Conrad. We dropped half a million dollars when Rothstein was killed. With money like that, an un-notarized IOU is pretty much worthless. Lillith was worried sick about the damage the loss would do to our businesses, and wanted to see if we could collect at least some of the debts in question. We'd have to get some corroborative evidence from Rothstein's accounts to back it up if we wanted to have even a chance of collecting. So, I hoped his black books would have a note in them that he owed money to Father. They didn't."

Igrat hesitated, turning the hesitation into a long pause.

"Conrad, I got in, I opened up the safe, which was a good one by the way, and read those books. I didn't take them. There was nothing of value to us in them. So, I put them back, closed everything up and left. If they're gone, somebody else took them."

"Probably Cantor. He made a big play of how he was trying to save as much of Rothstein's estate as he could for the people who needed it most. Personally, I think he sees himself as being the one most in need. Rothstein's alleged deathbed will is already being disputed in the courts. This will run and run. It could be a decade before everything gets sorted out.

"Once thing you ought to know. Rothstein was broke. His alleged fortune was a ghostly imitation of the real thing. Even if you'd found any paperwork to validate his IOUs, there is virtually no money to collect. You know, if the bullet wound had been in his head, I'd think that suicide to avoid bankruptcy was a definite possibility."

Conrad came to the decision that the burglary of Cantor's offices was of no great importance, other than a demonstration of Lillith's aversion to losing money. *In a strange way, she and Rothstein were very similar people.* It didn't affect his conclusion that McManus was being legitimately charged with the shooting of Rothstein or that he would be acquitted on grounds of self-defense.

"By the way, Conrad, what gave me away? I'm certain I didn't leave any evidence."

"You didn't. None that the police could find, anyway. But, a medal of Sir Thomas More was turned around. Cantor noticed, because it was of great sentimental value to him."

Igrat pushed her bottom lip out. "I remember that. I saw the medal and looked at it. I've always wondered if More was one of us; he had all the symptoms of the God-like delusions. It must have turned around when I let it fall back. Lesson learned. I'll be more careful in future."

That comment made Conrad choke on his biscuit. *The police forensic people are so impressed with the skills of the burglar, they call him, believing him a man, "the ghostly ghost". That Igrat believes her skills need constant polishing is absurd by comparison.* In truth, he understood the reason she was so skilled. She constantly analyzed and learned from the work she performed so expertly. She took notice of even tiny details, like leaving a coin turned around.

He finished his tea. After some polite conversation, which mostly consisted of inquiries after mutual friends, Conrad took his leave. Once the door had closed behind him, and Achillea had checked that the suite was secure again, everybody relaxed.

"Well, it looks as if the case is contained and closed. McManus gets arrested and acquitted. Conrad is happy and goes off to make a nuisance of himself elsewhere. We get back to ruining Nate Raymond.

"Progress on that front. He's cashed the check we gave him, and has approached a company we have an interest in for a consignment of machine tools for a new production facility he claims to be building in Chicago. Now, we can get to work on him."

The occupants in the room exchanged nods. Ten years earlier, the Great Influenza had swept across the United States, leaving havoc in its wake. The Daimones group had been hard-hit by the epidemic. Their usual defense against epidemics was to isolate themselves, cut off access to the outside world and wait until the disease had burned itself out. This time, it hadn't worked. The disease had spread too fast and was too infectious.

Almost two hundred of the Washington Circle had died, including two from Stuyvesant's inner circle. Semiramis and Scherezade had both been early victims of the pandemic, dying within a few hours of displaying their first symptoms. Most of the rest of the group has been desperately ill. Only Achillea hadn't gone down with the disease. The others favored the theory that she had taken the infection into a back alley somewhere and beaten it to death.

Lillith, Naamah, Nell and Inanna had been in San Diego on war work when the pandemic reached them. They'd been staying in a rooming house there when they had fallen sick. When the epidemic struck, it caused complete panic. Parents abandoned their sickly children, and vice versa, rather than risk contracting the Great Influenza.

In stark contrast to such craven behavior, Mrs. Timberley, the lady who owned the rooming house, had stayed with her guests and nursed them through their illness. In doing so, she had contracted it herself and nearly died. Nell had spoken for them all when she'd said that they wouldn't have survived without Mrs. Timberley's dedicated, unselfish nursing. The landlady had been added to the list of people to whom Stuyvesant's family considered themselves indebted. From that point on, things had gone right for the Timberley family.

Nothing particularly outstanding had taken place. There had been no sudden large inheritances or mysterious lottery winnings, but there had been a steady stream of guests for the rooming house and a profitable government contract for the metalworking business run by Mr. Timberley. One year, a particularly talented grandchild had won a Carnegie Scholarship to university. Not much, but enough to turn a marginal life into a comfortable one. Stuyvesant's family knew that sudden wealth was not a blessing to those who were accustomed to lesser standards of prosperity.

Then Nate Raymond turned up. He had managed to lure the Timberleys into one of his corrupt frauds. By the time he had finished, they had lost all of the money they had put aside for their old age.

Lillith had picked up on it when running a check on the people she supported. She alerted Stuyvesant to the problem. He'd set up a scheme that would see the Timberleys get their money back, while Raymond would suffer a just and dispassionate punishment. Lillith still hadn't quite worked out how it was going to happen, but she knew that it would and was reasonably confident that the expenses the family had incurred would be repaid, with a satisfactory overlap.

"What do we do next?" Lillith was intensely curious, but she knew that Stuyvesant preferred to play schemes like this close to his chest.

"Well, we start by substituting equipment that could be used for a brewery for the stuff that Raymond actually ordered. Then we tip off some of the syndicate in Chicago that Raymond is going to set up in competition with them and is boasting how he'll put them out of business. Oh, yes, we'll also tip off

Conrad's Other Eye

the Bureau of Prohibition in Chicago as to what is going down. Who's that young cop we met when we were last there, Nammie?"

"Eliot Ness?"

"That's him. We'll make sure that the Timberleys identify Nate Raymond as the man who defrauded them and they'll get the reward for putting his bootlegging business out of running. The money Raymond has from us will compensate the people he defrauded in San Diego."

"And us?" Lillith still couldn't work out how they were going to recoup their losses.

"Poor us. We were cheated by a vicious crook who used our good graces and public-spirited munificence to try and illegally purchase engineering equipment and then defraud us of the cost. We'll get all our equipment back, which you might note will be enough to equip several illegal breweries. We can then export it and sell to those who actually run such things.

"Of course, if Rothstein's paper was actually worth anything, we would be rolling in cash, but that isn't going to happen now. We'll come out of this a bit to the plus side of even, just not as much as I had hoped, though."

CHAPTER FOUR

RETALIATION

New York Central Railyard, South Loop, Chicago, November 14th, 1928

"Mister Raymond?" The shipping control clerk read the name off the shipping manifest he had received with the inbound consignment.

"That's me." Nate Raymond had his copy of the manifest. He also had almost a hundred and fifty thousand dollars in cash secreted on his person. On his way to collect his consignment, he had stopped at his bank and emptied his account. When the check he had given in payment for these boxcars of equipment was presented, it would be dishonored. By then, he, his money and the equipment would all be long gone. He'd carefully chosen the equipment on the order. It was all machine tooling and equipment that would be easy to transport and sell. Sometime soon, a less-than-scrupulous factory owner would buy this machinery at a price well below any reasonable market discount.

"Would you come with me please? We need to check your consignment against the purchase invoice." There was an odd intonation to the clerk's voice. It was a combination of excitement mixed in with a little trepidation. Raymond turned his overcoat collar against the cold and damp and followed the clerk out into the railyard.

The dank, dismal November day seemed to slice into Raymond's bones. "This is bad. How do you people live here?"

The clerk laughed. "This bad? You wait until we have a November Witch blow in. I've seen an inch of ice form in less time than it takes to pour a cup of coffee. You get caught out on the lakes in a November Witch and you'll be lucky to make it home. Michigan's like the other Great Lakes; she never gives up her dead. We're here now, Mr Raymond. How are you going to transport the goods?"

"I've got some trucks coming in a few minutes."

"Well, we'd better get to work then, hadn't we? First load. If you'd like to step into the boxcar, we have ten reels of copper wire."

"Check." Raymond ticked off an item on his list. "Next we should have . . ."

"Hold it right there." A young man stepped out of the shadows. "Eliot Ness, Treasury Department. I have a warrant to examine this cargo."

"No problem, Mr. Ness." Raymond was quite content to have his delivery inspected. His manifest showed that the shipment was entirely legitimate.

Ness took a crowbar from one of the two men with him. He levered open the crate that was supposed to contain a coil of copper wire. The contents were copper, but they weren't wire. They were sets of copper tubing, bent into spirals. Ness looked at them, then at Raymond. "These aren't wire, Mr. Raymond. These look more like coils from an illegal still to me . . . "

"What are you talking abou . . . "

"Hold it right there." A large black limousine pulled up. Three figures got out. One of them, a large, brutal-looking man, walked up to the boxcar. He was Frank "The Enforcer" Nitti, Al Capone's right hand man; a good runner for the most feared man in Chicago. He looked at Ness and screwed his face into an even more menacing scowl. "Who are you?"

"Eliot Ness."

"Never heard of you."

"Treasury Agent."

"Still never heard of you." Nitti's contemptuous grunt echoed around the boxcar before he turned to face Raymond. "That means you must be Raymond. Me and the boys heard you was coming to town, so we came to give you a real Chicago welcome. Always pleased to see someone new starting up in our city."

"Mr. Raymond is under arrest on suspicion of conspiring to make and sell alcoholic beverages in contravention of the Volstead Act." Ness was renowned across Chicago for completely lacking anything that might even vaguely approach a sense of humor. He glared at both Raymond and Nitti. Raymond was terrified. He realized who Nitti was and why he was here. Nitti was convinced he had the situation under control. The scene amused him.

"The Volstead Act? Why . . . that's bootlegging." Nitti sounded horrified. He threw up his hands in shock. "I'm in the dry-cleaning business myself. You gotta good case, Mister Ness?'

"We do now." Ness still was unable to see why Nitti found the situation so amusing. "We got a tip-off that a load of machinery for a vinegar plant was actually going to be used for an illegal brewery and distillery. All the stuff we can see could be used for a vinegar plant, but Mr. Raymond claimed it was electrical goods and machine tools. Shipping the equipment under a false description is pretty damning. We got a good case here, sure."

"Well, I feel I got to stand by a fellow businessman who's new in town." Nitti positively oozed bonhomie and good intentions. "Why don't I give you the money for his bail and we'll take him away to show him a really warm welcome to our city?"

"I don't think . . . " Ness knew exactly who Nitti was. He wasn't going to allow Al Capone's enforcer to walk away with a rival bootlegger. He had a strong suspicion that the warm welcome would be enhanced by the use of at least five gallons of gasoline, probably already stashed in the trunk of the limousine.

"Hold it right there." The new arrival got out of a Chicago city taxicab, holding up a badge. "Lieutenant Robin Locksley, Bunco Squad, Illinois State Police Department of Operations. I have a warrant for the arrest of Nathan Raymond on a California extradition petition. They want him on a charge of criminally defrauding a large number of elderly victims. Real charmer we've got here. Picks on old people who are a little short of readies, persuades them to invest in his enterprises and cleans them out. Leaves them destitute."

"Shocking!" Nitti rolled his eyes and again held his hands up in horror. He was genuinely, if only slightly, shocked. A hard, brutal, violent man who had never demonstrated a shred of mercy towards his victims, he also had a sentimental streak. He would shoot an old man dead without a qualm, but the idea of leaving the same elderly man destitute and starving really did disturb him. To Frank Nitti, taking the man responsible out to a piece of waste ground and incinerating him seemed perfectly justified by the circumstances.

The railway clerk quietly sneaked out of the boxcar and headed for a concealed corner in one of the maintenance sheds. In his opinion, it was a very good time to be anywhere else. This was, of course, an entirely sensible decision.

"Federal case takes precedence." Ness was a believer in the law, the whole law and nothing but the law. However much sympathy he had for the victims of Raymond's frauds, the law said that Federal offenses such as bootlegging took precedence over those against state and local laws.

"Not where the Federal law in question is for a much less serious offense. I'm sorry, Ness, but we're dealing with a felony here that could put him away for at least five years. The maximum charge you could get him on in Federal court is only three."

"Why don't you discuss this at leisure while I have him out on bail?" Nitti grew even friendlier. "Who knows? "By the time you come to an agreement, the whole thing might be irrelevant."

Now Raymond realized what Nitti really had in mind for him. Raymond lost control of his bladder. The stench of urine filled the boxcar

"Hold it right there." A State Police cruiser had pulled up and a man got out, showing a badge. "Trooper John McCabe, Gaming and Racing Control Board, Illinois State Police. I have a warrant for the arrest of Nathan Raymond on a charge of attempted fraud by race fixing, with attached Federal charges of wire and postal fraud. They're good for ten years at least."

Nitti, aware that the mounting list of charges against Nate Raymond precluded any chance of getting him away, threw up his hands yet again in exaggerated shock. "This display of lawlessness makes me feel quite faint. Gentlemen, you should be ashamed of yourselves. I don't know what our city is coming to when people such as this run loose. I fear that an honest businessman like myself should not be present at this kind of scene."

Nitti kept a straight face as he got back into his limousine. The jurisdictional dispute steadily increased in volume behind him. Once the door closed and the car had pulled away, he erupted into uncontrolled laughter. One of the reasons he had survived so long as 'The Enforcer' was that he could predict his boss's reactions very accurately. He knew that Capone was going to love hearing this story. "Oh, Big Al will have a ball listening to this."

"Sorry Boss?" The driver didn't know whether the remark was aimed at him. Having Nitti around was akin to juggling live hand grenades.

"Don't sweat it. Just drive."

Senatorial Suite 309, Park Central Hotel, Midtown, New York City, November 24, 1928

"So what happened next, ducks?" Nell Gwynne was dabbing her eyes, trying to control the effects of unbridled laughter.

"Having that state control board guy turn up was unexpected, but it all worked out in the end. Everybody knew Raymond was guilty by the way Frank Nitti had turned up to take him for a ride. Once Nitti had made a strategic retreat, Ness, myself and McCabe were left to argue the toss about who had Raymond. After some exchanges of jurisdictional pleasantries, things were nearly deadlocked.

"That's when I suggested that what California was really interested in was getting the old folks their money back. Now, Raymond had more than a hundred and fifty thou on him; the hundred thou we gave him and fifty-plus of his own. I happened to mention that, if he agreed to plead guilty to defrauding his victims and surrendered the money so they could receive compensation, California would drop its warrant before Nitti got back after putting up the cash for Raymond's bail. Raymond pissed himself again and agreed. The money went to California a couple of days ago and the Timberleys got their savings back a few hours later."

"Less ten percent to remind them that anything that seems too good to be true, is." Lillith added while Robin Locksley was refreshing his drink.

"They're happy and can't say enough nice things about the California police." Locksley took another gulp of his whisky. Stuyvesant had a working agreement with some of the best bootleggers in New York and his cocktail cabinet was well-stocked with high-quality drinkables.

"Anyway, we all agreed that the California warrant was settled and that left just McCabe and Ness fighting over who got Raymond. What settled it was the fact that Illinois had Raymond cold on fixing horse races, and ever since Rothstein fixed the World Series, they've been as hot as hell on that. Ness's case wasn't watertight, so he gave precedence to Illinois. The fact that the Illinois warrant had Federal charges as included other offenses helped as well. Raymond should be getting ten years; out in seven, probably. Only, I think Nitti has already passed word that he's to get a really special time in jail. The Capone mob pretty much control what goes on at Pontiac. Since Ness dropped charges, our machine tool shipment wasn't needed as evidence, so it reverted to our control. How's the money side of things looking, Lillith?"

Lillith leaned back in her seat and thought carefully. "So far, we're out for the cost of buying Rothstein's debt and the cost of the machine tools. That alone totaled nearly $200,000. Add in the cost of repaying the Timberleys and the other fraud victims, and our total comes to $350,000. Of that, we collected $150,000 back from Raymond. So, we're down $200,000, but we have the machine tools.

"Now, I had that machine tool shipment insured, of course. Once we had it back, we couldn't sell it at full price, since it was technically used. Things got a bit complicated there, but it all ended up nicely. I made an agreement with the insurance company that we'd sell it, and they'd only be liable for the difference. They jumped at that, rather than pay us off in full and having to sell it themselves. We sold it to Tommy Lynch up in Canada for $60,000 and the insurance company paid us another $60,000 to cover the claim.

"We're now down to $140,000 in the hole. Tommy then sold all the equipment to the Capone mob for $250,000, so we show a net profit of $190,000 on that deal. Put it all together, we made out by $50,000. If Rothstein hadn't got killed, we'd have raked in closer to $500,000."

"Doing well by doing good." Nell snuggled closer to Locksley. "Have we discovered how Rothstein found out about us yet?"

"I had a good look through Rothstein's books when I turned over Cantor's office and there's no mention of anything there. As far as I know, our paths have never crossed to any great extent." Igrat was genuinely puzzled. Given Rothstein's outbursts at their meeting, neither she nor anybody else who had been present had any doubts that he had discovered the Daimones secret, but the great mystery was how.

"No offense meant, ducks, but there's no way you could have missed any other records, is there?" Nell was reluctant to suggest that Igrat might have made a mistake, but the close relationship between the two women was based on knowing what was possible and what was not. Both understood that it was extremely hard to hide anything from a skilled thief, but it could be done. Just.

Igrat thought carefully about the offices she had visited and shook her head. "I turned over Cantor's offices, Rothstein's mortgage and finance companies and a few other places. There's no hints of anything that might point to us. Titanic says that Rothstein held a lot of business dealings in his head. I suppose he did the same with however he found out about us."

"He can't have tried to blackmail us with information he held in his head." Stuyvesant shook his head. "He has to have something somewhere. It could be as simple as a picture that shows us all an impossible time ago. Or some documents we can't explain. Or something. Whatever it is or was, it has to be something he could show people."

"There is another possibility." Locksley had a lot of experience of 'delicate' situations over the years, although his style of thievery differed dramatically from Igrat's. "We know that Cantor went through all of Rothstein's records and took out anything that was incriminating. I'd guess he started right after Rothstein died. It could be that he's already destroyed whatever it was that Rothstein had found, without realizing its significance. He might have thought that it was just some of his 'connections' and got rid of it on the basis of better safe than sorry."

Igrat nodded. "That's the most likely explanation. I've tried everywhere he might have had stuff tucked away."

"Perhaps we ought to ask Conrad to have a look around. He's supposed to be the experienced investigator." Lillith asked the question with wide-eyed innocence.

"Oh, no. No we don't. That's the last thing we want to have happening." The reply came in an almost perfect chorus from Naamah and Nell, neither of whom had any particular liking for Conrad. They'd run into him in London over forty years earlier and the meeting had not gone well. Their reaction gave Lillith cause for quiet amusement.

Stuyvesant looked up at the ceiling and thought for a second or two. "I don't think that's necessary yet. Not yet. Where is Conrad anyway?"

"He left town after he was reassured that nobody was going to be set up for the Rothstein killing and that McManus was going to be charged, but that he had a good, solid defense. I've no idea where he is now." Achillea had good reason to be relieved when Conrad had left town.

"Well, that solves that question, doesn't it? If he shows up again, we might ask him to do a quick check, but this whole affair seems to have been wrapped up now. Whatever Rothstein had has gone, and he's in no position to say anything to anybody. That's good enough."

Barber's Shop, West 42nd Street and Broadway, Times Square, New York City, November 28th, 1928

Inside the barber's shop, Detective Cordes found a man having a shave. This wasn't entirely surprising. The terms of this meeting had been very carefully negotiated the night before during a long telephone call.

"Hello, George," he said to the man under the lather.

"Hello," George McManus snorted.

"What ya doin', George?"

"Why, I'm gettin' a haircut and shave. Have one?"

"I've just had a shave, a pretty close one. How about you goin' downtown with me? You know you're in a pretty tough spot."

"Sure, I'll go downtown with you. Just give me a minute while I finish my haircut and shave."

Cordes sat back and settled down to read a copy of Life magazine, while waiting for McManus to finish his shave. He couldn't help reflecting that police work was so much easier when there was a little mutual respect between both sides of the law.

Interrogation Room, 9th Precinct Police Station, 345 West 47th Street, Hell's Kitchen, New York City

"We know you did it, George." Cordes was eminently reasonable. "You were in your apartment with Marion Roberts. Rothstein turned up to discuss his debts. Initially, the conversation was quite reasonable and Rothstein had taken off his overcoat and hat. However, he then started to become unreasonable and threatened you with a gun. In doing so, he endangered Miss Roberts and you went to her defense. The gun went off and Rothstein went down. You panicked, not realizing this was a clear case of self-defense and that no charges would be pressed, threw the gun out of the window and grabbed your overcoat. Then you left with Miss Roberts, not realizing you'd taken the wrong coat.

"As I said, clear case of self defense, and you risking your own safety to defend a young lady from possible harm. If you hadn't run, the DA would have simply closed the book, given you a quiet pat on the back for behaving like a real man, and that would have been that. But, you did run, so there'll have to be a trial. But, if you enter a plea of self-defense, the DA won't argue with it. You'll walk, probably with the court applauding you as you leave."

"That's a good explanation, a real good one. Only one problem with it. It ain't what happened. I never shot Rothstein, accidentally or otherwise."

"Oh, come on George, everything fits. You can't deny you had Rothstein's overcoat."

"No, I can't. But what you described didn't happen. Look, it went this way, see. I wasn't in my apartment with Kiki, I was in there with Ruth Keyes. She'd broken up with Nate Raymond. Truth is, he dumped her and left town. Rothstein came in and we talked business. Just as you said, we was all friendly, at first. I think Ruthie wanted to move in on him; everybody knows Inez was on her way out. Anyway, conversation drifted to things that outsiders shouldn't hear about. Arnie gave me the look; you know, 'things she shouldn't hear' look, and I told her this was going to go on late.

"I took her downstairs and got her a taxi back to her apartment. When I reached for my wallet, I realized I'd picked up Arnie's overcoat by mistake. No matter. There was cash for a cab fare in a pocket and I borrowed that. That's when I noticed there was no shooter. Always thought Arnie carried a rod, but no. Went back upstairs and the door was locked. Thought Arnie had locked it while he went to the can or somethin'. Pounded on it, but nothing happened. Then a maid came up and I told her I'd locked myself out. She let me in. When I went in, Arnie is on the floor, dead, head on a cushion. He looked dead anyway; guess he wasn't. Yeah, sure, I panicked and ran. Arnie had a lot of bad enemies who'd do me in as well, and a lot of powerful friends who might think I'd done him and get me for it. Just like you're doin' now."

The story made John Cordes hesitate. It sounded as plausible as anything else that had happened with this case, but it meant that a neatly-tied package had just come completely undone. That would not make Tammany Hall happy. They were very insistent that the Rothstein case be wrapped up fast and final. In fact, they were now at the point where they were calling him daily to remind him of their most heart-felt desires in that respect.

"Look, George, that may be true; it might not. What I do know is that Tammany Hall want this case wrapped up right now and they'll be really grateful to everybody who helps them get their wish. I'll tell you something else. Even Rothstein's friends wanted him dead. Why, only a week before he died, Meyer Lansky said that Rothstein looked as if he was suffering from some kind of sickness, the way he gambled so much. He said, it was only a question of time before Rothstein ended up dead.

"Gene Fowler, managing editor of *The Telegraph*, got a tip-off that Rothstein was to be hit. The words the tipster used was that 'Rothstein's number was up.' George we know you're not into the hit business, if you whacked Rothstein it was an accident or self-defense. You know the old saying about lemons and lemonade? Well, make some lemonade. You sign up to Rothstein's killing and stick to our story, you'll be acquitted on grounds of self defense.

"Think about it. You look good 'cos you took on an armed man to protect a lady. Tammany will owe you a favor for gettin' this wrapped up fast and quiet. We'll owe you a favor for helping us clear this off our books. Rothstein's friends and his enemies will owe you a favor for killing him and saving them the job. Tammany get what they want. We look good for wrapping this up. Nobody gets hurt 'cept those that have already come over all dead. It's the smart play, George. Everybody wins."

McManus sighed. "I know, it's the smart play. There's just one thing wrong, Johnnie. I didn't do it and I ain't putting my hand up to something I didn't do. Not with the chair in the background."

"What's the problem, John?" Patrick Flood had entered the room and heard the last few words.

"George here insists he didn't do it. We need that priest friend of yours. Where is he, by the way?"

"Left town a few days back. He reckoned since we knew George here did it, he didn't have to worry about somebody else being accused."

Cordes nodded wisely. "Since the priest knew George here did it. A priest speaks for God . . . George, even God thinks that you killed Rothstein. Are you going to call God a liar?"

McManus looked around desperately. "No, but . . . "

"There you are then. Stand up before the judge, tell him how Rothstein was threatening you and Keyes with a gun. How you tried to take it away from him and it went off in the struggle. The DA doesn't contest it, you walk."

"But I didn't do it. And what happens if the DA decides he'd rather have a conviction than let me walk? I could end up in the chair and nobody would care whether I denied doing it or not. No thanks, Johnnie. I'll stick to the truth. I don't know who shot Rothstein, but I do know it wasn't me or Ruth Keyes."

Cordes and Flood exchanged glances. Both detectives were familiar with accused prisoners making statements and both could tell the difference between a man who was telling the truth, or at least believed he was, and one who was consciously lying. As far as they could determine, McManus was telling the truth. They left the interrogation room together and leant up against the wall separating it from the Bull Pen.

"What do you think, John?"

"The timeline works. He and Rothstein were discussing the game; that's certain. Rothstein wanted the money McManus lost to him; that's also as certain as we can be. They both wanted Keyes out of the room because neither liked witnesses. McManus took her down, got her a cab and came back. Say what, 15 minutes? Five to go down, five to get the cab, five to get back to the room. I'll bet McManus didn't lock the door behind him.

"So, the shooter comes up, steps into the room. Rothstein sees him, starts to get up and gets blasted. That's why the bullet is angled down. He goes down. Gunman is going to shoot him again but the gun has jammed so he tosses it out the window. Then leaves, locking the door behind him. McManus comes back, finds Rothstein, panics and runs. After he's gone, Rothstein comes-to and staggers downstairs for help. Pat, it's as good as anything else. Enough to put reasonable doubt in a jury's mind. If I was McManus, I wouldn't plead guilty and rely on a DA keeping his word either."

Flood nodded in agreement. "We really need Conrad. We can hold McManus as a material witness for a while at least."

Penn Station, New York, December 1st, 1928

"Hey, Father, I'm glad we managed to catch up with you. We've got a real problem with the Rothstein case."

Conrad looked around and saw Detective Flood running across the concourse towards him. "Patrick, how did you know I'd be here?"

"We guessed you'd stay at the same hotel and checked their bookings. You were booked in for tonight, so we got a dozen uniformed patrolmen and staked out the entire station. There's another group down at Grend Central. I just got lucky."

Conrad looked at the panting detective and shook his head sadly. "Whatever your 'real problem' is, it's got to be bad for you to go to this trouble. Unless you're looking for divine absolution, of course."

Flood chuckled. "The entire New York City Police Department needs that. The problem is McManus. We picked him up, but we've hit a problem. District Attorney Joab Banton wants him charged right away so we can run the case and see McManus walk on self-defense. Only thing is, McManus won't play. He swears he didn't do it and won't even think about the self-defense plea."

"What do you think, Patrick?"

"Father, why don't you talk to him? Fresh eyes, fresh ears and all that. After you've done that, Johnnie and I will sit down with you and you can tell us what you think."

Four hours later, Conrad came out of the interrogation room, accompanied by two very impressed detectives. It was a myth that the Inquisition had gained most of its confessions by the use of torture. Mostly, inquisitors relied on their knowledge of human nature and their ability to trap the unwary in a network of their own words. There were few better than Conrad at that kind of gentle yet decisive interrogation.

Now, though, Conrad had met his match. Each time he cast his net of words over George McManus, it came back empty. The carefully disguised traps failed to snare him. To Conrad, there was only one possible explanation. McManus was telling the truth, the whole truth and nothing but the truth. There was just one point where McManus was evasive, and that related to Ruth Keyes. The explanation was simple. McManus hadn't wanted Kiki Roberts around for the meeting. She had become enamored of the dark world that surrounded gangsters. McManus believed she would be attracted to Rothstein, and, he had feared she might drop him in it. He'd brought Ruth Keyes to the meeting instead.

"What do you think, Father?" Flood was the one who finally summoned up the nerve to ask.

"He didn't do it." Conrad's decision was final and unequivocal. "He would have given himself away if he had, but he didn't. All he's guilty of is jealousy over Marion Roberts and using Ruth Keyes as a substitute. If you wanted to be really cruel, you could say he was pimping her to Rothstein. That's something he ought to seek absolution for, but it's a venal sin at most. It could even be argued he was protecting Miss Roberts, given Rothstein's reputation, and helping Keyes find a protector. We're going to have to start again."

Apartment occupied by Ruth Keyes, Broadway, Greenwich Village, New York City

"You know a Mr George McManus, Miss Keyes?"

"It's Mrs. Keyes." Ruth Keyes was very firm on that point.

"She's right, you know." Flood spoke to Cordes in an exaggerated stage whisper. "Her husband is Floyd Keyes, a brakesman on the Illinois Central Railroad. Ruth here works as a freelance clothing model, specializing in underwear. Usually, she's half way through her show when her husband gets home. Then her client gets shaken down for every cent he has. She likes to come to New York for 'shopping trips' while Floyd stays in Chicago."

"That's not true." Ruth Keyes was almost weeping. "Floyd and I broke up a long time ago. I want a divorce and came here until I got it. And we never did what you're suggesting."

Cordes slipped into the good cop role without real effort. "Detective Flood has a nasty mind. Why don't you just tell us what happened with Mr. McManus?"

"He invited me up to his place. He said he was having a meeting with Rothstein and if I wanted an introduction, this would be a good time. We waited around for Rothstein to turn up. George kept trying to amuse me, dancing, singing, catching ice cubes in a glass, that sort of thing. It was all quite silly, really.

"Then Rothstein turned up and they started talking business. George told Rothstein that he'd have to pay up eventually. Rothstein said he would, but he wanted to make them sweat a bit first. A bit later, though, he said the game was fixed and he wouldn't pay. Then they started talking about something else, a 'big deal.' That was when Rothstein wanted me to go.

"George took me downstairs, gave me a couple of fifty dollar bills and got me a cab for home. Last time I saw him, he was heading back to his room. That's all, I swear it."

"Was there anybody else there, other than Rothstein and McManus?"

"At first. There were a couple of other men there as well. I thought they wanted me to model my underwear for them, but they didn't. Nobody was out of line at all. They treated me a bit like a sister, I suppose. They stayed during the talk about the card game, then they left. Few minutes before I did."

"Would you recognize any of these men?" Flood was reinserting himself into the conversation.

Keyes shook her head. "I knew George of course, and Rothstein. But the others, I'd never seen them before."

Cordes produced pictures of Tom and Steve McManus. "Are these the men who were present?"

Keyes studied them carefully. When she spoke, she was uncertain of herself. "They might be. Everybody had had a lot of drinks and that makes them look different. They might have been the ones, I can't be sure. I'll do all I can to help, I promise, but I just don't recognize any of them."

"Do you remember anything else about the night? Anything at all?"

Keyes screwed up her forehead as she tried to remember. "There was just one thing. As I left in my cab, something hit it. There was quite a bang. The driver got out and started swearing, because there was a big dent in the side.

He said that somebody from a rival cab company had thrown a brick at us. I think he was guessing, though, because I didn't see anything."

The Bull Pen, 9th Precinct Police Station, 345 West 47th Street, Hell's Kitchen, New York City

"And that's it, Father, Keyes' story fits in almost perfectly with McManus's version. Only difference is McManus left out all the bits that made him look like a prize ass. Singing and dancing, for example."

"I wouldn't admit to that either." Flood was droll. "But, the fact is, the stories fit. Of course, they've had plenty of time to make sure they do."

"What I find interesting is that last bit about something hitting the cab. I'm pretty sure that was the gun. We're lucky it didn't go off when it landed." Conrad was depressed. He had been convinced McManus had killed Rothstein, albeit in self-defense. *And so, I come this close to convicting an innocent man – again.* "Somebody went to that apartment and killed Rothstein while McManus was seeing Keyes to her cab. That took some cold nerve."

Flood nodded in agreement. "We are dealing with a professional after all."

Cleaner's Utility Room, Park Central Hotel, Midtown, New York City, November 30, 1928

"A decenter, kinder man I never knew, and I'll be lighting a candle for him this very night. Bridget Farry looked defiantly at the priest and detective interrupting her work.

"What do you remember of the night Mr. Rothstein was shot?" Flood asked the question wearily. It was odd how quickly Rothstein was becoming some sort of romantic hero. If Bridget Farry had owed him money she couldn't repay, he would have had her beaten half to death without qualm or conscience. With George McManus dropping down the list of suspects, Flood increasingly believed somebody had applied the same logic to the 'The Great Brain.' Only they hadn't stopped at half-killing him.

"As much as happens every night in this place. That man you are asking about, McManus? Well, I went to his apartment, Room 349, because it hadn't been signed off on the list and that meant it hadn't been cleaned. So I went there and knocked on the door. Big feller, Irish as Paddy's Pig, comes to the door and says to me 'and what is it that you'll be wantin?' I tells him I'm the maid and I want to clean up the room. 'It needs no cleaning,' says he. My eyes can see different. There's empty glasses all over and ashtrays full, and there's a woman in the room. 'Ho, ho,' I says to myself, 'you're one for the walk of shame tomorrow.' But it's none of my business, and if he ain't wantin' the room cleaned, that's his business. Less work for me and the better off I am for it."

"Do you recognize this man?" Flood held out a photograph of George McManus.

"Sure I do. He's the man who opened the door to me that night."

"How about this woman." Flood held out a picture of Marion Roberts.

"No. She's not the one. She's blonde. The woman in the apartment had black hair. Olive skin too, not pale like this one. A Spic to be sure, and no better than she ought to be."

"Actually no." It took Conrad a serious effort to push down his anger at Bridget Farry's attitude. "The woman you're describing is Ruth Keyes. I believe she is of Irish descent."

"Well, to be sure she didn't look like a decent Irish girl. Funny thing. I saw her a bit later, walking in the corridor back towards the room. I thought she had left, but no."

"Thank you, Mrs. Farry." Flood and Conrad left the room with an unspoken air of relief. A little of Bridget Farry went a long way in the irritation department.

"What do you think now, Father?" Flood's association with Conrad was opening his eyes to the world around him in more ways than the obvious one.

"Well, most of the information we're getting confirms what McManus told us. We know Ruth Keyes was there, that there were others present, that they left early. He and Rothstein started to discuss something important, Rothstein didn't want Keyes overhearing, so she was sent home. The only question we have left is whether McManus went back to the apartment and found Rothstein had been shot or went back there and shot him. That's about as definitive as we can get."

"There's a third possibility, Father. Didn't it strike you as odd that Ruth Keyes was invited to that meeting? Even though she wasn't asked to perform any of her services for the other guests, McManus seemed desperate to keep her there until Rothstein arrived. Suppose her real role there was to make everything seem harmless and put Rothstein at his ease? Then McManus leaves him there. Ostensibly, to get Keyes safely off on her way home, but actually to leave Rothstein set up for a killer."

"Remember, McManus admitted he'd picked up Rothstein's coat by mistake. We know from the manager at Chesterfields that Rothstein kept his piece in it. So, McManus reached into the pockets to find the cab fare for Keyes and realized he had Rothstein's gun. That meant Rothstein was sitting up there unarmed. Here's another line for the third case. Suppose McManus deliberately took Rothstein's coat to disarm him? Perhaps McManus knew that

Rothstein's number was up; perhaps he didn't. But, we can put the gun from that coat in his hand. That's means. Rothstein alone in his apartment is opportunity. Add in the disputes over money from the big game, and we have motive. We got the Big Three, Father. He did it, after all. Or was instrumental in getting it done."

"That'll keep Cordes happy." Conrad felt relieved that McManus had swum back up to the top of the suspects list. That shamed him.

"Don't get Cordes wrong." Flood sounded a cautionary note. "Cordes is a da . . . very good detective. He's been awarded the Medal For Valor twice, only detective who's ever managed that. He once stopped an armed robbery while off duty and unarmed. In fact, he usually doesn't carry a gun, on duty or off. He's as tough as they come. Thing is, he grew up around here and he's a close friend of Jimmy Hines. They've known each other since they were kids.

"Hines runs everything in West Harlem, for good and bad. One of his people is in trouble, they go to Jimmy and he'll fix it. He gets up at five every morning so he's got the time to listen to his constituents' woes.

"Mostly, all he asks is you remember he helped you when you get to vote. But, Cordes is one of his people and, sometimes, that friendship costs him a bit more. Come to think of it, you know who else sometimes gets a few markers called in by Hines?"

"No?"

"Our friend, Assemblyman Maurice Cantor, attorney of record for Arnold Rothstein. And Rothstein's black books vanished while in Cantor's charge. Funny that."

Durkin's Speakeasy, 42nd Street, Hell's Kitchen, New York City

"Father, there were these two paddies diggin' the road directly across the street from a cathouse. Suddenly, they sees a wiseguy lurking around. He makes sure nobody is watchin' then ducks into the house. 'Would ye look at that, Mick!' said Pat. 'What a terrible thin' that is to be sure. A disgrace. That wiseguy must own the place and live off the shame and degradation of the poor girls forced to work in a house the likes of that!' They both shook their heads and continued working.

"Few minutes later, they watch as a copper looks around cautiously and then darted into the house when he was satisfied no one was looking. 'Did ya see that, Mick?' Pat asked in shock and disbelief. 'I just can't understand what the world is coming to these days. That copper going in there, shakin' down the place for a bribe and helpin' himself to the girls while he's there. T'is a cryin' shame, I tell ya!'

"Not much later a Catholic priest, was seen lurking about the house, looking around to see if anyone was watching, then quietly sneaked in. 'Oh no, Mick, look!' said Pat, removing his cap and crossing himself, 'One of the poor girls musta died'. . . ."

Conrad and Flood burst out laughing. Eventually Conrad dabbed at his eyes and shook his head. "That is good. I'll pass that one on to some of my brothers. Look, Mister . . . ."

"I'm Paul Quattrocchi, Father. Pauli Bagels, if you want to be one of the boys."

"That's quite an honor, Father. Not many outsiders get invited to use syndicate nicknames." Flood was impressed.

"Syndicate? Don't know what you mean. This here is a social club." Quattrocchi was grinning.

"Thank you, Pauli. I'm Conrad. We're still looking into the shooting of Arnold Rothstein."

"I thought you had The Hump for that?" Curiosity replaced amusement in the gangster's eyes. He glanced over to where Jack 'Legs' Diamond was sitting with his brother. Conrad followed the glance and saw Marion 'Kiki' Roberts sitting with the Diamonds. She saw Conrad notice her and her lips set in a defiant pout.

"We have him, and we've got him, but there's a few things worrying us. Our original theory of what happened hasn't panned out. We thought he and Rothstein had a fight over the big game and McManus killed him in self-defense. Now, it looks like we have something a lot more cold-blooded."

There was a sudden change in atmosphere at the bar. Quattrocchi looked over to the Diamond table again. There was a momentary pause. Then he nodded. "Father Conrad? My boss, Mr. Diamond would like to talk to you himself, and you, Flood. What he has to say comes from the top."

Conrad and Flood got up and made their way over to the table. To Conrad's guilty amusement, he saw Kiki Roberts unceremoniously shooed away. Then he took her seat.

For the first time, Conrad saw Jack "Legs" Diamond clearly. The man looked older than his thirty years. But there was a cunning calculation in his eyes that set him apart from the other gangsters in his bar. It also differentiated him from his brother, Eddie.

"First thing you got to understand. Rothstein had so many enemies, almost anybody could have done him."

"We'd already come to that conclusion. We still have to try and find out who did it, though." Flood was trying not to be impressed by the fact that the legendary Jack "Legs" Diamond was talking to him.

"Right. Well, something else you gotta understand. There's a war coming and everybody's pickin' sides. Rothstein was tryin' to play everybody off against each other and skim from them all. That's what got him killed. There was a contract out on him. Tried to warn him, but he wouldn't listen to nobody."

"We'd heard that the old-style Syndicate leaders and the new generation of leaders were on the outs." Flood was stunned by the fact that he, a policeman, was being told inside information on the world he dealt with, but actually knew very little about.

"Oh, that. Nah, that's just business. Moustache Pete's don't like competition and they don't like Italians and Jews teaming up. In fact, they don't like Sicilians teaming up with non-Sicilians."

"Important thing is, there's a war coming inside Tammany Hall. Same basic thing, though. The older guys like things the way they are and want them to stay that way. Newer generation, guys like Jimmy Hines, want to change things. And both sides are hiring muscle.

"Now, Hines has hired Arthur Flegenheimer, you know him as Dutch Schultz, to swing things his way. His enforcer is Joey 'No-Eyes' Noe.

"Rothstein was hooked up with the old school. Going right to the top, that means Mayor Jimmy Walker. He was the middle man; the one who fixed everything for Walker. McManus is hooked up with Jimmy Hines. Does for Hines what Rothstein did for Walker. Taking Rothstein out was a bad blow for Walker and a good stroke for Hines. You add up the bits from there."

"McManus set Rothstein up for a hit and Schultz, Noe, or one of their men went in to do the job?" Flood was now acutely interested in what had suddenly turned into a major political firestorm.

"I ain't saying' nothin'." Diamond grinned, well-aware that his denial was an eloquent comment all on its own.

Outside the speakeasy, Flood turned to Conrad and sighed. "Well, that sets it up. McManus was the man after all, even if he didn't pull the trigger himself."

"We'd better do some checking first. Remember the old rule. Nobody ever tells you anything because it suits your interests. They tell it to you because it suits theirs. And Diamond is an old Rothstein ally, which puts him into the Walker camp.

"It would suit him perfectly to hang this on Hines." Flood looked around the street, taking in the sleezy surroundings of Hell's Kitchen. "It would suit a lot of people for him to do that."

CHAPTER FIVE

CONSEQUENCES

New York Supreme Court for the First Judicial District, 60 Centre Street, Civic Center, New York City, November 30, 1928.

"Is the District Attorney's Office ready to press charges against George McManus in the case of the murder of Arnold Rothstein?"

Judge Charles C. Nott looked rather peevishly at District Attorney Joab Banton. The judge had every reason to be rather peevish. The night before, a newly elected magistrate, Judge Andrew Macrery, had failed to pay the agreed $10,000 bribe to Jimmy Hines; he'd been beaten to death by some of Dutch Schultz's men. Nott had spent a few anxious hours that morning before he's been able to confirm that his own payments had been safely received.

"No, Your Honor. We need additional time to complete our case." Banton looked apologetic. "Our case is circumstantial. But, in matters of this kind, circumstantial evidence is the strongest kind when the testimony of eyewitnesses is absent. Our case is a solid one. There are no weak links at all. Every link is a strong one, a sound one."

"If it is so strong, why are you not ready to press the charges?" It was, as everybody had to admit, a good question. "Is there a motion from the defense?"

There was a subtle intake of breath from around the court. If McManus's lawyer demanded his release now, the case would be over. However, McManus believed that would embarrass his captors and there was no need for acrimony.

After all, everybody was in this together.

Conrad's Other Eye

Conrad's Room, Savoy-Plaza Hotel, 767 Fifth Avenue, The Plaza, New York City

Reading the *New York Daily Mirror* that evening, Conrad had to admit the court correspondent had caught the atmosphere of the case perfectly.

And McManus, who might have seriously embarrassed his prosecutor by forcing him to show on what grounds he was being charged with the capital crime, smiled and agreed to the delay. He also smiled 20 or 30 times, nodded his head at friends and even waved familiarly at the detectives who were supposed to be trying to send him to the chair. And of course, District Attorney Banton smiled, the detectives smiled and all in all it was quite a happy occasion even though nothing had happened. And so McManus returned to his cell where he eats three meals a day of the best there is in the prison larder. He is being provided with special meals cooked by the prison chef – who is quite good. None of the institutional food for him. Tomorrow, he will go to the prison barber, as he goes every morning, to be refreshed by a shave, bay rum and scented talcum. His greatest hardship is that he has to read magazines because prison rules will not allow him books.

After he had finished reading the newspaper account of McManus' hearing, Conrad shook his head sadly. The story wasn't completely accurate. Something had happened at the hearing. Bridget Farry had been brought in should her testimony be needed. She had been voluble in her complaints about threats she had received. Apparently, strange men had stopped her in the hotel corridors and told her to keep her mouth shut or she would die. Another had suggested she take the first train out of town and reminded her of what happened to a squealer.

Judge Nott had been most disturbed by the claims. He instructed that Farry be held in detention as a threatened material witness and flight risk. While George McManus lived in luxury more appropriate to a guest at a fine hotel, Bridget Farry languished in a dank cell at the Tombs. Conrad had no doubt she would remain there until her memory suddenly deteriorated. He tried as hard as he could, but Conrad honestly couldn't feel too much sympathy for her.

Conrad was grappling with his interest in this case. *Why should I continue to be? There are multiple issues left unsolved, it is true. But I have little doubt George McManus pulled the trigger himself, or set Rothstein up for somebody else. There are no obviously innocent people in danger of being charged. Despite the original comments I heard, the police are doing the best they could to mount an honest investigation under nearly impossible circumstances.*

The only point that worries me a little is McManus turning down the self-defense plea offer so emphatically. It gives him a perfect way out. If he had set Rothstein up, it's as good a deal as he is likely to get. By refusing it, he forced the investigators to look deeper into the case. Now they've come up with another theory of the crime, one that accommodates both McManus's story and the evidence, such as it is. McManus had behaved foolishly, but my mission is to defend the innocent, not the foolish.

That thought decided him. *There is no work for me to do in New York.*

He would make his preparations to leave the next day. He had a yearning to take a trip across the Atlantic on one of the great liners. He would have to see about getting a ticket. Conrad wasn't short of funds; over his long life, the number of people who considered themselves indebted to him and had made sure he lacked for nothing was considerable. Lillith had once suggested to him that it was very hard for the Daimones, with their extended lifetimes, not to become well-off. That thought reminded him Stuyvesant had asked him to look into an unspecified matter. That fitted in neatly; he could do it while waiting for his voyage.

Senatorial Suite 309, Park Central Hotel, Midtown, New York City, December 2, 1928

"So, what's the inside scoop on the Rothstein killing?"

Lillith was busy setting the morning snacks out on the table that formed the centerpiece of the room. The Senatorial Suite wasn't as palatial as the Presidential, but it was certainly luxurious. A series of connecting doors turned the main suite into the centerpiece of a complex providing accommodation for up to a dozen people. At the moment, it was full to capacity as people had arrived for the Rothstein crisis.

"George McManus is waiting to be charged. Personally, I'm not sure whether he actually did the shooting himself or whether he simply set Rothstein up. But, either way, he's certainly an accomplice. The fact that he took Rothstein's overcoat, with his gun in it, does suggest that he would be the shooter. He's getting a fair hearing and a fair trial, as far as its possible in this city. So, I'll be leaving soon. I've got a ticket on the *Ile de France* in three week's time."

"Oh my, I hear she's beautiful." Igrat was impressed. She helped herself to some coffee and took one of the little cakes Nell had baked.

"Igrat, could you tell me something? One of the witnesses said that the girl who was in McManus's apartment was a candidate for the 'walk of shame.' What was she talking about?" It was minor, but it had Conrad puzzled.

"Oh. It's when a girl has been to a party returns home the next morning. She walks down the corridor to her apartment still wearing her evening gown, with her hair messed up, her make-up ruined and her panties in her handbag. And with all her neighbors watching."

"And, the incredible thing is, when our Iggie does the walk, she still looks beautiful." Michael Collins had joined the party as well, although he had come in from his home in Long Island rather than stay in the hotel. He was still feeling his way in the group and adjusting to his new status and that had mitigated his habitual brashness.

"Why, thank you, Mike." Igrat gave him a big, beaming smile and purred slightly at the compliment.

The room was filling up. Nefertiti Adams came in and took her place at the head of the table. Peter Stuyvesant sat on her right, Lillith on her left. Conrad was surprised at the formality being shown; it wasn't often that the precedence within the family was so clearly demonstrated. Whatever he had been asked to assist in, it was clearly much more important than he had realized.

"First of all, what's happening with Nate Raymond?" Nefertiti's voice was rich and soft.

"Illinois has him on charges of fraud and fixing a horserace. As soon as they've finished with him, California wants him for fraudulent misrepresentation and extortion. After that, if Prohibition is still around, the Feds want him for breach of the Volstead Act. The Syndicate are really annoyed with him and he is not due for a happy time in prison. At that point we're done with him." Peter Stuyvesant leaned back in his chair with a satisfied smile on his face. His favorite strategy to deal with hostile armies, suck them in, chew them up and spit them out, had worked perfectly on a cheap confidence man.

"Our friends, the Timberleys, got most of their savings back, as did most of the others Raymond defrauded. We think we may have missed a couple, people who were too ashamed to admit they'd been taken. Robin's going out to California to see if we can find any more victims." Lillith looked at her file on the incident. "At the end of the day, we are $50,000 better off and the Outfit are grateful to us for letting them have such nice new machinery for their breweries. Big Al sent us a case of his favorite Templeton Rye as a mark of his appreciation. I would say, we have done pretty well."

Nefertiti nodded in acknowledgement. "Well done, you two. Conrad, this is where you come in. We have a real problem that comes out of the Rothstein shooting."

"The money he owed you? I don't collect debts." Conrad was confused by his presence. Nefertiti looked down her nose at him. He shriveled slightly at the stare.

"Quite. We have a much worse problem than a mere half million that we viewed as a speculative amount anyway. Our sole and only purpose in being in that game at all was to hook Nate Raymond. The fact that we managed to win so big was purely a matter of luck. And luck it was, for if we hadn't taken Rothstein for so much money, we would never have found out that he knew about us. In fact, we would doubtless have found out later when the situation was entirely unfavorable."

"Rothstein knew about us? What do you mean?" Conrad asked the question almost by reflex and then suddenly realized the implications.

"About our gift. He made a series of threats that left it abundantly clear that he knew all about us. And that he would use that knowledge to destroy us all, unless we tore up the paper we held on him. That would only be the start of course. Rothstein was ruthless and he would use any sign of weakness on our part to our great disadvantage. That doesn't matter, though. The problem is, we can't find out how he learned about us or what evidence he had. That's where you come in, Conrad. We want you to find out how he found out."

"I've already searched his offices, his home and everywhere he does business." Igrat added the comment, her sleepy, heavy-lidded eyes focusing on Conrad. Conrad didn't like that. The truth was that Igrat made him very uneasy. Their meetings always left him with the feeling she could see right through him, down to the deepest depths of his soul.

"I couldn't find anything. We never really crossed paths with him. I couldn't find any pictures or documents in his possession that might give us away. Robin's looked around as well and he couldn't find anything that would link us to Rothstein or given us away. That really leaves only the possibility that Rothstein found out about us by a really freakish chance. We need to nail that down, though."

Conrad thought that over and glanced around the table and its carefully-ordered ranking. At the end sat Achillea. She was obviously bored and not particularly interested in the policy discussion. Conrad knew that her talents lay in places other than intellectual calculations. She was an expert at implementing decisions, especially ones that required carefully-applied violence. Since Semiramis had died, she had taken over as the family's primary muscle.

Suddenly, Conrad looked at her again. All the pieces started to fall into place. Rothstein finding out about the group, the mysterious woman who had been seen at McManus's apartment between the time he had left with Keyes and his return, the woman who looked so much like Ruth Keyes, the single, perfectly-placed shot that had killed Rothstein.

"My God. You killed him." The remark was addressed at Achillea, but it applied to the group as a whole. "He found out about us, so you silenced him."

"Isn't taking your God's name in vain blasphemy?" Igrat asked the question, but was obviously doing so to buy time while Conrad's outburst was absorbed. Conrad was taken aback by the remark. Before he could reply, Nefertiti cut in.

"Now why should you think that?" Her voice was still soft, rich and gentle, but there was a touch of steel behind it that hadn't been there before.

"Because it all fits in. Everything fits. I've always been uneasy about McManus denying everything so vehemently when the case against him is so weak. If he goes to trial, he'll certainly be acquitted. He denies it because he didn't do it and doesn't know who did. He sees himself being convicted despite his innocence, just to wrap the whole case up. And you would cheerfully see him hang for an offense he didn't commit."

"New York uses the electric chair." Stuyvesant made the note without any real emotion.

Conrad looked around the group. He expected outrage or offense at the accusation. There was none. Most of the participants seemed unaffected by his words. Naamah was looking at him with active dislike, Igrat with amused affection. He looked at Achillea. His stomach went cold. She was looking at him but her eyes were completely vacant. *The lights are on but there is nobody at home. I have often wondered whether she has a soul or not. Now I know the answer. There is no humanity left there. Not as I would define it, anyway.*

"Have you told anybody else about your suspicions?" Robin Locksley asked the question with apparent nonchalance.

Conrad jumped slightly, glad to be distracted from Achillea's stare. "No. No, I haven't. I only just realized it, myself."

"Oh good." Naamah started to get up. "I'll make some fresh tea."

"Sit down." Nefertiti kept her voice even. She and Naamah locked eyes. For a long, aching minute, they glared at each other. Eventually, Naamah glanced away. Nefertiti was the only person who could stare her down.

Igrat leaned forward slightly. "Conrad, a word of advice. When somebody asks, 'have you told anybody else about this?' they are really asking 'will this information die with you? Answering no to the overt question is saying yes to the implied one. That is very rarely a good idea."

Conrad felt his stomach clench again. The implications of the exchange between Nefertiti and Naamah made themselves apparent. Nefertiti was drumming her fingers on the table. Her long, intricately-painted nails tapped sharply on the glass that covered the top. The clicks echoed around the silent room. She looked at Stuyvesant, then back at Conrad, obviously weighing up alternatives. Eventually, she nodded slightly to herself.

"Now that you have got the idea in your head, you're going to follow it up and there would be only one way to stop you. No matter whether you are right or wrong, you will investigate further and you will endanger us all by doing so. There is also no point in telling you not to investigate or let this one pass. So, we'll tell you what actually happened that night."

Room 349, Park Central Hotel, Midtown, New York City, 10.30 pm, November 4th, 1928

"Make yourself comfortable, Arnie. I'll just get Ruthie safely into a taxi home and then we'll get back to business."

"Make it snappy, George. The deal I'm offering you and Jimmy won't be open all that much longer." As McManus closed the door behind him, Rothstein helped himself to a glass of McManus's whisky and settled back to read a copy of *The New Yorker*. It wasn't interesting enough for him to miss the sound of the door opening and closing behind him.

"George? That didn't take long." Rothstein started to turn around. He stopped in shock. At first, he thought the young woman was Ruth Keyes, but the resemblance was only superficial. The woman in the doorway was olive-skinned and had long black hair. The resemblance ended there. Her face was strong and showed character rather than the superficial glamour of the more conventionally beautiful but shallow Keyes. Of much greater interest to Rothstein, she was holding a gun. A snub-barreled .38 revolver. A second later, Rothstein realized it was his gun.

"Put that down. You'll hurt somebody."

"No, I won't." Achillea explained cheerfully. "You'll never feel a thing."

Rothstein began to panic. Oddly, despite his years in the rackets, he had never faced this situation before. He'd always done the violent end of his business through intermediaries. Threats against him had been dealt with the same way. "Look, you'll get your money. I was just trying to make you sweat a bit."

"Money don't mean nothing, Arnie. You threatened us. Nobody does that. How do you think we remained in the shadows all these years? That was really stupid of you. Nearly all the others who found out about us realized we are much better people to have as friends than as enemies."

The remark added confusion to his growing panic. Slowly it forced its way into his brain that the people he had threatened really did have something to hide, a secret so great they would kill to keep it. By sheer chance, he had managed to talk his way into this situation. With strength born of desperation, he tried to hurl himself out of his chair, towards the stocky woman with the empty eyes. A terrible blow took him in the side and dropped him to the ground. Somehow, he knew he was dying.

He looked up. The woman stood over him. "Who are you?"

Achillea misunderstood completely. She thought he was asking her name, not what about her caused her to kill him. "Achillea. Don't take this personally, Arnie. This is purely business. Now hold still."

She aimed at Rothstein's head. She pulled the trigger. Nothing happened. The gun was irretrievably and permanently jammed. She threw it away in disgust. It hit the window sill and slid outside.

"*Filius infirmabantur asinus et retro foramen meretrix*. Arnie, I'm sorry. Damned thing has jammed. I should have brought my .32. Here, there's no reason you should be uncomfortable." Achillea reached for a soft cushion and carefully slipped it under Rothstein's head. He smiled his thanks to her. She moved her hands to break his neck. The rattle of a key in the door stopped her.

"It just isn't your day is it, Arnie? Sorry."

She hurried out of the room, leaving by the small service door tucked away in the corner. Rothstein saw George McManus look in from the open main door. His face was white with shock. He slammed the door shut. Rothstein could hear him running down the corridor.

His vision started to darken.

A ferocious hammering on the door interrupted his growing peace. "Open up, you bastard Rothstein. You've been asking for this."

Rothstein recognized the voice. It was Joey "No Eyes" Noe, a vicious and sadistic killer and close associate of Dutch Schultz. He had little doubt Noe would make his last minutes as painful as possible. That prospect made him think kindly of the polite young woman who had just shot him.

Rothstein dragged himself across the floor and out through the service exit. Once outside, he managed to get to his feet and stagger down the service corridor towards the elevator there.

Senatorial Suite 309, Park Central Hotel, Midtown, New York City, December 2, 1928

"And that's it, Conrad." Achillea finished her story. "Noe pounded away on the door for a minute or two, but the hotel staff were already panicking because Rothstein had been found. So he ran for it. I slipped out in the confusion. Rothstein got carted away to hospital and that was that."

"So that's why he didn't reveal who the killer was." Conrad was amazed at how some mysteries had an unexpected explanation. "He was grateful for the kindness you showed him."

"Professional courtesy, not kindness." Achillea corrected him firmly.

"You'll have to turn yourself in. George McManus is innocent. We can't let him be convicted for something you did."

"You are remarkably free with convicting members of my family." Stuyvesant spoke quietly but with a decisive edge to his voice. "I do take that quite seriously, you know."

"Not to mention the fact that Achillea in jail would blow us just as effectively as anything Rothstein knew." Nefertiti was in agreement with Stuyvesant.

"That's a problem we'll have to solve, but I am not letting McManus be convicted for a crime he did not commit." Conrad gained in determination and his voice steadied.

"And I am not going to let one of my family go to jail for protecting all of us." Stuyvesant's voice was equally determined. His speech had never been anything other than steady.

"Preventing an innocent person from being convicted takes precedence over everything else."

"No, protecting my family takes precedence over everything."

"At the moment, the question does not arise." Nefertiti was decisive. "Igrat, you've got your finger on the pulse of things. In fact, you're the nearest thing we have to a court princess right now. What is the chance of McManus being convicted?"

Igrat thought for a second. "As close to zero as makes no difference. Titanic thinks the case against him is so weak that it might well get thrown out even before the trial. He's got a lot of money riding on an acquittal. If the case is thrown out by the judge after the prosecution rests, he'll clean up so much even I won't be able to spend it all. Titanic always wins his bets, Conrad."

"There we are then. Conrad, you'll do nothing until we find out whether McManus is going to be convicted or not. If it goes badly for him, we'll make sure the case falls apart. Without implicating any one of us." Nefertiti's voice was absolute.

At their end of the table, Nefertiti and Stuyvesant started having a quiet conversation. They glanced at Conrad every so often. As he was leaving, Conrad heard Stuyvesant speaking. "Achillea, could I have a word with you please?"

Conrad's Other Eye

"You do realize the trial starts in two days, don't you?" Detective Patrick Flood was exasperated with Conrad's suggestion that they give the evidence one last check before the trial commenced. "This isn't the only case in New York and it is probably the weakest I've ever seen brought to trial. Why the district attorney is even bothering with it is beyond me. We know that McManus did it, or at least was instrumental in setting it up, but the evidence of his involvement is all deduction and hypothesis. It wouldn't surprise me if Judge Nott throws the whole thing out."

Conrad was, quite literally, in agony, physical as well as spiritual. He knew that McManus was innocent, and that an innocent man was being put on trial for a crime he did not commit. The thought that he might be convicted, no matter how much the odds were against it, appalled him. Yet, he knew the only way to get the case quashed was to produce another, viable suspect. That would mean naming the real killer, Achillea. That caused another moral dilemma.

If he accused Achillea, the case against her would be even weaker than that against McManus. To a court, it would depend on her superficial physical resemblance to another woman, who might have been seen by a witness of highly questionable reliability on the same floor at the time. But, by accusing her, he put the whole secret that he and the handful of people like him held at risk. He was acutely aware that the majority of Daimones were not industry leaders or people of importance, but average men and women who were trying to cope with the unexpected problems presented by their inexplicable longevity.

Conrad's turmoil was further fueled by suspicion that McManus was involved in a scheme that would have killed Rothstein had Achillea not got in first. As a final piece of his dilemma, he had a feeling he was being followed. That, he could disregard, but he had been wrestling all night with the moral questions involved. The sleepless night had left him with a blinding headache. The only good thing he could think of was that a sleepless night had meant he hadn't suffered from the usual nightmares.

"Pat, do you have some aspirin in the station? My head feels like it's coming apart."

"Sure, Father. I'll get the desk to send some up." Flood picked up the telephone and rang down to the main desk. Conrad used the time to think of an angle that might be acceptable. By the time a packet of Aspirin powder and a mug of coffee had arrived, he had come up with a partial solution to the problem.

"Thank you." Conrad washed the powder down with the coffee and rubbed his eyes. The patrolman went away, happy in the thought that, having brought aid to a suffering priest, he had made valuable brownie points with the higher powers.

"Pat, I know the case is as shaky as it gets. Let's make one last effort to find something, anything, that will settle it one way or another. You don't want a guilty person to walk. I don't want an innocent man convicted. Perhaps another look will pick up something we missed before."

Two hours later, Flood tossed his file aside. "I can't see anything there. The supposition that George McManus did it is everywhere we look, but there just isn't any solid evidence. He's either the luckiest crook or the unluckiest innocent man I've ever run into."

Except that I know he is innocent. The thought tormented Conrad just as it had for all the darkest hours of the night. "There's one thing that still stands out to me. The card game. Not the big game where Rothstein took those losses. The other one, the one where Julia Barco was raped and her husband killed. Pauli Bagels made a big thing out of how wrong it was, that things just weren't done that way. I don't know about you, Pat, but I believed him. I think he really was genuinely shocked at what had happened."

Flood nodded slowly. "I won't disagree with you there. But, how would that link in with the main case? It seems an isolated incident."

Conrad frowned at that. "I know, but somehow it does seem to fit with the case. Let's try it this way. We've been told that there's a power-struggle going on in Tammany Hall and that Rothstein was associated with the faction behind Mayor Walker, right? Well, it seems to me to be unlikely that he would go to a game set up by the opposing faction, so let's assume that the big game where he lost all that money was associated with the Mayor Walker faction."

"That would fit in with the Diamond brothers and his gang providing security." Flood didn't really see where this was going.

"Right. But, the earlier game, where Julia Barco was assaulted, wasn't run the normal way. It was different; things weren't done that way. Suppose that game was run by Hines and his Harlem faction? That would explain the differences in attitude. The only problem is that's as much supposition and inference as everything else."

"Not necessarily." Flood was suddenly speaking very carefully. "Remember what your friend Quattrocchi said? That Dutch Schultz and his mob do the dirty work for Hines? Well, Schultz's right-hand man is Joey Noe. Do you know how he got the nickname 'No Eyes?'"

Conrad shook his head. "I'd assumed it was a play on his name. N. O. E."

Flood also shook his head. He gulped some coffee before continuing. "He's called 'No Eyes' because he just loves to blind people. There's a few women around here who won't go out until after dusk because Joey 'No Eyes' threw acid in their faces. You ever hear the story of the Rock Brothers?"

"No? Well hear this. John and Joe Rock started bootlegging here almost as soon as Prohibition was passed. About two years ago, Schultz and Noe decided to muscle in on their territory. The Rock brothers didn't want to be muscled so they told the Schultz-Noe mob to take a hike. Then, Noe picked up Joe Rock and held him for ransom. John Rock had to pay 35 grand to get his little brother back. Only, one of Joey Noe's boys had a bad case of gonorrhea. So Joey Noe had soaked a bandage in the discharge and taped it over Joe Rock's eyes. The poor kid went blind within a month. That's the kind of person Joey 'No Eyes' is."

Conrad felt an urgent desire to vomit but managed to control it. Desperately trying to persuade himself that the spasm had been a reaction to aspirin powder on an empty stomach, he carried on with his line of argument. "And Julia Barco was blinded. Her husband would have been if he hadn't choked first. That certainly provides some sort of tangible link between the game and Schultz and thus to Jimmy Hines. And McManus is definitively linked to Hines."

"Which, by the way, tends to put him out of the running for this. If Noe had killed Rothstein, he'd have thrown acid in his eyes first and then shot him where it hurts most. Rothstein would have died screaming. That single, expertly-placed shot, wasn't Noe's style and McManus doesn't have the skill to do it. That won't fly in court, though. Father, I'm as edgy as you are about this, but we've got nothing here we could present in court."

"Nothing you can present where?" Detective Cordes had entered the room.

"Father here has suggested how we could make a link between McManus, Dutch Schultz and the Barco assault, leading us back to Jimmy Hines."

Flood shook his head. "It makes sense. Hines wanted Rothstein dead because it would hit Jimmy Walker's revenue stream. So, he got Schultz to do it and McManus set Rothstein up. It won't fly in court, though; McManus is still going to walk."

I hope so, for whatever else he may have done, he is innocent of the Rothstein killing. But God must have been watching over Achillea that night. If she had opened the door, she would have fallen victim to the fate Joey No-Eyes intended for Arnold Rothstein. Conrad seemed impassive to the two detectives in the squad room with him, but his mind was filled with the ugly pictures of what might have happened in that room.

New York Supreme Court for the First Judicial District, 60 Centre Street, Civic Center, New York City, December 7, 1928.

Conrad found the prosecution of the Rothstein case quite unbelievable. Indeed, in the days when he had been a chief lieutenant for the notorious Tomás de Torquemada, he would have found the prosecutorial conduct so inexplicable that a presumption that they were in league with the Devil would have been the only reasonable explanation.

District Attorney Joab Banton had handed over the prosecution of George McManus to his chief assistant Ferdinand Pecora, and two of his deputies. James D.C. Murray was representing McManus. Pecora had opened the case by claiming he would show that McManus had killed Rothstein as a result of ill-feeling over the outcome of the card game at Jimmy Meehan's.

That hadn't been a bad start. Pecora had then gone ahead to produce a string of witnesses including Titanic Thompson, Sam and Meyer Boston, Martin Bowe and even an affidavit from Nate Raymond, now uncomfortably ensconced in Pontiac State Prison. All portrayed George McManus as a cheerful loser who laughed at setbacks and never displayed the slightest hint of anger.

Witness after witness spoke of how he always paid his losses with a smile. One journalist listening to the evidence being presented suggested that McManus had absolutely no cause for complaining about the fairness of the trial, since he there were two teams working for his defense and none for the prosecution.

Conrad did hold his breath at one point. The prosecution did manage to produce one surprise witness. Mrs. Marguerite Hubbell told of hearing a loud bang from Rothstein's room, followed by a hammering on the door. That fitted Achillea's story and meant that somebody had at least tried to get into Rothstein's room after the fatal shot was fired. Incredibly, it was a point that Pecora missed completely and failed to follow up.

The prosecution had also declined to call Ruth Keyes to the stand and thus lost the opportunity to place testimony as to McManus's character and behavior on the court record. They did, however, bring a much-chastened and humbled Bridget Farry to the stand. A week in the Tombs occupying a cell noted for its cold and damp, while being fed the worst food the prison kitchen could be persuaded to serve, had taught the former maid humility. Now, she claimed to be unable to recognize McManus as the man who had been in the room when she had knocked on the door. To make matters worse for the prosecution, she now claimed that McManus had left his room at 10pm and denied absolutely seeing a strange woman in the corridor. Having knocked a major hole in the prosecution's timeline, she then accused them of offering her a $10.00 bribe to implicate McManus. Finally, she swept off the stand in a fit of righteous indignation, tripped over the hem of her dress and fell flat on her face.

Once the court laughter had died down, one of the Assistant District Attorney's deputies, Jim Brothers, announced that the rest of the evidence would consist of police officers testifying as to George McManus's movements and the efforts to find him after he fled the city. Judge Nott was having none of that. He hammered his gavel on the bench and ruled the entire line of evidence inadmissible.

"If the defense denies the flight of George McManus, the State can put its evidence on that point, through the police officers, on rebuttal. It now appears, however, sufficiently clear that the defendant was indeed absent from his home between November 4th and the date of his arrest. Unless this absence, conceded by the defense, is now denied, there appears to be no reason for the additional testimony of police officers, since abundant evidence confirming his absence has already been introduced."

Conrad then watched the prosecution try to introduce a firearms expert, Detective Henry Butts. He would confirm that the murder weapon was the gun that had been found in the street and that it had been tossed out of the window of the murder scene. Once again, Judge Nott put a quick stop to that line of approach.

"To be very frank with you, I am at a loss to see you getting very far with that line of evidence, since, even if you prove a bullet from that gun killed Arnold Rothstein, I see no way you can link it to any particular person. Indeed, the evidence that you, yourselves have produced, links the gun in question to one person and to one person only and that is Arnold Rothstein."

By this time, Conrad had an odd feeling that he was completely wasting his time. Far from railroading George McManus into an unjust conviction, every effort was being made to ensure that he received a completely unjust, although actually deserved, acquittal. He had no doubt that Judge Nott believed that McManus was guilty of the crime of which he had been accused. Conrad was equally certain that Nott was not going to let any evidence be presented that might endanger the man's acquittal.

There was no sign that the police were making any attempt to find another suspect in the murder, so the chance of an innocent being accused of the crime was minimal. That meant there was no need for Conrad to expose his knowledge of Achillea 's involvement. Conrad felt a good deal of relief at that. He was well aware that Stuyvesant would do whatever was necessary to protect the people he considered his family. He knew he was still being followed, although he had yet to spot those trailing him. In his mind, those two considerations added up to only one thing; if he attempted to expose Achillea, his days would be severely numbered.

"My brother's on." Next to Conrad, Patrick Flood had seen his brother Dan take the stand and repeat the oath. Dan Flood explained that, when Rothstein's .38 had been found in the street by Abe Bender, the taxi driver had sworn that it was still warm. Bender had testified to that effect at the grand jury hearing earlier, but had now recanted.

"I have just one question for you, Detective Flood," McManus's attorney was feeling somewhat guilty about his participation in the whole affair. It wasn't often that a defense attorney had such whole-hearted cooperation from the prosecution. It made him feel as if he wasn't earning his fee. "Do you have any means of telling whether the gun found in the street was thrown from an upstairs window or dropped in the street by somebody in flight who remains unidentified to this court?"

"The damage to the gun was such that it was almost certainly thrown from a considerable height."

"Almost certainly. I see. And that certainty, such as it is, is reached based on the evidence of the damage to the weapon."

"That is so, yes."

"Could not the same damage have been caused by the gun being dropped in the street and run over by a truck or automobile?"

Dan Flood looked helplessly at the attorney. Honesty compelled him to give the answer he did. "Yes, I suppose it could have done."

At the prosecution desk, Pecora sighed noisily. Once again, one of his own witnesses had cast doubt upon the carefully constructed framework of circumstantial evidence. This was, however, a much more destructive piece of testimony. The previous witnesses had been friends of McManus. They were hostile to the prosecution and therefore could be expected to shade their testimony in his favor. Dan Flood, though, was an independent and unbiased witness, a homicide specialist. His word had much more weight than theirs.

Judge Nott obviously thought the prosecution case was fatally damaged. His gavel banged again and the courtroom quietened down. "Does the prosecution rest its case?"

Pecora stood up and adjusted his jacket. "Your Honor, when the prosecution commenced its case, we did so based on the evidence that was available to us at the time. From the start of the trial this morning, we have been confronted by a stream of witnesses whose sworn testimony is incompatible with that they presented to the grand jury.

"It is fair to say that they have all been hostile witnesses and that they have failed in their oath to tell the truth, the whole truth and nothing but the truth. We are thus faced with an entirely unexpected situation and one we need time to examine. I therefore would ask the court to adjourn until tomorrow morning so that I can discuss the situation with the other members of the District Attorney's office. If we have additional evidence to present, we can do so then."

"So ruled. The court will adjourn until nine am tomorrow. At that time, the prosecution will present any additional evidence that it may have and the court will entertain any motions from the defense." With that, Judge Nott gathered up his robes and left the courtroom.

"And that's it." Pat Flood sounded resigned. "Tomorrow morning, Pecora will state that he has no further evidence to present and that the prosecution rests. The defense will present a motion requesting dismissal on grounds that the prosecution has failed to make its case. Judge Nott will agree and direct a not guilty verdict. That's what the jury will give us and George McManus walks from the court a free man. More than that, he can never be tried for the murder again. Double jeopardy you see. Hey, Dan, Mom wants to know if you can make dinner tonight."

Dan Flood gave his brother a thumbs up sign as he left. Pat Flood nodded and then returned to Conrad. "Father, we should have known the case would go this way. Did you look at the court schedules?"

Conrad shook his head. "No. What did they tell us?"

"That Judge Nott had another case on December 9th. That was published a week ago. So, somebody knew that this trial wouldn't last for more than a day or so."

"Hey, you two, there's a message for the Father here down at the clerk's office." Cordes sounded positively cheerful. "A witness wants to speak to you. She says she can put Rothstein's killer in the chair and wants to see you outside the Chateau Madrid nightclub on West 54th Street near Sixth Avenue, at eight tonight. She says to come alone, because she doesn't trust us cops."

Outside the Chateau Madrid nightclub, 231 W. 54th Street, Midtown, New York City.

Conrad had a feeling that arriving for this meeting was a very bad idea. He had, at first, thought he was being set up by Stuyvesant and his family in case he exposed them. But Conrad dismissed that idea. It wasn't that they weren't capable of having a threat to their safety eliminated. In fact, he was well aware that they had done exactly that a number of times before. It was simply that, with George McManus set for an acquittal and no other arrests in prospect, he didn't represent any kind of threat to them. In any case, they wouldn't shoot him down on the street. He would either quietly vanish or go down with a regrettably terminal illness. Conrad wasn't sure if he found that thought comforting or not.

The woman who had left the message for him hadn't left a name. Conrad suspected she was linked in with Dutch Schultz and his gang. If that was the case, he felt sorry for her. From what he was learning about that group, it was best to keep well away from them. That was his real problem with this case. His mission was to protect the innocent, not to expose the guilty. The identity of the innocent people in this case worried him. As far as he could see, there weren't any.

A car skidding to a halt interrupted his train of thought. A blue Cadillac had swerved up on to the pavement in front of him. A man jumped out of the back seat. Conrad stopped dead in his tracks. He sensed something he had only felt a few times in his long life. Pure undiluted evil was surging from the man in waves. It was a metallic, rasping smell. Conrad gagged. *The Inquisition wasn't wrong when they said there was evil loose in the world. Full, pure, undiluted evil is rare, but it exists and this man is possessed by it. Tonight, I am in the presence of the Devil himself.*

"You should have kept your nose out of our business, Priest." The man started to take a step towards Conrad. His hand reached into his pocket. That was as far as he got.

Conrad experienced something he had heard Achillea talking about. When one's life was in danger, time seemed to slow down. The possessed man seemed to take his one step very slowly. He was arrested half way through it. A Tommy gun hammered out its burst as a series of single shots. They threw the man back against the Cadillac. His body seemed to make a slow-motion dance as the bullets hit it. It lurched and jerked with multiple impacts. Mixed up with the heavy roar of the Tommy gun were two single, light cracks. Conrad's would-be attacker slumped forward, rolling on the ground and leaving a great smear of blood across the sidewalk.

The driver of the Cadillac took a horrified look at the fate of his passenger and tried to escape. Conrad heard the metallic clash of the car being thrown into gear. It started to move forward fast. Not fast enough, though. The Tommy gun roared again. The glass on the car disintegrated into a crystal shower. The driver slumped over the wheel. The car smashed into a lamppost on the other side of the road. The silence that followed the impact was deafening.

Conrad looked around. Paul Quattrocchi calmly slotted another 100-round drum magazine into his Tommy gun. The gangster grinned at him and gave a friendly nod. "You know, Father, this is not the kind of place you ought to be right now. That's Joey Noe down there. My boss heard that he was going to deal with you, so he sent me to stop him."

Conrad felt weak at the knees. In the past, his cloth had protected him from much harm. The idea that he had come within seconds of death was a profound and unfamiliar shock. "Tell Jack that I'm profoundly grateful."

"Not Jack, Father. Charlie Luciano. I'm just keeping an eye on Legs for him. Charlie told me to tell you that you owe him a favor. One day, he might need a priest and, if he does, he'll call that favor in."

"You should know the rest." Achillea's voice came from a doorway a few feet away. She walked over to the body of Joey Noe and reached into the pocket the dead gangster had been trying to empty. It contained a bottle full of a yellow liquid. She poured it over Noe's body. It foamed as it struck his clothes. A bitter, acrid stench and a sizzling noise filled the air. "He was going to toss a bottle of acid in your eyes, Conrad. Peter knew that you were playing with fire when you tried to link Jimmy Hines and Dutch Schultz to the Rothstein shooting so he sent me to keep an eye on you. I didn't know my colleague here was doing the same."

"We've met before." Quattrocchi was speaking to Achillea but looking at the body of Joey Noe. The man's torso was riddled with .45 bullets, but the two shots that had killed him were .32s. Achillea had put one in each of Noe's eyes. He looked at her with respect, knowing they had met before but not quite sure where.

Achillea explained. "We met at the big card game. The one when the three ladies in our party stayed sitting?"

"Got you." Quattrocchi paused remembering the flash of recognition that had passed between them. "I didn't know there were women doing hits."

"There are a few of us. Mostly the really good ones. That's why you don't know about us." She gestured at the body and Conrad caught a glimpse of her eyes. They were still filled with the terrible emptiness he had seen earlier. "Everybody who sees that will assume it was John Rock getting revenge for what Noe did to his kid brother. Nobody will care about bringing him in for it."

Quattrocchi looked at the chaos in the street. Everybody who might have been in a position to watch had gone. Anyway, they were all well-educated in the philosophy of hearing and seeing nothing.

Achillea also looked around. Quattrocchi was checking the wrecked car and couldn't overhear. "Conrad, you tell Peter I shot Noe in the head and I will hurt you. I've been trying to break him of his habit of going for head-shots ever since guns were invented."

"I knew somebody was following me and I guessed it might be you. But, I thought you were going to kill me if I exposed you." Conrad was confused, bewildered.

Achillea wasn't, or, at least, not as far as Conrad could see. She just stared at him, her eyes still cold and empty. "Just what kind of people do you think Peter and Nefertiti are? Yes, we kill people who threaten us, but only as a last resort. We try everything else first. If we thought you were going to expose us, you would have gone to sleep and woken up in a remote monastery somewhere. One where the monks would have kept you as their spiritual advisor for a couple of decades until you'd thought everything over and come to your senses.

"Peter was really worried about you, especially because he held me responsible for the whole problem. According to him, I botched the job of killing Rothstein, so it was up to me to sort the resulting problems out. You ever hear of somebody getting their ass chewed? Well, my hip-bones still have his teeth marks in them. Making sure you didn't get hurt was just a part of making that right."

"But Naamah wanted to make me some tea and we all know what her cups of tea can be like."

"And she would have been chuckling to herself while she watched you trying to find an excuse not to drink it. Or drinking it and imagining yourself into getting the first symptoms. I don't like Naamah's sense of humor, nor does Nefertiti, but I can understand it. Now shut up. Pauli's coming back."

"Hadn't you two better get out of here?" Conrad was confused by the fact that they'd been firing machine guns in the street, there were two dead bodies and a wrecked car as a result and yet nobody seemed to care.

Quattrocchi laughed. "We've already told the cops and paid them off. They're waiting for us to go and then they'll hang the shooting on Noe's driver. They'll probably claim they shot him while he was trying to escape."

Years later, Conrad discovered, quite by accident, that was indeed what the police had claimed. He also noted that over the years the date of Noe's death had been moved forward by at least six weeks. The fact that he had apparently seen a dead man killed didn't disturb him. He knew a cover-up when he saw one.

New York Supreme Court for the First Judicial District, 60 Centre Street, Civic Center, New York City, December 8, 1928.

The shock in Cordes' eyes when Conrad entered the courtroom alive and unharmed was eloquent. Conrad, though, ignored it. He was much more interested in what Judge Nott would have to say. After the court had assembled and been called to order, the judge looked pointedly at the prosecution. "Does the District Attorney have anything to say?"

"Your Honor, the adjournment was requested to allow us to determine the advisability of calling certain experts to identify the bullet as compared with the weapon found in the street. We have concluded it would serve no purpose to call such witnesses. We think Your Honor's opinion, which coincides with ours, is sound. In the absence of further evidence, the prosecution rests its case."

Conrad's Other Eye

McManus's attorney got to his feet with alacrity. "Your Honor, the defense would like to make a motion for dismissal of the case against my client on the grounds that the prosecution has failed to produce any substantive evidence that would warrant the presentation of a defense."

Judge Nott nodded. "In presenting a case based on circumstantial evidence, the prosecution has the duty to prove that the chain of that evidence is not just sufficient to suggest the guilt of the accused, but to exclude all other possibilities. The prosecution has completely failed to meet that most elementary of requirements and I have no hesitation in stating that they have signally failed to make a viable case. Members of the jury, I am compelled by law and the rules of common justice to direct you to acquit the accused."

The jury conferred in open court for less than a minute. "Not guilty," said Jury Foreman Herman T. Sherman.

"Well, that's that." Detective Pat Flood shook his head. "He's free and clear. Whether he did it or not."

"I don't think he did." Conrad spoke very carefully. "I am convinced he set Rothstein up to be killed by Joey Noe or one of his accomplices. Whether Noe was the designated killer or not is something we shall never know now."

"You heard about Noe then?" Flood wasn't surprised. "He got rubbed out last night. One story is that Noe threatened his driver's girlfriend, a showgirl called Starr Faithful, when she wouldn't go to bed with him. Driver took out Noe with a machine gun and was killed by the uniforms while trying to escape. Another is that John Rock paid off the driver to kill Noe over what happened to his kid brother. Dutch Schultz is mad as hell about it, but nobody else cares. We've been told to investigate it only when we've solved every other case on the books. You got any plans, Father?"

"I'm heading for Europe soon, Otherwise, no. Plans seem to find me rather than me make them."

"Ain't that always the way. Look, Dan and I are having dinner this evening. You want to join us?"

Senatorial Suite 309, Park Central Hotel, Midtown, New York City, December 12, 1928

"Peter, I need to thank you for looking out for me." Conrad was awkward, speaking in a role for which he was unaccustomed.

Stuyvesant gave him a friendly grin. "Don't worry about it. Trouble with you, Conrad, is that you're so obsessed with protecting innocent people, you never think about the need to protect yourself. This case could easily have got you killed. Or worse."

80

"Noe was going to blind me." The enormity of the thought had caught up with Conrad during the night, when he had woken from his usual nightmare into a darkened room. *If the room was always going to be dark, if I never saw the sun rise again . . . dear God, would that mean the nightmares would never stop?*

"Version I heard is that he would probably have shot you afterwards. You might also reflect on the fact that he and McManus almost certainly got together and planned the same thing for Arnold Rothstein. Just how innocent does that make George McManus, Conrad?"

Conrad shook his head. "It's not my place to judge. I do not care to punish the guilty, only protect the innocent. I will say that Rothstein was fortunate Achillea got to him before Noe. If there is one image that will stick in my mind from this case, it is her putting a cushion under his head so he would be comfortable while he was dying. Peter, I truly think that of all the people in this case, she was the one who was innocent."

Only Stuyvesant's iron self-control that stopped him dropping his coffee in sheer shock. "How on earth did you come to that conclusion?"

"Peter, everybody involved in this case was playing their own agenda. The gangsters, the police, the witnesses, you, Lillith, everybody. They were all using the killing of Rothstein for their own advantage.

"The only one who wasn't was Achillea. She gained nothing from this. She received no reward, not even the satisfaction of a job well done. Death, her own or other people's, means nothing to her and she didn't even experience the joy of winning a fight. Nor was there any malice in her. Her sole and only interest was protecting your family and, by extension, all of us who share our gift. Her motives were purely altruistic and that makes her the nearest thing to innocent this case has."

Stuyvesant thought that over carefully. "Conrad, can I ask you a question, as a professional in spiritual matters? Do you think Achillea has a soul?"

The question took Conrad completely by surprise and he tried to buy time while he thought it over. "Why do you ask?"

"Just something I've wondered ever since she joined us."

"When I heard that story about her putting the cushion under Rothstein's head, I realized that she does. Only, it's different from what the Society of Jesus might define as a soul."

Conrad paused again, trying to put his thoughts in order. "Achillea is a Stoic, a real one. The philosophy of stoicism defines her outlook on life and her behavior, every aspect of it. It's a very harsh and unyielding discipline, one that has no room for compromises or evasions. There is no room in it for inventing excuses. I bet, when you discussed Rothstein's death with her, she simply said, 'I screwed up,' and left it there?"

Stuyvesant nodded. Achillea had simply stated that she had botched the job and took full responsibility for doing so.

"That would be what she believes. To a Stoic, a person's 'soul' is their ability to reason. It's everything that is responsible for thinking and planning. It means seeing the world the way it is and acting accordingly. As I said, a very harsh, very stern discipline, that must be very hard to live up to. It is mixed up with all the purely physiological life functions of a human including digestion, breathing, growth and movement.

"That 'soul' is nothing like our concept of a soul. There's no difference between it and the simple fact of existence; no distinction between the spiritual and the physical. Her soul is the same as her existence, no more and no less. She believes existence is the ultimate truth. That truth can only be determined by perceiving things correctly, and that depends on not letting herself be deceived by emotions or feelings. She believes that we can always avoid falling into error by being sufficiently disciplined enough not to be mislead into mistaking desires or illusions for reality. So, to her, excuses are meaningless. So are apologies. They don't change what is.

"The secret of Achillea's soul, as she might define it, lays within the very fact that she disciplines herself to accept what is reality without imposing her wishes on it. She's not that different from you, Peter. A lot of people think you haven't got a soul either. Achillea is just an extreme version of you."

"Is that a yes or a no?"

Conrad smiled sadly. "It's a maybe. For both of you."

POSTSCRIPT

The murder of Arnold Rothstein has never been officially solved, although many theories have been put forward.

Jack "Legs" Diamond spiraled out of control and was killed on December 18th 1931. Arthur Flegenheimer, AKA Dutch Schultz, was killed along with two of his associates in October 1935. Neither of these murders were ever officially solved.

George McManus suffered a severe heart attack two years after his acquittal, when his wife was killed in a car accident. He survived, but became an alcoholic. His health spiraled downwards until he died in 1940.

Marion "Kiki" Roberts became Legs Diamond's mistress. Some years after his death, she announced she was going to play herself in a theatrical production that would reveal what really happened the night he was killed. She was found dead in her rooming house the next morning. Ruth Keyes never found herself a rich daddy. She slipped into prostitution and died in the late 1930s.

Detective John Cordes was eased out of the police force during the La Guardia anti-corruption reforms. He became a private detective and died in 1955. Detective Patrick Flood continued working for the New York police until he died of natural causes in 1957.

Jimmy Hines was arrested for running a numbers racket in 1937. He struck a deal. If he plead guilty, the charges would be written down to misdemeanors and he would be sentenced to time served. He pleaded guilty, the felony charges were not written down and he got eight years. Hines' political career was ruined and he died in penury in 1957.

"Titanic" Thompson died of heart failure in 1978 at the age of 82. He was resident in a Fort Worth nursing home. The inquest revealed he had been visited by a known teenage prostitute just prior to his death.

Charles Luciano became the leader of organized crime in the United States, forming the "Commission" that has administered Mob activity even since. He was deported to Italy in 1946. He died of a heart attack in 1962. There is one mystery about his death. In his last days, he insisted on being attended by a specific priest who remains unidentified to this day.

EYE OF THE MARAUDER
Warminster, Pennsylvania, 1944

Conrad's Other Eye

CHAPTER ONE

THE MISSION

Final Approach, Warrington Field, Warminster, Pennsylvania, April 1944

"Don't let the speed drop; keep it above 135. You lose an engine now, speed is life. Keep her moving fast and you'll make it. Let the speed drop and she'll stall and spin in. Believe me on this. If that happens, nobody walks away."

Sitting in the pilot's seat of the TB-26G Marauder, Lieutenant Caleb O'Brien nodded diligently. The Marauder was a hot ship; nobody doubted that. Or, rather, nobody who had survived flying one doubted that. Those who didn't treat the Widowmaker with respect died. The official landing speed of the Marauder was 125mph, a good 20-30 mph higher than most other Army Air Force aircraft. It was that much faster than the official landing speed of the massive B-29. So many B-26 crews had been lost in training, the Army had ordered a special trainer version of the aircraft to try and familiarize the crews with their new aircraft. It was worth them doing so; the B-26 might be a widowmaker but its loss rate in Russia was the lowest of any bomber, light, medium or heavy and a higher proportion of the crew escaped from a shot-down B-26 than any other aircraft. The veterans coming back from the Volga Front said it loud and clear. 'Respect the Marauder and she'll fight all the way down to save you.'

Next to O'Brien, the instructor had his hands and feet ready to take control of the aircraft. If O'Brien made a mistake, there would only be seconds to save the situation. "All right, Caleb, ease the nose up and let the bird slow down a bit. You can drop her to 125 now. Try and put her down on the main wheels. Then, when she's rolling smoothly, drop the nose wheel on to the runway. Don't worry about bumping the tail; Martin put a wheel there just in case."

O'Brien watched the runway grow before him. Warrington Field had been a civilian airport before the war, but its adoption as a B-26 training base had seen it enlarged out of all recognition. The runway had been doubled in length, another tribute to the Marauder's landing characteristics, and a clutch of schoolrooms and training ranges built. However, the whole place was dwarfed by the nearby Brewster Aviation plant that had been built in 1941.

"Sir, why do I hold the nose high so long?" O'Brien hadn't quite lost the university habit of calling his professors 'sir.'

Captain Alexander Taylor smiled in satisfaction. He loved to have students who asked questions. It showed they were thinking about what they were doing. "It's called aerodynamic braking. We're using the undersurface of the wings as an airbrake to slow the plane down. It cuts down the landing run. This is a TB-26 with a landing parachute in the tail gunner's position; it should stop us in time without using the wings as brakes. In a standard B-26, you'd probably run into the Brewster plant. If that ever happens, do the war effort a favor and make sure you burn the place down."

"That wretched hive of scum and villainy never did any good for anybody." O'Brien agreed. The Brewster Aviation Company was notorious for its extensive vices and lack of any discernible virtues. Relations between the U.S.A.A.F and U.S. Navy personnel on one side, and Brewster Aviation employees on the other, were tense. As in 'waiting for the riot to start' tense.

O'Brien felt the bump and heard the squealing of tires as the main wheels hit the runway. The noise in the cockpit increased dramatically as the serenity of flying was replaced by cacophony of rubber rolling at very high speed down a rough concrete runway. There was another bump as the nose of the slowing aircraft dropped and left the Marauder thundering down the runway on its tricycle undercarriage. Finally, the aircraft came to a halt. O'Brien gunned the engines slightly and taxied the B-26 to the hardstand.

Taylor looked at his pad. "Well done, son. That was a damned good flight topped off by a first-class landing. As far as I'm concerned, you just qualified. The chief pilot has to approve, of course, and he may want to take you up for a check flight. But, fly the way you did this afternoon and it'll be a formality. You're done for the day. Any plans?"

"I've got an evening pass. Going off to see my girl, sir."

Taylor checked the time. It would be an hour or more before the shift at the Brewster plant changed shifts. That would give O'Brien time to pick up his girl and head into town.

"Well, watch your back. Those thugs would like to catch a serviceman on his own." Taylor wasn't certain whether he was referring to the Brewster workers or the union enforcers who hung around the plant. What he did know was that the looming air of menace that surrounded the Brewster factory didn't bode well for anybody.

Climbing out of the B-26 wasn't the easiest task in the world, but O'Brien managed it. He quickly changed out of his flight gear and into his uniform. His bicycle was stored by the flight line. It was a moment's work to release the safety chain and padlock before riding off.

Once out of the base gate, having logged his departure and told the base guard where he was going, he crossed East Street Road and set off for Willopenn Drive in Southampton. As he got further away from Warminster, the atmosphere of the area seemed to lighten and became much more friendly.

The surroundings became more pleasant as well. Warminster had been hard-hit by the Great Depression. Town development had stopped in 1929 and only resumed in 1941, when Brewster had opened its plant. The housing in Warminster reflected that; mostly the new construction was small, shoddy houses intended for the Brewster workforce.

Southampton was quite different. The housing reflected the prosperity and wealth of the 1920s. The individual buildings were much larger and were solidly built out of brick rather than cheap clapboard. Once intended for the large families that had been commonplace three decades earlier, they had mostly been divided up into apartments.

O'Brien's girlfriend, Melba Ramsey, rented one of those apartments. A small one, of course; she was the manager of a local diner and her salary was hardly that of a princess. She could make a lot more if she'd got a job at the Brewster plant, but she had dismissed the idea with the comment that she wanted to do something useful with her life.

O'Brien pedaled his bicycle into the drive of her apartment house and carefully secured it to a nearby lamppost. With gasoline rationing in place, bicycles were the preferred form of transport. The shortage of them made bicycle theft a growth industry. He knew that the irony was that gasoline rationing was in place to save tires, not fuel. Supplies of gasoline were adequate, although diesel fuel was another matter. Rubber for tires was desperately short.

"Good afternoon, Cal." One of the neighbors saw O'Brien and gave him a friendly wave. "Here to see Mellie?"

"Sure am, Mr. Sullivan. How's things going?"

"Pretty well, thank you. Yourself?"

"Just got back from a training flight." That wasn't a breach of security; everybody in the area could see the B-26s flying overhead all day.

"Well done, Cal. We're all proud of you here. Now, go see your Mellie." Sullivan smiled at him and set off for his late-afternoon walk. O'Brien noted the remark. A few years before, Mellie would have been described by her neighbors as 'fast' or 'loose,' with the more puritanical using far less complimentary descriptions. Then the long casualty lists from the Russian Front had started to come back. People now understood that all too many of the young men who were leaving for the front would never come back. So tolerance for the 'live life while you can' philosophy had grown.

Mellie's apartment was on the second floor, at the front. Although small, it was solidly built, as befitted the building's age. The conversion into apartments had been done properly as well. Some conversions had used cheap plywood or plaster-board for the divisions, but here even the interior walls had been well-built. That gave the residents a lot of privacy, something for which O'Brien was profoundly grateful.

Having finally mounted the stairs, something that came easily after getting into a B-26, he knocked on Mellie's door. There was no answer. Normally, she was in a hurry to answer his knock, so they could make the most of their time together. There was something else as well. Her door had given slightly under his knock, telling him that she hadn't fastened the lock. That was very unlike her. O'Brien pushed slightly and the door opened.

"Mellie? Darling?"

His voice echoed around the apartment, telling him that it was empty. He stepped in and looked around. O'Brien began to realize there was something wrong. The place had four rooms, a bedroom, living room, bathroom and kitchen, although the last two were closer to being glorified closets. When he stepped into the bedroom, his first glance missed the crumpled figure on the floor and he only saw her when he moved away from the door.

He ran over to her. He saw torn, blood-stained clothes. Bruises were visible on her back. He took her body in his arms and turned her over. The sight nearly made him sick. She had been so badly beaten that she was unrecognizable. Her mouth had literally been torn apart. The way her clothing had been ripped open was mute evidence of what else had happened to her. Shocked to his core, he laid her lifeless body down and went over to the telephone to call the police.

Room 650, Hotel Astor, Broadway and West 44th Street, Times Square, New York City

The telephone in Conrad's room rang insistently. He left his shower and picked up the receiver with a degree of reluctance. A good shower was something to be valued when such things were restricted. Even when living in hotels, as Conrad always did, the fuel used to heat water was rationed, and so hot showers were available only at certain times. Without saying so, Conrad privately felt that the rationing was going a little far.

"Good morning, Father Lorenz. Reception here. We have a military officer to see you. Captain Taylor from the Army Air Force. He says he hasn't an appointment."

"Thank you, Joan. Please ask Captain Taylor to wait in the lounge and tell him that I'll be down shortly. If he'd like a cup of coffee, please put it on my account." Conrad had no illusions. This was going to turn into another case for him. The only thing that he wondered about was how the Army Air Force had got itself involved.

A few minutes later, he stepped out of the lift and greeted the Army officer who had been waiting. "Captain Taylor, I believe? How may I help you?"

They sat down, Taylor taking a sip of his coffee. Another thing that was in short supply and rationed. "Father Lorenz, please call me Alex; everybody does. We have a problem at our airfield. One of our trainees, a young man named Caleb O'Brien, has been arrested and charged with the murder of a local woman."

The waitress had brought Conrad a coffee and a small plate of cookies. Conrad thanked her and looked at the captain. "Alex, please call me Conrad. I have a hunch we'll be working together. Now, let's start at the beginning. What happened?"

"Very well. I am an instructor-pilot at a training base in New Jersey. We train pilots for multi-engined aircraft. Caleb O'Brien is one of my students. One of my better students. Good kid; works hard, is very careful and meticulous. Some students leave me with white knuckles and the shakes. O'Brien never does. A few days ago, we were up for a qualification flight. Nothing complex, just what we call circuits and bumps. The only new thing was I showed him how to do a high-speed landing with an engine out. Only we didn't cut the engine. Did it well. Anyway, he had an evening pass and went off to spend it with his girl. Just like ten thousand other guys, I guess."

Conrad nodded. He could see where this was going. By the distress on Taylor's face, the Captain wasn't happy with the situation. "When he got to her apartment, she found her dead. She was in her bedroom. She had been raped and beaten to death. It was bad, really bad.

"O'Brien called the police, of course. They turned up, took one look at the scene and arrested him for the girl's murder. We managed to get him into our custody; but, before that, the local cops really worked him over."

"This O'Brien is a serving Army Air Force officer? So, he's under the jurisdiction of the Armed Services?" Conrad looked straight at Taylor. "And subject to trial by court martial?"

"That's correct, yes. I've been appointed to act in his defense. Before you ask, yes, I was a lawyer in civilian life. I have, though, come to the conclusion that bomber pilots do less damage than lawyers."

"And how can I help you?" Conrad knew by now that his footsteps had been steered to another innocent person who needed defending.

"I believe my client is innocent. I believe the case against him is very weak; almost ghostly, in fact. But the Army's taking jurisdiction away from the local police has stirred up a lot of ill-feeling. The police won't help us investigate and they refuse to look into any of the discrepancies we want to resolve. A far as they are concerned, O'Brien did it, and that's that.

"I was discussing this with our chaplain and he mentioned he'd heard of a Jesuit priest who investigated crimes where an innocent person might be accused. I found you here and came to ask your help. This case, and simple justice, need an independent, impartial, investigator."

"You do realize that means I might find your man did it?" Conrad looked severely at Taylor. "If he's guilty, what then?"

"If he's guilty? Then, after what he did to that girl, we hang him and good riddance. From one perspective, not mine, I hasten to add, that would be a good solution. You see, there's a political dimension to all this. People don't like the idea that the Army has taken the case over and are trying the accused. There are already accusations of cover-ups and whitewashes. If O'Brien is found guilty and hanged, all that potential grief goes away. If he gets acquitted, then we'll really have trouble.

"There's already a lot of tension between the Armed Forces personnel and the local community, especially where the Brewster plant is concerned. We could be looking at rioting, and the local police turning their backs. There's an old military tradition of taking one for the team. I don't want my client to be doing the taking."

"And there is the other point of course." Conrad knew he was hooked. "If O'Brien is wrongfully convicted, then the real murderer walks away."

"There's that." Taylor looked grim. "Frankly, you'll be doing a big service to everybody if you can sort this out. Nobody's going to accuse a priest of wrongdoing."

I'm not so sure of that. "And, I suppose it would help the war effort?"

"Not as much as you might think." Taylor sounded grimly amused. "The major war industry in the area is the Brewster Aviation Corporation plant in Warminster Township. They started off building Buffalos for the Navy, then shifted to the Buccaneer. Recently, they got a contract to build Corsairs for the Navy and Marines."

"I've heard of the Buffalo and Corsair, of course. Never heard of the Buccaneer."

"I'm not surprised. The Brewster SB2A Buccaneer is a truly terrible aircraft. Overweight, underpowered, and lacking maneuverability.

Workmanship is extraordinarily bad and they're years late. The Navy won't fly them and is using them to test catapults. There's a reason why the Army won't do business with Brewster. I doubt if the company has produced single aircraft of any value to the war effort."

"That's harsh. And I suppose the problems with Brewster are exacerbating the tension between the local people and the service personnel?"

Taylor hesitated. "I don't know if that's true. All I can say is that if our personnel go off-base, we suggest they stay in groups of four or more or get out of Warminster Township as fast as they can."

"Where did this murder take place?"

"Southampton. It's down Route 132. Technically, Southampton is the old part of town, Warminster Township is a sort of outgrowth. They share a police department, by the way. The whole community is about 15 miles due west of Trenton. Just on the Pennsylvania side of the state line."

"I suppose the police department recruits mostly from Warminster?"

"They surely do."

"Thank you, Captain. I'll come down to the area later today and have a look at this. By the way, what was the victim's name?"

"Melba Ramsey. Nice girl by all accounts, although a little too friendly with the men around her, if you get my drift. O'Brien fell for her pretty hard. Kept a picture of her in the cockpit of the aircraft he was flying.

"Oh, one more thing you should know. She was six weeks pregnant when she was killed. Baby died with her, of course. The local police are claiming that as the motive. Say she told O'Brien she was expecting and demanded he marry her. He decided killing her would be easier."

"It happens." Conrad was sadly aware of how often. "You say he was smitten with her, though?"

"Sure. And I'll tell you something else. This kid is cool.

"The Marauder is a tricky bird to fly. When things go sour, they go very sour very quickly indeed. Couple of times, that happened when O'Brien was at the controls. He stayed cool and did the drills to get out of the coffin corner. Just like his is supposed to do.

"If Ramsey had been found as the victim of a carefully planned, regrettable accident, I'd say there was a chance he did it. But this kid doesn't panic. A clumsy, stupid murder like this just doesn't ring true."

Conrad's Other Eye

"And just who the hell are you?" Police Chief Bernard Schultz was nearly purple with rage.

"My name is Conrad Lorenz and I am a member of the Society of Jesus. I also work for the Clarkson Foundation. It's a charitable group dedicated to defending people who have been wrongly accused of a crime. Our founder was a very wealthy man who was wrongly accused of murdering his wife. He would have been executed for doing so; only, two days before the execution, she was arrested for speeding in another state. Our representatives have a lot of discretion in the cases we take on and the circumstances surrounding the rape and murder of Melba Ramsey concern me greatly."

The story came out with the benefit of much practice. It had the advantage of being true. It had to be. Conrad very rarely lied, and always paid penance for the times he had to, although he had to admit that he was sometimes economical with the truth. The Clarkson Foundation did exist, and it was named after a man who had been nearly executed for murdering his wife, only to be saved by her being arrested in another state.

The singular problem was that Conrad was the only member of said foundation.

Lillith had created it to cover his expenses and guarantee him an income. Conrad had saved so many people over the years, and they had remembered him so generously, that his foundation was quite wealthy. Lillith's inspired money management had made him more so. This had conflicted with his vows of poverty. *Igrat convinced me that my stipend from the foundation really was poverty compared with the money my benefactors had given me, but I suppose Igrat can convince anybody of anything. She can talk the Devil out of his horns and probably has.*

"Me too, and I'm not going to let the bastard who did for her walk away. You know she was pregnant? That swine killed the baby as well."

"I have heard the tragic fact that the most common cause of pre-natal death for infants is murder of the mother by the father." Conrad thought he had heard that somewhere, but he wasn't sure if it was true or not. *If I don't find out, it's not lying if I repeat it.* "If Caleb O'Brien really is the killer, then his soul has a terrible burden on it. But is he?"

"I don't know how you amateur detectives think, but, round here, we find a man standing over the body of a butchered woman, soaked in her blood, it's certain odds he did it. You see what he did to her? Every bone in her face was broken and most of her teeth knocked out. I promise you this, Father, that bastard is going down."

"He claims she was already dead when he found her; his uniform was bloodied when he turned her over to see if there was anything he could do for her. Air crew are all trained in first aid, you know."

"First aid." Schultz shook his head and sighed. His temper seemed to subside a little. "Will you come with me? The coroner's office and the morgue are just around the back."

It was plain from his tone that his words were not a request. He led the way out of the police station, across the parking lot at the back and into another modern building behind that. Conrad looked around; everything seemed new, as if it had been built just before the war had started.

"We just squeezed by the construction halt." Schultz must have guessed what Conrad was thinking. "The old police station was built in 1870 and the Coroner's Office was a single room in the hospital. Now, we have a proper facility and a real morgue."

"Coroner is in the examination theater, Chief Schultz." The receptionist looked up with a bright smile on her face that quickly faded when she saw Conrad.

"This is Father Conrad Lorenz. He's a visitor. Give him the correct ID pass please, Monica."

Conrad hung the badge around his neck and followed Schultz into the examination theater. "This is Doctor Fischer, our Chief Coroner for Bucks County. He did the work on Melba Ramsey himself."

"Conrad Lorenz. I've been asked by the officer defending Lieutenant O'Brien to look into the evidence being presented against him."

"Goddamned Army, trying to get one of their own off." Chief Schultz was working himself up into a temper again. Conrad glanced at Fischer, seeing him catch his breath slightly. *There is more going on here than it appears.* It seemed to Conrad that the coroner had a lot more to say than he was willing to reveal.

"What was the cause of death, Doctor?"

"Asphyxia, combined with massive blunt force trauma. In simple terms, her broken ribs lacerated her lungs and she drowned in her own blood. That was exacerbated by bleeding from her facial wounds. Both cheekbones broken, her jaw broken in several places, most of her teeth knocked out. All the blood from those wounds went down her throat and accelerated her drowning. That was a mercy, in a way. She'd suffered enough by then."

"What was the time of death?"

"We think around four." Fischer glanced for support at Schultz and received a slight nod in return. "Yeah, about four."

Schultz reached out and pulled the sheet covering the body back. The head and face were hideously distorted by the beating the victim had received. One of Conrad's deep regrets was how novels and films trivialized beatings. Somebody would be hit over the head with a club or a gun barrel and a couple of minutes later they'd be none the worse for the experience. He believed if people knew what that sort of attack really did to its victims, they'd be less keen to swing the blows.

Schultz looked at him with something very close to derision on his face. "You think first aid will fix that?"

"In his statement, O'Brien said that he saw injuries on her back. Could you turn her over please, so I could see those?"

"Why should we help you?" The brief burst of comparative amiability from Schultz had gone. He was back to his previous hectoring demeanor.

"There is nobody left to speak for Melba Ramsey but her body, the coroner and myself. It is the duty of every priest to speak for those who cannot speak for themselves. Just as it is the coroner's duty to allow her remains to speak for her."

Conrad's words had put some steel into Doctor Fischer. He ignored the protests from Schultz and rolled Ramsey's body on to its side. The thick stripes of heavy black bruising across her back were clearly visible. Conrad looked at them carefully, noting their thickness and even spacing. "I'd say some form of round club, wouldn't you? A baseball bat perhaps?"

Fischer nodded. "She was hit repeatedly across the back. This was a prolonged, vicious beating."

Conrad looked sharply at the Doctor, realizing he had been given a distinct hint that there was much more to be told. "Did she put up a fight? Anything under her fingernails?"

"There were traces of blood and tissue. She scratched her assailant, quite badly I would think."

"So she was attacked, fought back, was beaten to the ground, then raped. When the rapist finished with her, he took the bat he had used before and pounded her head until she died. Do you think that sounds reasonable?"

Schultz tried to protest. Conrad simply stared him down. Fischer thought carefully. "The wounds on her back are definitely pre-mortem. The rest took place about the time she died. I can't be more accurate than that."

"So there was enough of a time interval between the first set of injuries and the ones that killed her to be able to distinguish between them?"

"Oh, yes. At least an hour."

"Which, based on your time of death estimate of four o'clock, means that the attack on her started no later than three. At which time, Lieutenant Caleb O'Brien was performing a training flight in a B-26 Marauder." Conrad stared very hard at Chief Schultz. "Your case has a problem."

Detention Block, Warrington Field, Warminster, Pennsylvania

Caleb O'Brien had a black eye and heavy bruises on his cheeks and mouth. He also had surgical tape over his nose. He was sitting at the table in the interrogation room and was a very angry man. "Thank you for coming, Father. Can you really help me?"

Conrad smiled at the sight of a young man who had tried to put his anger and resentment to one side in order to be polite to his visitor. "From what I have seen to date, I don't think you need much help. However, we have to take this logically. The first thing we need to do is to construct a timeline for the events of the afternoon. One that we can prove, step by step."

"The Air Force Police here will be at your disposal, Father." Colonel Clifford Reyes had followed Conrad and Taylor in. "Just tell them what we need to do."

"We do need to make sure the local police are involved in the investigation. All the way, at each step. That way they won't be able to claim we've been covering things up." Taylor looked at the group defensively, expecting to be howled down. In Army eyes, the local police had hardly put on a convincing performance to date. Conrad could sympathize. *In fairness to the Army, the local police have been negligent to the point of co-conspiracy.* That thought made Conrad look at things a different way.

"They'll block us every step of the way. They've made their minds up." O'Brien didn't add 'just look at me' to illustrate that, but he might as well have.

"Well, we'll have to make sure they don't get the chance." Conrad sounded grim. He touched his priestly collar. "This tends to make people a bit more honest. Anyway, when did your aircraft land?"

"We were on the parking stands and shutting down at 1530." Taylor had the flight log to hand. "We'd been up for almost four hours. We were doing a simulated mission that ended with bringing in a damaged aircraft. O'Brien landed fine. We have the flight log, the tower log and the CAA civil record, all agreeing on 1530."

"CAA?" Conrad was confused. Government agencies weren't in his area of expertise. With the war roaring along at full force, there were so many now even the expetrs lost track of who did what.

"Civil Aviation Authority. Warrington was a civilian field pre-war and there are still civilian flights out of here. So, the tower has a CAA log as well as a military one."

"That's convenient. What happened then?"

"I went to my quarters, changed quickly out of my flight gear and took my bicycle to ride down to Mellie's place. I logged out of the base at the main gate and cycled down to Southampton."

"Didn't take a shower or anything first?" Conrad knew very few men who would go to meet their girls without cleaning up first.

O'Brien went brilliant red. "Ummm, Father, we'd take a shower together when I got there. I'd take a clean shirt and skivvies with me."

He looked up, expecting to see a thunderous look of disapproval on Conrad's face. Instead, Conrad was smiling gently. "Saves hot water, of course."

A laugh ran around the room. Conrad saw O'Brien's anger fading. *Time for the sensitive questions.* "When did you get to her rooming house?"

"About ten past four. It's a 25-minute bike ride, assuming nothing goes wrong. After sitting in a B-26 for four hours, it's good to get the kinks out of my back."

"Did anybody see you arrive?"

"Yes, Mr. Sullivan. He lives in a ground floor apartment at the back. That's how I know I arrived after four. He likes to listen to the radio, but he really doesn't like *The Falcon,* so he goes for his afternoon walk while it's on."

"We'll have to talk to Mr. Sullivan." Conrad made the remark and Taylor noted it down for action. "What happened then?"

"I went in, went upstairs. Mellie's door was open and I went in. She was on the floor, face down. I saw she was a hell of a mess, but there was a chance she might be alive. I could see what had happened . . ." O'Brien's voice cracked and he dropped his face into his hands.

"This is a delicate question, Caleb, but did you know she was pregnant?" Conrad asked gently and the switch to using O'Brien's first name was deliberate.

"Yes. Well, she told me the previous week that she was late and she thought she was."

"What did you do?"

"I bought a ring and asked her to marry me." O'Brien's voice had picked up again and he was defiant. "She wasn't sure. The test result hadn't come back yet. She put the ring in her bedside drawer and said she'd give me her answer when we knew one way or the other."

"Are you sure you are the father?" Taylor made the query to Conrad's annoyance. It had broken his carefully-constructed stream of questions.

"Caleb, there is an old saying. Motherhood is a fact, fatherhood is an opinion. What is your opinion?"

"I think the child was mine. Mellie had a reputation, I know that. She told me I was the only candidate and I believed her. I put the paperwork in for permission to marry a few days ago. And, the baby was a gift from God. You know what the casualty rate on the Russian Front is like? A baby already on the way, it means that I had a legacy even if . . . "

Colonel Reyes picked up the telephone and called personnel. He spoke quietly for a few minutes, waited for an answer and hung up. "Checks out. O'Brien put the papers in two days before the murder. They're marked RFP."

"RFP?" Conrad hadn't heard that one.

"Officially, and if civilians ask, it means Russian Front Priority. It really means Reports Fiancée Pregnant. Means the same thing: 'get this paperwork through the system fast.' We had to check the girl out, of course, but we'd run the whole process in a week or two. So the couple could be married before the baby started to show."

"Colonel, the paperwork you asked for, sir." A military policeman had brought a couple of files in. One was O'Brien's request for permission to marry; the other was the main gate log. Reyes flipped through both and gave them to Conrad who read them more carefully.

"The log shows you checked out through the main gate at 1546. We need to find out if you could have made that bicycle ride in less than 25 minutes. It could be argued you rode like hell, got there in ten minutes, slipped in, killed Mellie, slipped outside again and then pretended to arrive a few minutes later."

"That's impossible." O'Brien's outburst was quite genuine. "Nobody could do that."

"We have to discount it as a theory. It is a very bad theory and it doesn't address the main problem, which is that the attack on Mellie started while you were airborne. But, we need to prove it couldn't be done."

"I've looked at a map. It looks impossible to me." Taylor sounded thoughtful.

"I'll look as well but we'll need more than that."

"What have you in mind?" Taylor was curious.

"A bicycle race. Four airmen against four policemen. The course extends a bit beyond the murder scene to make it less obvious what we're up to but we time how long the contestants take. That'll tell us."

"The police will never agree to that. Chief Schultz won't allow anything that will compromise his case." O'Brien sounded bitter.

"Oh, I think I can motivate them." Conrad seemed to be almost smirking. "I'll need to be in Washington tomorrow. If you've got a liaison plane going that way, I'd like to thumb a ride."

Colonel Reyes picked up the telephone again and spoke briefly. "If you don't mind riding on a B-26, we've got one going down to Camp Springs Army Air Base tomorrow morning. Leaves here at 0800, return flight at 1730."

Lillith's Office, Economic Intelligence and Warfare Department, Blair House, Washington, D.C.

"Will ribeyes do? On the bone?" Lillith looked at a file marked Top Secret. It contained details of the beef output from a farm in Kansas owned by the Washington Circle. "I can let you have eight twelve-ounce steaks."

"That's just what we need." Conrad was relieved. A box containing six pounds of chilled ribeyes would be a prize that would cause any team of bicyclists to strain themselves to the utmost. It would also cause Chief Schultz to be lynched by his officers if he tried to prevent them from winning it. "Are you sure this will be all right?"

"You mean, cause us problems with the OPA?" Lillith thought for a second. "Not really. We're fulfilling our beef delivery contract with the Army and technically what's left over is ours. The Office of Price Administration knows we're donating beef from that surplus to military hospitals and so on, so the amount we use ourselves is small. If we were selling it, that would be different, of course. OPA is really concerned with prices and black marketeering, and we're giving the stuff away, so they're not interested in us."

Conrad wasn't surprised at the explanation; he was well-aware that Lillith had not found a financial regulation yet she couldn't drive a whole wagon train of coaches and horses through. Meat rationing was one of the things that most upset civilians in America; being limited to buying two and a half pounds of meat a week at controlled prices was a constant source of complaints.

That was the logic behind the prize for the bicycle race he was organizing. People could buy more than the two and a half pounds, but they had to pay uncontrolled prices; those were many times higher than the controlled price. The prospect of six pounds of free, off-the-ration steaks would make mouths water.

"What are you up to anyway, Conrad?" Lillith was curious.

Conrad took a deep breath and explained the situation. "So, if we want to avoid political problems, we have to dot every I and cross every T. I know O'Brien didn't do it, and so do the local police, but they went public with the arrest and now don't want to admit they jumped the gun. They'd rather allege an Army cover-up than tell people they made a mistake.

"We need to find out how quickly O'Brien could have got from his base to his girlfriend's home. The best way to do that is a bicycle race involving the local Warminster police. We're pitching it as a challenge from the enlisted airmen to the local police officers."

"Warminster." Lillith looked up sharply. "That name's familiar. Is there an aircraft plant nearby?"

"Brewster Aviation."

"Well, now isn't that interesting. I've been looking into that company recently." Listening to Lillith, Conrad got the distinct impression that accountants across New Jersey and Pennsylvania had just started whimpering.

"Fraud?"

"That would be a polite name for it." Lillith was rooting through a filing cabinet. "Here we are. Brewster Aviation Company. Winner of the 1944 Biti-Anat Award for the worst-run company in these here United States. Or, so I thought at the time. I've changed my opinion since then. The problems with Brewster go far beyond just being badly run, although that's a large part of it. Conrad, you haven't asked the important questions. If your friend O'Brien didn't kill the girl, who did? And why?"

"I just want to make sure an innocent man is exonerated." Conrad recited the phrase with the certainty of dogma.

"But you won't have, will you? If you don't find out who, and why, he'll always be the man who beat his pregnant girlfriend to death and got away with it. Talking about pregnancy, wasn't the child she was carrying innocent as well?"

Conrad knew that the discussion was taking them into sensitive ground. Lillith's own three children had been brutally murdered as infants and the assassins had made a good try at killing her as well. That was why she limped when she walked and sat down whenever she could. "The child is the ultimate innocent, yes. Which is why its death makes me all the more determined to see an innocent man is not charged with its killing. For that would mean the guilty man has walked free."

"Have you any idea why Melba Ramsey was killed yet?" Lillith's eyes showed that Conrad's comments had struck a chord with her. Now she was determined to help him.

"There are the classic murder motives for the 'why' question. Killings always boil down to one of money, sex, revenge and silence. Anything outside those is very unusual. We know that Melba Ramsey wasn't robbed. There was money and jewelry in her rooms. Including, by the way, the engagement ring O'Brien gave her. The police had found it, but they didn't realize its significance. That leaves sex, revenge or silencing her." Conrad hesitated slightly. *No matter how one moves in this case, the focus always shifts to Brewster Aviation.* "What's the matter with Brewster anyway?"

"Other than the fact that their aircraft production per employee is thirty times lower than the national average? *Thirty times!* Or that the aircraft they do manage to produce are useless? They're becoming a services-wide scandal and a stain on the entire war effort." Lillith drove the passion out of her voice with obvious effort.

"Look, Conrad, I don't know much about military aircraft, but I know somebody who does. He works with me on the Brewster investigation. Why don't we go and see him while I get your steaks sent over? When do you have to leave?"

"Five-thirty this evening. I got a lift on a B-26."

"That's brave of you. We got plenty of time, then. I'll take you to see Timmy and he can give you an insight into what is going on in that Warminster plant."

CHAPTER TWO
CORRUPTION?

Washington Field Office, Investigations Division, War Production Board, Washington, D.C.

"Timmy, can you spare a few minutes to tell Father Lorenz here about Brewster Aviation?" Lillith limped into Colonel Timothy Hammond's office. She had, in fact, called in advance to arrange the meeting.

Hammond jumped up with a beam of pleasure on his face and seated her. Then he took note of Conrad's cloth. "Oh my. Please tell me the entire management and workforce of Brewster Aviation are about to be excommunicated? They certainly deserve it."

"I think that's a bit beyond my authority." Conrad was getting the distinct impression that Brewster Aviation had all the popularity of a turd floating in a swimming pool. "What did they do?"

"Where do I start?" Hammond seemed to be a bit bemused by the question. "Well, they had a problem with foreign objects being left inside completed aircraft. So, instead of improving supervision of the workforce, they designed *and built* a rig to turn the completed aircraft upside down and shake them. We've had sabotage on the line, including aircraft with important components such as control runs cut and landing gear compromised.

"I'll give you an example. A Navy fighter called the Buffalo had a series of problems when it entered service with the hook refusing to catch the wire. This was new; it hadn't happened when the Navy qualified it to operate off carriers. Investigation found that knife cuts were being made in a rubber grommet that was part of the arresting system. The cuts let the grommet expand and the hook would disengage after the initial capture.

"When the Navy went after Brewster with murder in its heart, they found that the way they were building the airplanes, nobody knew who was responsible for what part of the construction process. That particular case of sabotage ended up being blamed on a disgruntled, departed employee, and the problems stopped for a while. There were also problems with landing gear collapses being blamed on weakened/damaged parts, but the Navy still hasn't sorted out whether this was sabotage, incompetence or just bad suppliers.

"Things got really bad when Brewster got orders for a new dive-bomber. The Navy call it the SB2A or the Buccaneer. Once that started to enter service, the problems returned. Inspectors, and worse, aircrews in flight, discovered cuts in control and throttle cables, tools and scrap jammed in controls and moving surfaces, intentional omission of parts and work left undone. No matter how you classify it, there are people working hard to keep Brewster planes from being safe."

"One thing I don't understand about this. If all these problems affected Navy aircraft, how did the Army get involved?"

"Firstly, contrary to many opinions, we and the Navy do speak to each other. Sometimes. So, when the Navy started hitting problems with Brewster, they unofficially asked us if we had similar problems with any of our contractors. You see, the Navy primarily deal with Boeing, Curtiss and Grumman, all solid, reliable people. Our people are pretty solid as well. We have workmanship problems sometimes, everybody does, but even our new contractor, Bell, has worked out pretty well. That's what we told the Navy. But, when Brewster approached us with an offer to build dive-bombers for our attack squadrons, the questions from the Navy made us very suspicious very quickly. They wanted to build a land-based version of the SB2A.

"We played along. Gave it the designation A-34, then started to ask awkward questions about how, if they couldn't keep up with Navy orders, how could they build for us as well? They told us that they would back-burner Navy orders in favor of ours. Now, that really told us something bad was happening, because prioritizing orders is done here, not at the factories. We were quite surprised to find that the Navy weren't too upset. They'd pretty much given up on the SB2A and were firing the ones they'd received over the side to test the catapults on new carriers. Their attitude was that they'd take them if they got any, because they could use them for hack work and free up a more useful airframe for important duties, but that was it.

"By that time, we were getting acquainted with the Brewster production facilities and what was going on in them. The first day we had people on-site, the United Auto Workers Local 365 struck the plant for four days, at a cost of 240,000 man-hours, the time it would have taken to build 20 planes. The cause was that the security guards had not been allowed to choose their posts, front gate or bathrooms. We found out why that was an issue. Male employees at the plant were using the bathrooms to have sex with women workers. Inside aircraft fuselages as well, and not all the women were willing. Some were carrying sharpened screwdrivers to protect themselves.

"When we took the issue up with the union local's president, Thomas V. DeLorenzo, he told us that he would let American kids on the front line in Russia die, if necessary, as long as that meant he got to 'preserve the rights of his union.' The whole plant was ludicrously overstaffed, and it seemed to us that the union and management were colluding to put draft-aged relatives of their workforce into the plant to keep them out the Army. When pressure was applied to increase production rates, rival shifts started hiding parts from each other. Stealing parts and equipment was rampant."

"Anyway, we told Brewster that their A-34 wasn't wanted by us and we could see no use for it. They then tried to get us to order it as aid for the Russians. That's when their president, a man called James Work, really stepped on his dick. Sorry, Lillith. He tried to bribe our people to place aid orders for the A-34. That did it. We told the Brewster Aviation Company that we wanted no part of them or their products. The hostility from the plant we've had since then is overwhelming. Army personnel leaving the Warrington Field base are advised to stick together in groups of four or more or they'll get the . . . stuffing . . . beaten out of them."

"I do know the words, Timmy." Lillith sounded amused and slightly bored.

Hammond flushed slightly with embarrassment. The Economic Intelligence and Warfare Department was notorious for both the number of women in its ranks and their seniority. It was also now accepted that they held those posts because they were exceptionally capable at their duties. Even so, the idea of women working in senior positions of a government agency was still new enough to cause etiquette problems.

"I know, but . . ." Hammond smiled. "Every time I think of using one in front of you or your colleagues, I can feel my mother boxing my ears."

Lillith gave him an amiable smile. "Can't argue with that."

"Something occurs to me." Conrad had been putting the pieces together in his mind. "We have a plant that has a history of demonstrating a serious sabotage problem, one that is consuming resources without any real output to justify them. Are you sure there is no hostile involvement here?"

"I told you he was good." Lillith had the insufferably self-righteous tone she adopted sometimes when she had been proved right after promoting an unlikely idea.

"By hostile, you mean German fifth columnists? What makes you think that?" Hammond leaned forward a little.

Conrad marshaled his thoughts for a second. "The sabotage, mostly. It's way beyond anything bad industrial relations would induce. Also the hostility towards servicemen. The two together suggest that what's going on in the Brewster plant is being induced from outside."

"That's exactly what we thought. Father Lorenz, our country is at war and we need every skilled expert we can find. While Lillith was bringing you down here, I looked up some references she gave me. You have quite a reputation as a skilled investigator. We could use your services in our Investigations Division. That would put your working with Captain Taylor on an official basis."

"I'm sorry, but I can't do that. I will help you as much as I can, but I can't become part of a government investigations branch."

"Come on, Conrad. We're all doing what we can to help the war effort." Lillith was doing her best to imitate Igrat's persuasive manner and failing dismally. It wasn't surprising; Igrat was unique. "Look on it as becoming an inquisitor."

"Lillith, that's unfair." Hammond seemed embarrassed. "I don't expect the Spanish Inquisition. Just some help investigating disruptions to the war effort.

"Nobody expects the Spanish Inquisition." Conrad sighed.

"We could draft you into the Chaplain's Corps." Hammond made the proposal tentatively.

"Wouldn't help much, I'm afraid. Look, my over-riding objective is to protect the innocent and ensure that people who are charged are not being falsely accused. I'll do whatever I can to help you, but not as an employee. If you'd like to use me as a consultant, fine, but that's as far as I can go."

"That sounds fair, Timmy. A lot of us at the Economic Intelligence and Warfare Department work that way. Even The Seer. We have contracts that pay us a dollar a year retainer until the war is over."

"I'll have to talk to our paymasters about that. In the meantime, could you please help us on this, Father Lorenz?"

"Certainly. We have a congruence of interests on this. As Lillith pointed out, if we don't find who killed Melba Ramsey and why, Lieutenant O'Brien will spend the rest of his life with that shadow hanging over him. Now, can you tell me if there has been any other record of sabotage in US aircraft factories?"

"No, none. It sounds incredible but there have not. The Germans tried to organize a sabotage attack last year. They landed two teams of four saboteurs, one on Long Island, the other in Florida. They really weren't very good. The team in Florida was caught when one of them gave a fellow traveler on a train a match. It was a Belgian box of matches.

"The Long Island team included two members who had independently decided to defect to us and handed over the rest. They got life inside; the other six went to the electric chair. And that's all she wrote. We got both U-boats that landed the teams, by the way. Well . . . we got one; the Canadians got the other one."

"So, if the Brewster business is political sabotage . . . ."

"The word you are looking for is treason." Hammond was very firm and emphatic.

"Fair enough. Treason. If production there is being disrupted for treasonous motives, it's a home-grown business." Conrad's eyes hardened. "From what I've seen, there's a lot of German ancestry up there."

"There is, and you don't have to worry about them." Hammond was very firm. "Their sons are lining up outside recruiting offices to volunteer and, even before the war, any German-American Bund people who tried peddling their ideas in that area got their asses handed to them. The ones we have to worry about are recent immigrants. We had a lot of Germans coming into the country in the 1920s and they still have 'ideas' about their homelands. That's where the German-American Bund got its support."

Centuries of practice kept Conrad and Lillith from smiling. The terrible fate that Igrat had handed out to one German-American Bund leader had become the stuff of legend. Overnight, she had reduced the man from a swaggering political rabble-rouser to a destitute street bum in Mexico. Mexico was not a good place to be a destitute street bum.

"So, why doesn't the Army or Navy intelligence services put somebody in there to find out what was going on?" Lillith was feeling a bit left out.

"Not our jurisdiction." Hammond shook his head. "The Counter-Intelligence Corps is tasked with investigations of possible sabotage and subversion and allegations of disloyalty, especially those directed against Americans of Japanese, Italian or German ancestry. Anyway, CIC sent an agent in with orders to make contacts throughout the area and gauge the possibility of illegal activities."

Conrad put all the bits together and came up with an answer to one of the questions that had plagued him. "Melba Ramsey was your agent, wasn't she? That's why she was killed."

The nod from Hammond was enough. "Did Melba Ramsey know what she was getting herself into?"

Conrad was perturbed by the news about the woman. In his initial investigations, he'd found she was considered promiscuous and had too many male 'friends' for local acceptance. If the information he had been given was accurate, it would appear that she had deliberately sacrificed her reputation, and probably her self-respect, in order to aid the war effort.

"She did. She was a very brave and dedicated young woman. When she accepted the assignment, we told her that if she wanted out, it would take a single telephone call. She'd be extracted, no questions asked.

"We got that call about a week before she was murdered. She'd met an Army Air Force pilot and genuinely fallen in love with him. She'd stopped sleeping around already; and, when she found she was expecting, she decided to end the operation. We were looking for her replacement when the news of her death came in."

Colonel Roy Cooper had the file on the Brewster Aviation investigation opened. "I know it's distasteful and I deeply regret having to order an operation of this kind. I have daughters of my own. But, sometimes this kind of operation is the only way to get to the truth of what is going on."

"Did she give you any idea of what she had discovered?"

Cooper shook his head. "She made regular reports, of course, and we would have given her a thorough debriefing when she had been brought in from the cold. We never got that of course. She said that the rot in Brewster Aviation went far deeper than anybody had thought but didn't elaborate."

Privately, Conrad thought that Melba had been poorly trained for the work she had been undertaking. *If Igrat had been in her position, she would have made sure everything she'd found out was on record somewhere. Not to mention the fact that if somebody tried to rape and murder Igrat, the attacker would have been found stretched out on the floor with some small but very lethal knife wounds in him.*

"I would have thought she would have left some messages or logs somewhere?"

"So did we. Our agents are trained to, but she didn't. Not that we haven't looked." Cooper looked suspiciously at Conrad. "You know the intelligence business well?"

"I'm a member of the Society of Jesus, a Jesuit. We've been doing intelligence stuff for centuries before the USA was even founded."

"Ahh, yes, that would explain it." Cooper was being facetious but then started to think it over and decided Conrad was probably telling nothing but the cold, hard truth.

"There's a reason why we might not be able to find her messages. We've assumed that her injuries were sustained while she was being assaulted. Perhaps, she was interrogated, broke under the pressure and told her attackers where she'd hidden them. The subsequent rape and murder were just to cover that up."

"That," said Cooper, "sounds depressingly probable."

Main Gate, Warrington Field, Warminster, Pennsylvania

"And the winner of the grand prize for the 5-mile bicycle race from the Nativity of our Lord Church to the Bible Baptist Church is . . . Officer Thomas Banks, with a winning time of 18 minutes. Tom, please come up and collect your prize donated by the Kansas Cattle Ranch Company."

The police officer, still panting after his efforts, stepped up and took the box from Chief Schultz. He opened it to display the contents to the crowd before giving each of the other three members of the Police Team one of the four packets of two steaks. Conrad saw that Lillith had done them proud; if those were twelve-ounce steaks, they were the largest ounces Conrad had ever encountered. The two teams were exchanging handshakes in probably the friendliest exchanges there had been between Warminster Police and Warrington Army personnel in months.

Chief Schultz made his way over to where Conrad and Captain Taylor were standing. "All right. You win. There's no way in hell O'Brien could have made it from the main gate to the girl's apartment in the twenty minutes he had and still have had time to do the killing. He must have pedaled like mad to get there as fast as he did."

"We all won, Chief Schultz." Conrad was gently reproving. "Now that we have O'Brien excluded, we can try and find out who really killed Melba Ramsey. And why."

"We know why. It was a rape-murder. We're looking for a pervert." Schultz was back to his aggressively hectoring manner.

"Are any such men known to you in this county?" Conrad asked the question in his normal, soft and polite tones, but there was an unmistakable hint of steel in his voice.

"Of course not, this is a peaceful community of good people. Are you trying to suggest one of them could have done this?"

"No," Conrad said, still keeping his voice soft and polite. "You just did."

"What?" Schultz was stunned by the comment.

"Has to be somebody from the community." Captain Taylor was enjoying watching how Conrad handled the aggressive police chief. "There's a war on, you know. People have a real hard time travelling outside their immediate vicinity. Whoever did this to Melba Ramsey lives right here. Now, you know the area, Chief; who should we be looking at?"

Conrad actually felt sympathetic towards Chief Schultz as that huge anvil descended from the clear, blue skies and struck the police chief soundly on the head. *He has just realized that, if O'Brien didn't kill Melba Ramsey, somebody from this community did and that person is still out there. To murder a young woman so brutally means he is a very dangerous person and he could very easily kill again. He's a danger to everybody, and that includes the chief's own family.*

Schultz was looking very thoughtful as the implications of the situation sank in. "There are a few men here I'd look at. You probably can guess the type. The ones whose wives are accident-prone, after their husband has been drinking. In fact, we had better start talking to them. I heard that Mellie Ramsey was a little too friendly with the men of her acquaintance, if you get my drift. Perhaps, when she was late and found out why, she threatened to tell the father's wife? And he silenced her."

"There's a problem with that theory." Conrad's dedication to protecting the innocent wouldn't allow him to let the false assumption pass. "O'Brien was the father, she had already told him and he was going to do the right thing. He'd already bought her the ring."

"So he says." Schultz was reverting to his original persona again, to Conrad's annoyance. *Every time I think I have made some progress with this man, he reverses course. Truly, two steps forward and three back.*

"I believe the engagement ring was actually found in her apartment." Captain Taylor also sounded frustrated with Schultz's obduracy.

"A ring was found." Schultz made the admission grudgingly.

"Please deliver it, and any other evidence you may have found to the Army Air Force Police." Taylor had had enough and Conrad didn't blame him in the slightest. "We are the investigating authority here now."

"Not any more. O'Brien is off the hook. You said so yourself. So this reverts to us."

"Not correct. Melba Ramsey was engaged to be married to an Army pilot. The paperwork had been filed and she was already listed as his next of kin. Therefore, she was an Army Air Force dependent, and, therefore, falls under our jurisdiction. So much so that obstructing our investigation is a Federal offense and, if it continues, you'll have the FBI down here in our place. And, I can assure you, the FBI will not give up this investigation until every stone, no matter how tiny, has been turned over."

Schultz went white and stomped away. Taylor watched him curiously. "Now, I wonder what he is hiding."

"Is that true?" Conrad was curious.

"Which bit, Conrad? About us treating fiancés as dependents, it's true. We're losing so many young men on the Russian Front, we had to do something about looking after their loved ones." Taylor hesitated and looked around carefully. "And not all the significant others are women. A few are men married to or engaged to servicewomen but the rest . . . Well, the Army needs men to fill the ranks and they aren't asking as many questions as they used to.

As long as nobody actually says anything. . . The bit about us retaining the case though, that's a misstatement of fact. In fact, local police can retain jurisdiction, although for how much longer is another matter. And there's no way the FBI would get involved."

"This war is changing the country." Conrad was thoughtful. "It'll never be the same again."

"It's not the war, Conrad. It's the Russian Front. That bloodbath is changing everything and not all the changes are for the worse. Have you spoken with the veterans coming back? They call themselves the Frontoviki. We get a lot of them as instructors; tour over there has finished, so they come back to pass on the lessons to the students, then get tour or two in the Pacific.

"All they care about is whether you're one of them or not. If somebody has been on the Russian Front, they don't care who or what they are. They're one of them, a Frontoviki. If they haven't been on the Russian Front, they're not worth worrying about. Anyway, where do we start?"

Conrad thought carefully. "I want to see the room where Ramsey lived and where her body was found. I assume the crime scene has been preserved?"

"I hope so." Taylor didn't sound convinced. "We're about done here. Why don't we go and see?"

Melba Ramsey's Apartment, Willopenn Drive, Southampton, Pennsylvania

To Conrad's surprise, the apartment had been taped off and the door locked. O'Brien had given them his key. Even if he hadn't been confined to base, he'd said he didn't want to go back there. Conrad could understand that.

"Excuse me, what are you gentlemen doing here? Oh, sorry, Father."

"And you are?" Captain Taylor looked at the man who had approached them. Behind Taylor, two burly Air Force Policemen edged slightly forward.

"I'm Frank Sullivan. I live here."

"Thank you for coming over, Mr. Sullivan." Conrad sounded sincerely grateful, although his gratitude was directed at God for dropping this highly convenient meeting into his lap. "If you have a few minutes, I wonder if you could help us clear up a few points about the terrible events here."

Sullivan frowned slightly. "I've told the Warminster Police everything I know. Do I have to go over it again?"

"If you wouldn't mind, sir." Taylor's manner had all the grace and courtesy one might expect of a man descended from noble Spanish ancestry. Conrad, who knewn real Spanish aristocrats and what they were capable of doing, wasn't fooled for a minute. "We have to make sure that the information passed to us by the Warminster Police is as complete as possible. Since we're Army Air Force, some things that are important to us are meaningless to them, and vice versa. You know how these things are."

"Ah, I see. Of course."

"You're retired now, Mr. Sullivan?" Conrad was applying the first rule of interrogations. 'Thou shalt start off with questions that the subject feels comfortable in answering and on subjects in which he is both confident of his knowledge and happy to discuss. Thus shall his spirit be set at ease and the habit of answering established.' The advice had been given to him by his first mentor, Tomás Don Pedro Ferdinando de Valladolid, Archbishop of Seville, a man better known to history as Tomas de Torquemada.

"I am. I used to be an accountant and, for more than forty years, I woke up every day looking forward to the time I could retire. Then, finally, that day came and now all I can do is sit in my rooms and listen to the radio. I'd give anything to be working again."

"Contact the Army, Sir. We'll find a place for you. We've got more billets to fill than warm bodies to fill them. We're pulling in anybody and everybody who can help out."

"I thought fighting was for the youngsters."

"We've got plenty of jobs that require skills the youngsters usually don't have. I'll tell you what I tell everybody who we could use. If you're young at heart enough to want to work, we'll find a job for you."

"Were you at home when Mellie was killed?" Conrad wanted to get back on track. The distinguishing feature of this case seemed to be people's determination to cut across his lines of questioning.

"I must have been, yes. I was listening to the news, of course, then a New York Philharmonic concert, a pre-war recording of one of my favorite concertos, then *The Adventures of Ellery Queen*. The four o'clock show was *The Falcon*. It's not one I like, so I use the 30 minutes it's on to take a walk around the neighborhood. I left at four and met that young lieutenant about ten or fifteen minutes later. He was just riding his bicycle in through the gates. He and Mellie have been walking out for three or four months now. He must be a forgiving sort of guy, going steady with a girl like that, knowing her reputation."

"You didn't hear anything, did you, before you went for your walk." Conrad asked the question with an air of a man checking off the boxes on questions he had to ask.

"No, nothing. The walls here are pretty thick and I did have the radio on pretty loud. I'm a little hard of hearing, you know."

"How long have you been living here for, sir?" Conrad was still giving his 'wearily checking the boxes' impression.

"About three or four years."

Conrad frowned very slightly. "Well, thank you very much, sir."

Once inside the room, Conrad looked around. It was a chaotic shambles. Drawers had been pulled open and their contents scattered across the floor. Cushions and mattresses had been cut apart. Even the cistern for the toilet had been broken open.

Taylor heaved a deep breath. "This wasn't the police, that was for certain. They don't have this kind of energy. Well, not unless they've been very well paid."

"This confirms something I've suspected. Melba Ramsey wasn't killed by happenstance or by a maniac. She was targeted very deliberately because she either had something somebody else wanted, or knew something they believed she shouldn't know. She wasn't beaten and raped as part of a sexual attack. The assaults were intended to force her to reveal where she had hidden something.

"She knew she was going to die anyway, even if she told them what they wanted to know, so she kept her mouth shut. It was the only way she could make her death, and that of her baby, mean something. Captain, we need to honor her sacrifice by finding what she died to protect and using it to complete the work she was assigned."

"How do you know she had something rather than knew something?" Taylor agreed with Conrad's analysis of the situation, but wanted to dot all the Is and cross all the Ts.

"This room was turned over between the time the police removed her body and us arriving today. There's no mention of this kind of damage in the police report. There would have been if it had been like this, even if it was only attributed to an alleged fight between O'Brien and Ramsey. By ripping this room apart, the criminals have admitted they were looking for something and haven't found it yet."

Conrad looked at the floor of the room and the crumpled carpet where her body had been found. "You know, it seems to me that a girl who was beaten to death there and suffered a sexual assault as well would have bled into the carpet a lot more than that."

Taylor nodded. "I was thinking the same. And I have never known of a woman being the victim of that sort of attack who didn't scream loudly enough to wake the entire neighborhood. You think she was killed elsewhere and her body brought here?"

"I do; the problem is we have a really tight time-line already. How that could have been fitted in is beyond me."

Base Commander's Office, Warrington Field, Warminster, Pennsylvania

"We're right back where we started, aren't we?" Taylor believed that the day's work had been just about as depressing as it got. "Talk about two steps forward and three back."

Conrad felt tempted to try and cheer him, but he was firmly of the opinion that false hope was worse than none. "We are, yes. We have no idea who killed Melba Ramsey. We have no idea when she was killed or where. We have no timeline for this crime. But, we have exonerated Lieutenant Caleb O'Brien, and we now know that the previous theory of the crime had no substance. So yes, we are back where we started. The difference is that we are now on solid ground and, if we take a step, our footing will be sure."

"Oh well, let's take that first solid step. We need a timeline for Melba Ramsey's activities that afternoon. Do you find it quite incredible that the police didn't do that?"

Conrad hesitated before answering. *It is not my role to judge.* "I suppose they thought they had their man and they looked no deeper. It is a dreadfully easy trap to fall into. I would say that at least half the cases the Clarkson Foundation takes on have that feature in common. Since we have to start somewhere, we might as well start there. Do we have one or more corkboards around?"

Taylor snorted with laughter. "This is the Army Air Force, Conrad. We have corkboards coming out of the wazoo. I'll tell you this, if somebody figures out a way to put a corkboard on a radar screen, they'll make millions off us."

Conrad chuckled at the thought of his beloved corkboards being replaced by anything. "Right, well, let's get started. Where did Ramsey work?"

Taylor looked at the file that had been compiled when O'Brien had applied for permission to marry. "The Buffalo Diner. It's not that far from here; if O'Brien hadn't been flying, he'd probably have met her there and walked her home and we wouldn't be having this meeting. It's a popular place with the Brewster people; its rumored they like it so much they named one of their aircraft after it. If I owned that diner, I'd be offended."

Conrad snorted slightly. He was getting a strong feeling that the Brewster Aviation Corporation was seriously loathed by everybody except the people who worked there. "Well, let's start at the Buffalo Diner."

"Can you give me a couple of hours? Now that O'Brien is off the hook, my instructor pilot duties are back on the roster. I have to take a kid up for a check-ride."

"Graduating him?"

Taylor shook his head sadly. "Washing him out. Unless he pulls a hat out of a rabbit, he's done. He's afraid of the aircraft and you just can't be that way with the B-26. Give her a chance and she'll walk all over you. He's good with figures and good with maps, so he'll go to navigator school. Odd thing is, we'll probably be saving his life."

"Can I come and watch?"

"Sure. There won't be much to it, though. Just take off, fly around a bit and land."

Conrad and Taylor walked out of the offices and over to the runway. Halfway there, Taylor stopped. There was a dark blue fighter sitting on the parking stand with men around it. "Conrad, that's the first of the Brewster-built Corsairs. I forgot they had scheduled her for a test-flight today."

"So that's a Corsair." Newsreel film of the Thunderbolts and Airacobras in Russia was a feature of every cinema presentation. The Navy's carrier strikes were only just beginning to bite home and the Navy Corsairs, Helldivers and Avengers were unfamiliar sights. The youngsters knew them all, of course, but adult civilians weren't so well-informed. "It's got a vicious look about it."

"It's a vicious bird. Fast as a thief, well-armed and built like a tank. The first ones had problems flying off carriers, but the Navy fixed that. All the Corsairs are going to the Atlantic Fleet. The Navy is sending the Grumman Hellcats to the Pacific. Hello, they're starting her up."

Conrad watched as the Corsair was suddenly wreathed in blue-white smoke, while the prop started to turn in a series of jerks. The engine was coughing and spluttering as it picked up speed, then it settled down into a steady snarl. The pilot was obviously testing the controls, since the ailerons and elevators were moving. Then, the wings started to fold just where the downward pointing section joined the flat outer panels. The left wing went up, then the right, before both returned to their down position.

"I hope they don't do that in mid-air." Taylor sounded a bit amused. "In the Army, we tend to think that the wings shouldn't bend like that."

The Corsair was taxiing forward, heading down the parking stand towards the runway. "Alex, how does the pilot see over that long nose?"

"That's one of the problems the Navy had to solve. They did it by lifting the pilot's seat a bit. See how the cockpit on that one is bulged? Also, they changed the approach from a straight line to an S-shape. Our Thunderbolts in Russia had the same problem, but the Russians solved it by ordering one of the ground crew to lie on the wing and slide off just before the aircraft took off. They think a bit differently from us."

"Thank God they're on our side." Conrad looked at the Corsair as the engine note picked up and turned from a snarl into a full-throated roar. "There she goes."

The Corsair made its take-off run and soared into the air. Its undercarriage retracted as the aircraft climbed away. It was a stirring sight, and one that made Conrad finally understand the thrill of flying a fighter. He watched, entranced, as the dark blue aircraft made repeated runs over the airfield, each one a little faster than those before. "What's he doing?" Conrad had to shout the question.

"Speed checks. He's working up to the maximum speed of the aircraft. Also, he's a Navy pilot showing off to the Army. That last pass was about 320 knots."

The Corsair was pulling away in a tight turn. Conrad clearly heard a bang over the sound of the engine. He saw one of the wings separating from the fuselage at the point where it had folded just a few minutes earlier. The aircraft was obviously out of control and rolling over on its back. A small black object detached and fell clear. The aircraft completed its roll and simply fell out of the sky. The black spot continued to tumble down. The sigh of relief as a white canopy mushroomed over his head was profound. An Army ambulance was already racing towards the point where the escaped pilot was about to land. Conrad managed to get his mouth working. He hadn't realized it was hanging open in shock at the sudden end of the test flight. "What happened?"

Taylor's voice was terse and it was obvious he was controlling his anger with great difficulty. "Structural failure. The wing just crapped out on him. There'll be hell to pay over this. He wasn't even pushing the bird that hard. Jesus, and I said I hoped the wing wouldn't come off. I hope I didn't jinx the bird."

"You didn't." Conrad took his arm and turned him so the two men were facing each other. "From what I have heard, that problem started over there."

He gestured at the Brewster factory. "And nowhere else. Don't you dare blame yourself."

Taylor smiled weakly. "Thanks, Conrad. Look, I've got to get my bird up. We need to fly something right away, before alarm and despondency start to spread. Say a few prayers for the Navy gob, will you? That wasn't much altitude for a bailout."

CHAPTER THREE

SABOTAGE

The Buffalo Diner, Warrington, Pennsylvania

Conrad and Taylor parked their bicycles by the diner, locked them securely to the bicycle frame, and went in. It looked, and smelled, like a normal diner. The same sort of low-cost family restaurant that featured in virtually every town in America.

"Did you wash out your pilot?"

"I'm afraid so. The crash this morning was the last straw. After watching that Corsair go in, I think he'd have joined the infantry given half a chance."

"What's the word there?" Conrad had a feeling the crash was related to this case somehow.

"Still structural failure. The Navy moved like greased lightning when they heard. All Brewster-built Corsairs have been grounded until further notice. There's something else going on as well, but I don't know what it is . . . yet."

Conrad looked at the menu. "Prices are going up. Peanut butter sandwich for 25 cents. How are you fixed for coupons, Alex?"

"I'm fine. Got a pound of meat left to last until Saturday. The fried ham sandwich looks good and I like kidney bean salad. What you going to have?"

"Virginia corned beef hash sandwich, I think. And two coffees please?" The last remark was directed at the waitress who had started hovering over them.

"I'm sorry, sir, we can't do coffee right now. We've used up our ration. How about a pot of tea?"

"That'll be fine."

"Fried ham, corned beef, pot of tea." The girl called out the order with the assurance of a seasoned professional waitress before turning to Taylor. "There's no need for meat coupons, sirs. As long as a sandwich contains two ounces of meat or less, it's exempt from ration limitations. We're offering two ounce hamburgers now to take advantage of that. Sir, the pilot from the crash this morning? Is he all right?"

"Sure." Taylor smiled. "He broke a leg landing. He bailed out pretty low and his chute only just opened in time. But, he's Navy and they break things all the time. He's Lieutenant Andrews, do you know him?"

"No, sir." The girl looked around to make sure nobody could overhear. "But there were some union people from over the plant here. They were laughing about the crash. Made me feel right sick. I'm glad he's all right. Makes me feel a bit better."

"Did you know the girl who used to manage here? Melba Ramsey?" Conrad couldn't help but feel that somebody somewhere was dropping the right people into his lap and the right time.

"Poor Mellie." The waitress was nearly crying. "That Army pilot what done her, I hear he got off. She was such a nice girl too. A bit free with her friendship, if you get my meaning, and she chose some odd friends but there was no harm in her. She was always nice to everybody."

"Odd friends?" Conrad picked up on that.

"Yeah, she used to go walking out with some of the Union people from the plant. One of them was one of the men laughing today. I don't know what she saw in him."

"We need to talk to the owner about Mellie. Is she here?"

"Oh yeah. Now Mellie's gone, she has to be here all day. Not pleased about that at all."

"If we could see her please? By the way . . . " Conrad fumbled for the girl's name.

"I'm Liz, sir."

"Thank you, Liz, you've been very helpful. You should know, though, the Army pilot who was accused, he was flying at the time Mellie was killed. He couldn't possibly have done it."

The relief on the waitresses' face was unmistakable. "That's so good to hear. She was really taken with him. She gave up all her other 'friends' when they started walking out together. I'll get Phyllis, that's Mrs. Barnes. She's the owner."

The owner of the diner was a late-middle-age woman whose face combined motherly concern with piercing eyes that could be counted on to reduce any potential problems to gibbering compliance. "I'm Mrs. Barnes. Liz says you wanted to speak with me?"

"Thank you for your time, Mrs. Barnes. Perhaps you could sit with us for a few minutes? How long had Mellie Ramsey been working for you?"

"About four or five months. She was a very good manager; kept on good terms with all the staff. Place like this, sometimes the girls will have a dispute over tips or favorite customers. Mellie always used to smooth things over. She arranged the work schedules so that everybody got a fair share of the hours and they were all happy with their shifts. That's unusual. She was a bit too friendly with the customers, though, if you ask me. To tell you the truth, I thought she was on the game at first, but no. She just didn't realize that men won't buy a cow if they get free milk. Then she got caught, of course."

"Caught?"

"Lord love you, Father. She was in the family way. She didn't say anything to anybody about it, but us old ladies know when a young'un is in trouble."

"Mrs. Barnes, I suppose you must have heard that the Army pilot who was accused turned out to be flying when Mellie was killed?"

"No. Glad to hear it though."

"We worked it out. He was northbound over LeHigh when the window for Mellie's murder opened and southbound over Scranton when it closed. So, we're trying to find out who might be of interest to us. If we don't find out who really did it, that poor kid will have suspicion hanging over him for the rest of his life." Taylor had decided to make himself useful.

Conrad wished he hadn't. *Still, what's done is done and Alex means well.* "Do you know anybody who comes here who might have wanted to hurt her?"

Barnes shook her head. "Nobody meant her any harm. To be honest with you, she was a bit of a joke with some of the men. Especially the Union ones. They said she was a communist; from each according to his ability, to each according to his need. Then they'd laugh and not in a nice way. I think Mellie realized what they really thought of her, because I would see her staring into a mirror sometimes for minutes on end. Then she met her pilot and she got back on the right path. Bit late, of course."

"Not really, Mrs. Barnes. When she told Lieutenant O'Brien she was expecting and the baby was his, he proposed to her on the spot and even bought her a ring. The Army were expediting the paperwork so she could marry before she showed." This time Conrad approved of Taylor's contribution; he had said the right thing at the right time. *Interesting; he's stopping thinking like a lawyer and beginning to think like an investigator.*

"Well, doesn't that beat all." Barnes shook her head. "Most men would have run a mile when a girl with Mellie's reputation said they'd been caught and it was his. So he stepped up and did the right thing instead. And then she got killed."

"The day Mellie was killed, Mrs. Barnes, when did she leave here?"

"She was on the morning shift. Seven 'til two. She liked doing mornings but I knew that wouldn't last. Morning sickness would have seen to that. Evening shift is two 'til eight. We close then. She rode off on her bicycle just after two. Say two-ten at the latest."

"Was anybody else here?"

"Mostly people from the Brewster plant. Union men, mainly. They are in here all the time. I don't think they ever work. A few locals, that's all. Usual crowd."

"Anybody in particular you remember?"

"Just locals. Mostly regular; Liz will remember their names. It's her job to, after all. I'll talk to the girls and make out a list for you. Say, were you on the base for the crash this morning?" Conrad and Taylor both nodded. "I heard you say the pilot bailed out OK. Those union guys, they said something very odd. They were laughing over the crash, the bastards, and one of them said that it would screw the other shift over. Can you make some sense of that?"

Hangar Number Three, Warrington Field, Warminster, Pennsylvania

"How's this?" Taylor looked around proudly. The office space he had arranged was small but it had a desk, a telephone, four seats and, to Conrad's delight, four corkboards. It was a bit noisy, due to the Navy and Chance Vought personnel in the main part of the hangar bringing in the wreckage of the crashed Corsair. Already enough parts had been brought in so that the vague outline of the aircraft was apparent. Conrad saw that the section of the port wing that appeared to have collapsed was surrounded by red tape.

There was something else about the hangar; there were a dozen or so marines guarding all the entrances. It was apparent to him that the security offered for his investigation by their presence was one reason why the office had been made available to him.

"Excuse me, are you Father Conrad Lorenz?" A Navy commander had bustled over, clipboard in hand.

"I am. May I help, somehow?"

"Yes, sir. We have you on the list of people who saw the crash. An investigator from the Accident Investigations Board would like to interview you at your convenience."

"That means right now." Taylor made the remark with what could only be described as over-emphatic innocence.

"We do have an investigator free now, a Lieutenant Kepford. If you could speak with him now, that would be best. The less time that elapses between what you saw and relating it to us, the better."

"That is very true, Commander. Please take me to him."

Conrad followed the commander down the length of the hangar. On the way, he passed an odd scene. One of the marine guards was standing at attention in front of the duty officer, who had a civilian with a bandaged foot beside him.

"Private Barton, why did you strike this man's foot with the butt of your rifle?"

"Sir, I was standing my watch when this man tried to enter the secure area. On being instructed that he was not allowed access to the hangar, he tried to push past me. Sir, the Rifle, .30-06, semi-automatic M2A1 Johnson does not have provision for a bayonet, so I improvised, sir."

The Marine officer nodded at the injured civilian. "There we are, sir. I told you there would be a reasonable explanation."

"I'll have you know I am Thomas V. DeLorenzo, President of United Auto Workers Local 365."

"I'll be sure to enter that on the charge sheet, sir. Private Barton, escort this person from the base."

"Father Lorenz? I'm Lieutenant Kepford. Please excuse our little melodrama, but we've had people from the Brewster plant trying to take parts of the wreckage. They're in the brig, of course." The Navy lieutenant led the way to another of the offices surrounding the working area of the hangar. "Can I offer you a cup of coffee? It'll be the real Navy stuff, not the Army's imitation."

"That would be very kind of you. Thank you."

Conrad was a master at the art of questioning people but being on the receiving end of the process was less familiar to him. So, he mentally reversed the process, working out what Kepford was trying to learn from the questions and gaving him as accurate an answer as he could. It didn't take long before he was teaching the Lieutenant how to ask the right questions. Eventually, they came to the key issue.

"Did you actually see the wing detach from the aircraft?"

Conrad thought about that carefully. "No, I didn't. I head a bang. Obviously, it was loud enough to be heard over the sound of the engine. Then I saw the outer part of the left wing when it was separate from the Corsair and the aircraft already beginning to turn on its back. But I didn't actually see the wing come off."

"I see. Did you see smoke where the aircraft was? A puff or a cloud?" Conrad thought about that even more carefully. *Kepford is suspicious that some sort of explosive device blew the wing off. The trouble with that theory is, apart from the bang I heard, there is no evidence of an explosion.*

"No. There was a sort of black streak from the engine as the Corsair accelerated away and started to climb, But no puffs or clouds."

"That was probably just the engine adding power. The R-2800 does that. Let me show you something. These are drawings of an F4U-1 Corsair. The aircraft made by Brewster is called the F3A, but it's identical. Or it should be. Could you put your finger on where the wing broke off?"

This time Conrad didn't hesitate. The Corsair had one section of wing that sloped steeply down from the fuselage and a sharp bend where it started to slope upwards. *That is where the wings had folded.* He put his finger on that joint. "Here."

"Are you sure?"

"Very. It's the same place where the wing folded when the pilot put them up and down before taking off."

"This is called a gull wing. The idea is that the downward-sloping inner panels lift the nose and give the propeller enough room to clear the ground. The bend where they join the level outer panels is a stress point, but the designers at Chance Vought used it as the point where the wings fold for storage on an aircraft carrier. So far, we think that the wing failed there. Wherever it did fail, it did so because of either poor design, poor construction or sabotage."

"May I ask a sensitive question, Lieutenant Kepford? Have any other Corsairs crashed from wing failure?"

"Call me Ira, please." Kepford hesitated. "There are three factories making Corsairs. Chance Vought makes F4Us, Brewster makes F3As and Goodyear makes FG-1s. The F4U and F3A should be identical. The FG-1 has been modified to improve low-altitude performance at the expense of speed higher up. Corsairs have a high accident rate. They have a tendency to go into a flat spin if handled unwisely and their stall is brutal. They're rough to land. But, we've never had a Vought or Goodyear break up like this."

"I'm Conrad. Please excuse a rank amateur from butting in, but doesn't that rather suggest that the design isn't at fault?"

"It does. That's both a relief and a major worry. The Corsair is the aircraft we need to take off from carriers and fight the best the Nazis have. A design fault would have been crippling to the Navy's war effort. On the other hand, we wouldn't be surprised if the Brewster-built aircraft were badly built; all the other aircraft we've had from them are. As to sabotage, well, it's hard to credit but we've only had one case of sabotage at aircraft factories since the war began. And it took place there." Kepford jerked his thumb at the Brewster plant. "But you know that of course. Colonel Hammond told you all about it."

Conrad controlled his shock at the comment manfully. "Uhh, Colonel Hammond?"

"Head of the Washington Field Office, Investigations Division, War Production Board? They're heading the investigation into Brewster. He advised us that you were down here on another matter and suggested we might try and enlist your help. Another cup of coffee? We have some fresh-baked cookies. Even the Army admits our cooks have theirs beat hollow there."

Before Conrad could reply, one of the Marines knocked and entered. "Sorry to trouble you, sir, but the recovery team has brought the port wing in. It's almost intact."

Kepford beamed. "I was hoping it would be; it detached before the crash. We've really got a break. Now, we can see what the wing looked like just as it separated."

Conrad saw the wing section being brought in on a trailer. He had expected it to be tangled wreckage like everything else in the hangar, but it was indeed surprisingly intact. Taylor had come over to see what was going on.

"When it detached, it didn't quite float down, but it didn't fall out of the sky the way the rest of the aircraft did. This is what everybody has been hoping for. See the man over there, fair hair, glasses? That's Rex Buren Beisel, the man who designed the F4U. He's currently the general manager of Chance Vought. Effectively, he runs the whole company."

Conrad looked at the man Taylor had indicated. He was wearing the same white overalls with 'Chance Vought' printed on the back as all the other company personnel, and was struggling alongside the rest of his men to unload the wing section without causing further damage. Kepford was on his way over to him. "Thank you for coming, Mr. Beisel."

Beisel straightened up and looked at him. "Lieutenant, it's Rex. *I* work for *you*. Have you got all the statements in?"

"We're still working on that, si . . . Rex. We got one perfect eyewitness though. Knows nothing about aircraft, but does know how to give evidence. Tells us what he saw and that's that."

"Once we've got this unloaded, I'd like to speak with him." Beisel paused and looked at Conrad. "This him?"

"I'm Conrad Lorenz, sir. Any time convenient to you."

There was a dull, muffled thud as the detached wing portion was lowered to the concrete floor in roughly the same relation to the rest of the wreckage as it would have been on an intact aircraft. Another marine came running up. "Engine coming in, sir. They found it and dug it out."

"Ten feet down?"

"Twelve, sir."

Beisel cursed, then apologized to Conrad. "Charlie? You won the pool. Twelve feet down. Ground must be softer than I thought. Father, could we speak now?"

"Certainly."

"Thank you, Father. We'll go back to the investigation office. There, you'll sit down, close your eyes and go back to the first time you saw that F3A. Then go forward in real time. Don't jump forward or miss anything, and tell me everything you see. I won't interrupt you until you finish."

"Got it." Conrad smiled. *Beisel would have made a great detective.* "You've done this before, haven't you?"

Beisel suddenly looked incredibly sad. "All too often, I'm afraid. It was bad during the early days, when we were designing aircraft without really knowing what we were doing. Then things got better as we learned from our errors. Now, they're getting bad again, as we push for warplanes with the highest performance regardless. All of the new, really high-performance fighters are rough on their pilots. The Nazis are having the same problems. Our people are reporting that the FW-190D has a habit of diving straight into the ground for no apparent reason. Anyway, I hear you have another investigation in hand, so let's get started."

Twenty minutes later, Conrad opened his eyes and saw that a stenographer had quietly entered the room and taken down everything he had said. Beisel was reading one set of notes and looked up. "Father, you said when the pilot was testing the wing folding mechanism, the left wing came down first, then the right wing. Are you sure of that?"

"Quite sure, I remember thinking that I would have expected the wings to go up and come down together."

"They're supposed to. We better have a really close look at that folding mechanism."

Back in his own investigations room, Conrad looked at the blank corkboards and felt at home. *It is long past time to try and make order out of chaos.*

"All done with the Chance Vought people? And if you want coffee, scrounge it from the Navy. Theirs really is much better than ours."

"Had some, Alex, but thank you for the tip. Now, let's get sorted out. We can start a timeline on one of these boards." Conrad stretched a line of red ribbon across the first board and pinned it into place. "We should start with Mellie arriving for work at 0600. She's pretty much accounted for from there until she left for home at 1410. We'll put her above the ribbon and O'Brien below it."

"Why? We know he didn't do it?"

"He's involved somehow. No, he didn't do it, but he may be why it was done."

"OK. Well, we know what he did from reveille up to takeoff. That's the same everybody does when they're flying. I took the liberty of checking and we can confirm he was at each one of these steps." Taylor wrote them under the ribbon. "You know, it's really odd, isn't it. At the time Mellie was working in the diner, like any good American girl, Caleb was learning how to bomb people. And, over in Russia, his equivalent was doing it for real. Yet Mellie was the one who died."

"War is full of strange ironies." Conrad sounded infinitely sad. "When did he take off?"

"According to the tower, 1128 on the nose. The crew called in at each checkpoint, all the way until they landed at 1530. He was sitting next to me all that time."

"Never out of sight?"

Taylor blinked at that. "Not on this flight, no. If it had been an operational flight, the navigator would have moved to the nose to operate the bombsight and nose gun, the flight engineer to the upper turret, but the copilot stays put. We do radio checks every so often, in which each crewman gives his position. But, where would he go? He can't leave the aircraft and rejoin it."

Conrad felt a little foolish. He had asked the question almost as a reflex, since he knew of enough cases where a person with an alibi had slipped away just long enough to commit the crime. "Sorry. So, we have the B-26 landing at 1530 and he was off the base at 1546. He arrived at 1610 at which time he found Mellie dead. So she was murdered sometime in a two hour window, 1410 to 1610."

"Did the coroner give a time of death?"

"1600, but that was just him repeating what Chief Schultz had said. I get the distinct feeling it's not wise to disagree with Schultz. There's no reference to the coroner taking a body temperature, so we have no idea when she really die. We can close the window a bit though. The coroner did say that the murderer took an hour or more to kill her."

Conrad stopped speaking for a second. Mental pictures of what Mellie Ramsey's last minutes had been like flooding his mind. He had little doubt that the greatest agony she had suffered was the knowledge that her baby was going to die with her. "That would suggest she died sometime between 1510 and 1610."

"We could push that back a bit. We've got a good case that he body was moved to her apartment after she died; so, depending on how long that took, we can move the actual time of death back towards 1510."

"Wait a minute. We've got a problem." Conrad was annoyed with himself for missing the obvious. "Forget about when her body was brought to her apartment; ask yourself, how? Everybody around here is riding bicycles. Gasoline rationing means seeing cars are so rare these days that people remark on them. And nobody has. A killer can't move a body on a bicycle. Not without causing comment."

"I'll push that further." Taylor's eyes were flashing as the message sank in. "She can't have been taken to where she was killed by bicycle either. If the local people see a bound and gagged woman being carried on a bicycle, they'll probably do something about it. Even if they don't, they'll remember it. So we have a double problem. How was Mellie taken from where she was abducted to where she was killed and from there to her apartment. If this was before the war, we'd say in the trunk of a car but, gasoline rationing means very few cars around. So how? If we can solve that, we've fixed the time of her death."

Warminster Police Station, 401 Gibson Avenue, Warminster, Pennsylvania

"My officers have better things to do than this." Chief Schultz was back in fully-fledged aggressive obstruction mode again. Conrad wondered what lay behind his attitude and the mercurial changes in it and why he tended to default to blustering and hectoring everybody around him.

"We need to know if any vehicles were seen on Route 132 between 1410 and 1610 on the day Melba Ramsey was killed. Your officers are the most reliable source of information on that matter."

Conrad was about to tell him why, but suddenly stopped himself. *The less Schultz knows about what was really going on, the better.* "1410 to 1610 is the window during which Mellie was killed. We know she was alive at 1410, we know she was dead at 1610. We must trace her movements during that period. We also need to find what traffic was in the area she was known to have been riding her bicycle. If your officers can identify the vehicles that were driving in the same area, we can eliminate the ones that are uninvolved and narrow down to the subjects of interest. A vehicle that is from outside this area would be a primary subject of interest."

Watching Schultz carefully, Conrad saw a gleam of crafty delight in the Police Chief's eyes. *He sees an opportunity to shift suspicion away from Warminster and its inhabitants. Or, away from the Brewster Aviation factory. Is there a difference?*

"All right then, if it's important to the case. You need to talk to patrolmen Timmins and Lane. Their beats cover that area."

Hangar Number Three, Warrington Field, Warminster, Pennsylvania

"So, what did they say?"

"There were a handful of vehicles around. According to the patrolmen, anyway. Mostly Army, and a few Navy, trucks and jeeps from here. A couple of cars that went into the Brewster plant. Officer Lane thinks that one was owned by James Work himself. If that is correct, we can be reasonably sure that isn't involved. People like Work don't do the dirty work for themselves."

"Somebody else might have been driving the car." Taylor sounded tentative, as if he was raising objections simply for the sake of doing so.

"That is a possibility. Anyway, Lane had noted the numbers on the cars so he could check them for possible black market gasoline purchases. Can we check them out?"

"We certainly can." Taylor hesitated. "I'll as the Pennsylvania State Police to run them for us. I don't believe we'll get an answer from Chief Schultz if it's inconvenient."

"Thank you. Now, I also spoke with Doctor Fischer again. He was a lot more communicative once Schultz wasn't around. He confirms that the body was moved after death. Apparently after death the victim's blood pools in the lower portions of the body and stays there. That tells him Mellie Ramsey died lying on her back and stayed that way for at least ten or fifteen minutes but was then moved before being dumped in her apartment. So that moves the back end of our time window to sometime before 1600."

"That would explain why Mr. Sullivan didn't see anybody. He was still listening to his radio then."

"Ahh yes. Mr. Sullivan." Conrad sounded very thoughtful.

Taylor caught the intonation. "Something wrong there?"

"Something odd. Sullivan claimed to be an accountant for over forty years. Yet every number he gave us was inexact. Forty years. Ten or fifteen minutes. Three or four months. About three or four years." Conrad counted them off on his fingers. "Alex, I know quite a few accountants of long standing and they never use inexact numbers. It would be 43 years or however long it was, ten minutes, three months, three and a half years or even three years four months, again whatever the time was.

"Alex, accountants don't guess or give vague information. To them, a number is what it is. If there is doubt they'll say 'approximate' or 'estimate' or some other qualification but there will be a solid number there. 'I'd estimate ten minutes.' To an accountant, an inexact number is like saying that Corsair out there is nearly flying."

Almost on cue, Lieutenant Kepford knocked on the door. "We got it! You guys want to come over and take a look?"

A steadily growing crowd was gathering around the wreckage of the Corsair. In the middle of it, Rex Beisel was holding up a part of the wing-folding mechanism. "Here it is, people. This is the latch that holds the wing locked down. There are two female lugs on the inner stub wing, with an actuator behind them. There's a male lug on the outer folding panels. When the wing drops down, the male lug slides between the two female ones and the actuator pushes a bolt through holes in those lugs, locking them in place. This is a critical assembly. The position and fit of the lugs and bolt has to be accurate and precise. The tolerances are extremely tight."

There was the sound of multiple teeth being sucked. Accurate and precise were rarely used with reference to work carried out at the Brewster plant.

Beisel looked around and nodded. "So, what went wrong? We owe our priestly friend there for the key information. His evidence pointed us in the right direction. When we look at this locking mechanism, it is apparent that the holes in the lugs do not line up properly. In fact, the holes are a total of almost a quarter of an inch out of position. Given this assembly as made, it is impossible for the wings to be locked in the down position.

"So, those geniuses over the road fixed the problem by drilling out the holes so they do line up. In doing so, they enlarged them significantly over spec. Also, the locking rod was made significantly under spec. This had two effects. One is that the outer wing panels were not properly locked into place and so vibrated as the aircraft flew. The Navy is sending an emergency message out right now, red-lining all F3As at 300 knots and ordering a check on all F4Us and FG-1s to ensure that the locking mechanism is safe. The other problem is that the oversized holes severely weakened the lugs. When the vibration reached a critical level, they failed. There's something odd about the failure that we must look into."

Beisel paused. "Father, it was your comment about the wings folding and unfolding that made us look at this. The left wing failed first because of the torque and prop wash from the R-2800. Your comment about the port wing lag made us look harder at the folding mechanism. You see, when we designed this part of the wing, we knew that the lug locking system might fail. So we designed a back-up that would hold the wing in place long enough to give the pilot a chance of getting home, or at least getting out. See this part here? It's part of the hinged bar that joins the folding mechanism to the outer panels. It's deliberately over-engineered to hold the wing down if the latch fails.

"Brewster aircraft are all overweight and the company has been repeatedly penalized for that. So, they cut weight by drilling this bar full of holes. Of course, in doing so, they weakened it drastically, causing it to bend, and that slowed the extension of the port wing. When the latch failed, that threw stress on this weakened bar, which snapped under the load. The wing folded in flight and aerodynamic stress snapped it off. Luckily, the test pilot was flying with his canopy open and got out. We need to talk to the people at Brewster and find out who authorized these actions. Father, you're a Catholic, do you have any old text-books on the Inquisition tucked away?"

That caused a round of laughter that dispelled the anger that had built up during Beisel's explanation of the crash. As a result, nobody noticed Conrad flinch and go white. By the time attention had focused on him, he had regained control of himself. "I'm sorry Rex, the Inquisition only covered blasphemy, heresy and satanic practices. That's nowhere near adequate for Brewster Aviation."

"Satanic practices might be close." Conrad couldn't tell who had shouted out the comment, but it caused another round of laughter.

Beisel nodded in appreciation. "We've sent a preliminary report to the Navy. What they'll do, I don't know, but I guess we'll find out soon. Colonel Reyes, could you assemble everybody on the base who worked on bringing the wreckage in? I want to thank them for their efforts."

Conrad slipped away and made for the washroom at the back of the hangar. Since it dated from the civilian days of the airfield, it was better equipped than the spartan military equivalents. He went to a stall, shut himself in and then slumped down with his face in his hands. His memories of the Inquisition came flooding back to haunt him and he knew there would be no rest for him in the nights to come.

Investigation Office, Hangar Number Three, Warrington Field, Warminster, Pennsylvania

"A Colonel Cooper of Army CIC called me. Briefed me on what is going on. You knew Ramsey was a CIC operative?"

Conrad nodded. "I'm sorry I didn't tell you, Alex; but I was told in confidence."

"And priests take that seriously. So do Army officers, so don't sweat it. You done right. This puts a whole new complex on things, though. It looks to me as if she was killed to silence her."

"That seems most likely, yes." Conrad was staring at the board with motivations on it. Robbery was far over on the right, placing it as the least likely of the options. He picked up the card marked "silence" and put it on the left. That left sex and revenge in the middle. He wasn't quite sure which way round they should be going. "Revenge would be that she turned somebody down and they punished her for insulting them. The other possibility is that we are dealing with somebody really sick. I'd make that the more likely of the two myself."

"Agreed." Taylor thought for a moment. "There is something odd here, Conrad. Everybody knows that Brewster is rotten to the core. Why weren't they closed down or taken over a long time ago?"

"Probably because the people in charge of the investigation thought there was something much worse going on and wanted to find out what that was. So they allowed the Brewster management and unions enough rope to hang themselves, while they sent Melba Ramsey in to tie the knot."

Conrad felt as if he was handling a straw bale soaked with unspeakable filth. He always felt that way when dealing with this kind of counter-intelligence work. That was why he had turned down the opportunity to work for Army CIC. "There is another side to that, you know. The Brewster people knew the game was up, that it was only a question of time before the axe fell. Why make things much worse by killing a CIC agent in such a brutal manner? Disappear her, certainly; although, it was probably too late for that to make much difference. But, by killing her the way they did, they made certain all hell would break loose."

Taylor closed his eyes and put the pieces together. "Killing Mellie wasn't a part of the plot, it is a distraction from the plot. There's something else going on here that we haven't even begun to pick up on."

"If that's true, it means that she was a target of opportunity. Somehow, the people behind this found she was a CIC agent and decided to make killing her a distraction from their activities. That means that they were quite sure that the firestorm from her death would not spill over into their primary scheme. Everything falls into place from that. The clumsy attempt to frame O'Brien; the obstruction from the police. Everything fits the image of this murder as a decoy from the real situation." Conrad shook his head sadly. "This means that Mellie and her baby died simply because they were a convenient distraction."

"I hate to say this, but that fits in with why Brewster hasn't been closed down much earlier. I bet CIC knows there is something much more serious happening, and held off while Mellie investigated. I think we're both being manipulated here."

"I don't doubt it." Conrad was tired and dispirited. *I came here to clear a young man of the brutal murder of his girlfriend and now I'm getting involved in a sleazy counter-intelligence plot.*

Main Gates, Brewster Aviation Corporation, Warminster Township. Pennsylvania

Normally, the watchman on the main gates of an industrial plant is an elderly man; a man who has received an easy job to support his retirement as a reward for years of faithful service. In the case of Brewster Aviation, Adam Morris was a young, fit man in his very late teens. He had paid the management of the company a substantial fee to be employed by the aircraft plant and thus secure the draft exemption he sought. He was well aware that the job had few prospects for advancement, but the one thing he did not care for was the prospect of advancing on the Russian Front.

The roar of truck engines approaching his gates drew him out of the watchman's hut. The cause of the noise was a column of military trucks advancing down Route 132 towards the entrance. Morris had specific orders for this eventuality; alert the management, close the gate, stop the military personnel there and hold them for as long as possible. So, he lowered the pole that marked the entry and stood in front of it with his hand raised. Then he jumped for his life. The lead truck smashed straight through the checkpoint, sending splinters of fragmented timber dozens of feet into the air. By the time he got to his feet, the column of trucks had reached the front of the main buildings and dozens, if not hundreds, of men in mottled uniforms were pouring out. Some formed a perimeter around the Brewster building, others forced their way inside.

"Morris?" One of the intruders barked the word at him. Close up, Morris realized that the man was a marine. The mottled uniforms weren't used in Russia, since they looked too much like the ones worn by the SS, but stateside units still wore them.

"What if I am?" Morris had meant the words to assert his authority as an essential military production worker over mere marines. The phrase was choked off when a rifle butt hit him in the stomach. He collapsed on the ground, sobbing for breath.

"We'll try again. You Morris, Adam?" Mossis nodded. "Your draft exemption is revoked. The Army wants you; why, I do not know. They have been kind enough to offer you a choice of duty. Infantry or ordnance disposal. Take him away."

131

Conrad's Other Eye

President's Office, Brewster Aviation Corporation, Warminster Township. Pennsylvania

James Work, President, Chief Executive Officer and Chief Financial Officer of Brewster Aviation Corporation, heard the roaring of engines and the crash as his front gates were crushed. He then heard the shouting and chaos as marines poured into his building and started rounding his workforce up. Although he didn't know it, the same thing was taking place at the Brewster buildings in Long Island City, New York and Newark, New Jersey.

He also didn't know that a major row was going on behind the scenes between the Army and the Navy over the action to be taken over Brewster. The argument hadn't been resolved in any meaningful sense. The Navy had simply gone ahead and done what it wanted. Most of what it wanted, anyway. After reading the accident report on the crashed Corsair, Admiral Ernest Joseph King had wanted to hang James Work and his entire staff from the highest trees that were conveniently located to the plant. What was happening now was the nearest thing to that he could legally justify.

"You Work?" A sour-faced elderly man in the mottled Marine Corps uniform had thrown the door open and stalked in. He looked at Work as if the man was something that would normally be scraped off the sole of his boots.

"I am James Work, yes."

"That's nothing to be proud of. I am Marine Corps General Holland M. Smith and I have been ordered to secure this facility and all the records of the Brewster Aviation Corporation. I have also been ordered to place you under arrest and also to arrest some or all members of your workforce at my discretion. Now get your ass out of that chair."

"How dare yo . . . "

"Listen to me, you son of a bitch. I am facing a sniveling . . . creature . . . that has not only failed to do his duty, but has sought to profit from the lives of men who bravely serve their country. Gunnery Sergeant, place this man in detention. If he resists, shoot him."

Smith heard the door open behind him. Lillith entered the office, followed by two Marines. One carried her adding machine, the other a pile of ledgers. She limped over to what had once been James Work's desk and sat carefully in the seat. "Thank you, marines. I'm Lillith biti-Anat, General Smith. I've been asked to go through the books of this company."

Listening to her soft voice, General "Howlin' Mad" Smith could have sworn he heard wolves baying at the gates.

CHAPTER FOUR

TREASON

Main Gates, Brewster Aviation Corporation, Warminster Township, Pennsylvania

"Thank you for meeting me here." Colonel Cooper had arrived in a jeep with a mass of files in the back. "The Navy's actions here are causing our investigations a lot of problems. In fact, we wish they hadn't done this, although, given the accident report yesterday, I can see their point."

"They're talking of charging the entire workforce with attempted murder. Speaking as a lawyer, I don't think they'll get away with that, although they might have got the people who worked on that Corsair with manslaughter had the pilot been killed. But then, the company probably doesn't know who worked on that Corsair." Taylor looked at the Brewster plant, now with marines guarding every exit and an increasing number of workers being led away to the waiting line of trucks. "In fact, I'd have to ask whether what is happening here is legal."

Cooper looked at the scene with the same jaundiced expression. "I think the Navy are taking a hell of a chance, frankly. If they don't find some pretty solid evidence of wrongdoing, they could be out on a limb while sawing it off behind them. Supreme Court material, Captain?"

"If this goes bad, could be, sir. Depends on the exact circumstances but it is arguable there could be a Fourth Amendment breach here. Unless the Navy got a search-and-seizure warrant, of course. What's happening at the other Brewster locations?"

"Much the same thing. The Navy has taken the plants over and is confiscating everything in them. This is the center, though. All the paperwork is being shifted here."

Conrad's Other Eye

"Sirs, would you please accompany me inside, sirs?" An earnest young marine was standing at attention. "General Smith asks that you attend his staff meeting for a briefing."

"Not Howlin' Mad Smith?" Taylor seemed slightly awed.

"Sir, General Holland M. Smith, sir. And if I may say, sir, he is not a happy general right now."

Inside the factory, the production lines were at a standstill while engineers from Chance Vought and Grumman swarmed over the half-built aircraft. Conrad saw Rex Beisel sprawled over the nose of a semi-complete F3A-1 working on the engine. He straightened up, and then saw Conrad standing below him. "Father, we've struck gold up here. Charlie here and the boys have just finished stripping this engine. All the sparking plugs on this R-2800 are reconditioned units. Run this engine up and down, idle to full power and back again for a few hours, throw in a few tight turns and bunts and it will foul and die. Satanic practices, definitely satanic practices."

The Chance Vought engineers burst laughing and waved at Conrad. The Grumman and Pratt and Whitney personnel looked confused, until the basis of the joke was explained to them. Then they gave a friendly wave to Conrad as well.

"Damn, if that don't beat all." Taylor shook his head, then saw that Cooper and Conrad were bewildered. "The R-2800 used in fighter aircraft has to have its sparking plugs changed every other flight. The old ones are replaced by newly-made ones and the old ones sent back to the factories to be refurbished. We have aircraft on the Air Bridge that do nothing but take out replacement sparking plugs. The used ones come back by train and ship; they aren't so time critical."

"What happens to the refurbished plugs?" Conrad had the slightly light-headed feeling that he got when suddenly a key piece of information had fallen into his lap.

"They get supplied to manufacturers for use on aircraft that have more sedate life-styles than single-seat fighters. I know what you're thinking, Conrad." Taylor was irate. "The people here are taking delivery of R-2800s as government-furnished equipment, removing the new sparking plugs and replacing them with refurbished ones. Then they sell the new plugs and pocket the difference."

"And that's probably what Mellie was on to. She found out about that racket, and probably others, and they killed her for it. They made a big thing of it as a sex killing so we'd spend our time looking at that side of things instead of thinking there may be other things going on. We have to find her notes." Conrad was irate as well, but for different reasons. *The idea of deflecting blame by making Melba Ramsey's murder look like a sex-crime was sound and it had nearly worked. If I had followed my usual pattern, once O'Brien had been exonerated, I would have stopped looking into the case and the killers would have got away with it. If Chief Schultz hadn't offended me and if that Corsair hadn't crashed in front of me, Mellie Ramsey's murder might have been written off as another unsolved case.*

Taylor nodded. "This has to be it, only it can't just be a few sparking plugs. It has to be bigger."

"How about whole engines?" Conrad was assembling the pieces quickly. "Take the new government-furnished engines supplied, replace them with reconditioned units and sell the new ones to people who can't buy them from the manufacturer for some reason."

"You know, there were always rumors that some of the Brewster F2As had reconditioned engines." Ira Kepford had joined the group. "That was always an odd aircraft. Every type of aircraft has good and bad examples. Some of them want to fly and try hard for their pilots; other ones don't. The variations in the F2A were remarkable though. The original prototypes were sweet birds, fast for their time and pretty damned agile. Then performance went to hell. People said it was the Navy loading them down, and there was some of that, but the pilots didn't swallow it. There was something wrong with those birds; they just didn't respond or fly like they had. A few flew like the originals, but not many."

Their marine escort showed them into what had been James Work's office. Lillith was working with a pile of ledgers, an expression of pure bliss on her face. "Hello, Conrad. How's the investigation going?"

"We think we know what Mellie found and what got her killed." Conrad quickly explained the latest developments.

"Don't worry about the legal side of this. We got search-and-seizure warrants for the books and property. Found the evidence too. Work was the CEO of Brewster Aviation but had hired himself as a consultant for all three manufacturing locations. By the way, he owned those sites personally and was renting them to his own company. That's just the top of an iceberg. As I suspected, Brewster Aviation has been thoroughly looted over a period of years. I'd say over ten million dollars has vanished from this company, one way or another." Lillith looked like a cat that had just inherited a cream factory.

"Might I make a suggestion, Lillith? You might want to check the receipts of government-furnished equipment against the use of that equipment. We've already identified some irregularities and, where there's some, there will be more."

"Too right." Lillith agreed.

"Lieutenant, is it possible to get the engine numbers from the F2As? I assume each engine has an individual serial number?"

"I'm not sure there are any F2As left. I suppose some might be around as hacks and target tugs. I'll check. We could do the same for the SB2As. They have Wright R-2600s. Only problem is that we fired most of them into the sea off Norfolk."

"No, you didn't." Lillith smiled. "We have three hundred incomplete airframes here and at the other two plants. The General wants to personally beat James Work over the head with each and every one of them."

"Wait a minute." The operation had snapped into focus as Conrad had thought about it. "Three hundred incomplete airframes means there should be three hundred engines waiting for them. Is that correct?"

"And three hundred sets of radios, six hundred .50 caliber machine guns and twice that number of .30s." Kepford had followed Conrad's line of logic. "Plus a lot more stuff. To the GFE Vault!"

Government-Furnished Equipment Vault, Brewster Aviation Corporation, Warminster Township, Pennsylvania

"Well, that's not a surprise." Conrad looked around the GFE Vault. Despite its name, it was not some small room but a large warehouse space. It wasn't quite empty, although its capacity vastly exceeded its contents. There were small numbers of crated R-2600 engines for the SB2As and larger numbers of R-2800s for the F3As, but that was it. The stockpile of equipment waiting for installation on the undelivered aircraft was conspicuous by its absence.

"Mice?" Lillith's comment echoed around the nearly empty room.

Investigation Office, Hangar Number Three, Warrington Field, Warminster, Pennsylvania

"We really need Mellie's notes. She found out what was going on and was killed for it. That we know. We're pretty certain that her death was made to look like a sex crime to deflect our investigation. You know what really worries me, Conrad? The engine stuff? Well, that sort of thing happens in every industry. Buildings get erected with sub-standard cement, bridges have inferior-quality steel, automobiles are delivered with remolded tires. Despicable, I know, but not unusual. What is unique about this case is that we know of nearly two thousand .30 and .50 caliber machine guns that have vanished. The boys on the front need those guns. You probably haven't read the confidential 'lessons learned' reports we get back. As an instructor, I get them. The Army says the .50 machine guns are the things that really make the ground fighting break our way. The Nazis are terrified of them. Our boys need them and these bastards sold them to line their pockets." Taylor smiled apologetically. "I'm sorry, but that really burns me up."

"I find the thought of two thousand heavy machine guns on the loose a bit chilling as well." Conrad thought it over. "Who would buy a machine gun like that?"

"I doubt if a private citizen would. Too heavy and the ammunition is too hard to get hold of. I bet they've gone abroad."

"I'll bet that was what Mellie found out." Conrad stared at the timeline again and his eyes focused on the narrow window in which she had died. "Fifty minutes. That's all the time there was to take her to where she was murdered and then take her body back to her rooms. And the killers didn't have a car. The crime scene can't have been that far from the house she lived in."

"We know it was about half an hour's bicycle ride from her home to the diner." Taylor was looking at the timeline as well. "Probably longer, she wasn't going to pedal hard in her condition. And there were no cars of note around. You're right; she must have been killed close to her home."

"Suppose she was killed in that building? Not in her own room, but somewhere else. She reached her home, was probably feeling safe because everybody does when they get home, and was snatched at the door. The killers took her somewhere else, killed her and then took the body back for O'Brien to find."

"That works. In fact, that fits better than anything else we've found. But, we're still left with the critical question. Where did she hide the notes?"

Conrad thought about that. "We know they weren't in her apartment. The way that place was torn apart, the killers would have found them. It's a myth that people will hide something somewhere remote and isolated, like burying it in the woods. That leaves it unguarded. No, she would have left it with somebody she trusted. And there's only one person I can think of like that. O'Brien. The moment he found out about her condition and proposed, she knew he could be trusted. She left her notes with him. Although he probably doesn't realize it."

O'Brien's Quarters, Warrington Field, Warminster, Pennsylvania

Conrad knocked on the door and waited for it to open. O'Brien looked out. "Oh hello, Father. I'm glad you came by. I didn't get a chance to thank you for everything you did. You're an ace."

"I'm just glad everything's working out, Caleb. You've heard what's going on over at Brewster's?" O'Brien nodded. "Well, there's an aspect of that which ties back to Mellie's murder. You know she was an Army CIC agent?"

O'Brien shook his head vigorously. His face showed serious shock. "You mean she was using me?"

"No, quite the reverse. When she fell for you, she asked to be pulled out. Another day or so, she would have been safe. Point is, we need her investigation notes and we couldn't think where she hid them. Then we realized you were the only person she trusted. Did she ever give you something? A gift or keepsake?"

O'Brien glanced around. "We had a picture taken one day. I sent a copy to my folks. Mellie framed another copy for me. It's over there."

He went over to his bunk and picked up the framed picture. Conrad looked at it, seeing the liveliness and intelligence on Melba Ramsey's face, and reflected on the tragedy of loss. "Caleb, there's something you should know. With other people, Mellie was playing a part. One she needed to play in order to get the information she needed to do her job. She wasn't really like that and I think she hated the person she was playing. I think she saw you as her link to decency, an anchor that kept her attached to her real self. When she asked to be pulled out of this job, she told CIC that it was because she loved you and wanted more than anything else to be honest with you. When you proposed to her, she was truly happy. Not just because you stood up for her, but because you'd confirmed the faith she had in you."

O'Brien turned away so Conrad wouldn't see the tears in his eyes. When he finally spoke, there was a catch in his voice. "I think there's a tab on the back, one that holds the backboard and picture in place."

Conrad looked carefully. A metal square was nailed to the wood at one end with a tiny pin. He rotated it carefully and lifted the back panel off. Between the panel and the picture was a small wad of notepaper, covered in very small but carefully-formed handwriting.

"That's it, isn't, it?" O'Brien was looking at the notes. "That's what got Mellie killed."

Conrad shook his head slightly. "No, not quite. What she knew got her killed. These notes saved what she knew. Your guardianship of them meant you saved them. Now, we can get the men who killed her."

"And, rest assured Cal, they'll pay for it." Taylor spoke with utmost sincerity.

"That won't bring Mellie back." O'Brien sounded bitter. "Nothing will do that."

"Caleb, you bring her back every time you remember her." Conrad put his hand on the pilot's shoulder. "She knew that as well. I believe that it was the one thing that comforted her and gave her the strength to hold out."

Behind them, Taylor was reading the notes. "These aren't encrypted; I think she was in a hurry to get what she had found down on paper and safely hidden. If a quarter of what she says here is correct, there's going to be a scandal of monumental proportions. We'd better head back to the Brewster plant. Colonels Hammond and Cooper need to see these, right away."

Conrad nodded in agreement and the pair set off for the road leading to the Brewster plant. On the way, they passed a set of steps leading downwards. "Alex, what's down there?"

Taylor took a single glance at the steps. "Leads to a bomb shelter. All Army bases have them, but they don't get used much. Really, it's just a cellar."

"All the old houses have one, don't they?"

"The older ones, sure. I've heard that the people living on the coast started using them as shelters when U-boats started lobbing the odd shot from their deck guns at houses. The new ones don't though. Adds too much to construction costs."

Conrad looked grim. "We need to see the plans of Mellie's house. If it's got a cellar, or a basement as well, I think I know where she was killed."

Investigation Office, Hangar Number Three, Warrington Field, Warminster, Pennsylvania

"Conrad, have you finally decided to surrender your virginity after all these years?' Igrat's husky voice seemed to ooze seduction. Behind Conrad, Taylor's eyebrows met his hairline.

"If I had, Ingrid, you'd be my first call. But, this is business. Do you know any of the executives at NBC Radio?"

"The New York, New Jersey and Pennsylvania networks, sure. New England has a different family of stations and I'm not so hooked into them."

"That's perfect. I assume you have lots of favors you can call in?" Conrad was being careful to make sure that Taylor wouldn't get more suspicious than he had to be about who he was speaking to.

"Of course. What do you need?"

"A recording of the episode of *The Adventures of Ellery Queen* that went out ten days ago. It's for an investigation I'm on."

Conrad heard Igrat grunt. "Shouldn't be a problem. Ten days ago? That'll be 'Dead Man's Cavern.' You jealous, Conrad? Or looking for some professional tips?"

"Sorry?"

"You'll work it out when you hear it. Can you play reel-to-reel tapes where you are?"

Conrad glanced at Taylor who nodded. "We can, yes. Could you get it sent to Warrington Field, outside Warminster Township?"

"I can do better than that. I'll bring it down. Lillith has asked me to bring down some material for her so yours can come along for the ride. See you."

"Wow, Conrad. Who *was* that?"

"A friend of mine with a lot of really useful contacts. The more I think about our Mr. Sullivan, the more suspicious I get of him. And, if we're right about where Mellie died, he was at the scene at the right time."

Conrad was going to continue further, but was interrupted by knocking on the door. Taylor opened it. An Army Air Force Police sergeant saluted, then gave him a roll of blueprints. "Architects plans for the building you wanted, sir."

"Very good, Sergeant. Thank you." Taylor closed the door and opened up the roll. "Well, Conrad, there we have it. Mellie's building does have a basement; a good, solidly built one. Not a crawlspace with a thin wooden floor over it. This one has brick walls and a solid brick ceiling. I'd guess this was built to tornado or hurricane standards. I doubt if they get that many of either here, but if one came this way, this would prove a good investment."

"I think we better have that building searched thoroughly, don't you? All of it."

"I'll talk to Colonel Cooper and get some CIC people to accompany us." Taylor hesitated for a second. "Conrad, has anybody ever told you that for a priest, you have some very odd friends?"

Melba Ramsey's Apartment Building, Willopenn Drive, Southampton

"According to the blueprints, the entrance to the basement should be from the kitchen area." Conrad had the roll of plans open and was orientating them so they matched the building.

"That makes sense. Most people used the cellar as a root vegetable storage area for the winter. Even in the summer, those old cellars stayed cool."

"The owners kept the kitchen and the rear of the house as their own area when they divided the rest up into apartments." Conrad had another set of plans open, but he was beginning to lose control of all the bits of paper in his hands. One of the CIC soldiers reached out and helped him steady the unwieldy documents. "Thank you. They did a good job of the conversions. Proper walls, and the apartments had their own bathrooms and kitchenettes. Lot of these places were converted into apartment houses on the cheap."

"They probably looked on this place as their retirement income, so wanted to make sure it was solid. Kitchen's through here, I think."

Taylor opened the old-fashioned door and looked around. "Can't see an entry to the cellar. According to the plans, it's over there, where those cupboards are."

"Who are you? What are you doing here?" An elderly man had pushed past the Army police and CIC personnel.

"Army Counter-Intelligence Command. We have reason to believe that activities damaging to national security and the war effort were conducted here."

"Get out of my house." Anything more the man might have said was cut off when two CIC men pushed him out of the kitchen. Taylor went out of the door and held up a document he had been very careful to get properly authorized. It was a Federal search warrant.

"Sergeant. Detain this man."

Conrad heard Taylor give the order and agreed with it. The fact that the entry to the cellar wasn't immediately visible showed that it had been concealed. That implied the owners of this house had something to hide. What exactly that was would be revealed soon enough. "Alex, this must be Frederick Sherman. His wife will be here as well; they both need to be detained."

"You heard the Father, Sergeant. Find Martha Sherman and detain her."

The sergeant nodded wisely. "Very good, sir. I think there are satanic practices going on here."

There was a ripple of laughter that spread around the group of police and CIC men. Conrad's earlier quip about the jurisdiction of the Inquisition had spread quickly and become a standard description of any apparently illegal activities connected with the dealings of Brewster Aviation and, now, the murder of Melba Ramsey. As word of her real identity as a CIC agent had spread, the attitude of everybody on the case had changed. Now, they were looking for the killer of one of their own.

Conrad was looking at the cupboards that were located where the entry to the cellar should have been. "We need to look behind those."

"I'll get a sledgehammer." The head of the CIC detachment sounded grim. The general attitude that Melba Ramsey was one of their own had special emphasis for the CIC men. They now understood the sacrifices she had made and the final cost she had paid for the information she had gained.

"We may not need one." Conrad sounded reflective. "In films, things like this always have some carefully-hidden and fiendishly complicated locks, but I've never seen that in real life. Usually, the fact that the entry is concealed is enough and the way to open it is quite simple. The lock is more to stop it opening by accident. Now, look. There's scrapes on the floor beside this thing. That's where hidden doors always fall down. They may be perfectly built to start with, but when they are used, they start to show themselves. The cupboard goes sideways, so . . . ."

He pushed at the cupboard and felt the resistance to his pressure. "I can feel the top move slightly but not the bottom. Therefore, the lock is low down. Now, if we look inside that cabinet at the bottom of the cupboard . . . I can't see why there are two extra reinforcement bars at the back, can you?"

He reached out and tried to lift one of the pair of two by fours that were at the back of the cabinet. It resisted for a second and then lifted. The other did the same. With them out of the way, the furniture slid easily to one side. That exposed the original door to the cellar. The sight took Conrad back through the centuries, to times when he had seen similar doors leading to the cellars of the Inquisition. That gave him a terrible presentiment of what he might find.

The cellar was dank and had a distinct smell of mold about it. Beneath that, though, Conrad could detect a faint coppery smell; blood. It was faint enough that he could almost dismiss it as a figment of his imagination, but his instincts all told him that they had found the place where Melba Ramsey had died. One of the men behind Conrad found a light switch. He flipped it up. The room suddenly grew bright.

Conrad looked around. He saw a line of filing cabinets by a desk that had an odd-looking typewriter on it. He could also see where one of the walls had been scrubbed. There had been an attempt to clean it up, but bloodstains were clearly visible on the wall, where they had soaked into the brick. There were more stains on the floor, mute evidence of what had happened there.

"Conrad, look at this. Don't touch; there may still be fingerprints on it." Taylor was pointing at a pair of heavy-duty pliers on the floor. They looked like they too had been scrubbed, but blood had found its way into every crack and groove.

Conrad felt hideously saddened. "Mellie didn't have her teeth knocked out. They pulled them out using those pliers. I wondered why her face had been so badly battered. It was to hide the fact her teeth were torn out. That's inconsistent with the kind of sexual assault they were trying to suggest."

"Oh my God." Taylor looked as if he was about to be sick.

"Alex, Caleb doesn't need to know that. The pictures he must have in his mind are bad enough. He doesn't need worse ones." Conrad shook his head.

He knew that when he was alone that night he would weep for Melba Ramsey and her child while he prayed for their souls.

"Sirs, we have arrested Mr. Frank Sullivan while he was attempting to leave the building, sirs." One of the representatives from the War Production Board had obviously been seconded from the Marines.

"That's good. We have a lot of questions to ask Mr. Sullivan. Would you gentlemen kindly secure the filing cabinets back there? I suspect the information they contain might be the key to what is going on here. And that odd-looking typewriter in the corner?"

Detention Block, Warrington Field, Warminster, Pennsylvania

"I've told you everything I know." Sullivan sounded aggrieved.

"I know, Mr. Sullivan. I'm sorry about this, but I'm afraid the situation has changed significantly since we last spoke. The whole Mellie Ramsey killing has been connected with the scandals up at the Brewster plant. It appears that the original appearance of the killing was concocted to cover up the fact that she was really tortured and killed because she had found out what was going on there. We now know she was killed between 1430 and 1600 in the apartment house where you live. You were there at that time. Given what was being done to her, it's likely that her screams would have been clearly audible. So we have to go over your evidence again. Are you sure you heard nothing?"

"Quite sure. I had the radio on all the time and I was listening carefully. I like to see if I can solve the mystery when the armchair detectives do not."

Conrad gave Sullivan a friendly grin. "Of course. So do I, and a lot of professional detectives I could name. The writers stack the deck though, making the evidence misleading enough to fox professionals. It's not surprising the armchair detectives never get the right answer. Did you deduce the answer to the riddle of the 'Dead Man's Cavern?'"

Sullivan shook his head. Conrad gave him another, even more friendly grin, not hinting that he had only listened to the episode a few minutes before. "Nor did I. What did you think of the armchair detective's solution?"

"They were way off as usual. I'm glad they're not on this case." Sullivan seemed to relax at that point.

"I suppose you would think that." Conrad's voice was mild. "You see, Miss Marjory Lawrence and Mr. Beverly Kelly were the first pair of armchair detectives in over a year to solve the case correctly. That's so rare the script didn't cover it and Santos Ortega had to ad-lib his response. He did very well, by the way. Everybody who was listening to the show remembers that. So, what were you really doing between 1430 and 1600?"

Sullivan said nothing and just stared at Conrad. *That is usually phase two of them folding,* Conrad thought. *He's trying to buy time to come up with a plausible explanation. So, let's give him something else to think about.* "We have another problem with your testimony. You met Lieutenant O'Brien at 1610. Ten yards from the front door of your house. What did you do in those ten minutes? Are you so infirm you can only walk at one yard per minute?"

Conrad watched the panic spreading in Sullivan's eyes. *He is trapped and he knows it. The fact that the armchair detectives got it right for once was so unpredictable that he had every reason to assume that the normal pattern of them blundering, and Ellery Queen rescuing them, would hold good. But, even if it hadn't, it would have been something else. It doesn't really matter what the trap is; he will step into one or another. If he comes up with a convincing answer over the hour the Adventures of Ellery Queen was being broadcast, he is then faced with explaining those ten minutes. And there are more pitfalls behind that.*

There was a knock on the door and the single word "Ingrid."

On hearing Conrad's response, Igrat walked in with a note in her hand. "Colonel Cooper wanted you to have this right away, so I brought it down. We've identified the couple who owned the house; Frederick Sherman is actually Friedrich Schumann and his wife 'Martha' is really Marta. Both long-term members of the German-American Bund. They arrived here in 1932 and are currently tagged as people of interest. They say they weren't involved in what happened to Mellie; that it was all this person's doing."

"They might be telling the truth, Ingrid. This may well be the man who raped Mellie."

Igrat stared at Sullivan with acute loathing that was quite genuine. "I castrated the last man who tried to do something like that to me."

Igrat stalked out. Neither she nor Conrad any any indication a little bit of theater had been set up between them. In fact, the Schumanns were doing the sensible thing and were keeping their mouths shut. Conrad stared at Sullivan with genuine disgust on his face. "And so, we have it. You'll be charged with the first-degree murder of Melba Ramsey and her baby. You will also be charged with collaborating with agents of a foreign power, to whit the German-American Bund acting on behalf of the Nazis. In time of war, that's treason. Ordinary, decent criminals are oddly patriotic and they really hate men who abuse women and children. I think you'll have a very, very bad time in prison before you fry."

"We weren't working for the Bund. I told you, I was an accountant. That wasn't really true. I worked for the State Department, a clerk processing export permits. Every time a company in America wanted to sell specific equipment to somebody, I had to check to see if the buyers were authorized to receive that equipment. I saw there how many countries aren't allowed to buy military equipment. When I was coming up to retirement, I saw how prices were going up and asked for an increase in my pension. They never even bothered to reply.

"Then two people from Brewster's came to me. Two brothers, Alfred and Ignacio Miranda. They had a whole clutch of potential customers in South America, but they'd already been to prison for selling illicit arms to Bolivia. Their name would be poison on any export permit. Not that one would be permitted anyway; not with the war on. So, they asked me to navigate them through the export maze, so they could smuggle weapons to their clients. That's all I did, told them how to avoid the checks and security precautions. I wasn't involved in the rest. The Schumanns are lying. I was never in that cellar."

"Who said anything about a cellar?" Conrad's question was mildly-worded, but had all the qualities of an armor-piercing shot from one of the dreaded German 88s.

Investigation Office, Hangar Number Three, Warrington Field, Warminster, Pennsylvania

"Did he do it?" Taylor had been trying to get information out of the Schumanns and finally succeeded. Almost. They had finally broken down when they'd been told about Sullivan's statement implicating them. As the note, which Conrad had faked and Igrat had brought in, had suggested, they'd blamed Sullivan for the killing. Although the husband and wife had been separated, their stories had coincided on that point.

Some might think that supported their statements as being the true version of events, but I am not so naïve. To me, that tells me they had agreed on their stories beforehand and always intended to throw Sullivan to the wolves.

"Oh yes, he did it. Some of it. All three of them worked on Melba Ramsey; it would need all of them to make sure she didn't manage to get away once they got started."

"That'll do it." Taylor had his pre-military service lawyer cap on. "Common purpose. It doesn't even matter if he wasn't in the same room. He shared their purpose and he'll go to the chair along with them. Perhaps they'll be holding hands when the warden throws the switch. Do you think they knew she was pregnant?"

"I think so. Even if they didn't at the start, Mellie would have told Marta Schumann when she understood what was about to happen. She'd have thought another woman would understand and have pity on her. Obviously, she was mistaken. We're not done with this yet. We have the mess at Brewster's to clear up. You got a date with Ingrid, by the way?"

Taylor's jaw dropped. "How did you know?"

Conrad's Other Eye

Conrad smiled at him. "I didn't. But I do know Ingrid."

"Will we ever know who actually killed Mellie?" Taylor sounded despondent.

"All three of them." Conrad was brusque. He really didn't want to think about what had happened in that cellar. It was too much like things he had seen in other cellars at other times. "Two of them held her down while the third raped her. Then . . . "

Conrad stopped; he simply could not go on. Taylor had waited patiently for him to recover his composure. When Conrad had, he resumed the discussion. "I'm sorry, Alex. This case is getting to me. How's Lillith getting on with her financial investigation?"

"She sent a message over; she wants us over in the plant as soon as we're finished up here. Apparently Thomas DeLorenzo is in custody again and she wants us to talk to him."

Conrad smiled at that. *After all these years, Lillith and Naamah still forget themselves sometimes and bark orders at people.* "Alex, can you give her a call and ask her to send DeLorenzo over here? Tell her it would be better if we spoke to him when he's in strange surroundings."

CHAPTER FIVE

JUSTICE

Investigation Office, Hangar Number Three, Warrington Field, Warminster, Pennsylvania

Taylor had just finished on the telephone and hung up when it rang again. Conrad found himself looking back on the days of long-delayed communications with affection. When Taylor had finished that call he took a deep breath. "Well, that's a new twist. Army CIC have started going through the records we confiscated from the filing cabinets in the murder-cellar. Apparently that typewriter thing was a decoding device. Don't ask me how they got it working so quickly. The Schumanns were setting up a spy-and-sabotage ring here.

"It looks like the Nazis have given up on trying the infiltrate agents in from outside and are trawling ex-members of the German-American Bund for recruits. One of the first things they found was a list of active members of said ring. The list includes an engineer and a plant manager at Brewsters. They also have a list of sympathizers, including Work, DeLorenzo, the Miranda brothers and Chief Schultz. CIC caution us that previous experience suggests that 'sympathizers' may not be aware they were considered to be such."

"Useful idiots." Taylor looked at him curiously. Conrad hastened to explain the reference, knowing that the burgeoning American-Russian alliance meant that many inconvenient things were being politely forgotten. "Lenin. He used to describe people who would further the communist cause without realizing it as 'useful idiots.' I suspect the same applies here. Let us speak with Mr. DeLorenzo of such things."

Conrad had seen DeLorenzo being marched in by two marine guards. He was amused to note that the union president was being very careful where he put his feet. "Thomas, Thomas, this is a sad day for organized labor."

"When the military take over the livelihoods of honest workers? You understate things, Father."

"No, Thomas. When the head of a union, designed to protect the working men and women of this country, stands charged with the rape, torture and murder of a pregnant woman, and of committing high treason by levying war against the United States and adhering to its enemies, giving them aid and comfort. If any man has ever put deadly weapons in the hands of those who were undermine the representation of working people, you have. Every time now, when workers wish to organize, the company management will simply say 'Thomas V. DeLorenzo' and the worker's cause will be lost. "

DeLorenzo had gone white with horror. "Rape? Murder? Treason? I never . . . "

Conrad was quiet, polite and remorseless. "Melba Ramsey was carrying the child of an Army officer when she was abducted, beaten and raped. Her teeth were torn out and her head so crushed she could not be recognized, even by the man who loved her. You shared a common purpose with the people who did that, and so the State of Pennsylvania will charge you with the crimes committed against a woman who had every right to expect protection and every citizen of this country has an absolute duty to protect.

"You also gave aid and comfort to a group of Nazi saboteurs who were planning an insurrection against the United States, and you aided in supplying them with the weapons and equipment they needed. You enabled them by directing financial resources to them, and you sabotaged the production of the equipment needed to fight their cause. You shared a common purpose with those people, and so the Federal Government will charge you with high treason. I do not know whether you will be executed by Pennsylvania or the Federal Government, but surely executed you will be. If you live that long."

"In civilian life, I was a defense attorney." Taylor spoke equally quietly and politely. "I would offer to act in that capacity for you, only I can think of no defense to offer on your behalf."

"But . . . But . . . All I wanted was . . . "

"What did you want, Thomas? What was so important that it was worth all this?"

"My members. They were in reserved occupations, but their brothers and cousins weren't. So, I struck a deal with Jimmy Work. If the union paid him a hundred dollars each, he'd employ as many people as we wanted. There was another aspect to that, of course. The company would have to pay the workers it had hired and they needed to generate income to do that. So, we agreed to slow down production as much as we could, while Jimmy and his boys sold the GFE for the unbuilt aircraft on the black market. The profits from that paid the extra workers."

"Do you know what was really happening, Thomas?"

"Yeah, we were keeping our people off the Russian Front."

"No, most of the money from the equipment that was being sold went to Friedrich and Marta Schumann to subsidize their nascent sabotage ring. The Miranda brothers were selling the weaponry and engines to Argentina, Paraguay, Ecuador and a few others. You know what they all have in common? They're either Nazi allies or sympathizers. Or, at the very least, they have large German minority populations. Arm them, and there is the possibility of a coup that would flip them into the war on the German side.

"You were enabling the Miranda brothers to supply military equipment to the enemies of this country and, quite possibly, allow our enemies to bring their war to this continent. You weren't keeping your people off the front line, Thomas. You were bringing the front line home to them." Conrad quietly blessed Melba Ramsey who, alone and unassisted, had put all of this together and made sure the records of her findings were preserved. Silently, he asked forgiveness of her for having doubted her capability in this work.

DeLorenzo slumped in his seat, his face buried in his hands. "I didn't know."

Conrad was still quiet, polite and pitiless. "All the evidence was there for you to see, had you wanted to see it. You didn't know only because you didn't want to know. Melba Ramsey, working as the manageress of a local diner, put it all together. That's why she and her unborn baby died a horrible death. All you saw were the five hundred dollars you charged each of your union members for a draft exemption certificate. Four hundred dollars of which went into your own pocket."

The telephone rang in the background. Taylor answered it. He simply thanked the person on the other end. "Sorry to interrupt, Conrad, but that was Colonel Cooper. The Miranda brothers have just been arrested crossing the state line. They were heading south, probably for Mexico. They're being held on charges of purchasing black market gasoline. Just to hold them, of course. He's on his way over now. Just out of interest, DeLorenzo, is there any depth to which you are not prepared to sink?"

"What can I do to make this go away." There was a gleam of calculation in DeLorenzo's eyes. Conrad read what the man was thinking as clearly as if he was speaking the words. *"What will it cost to pay these people off?"* He *doesn't realize it, but he just answered Alex's question with a single word: none.*

"You can't. All you can do is to try and mitigate your offenses. You might, might, be able to buy yourself a lifetime in a Pennsylvania or Federal prison without possibility of parole instead of the electric chair. But that entirely depends upon how completely you cooperate with the authorities." Taylor was

Conrad's Other Eye

speaking as a lawyer now. "In your shoes, I would start making a very complete and very thorough statement. And woe betide you if we find even the slightest evasion or distortion when we corroborate it. Just remember, we have all the paperwork and eight other people also making confessions."

Police Station, Gibson Avenue, Warminster, Pennsylvania

Police Chief Bernard Schultz read the report that had been given to him with despair. *It seemed so simple when we started. I had to investigate the people who were being given draft exemptions and demonstrate that their work really was essential to the war effort. Instead, I took the payment per man and signed off on them. Then, when the Ramsey woman was found dead, I took the obvious solution that was presented to me. I should have known it was just too convenient. Sullivan had told us about the Army pilot coming over every day after he had finished duty. I just never made the connection between him knowing that and her dying. I didn't make it because I didn't want to make it.*

Schultz read everything he had written down. It was as professional a statement as any police officer could make: accurate, detailed and completely true. *How they must have all laughed at me. The blundering flatfoot too stupid to see what was in front of his nose.* He was well aware that everybody else who had been arrested would be making statements that minimized their own part in the atrocity of Melba Ramsey's death and accused others. *There is only one way I can make sure that the truth is recognized. By making sure that mine is the only statement that cannot possibly benefit its author.*

And so, Police Chief Bernard Schultz carefully signed his statement and put it into an envelope along with his badge. He sealed it, wrote Conrad's name on the front and carefully placed it on to his desk.

Then, he took his service revolver, placed the barrel under his chin and shot himself.

Detention Block, Warrington Field, Warminster, Pennsylvania

"Frank Sullivan, Friedrich Schumann and Marta Schumann are all to be charged by the State of Pennsylvania with the abduction, rape and murder of Melba Ramsey and the murder of her baby. The full details of what happened at the Brewster plant will remain classified. That applies to you, Father. You must continue to say nothing about this."

"I understand."

Hammond looked up. "As far as the public is concerned, the Navy is cancelling all outstanding orders with Brewster Aviation due to failure to comply with delivery schedules and defective workmanship. James Work will

150

be charged with fraud, malfeasance, theft of company funds and defrauding the United States Navy. The Miranda brothers are being charged with fraud and the Brewster shareholders are suing them for $10 million."

"They're literally getting away with murder." Conrad shook his head.

"Work and the Mirandas? I agree, but there is more in play here than it seems. If it's any consolation, the workforce members are having their draft exemptions revoked and will be on their way to the Russian Front, as infantrymen, as soon as they have received the necessary training. A few men who seem genuinely skilled and the women employees, most of whom worked in the plant for all the right reasons, will stay on when the plant is handed over to the Navy for use as an experimental weapons establishment."

Colonel Hammond once more looked up from the file he had been given. "Conrad, I really have to thank you for this, both on behalf of the US Government and my department. We've made an example of a badly-run plant and the Great American Public know that we are watching how their tax money gets spent. Which we are, to the best of our ability."

"I wish, Colonel Hammond, that I could take comfort from that. A victory has a sadness all of its own."

"This wasn't a victory, Conrad. We won a skirmish, but the Nazis won a battle. They've reduced the production capacity we have available for Corsairs by a quarter. We need every one of those bent-wing bastards to beef up the attacks on Europe. Now, we'll have to keep the Grumman Hellcats in the North Atlantic longer and that means the carriers in the Pacific will have to continue flying Wildcats for a bit longer. This is a production war, Conrad, and we just took a bad hit."

"I have one question to ask," Conrad looked accusingly at Colonel Cooper. "Did you know the Schumanns were German-American Bund members when you sent Melba Ramsey in there?"

Cooper shook his head. "No, we did not. We should have done, I agree; and that will weigh on my conscience. If it's any consolation, Army CIC has not come well out of this business. We missed what was really happening completely, got our agent killed and had to be rescued by an amateur detective, an accountant and an instructor pilot who happens to be a lawyer in his civilian life.

"Anyway, few people in CIC came out of this well. To tell you the honest truth, we ended this looking like a bunch of incompetent clowns. I have been told that most of our functions, including all those taking place in US territory, will be assumed by the FBI."

"I'm sorry to hear that, Colonel."

"I'm not." Cooper looked strangely satisfied. "Army CIC is being reorganized as a behind-the-lines security force aimed at detecting and preventing espionage and sabotage. Those are bad problems and doing something about them in the US sectors of the Russian Front is beyond urgent. I'm told, the alternative to retasking CIC is to ask CheKa to take the job over. I like to think we would be a little more . . . discrete . . . in how we do things."

Room 650, Hotel Astor, Broadway and West 44th Street, Times Square, New York City, three months later

When Conrad came out of his shower, he found Igrat sitting in his suite, reading his newspaper. She had not, however, stolen his toast and jam. Yet.

"Hello, Iggie. What can I do for you?"

"Official business, Conrad. I've got some messages for you. All by word only."

That told Conrad this was serious. Igrat's abilities as a courier were many and varied, but the most important was that she could remember long verbal messages and repeat them word-perfect. More than word perfect; she would even include the pauses and intonations the speaker had used and pass those on as well. Conrad watched while she half-closed her eyes.

"The Brewster business is all wrapped up now. Eight members of the production staff, including the F3A acceptance officer and the test squadron maintenance chief, have been arrested for sabotage or failure to detect the results of sabotage. In the last two cases, they have been assigned to the weather station at Anadyr, where they will have nowhere to spend the bribes they accepted.

"When the FBI took the case over, they went over the cellar where Melba Ramsey was murdered with extreme care. She was a fellow Federal agent, after all. They used a new stuff called luminol that glows blue if there is a tiny trace of blood present. They found huge areas of blood trace where she died. It appears that one of the murderers stepped in that blood and tracked it over the floor. The Schumanns washed up, but they couldn't beat luminol.

"The FBI were able to determine the shoe size of the person who stepped in Melba's blood. That positively identified Frank Sullivan as being in close proximity to her when she died. Not that it changes much, but it makes it probable he was the rapist."

"So he goes to the chair?" Igrat had opened her eyes, which was permission for other people to speak. Conrad had jumped at the chance.

"The Schumanns will, for a vicious, perverted rape-murder. Sullivan won't. Somehow, Lieutenant O'Brien got told what had been done to Mellie and their child. Probably, somebody took it on themselves to decide he had a right to know. Whatever. He found out and, when Sullivan was walked from the courtroom, he pumped eight shots from a .45 into him. Hit him in the stomach and balls. Sullivan died screaming."

"God have mercy on Caleb. And on me for the part of me that cheers his action."

"Me too. Both parts. Caleb was court-martialed, of course. After a few minutes deliberation, he was found not guilty on grounds that the awful murders of his fiancé and child had temporarily unhinged his mind. That, of course, makes him unfit for duty and, equally of course, he was given a medical discharge from the Army."

"That's a loss for the country. He's a good man and Alex told me he was a good pilot."

"He still is. General Chennault has hired him for the Flying Bears. He'll be flying B-25s on the Russian Front."

Conrad smiled slightly. The Flying Bears, the original American Volunteer Group in Russia, hired pilots and aircrew who, for some reason, didn't qualify for the US Army Air Force or the US Navy. Too old, perhaps, or sometimes too young, men with a criminal record or men for whom the legality of their residence in the United States was doubtful. Other recruits came from countries occupied by the Nazis and included substantial numbers of their national air forces. As a result, the Flying Bears were a skilled and motivated force. They mostly flew P-40s and B-25s, aircraft otherwise relegated to the Pacific and the Continental US. It would be a good home for Caleb O'Brien, who had more than his fair share of demons to exorcize. *The busybody who told him things he shouldn't know has much to answer for and will, in time.*

"I hope he does well there and finds some peace. The way he immediately did what was right when Mellie told him of her condition spoke volumes of his character."

"I agree." Igrat settled back in her seat. "Caleb is one of the good guys. Talking of good guys, Alex sends his regards. I guess you've worked out that he defended O'Brien at his court-martial?"

"I expected that would be the case the moment you told me what happened at Sullivan. How are you to getting on, by the way?"

"Casual, but friendly." Igrat smiled warmly. "He doesn't seem to think that, because he's had me, he owns me. That's nice. We don't meet often but when we do we're pleased to see each other and sorry when we have to split again.

Conrad's Other Eye

"Anyway, Conrad, I've got to run. But I've got one more message for you, this time from The Seer. He says the Pope claims that he badly needs your help and wants to see you over in the Vatican. You've got tickets on a Pan Am Constellation any time you want them. Which means right away, of course. The Seer says, watch your back; that place is a snakepit. He's right. Rome is one of my standard stopovers and it's almost as bad as Cairo. Food is better and the people are nicer though."

Igrat picked up her handbag, snagged a piece of Conrad's toast and headed for the door. "Bye, Conrad, and don't do anything I wouldn't. Which gives you almost infinite scope!"

The door closed behind her and Igrat was gone. As always, she left the room feeling strangely empty.

Conrad sighed gently and ate his remaining slice of toast and its thin skim of jam. As he drank the last of his coffee, he stared into the mirror..

"Now, what does Eugenio Maria Giuseppe Giovanni Pacelli, better known as Pope Pius XII, want this time?"

EYE OF THE CONFESSOR
The Vatican City, 1944

Conrad's Other Eye

CHAPTER ONE

THE SACRIFICIAL LAMB

Basilica of Saint Peter, Vatican City

"May God have mercy on us all!"

Wachtmeister Julian Hüber's rank in the Vatican Swiss Guard was the equivalent of sergeant in other armies, and he had an assignment of awesome responsibility. Every night, he patrolled the rearmost passages of the palace until he came to an alcove in the wall that formed the southern boundary of the Basilica of Saint Peter. There, between the statues of Saint Veronica and Saint Andrew was a heavy wooden door, secured by a heavy lock.

Wachtmeister Hüber took a ring of keys from underneath his tunic and solemnly opened the door. It opened the way to a tunnel leading to another door, an ancient one that was secured by three very large and intimidating locks. Each had a different, equally large, equally intimidating, key. Once the door was open, Hüber passed through and gravely locked it behind him. Having checked that the entry was indeed secure, he made his way down a metal staircase that took him into the deepest part of the Vatican crypt.

Rome in midsummer was not the most pleasant of cities to live in. When a heat wave struck, the city would swelter in excessive temperatures and humidity until a cool breeze from the mountains eventually brought relief. Logic might suggest that the Vatican crypt, being deep underground and surrounded by rock, would remain cool, but it did not. It was perpetually hot and kept excessively humid by the nearby river Tiber. It was, in fact, a rather unpleasant place; one made worse by a vague but unpleasant smell. Hüber continued his regular patrol down a long curving corridor. The lamp he carried illuminated alcoves, from whence he was flanked by dead popes and kings.

Eventually, the passage brought him out into a vault. Normally, the centerpiece of that room was a long, low, box-like structure, one that covered excavations investigating the possible gravesite of Saint Peter. Originally, the site of the box had been a pile of masonry some 20 feet long by 40 wide. In the process of enlarging the crypt in the 1930s, the rubble had been cleared and the floor lowered by two and a half feet. In doing so, the Papal engineers had discovered a mausoleum that had been untouched since the times of the Caesars.Pope Pius XII had decided to proceed with the excavations, much encouraged by the discovery of an inscription *Petros eni*, 'Peter is within,' on the mausoleum roof. Convinced that the archeologists were on the right track, work had continued in secret, despite the outbreak of war.

Now, though, the box had been roughly and crudely moved to one side, exposing the pit beneath. It was not the sight of the excavation that had forced Hüber's cry. It was that of a man hanging by his feet over the pit that formed the center of the excavations. Even in the dim light, it was apparent that the man's throat had been radically cut, the slash carving his neck open from ear to ear and laying bare his spine.

Pan-American Lockheed Constellation Clipper Freedom, *on route to Rome, September 1944*

Conrad was enjoying the rare privilege of sitting in the copilot's seat of the Lockheed Constellation as it made its way from Casablanca to Rome. Having his ticket supplied by Pope Pius XII's private office was one factor that went towards that; another was that he was the only first-class passenger on board. That wasn't surprising, since the first-class compartment held only a single row of four seats. The copilot himself was in the passenger cabin, chatting to the occupants of the coach class seats. They were mostly government officials travelling as part of their duties. Captain Jeffery Franklin had finished showing him the controls of the airliner and the two had been chatting about Pan-American operations in general.

"Frankly, Jeff, I'm surprised we're flying in daylight. I thought we would be flying into Rome at night."

"Because of the krauts? We're all right down here and we don't normally fly north of Rome. We've flown to Bologna a couple of times but that's as near to hostile airspace as we get. Milan is definitely out. The rule of thumb is single-engine fighter range. This lady can pick up her skirts and run if she needs to. We can do 330 knots if we have to, although the accountants hate us afterwards. That's not enough to get away from 109s and 190s, but if we're far enough south, the Hitlerites would have to use Me-110s to come after us and we're 10 knots faster than them. And, there are Italian fighters based in Northern Italy who would nail any Nazi fighters intruding on their airspace. Or any of ours come to that; they're serious about being neutral. That's why we're flying this route as civilians."

That and propaganda, Conrad thought. *Showing off that the avalanche of American war production is so great, they can afford to divert four-engined aircraft to civilian airlines. That's why the names have changed. The Clippers used to be named after far-away exotic places but now the great airliners carry names like* Clipper Freedom *and* Clipper Liberty. *It's manpower that is in short supply. Captain Franklin must be in his fifties and his co-pilot is the same age. It is even rumored both Pan-American and TWA are training women to fly the airliners. All because the younger men are flying bombers.*

"It's hard to remember when flying cross the Atlantic was an adventure. This time, it took us eight and a half hours to the Azores, four hours to Casablanca and another four hours from there to Rome. Less than a day to go half way around the world."

"It still would be an adventure if you were on a C-54. The first leg alone would take you nearly 14 hours. Those Douglas DC-4s are slow. They cruise at 190 knots compared to our 270. They're all on the Air Bridge to Russia, though. Not many Connies on that route."

"I saw a newsreel on the Air Bridge before I left. One aircraft landing in Russia every fifteen minutes, with ten tons of cargo or forty men per flight. Why don't they use Connies up there if we're so much faster?"

"Connie is mostly a passenger aircraft. We're not so good at hauling cargo. The doors are too small and the fuselage is the wrong shape. Then the Douglas is a lot cheaper; like three quarters of the price. That's a big thing, considering there are more than a thousand of them now. It's also much faster to build, which is also a big thing, since a thousand is nowhere near enough." Captain Franklin leaned forward slightly in his seat. "See that shadow on the horizon ahead? That's Italy. I'm sorry, Father, but I'm going to have to ask you to return to your seat now. I'm going to need Jim up here for the rest of the flight."

St. Peter's Square, Rome, Italy.

It was 294 steps from St. Peter's Square to the main office of the Sacred Congregation for Extraordinary Ecclesiastical Affairs, the convoluted name for what was effectively the Vatican's combined foreign office and secret service. Conrad had to pause for breath twice on the way up. Each time, he reflected on his need for more exercise. When he finally reached the landing and the nondescript door that it was host to, he needed another minute's rest to compose himself. Once inside, he found Lotario dei Conti di Segni waiting for him. With him was Eugenio Maria Giuseppe Giovanni Pacelli, better known as Pope Pius XII. That would have been impressive enough, even for a member of the Society of Jesus. However, Lotario of Segni had once been known as Pope Innocent III, and he had been alive a very long time. He had been that even when Conrad had been born.

There was an elaborate protocol that had to be completed when meeting the Pope, although it had hardly envisaged the situation when two Popes were in the same room. Pope Pius waved it aside. "Conrad, thank you for coming. We need your help urgently. Lotario, could you please brief Father Conrad on the situation here?"

Conti di Segni nodded. "Conrad, first you should know that His Holiness is aware of our secret. That indeed is a large part as to why you were summoned here so urgently. We are used to secrecy, even more so than the Society of Jesus. You, being both long-lived and a member of the Society have unique qualifications to handle this case. Let me explain what has happened and you will see why extraordinary secrecy is essential."

The story told by Conti di Segni was a familiar one to Conrad. It was reminiscent of many English detective stories, the body found in a locked room with no apparent means of access. As the details piled up, Conrad found himself puzzled by the mystery. *There are only three solutions to this: either there is another entrance to the room, the door was not locked or the murderer was already in the room when the victim entered it. Diabolically complicated murder machines really don't exist.* By that time, Conti di Segni had finished his review of what had happened and was looking at Conrad hopefully.

"My first question." Conrad knew that the Pope's daily workload was immense, and he needed to be elsewhere. At this point, the highest service Conrad could perform was not to waste his time. "Has the victim been identified?"

"He was Doctor Ermes Parrino, a doctor of archeology, not medicine. He was supervising the dig in the Vatican Crypt. His body is in an autopsy room at the Santo Spirito in Sassia Hospital, protected by the Swiss Guard."

"Was the crime scene photographed?" Conrad knew there was no chance that the scene had been left untouched, but thorough photography would be invaluable.

"It was." Conti di Segni passed over a file, bulging with pictures. "We photographed everything and also drew diagrams of the crypt and surroundings."

"Third question. Who has keys to the crypt?"

"That is the problem. There are only three sets of keys. One is held by His Holiness, the second by the Swiss Guard and the third by the archeology team. At the moment, we are holding *Wachtmeister* Julian Hüber, who had custody of the Swiss Guard set of keys, as a suspect. Frankly, we can't think of anybody else who could have done it."

Conrad thought that over. "Could we go down and see the crime scene? These pictures are very good, and tell us much, but I'd still get a better feel for the case if I can see where the killing took place."

"There might be a problem there." His Holiness looked worried and embarrassed at the same time. "The few records that exist of Saint Peter's martyrdom and burial all state that a dreadful curse was placed on his burial chamber. Anybody who disturbed it would suffer an awful fate in this world and the next. I like to think of myself as a man of science as well as one of religion and an agent to bring the two together. As such, things like curses have little credibility with me. Only, with this murder, I have to ask if I can be so sure of that position now."

"I have come across many such curses over the years, Your Holiness. My experience has always been that they are there to hide something. Usually they are started by the ones guilty of the crime so that they conceal their act. Once the light of truth is shone upon them and their deeds, the curse shrivels away."

"There is written evidence for this curse that goes back to the fifth century." Conti di Segni also sounded disturbed. "It really is blood-curdling. I have never read or heard such foul and threatening language."

You should listen to Achillea in full flood. Conrad thought with a degree of amusement. *You'd have to come up with an entirely new definition of foul language. She told me that it was just the way people spoke back then. Foul curses and obscene language were the normal way somebody expressed themselves. She says that Latin was a language that came from the gutter and carried that legacy proudly. Its exalted position, and the pretensions of its users today, amuses her. Back then, she says distinguished people spoke Greek when they wanted to impress others with their erudition and culture.* "That isn't unusual either. Most cursers made a point of expressing their intent using violent imagery and exploiting cultural taboos."

"There's another side to the same thing." His Holiness was about to reveal a secret that was as carefully kept as that of the Daimones. "You know the story of Saint Peter, of course. How Peter, fleeing Rome to avoid execution, asked the question of a vision of Jesus, to which Jesus allegedly responded that he was 'going to Rome to be crucified again.' On hearing this, Peter decided to return to the city to accept martyrdom.

"What that story does not add is another legend. That, because of his willing acceptance of martyrdom, Peter's remains became infused with the Holy Spirit and thus they granted absolute protection to wherever they lay. According to this legend, the burial of his body here is why the Vatican has survived for nearly two millennia, despite all the odds against it doing so. That is why, also, the hideous curse was laid upon anybody who attempted to interfere with them."

"The point is, there is a whole complex of legends and curses that encircle this single site and they all focus on that crypt." Conti di Segni looked very seriously at his companions. "When there is that intense a concentration of legends about a single place, there must surely be something behind them?"

Conrad's Other Eye

Conrad was about to shake his head when a very disturbing thought struck him. *We are in the middle of the most destructive war in history, one that has already killed more people than any other and has embraced the whole world. It shows no sign of ending; indeed, the bloodshed and horror grows worse every day. By His Holiness's account, the excavations started in earnest during 1939. Could this whole dreadful war be the result of that curse? And, if so, where and when will it end?* "Nevertheless, we should start there. From there, I will need to see the body and speak to the doctor who performed the autopsy. Your Holiness, perhaps I should report back to you after these first steps have been completed?"

Mausoleum Crypt, Underneath Basilica of Saint Peter, Vatican City

"Four locks, four separate keys." Conti di Segni looked around the crypt with palpable unease. Conrad could understand why. The peculiar heat in a room that should be chilled, the humidity that made everything damp and the strange, disturbing smell all made for a location that was profoundly uncomfortable. Added to that, Conti di Segni was more than three hundred years older than he was and came from a time when curses, both spoken and written, were taken very seriously. Conrad blessed himself for being a Renaissance man, one of the many clerics of that time who finally understood that curses and spells were just superstitions and their only powers were those that people allowed them to have by their belief in them. Conti di Segni predated that era by a wide margin and old habits died very hard.

"Originally, the headroom here was very limited, but His Holiness ordered the floor to be excavated to a depth of one meter so that people could stand erect. That's when we started finding the relics down here." Conti di Segni pointed at the excavation area.

"The box is supposed to cover the excavation site when it isn't in use?"

"That is correct, yes. It should be placed over the pit every night and lifted aside when the team starts work. It's to prevent the excavation being contaminated by debris falling in."

"And, apart from removing the body, nothing has been touched here?"

"With that exception, the scene is untouched. We had to remove the body, otherwise the decay would have been very rapid."

"That's understandable. In this case, I think it makes little difference. It seems to me that the key to this mystery lies in the where and the why. Once we have found the motive for this murder, the rest will fall into place."

Conrad walked around the room, looking for any sign of another entrance. There was none. His nose wrinkled slightly as he passed the south wall; the odd smell of the room seemed a little stronger there. His inspection ended at the pit. Looking down, he could see the stone slab that covered the mausoleum and the remains of the great pool of blood that had drained from the murder victim.

"If the cover was placed over this pit every night, then it must have been removed prior to the murder. That would suggest the circumstances of the murder were pre-planned. If Doctor Parrino had disturbed one or more intruders, he would have been killed in a hurried, extemporized manner. Hit over the head, strangled or stabbed, perhaps. Or shot. Uncovering the excavation, hanging him over the pit and then cutting his throat so decisively all speaks to the attack being premeditated. Which, of course, raises the question of what he was doing down here when the excavations had finished for the day. That brings us back to the question of motive."

"We had assumed that the killers were grave robbers and the Doctor was killed because he disturbed them."

Conrad shook his head, the gloom of the crypt making the movement almost indiscernable. "If that is so, why wasn't the grave robbed? And why the elaborate killing of the man? Whatever happened down here was what the murderers intended to happen. The question I would ask is did Doctor Parrino come down here by happenstance? Or was he lured down here specifically, so he could be killed? Then, that leads to other questions. If he came down here by happenstance, why? If he was lured down here, then, again, we have to ask why. Was it because he knew something he shouldn't and had to be silenced?"

"Given the elaborate preparations for this murder, I would say he had to be lured down here." Conti di Segni looked around the gloomy expanse of the crypt.

"Not necessarily." Conrad's mind was running through permutations while he compared the scene in front of him with the pictures that had been taken a few days earlier. As far as he could see, the room hadn't been touched between the two events. "The killers knew that somebody was coming down here. The Swiss guard who does his routine patrol of these crypts and vaults. Perhaps he was the target. A convenient visitor to these crypts, on a known and regular schedule, with a key that would permit access to this particular part of the crypt.

"We have to look at the possibility that *Wachtmeister* Hüber was the intended victim and that Doctor Parrino simply presented a convenient target. He arrived unexpectedly, he also had a key to the crypt and he found the killers in wait. So, they attacked him and, realizing that they had an opportunity to carry out their intent without trying to attack a trained and equipped soldier, they used him instead of their intended victim."

"But what was their intent?" Conti di Segni had a strange idea that he knew what Conrad was going to say.

"The victim was suspended, upside down, over the entry to this mausoleum and killed by having his throat cut. His blood drained out as he died and sprayed all over the stone. Doesn't that sound familiar to you?"

"A human sacrifice." Conti di Segni spoke heavily, now that the thoughts he had studiously excluded from his conscious mind were spoken. His words hung heavily in the air.

"Exactly." Conrad looked around. "Earlier, we spoke of curses and prophecies. Is not a human blood-sacrifice an integral part of the same fertile ground?"

Autopsy room at the Santo Spirito in Sassia Hospital

"It is quite clear that the victim was alive and fully conscious when his throat was cut. Although that hardly describes the massive injury we see here." Doctor Massimiliano Agostini looked at the nearly severed neck and shook his head. "Cause of death was extreme exsanguination, but that simply led the pack, as it were. There were numerous fatal injuries resulting from the damage to his neck. Blood loss just killed him before any of the others did."

"Have you any idea what kind of weapon inflicted this wound?" Conrad looked down on the dead archeologist and quietly prayed for his soul.

"Something much more than a normal knife." Doctor Agostini thought carefully. "A sword, perhaps; but it would have to be a heavy-bladed longsword or broadsword, not a proper sword like a rapier or estoc. An axe could do the same job, of course, or a hatchet. Even a spade, if its edges had been properly sharpened. Every soldier knows how deadly an entrenching tool can be once properly prepared."

"How about a halberd?" Conrad had in mind the Swiss Guards he had seen scattered around Vatican City. They carried halberds as part of their ceremonial equipment. He was also suddenly conscious of the fact there were two Guards outside this room.

"You mean the ones carried by the Swiss Guard?" Doctor Agostini caught on fast. "The blade of a normal halberd would do this kind of damage, yes. Very easily, in fact. The problem is the ones carried by the Swiss Guards are not normal halberds. They have the long central spearpoint, and the counterbalance on one side of that, but the main cutting blade is concave, severely so. If one was swung to cut the throat like this, the wound would be very different. Also, the long pole handle would impede the user. A heavy-bladed sword? Yes. An axe or hatchet? Yes. A normal halberd? Possibly yes. But one of the halberds carried by the Swiss Guard? Not quite no, but unlikely."

Conrad looked at the ghastly wound that had ended the archeologist's life. "Doctor, this is purely speculation, of course, but I have to question whether the actual intent here was to decapitate Doctor Parrino."

"Why do you think that, Father?"

"The depth of the wound; the fact that it is a single cut. There are no hesitation marks or restarts. This wound was inflicted in a single swing, probably, as you say, by a heavy sword. There is much that is ritualistic about this murder. Hanging the victim over the entrance to the mausoleum, draining his blood over the entry stone, all these things point to some kind of foul ritual. Such rituals may be accompanied by slitting the victim's throat, but decapitation is also common in such circumstances. The killer, or killers, may have neglected to allow for the fact that the suspended body would swing with the impact and that would absorb much of the blow. Probably enough to convert a clean decapitation into the kind of wound we see here."

"You're quite right, Father; there are no hesitation marks at all. There was one continuous sweep that was fast and certain. I think you are right, the wound is consistent with an attempted decapitation."

"Other marks on the body?"

"Ligature marks on the ankles, of course, and around the wrists. The bruising there is very bad and the skin is torn open. I would say the victim struggled for several minutes before the deathblow. I found fragments of cloth between his teeth, which would explain why nobody heard his cries for help."

Conrad reflected that the crypt, deep inside the bowels of the earth and under a massive stone building, was probably as close to being soundproof as any building came. The scene bore an unpleasant similarity to the circumstances in which Melba Ramsey had died just a few weeks earlier. "Are there any signs of the victim being hit on the head? Or drugged?"

"There is an impact wound on the back of his head, yes. I cannot say whether he had been drugged yet; I will pass through the results of the blood tests as soon as possible."

"I assume that the victim's personal possessions have been collected and preserved as evidence?" Conrad was aware that he was sounding officious, but the corruption and sloppy police work he had seen during the Melba Ramsey case caused him to be suspicious of everything and leave nothing unchecked.

"We have, yes." Doctor Agostini showed no resentment of the checks. In fact, Conrad got the distinct impression that he was relishing the chance to show how meticulous and careful he had been. "He had in his possession the usual things any man carries. His wallet, identification papers, house keys, some loose change, a penknife, pens and some papers relating to the dig. That is all."

"He didn't have the keys to the crypt with him?"

"Not when the body was brought here, no. Either he didn't have them with him when he was killed or the killers took them away when they left."

Swiss Guard Barracks, Vatican City

"*Wachtmeister* Julian Hüber is a good man." *Oberst* Ludwig Herrmann was emphatic. "He has been in the Guard for seven years and is one of thirty *wachtmeister*. That's a sergeant. He is a good, practicing Catholic of course, a single man of Swiss citizenship who completed basic training with the Swiss Army prior to joining the Pontifical Swiss Guard. His credentials on joining the Guard were irreproachable; he had the required certificates of good conduct from the Swiss Army and a letter of recommendation from the Papal Legate in Bern. The latter is a rare distinction.

"Of course, he complied with the requirement to have a high school diploma and he had a glowing character reference from his headmaster. He was twenty years of age when he joined us and is 184 centimeters tall. That is an important thing for the Guard, since most of our responsibilities are ceremonial and carrying a halberd with style needs a tall man. In fact, I would say, he is not just a good guardsman, but one of our best. I place the utmost trust and confidence in him."

"Is that why he was assigned to patrol the Vatican vaults?" Conrad was slightly suspicious of praise so all-embracing.

"It was. He is one of five *wachtmeister* who share that duty on rotation. All are the most trusted of our NCOs. We know the importance of that area and watch it well."

"I see. I assume he doesn't carry a halberd down there? A sword, perhaps?"

Herrmann laughed at that. "No, and he doesn't wear the blue and yellow striped uniform either. I'm sorry, Father Conrad, but most people think the Swiss Guard is a remnant of the Renaissance era. Only here to amuse visitors to the Vatican. I must tell you that we are a real army, although a very small one. *Wachtmeister* Hüber would have been wearing his dark blue fatigues and carrying a SiG MKPO submachine gun every time he did his rounds. Not a broadsword. He would have been carrying a pistol as well, a Dreyse Model 1907. Both are chambered for 7.65mm kurtz. If you like, I can take you to the armory and you can see these weapons. Before you ask, both were signed out to *Wachtmeister* Hüber and signed back in when he returned to the barracks."

"Ammunition as well?"

"All accounted for. A total of eighty-one rounds; two 30 round magazines for the SiG and three seven round magazines for the pistol."

Conrad couldn't help but reflect that the administration side of this affair had been conducted with admirable efficiency. "Thank you very much, *Oberst* Herrmann. I would like to speak with *Wachtmeister* Hüber now."

"You are welcome to do so. However, I must insist on being present at the interview. These guardsmen, and their actions, are my responsibility. If there are any irregularities uncovered, the blame rests with me."

The barracks weren't like anything Conrad had seen before. They didn't seem to have sleeping quarters attached, but did have ready rooms, briefing areas, an armory and a room that could only be described as a giant walk-in wardrobe. *If Igrat saw that, she would go green with jealousy.* The room contained the striped renaissance-style uniforms worn by the Swiss Guard on its ceremonial duties. Each uniform was marked with its wearer's name.

"Those uniforms are individually tailored for each Guardsman, They are made from 154 pieces and takes nearly 32 hours and 3 fittings to complete." Herrmann explained when he saw Conrad looking curiously at them.

"There doesn't seem to be a sleeping area here?"

"Most of the guardsmen live in apartments close by, provided by the Guard. Although they must be unmarried when they join the Guard, many marry once they have been here a while. To Italian girls mostly, of course. The average tour of duty with the Guard is 25 months, but most of the men re-enlist many times, assuming their service in their previous enlistment was satisfactory. There is a medal awarded to those who re-enlist, the Benemerenti medal. *Wachtmeister* Hüber has received that award.

"Now, we may use a small interview room here. It is usually where men applying to re-enlist are interviewed and their application granted or rejected. There are very few rejectees, a matter of great pride to the Guard."

The room was typical of its kind, sparsely decorated and furnished. *Functional is the most appropriate word. It is exceptionally clean though, something I have noticed before in military barracks but found sadly absent in most police interview rooms.* When *Wachtmeister* Hüber came in, Conrad took in his appearance. *Tall, fair-haired with blue eyes set in an open, honest face. He has not been arrested, nor is he under guard. He is, however, accompanied by a comrade.*

"Good afternoon, *Wachtmeister* Hüber. Thank you coming here so promptly. I am Conrad Lorenz, of the Society of Jesus and I have been asked to look into this terrible business. Could you start by telling me exactly what happened the night you found the body of Doctor Ermes Parrino? Don't worry about wandering. If you think you have missed a point, go back to it, then continue."

Despite that authorization, Hüber told the story in a straightforward yet painstakingly complete manner. *Listening to him, I begin to understand why his commander has such a high opinion of the man.* By the time he had finished, Conrad had a very clear picture of what had happened. "*Wachtmeister* Hüber, that was an excellent account of what must have been a most disturbing experience. I'd like to ask just one question about the crypt. When you got to the door leading into the crypt, are you sure the door was locked? Some of those old locks are made so that one can turn the key to "unlock" them when they are already opened."

Hüber was about to confirm that he had unlocked the door to the crypt when he suddenly stopped. "I thought I had, but now I'm not sure. I put each key into the correct lock and turned it. I am sure I must have felt the tumblers move but I honestly can't actually remember them doing so. You know how it is when we're doing something we've done many, many times before. I can't remember if I felt the tumblers move, remember it from other times or just believe that I must have. I didn't try the door before I unlocked it, so I can't be sure it was locked before I opened it."

Conrad knew exactly what Hüber was getting at. *This is why people go back and check their front doors because they couldn't remember locking them, even when they had.* "That's very helpful, *Wachtmeister*. Tell me, have you noticed anything strange in recent days? Things that have been moved, perhaps? Or people who were not where they should have been?"

Once again, Hüber thought carefully before answering. "There are always things that are moved sometimes. It is inevitable, given how many people work here or are visiting. People out of place, though? Certainly not. We are constantly on guard against people who are trying to get to places they should not be. If we had noticed anybody like that, they would have been reported and, if possible, detained for investigation."

"Do many people try and get into the official buildings here?"

Both *Oberst* Herrmann and *Wachtmeister* Hüber burst out laughing, giving a welcome air of relief to the tension that had inevitably accompanied the interview. Herrmann took the lead in answering. "Oh yes. There are people who believe that the Vatican buildings are full of objects of great value just standing around waiting to be taken. There are objects of great value here, but they are well protected. No casual thief would be able to steal them."

You haven't met Igrat, Conrad thought. *If she wanted to, she would have the place stripped to the bare walls in a few hours. No, that's unjust. She would just walk straight to the portable object that had the greatest value and steal it without leaving a trace.*

Herrmann was still speaking. "Then there are those who wish to speak with His Holiness for some reason. This may sound strange to you, but sometimes these are people who have a genuine need and are in great spiritual anguish. When we detain them, we listen to their stories and, once in a while, under conditions of great secrecy, we mention the matter to His Holiness and he will make time for them. Obviously, this is something that is never mentioned in public, since if people thought there really was a chance of getting a private audience that way, the lines of would-be intruders would stretch all the way to Cortina d'Ampezzo."

Herrmann looked innocent, but something about what he had just said struck Conrad as deceptive. *This is the first time my senses have told me that either of the guardsmen have hidden something. I don't think the* Oberst *is lying, so much as telling only a portion of the truth. So there are people who come here in secret and have clandestine meetings with His Holiness. Suddenly there is the smell of politics here.*

"Have you any idea why Doctor Parrino went down to the crypt after the dig had closed for the day?" Conrad was reasonably sure that *Wachtmeister* Hüber wasn't the killer, although he was still open-minded about whether he might have been the intended victim.

"None at all, Father. I was unaware that he was there until I opened the door to the crypt and lifted my lantern to see inside. I have thought about this much since I found his body and I can only come up with two possibilities. One is that he had either thought of something very important that excited him so much he couldn't wait until morning. The other is somebody had told him something that was so important it required his immediate presence."

"So you think his presence there was either accidental or he was lured down there?"

"They are the only possibilities I can see." Hüber sounded apprehensive, as if he was afraid that he had made himself look foolish by missing the obvious.

"I agree. I can't think of another. However, there are some deductions we can make from those assumptions. If we assume that Doctor Parrino was lured down to the crypt, then he was specifically targeted for murder. That raises the obvious question of motive. Why was he made the target? What did he know? Or, what had he seen? If he was there by accident, then either he disturbed something, perhaps tomb robbers trying to steal things of value, and was killed to silence him or somebody else was intended to be the victim and Doctor Parrino took his place."

"But, the only other person who would be down there that particular night was me," Hüber objected. As he did so, the cause for the objection shifted from the idea itself to the sudden realization of its implications.

"Quite." Conrad smiled at the *Wachtmeister.*

"You are saying that I could have been the intended victim." Hüber was struggling to come to terms with the idea that somebody was trying to kill him. *"Ach je."*

Oh dear is a remarkable understatement, given the circumstances. "Have you any idea why anybody might want to kill you? I know you are a soldier, and that this war is killing millions of young men like you, but why you in particular?"

"The Vatican is neutral and the Swiss Guard, as the Vatican Army, is neutral also. Our role is to protect His Holiness from those who would harm him." Conrad again got the feeling that Herrmann was repeating the official line and that omitted some key facts. "I can't think of any reason why anybody would want to kill *Wachtmeister* Hüber."

"Nevertheless, it is a possibility that we will have to bear in mind." Conrad looked at the other Swiss Guard who was accompanying Hüber. "*Wachtmeister*, I fear your responsibilities have just grown much heavier."

CHAPTER TWO

THE ORDERS COMMITTEE

Sacred Congregation for Extraordinary Ecclesiastical Affairs, Vatican City

"What is it that you are not telling me?" Conrad put the question in slightly more heated terms than he had intended. "This isn't just a simple murder. There's a major political aspect to the situation we have here. I'm just not sure what it is. Yet."

"I told you he would work it out in less than a day." Lotario dei Conti di Segni, once Pope Innocent III, looked at His Holiness Pope Pius XII with resigned good humor. "Tell me, Conrad, what do the words 'orders committee' mean to you?"

Conrad frowned, remembering several very long and almost indecipherable lectures from Sir Humphrey on the niceties of proper, orderly government. Usually, those lectures centered around Conrad's actions making the desired objective hard, if not impossible, to attain. "It's a governmental committee that usually determines things like the agenda of government business and the terms of reference of departments and thus of their ministers. I don't think that applies here, though."

"It doesn't. The Orders Committee is a secure and secret operation that carries out actions to protect our Church that cannot be acknowledged or admitted. It has the fundamental rule is that, if discovered, the Vatican will disavow any knowledge of its actions.

"The Orders Committee includes a worldwide network of informants, backed up by handwriting experts and code breakers. In very real terms, it is a secret espionage association outside and above the normal, overt hierarchy of the Church. It draws from all experts, all orders, and even includes qualified members of the laity, something unheard of in ecclesiastical history. Its unofficial motto is 'to do those things that must be done while leaving undone

171

those things that must not be done.' This is intended as a reminder to its members that they must always act in strict accordance with the teachings of the Church.

"Being made a member of the Orders Committee is not blanket permission to do whatever the member wants. Rather, it is a sign that said member can be trusted to find a way to do what is needful without breaking the laws of God."

Conti di Segni caught his breath for a second, "At the moment, its members form the pipeline that links the Vatican, and His Holiness in particular, with the religious orders in Germany that form the backbone of resistance to Hitler and the Nazis. The Jesuits, the Dominicans and the Benedictines are all key parts of that resistance. They do not report to their local bishops, many of whom are compromised by the Nazis and, in some cases, actively support them; instead, they report directly to their Order's leaders here. One part of the duties assigned to the Orders Committee is to be the conduit down which those communications flow. The Dominicans and the Jesuits, in particular, have shown an enterprising and martial spirit that has earned them the proud title of 'Enemies of the Reich'.

"This is only part of their work, though. They travel Germany, collecting information about German plans from secretaries, telephone operators, government clerks and their equivalents in armaments companies, military officers, even members of the Gestapo. That information is sent to a central point in Geneva for analysis. We do not know who, or what, that point is and we have no desire to find out.

"On the same principle of compartmentation and secrecy, the Orders Committee in Germany is divided into seven-person cells and none know the identities of the others. Also, as a matter of secrecy, the members of the Orders Committee have privileges granted to them to enable them to continue their work. They are allowed to wear non-priestly garb and to live outside the regulations of their orders."

Conti di Segni smiled at Conrad. "Privileges that you have taken for yourself more than once, of course. His Holiness and I think that it's about time your peculiar position in your order was regularized, before you get accused of heresy. Before you can go further into this mystery, we are inviting you to join the Orders Committee as a member at large. Normally, your life will continue as before but sometimes, as now, when your talents are needed, we will call on you."

His Holiness sighed deeply. "The existence of the Orders Committee and its actions are highly secret, of course, and have been since it was formed more than three centuries ago. Most of its members are clergy for a simple and terrible reason. They have no families that can be used against them. Have you heard of Hans and Sophie Scholl?"

Conrad shook his head. His Holiness continued, his voice softened by sadness. "They were brother and sister, Munich students who printed anti-Nazi leaflets in a shed behind their home. They called these leaflets 'White Roses' and they denounced Hitler in the most scathing of terms. They then scattered them in the streets of Munich and in stations all over Germany. It couldn't last, of course, and they were caught. The Gestapo made Hans Scholl watch while they tortured his sister. For all the brutality to which they were subjected, the two would not confess to anything other than printing and distributing the leaflets. For which act, they were both beheaded."

Conrad's head snapped up at the last word. His Holiness nodded. "Normally, the Nazis behead criminals using a guillotine similar to that used by the French. That was how they announced Hans and Sophie Scholl had been executed, but we know the reality; they were hung by their feet and had their heads cut off by a sword. There is a ritualistic element to that which we do not yet understand. But one thing we do know; they died without revealing their links to the Catholic resistance to the Nazis or the existence of the Orders Committee."

Conrad thought carefully about what he was hearing. "I need no convincing that the Nazi government of Germany is, if not the ultimate expression of evil, perilously close to it. I have often wondered if their leadership is possessed by Satan. But, is not what you are suggesting perilously close to taking up arms against them? Quite apart from anything else, once the Holy Church is committed to such a policy, they may take up arms against us. And the Germans are very good at taking up arms against those they see as their enemies."

"This is a path fraught with peril, yes." His Holiness oddly seemed to gain strength as he explained the logic behind the policies upon which he had decided. "Hitler has already made it clear that he is implacably opposed to us and seeks our destruction within Germany and the territories that it occupies. As soon as he assumed power in 1933, he started to lay the foundations of a 'National Socialist Church' that would replace the True Faith in Germany.

"I fear that many Gemans, offered the choice between that creation and the true Church, would choose the former. Even before the war started, they had already introduced their own sacramental rituals for baptism, confirmation, marriage and funerals. They have changed Ash Wednesday into Wotan's Day, Ascension Day into the Feast of Thor's Hammer. German families now crown their Christmas trees, not with a star, but with a swastika. The Nazis have thwarted our teachings, banned our organizations, censored our press, closed our schools and seminaries and seized their properties and dismissed our teachers. The Nazi leaders have openly boasted that after the defeat of Bolshevism and Judaism, the Catholic Church will be the only enemy left.

"We cannot, we must not, allow our Church to be destroyed without resistance. Yet, beyond that, we must rescue as many Jews as we can. The Orders Committee is organizing the evacuation of Jewish people from Germany into Switzerland, from occupied France and Britain into Spain and Portugal. For your information, this is called Operation U-7."

Conrad nodded, remembering his own part in such a rescue mission that had followed the occupation of the remaining areas of France in 1942. "There has always been a fundamental contradiction between the Church's essential role of saving souls and achieving the political conditions under which souls could be saved. Priests must baptize, say Mass, and consecrate marriages without interference from the state. It has always been so, whether at the time of the Albigensian Crusade or the Inquisition. The existential problem of the Church has been how to remain a spiritual institution in a physical and highly political world."

"Spoken like the true Jesuit you, at heart, are. And now we face the essence of that problem in its most distilled and concentrated form." His Holiness suddenly looked much older than his years. "In the Nazi regime, our Church faces an existential threat. This is not a dispute over doctrine or the ruling principles of the Church. It is a direct assault upon our Church's very existence. Already, Hitler himself has stated that 'the Reich does not desire a *modus vivendi* with the Church, but rather its destruction.'

"In Poland, hundreds of priests were arrested and shot by the Germans, while Catholic intellectuals, clerics and laity were arrested and sent to concentration camp Oranienburg near Berlin. With every month that has passed since then, the attacks on our Church have increased in severity. The Nazis constantly look for excuses to send more of our people, priests, monks, laity, before show trials. That is why every statement that comes out of the Holy City must be carefully worded and discreet.

"The only hope for our brothers and sisters in Germany, and the territory occupied by the Germans, is to engage with the German military resistance and encourage a counterrevolution not just to stop the war, but to eliminate Nazism by removing Hitler."

Conrad had listened to the explanations with a growing level of shock. He appreciated the need for organizations such as the Orders Committee, but they sounded unpleasantly like the Inquisition to him. Also, that the existence of such an organization had been kept so secret for so long that he had been completely unaware of its existence.

"I am deeply discomforted by the thought that we countenance the sort of actions that will be needed to do that. The only way to remove Hitler from power is to have him killed. Either by direct action, or to put him in a position where the normal hazards of war will do the deed. Do we condone the assassination of a head of state, or anybody else?"

Conti di Segni didn't seem older than his years, but he suddenly looked every one of them. "Church teaching states the conditions under which citizens can kill tyrants. Catholic doctrine permits capital punishment; and though a priest himself cannot shed blood, a Christian knight may do so at the bidding of a priest. You know very well that Catholic theologians have developed a nuanced doctrine of tyrannicide, covering virtually every conceivable context. They divided tyrants into two classes: usurpers, who seized power illegally, and oppressors, who used power unjustly. We have determined that Hitler, who holds office legally but rules unjustly, has become an oppressor and falls into the class of tyrants whom citizens could assassinate.

"Aquinas argued, and Jesuit theologians demand, that the tyrant's executioners must have good grounds for believing his death would improve conditions and would not cause a bloody civil war. The tyrant himself must not merely stand revealed as the primary instigator of unjust policies; his assassins must have sufficient reason to believe that those unjust policies would end with the tyrant's life. If another tyrant would likely continue those polices, the assassins had no moral basis to act. Finally, the assassins must have exhausted all peaceful means for removing the tyrant. Our objective is not to carry out the act, but to provide the spiritual rationale that allows them to do so without imperiling their mortal soul."

"There is another side to this." His Holiness seemed to have recovered his composure. "This war must end. Every minute that passes sees two or three young men, Russian, American and German, dying on the Russian Front. Their lives are blood on the hands of us all. But, we cannot end the war while Hitler still lives. The Allies will not countenance that. Hitler's death is the precondition upon which any and every peace agreement must be founded. Father Conrad, you have devoted your life to protecting the innocent victims of the world. Surely, you can see here that the innocents needing protection number literally in the millions? Because if we do not end this war, the Americans will do so in ways whose devastation will be beyond imagining."

Conrad remembered The Seer speaking once about Americans and war. *First, they get really enthusiastic. Then they get really bored. Finally, they get really angry and then may the gods help their enemies.* "How does this relate to the case we have today? Was Doctor Parrino a member of the Orders Committee?"

His Holiness held up a hand, "Conrad, will you join the Orders Committee? Before we go any further, we must know the answer to that question."

"Holiness, I must ask one question before giving you an answer. To whom does the Orders Committee answer?"

"To me." Conti di Segni gave the answer immediately. "And I answer directly to His Holiness. The existence of the Orders Committee is one of the secrets that each Pope is briefed upon when he assumed the office. Another is the existence of us, the long-lived, and the curse that lies upon us."

"Why do you say that our gift is a curse? I do not disagree with you, but the reasoning interests me."

"Ever the Jesuit." Conti di Segni shook his head. "Centuries ago, during the Albigensian Crusade, we took the town of Béziers. The defenders and the local population were mixed together and the latter would not identify the former. The Papal Legate, on my authority, gave the command. *Caedite eos. Novit enim Dominus qui sunt eius.* Kill them, for the Lord knows those that are His own.

"Soon afterwards, I felt the beginning of what we now call transition and eventually I realized the message. Because of what was done at Béziers, the Lord does not know me, and will not recognize me as one of his own, until I have properly made amends for that foul crime by protecting our Church without recourse to such methods. Only then will I be allowed to die."

"That is the same belief that drives me. I must protect the innocent until such time as I have paid penance for the innocent who died in the Inquisition." Conrad thought carefully about the situation. "Very well, I will do as you ask."

His Holiness nodded in satisfaction and relief. "The Almighty be praised. Conrad, Lotario, you both do yourselves much injustice. God's mercy is always there for you; all you need do is accept it. But your mutual need to protect the innocent is the one thing above all others that qualifies you for the Orders Committee. Now, I have other duties and must withdraw. I place this matter in your hands and feel great relief that you are both here to bring it to a proper and moral conclusion."

Once His Holiness had left, Conti di Segni looked at the empty seat. He spoke quietly. "There is the man for this time and probably also the most widely misunderstood man in the world today. Now, Conrad, what made you think there is a political dimension to this murder?"

"Right at the start, I saw this as a sealed room murder. You know the situation; a body is found in a room with no windows and the doors locked. How did the victim die? There are only a limited number of realistic answers to that question and each requires the killer to have access to the room. To get to it, to gain entry to it and, most importantly, to leave it, all require the killer to be familiar with the room and its surroundings. As soon as I interviewed *Wachtmeister* Hüber, it became apparent that the Swiss Guard would have found any ordinary intruder and, ahh, escorted him from the premises. So, we have to have a skilled intruder, deeply familiar with the arts of getting into places unobserved and finding, then removing, the contents that interest them. Such people are rare."

"And Igrat Shafrid is in New York." Conti di Segni laughed as he saw the expression on Conrad's face. "We know Igrat well; why, you will soon find out. Anyway, this crime is not her style. If some extremely valuable objects had been removed without a trace of how it was done, then we might be suspicious of her. Not this."

"Igrat is not vicious." Conrad instinctively went to Igrat's defense, something that made Conti di Segni smile quietly to himself. "Or, rather, she is vicious, but only when threatened. The point is, even a person of her skills would have to be intimately familiar with the scene of this crime and it requires significant organization plus commitment of resources. All that to get into a largely empty room? A thief would use the same access and skills to get into one of the galleries here and steal objects of great value. So, here, there must be motivations other than the enterprise of conventional criminals. And that must mean political objectives. And we return to my original question. Was Doctor Parrino a member of the Orders Committee?"

Conti di Segni shook his head. "No, he was not. He was just an archeologist. The crypt where the dig is taking place is used, sometimes, for covert meetings that must remain secret, but he was not part of them. His Holiness uses taking people down to the crypt as a cover for such meetings. It is well known he is obsessed with finding the remains of Saint Peter and is very proud that the excavation of the site is taking place under his auspices. So, it is hardly surprising if he takes some people down to see the dig."

"So, it is apparent that it is the location that is of political significance, not the identity of the victim. This is reinforced by the way in which he was killed. It is ritualistic, a sacrifice. His Holiness indicated the similarities it shares with the way those two unfortunate students were killed in Munich. That was hardly an execution practice. The connection there is too strong to be ignored. But, if the Orders Committee is not involved, then what is that link? There is little connection between two young German students and a middle-aged Italian professor of archeology, so, logically, the link must be the people who did the killing."

"You are assuming that Doctor Parrino was the intended victim. Suppose he was not?"

"I had taken that into account. It is quite possible that Doctor Parrino was not the intended victim. But, if that is the case, the only other candidate is *Wachtmeister* Hüber. The same arguments still apply. Unless, of course . . ."

Conti di Segni shook his head again. "He is not. None of the Swiss Guards are. They are all good men who hold many secrets, but the Orders Committee is entirely separate from them."

"So, no link between the German students and the Swiss Guardsman, except, of course, the way they would have been killed, had *Wachtmeister* Hüber been the intended victim. We are back to the same place. The only link is the way the victims were killed and that is unusual enough to suggest the same people did it."

"Could it just be coincidence?" Conti di Segni was playing Devil's advocate and they both knew it.

Conrad thought about that. "No. If it was not planned, if Doctor Parrino had been killed because he had stumbled in on something, then he would have been bashed on the head with a rock, shot or stabbed. It would not be hard to have disguised his death as an accident. An unfortunate fall, perhaps? Or a rock that toppled and sadly killed him? Either would have made sure this discussion never took place. No, the way he was killed was so important that it was worth the killers making sure there was an investigation just to carry out their crime that particular way.

"Again, we come back to the identity of the killers. Whoever they are, that particular way of killing, hanging the victim upside down and removing their head, is very important to them. Why may well be the key to finding out who they are."

Conrad's Room, Domus Sanctae Marthae, Vatican City

The *Domus Sanctae Marthae* wasn't a hospice, despite its name. Saint Martha's Hospice had been built to protect the Vatican against a cholera pandemic in the 1890s, but it hadn't been needed. Now it was used to house guests who were on official business in Vatican City. There was a strange ritual when a new tenant arrived; they would draw their room number from a large vase. Thus, a simple priest might get one of the largest rooms and a high dignitary of the Church one of the smallest.

Conrad had been lucky, although his always-cynical mind wasn't quite certain whether luck had much to do with it. He not only had one of the larger rooms, it had a spacious private studio where he could set up his case study equipment. That seemed all too convenient to be entirely a matter of a lucky coincidence.

Although his travel bag was small, he was loaded down with packages he had bought locally. He had delighted the owner of a stationery store by stocking up on display boards, index cards and other office supplies. Cards, notepads and other stationary were in short supply in America due to rationing of paper. He had also bought a selection of pencils, pens and other needed materials. *Looking back with hindsight,* Conrad thought, *Mussolini showed immense foresight by folding when he did in 1940. Italy is prospering as a neutral trading point in a world at war. The country's long-term future is going to be as wealthy as any in Europe once this madness ends.*

Conrad took a deep breath and set his display boards up. In his eyes, this was the point where a serious investigation began. The first consideration was who had been the intended target of the murder? He wrote out two cards, one for *Wachtmeister* Julian Hüber, the other for Doctor Ermes Parrino. He pinned them to his brand-new boards and stood back.

To him, this was the beginning of the process. The available facts were organized, significant information identified and the irrelevant discarded. This was also where, in a normal case, suspects would be listed and ranked according to the strength of the case against them. Only here, there were no suspects. *Where do I start? The answer has to be the obvious; at the beginning. Why was Doctor Parrino killed? In fact, was he killed at all? And, if he was killed, had he been done to death elsewhere and his body brought to where it was found?*

Conrad considered the facts that he had at his disposal. Despite the copious quantities of blood at the scene of the death, there was no blood trail to that point; nor were there any signs that of another scene-of-crime. The sheer quantity of blood in the pit also tells us that Parrino died there. *No, we can be sure that he died hanging over the excavation. That leaves suicide. Quite apart from suicide being a mortal sin, all the more so given where this would have taken place, there is no sign of a weapon. Suicides do not nearly decapitate themselves, put the weapon away, then suspend themselves by their feet before expiring.*

With those two possibilities excluded, there were only three reasons Conrad could think of. *The doctor had stumbled across something he shouldn't have, he had something that the attackers wanted or those attackers had mistaken him for Hüber.* He wrote a card out for each and pinned them under the doctor's name. He realized they all raised the same question, *why was the doctor in the crypt to start with? If he had gone down their unexpectedly for some reason, then it was certain that he had either found something he could not be allowed to know or he had been mistaken for Hüber. If he had gone down there deliberately, either he had been lured down there or he had made an arrangement to meet somebody.*

Suddenly, he realized the common thread that joined all three situations. No matter why Parrino had gone down to the crypt, the killers had to have been down there first, and they couldn't be. Right up to the time of the killing, all the keys were accounted for. Only now was one set missing, the set used by Parrino.

Conrad visualized the doctor unlocking the outer door and walking down the corridor that led to the crypt. That was when he realized it was impossible to ambush somebody in that corridor. Even in the uncertain light of a lantern, there was simply nowhere to hide. The killers had to be lying in wait inside the crypt itself. *There has to be another way into that crypt.*

That was when a great light suddenly dawned on him. *Nobody can get into that crypt without one of a limited number of sets of keys; but, if the doors are locked, nobody can get out of it either. It's a dead end unless somebody gets hold of that set of keys. But, once those keys are in hand, the people responsible can leave the crypt and enter the main Vatican complex at will, inside the perimeter formed by the Swiss Guard. They may not be completely safe, because the Swiss Guard does carry out random patrols of the area, but they are a lot better off than they would be trying to penetrate from the outside. Both Parrino and Hüber had the sets of keys that the intruders needed.*

The room was beginning to darken as dusk started to fall. Conrad wrote out more cards for his display, labelling three motives for the killing of Parrino and two for Hüber. Four of the cards formed two pairs, one for each potential or actual victim. In each pair, one was labelled "something he knew" and the other "something they wanted". Now, Conrad placed a single card under each of the latter. It read, quite simply "Keys."

Looking at the display, Conrad realized that it was telling him who the intended victim was. He knew, from centuries of experience, that skilled criminals kept things simple. Simple plans confounded the police because they gave them only restricted resources to work with and limited the scope for the element of chance to work its ways. The more complex the plan, the more there was to go wrong and the more information the police had to exploit.

The simplest of all homicides was a random murder with the body left in a back alley somewhere and that was those were the ones that got solved least often. *Why should the criminals go to the trouble of luring Parrino down to the crypt to rob him of his keys when they know Hüber will be coming down there anyway, at a more or less predictable time? If they wanted a set of keys, they merely had to wait inside the Crypt until Hüber arrived. Only, for some unknown reason, Parrino came down and found them. They killed him to hide the fact they were there at all, then realized that they had acquired the keys they needed. They didn't need to kill Hüber after all, so they set up the scene for him to find and left. That Swiss guard is a very fortunate young man. The question left is why set up such an elaborate scheme?*

Home of Doctor Ermes Parrino, Via Degli Ombrellari, Vatican City

"Why did they have to kill poor Ermes in such a horrible way?" Unknowingly, Marianna Parrino asked the same question Conrad had earlier.

She was trying heroically to keep her composure while her world was crumbling around her. She looked around for some source of comfort and familiarity in a situation that was completely strange and unexpected. Sitting next to Conrad, Julian Hüber was in civilian clothes, but his build and bearing immediately identified him as a soldier. In Vatican City, that could only mean he was a Swiss guard. Madam Parrino was comforted by that, since it was obvious proof that the Church authorities were taking this matter very seriously indeed.

Earlier that morning, Conrad had held another meeting with Hüber and *Oberst* Herrmann and explained his deductions of the night before. Even in the cold light of morning, they made perfect sense. Both men had seen what he was driving at before he had even finished his presentation. Hüber had, of course, been cleared of any suspicion that might have attached to him and Conrad had respectfully requested that he join him in the hunt for the killers of Doctor Parrino. After all, they had killed one person without any hesitation and could just as easily kill a second. *Oberst* Herrmann had made some other changes as well. Effective immediately, the patrols in the Vatican buildings would be carried out by two guardsmen rather than one. The frequency of the patrols was also increased, the only limit being knowledge that the strain on the limited force of Swiss Guards would quickly become unacceptable.

Now, it was the part of the investigation that Conrad knew would distress him most. "Madam Parrino, have you any idea why your husband was down in the crypt that night? Did he often go down there late at night?"

She nodded. "He did. At first, I thought he was using it as an excuse for . . . for . . . something else, but when he realized that I was suspicious, he started taking me down there as well. He swore he could hear running water when he was down there. Not all the time, but just sometimes. We would sit there in the darkness and silence, just listening for anything. Most nights, neither of us would hear anything. But, once in a while, Ermes would claim he could hear water flowing. Mostly in winter. I remember that because the crypt would be bitterly cold and I would wear my warmest coat. I never heard anything though."

Conrad frowned at that, remembering how unpleasantly warm and humid the crypt had been. *Cool or even cold would have been more typical for a stone vault, and that is what Madam Parrino had described.* "Were you down there in summer as well?"

"Oh yes, we went down there together for more than a year. We still go down together, I mean we did until . . . It was quite different in summer. Unpleasantly hot. But, we never heard anything in summer. Well, I never did, but Ermes did claim he heard flowing water once in summer. I remember it well, because it was just after a terrible storm that hit the whole city. It was so bad parents kept their children home for the day, because classrooms were flooded and roads near schools impassable. Early in the morning, a massive lightning bolt hit the dome of St. Peter's Basilica. We could see it clearly from here."

"I remember that." Hüber spoke up for the first time. "0920. The shock was so great all of us on guard could feel it. A storm like that is very unusual; usually there is only six or seven millimeters of rain in July and August and storms are very heavy but short. This time though, the rain started before dawn and continued until after dusk."

"We had planned to go down to the crypt that night but the weather was so bad we had called it off. Then, the rain stopped so we decided to go after all. Ermes said he heard water very clearly that night, but I heard nothing."

"Men and women hear most acutely at different frequencies." Conrad was very thoughtful. "That is why women wake up when babies cry and men do not."

"I thought it was just because they were lazy." It was the first glimpse of humor from Madam Parrino since the meeting had started.

"That too," said Conrad. "Did you notice anything else down there?"

"The smell." Madam Parrino was emphatic. "It smells bad. Sometimes worse, especially after a dry spell, but there was always a bad smell, like a toilet that had not been properly cleaned."

Conrad looked at Hüber. "There's a sewer down there somewhere."

Mausoleum Crypt, Underneath Basilica of Saint Peter, Vatican City

"Thank you all for coming down here to help us." Conrad looked around at the group of school students who had been given the afternoon off to help with the exploration of the crypt. The covering box had been replaced over the excavation and any evidence of the murder had been removed. There was nothing to be seen that would reveal the crypt had been the scene of a foul murder and the story had been kept confined to a very limited and extremely discreet circle. How long that would remain the case was an interesting question.

Conrad took a deep breath before continuing. "The exploration of this crypt is something that is very close to His Holiness's heart and he is very grateful for your assistance. First thing I must explain is that is not a competition to find something. Instead, we are trying to map the peculiar smell that seems to be everywhere down here. Secondly, accuracy is the most important thing. We are trying to measure how strong the smell is in various parts of the crypt.

"What we will do is start off along one wall and walk slowly across the crypt to the opposite wall. As you go, draw a line on your paper to represent the strength of the smell. The line should go up if the smell gets stronger, down if it gets weaker. If you cannot detect any change in the strength of the smell, then the line should remain level.

"After we have done the first pass, we will go upstairs for some cakes and sandwiches, then come back down and do it again at right angles to our first inspection. Please remember because this is most important, there are no right or wrong answers here. Every bit of information, even negative information, is equally valuable, as long as it is accurate."

Hüber had added formality to the event by changing into his ceremonial blue and yellow uniform and was carefully marshalling the youths into a line, evenly spaced along the east wall. "Now, please keep in a straight line and hold the same spacing between yourself and the lads on either side of you."

One of the schoolgirls coughed politely. Hüber immediately made a small gesture of apology. "I am sorry, miss. I meant between yourselves and your fellow students on either side of you. Now, there is no hurry; we have plenty of time."

Conrad watched the students cross the crypt with admiration. Although they had not been specifically told to do so, they were more or less keeping in step and moving forward in unison at the speed of the slowest. They were also taking careful sniffs with each step. *Children are much better at this sort of thing than adults are. Adults will try and theorize or make speculation about what the answer is and that will unconsciously distort the results they get. Or, sometimes, consciously distort their answers. Children won't do that; as long as they are asked the right questions and their answers are properly understood, their information is much more reliable. The problem is that we can't do this often with the same group. Their attention will wander and, as they get bored, they will rush the process.*

Once the line had reached the opposite wall, Conrad collected the paper charts. He noted immediately that his confidence in the youngsters had been well placed. Without being told to do so, every one of them had either written the word "top" on one edge or placed an arrow there so the papers wouldn't get turned upside down. A satisfying number of the lines were straight, indicating the author hadn't noticed any change in the smell. He nodded in satisfaction, a gesture noted by the students who visibly swelled with pride.

"Very good work, very good indeed, all of you. Now let us go and have some refreshments and then we'll do the other set."

The Vatican kitchens had done the investigation proud. There were plates of cheese and cold meat sandwiches, small meatballs and sausages on sticks, all accompanied by iced cakes and fruit tarts. A tea bar had been set up in one corner and there were jugs of fruit juice for those who preferred cold drinks. It was something that would have been commonplace at a birthday party in a middle-class, pre-war American home and it drove home to Conrad how much that country was sacrificing in the drive to win the war. The sheer volume of American war production was the subject of awed admiration from her allies and, Conrad had no doubt, was causing concern, if not outright dread, from her enemies. Yet, there was a price being paid for that flood of weapons and equipment and this simple tea highlighted how high that price was.

Conrad's Other Eye

"You had better eat well, Conrad. The way things are going, we will soon have to start tightening our belts as well." Conti di Segni had entered the room and helped himself to fruit juice and a plate of small cakes. He looked slightly guilty at the indulgence but, in Conrad's eyes, he had earned his share by arranging the party. *Dipping his beak, the Italians call it*, Conrad thought. The sudden silence that fell on the room stopped him from responding. To everybody's surprise, Pius XII had entered the room and was quietly making his way around the students, thanking them for their help this afternoon and distributing small religious items to each. Conrad knew that those small gifts would become treasured family heirlooms.

"Some people say that Eugenio Maria Giuseppe Giovanni Pacelli is a formal man who lacks the common touch and is remote from the real needs of his people. Those who make that judgement do not know him." Conti di Segni looked at the scene with the students crowded around His Holiness while photographers took pictures of each guest with the Pope. "Last year we had a reception here for 800 students who graduated from their *scuola media superior*. His Holiness was encouraging them to go on further, to the *Liceo Scientifico*. He believes that science and religion should be partners, each answering the questions that the other, by its nature cannot."

Conrad couldn't resist it. Looking carefully around to make sure that the conversation could not be overheard, he spoke very softly, "Didn't we once put people on trial for their lives when they said things like that? But then, we of all people know how much times change."

The presence of His Holiness at the party had extended the length of time it had taken, since nobody could leave until the Pope did and he was obviously enjoying himself. That wasn't a problem to Conrad; the whole point of this interlude was to get the students away from the smell in the crypt so that their noses wouldn't become too deadened. Eventually, His Holiness left, leaving the staff to make the leftover food into packages that the students could take home with them. Conrad suspected that in many cases, the contents wouldn't be eaten but kept as a form of remembrance of an extraordinary day. Then, once everything was sorted out, he and Hüber took their mapping team back down to the crypt. The procedure was the same as before, only this time the path of each student was at right-angles to their previous one. Once again, the students moved slowly and deliberately. In fact, to Conrad's eyes, they were taking even more care than in the first pass; probably inspired by the honor they had just received. Eventually the job was done and the papers collected. Now, they would be delivered to one of the technical artists in the Vatican architect's office for conversion into a 'smell map' of the crypt floor.

Conrad's Room, Domus Sanctae Marthae, Vatican City

"We have the drawings." Hüber was back in civilian clothes and had the rolled art paper in one hand. Heroically, he had managed to refrain from taking an advance look at the results of their afternoon's work.

"Let's spread them out and see what we have." Conrad took the roll from the Swiss guard and spread it on the table, weighting the edges down with boxes of pencils. One glance told him that the experiment had been a success. The artist had prepared a graphic in which the paths walked by the students were represented by single lines forming a grid covering the whole floor. Their perceptions of the strength of the smell were shown by the rise and fall of those lines. The artist had "normalized" them so the baselines were consistent and obviously, there was substantial variance in each individual line. Nevertheless, despite that experimental noise, there was a clearly defined pattern across the floor of the crypt.

Conrad looked at the pattern and raised his eyebrows. "Well, Julian, I didn't expect that."

Mausoleum Crypt, Underneath Basilica of Saint Peter, Vatican City

Conrad had spread the drawings out again and orientated them to the layout of the room. Now, everything made a lot more sense. As he had expected, there was a distinct hump in the middle of the crypt where the odd smell that permeated the place was strongest. It showed up in both the east-west and north-south traverses with a surprising level of consistency. Conscientious students who had taken pride in their responsibilities and talented technical artists had combined to make sense of a highly unusual situation. What had surprised Conrad was that, in addition to the hump he had expected, there was a long ridge of more intrusive smell running the whole length of the south wall.

"If I had to guess, I would say that, if there is a sewer here, it runs along by the south wall. I think that there must be a branch line or perhaps a leak from the sewer towards the middle of the crypt. It may even be leaking into the mausoleum down there. If that is so, I do not envy the archeologists their job once they get the stones open. If they get the stones open." *Wachtmeister* Hüber shook his head.

"There is a problem with opening up what is down there?" Conrad was getting an insight into the strange situation that existed in the crypt.

"There is a complex of pagan mausoleums down here. About thirty or more of them. Together, they are called the Vatican Necropolis. One of the responsibilities of the Swiss Guard is giving distinguished visitors a tour of the necropolis, so we know quite a bit about it. Once of the things is that all the crypts were originally buildings, but they were levelled by the Emperor Constantine I and only the belowground portions remain. The stones that roof the remains are typical floor stones; they can be lifted up very easily. The crypts were filled with soil and building debris that yielded much archeological information of value. We even know the family names of the owners of the mausoleums. The larger and more important of them have been cleaned out and they are interesting places. I can take you there if you wish."

"I would enjoy that, Julian; thank you for the offer. This archeology work is a particular interest of yours, isn't it?"

Hüber flushed slightly. "It is, yes. I sometimes help with the excavation when I am not on duty. Nothing skilled, just sifting the dirt for relics. A friend of mine is in charge of that. Doctor Albina Caito."

Aha, Conrad thought. *Do I detect a romance here?* "How does that stone floor work?"

"There was a framework on which the stones were laid and then a light mortar brushed across the joints to seal them. All we have to do is to break up the mortar seal; it's usually in bad condition anyway, and we put the bits aside for analysis. Then the stone just lifts straight up. The archeologists are very insistent that the stones remain unbroken. That's what makes the problem here so difficult. The construction is entirely different. The stones are tongued and grooved, so they lock into each other and they can't be lifted up. The archeologists think the floor fits together like one of those children's puzzles, where pieces have to be slid around to form a picture. They think the stones have to be slid around so that they allow one to be lifted up and that allows the rest to be moved."

"There's another possibility." Conrad was looking around at the floor. "I can't see how the stones could be slid around like that. The floor paneling runs all the way to the walls. The only way I could see one being removed is to drop it downwards."

"It would have to have a lock somehow; otherwise, it would collapse when it was stepped on. There's no sign of a mechanism on any of these stones."

"Which raises an interesting question. How did people get down to the mausoleum? Once all the stones were in place and the walls built to contain them, how did people up here get down there?"

"It raises another, even more interesting question, Conrad. Is this really a mausoleum down here? Or is it something much more interesting?"

"Of course it is a mausoleum!" One of the people working to clean up the excavation site after the murder had stormed over, bristling with indignation. "This is the Vatican Necropolis! And how could anything be more interesting and important than the tomb of the Blessed Saint Peter?"

"And you are?" Hüber asked politely.

"Doctor Sergio Alinari. I am the head of the excavation team here now Doctor Ermes Parrino no longer holds that position."

That's an interesting way of putting it, thought Conrad. "Doctor Alinari, perhaps you could enlighten me on something? Why is everybody so sure Saint Peter is buried here?"

"Because we found his name on the mausoleum, that's why. Look, I'll show you." Alinari led the way over to the pit. "See, on the stone in the middle? The one that had the most blood on it? The words are '*Petros eni*', the inscription *eni* being a contraction for *eneoti*. So, it translates to 'Peter is within.' Other inscriptions ask St. Peter to pray to Christ for deceased people, and yet more are common Christian symbols, like the alpha and omega, or the chi and rho."

"It doesn't actually say *Petros eni*. The supposed letters o and n are completely illegible. It could say *petras edi*. Which would translate to 'this stone.'"

"And that would indicate it might be the keystone we are looking for." Hüber was running ahead with that idea. "If it is, I wonder how it would work. And why the killers of Doctor Parrino made such a point of pouring his blood over it."

"Of course it is blessed St. Peter's tomb. Everybody knows it. After his death, the faithful recovered St. Peter's body and buried it in a necropolis somewhere around here. The faithful secretly venerated the grave and protected it from pagan desecration. Pope Anicetus built a memorial, or *tropaion*, to mark the grave, and other popes were buried nearby. In 330, Emperor Constantine began building a huge basilica at the gravesite to honor the first pope.

"The builders had to level the land, thereby filling in the necropolis. They purposefully positioned the altar over the burial site of St. Peter. In other words, here. When Pope Julius began construction on the present St. Peter's Basilica in 1506 to replace the decaying original basilica, the high altar purposefully remained over the burial site. So, of course this is St. Peter's grave." Alinari's voice had risen so that it was echoing around the crypt and he was speaking much faster.

"His tomb is probably, indeed almost certainly, here somewhere." Hüber maintained his polite and cautious demeanor. "But this is a very thin thread to hang the claim on this particular area. This is a large crypt and the excavations have been very slow. At the other mausoleums, the archeologists have found many bones, not all human, dispersed over a wide area. This was, after all, a pagan mausoleum at first and animal sacrifice during the interment of a family member was not uncommon. A suitable gift to the Gods was considered a useful investment in gaining advantage for the deceased in the afterlife. An advantage for which the dead would be expected to exploit on behalf of the living."

Conrad thought about that and had an ugly feeling as to where that belief could end. "I need to speak with an expert on ancient Roman religion."

Conrad's Other Eye

Hotel Pierluigi Piazza de Ricci, Rome

"*Linguine ai ricci di mare e nocciola tostata*. That's linguine with sea urchin and toasted hazelnuts, Conrad. This is by far the best seafood restaurant in Rome and probably the best one in Italy. I eat here every time we come through. You can get steak and lamb here in Rome but they're mostly Australian. Brought here in Japanese ships by the way. Neutral ships, you see, delivering cargo to a neutral country." Igrat handed the menu to the owner. "And a bottle of your 1937 *Chardonnay e Grechetto Marchesi Antinori, per favore*."

"Certainly, madam. And welcome back to Pierluigi's."

"I'd hate to see your expense account when you get back."

Igrat smiled at Conrad. "It's money well spent. This is good for our cover, you see. Henry is my daddy and he had better look after his baby well, or baby might go off and find somebody else who will. And he can afford to, because he is into selling black market products from the US to occupied countries. He banks all the profits I don't spend in Geneva. You can guess where. And what else I get while he's doing so."

Conrad shook his head. "Is the black marketeering legal?"

"In America, of course not. Trading with the enemy and all that. In Italy, nobody cares. This country survives by trading with both sides. Germans, we don't really know." Igrat looked puzzled for a moment. "We've never had any problems with the Gestapo, but they must know that we're black marketeers. So, I guess they don't care either. The thing is, since they know we're up to things that could get us thrown into jail for a ridiculously long stretch, they don't ask what else we could be doing. Anyway, how can we help you?"

"I need some advice on Rome, so I need to speak with Achillea. I'd like to talk with Messalina as well, but I don't know where she is."

"Sorry, nor do I. Sign of the times I guess."

Conrad reflected that the statement might or might not be true. Igrat was capable of lying with a convincing fluency that could fool even him. "A pity, but I need some advice on Roman religious matters very quickly."

"All right, why don't you settle back and enjoy lunch. You can speak to Achillea after we've eaten." Igrat paused, "You like opera, don't you, Conrad?"

"Very much so."

"Well, there's a performance of Marco Marazzoli's *Dal Male il Bene* at the *Teatro Argentina* tonight. It's one of the oldest known Italian operas. Henry is taking me to see it and we have a box that seats five. Want to come along?"

"I would love to. But . . . " Conrad wasn't quite sure how to phrase the next bit. "Won't being seen in public with a priest endanger your cover?"

Igrat laughed at that. "Of course not; they'll just assume that you are acting as an intermediary for a really big deal on behalf of the powers that be around here and we're greasing the wheels of commerce a little. If anything, it will strengthen our cover by showing how important we are in the black market world. Ah, lunch. Enjoy yourself, Conrad."

Two hours later, Igrat had joined Henry McCarty at a table some feet away while Achillea had taken her seat with Conrad. It was noticeable that she was still positioned so she could watch everything that was going on around her. "So, Conrad, what do you want to know?"

Conrad gave a quick background to the case, concentrating on how the body of Doctor Ermes Parrino had been found. "It was so ritualistic, we couldn't help but think it was some sort of sacrifice. Then, when I found out that those two students in Munich had been killed the same way, it seemed to me to link the murder of Parrino with the Nazis. So, first question is, 'Lea, what was the significance of sacrifices in general in Rome? Why would animals be sacrificed at a burial, for example?"

Achillea's eyes looked remote as she thought back over the centuries. "We saw the relationship between the Gods and humans as sort of contract. It was a two-way deal; each side would provide as well as receive services. If one side or the other broke the deal for any reason, then the agreement was off. In a funeral, the request to the gods was please look after this person and give him a good time in the afterlife. The role of the humans in this partnership with the gods was to worship the gods with prayer and sacrifice for which there were firmly defined rituals. A big part of the deal was that we had to perform these rituals correctly. One mistake and the priest would have to begin all over again.

"Prayer and sacrifice always went together, and even a routine prayer was made together with a small offering to the deity. Such sacrifices did not always need to involve the killing of an animal, although this was very often the case. For us, you see, the sacrifice had to be a symbol of life. Milk, fruit, cheese, and wine were often used as less bloody offerings to the gods. I don't know if you noticed, but before I ate lunch, I tipped a small amount of wine out. That was a gift, a sacrifice, to the Gods. In the old days, it would have gone on the ground; but, out of sympathy for the poor schmuck who has to clean the floor, it went into a plant pot. Note there is one within easy reach of every table. The old religion dies harder than most people believe.

"When we did sacrifice a live animal, it was an elaborate and bloody affair. The animal had wine and sacred bread sprinkled over it, before it was killed by having its throat cut. Its blood was drained out and either poured on the ground or over the head of a participant. Its guts were inspected to ensure that the god had not been offered an animal bearing a bad omen. Should indeed something be found wanting about the animal's entrails, then it was not only a bad sign, but a new animal would have to be sacrificed in its place. After that, the animal's body was roasted on the altar and eaten as part of a feast. It was important that nobody should hear or see anything evil while the sacrifice was carried out. For example, when the priest was saying prayers, he would be wearing some form of mask or blindfold to protect his eyes from seeing any evil and a flute would be played to drown out any evil sounds."

"It sounds almost like a good American backyard barbeque." Conrad hoped he hadn't offended Achillea and was relieved to see her smile.

"I've often thought that. The important thing is, Conrad, the god was supposed to come through on his side of the deal. There was none of this his ways are inscrutable nonsense. If a god didn't deliver on his side of the deal, then the worship would stop and often another god would take his place. That's why so many gods fell out of favor and were forgotten. That's why Christianity replaced the Olympian gods; the old Gods hadn't delivered, so they were abandoned." Achillea took a gulp of her wine. Conrad noted it was a rough red, not the fine vintage white that Igrat had been drinking. Achillea caught his look. "This is closer to what I used to drink. I'd put water in it, but it makes the vintner here cry."

"So, I assume that, for a really big favor from the gods, you'd sacrifice a human?"

"Like hell." Achillea smiled again to take the sting out of her words. "We were as horrified by the practice of that sort of thing as any modern society might be. The practice of human sacrifice was prohibited in the year of the consulship of P. Licinius Crassus, whenever that might have been. Long time before I was born. We always stopped the practice whenever we conquered somebody and ending their practice of human sacrifice was one excuse used to justify taking them out. Our hatred for the practice was something we saw as distinguishing our own civilization from the barbarians outside the empire."

"What about the Christians?" Conrad was fascinated to hear the inside story from somebody who had been there. He couldn't help contrasting it with the stories he had heard.

"They weren't sacrificed; they were criminals and they were punished." Achillea glanced around. "You do realize I knocked off quite a few of them myself? I remember one of them telling me he would pray for me while I killed him. He did, too. Clever move on his part; he must have guessed I would reciprocate by making sure he died quickly. It was all part of the job, being a gladiator and all. Most of those killed in the Arena were criminals; putting a man or woman who needed execution up against a professional like me was a death sentence, but it gave the victim a chance of an honorable death. The Christians were denied that, unless there was something odd about the case.

For all that, the gladiatorial games did evolve from a human sacrifice and the crowd really loved seeing the blood, but the Arena was always something else. There was no deal with the gods there you see. A sacrifice was the price paid for aid from a god. The Arena was sport and spectacle."

Conrad frowned as he processed all this information. "So the death of Doctor Parrino doesn't sound like somebody trying to recreate a Roman ritual?"

"No. Although it may have been somebody trying to recreate what they thought that a Roman sacrifice may have looked like. They missed vital details, though, and do not understand the reasons why a sacrifice took place at all."

"Is it possible they believed that a blood sacrifice might have opened up the mausoleum?"

Achillea thought about that very carefully. "The deal being that the gods reveal the way to open the entrance to the mausoleum in exchange for a human life? I don't think so. The gods want worship and sacrifice is only a part of that. It's a gesture of sincerity. There's no sign of worship down there, is there? I don't mean Christian worship."

Conrad shook his head. "No."

"Then this isn't a Roman sacrifice. It could be that they were trying to desecrate the tomb of St. Peter. Take away its power or something. You know who was big on human sacrifices?"

"The Germans?"

"The Nordic and Celtic tribes generally, but yes. The Germans. And aren't the Nazis trying to recreate the old pagan religions?"

Teatro Argentina, Via di Torre Argentina, Rome.

Dal Male il Bene was a comedy of romantic misunderstandings. Don Diego believed his beloved Donna Elvira had been unfaithful to him with Don Fernando. Poor Don Fernando was simply a good-hearted stranger who was only trying to help her with some family problems. Don Diego's sister, Donna Leonora, really was in love with Don Fernando, recognizing his qualities as husband material. Of course, Don Diego intended to wreak terminal physical harm on Don Fernando for his presumed attentions to Donna Elvira and would be enraged if he knew where his sister's true affections lay. Equally naturally, Leonora believed that Elvira was trying steal her beloved and was trying to divert her towards Don Diego, not realizing that was where Elvira's true affections already lay.

It was now half way through the opera. From those simple beginnings, the plot was getting complicated. Don Diego's servant, Tobacco, was secretly having an affair with Donna Leonora's maid Marina, who returned his affections wholeheartedly. Their constantly foiled attempts to meet secretly formed a comic sub-plot. Meanwhile, Donna Fortuna, a character who showed that gold-diggers existed in 1654, was trying to seduce Don Diego in hope of getting her hands on his fortune. Igrat, of course, approved of her objectives. Conrad's sympathies lay with Don Fernando, who was the innocent victim of the swirling plots and misunderstandings.

Don Fernando was on stage now, singing a whole-hearted lament. "Why is this happening to me? What did I do to deserve this?" The stage had been set up brilliantly. Most of it was in total darkness. A single spotlight illuminated Don Fernando perfectly and riveted the audience's attention on him. The singer was doing a near-perfect performance of a man bewildered by why his acts of kindness were having such disastrous results mixed with anger that his honorable and decent motives were being so comprehensively misunderstood.

"This was the original purpose of the solo. Everybody's attention is fixed upon the singer putting on his performance while, in the background, the stage hands and others switch the scenery around for the next act. So, when the lights come back on, everything has changed and nobody knows how it was done." Igrat was speaking very quietly; her voice would not have carried beyond the confines of the box. Conrad was on one side of her. On the other, Henry was putting on a superb act of a rich sugar daddy indulging his baby, while trying not to let her know her choice of show was boring him into catatonia.

Conrad glanced across the theater to the box opposite, where a very familiar figure sat. Nobody had expected Benito Mussolini to watch the performance, but he had arrived with his wife Rachele and mistress Clara. The orchestra had struck up "Giovinezza" to welcome him, but the music had almost been drowned out by the applause. Conrad reflected on the change, both in the man himself and public attitude to him. Pre-war, people had gone through the motions of respecting him in public but privately ridiculed him as a pretentious blow-hard. Then, following his stroke and the resulting withdrawal of a defeated Italy from the war, he had been pitied as a man whose dreams had crashed in ruins. Now, he was respected, almost loved, as the man who had saved his beloved Italy from the slaughter that was decimating the youth of Europe.

"People can change, Conrad. Always remember that. All they need is the chance and the motivation." Conrad knew she was speaking about herself. Igrat had consciously and very deliberately changed herself from a vicious, sadistic street criminal to the warm, good-humored, tolerant person she was now. He looked back across at where Mussolini was sitting, watching the performance. In doing so, he saw the stage hands quietly moving the settings around for the next act. The spectacular setting of the Don Fernando solo had completely distracted attention from them. That was when Conrad realized why Doctor Parrino had been killed the way he had.

CHAPTER THREE

THE OPPOSITION

Mausoleum Crypt, Underneath Basilica of Saint Peter, Vatican City

"Have you ever heard of a priest hole, Julian?" Conrad was staring at the pit that marked the excavation site and, possibly, the grave of Saint Peter.

Hüber blinked, nearly said something, changed his mind and then tried to stop himself laughing. "Uhh, in what context?"

"I've just stumbled into a soldier's joke, haven't I?" Conrad didn't wait for an answer. "In this case, a priest hole is a hiding place. You see, in England during the reign of Queen Elizabeth, the Catholics were seriously persecuted. Frankly, they had only themselves to blame. There were several Catholic plots designed to remove her and severe measures were taken against Catholic priests and they were forbidden to hold services.

"As a result, the number of secret chambers and hiding places increased in the houses of the old Catholic families. These were carefully designed hiding places, not only for the priest to slip into in case of emergency, but also to provide a place where the vestments, sacred vessels, and altar furniture could be stored on short notice. The key point about the most carefully designed hideouts was that they could be opened easily at first but, when closed from the inside, they could not be opened from the outside."

"Just like the stone panel here." Hüber was looking down at the stone marked with the *Petr.s E.i* inscription. "We can't open it from up here, but if somebody was below, they might well be able to. And being a pope was a dangerous place to be in that era. You know, of course, how many of the early popes were martyred?"

"All of them?" Conrad had a curious feeling he knew who had martyred Pope Evaristus. *From what little is known about the man, him praying for his killer at the moment of his death was entirely possible.*

"There is dispute over some of their claims to martyrdom, but mostly yes. Not a safe position to be at all. Wouldn't it make more sense to have an emergency exit than a hiding place? So that an escape from pursuers was possible?"

"It would." Conrad found the idea much more than plausible. *It would explain why this crypt was built the way it was.* "One of the things about priest holes was that they were disguised to look like something they were not. An ambiguous sign on a stone, suggesting it led to a mausoleum would do that wouldn't it?"

Hüber nodded, looking down at the stone in question. He also noted that the archeologists working around the crypt were keeping as far away from them as they could. This meant they were digging up the two meters of dirt that covered the flagstones. "An escape route would have to go somewhere. Suppose there was a sewer just over there, where the smell is bad, and the escape route is a tunnel leading into that sewer. That would work, wouldn't it?"

Conrad also nodded. "And an escape route leads both ways. It is a secret way in as well as an emergency way to escape. If this really is a priest hole or an escape route, and somebody found a way into it from the other side, they could close the entry from the inside and nobody could open it from up here. I'd bet they jam the lock as well just to make sure."

"Then why draw attention to the entrance the way they did?"

"I got the answer to that last night when I watched a solo at the Opera. This whole sacrifice thing is a distraction. It's intended to focus our attention on the stone, but also on the victim, so that we ignore everything else around it and who else might be the real target. We would be so obsessed with the obvious victim, why he was killed the way he was and where his murder took place that we would ignore the really important issues. And it worked. If I hadn't gone to the Opera last night, we'd still be looking at Doctor Parrino and why he was sacrificed. Just to add a detail to that, the killers knew that drawing attention to that stone was safe because it had been comprehensively misunderstood and it couldn't be opened up without ripping up the whole floor - which the archeologists wouldn't allow."

Hüber nodded in agreement. "It makes more sense than anything else we have come up with. But there is one question left. Why would somebody want a secret entrance into the Vatican?"

"Think about it this way. Let us assume that somebody found the way into this escape tunnel, found and operated the mechanism that opens it from the inside. But, it's a dead end. They can't get out of the crypt without the keys.

So, one night, they set up an ambush, intending to kill you and take your keys. They came up with an elaborate scheme, too elaborate for its own good, by the way, to explain the crime without involving those keys. At a guess, they intended to copy them and then put the originals here so they could be 'found' a day or too later. Now, they have unrestricted access to the Vatican and its treasures. But, Doctor Parrino came down unexpectedly and found the killers waiting for you. They killed him instead, recognizing that his keys were as useful as yours. In passing, it is a mercy that Doctor Parrino did not bring his wife down here with him. They would have killed her as well."

"Which leaves us with an awkward question, or rather, two. Who are they and where does the escape tunnel end?"

"Given the smell, it ends in a sewer. That would explain the unusual warmth down here in summer and the bitter cold in winter. Water flowing in the sewer draws down hot, humid summer air from outside. It builds up in the sewer and rises. The escape tunnel must slope down, so the warm air rises up it and fills the room. In winter, cold air sinks, flows down the tunnel and again draws cold winter air in from outside. Now, do we know about sewers near here?"

Hüber laughed. "This is Rome, Conrad. There's more archeology down here than anybody can comprehend. Tunnels, mausoleums, buried rooms, everything. Every year the Tiber would flood and deposit a foot or more of alluvial mud in the lowest-laying areas, like here. People just built up to keep ahead of it. Sometimes, you can go down three or four layers of buildings, one on top of the other."

"The obvious suspect is the *Cloaca Maxima*, the great drain that carried flood water and sewage out of Rome." Doctor Sergio Alinari had finally condescended to come over and join them.

"I still think you are quite wrong and this is the tomb of the Blessed Saint Peter, but your speculation is plausible. The *Cloaca Maxima* was formed by three streams, Esquiline, Quirinal and the Viminalis, running from the hills of Rome down to the Tiber. They were first channeled into an open culvert, then that was roofed over. The constant stream of running water keeps it clean and sweeps debris out. There are also many side-branches. All seem to be official drains that would have served public toilets, bath-houses and other public buildings, but many of them have never been properly mapped. Even today, the *Cloaca Maxima* is the main storm drain for the City of Rome. Now, it goes the wrong way to do the same for the Vatican, of course. But there is a westward equivalent that has never been properly explored. It could easily run close to here.

"That sounds like the best place to start." Conrad was thoughtful. "We need to investigate this western *Cloaca Maxima*. Are there any maps of the known portions?"

"Of course." Alinari sniffed the response, although he was obviously pleased to be able to demonstrate his knowledge of the city. "The entry to the western sewer is close to the *Ponte Principe Amedeo Savoia Aosta*. It was covered when the bridge was built but there is still a small entrance leading to it. You'll find a map of the known section in the Geological Museum."

Conrad's Room, Domus Sanctae Marthae, Vatican City

The next morning, Conrad had woken with a terrible sense of impending doom. It was heightened by a message from the Holy See, asking him to attend an audience at his convenience. That meant immediately, preferably sooner, and right now would be too late. Conrad set out without waiting for breakfast, blessing the fact that the small size of Vatican City meant that it took only a few minutes of walking to get anywhere significant. Even so, he felt himself beginning to sweat profusely. The sky had a yellowish tinge to it. The combination of heat and humidity had hit him with all the force of a hammer blow. He got the distinct feeling there was another abnormal thunderstorm on the way. He was relieved to get to the Vatican offices without it starting.

Once in the *Palatium Apostolicum*, Conrad was conducted to the Borgia Apartments. Conrad had always believed that they had been sealed off and neglected following the death of Pope Alexander VI but now knew that they had instead been used for the secret works of the Orders Committee. Only when the Committee had outgrown them had the apartments been "reopened" by Pope Leo XIII in 1889. Then the existence of the apartments been recognized and they had become part of the Vatican Library. Now, they had returned to the world of shadows.

He had a presentiment of what awaited him when he saw Achillea and Henry McCarty waiting in the *Quadrivium*. Their presence meant that Igrat had to be around somewhere close by. That presumption was correct. Igrat and Conti di Segni were waiting for him in the Hall of the Mysteries of the Faith. Any idea that the meeting was anything other than damage control for a major problem was immediately dismissed by her first words.

"Hello, Conrad. We've got a problem here."

Conrad looked confused, but something told him that whatever had gone wrong was intimately linked to the case he was handling. "What's happening, Iggie?"

"I was on my travels and I picked up a package that had to come straight here. Conrad, there was an attempt to assassinate Adolf Hitler about a month ago. An unsuccessful attempt. The details are in one of the packages I brought." Igrat glanced at Conti di Segni who nodded slightly. "It appears a group of Army officers, headed by Colonel General Ludwig Beck, Chief of the German General Staff, wanted to stage a coup to get rid of Hitler, establish a new German state and negotiate a separate peace with the United States. One member of the conspiracy, a Colonel Claus Graf Schenk von Stauffenberg, took a bomb into Hitler's military headquarters at *Wolfsschanze* in the Masurian Forest. Eight people were killed and everybody was injured but Hitler survived."

"We've heard nothing about this." Both Conti di Segni and Conrad were stunned by the news. It was Conti di Segni who continued. "Are you sure? Where does this come from?"

Ingrid just gave him a slightly condescending smile. "It's true, but you're not alone in not knowing. The assassination attempt is probably the most closely-guarded secret in Germany right now. The Seer says looking at who knows about it and who doesn't is a very good guide to who is really in power and who isn't. Goebbels knows, Goering does not; Heydrich knows, Himmler does not. Despite the attack taking place in what is essentially an Army base, almost nobody in the Army knows about it."

"Wait a minute. If you came straight here from where you got the information, how does the Seer know about it?" Conti di Segni was confused. Conrad reflected he clearly didn't understand much about the relationship between Igrat and the Seer.

"He knows everything." Igrat left that issue there. Conti di Segni was perceptive enough not to press the issue further.

"How does this affect the Vatican?" Conrad guessed there had to be a reason why Igrat had stopped here. Her role as an utterly reliable courier made every demand placed on her time subject to strict prioritization. She made her occupation look easy, but it required great skill and, despite her laid-back attitude, she was seriously over-worked. There was something about her eyes that told him she had been travelling continuously since they had left the opera two nights before. She had probably gone from the *Teatro Argentina* to the station and caught the overnight express to Geneva. Since she had been in an evening dress at the opera, she'd probably changed in the taxi to the station. Once she had picked up her packages, she must have come straight back. *There must be a momentous problem that she hasn't told us about yet.*

"The Pope has been in contact with groups of resistance leaders in Germany," Igrat lifted a hand to pre-empt the denial. "Don't try and deny it. His objective was to organize the resistance in defense of the Catholic Church there. In doing so, he met with a number of leading anti-Nazi figures. Josef Müller, for example; you probably know him as Joey Ox. More importantly, the Pope was in negotiations with Helmuth James von Moltke over the structure and organization of a post-Hitler Germany.

"Joey Ox pretty much did the same work I do; he carried information backwards and forwards. Only, his route ran from Munich to here and back. Von Moltke was the effective head of something called Decent Germans, a group aimed at replacing the Nazi government with a civilized civilian administration. Pope Pius was negotiating with him on that and was trying to get American support. I took some of the papers back to Washington."

Igrat paused and when she spoke again her voice had the unmistakable accent and inflexions of Franklin D Roosevelt. "I've been authorized to tell you that there is not now, has never been and will never be any chance under any circumstances of a separate peace agreement that excludes either member of the Russian-American alliance being negotiated. In fact, the United States government would regard any such proposal as a diplomatic insult of the highest order and take due and dispassionate action against anybody proposing it. We cannot speak for the Commonwealth countries but we believe they also feel strongly on that point."

Conrad realized that was a direct and unambiguous warning aimed directly at the Holy See. Igrat looked around, privately noting whether that comment had sunk in before continuing. From the expression on Conti di Segni's face, he was already envisaging Superfortresses unloading over Vatican City. Personally, Conrad doubted it would come to that.

Igrat looked satisfied at the impact her words had made and continued. "Be that as it may, the problem is, von Moltke wrote everything down in detailed files, naming Pope Pius as a leading supporter. To make matters worse, von Moltke was also involved with the assassination attempt planned by Beck. When Heydrich's people started arresting everybody concerned with the attempted assassination, they included von Moltke and ransacked his home. They found those files."

"Oh my God." Conti di Segni was horrified. *This is exactly what he was trying to avoid.* Conrad thought. *The Orders Committee was set up to insulate the Pope against involvement like this and His Holiness has by-passed the whole system. That was . . . unwise.*

"Precisely." Igrat sounded openly contemptuous. "Have you people never heard of tradecraft? I suppose you thought that your God would protect you. Be advised, the gods don't give a damn about us, one way or the other. Anyway, put those things together and it looks like Pope Pius XII is directly involved in the attempted assassination of Adolf Hitler. I am advised that *Der Führer* is not a forgiving or magnanimous person."

Oberst Ludwig Herrmann's Office, Swiss Guard Barracks, Vatican City

"A plot to kill the Pope? You surely cannot be serious." *Oberst* Herrmann looked stunned at the enormity of the suggestion. "But, I see you are and therefore I must take what you say seriously. It is the oath taken by the Swiss Guard that they will protect the Pope at all costs. What do we need to do?"

Conrad had already ordered his thoughts into a clear, consistent exposition of the possible German plan. He ran through it now, proposing that somehow, the Germans had found the secret escape route leading into the western *Cloaca Maxima* and followed it back. When they had opened it up, they had found themselves in the crypt under St Peter's Basilica. They had also found it was a dead end and they couldn't explore further without the keys to the crypt doors. Probably, and Conrad made it clear this was an assumption, the old, heavy locks had proved resistant to lock-picking techniques designed for much smaller, lighter locks.

"Whatever the reason, they had decided to ambush *Wachtmeister* Julian Hüber or one of his colleagues, steal his keys, copy them and then dump the originals in the crypt so nobody would know a fake set existed. Now, the attackers would have had access to the Vatican itself. Only, Doctor Parrino had turned up and walked into the ambush. The attackers had killed him in a spectacular fashion, so that the very flamboyance of the crime would divert attention from what was really going on. By that time, the attempt to assassinate Hitler had taken place and the Pope Pius's apparent involvement discovered. Hitler, quite probably personally, had ordered Pope Pius XII killed in retaliation and the entry tunnel was the obvious way in.

"I would expect that the assault team would be either *Heer* paratroopers, members of the Brandenburg Division or part of an SS commando unit. All would have the skills and ruthlessness needed for this attack." Conrad summed up his presentation. "We are running against the clock here. The Germans must guess that we are on to them, so they will be moving ahead with little delay."

"We will move additional guards on to the entry to that crypt immediately. But, Father Conrad, you must realize that all you have laid out before me, logical though it is, bases itself on assumptions. There are many, many ifs in there."

"There is one other piece of evidence. I had a telephone call from Doctor Massimiliano Agostini. He was inspired by a Sherlock Holmes story to inspect the wound in Doctor Parrino's neck. His attention paid off; he could see fragments of dirt and soil in the wound. He believes, and I agree with him, that this makes the most likely weapon used was a spade or entrenching tool with its edge sharpened. That is a soldier's weapon."

"A good point; a very good point." Herrmann nodded in agreement.

"We can reduce the uncertainty still further by entering the western *Cloaca Maxima* and exploring it as far as we can. If we can also find the end of the escape tunnel, or, more importantly, if we can find traces of work made to ease access in there, then we have a much more solid case." Conrad paused and took a deep breath. "We need to get in there."

"I keep telling you, the Swiss Guard is a real army, albeit a small one. We even have an engineering unit. I would like to introduce him to you. *Korporal*

Felix Freytag." Herrmann picked up his telephone. "*Korporal* Freytag, report to my office immediately."

The *korporal* was a heavy-set man who had the hands of a man who had spent his life handling working tools before taking up the halberd. Herrmann explained the need to investigate the western *Cloaca Maxima* without explaining why, merely saying that it was a possible security concern. Privately, Conrad doubted that Freytag would not make the connection between the gruesome murder in the crypt and the sudden interest in the ancient sewer.

Freytag looked thoughtful. "That sewer was deliberately sealed off in 1939 when the city authorities started to build the *Ponte Principe Amedeo Savoia Aosta*. The sewer has never been properly explored, since it is too dangerous. Every so often, some children, more adventurous than the average, would go down there and look inside. Some, who went in too deeply, would die. That is why the City built the bridge just there. There is a door to allow access, but it is tightly locked. If we go in there, we will have to prepare very carefully."

"What are the dangers?" Conrad asked.

"Cave-ins. The stones have collapsed in many places and the rocks are loose. They are usually very wet and slippery. It is easy to fall and injure oneself quite badly. Then there is the air. The sewer is quite different from the *Cloaca Maxima* on the other side of the river. That more famous sewer has a strong flow of water and the air is circulated as a result. So, the sewer is relatively clean. The flow of water in the western sewer is much slower, so the waste and filth has time to build up and turn to poisonous gas. If we go in there, we will need to take breathing equipment. Also, the sewer is, we think, a dead end and does not reach the surface anywhere. We will need lights as well."

"It sounds like a hazardous enterprise." Herrmann was concerned at the risk to the men under his command. "Are you sure of this?"

Conrad nodded. "As you point out, all the evidence is circumstantial, but it does fit together. We must make sure, one way or the other. And if this revenge assassination is real, then the results would be catastrophic, for everybody. The Church, the people, everybody."

"Not least His Holiness." Herrmann made the remark dryly. "*Wachtmeister* Hüber, pick six of your best men for this work. *Korporal* Freytag, get together all the equipment you need to make sure our fellow Guardsmen are as safe as possible. You may draw upon our special fund to get any equipment you need. Just remember to get receipts for the payments. And, *Wachtmeister* Hüber, take submachine guns and pistols with you. There may be rats down there."

Entrance to the Cloaca Maxima Occidentalem, Ponte Principe Amedeo Savoia Aosta, River Tiber, Rome

"We are 900 meters from Saint Peter's Basilica. The Basilica is west of north west from here." *Korporal* Freytag had led the way down from the road that ran alongside the banks of the Tiber, down a narrow flight of stairs to a constricted footpath that bordered the river itself. The group of nine men had followed that path almost six hundred meters along the bank until they came to the *Ponte Principe Amedeo Savoia Aosta*. Conrad had been half-expecting them to be wearing blue and yellow ceremonial uniforms but, instead, they had on a modern-looking dark blue battledress. The path narrowed still further as it rounded the bridge abutment to reveal a small steel door set in the stonework. Now, they were about to open that door when Conrad stopped him.

"A moment please, *Korporal*. I'd like to have a look at the lock." There was a pause while Conrad inspected the lock. "I thought so; look, there are some recent scratches on the metal. Somebody has been trying to open this door."

"It could be children." Freytag peered at the scratches, "but I think you are right. We are on the right track."

He unlocked the door and it swung open smoothly, with no creaking or squeals from the hinges. Despite the glare outside, the opening behind the door seemed to be pitch black. Freytag lit a candle on the end of a pole and then pushed it into the space. It continued burning evenly. The faint light helped to reveal a semi-circular vaulted area, one where the floor was submerged by a foul-looking layer of water. "Everybody, put your waders on now. And keep your gas masks handy. You might need to put them on quickly."

Freytag had bought pairs of one-piece rubber waders from a hunting store. Once again, Conrad was struck by the fact that Italy had goods available that rationing had long removed from American stores. Rubber in America was a strategic commodity, strictly reserved for military use. He adjusted the shoulder straps so they fitted comfortably.

Hüber finished putting his own pair on then glanced at Conrad to make sure he had his on properly. Satisfied, he looked at his group. "Blosch, Dietiker, go with Freytag in front. Fassnacht, Guidroz, you two stay with the Father and me. Montandon and Staheli, you bring up the rear. One of you, Montandon, stay back here in case somebody else comes in. Everybody, take great care. We are in no hurry, but we do need to search this place thoroughly. Now, electric lanterns on; we do have spare batteries, so do not stint their use."

Conrad wasn't carrying a Sig MKPO, but did have a pad taken from his art supplies and some pencils. He also had a Swiss Guard issue compass, which he used to take bearings on the orientation of the tunnel. He had been offered one of the MKPOs, but had declined, pointing out that an automatic weapon in the hands of somebody untrained in its use would endanger everybody but the people he might be shooting at. The laughter at his comment and respect for his honesty had welded the group into a single party very quickly.

Now, he turned to the man next to him who had the maps. "This tunnel looks like it heads due west to me. That means it will run south of the Basilica."

The first steps into the sewer tunnel made it clear just how old it was. Multi-colored deposits covered the stones, sometimes forming into stalactites that hung from the roof. The initial two or three meters were at least three meters high, but then the tunnel contracted to a bare couple of meters in diameter. Conrad could feel the rocks that had fallen from the roof under his feet. As Freytag had warned, they were loose and moved easily. Suddenly, Conrad realized how right Herrmann had been when he insisted on the party containing the extra men. If somebody slipped and tore up a knee on the stones, it would take three or four men to carry them back to the entrance. He could also feel a pull on his ankles and calves from the flowing water. The current seemed to be much stronger than Freytag had suggested earlier.

It was also deeper. Conrad had been expecting the water to cover his ankles, or reach his knees at most. However, it was already up to his thighs and promised to continue rising. The shoulder-high waders that Freytag had procured had seemed to him to be overkill, but already he was seeing them as a wise precaution. *Remember, Conrad, military personnel usually know what they are doing where practical issues are concerned.* He noted that Guidroz, the man he had spoken to over bearings, had hitched the sling of his submachine gun higher to keep it out of the water. Most of the other men were doing the same.

"The current seems much stronger than I was expecting." Freytag gave the warning quietly. "Everybody, take care."

"Felix, where is this water going? The entrance we came in by was completely blocked."

"It flows into a sump, Father, and then through a stone grid deep under the bridge into the Tiber. Nobody can get through there."

Conrad waved a 'thank you' and got a quick salute in acknowledgement. The state of repair of the tunnel was quickly getting worse as the party moved further in. The stones were becoming more ragged, many more were cracked and flaking while the staining on the walls, now predominantly white, was everywhere. Off to the right, Conrad saw a large square opening out of which water was trickling. Downstream of the branch, there was a brown, soggy-looking strip of debris that had obviously come out of that side-tube and been deposited on the main tunnel. With common, unspoken assent, everybody stayed well clear of it.

"Air is still fresh. There must be a lot of clean water coming in from further down. The stuff we have just passed was definitely sewage." Freytag was looking around. "The shape of the tunnel is changing; it's becoming flat-sided rather than a perfect circle."

"I make it we are about a hundred meters in." Guidroz looked around. "That'll put us under the *Rampa del Sangalio*."

A minute or two later, the lanterns carried by the party showed what seemed to be a major dam crossing the tunnel. To Conrad, it looked like the roof had fallen in completely and partially blocked the way forward. Obviously, the blockage was nowhere near complete, since water was flowing through and past the pile, but it effectively stopped any further movement forward. *Or does it?* Conrad thought.

He took a few steps forward and looked at the way the stones had fallen. *It seems as if, assuming somebody could climb the pile, there is enough room between the top and the roof to get through quite easily.* He looked harder and it suddenly seemed to him that many of the larger square stones were ideally placed to help somebody climb the pile and the smaller ones made good handholds. He took and experimental step up and found that the going was even easier than it looked.

"Careful, Conrad." Hüber called out, the concern in his voice obvious.

Conrad nodded in acknowledgement but kept going. Although it hadn't been immediately obvious, the stones formed an almost perfect staircase up the pile and it was easier than he had thought to swing over the top. There was another hard-to-see staircase down to a deep flood the over side of the pile. There, the water came up almost to his chest and he had to hold his papers up to keep them dry. "Come on over; be warned though, the water this side is deep."

"Well done Conrad, my friend. That was good work!" Hüber followed Conrad over, realizing as he did so that the way the stones were placed made crossing the barrier easily. Once on the upstream side, he looked back at the barrier where his men were following him over. "That stone staircase is far too convenient."

Then, Hüber dropped his voice so they could not be overhead easily. "Next time, Conrad, I put people out on point, let them do their job. You had no place going over that pile first. Suppose there had been an ambush here? Or the rats had booby-trapped the crossing-point? You would have been killed and I would get writer's cramp doing the paperwork. Are we clear on that?"

Conrad, abashed, nodded. "I'm sorry, Julian, I just didn't think."

"Not thinking has killed more people than most anything. Just don't do it again. Let the men on point do their work."

Behind them, Freytag had seen their *wachtmeister* speaking quietly to their civilian and guessed what was being said. Accordingly, he stayed back and, like any good junior NCO, made sure the rest of the guardsmen did the same. Once the *wachtmeister* had finished, he made his way forward.

"This water is clean, relatively speaking. The archeologists asked me to get samples once we were into the unexplored section, but I think this is groundwater."

"That would make sense; this area was all marshland back then, and a prime breeding ground for mosquitoes. I think this tunnel isn't primarily a sewer as such but a part of the system intended to drain the Tiberium marshland." Conrad looked around at the old tunnel, lit now by the electric lamps carried by the Guardsmen. "I wonder if this stone pile was intended to stop the sewage from lower down flowing back and contaminating the cleaner water from the underground springs that fed the marsh?"

"A more important question might be how long the Germans knew about this tunnel." Freytag was looking around at the tunnel as well.

"There was an archeology team from Heidelburg University here in 1938." Hüber remembered them well. "They probably found this tunnel then and kept it to themselves. Quite possibly because the Germans knew they might need secret access to the Holy See one day."

His words caused a reflective silence in the group. Eventually, he broke it. "Back to work. Blosch, Dietiker, Freytag up front again. And keep a keen eye open. We have to assume the intruders are down here. Also, we are well into the unexplored area of this tunnel and we might find anything down here."

Despite his words of caution, the going was considerably easier than it had been before the stone pile. The depth of water in the tunnel shallowed quickly, the walls were in much better condition and everything was cleaner. The outfalls of water from openings in the wall were much more common though and, despite their waders, the team members were getting steadily wetter. Conrad guessed that there would be a careful gun-cleaning session that evening. Eventually they came to something nobody had expected. The tunnel forked, one limb continuing to head westwards, the other heading northwest. Conrad carefully noted the position on the chart he had been keeping.

"I make it that we are exactly 200 meters south east of St. Peter's." Conrad showed his chart to Guidroz who nodded in agreement.

"If my figures are right, 200 meters on that bearing take us directly under the center of the cupola at Saint Peter's Basilica. That can't be a coincidence."

"And the water in that branch is septic again. Obviously, the main line isn't quite as clean as we thought." Freytag gave the warning before setting off down the branch tunnel.

It was smaller than the main tunnel, circular again and the headroom was restricted. Fortunately, the water was shallow and the party made good time.

Unlike the main tunnel, the walls of this branch line were slimy and Conrad could see traces where somebody had brushed up against them while making their way through. This tunnel had been used and used quite recently. As in, within the last few days.

200 paces later, Freytag raised his hand. Movement forward stopped. Off to the right was a small tunnel, obviously hewn through rock and never lined with stones. It was barely high enough for a man to walk down without stooping uncomfortably low, and narrow enough to cause a broads-shouldered man to walk sideways. A portly man would have extreme difficulty in making his way through.

The branch line continued northwest, but it was obviously the small tunnel that was the entrance they were looking for. It was only a few meters long and sloped steeply uphill, but it led to a small room with an odd mechanism in the roof. Conrad saw a bronze bar that held a roof stone firmly in place. The bar was obviously arranged so that it could pivot sideways to release the stone. A piece of wood had been jammed into it to make sure that, if there was a mechanism by which it could be moved from above, that mechanism would be frozen. It was obvious from the size and shape of the stone that it was the *Petr?s E?i* stone he had seen in the crypt. Once the bar locking it was released, it could easily be removed downwards.

"By my calculations, we are exactly under the Basilica." Guidroz looked up from his map. "That's the way in."

Conrad was looking at the bar. He could see scratches on the roof stone where it had been moved. "Somebody has opened that entrance very recently. See, the scratches in the stone are still bright."

"Very good." Hüber thought very carefully. "We leave everything untouched. Nobody should know we have found this place. As we back out, make sure any sign we were here has been erased. Our presence upstairs will be a surprise for anybody who comes in this way."

Sacred Congregation for Extraordinary Ecclesiastical Affairs, Vatican City

"Before we think about sealing that escape route up, please reflect on the fact that I might need it one day." His Holiness Pope Pius XII wasn't joking. "How did it work by, the way?"

"I think the tunnel was kept open all the time, so that a Pope fleeing a raging mob could immediately get inside, lift the stone up and rotate the support bar into place. Once that is done, there is no way to get inside the tunnel and he can make his way to the drainage sewer in perfect safety. We don't know, yet, where that sewer goes, but I suspect it ends somewhere to the

Conrad's Other Eye

west of the Tiberium. Or, he could go to where that branch line joins the main sewer and either head for the Tiber exit or one inland." Conrad had taken a long shower after leaving the *Cloaca Maxima Occidentalem,* but still felt dirty. He shuddered slightly at the memory of the hours spent walking through those tunnels.

"I wonder how many more tunnels are down there that we know nothing about." His Holiness sounded reflective, probably only now realizing the possible impact that his involvement in the German resistance to Hitler could have caused.

"Probably a lot." Conti di Segni had already started a very quiet investigation into exactly that issue. "The archeologists say there are layers and layers of ruins under the ancient city and we've only begun to understand what was built where and why. This whole drainage network under the west bank of the Tiber was completely unexpected and we are keeping very quiet about it. In fact, bearing in mind how dangerous this whole situation is, we should be very careful indeed what we say about the events here. And those to come of course."

"Those to come?" His Holiness painfully obviously did not want to think about that issue.

"There is a German assassination squad coming to kill you in revenge for your involvement in the attempted assassination of Adolf Hitler. They might be here right now, they might be on their way here, but they will come. Thanks to Conrad's efforts, we will be waiting for them but we must decide what we have to do when that issue is decided." Conti di Segni had been thinking about that a lot and was coming to the conclusion that the less said about it the better.

"Have we any idea when?"

Conrad had thought about that as well and come up with some conclusions that would ease things a little. "It really doesn't matter whether the assassination squad is here now, although I think they are, or whether they are coming. There will only be one way out for them and they must use it quickly because, after the assassination, the entire city will be up in arms and hunting down every shadow. They will have to get to Ciampino Airport and fly out.

"Now, *Lufthansa* has a Kondor that comes into Ciampino on an irregular schedule. The attack will come just before that aircraft is due to leave on its return flight to Berlin. We need to watch the aircraft when it arrives and see if there are any likely passengers on board. That will tell us whether the assassination squad is already here or not, although it makes little difference. It is the flight out that is critical. It will decide the timing of everything else."

"The *Lufthansa* flight isn't like the Pan-American service. The people who live near Ciampino joke that they can set their watches by when the Pan-Am Constellation comes in. We'll have to find out when the next German flight is due to arrive." Conti di Segni looked at Conrad curiously. "The assassination team is already here, you say?"

"Of course." Conrad felt irritated at having to say something so obvious. "We know that they were in the crypt when Doctor Parrino was killed. The actual killing was soldier's work, although I wonder whether they did the setting for the scene. It's too complex and elaborate for its own good."

"I accept your first assumption, not the second." Conti di Segni had picked up on Conrad's irritation and was equally vexed by it. "You are used to dealing with criminals who have a realistic perspective on their actions and the police response. That realism means they know they must keep things as simple as possible. It's amateurs who go in for complex, elaborate schemes and the people we are facing here are soldiers.

"They may be very skilled soldiers, but they are soldiers, and thus amateurs when it comes to criminal acts. They will see elaborate plans as being clever. Not only that, they are *German* soldiers and, if we have learned anything from this war, it is that the German command likes horribly over-complicated plans. Remember the battle over that island in the Volga last year? A simple job like taking a small island outpost and they ended up with an operation that had as many layers and as much overwrought decoration on it as one of those hideous Austrian cakes. But I do agree with what you say. That assassination squad is already here."

Ciampino Airport, Via Appia Nuova, Metropolitan City of Rome

"It's tonight." Conrad looked across at the surreal sight in front of him. A few dozen yards to his left, the daily Pan-American Constellation *Clipper Democracy* was loading up her passengers for her flight to Casablanca, the Azores and then to Washington. What made the situation surreal was that just over a hundred yards away, a *Lufthansa* Focke-Wulf Kondor, its tail painted bright red, with the Swastika boldly displayed on a white circle, was unloading her passengers after coming in from Berlin.

There was a prominent presence of Italian troops with armored cars and motorcycles between the two aircraft. Conrad couldn't help but feel that the German airliner looked painfully outdated compared with the sleek Constellation. The fact that there was only a dozen or so passengers coming from the German aircraft while the Lockheed was loading nearly eighty also told its own story.

The scene was completed by a third airliner, also isolated from the German aircraft by a ring of heavily-armed Italian troops. A De Havilland Australia Flamingo, belonging to Falcon Airlines, was on the hardstand waiting for her passengers for a flight to Tobruk and then Cairo. A twin-engined, high-winged aircraft, she also looked old-fashioned compared with the Constellation. Looking at them, Conrad suddenly realized that the German and Commonwealth aircraft both had tailwheel undercarriages and that was what made them look so outmoded.

He also noted that there were only four Italian soldiers between the Commonwealth and American aircraft. *That makes sense. Technically, Middle East Command under General Wavell still answers to Britain, nominally a German ally and now occupied to make sure it stays that way. But, in reality, Middle East Command and London parted ways four years ago and General Wavell now owes allegiance to the Commonwealth. So, what is the status of Falcon Airlines? On paper, it's Egyptian, so what does that make them? Neutral? Commonwealth ally? What interesting times we live in.* Conrad glanced at Hüber standing beside him. The Swiss guardsman was in civilian clothes again; after all, on paper Italy and the Vatican were different countries. "An unusual sight, Julian, for the middle of a war."

"It is, Conrad, but I find eight of the passengers who have just left the Kondor much more interesting. They remind me of me."

"I see what you mean. Eight very fit young men, all with close-cropped hair and trying not to march in step. They could, of course, be members of a church choir."

"That is true, my friend, but they look more like members of the local chess club to me. We must not jump to conclusions; after all, the stewardesses on that Lockheed are all walking in step."

Conrad noted that it was true. The five stewardesses who would look after the passengers of *Clipper Democracy* were walking to the aircraft in step. They split up between the stairs leading into the cabin and started to get the passengers on board. Conrad noted that Igrat, Henry and Achillea were amongst the handful of first-class passengers. One of the stewardesses looked sharply at Henry but said nothing, presumably having been briefed that somebody coming on board would be armed.

"We can drop the Church choir and chess club possibilities, Conrad. None of those eight checked out those stewardesses. That suggests they are disciplined and under orders. The other possibility . . . "

Hüber looked innocent, making Conrad chuckle. "What's your opinion as a soldier, Julian? Do you think they are reinforcing the team already here."

"No, they are here to make sure the retreat of the assassination squad is secure. We are just 15 kilometers from the scene of the assassination. The time-consuming bit will be getting out of the Vatican. Once they are out, a fast car can have them here in ten to fifteen minutes. The troops who have just arrived will make sure the airliner is secure and waiting for them."

"It might not take so long for the team to get out of the Vatican. They have to make their entry quietly but, once inside, they can do their mission and escape through the normal exits. All they need to have is a fast car waiting for them. In fact, that fixes the size of the squad for us. They must be able to get into one or two Mercedes limousines."

"Six men." Hüber thought for a moment. "Possibly eight, but six or seven most likely. Well, it all goes to prove the old joke was right."

"Old joke, Julian? Or shouldn't I ask?"

"Soldier's humor, Conrad. What is the similarity between a Mercedes and a condom?"

"I don't know."

"Sooner or later, each has a dick inside it."

Conrad burst out laughing and shook his head. "I wish that wasn't true. Look, the Constellation is leaving."

The three-man flight deck crew had walked out from the departures building and boarded the Constellation. Conrad guessed that the fourth man would be the flight engineer and was already on board, getting the aircraft ready for departure. As he watched the three men walk to the aircraft, he got an uneasy feeling he recognized one of them, but he couldn't say how or where. He still hadn't solved that when the crew entered the aircraft, the doors shut behind them and there was a sudden silence.

It was broken by the sound of the number three engine starting to turn its propeller. The blades seemed to be moving very slowly and not picking up speed. Watching them. Conrad began to feel concerned that the Constellation was going to break down on the parking strip. With a *Lufthansa* crew watching, that would be embarrassing. It could also be dangerous for those on board. Grimly, he knew that one of the duties of Henry and Achillea was that, if something bad happened, their only responsibility was to get Igrat out of the aircraft alive. No matter who got in the way and, if necessary, at cost of their own lives. The information she carried in her head and on her person was that important.

He was just beginning to believe the worst when the propeller on number three engine suddenly started to spin faster. There was a loud cough, a bang and a cloud of gray-black smoke from the engines accompanied by a sudden burst of orange flame from the top of the cowling. It quickly flared out and number three settled down to running smoothly.

A few seconds later, the outboard engine on the same wing, Conrad guessed it was number four, started the same procedure, first turning slowly and then speeding up and bursting into life with the same cloud of smoke and burst of flame. That struck him as odd; he had assumed the engines would be started alternately between the left and right wing. By the time the thought had passed, the inner engine on the other wing was going through the start-up

Conrad's Other Eye

sequence. *Number Two?* Conrad thought. *It seems to me to be taking each engine less time to start and the smoke and flame is getting thinner each time.*

By the time the fourth engine had started, the other three were running smooth and smoke-free. The aircraft paused for a minute or two; obviously, the crew was making sure that everything was running smoothly and the engines were properly warming up. Then the Lockheed began to edge forward. The nosewheel was already turning to help the aircraft start its move down the taxiway to the runway. As the Constellation edged forward, two Italian Army trucks took station, one on either side of its nose. Conrad glanced over to the *Lufthansa* Kondor and saw that the armored cars had moved to block the German aircraft's route out of its parking area.

He was also surprised to see how tightly the Constellation had turned. The aircraft was giving out groans and squeaks as it made its way out of the loading area, all them drowned out by the deafening squeal as the pilot applied the brakes. The squeaks, squeals and whines continued all the way to the runway. There, the Constellation paused for a second, undoubtedly getting their final takeoff clearance. Then the airliner started accelerating forward.

Conrad noted that the silver finish on the tops of the wings, carefully cleaned and polished before the flight, was already stained with exhaust from the engines. By the time it was halfway down the runway, all of the other noises faded away, replaced by the deep drone of its engines. The nose lifted. The main wheels cleared the runway and the Constellation was airborne. Conrad got the absurd feeling the aircraft sounded happy. The undercarriage retracted. The wings tilted slightly as the aircraft started its climb to cruising altitude and it headed south, away from any threat that might come from German airspace to the north.

"That's the end of the big flying boats you, know." Hüber looked at the departing Constellation with longing in his eyes. "BOAC fly them out of Naples on the route to India, but they can't compete with landplanes for economy. Now the war is causing great airports to be built all over the world, the flying boats are doomed. That's sad. They were beautiful aircraft."

Conrad nodded, more from politeness than anything else. To him, aircraft were a means of getting around and flying was a lot more convenient than walking. "I suppose that means that people will travel a lot more. That'll cause problems all of its own. But we have a more pressing problem on our hands and it also links to air travel. An attack like the one we are expecting couldn't happen without air transport."

"I'm not sure that's right. An assault team like this could come from ships. You're right though, civilian air transport will make doing this sort of thing much easier. At least we understand what we are facing here and now."

"We do indeed; we know the when, the how and the how many, Julian. We had better get back home and find out what we can do to stop them."

Eye of the Confessor

Sacred Congregation for Extraordinary Ecclesiastical Affairs, Vatican City

The sun was setting, casting a red glow over the rooftops of Rome. Conrad had a strange thought that would not leave his head. *The most common cause of death for a Roman emperor was assassination. How many emperors stood in their palace on the Palatine Hill over the Roman Forum, looking at this sunset and knowing that an assassination was on the way? Did they stand there, calculating odds, wondering which of their bodyguards, which of their family, would be loyal? Which were involved in the plot to kill him and which would fight for his life? Pope Pius doesn't have many of those questions to answer. He has no family to betray him and his Swiss Guards are as loyal as any group of bodyguards in history. And yet, even in thinking that, I am doing the same thing as so many Roman emperors. Calculating odds, deciding on loyalties, trying to predict the future. It is not as if other Popes have not been murdered. Alexander VI died by poison at the hand of the man who became Pope Julius II. John XII was beaten to death by an outraged husband.* Conrad reproved himself for remembering that. *But this one, Pius XII, is at risk of his life; not because of his own failures or ambitions, but because he tried to be of service to humanity.*

"Looking back over the years, Conrad? That can be hard for us." Conti di Segni had entered the room and was standing beside him.

"I think every man must stand at a window like this sometimes, and stare out as he thinks back over his life and looks at the decisions he made. And, of course, marvel over how the young man he once was managed to survive, despite looking at the world with the eyes of a child, when childish things should have been left in the past."

"And yet, how often have those awful mistakes led us to places that we would never have reached without them? You, Conrad. Your work defending the innocent has done far more good for the world at large than any alternative I can think of."

Conrad was about to disagree with that when the telephone rang. Conti di Segni picked it up and answered briefly. "That was our observer outside the German Embassy. Four Mercedes limousines just left there, in this general direction."

"Four? We could be seeing a larger attack than we expected."

"Perhaps; or the vehicles intend to scatter once they have picked up the assassination team to foil any likely pursuit. I've had the message passed through to *Oberst* Herrmann. We'll know more when the next observer calls in. In a situation like this, information is king."

"I thought that when I was watching the Constellation take off this afternoon. Igrat was on board with 'Lea and Henry. Their job is to make every

211

effort humanly possible to protect her life. It's a recognition of how important the information she carries really is."

"And of how dangerous her work really is." Conti di Segni spoke softly. "She makes it look easy, but it isn't. She is in great danger all of the time and the risk may not come from obvious places."

Conrad looked at him sharply. *What does the head of Vatican intelligence know that I don't? The answer must fill volumes, but there was a specific warning there.* Instead of pushing it further, he changed the subject. "Before you came, I was thinking about previous Popes. Many have died of violence, but this one is under threat for doing good deeds."

"Much more than you think." Conti di Segni looked at Conrad. "We've noticed something over the last few years. A lot of scientists in America have disappeared, gone on leave of absence from their research positions in the great universities, and then just vanished. They all have one thing in common. They all work in nuclear physics. It could be that His Holiness, who understands nuclear physics, by the way, has seen something coming that is more terrible than you or I can imagine."

CHAPTER FOUR

THE BATTLE

Mausoleum Crypt, Underneath Basilica of Saint Peter, Vatican City

"Remember, don't throw hand grenades. This crypt is underneath the dome of Saint Peter's Basilica and the explosions could bring everything down." Doctor Alinari and his archeologists were helping the Swiss Guardsmen dig foxholes in the dirt that covered the stone floor and fill sandbags to provide strongpoints. There were ten Swiss Guardsmen in the crypt, two gun crews with MG30 light machine guns and six submachine gunners. Their commander, *Feldwebel* Christen Buchmüller, was urging everybody on to have their positions finished as quickly as possible. The aid from the archeologists had been invaluable, but it was time for them to go.

"All right, it's time for you civilians to get clear. Remember, you are sworn to eternal secrecy about what is happening here tonight." Buchmüller looked around the crypt, checking to see that the positions of his men would cover the entrance to the tunnel with a murderous crossfire. Reassured that they were ready, he went to the door and called out.

"Civilians coming out now. Hold fire. Say again, hold fire."

The warning was timely. Buchmüller was a sincere believer in what can go wrong will go wrong and, if it can't go wrong, it will anyway. There was a second line of defense outside the crypt; the corridor leading to it had another machine gun crew at one end, also behind piles of sandbags. If the attackers got past that, there was a final reserve of submachine gunners outside the first door. In all, two-dozen guardsmen were waiting for the attack. Every man was anxious for the chance to prove that they really were soldiers, not just quaintly dressed guides for the faithful.

The archeologists trooped out and down the corridor, looking apprehensively at the machine gun nest they faced on the way. Behind them, Buchmüller closed the door and turned off the lights in the crypt. It was time for his men to get their eyes adjusted to the dark. Quite apart from anything else, the darkness would hide the lethal trap that had been prepared.

Sacred Congregation for Extraordinary Ecclesiastical Affairs, Vatican City

The telephone rang again. Again, Conti di Segni answered it. "Another observer. The cars are definitely heading this way. They're crossing the bridge now. All four of them."

Conrad found it reassuring that the stream of information from observers was keeping them well-informed on the situation as it developed. However, for all that, he was growing increasingly disturbed by facts that didn't seem to fit the general pattern of expectations. *We expected the Germans to send cars to pick up the assassination squad when it had done its work. But why four cars, when two would have done the job?*

Another telephone came in. Conti di Segni picked up on it and listened. "Ciampino. The *Lufthansa* ground crew is getting the Kondor ready to depart."

"The cars are on the *Borgo San'Angelo*." Conrad had picked up a call on the other line. "They're heading right for us, no effort to try and stay back until the team have made their attack from the tunnel."

Suddenly, the truth dropped in on him. He felt the crushing despair of a man who had got the most critical decision of his life completely wrong. "We've got this all wrong. They're not coming through the sewer tunnel at all! That was a diversion, intended to draw our defenses away from the real point of attack. That's why everything they did there was so spectacular. It was intended to focus our eyes on the crypt under the Basilica to the exclusion of everything else.

"They knew if there was a brutal murder down there with mystical overtones, we'd look into it and we would find, or guess at, the tunnel underneath. We would realize that, without keys to the crypt, the entrance through the sewers was a dead end. So, when we saw a German plan to get those keys, we assumed that proved they were coming that way. That's why they made getting the keys so obvious when simply getting a wax impression would have been enough. The whole thing is a calculated diversion, and it worked. The Swiss Guard is the other end of the Vatican Complex and we're completely helpless here."

"Oh ye of little faith." *Oberst* Herrmann had entered the room halfway through Conrad's tirade of self-recrimination. "I keep telling you the Swiss Guard is a real army, even though it's a very small one. Real armies keep reserves for just this reason and position then where they can do most good. We have detachments at all key points to make sure the intruders don't get anywhere near His Holiness. We're ready for this."

"They won't just try and kill His Holiness." Conrad was still distraught at how easily he had been tricked and mislead. "They'll destroy everything they can. They'll smash the statues and frescos, rip the paintings apart, burn the tapestries. That's what they've always done. Remember what they did to Louvain? Twice? They openly say that if anybody resists them, they'll destroy everything their enemies hold dear. This is the greatest treasure-house in Europe and they'll destroy it all."

"Calm yourself, Father." Herrmann sounded both severe and reassuring. "We are waiting; they shall not pass. And we have reinforcements already on the way. There are many veterans who have elected to stay in Rome after their enlistment was finished and they already rally to the sound of the trumpets. A company of the 8th *Bersaglieri* Regiment is coming to help us. They can't enter the Holy See, of course, but they can block the way out. And they have already loaned us some added weapons. We are ready and the barbarians will not pass."

He was interrupted by the sound of a large explosion from the vehicle entrance to the Apostolic Palace courtyard. A few seconds later, the four cars pulled up outside the main entrance and started to disgorge men.

Largo el Colonnato, Vatican City

The cars had threaded the narrow gap at the vehicular entrance to the Vatican's Apostolic Palace. That was the first sign that the diversion had not been successful, for those with the insight to see it. The heavy wrought iron gates had been closed and locked. Less astute drivers might have rammed them in the hope of crashing through. The men driving the Mercedes limousines knew that, if they tried that, they would end up with crushed radiators and still-closed gates. Quite apart from anything else, those gates opened outwards and the combination of wrought iron and stone support made a formidable obstacle.

"Take those damned things out!" *SS-Standartenführer* Stephan Bähr roared the order at the men in his squad. What had been the old *SS-Jagddivision* 502 had been drastically cut back and was now barely a company in size. All the rest of the division had been transferred to other SS units in an effort to bring them back to something resembling full strength after the dreadful casualties experienced in the fighting for Stalingrad and Moskva. Bahr had approved the retention of every man selected for the remaining group himself and liked to think they were the best of the best.

One of those men aimed a *Faustpatrone* at the gates and squeezed the trigger. The clumsy projectile left the barrel, wobbling slowly towards the target gates. The explosion in the quiet of the night seemed deafening. It was effective. The gates swung slowly open, allowing the four cars to race through into the courtyard beyond. They swerved to a halt outside the main doors to the palace. Bähr led his assault team towards the elaborate portal.

His *Faustpatrone* gunner didn't need to be ordered. He had already picked up a replacement launcher. Now he fired a second projectile at the doors. The explosion ripped them from their hinges, sending fragments spiraling through the air amid a very satisfying cloud of smoke. A few of the men had to duck to avoid debris. Bähr and the other eleven men in the assault team burst through the ruins into the entry hall of the palace. Behind them, the four drivers remained to act as a rearguard, securing the line of retreat for the assault team when its work was done.

Swiss Guard Barracks, Overlooking Apostolic Palace Entrance

The Swiss Guard wasn't supposed to have light machine guns. They were supposed to have their traditional weapon of sword and halberd, plus light arms for policing duties. Accordingly, the small number of machine guns they had were always referred to as Mark II halberds. In fact, they were Swiss Army MG30s, with a slightly apologetic note that they were light machine guns.

When the telephone warning had arrived from *Oberst* Herrmann, *Korporal* Freytag took an MG30 from the armory, reminding himself that he really ought to sign for it when he had time, and made his way to a second-floor window overlooking the entrance to the Apostolic Palace. On his way, he was joined by *Hellebardier* Raphael Scheller, who had a carry-case full of loaded 30-round magazines. Together, they set up the gun inside a small office and opened the window to fire out.

Freytag was about to open fire on the lead car when inspiration struck him. There was no way out of the courtyard for cars other than the gates they had come in by. Therefore, if they were blocked, the escape route for the attackers would be cut off. There were other ways for the men on foot to leave, of course; the whole of Vatican City was a warren of entrances, exits, corridors and secret passages. Very, very few people had even a rudimentary knowledge of the full extent of the maze and that number certainly did not include the attackers. Freytag switched his aim before opening fire and raked the rearmost car with a full 30-round magazine. Bullets exploded the fuel tank and sent a ball of fire upwards.

In the light of the fire, he saw the men standing near the cars dive for cover. They swung what looked like rifles upwards. Freytag qualified that. The muzzle flash from the weapons was much greater than he'd seen from a rifle. The hail of bullets that shattered the window was more like the fire from machine guns than rifles.

"What the hell are those things?"

Beside him, Scheller slammed another magazine into the side of the MG-30. "Don't ask me. I suggest we find somewhere else to shoot from. We'll get our heads blown off if we stick them up here again."

"Good thought, Rap. Let's get out of here." As they wormed their way backwards, they heard more gunfire erupting from the windows of the barracks.

The Battle of the Apostolic Courtyard had started.

Sacred Congregation for Extraordinary Ecclesiastical Affairs, Vatican City

"I'm assigning four men to guard this office." *Oberst* Herrmann was coordinating the defense of the palace by telephone, but he knew he would not, could not, leave these civilians unprotected. "They are Swiss Guard veterans who have volunteered to help us this night. Fortunately, they live just a few yards away, across the border. As soon as they are here, I must go to the Palace."

Conrad listened to him, but the words hardly meant everything. He had heard the gunfire and explosions from the Apostolic Palace and guessed that the members of the enemy assassination squad were already inside, destroying everything and killing everybody in sight. He blamed himself for that. The weight of the self-condemnation was crushing his spirit. In his eyes, he had fallen for a simple, albeit well-planned decoy operation that should not have fooled him for a moment.

"Snap out of it." Herrmann had caught his misery and had no time for it.

"This is my fault. I fell for a diversion. I should have recognized it earlier."

"You told us what to expect and when. No civilian could have done more than that. We are ready and waiting because of you. If it hadn't been for your warning, we would all have been caught sleeping in our beds. Now stop whining and start thinking." Herrmann glared at him with all the considerable power than his rank and position of command could give him.

"*Oberst* Herrmann, sir." A group of six Swiss Guardsmen trooped in. They were all middle-aged or even elderly, although their dark blue uniforms still fitted them. They were carrying hunting rifles complete with telescopic sights rather than the submachine guns most of the Swiss Guard had.

Herrmann recognized them instantly. "Willi, Oliver, Berti, Nevio, Pirmin, Alex, welcome back to the Guard. We're outgunned here. The attackers have some sort of rifle that acts like a machine gun. We'll need those rifles of yours."

"Good to be back, sir. There's another group a few minutes behind us." Willi Schaffner had obviously something more than a simple gardist. A *wachtmeister*, or possibly a *feldwebel*. "What do you want us to do?"

Herrmann looked around and changed plans. Six veterans with very accurate rifles had more important roles to play than just guarding some civilians. He called out to a pair of regular guardsmen who were making their way towards the fighting. "You two, Gertsch and Klein, stay here with these civilians. See they come to no harm. The rest of you, come with me."

He paused for a second. "Father Conrad, stop blaming yourself for this mess and get your brain working. That's an order. We need you to work out what's coming next."

As they were leaving, Schaffner looked comfortingly at Conrad. "Don't take on so, sir. We'll sort this out. Old age and treachery will beat youth and skill."

Mausoleum Crypt, Underneath Basilica of Saint Peter, Vatican City

"You in here, stay here. Nobody must get past that entrance. Use grenades if you have to. If the Basilica falls down, so be it." *Feldwebel* Buchmüller paused for a second. "It would be a chance to put the stones the builders took from the Colosseum back. I'm taking the men from outside with me to the Apostolic Palace to help fight the invasion there. *Wachtmeister* Mauchle, take command here. All of you, remember you're guarding everybody's back. Remember Caspar Röist and his 147 men who died holding off a hundred times their number while protecting Pope Clement VII. Don't let them down."

Buchmüller went to the crypt door. "Coming out. All of you out here, come with me. We need to reinforce the guard at the Apostolic Palace.

By the time he had assembled his force, he had fourteen men with two machine guns. Then, he did what every good commander should do. He marched his men, at double-quick time, to the sound of the guns.

Vestibule, Apostolic Palace, Vatican City

"They're awake. They weren't supposed to be, and the ones that are on guard were supposed to be down the other end of the Vatican." Bähr was confused and angry. He had spent years watching Skorzeny planning special forces operations like this and had assumed that, when he took over the unit, he would be able to do the same. Now, he was beginning to realize that, like any expert, Skorzeny made the difficult look easy. He was also beginning to understand why so many operations like this one hit problems.

The problem facing him was, in essence, quite simple. The Apostolic Swiss Guard detachment on the scene had been reinforced. They now held the great spiral staircase that led up to the apartments on the next floor. Bähr had been expecting the few guards present to have the ceremonial halberds and striped renaissance uniforms. Instead they had guns and were wearing a dark blue that blended well into the shadows.

The spiral staircase had no center, so the cover it offered was limited; but that worked both ways. The familiarity of the Swiss Guards with the building was another advantage the defenders possessed. The result was that Bähr and his eleven men were unable to get up the staircase towards the Pope's private quarters. He was also beginning to suspect that the Pope might not be there.

Bähr cradled the StG-44 rifle in his hands and edged forward towards the staircase. His movement drew the attention of one of the guards above. He fired a submachine gun burst downwards. That gave Bähr the man's position. It took no more than a second to line up the shot. He fired a return burst. It ricocheted off the wall towards the Guard's position. Bähr heard a scream from above. At least one of his bullets had struck home. Even better, from his point of view, the burst had left a series of large craters across a fresco by Raffaello Sanzio da Urbino. Destroying as many as possible of the treasures stored in the palace featured heavily in Bähr's orders. As his orders put it, burning down the entire building would be considered entirely satisfactory.

One of his men ran past him and around the first curve of the spiral staircase. There, he was sheltered from gunfire from above by the structure of the stairs. The Swiss Guards couldn't move to fire on him without exposing themselves to Bähr's StG-44. A shattering crash filled the atrium. A display cabin of priceless ancient Corinthian, Iaconian and Attic vases was broken open and its contents smashed.

Some of Bähr's men had tried to move out from the Atrium via doors on either side of the spiral staircase. They had found the doors were wedged shut from behind. They tried to fire through them. The sturdy wood withstood the assault; the intricate carvings, made centuries before, had been destroyed beyond any hope of redemption.

That meant going up the stairs was the only way forward.

Swiss Guard Barracks, Overlooking Apostolic Palace Entrance

One of the attackers was already down. A second Mercedes limousine was burning furiously. Freytag had a guilty feeling about thoroughly enjoying himself. He had never liked the Germans, and severely resented it when visitors assumed from his name that he was German rather than Swiss. Blowing up the property of the German Embassy pleased him greatly.

Conrad's Other Eye

The gunfire from the three remaining men down by the two surviving cars had slackened slightly. *They must be running short of ammunition for those machine-rifles,* he thought. This had allowed some of the guardsmen to take more time over their shots. That allowed them to offset the inaccuracy and lack of power of the weak cartridges they were using. One more of the attackers slumped as some bullets finally bit their target. From his firing position, Freytag saw blood spreading across the man's shirt. *He's in civilian clothes down there. We can hang him for that.*

With that comforting thought in mind, Freytag settled the butt of his MG30 into his shoulder. He checked that Scheller had inserted a new magazine into the side of the machine gun and proceeded to do more damage to German Embassy property.

Upper Floor, Apostolic Palace, Vatican City

"Keep the *Sauschwabes* pinned in the staircase." Hüber had brought his six men through the maze of apartments and reception rooms on the upper floor to where the spiral staircase well emerged. There had been four guards on this floor. They would be preventing the invaders from getting any higher in the building. *If they are still alive.*

As it happened, one of the four guardsmen had survived. Although wounded, he was still firing across the sweep of the steps. That pinned down the men trying to come up the stairs. He hadn't stopped them, but he had delayed them long enough for Hüber's team to arrive. He heard the reinforcements arriving and called out a desperate warning.

"Be careful, my friends, the *Sauschwabes* have machine guns."

The warning had been timely, but it cost the man his life. One of the SS men moved a bit further up the stairs, where he could get a good shot at the lone survivor. The burst from the StG-44 stilled the guardsman's voice although its work was done. Instead of Hüber and his men running through the door into the machine gun fire, they held back and laid down a barrage of fire from their submachine guns. The exchange of fire drove home just how pitifully outgunned his men were. *The* Sauschwabes *don't just have rifles; they really do have rifles that fire like machine guns. Against them, our MKPOs are weak and useless toys.*

It wasn't just machine rifles as Hüber quickly learned. The Germans must have heard the reinforcements arrive. Hüber heard a bang and clatter. A hand grenade was thrown at the open door. It hit the door and spun around as it rolled into the group of guardsmen.

Only one thing saved them.

Before joining the Guard, *Hellebardier* Lukas Montandon had been a mighty athlete and the champion footballer for his gymnasium team. His fellow students still talked of the time when he had scored four goals in a single game. By chance, or as the Guardsmen saw it, by the Grace of God, he was standing to one side. He ran out and kicked the grenade back from whence it came. Everybody in the Palace could hear the blast. It went off in the staircase. The men it wounded screamed. Only one of the Germans was killed; by chance, it was the same man who had shot the guardsman at the top of the stairs a few seconds earlier.

The progress of the assault team up the spiral staircase was halted. Hüber and his men couldn't drive them down, they were far too outgunned for that. Their gunfire could stop the SS men from coming up. With the side doors from the vestibule blacked and barricaded, the killers were trapped in the entry room. From Hüber's point of view, the problem would now be driving them out.

Sacred Congregation for Extraordinary Ecclesiastical Affairs, Vatican City

"The *Bersaglieri* have moved to block off any further access to the area. What's in, will stay in; what's outside, will stay outside. The Swiss Guard have pinned the intruders inside the vestibule of the Apostolic Palace. They've also engaged the escape force in the courtyard, destroyed three of their cars and damaged the fourth. All the intruders are in civilian clothing, so they can be treated as common criminals." Conrad had managed to recover his composure and was watching the developing situation carefully.

"They can be executed for attempting to assassinate the Pope. It's the only capital offense on the books in Vatican City. Italy, now that's different. They have capital punishment for several offenses. Death by firing squad, if I remember correctly." Conti di Segni was already calculating the political implications of the attack on the Holy See. At this point, he couldn't really see any good ones.

"Under military law, simply opening fire on combatants while in civilian clothes is a war crime, punishable by death. The only defense is that those firing must be wearing insignia distinguishable at a distance. We have had no reports of them doing so and, as *Oberst* Herrmann has been at pains to point out, the Pontifical Swiss Guard is a real army. If there are any prisoners taken, they could be tried by court-martial. As the military commander on the spot, that would be for *Oberst* Herrmann to decide.

"I think. You'd better get some lawyers to look at the situation. The big problem in a civil trial would be proving that the attackers were intending to kill the Pope. We're certain they do, but that isn't proof. They could claim that their intent was to kidnap His Holiness and take him back to Germany for trial on charges of complicity in the attempted assassination of Adolf Hitler." Quite without realizing it, Conrad had dropped into his defense mode.

"Ouch." Conti di Segni had suddenly realized another set of implications for the situation existed. "If they use that defense, they'll be admitting there was an assassination attempt on Adolf Hitler, something they have kept extremely quiet to date. In fact, the only way out the Nazi Government has for this situation is to deny the attackers have anything to do with them. They could accuse them of being anti-religious Communists, of course, and use the situation as a lever to try and break up the Russian-American alliance. That won't stick, although it may have figured in their planning for this operation."

"I doubt it." Conrad's brain was back in full gear again, the lights were on and he was putting the pieces together. "I think this was a turbulent priest case. Hitler had one of his rages and was ranting about His Holiness's involvement in this case and was screaming that he wanted His Holiness dead. Somebody, I would guess Heydrich, overheard him and set wheels in motion without thinking through the consequences. Then planning the attack was handed to some over-promoted junior officer who came up with this plan.

By the time people had realized the demand had been taken seriously, it was too late to stop it. For a serious plan to assassinate the Pope, all it would need would be a sniper on a convenient rooftop or behind a window. This commando raid, with its elaborate decoys and diversions, is the product of a junior officer who has spent his career doing commando operations and can't think of anything else."

"So, what are you recommending?"

"We play this quiet. We can't deny that something has happened, but we can obfuscate. We can bury it under a heap of allegations and theories until nobody can work out the truth. If we try and expose this, the Nazis will take horrible reprisals against our brothers and sisters in Christ who live in the territories that are Nazi-ruled. I hate to say this, but, this one time, our overwhelming interests, our absolute need to protect our innocent fellow Christians who are guilty of little more than trying to survive a reprehensible regime, coincides with the political needs of the Nazis."

Conti di Segni nodded in agreement. *I wonder if Conrad realizes that he has just explained why we can't take any prisoners from tonight's affair?*

Swiss Guard Barracks, Overlooking Apostolic Palace Entrance.

For some reason, the last of the four Mercedes in the courtyard was resolutely refusing to burn. It had been parked so that its bulk was shielding its fuel tank. 6.5mm bullets from Freytag's MG30 didn't have the power to penetrate through all the bodywork. In fact, the lack of hitting power exhibited by the weapons issued to the Swiss Guard was a major problem across the whole battle. Three of the four Germans who formed the rearguard to the attackers in the Palace were still alive because the 7.65mm Kurz rounds from the MKPOs lacked the range and penetrating power to deal with them. On the other hand, the rifle bullets the attackers were firing did have the range and power needed. Casualties amongst the guardsmen firing from the windows of their barracks were steadily rising. In fact, Freytag's MG30 was the only weapon disputing the German riflemen's dominance in the courtyard.

That situation changed suddenly with a single shot. The full-throated crack of a rifle being fired echoed around the courtyard,. Freytag easily distinguished it from the rattle of the submachine guns or the rhythmic thumping of the machine rifles. Below him, one of the three surviving attackers slumped to the ground. He lay still in a spreading pool of blood. *A lucky shot struck home!*

Another rifle shot rang out. A second man crumpled. *Snipers,* Freytag thought with profound relief. *Somehow, we've brought up snipers.*

"Hey, Felix. I might have known you'd be behind that machine gun."

"Oliver Leuzinger! Old Herrmann must be scraping the bottom of the barrel!" Despite his words, Freytag was delighted to see his old friend. He would have jumped up to give the man a firm embrace, but there were far too many bullets flying around for that. "I see you brought your hunting rifle. We need the firepower."

"All the old gang are here and we brought our hunters. With scopes. Now, let's get rid of that remaining *Sauschwabe* down there before he hurts somebody else."

Leuzinger took up a sniper's position carefully, well inside the room so the muzzle blast from his rifle wouldn't give his position away. The German down below had moved around the single remaining Mercedes. Now, it protected him from the source of the first pair of rifle shots. Unfortunately for him, doing so exposed him to Leuzinger. There was a loud blast, amplified by the small room. The last German in the courtyard crumpled to the ground. "Got the Sauschwabe!"

"Well done, Ollie! We'll get them out of there now."

"Not yet, Felix. Those machine rifles will cut you to pieces if you try and cross that courtyard. Leave this to us."

Vestibule, Apostolic Palace, Vatican City

Bähr was beginning to feel desperation tug at his mind. The four men outside were dead. One of the men he had brought into the vestibule had been blown up by his own hand grenade. A third of his men were already dead. Two more had been wounded, although the weak rounds fired by the Swiss Guard had left both of them capable of continuing the fight. On the other hand, his men had killed at least a dozen of the Swiss guardsmen. They would have done the same for many more, but they had run out of targets. The guardsmen had been brave and dedicated, but they were no match for the elite members of *JagdKompanie* 502. The men guarding the vestibule had been shot down without loss.

What do I do now? Where do we go? Our target is upstairs at best. More likely, has abandoned the building completely. Isn't there a castle near here where a Pope is to take shelter in the face of physical attack? We can't even burn the palace down; we brought thermite charges, but they are in the cars. Were in the cars. At least we know they would have worked. We've smashed or torn up everything left in here. What do we do?

"Sir, orders?" *Scharführer* Paul Schoenfeld knew from his experience, which vastly exceeded Bähr's, that this operation had gone completely pear-shaped. The barrage of submachine gun fire peppering the front of the building convinced him that there was no hope of escaping the way they had come in. Anyway, the men outside were dead and the cars burning.

Bähr looked around, trying to find a way out. Neither he, nor anybody else, knew exactly what the layout of the Apostolic Palace was. That knowledge was confined to a small group of people high up in the Church. The only information that reached the public was contradictory and wildly inaccurate. From the number of guardsmen slowly increasing the ring around his position, Bähr guessed there had to be a way through the maze to the outside. "All right, Schoenfeld, we'll have to go up the stairs again, to the first landing. We know there are Swiss Guards to the left, so we will go right and make our way along the floor that way. With luck, there'll either be a way out there or another set of stairs leading to one."

Bähr heard a very quiet, odd, wet-slap noise. He glanced up in time to Schoenfeld's head suddenly start to swell. His forehead burst open with a spray of blood and debris that splattered the front of Bähr's clothing. Instinctively, Bähr dropped flat. Schoenfeld crumpled to the floor. A few feet to his left, another one of the raiding party fell. Another sniper's bullet struck home.

"Turn off the lights, keep away from the windows. Make your way to the staircase, we have to get out of here."

Upper Floor, Apostolic Palace, Vatican City

"Here the *Sauschwabes* come again."

Hüber had made good use of the brief respite. He and his men had piled cushions and furniture up against the door to make the best barricade they could. They had also collected some halberds from the displays on the walls and placed them within easy reach. It had occurred to Hüber that, if it came to fighting hand-to-hand, the extra reach of the halberds might be useful.

One other improvement had not been so useful. *Hellebardier* Guidroz had crawled out and managed to salvage the machine rifle the now-dead grenade-throwing German had been carrying. He had brought it back in triumph and found out how to release the magazine. It was empty and the weapon was useless.

The Germans came up the stairs in a series of leaps. One group hosed down the position held by Hüber and his men. Others ran up the stairs and around the curve, to the next position they could use to provide covering fire. Once the attackers were close enough, they threw hand grenades at the Swiss Guard position.

Fortunately for Hüber and his men, the heavy antique furniture took most of the blasts. Some of the guardsmen went down, and the rest were stunned. The explosions and automatic weapons fire filled the landing with heavy blue smoke. The raiding party ran through the cover it provided into the landing and across to the doors opposite Hüber's position. The doors weren't locked. The Germans piled through them, into the Pope's private library.

They also ran straight into the concentrated gunfire from *Feldwebel* Christen Buchmüller and his men.

Private Library, Upper Floor, Apostolic Palace, Vatican City

When *Feldwebel* Christen Buchmüller finally made it to Fiddler's Green, he and his men would undoubtedly be made honorary members of the U.S. Cavalry. In the finest of Hollywood traditions, they made it to the rescue just in time to save Hüber's men and the contents of the Papal Library from death and destruction. His MG30 crews had set up along each wall; they could fire obliquely into the doorway without hitting each other or endangering Hüber's men on the other side. Buchmüller had set the rest of his men to turning the heavy antique reading desks over and padding them with books. A few of the Swiss guardsmen had even found time to move some of the valuable relics to cover.

Fortunately, the library not only contained ancient tracts of great historical value but also a large number of modern works that had been featured on the *Index Librorum Prohibitorum*. His Holiness had been heard to remark that it was necessary for a devout man to read such books every so often to remind himself how horrifying they were. For some reason, a major consignment of copies of *The Myth of the Twentieth Century* by Nazi ideologist Alfred Rosenberg had been received. Now they performed useful service as quasi-sandbags. At least one guardsman had been heard to mutter that it was a pity Rosenburg's books would be shot to shreds since they had been printed on such nice soft paper.

The first of the Germans to burst in did so while firing long bursts from their StG-44 rifles. The bullets went everywhere; they were firing from the hip while running and slamming the doors open. There were four men in the initial breaching team. Two of them were shot down before they realized how many Swiss Guards were in the room. The other two dived to each side of the doors, seeking cover from the hail of submachine gun fire that enveloped them.

The Swiss Guards were now fighting their enemies on even terms. At ranges of a few feet, the small 7.65mm rounds they were as effective as any pistol round could hope for. The Germans were cut down. The defenders of the library paid dearly for that achievement. They had expected nothing else. As experienced soldiers, they knew butchery resulted from automatic weapons in a confined space. None of the survivors would leave the library without severe damage to their hearing.

Bähr and the remaining six men of his assault group were pinned down outside the library. They tried throwing grenades inside. The stout tables and stacked copies of Rosenburg's books absorbed the blasts. One of the Swiss Guards even emulated Montandon's feat and kicked a hand grenade back. Two more of Bähr's men went down. The position of the rest was even more precarious.

They were now taking fire from Hüber's men behind them. Below them, Freytag and the rest of the men from the Swiss Guard barracks had stormed back into the vestibule. They were working their way up the spiral staircase. They were moving a lot faster up the stairs than the Germans had done. They were, after all being supported by fire from two other directions. The few surviving SS commandos were pinned down and unable to protect themselves.

Bähr knew the situation was hopeless. He guessed there were more Swiss Guards on the floor above him. All other escape routes had been cut off. The Swiss Guards behind him were closing in fast. Those in the library were being more circumspect, but were still moving forward. He also understood enough Swiss to understand that the guardsmen coming up the stairs had seen the destruction his men had caused in the vestibule. They were in a bloody mood.

A loud scream from behind finally decided him.

Wachtmeister Hüber had run out of ammunition for his MKPO. He picked up one of the halberds he had placed conveniently available. One of the last surviving Germans had seen Hüber and his four surviving men moving to attack the rest of the SS team in the rear. He tried to stop them. Hüber ran him through with his halberd. Huber's men finished the mortally wounded man off with their submachine guns and pistols.

Bähr understood that he and the three survivors were about to be engaged in hand-to-hand combat. Halberds, with the Swiss Guard's determination behind it, would easily trump the bayonets available for the short, stubby StG-44s. He stood up, hands raised, and shouted out "Don't shoot, we surrender."

Ten minutes later, Bähr and the two surviving SS men were standing against a wall, surrounded by Swiss Guards with weapons, including Hüber's leveled halberd. Conti di Segni arrived and looked at the prisoners, realizing the full implications of their presence. *Oberst* Herrman had come with him. He also knew the dilemma that this caused. "What are the orders for the Guard, Eminence?"

Conti di Segni found the old words coming back to him. He felt a mortal despair as they left his lips. "*Caedite eos. Novit enim Dominus qui sunt eius.*"

"I cannot order my men to do that." Oberst Herrmann shook his head firmly. "I am sorry, Eminence, but as the commander of the Pontifical Swiss Guard, I am in sole charge of the military assets of Vatican City. And I will not order my men to do what you ask."

Joining the group gathered in the vestibule, Conrad heard the small but emphatic emphasis on the word ask. *Oberst* Herrmann was quite correct, of course. Conti di Segni was not in the chain of command and had no authority to give binding orders or even issue requests to anybody, let alone the commander of the Swiss Guard. Conrad guessed that the man who, as Pope Innocent III, had once exerted almost unlimited power had just found the limitations of a truly secret organization. *He can make suggestions, but only issue orders to people if they are ready to agree to the content of those orders. Here, they obviously are not.* Oberst *Herrmann suggested that he would obey a reasonable order, but not ones he regarded as illegal or immoral.*

He took the chance to look around the scene of devastation in the vestibule. Much of the damage had been inevitable, the result of indiscriminately using modern infantry weapons in a room filled with precious artifacts. More, though, had obviously been the result of deliberate, planned vandalism. A case full of Etruscan vases, made before Rome had even been founded, had been pushed over and its contents shattered. The vandals hadn't stopped at breaking the pottery; they had ground the fragments underfoot, to make sure the antiques could never be restored. Behind him, Conrad heard Conti di Segni gasp in acute misery.

"Conrad, look."

Conrad turned to see him staring at a small section of wall, an unobtrusive area shadowed by the staircase. It had been the location of Raffaello Sanzio da Urbino's least known work, a small fresco he had called "The Adoration of the Madonna." Conrad had, over the years, spent hours studying it, delighting in the subtle interplay of light and color that characterized Raffaello's work. It depicted a simple scene; a young woman looking at her newborn child, while her husband proudly watched over them. The ambiguity of the title fascinated the few people who had found it. *Was the adoration, the love of the mother for her child or was it the adoration of the mother by her husband? Or did the adoration in question lie in the hearts of those who looked on the work?*

Now, the mystery would never be solved. Somebody had fired one of the machine-rifles into the fresco at point-blank range. A normal painting might have splintered, giving restorers something to work with. The plaster on which the fresco had been painted was powdered by the impacts. "The Adoration of the Madonna" was gone forever.

"I stood by Raffaello the day he completed the work. He thought it was his masterpiece." Tears were streaming down Conti di Segni's face as he looked at the ruin.

"We had just enough warning to get the most valuable relics out of here. Some were damaged due to haste, but nothing that cannot be restored. Nothing like this." Cristoforo Romano, *Inspettore Generale* of the *Corpo della Gendarmeria dello Stato della Città del Vaticano*, was busy trying to restore order to the situation. "You are the two who realized what was about to happen? Then we all owe you a great debt."

Behind him, the surviving Swiss Guards were bringing the bodies of their dead down to the vestibule. They had lost 22 of their number, a massive death toll for a force that only numbered 130. Each new body was placed at the end of the line, respectfully covered by a white sheet.

A familiar figure in white was walking down the line, personally blessing each casualty. "*Oberst* Herrmann, please make sure we have the full details of the whole family for each of these brave men. They will all be in our care as a sacred duty and we will make sure they want for nothing."

"It will be done, Holiness. What shall we do with these three?" There was no doubt whom Coni di Segni meant by these three, nor what he wanted done with them.

His Holiness thought carefully about that. "The law must take its course, but we must remember secular power can execute punishment even unto death, without mortal sin provided that it punishes with justice, not out of hatred, with prudence, not precipitation and we must offer every chance for reconciliation with the church."

Conti di Segni sighed quietly. "Holiness, you have done what is right, but I greatly fear that the results may be a calamity. If what has happened here tonight gets out, the repercussions could be worldwide. Sometimes, the choices we face are not between a good thing and a bad thing, but between bad and worse."

Pius XII looked at him with reproach. "That is something we must leave in God's hands. Surely you, of all people, must understand that?"

Ufficio dell'Inspettore Generale, Corpo della Gendarmeria dello Stato della Città del Vaticano, Vatican City

Inspettore Generale Cristoforo Romano brought in a sheaf of papers that had just arrived. "We have had word from the German Ambassador to Italy. He reports that four Mercedes limousines were stolen from the Embassy grounds overnight and has provided details of the vehicle's registrations. They are consistent with the four vehicles that were later destroyed outside the Apostolic Palace. The Embassy, of course, denies all knowledge of the attack itself."

"How convenient." Conrad was dry. The destruction in the vestibule of the Palace, and the constant nagging fear that his failures had contributed heavily to it, still weighed upon him. "I suppose he denies any knowledge of the men as well?"

"He does." Romano hesitated, afraid that he was about to make himself look very foolish. He knew well that he was out of his depth here. The Papal Gendarmerie Corps dealt with crime in Vatican City, but that was almost always confined to pick-pocketing and bag-snatching. The Vatican also had no working prison and only one judge. The previous night was far outside his experience. "This will sound foolish, I know, but I believed him."

Conrad thought about that carefully, putting all the pieces together. "You might well be right. What happened here may have been as much of a surprise to the ambassador as it was to us. The same might not go for his staff, of course. Do we know who runs the German intelligence section here?"

"I believe it is an *Abwehr* operation. I am not sure of that; we are far beyond anything I normally deal with now."

"Then I think we can be sure that the ambassador was telling the truth." Conti di Segni spoke up for the first time. In a way, he had experienced as bad a shock as Conrad had. Used to operating from the shadows, where his authority was unchallenged, he had watched that authority shrivel in the light of day. "*Inspettore Generale*, could you arrange for us to interview the prisoners?"

Romano nodded and left to make the arrangements. As soon as he was gone, Conti di Segni, looked up at Conrad. "Conrad, the *Abwehr* is a major part of the resistance to Hitler and the Nazis. That is how the resistance has survived so long. If the SS and *Gestapo* have captured records, they must know how deeply the *Abwehr* is implicated in the coup attempt. The *Abwehr* section here has certainly been cut out of the loop and that means the ambassador has also been isolated from whatever was being planned in Berlin. That does not, of course, preclude them from being set up as scapegoats for what has happened here."

"It is reasonable then to assume that the cars genuinely were stolen, albeit with the complicity of a member of the German Embassy in Rome. We can also assume that the people who took part in the attack are unknown to most of the Embassy staff." Conrad thought through the implications of that. "If we assume that the *Abwehr* is present in the Embassy, as they surely must be, and that they are also a major part of the anti-Nazi resistance in Germany itself, then we can assume that the resistance is aware of what happened here last night. It won't take them long to put everything together and they'll know that there was an attempt to assassinate the Pope and who was behind it. You told me that the Catholic Church is the best-organized and most dedicated part of the resistance and that even the Protestants admit that. So . . . "

"So, some hotheads over there will take it into their heads to take their revenge by killing the people they hold responsible for the attack." Conti di Segni shook his head in horror at the picture forming. "This could go out of control very easily. Why did His Holiness have to involve himself in this? And, even worse, put everything in writing?"

"That was indeed . . . unwise." Conrad also was horrified at how fast and how far this chain of events could spread. Before he could develop his thoughts further, Romano had returned.

"We have the prisoners in an interview room now. If you would follow me, I'll take you to them. They're keeping their mouths firmly shut, though."

"They usually do. We'll have to persuade them to do otherwise. Can you split them up so we can interview them separately?"

"Of course. I'll see to it right away."

Interview Room, Corpo della Gendarmeria dello Stato della Città del Vaticano, Vatican City.

The so-called interview room looked suspiciously like a staff break-room, where tired gendarmes would rest their feet and sip an expresso to recover from the day's ordeal of shepherding the faithful around the Holy See. Conrad felt his sensations of guilt and remorse return as he realized those hard-working men were being deprived of richly deserved comfort. "This will be perfect. Do we know who these men are?"

To Conrad's secret delight, the prisoners were in *Wachtmeister* Julian Hüber's charge. He was obviously exhausted, but outrage at the night's work drove him onwards. He still had his halberd; the three men with him had the machine-rifles picked up from the vestibule. He peered at the men in his charge with something very close to a sneer on his face.

"I am sorry, Conrad; they will not say anything. We have searched them, thoroughly and not gently. They have civilian clothes without markings or labels. These rifles have no identifying marks. The only distinguishing feature is that each has a tattoo on his arm, above the elbow. It appears to be his blood group. I would say, given the skill with which they fought, they have been trained as soldiers." Hüber hesitated, then continued. "They do, of course, lack the honor of real soldiers."

Bless you, Julian, Conrad thought. *That will start the process of making them break their silence nicely.* "Julian, please use your expertise to pick the one you think is the most junior and bring him in. And, if your men need coffee or something to eat, I don't think the *Gendarmeria* will begrudge them to you."

"Thank you, Conrad. But, after last night, none of us feel like eating. I will bring the first prisoner in." Hüber disappeared outside. He reappeared with a young man in handcuffs. As he had told Conrad, the man was in untidy civilian clothes, a dirty white shirt and a pair of black workman's trousers.

Conrad smiled at him. "I am sorry for these unorthodox surroundings, but the Holy See doesn't have the proper facilities for this kind of thing. Please take a seat; the chairs are quite comfortable for a break-room. *Wachtmeister* Hüber, please bring the prisoner a comfy chair."

The prisoner was reluctant to sit down, until he was helped to do so by a firm push on his chest. To his obvious astonishment, the padded chair was surprisingly comfortable, given the spartan facility they were using. The Holy See obviously did not stint on the small comforts it provided to those in its service. "Now, let's get started. What is your name?"

The man said nothing. By doing so, he told Conrad much more than he realized. "Come now; you can't expect me to address you as prisoner, can you? And we have to put a name on your tombstone; something other than *Milite incognitus*. Don't you want your family to know where you are buried? If they are Catholic, it may even console them in their loss to know that you are interred here."

The prisoner still said nothing. He was unaware that his body language and expressions were speaking for him. Conrad had not expected him to speak; later, perhaps, but not now. Instead, his questions and comments were intended to provoke the reactions he was now getting. "Listen, soldier, you are allowed under the terms of the Geneva Convention to give me your name, your rank and your serial number. That's so we can tell your government and your family where you are. Unfortunately, and I must be honest with you here, you will be placed on trial for your actions last night. You see, you are in civilian clothes, not your uniform. Therefore, the killings which you took part in last night were acts of murder, not of war."

Conrad paused. He was telling the truth, and he knew it, but he didn't want to admit, even to himself, that he had been pleased when Conti di Segni had issued those dire words. "Several people here wanted to have you and your comrades summarily executed. His Holiness himself stopped that, even though the executions would have technically been legal. You see, you are in Vatican City here and the His Holiness is the sovereign of Vatican City State with full legislative, executive and judicial powers. The commander of the Swiss Guard has his authority to act in in his stead where matters concerning the security of the Holy See are concerned so, if he had decided to have you shot for killing his men, that would have been entirely in order.

"Even if that were not the case, Vatican City has not signed the Hague Convention. So the authorities, meaning His Holiness, can treat prisoners in any way he pleases. Of course, His Holiness does believe that, this being the Holy See, the standard of morality, justice and personal honor is set for the Catholic World here. So, in His eyes, it is essential that an example of morality should be established. So you will get a fair and just trial. The verdict, though, is hardly in doubt."

Still the prisoner said nothing. His sideways glances and nervous movements in the chair showed that he hadn't realized just how bad his situation was. "Still nothing to say? Well, think about it while we speak with your comrades."

Carefully watched by Conrad, Hüber escorted the prisoner back to the holding area. The glances the prisoner exchanged with one of the other prisoners clearly told Conrad which one of the three was in charge. "Julian, bring the middle one in next."

After having gone through the same preliminaries as before, Conrad leaned back in his seat and surveyed the man in front of him. "Tell me, *SS-Standartenführer*, aren't you a little high-ranking to be in charge of a penny-ante little operation like this?"

GOT HIM! Conrad's expression showed none of the flood of glee that flowed through him when he saw the quickly-masked shock on the prisoner's face. He had heard that members of SS units had their blood groups tattooed on their arm. It was a logical assumption that this attack had been carried out by a specialized commando unit. Such units had always been over-ranked. So, he had looked up the ranks of the SS and picked one that was significantly higher than he would have expected. *A general grade rank was too high, but a colonel seemed about right. It was a gamble, but it has paid off better than I had expected.*

"After all, *Herr SS-Standartenführer*, in any normal army, a man of your rank would be commanding a whole regiment, not an understrength platoon. Perhaps you are not too highly regarded by your superiors. After all, last night's attack was a fiasco. A British officer from Middle East Command described it as a cake and arse party. I don't understand the British sense of humor, so perhaps you could explain that to me? You were in the invasion of

Britain, I believe? Now that was a well-planned operation. It seems strange to me that it could have been the product of the same minds that came up with this *polnaya katastrofa*."

The prisoner's eyes were bugging out with shock. Conrad could read the man's mind from his expression. *How did they know I was in Britain for the invasion? How much about me does he already know?*

Conrad let no hint of his thoughts show in his face, a skill he had picked up from the Inquisition. *It was easy enough to guess. You have already confirmed, without realizing it to be sure, that you are Germans, a member of an SS Commando unit and the equivalent of a colonel. Now, all such members of units like that were involved in the invasion of Britain. So, the odds are overwhelming that you were. And you understood me when I spoke in Russian. So you almost certainly served on the Russian Front. Again, not surprising; most of your kind did.*

It took longer than for most. But, eventually, the prisoner confirmed that he was a member of the SS and was *SS-Standartenführer* Stephan Bähr. It was the first crack in the wall he and his men had erected around themselves. Like most such walls, once the cracks started to form, they spread quickly. It took Conrad all day, and most of the following night. But, by the time he had finished, he had assembled an accurate account of the attack. None of it really surprised him. It was more or less what he had already deduced, but deductions were one thing; solid statements of fact were quite another. These statements could be produced at a trial.

Towards the end, Bähr had made a key statement, one born of despair, exhaustion and a crippling sense of complete failure. "It was the *Führer* himself who was ready to get things started. 'I'll go right into the Vatican. Do you think the Vatican embarrasses me? We'll take that over right away. For one thing, the entire diplomatic corps are in there. It's all the same to me. That rabble is in there. We'll get that bunch of swine out of there and kill them all. Later we can make apologies.' In the end, he was persuaded to settle for just killing the Pope."

Sitting quietly in a corner, listening to the interrogation, Conti di Segni had observed Conrad at work with awed respect. Without a single act of violence or even an angry word, by sheer force of character and skilled deductions, he had persuaded the hardest men in Europe to confess. As the Germans were led away to a detention area, he caught Conrad's eye. "Now, we have something to work with. Now, we can begin to try and limit this disaster."

Conrad's Room, Domus Sanctae Marthae, Vatican City

Conrad had uncharitable views about the press in general and newspapers in particular. He was firmly of the opinion that the only reason why a newspaperman wouldn't sell his grandmother in exchange for a good

233

story was that he had already traded the poor old lady in for a clever headline. The newspapers in front of him were merely serving to confirm that opinion. All were leading with the attack on the Vatican, of course. *La Stampa* was decrying it as an attempt by the fascists in Italy to take over the Vatican City enclave. The newly-established *Il Tempo*, on the other hand, was accusing local communists of trying to steal priceless works of art from the Vatican museums and sell them to finance their revolutionary activities. *Il Gazzettino* was pointing its collective finger at Sardinian separatists while *Il Piccolo* was doing the same at the organized crime families of the Mafia and the Camorra.

About the only thing they all agreed on was that the Swiss Guard had fought heroically to defend the Apostolic Palace and suffered heavily for doing so. It struck Conrad as odd that not one of the newspapers had picked up the fact that the Swiss Guard, picked men forming a force trained by the Swiss Army, had been really roughly handled by their enemies. *Surely that should imply that they were up against trained soldiers?* Reading the stories carefully, he also began to pick out a few other common factors. They all stressed that the attack had been on the Apostolic Palace and the treasures it contained, not on the Pope himself. In fact, some of the stories managed to suggest, without quite saying so, that His Holiness had been in the *Castel San Angelo* at the time and thus well protected from the attack. *The well-protected bit is true enough, although whether it was well-enough is another matter.*

Another common factor was that, to whomever they attributed the attack, it wasn't the Germans who were identified as being those really responsible. Conti di Segni had been working overtime to create that situation. There were so many different stories about what had happened that they provided an almost opaque smokescreen for reality. *Somebody once said that, in war, the truth has to be guarded by a bodyguard of lies. Who was that?* The fact that they had the three survivors identified and on ice, awaiting further use, was something that had to be kept secret, for a while at least. That secrecy made them a useful bargaining chip in containing the consequences of this situation. Conrad was quite sure that the authorities in Berlin were beginning to realize the full scope of the disaster and where its aftermath would lead. *The question is, what are they going to do about it?*

Conrad tried to piece the situation together, acutely aware that in political areas, he was little more than a local priest, without a nuanced view of what was happening in the broader arena. He did, however, know that the Nazis, and the Kaiser's government before them, had a built-in preference for doubling down on their bets. *If they planned something and it failed with disastrous consequences, they would try the same thing again on a bigger scale. The question is, will they invade Italy? Or launch a bombing raid on Rome? Surely not. Even the news of the assassination attempt on the Pope would create a massive wave of hostility across the entire Catholic world. Any hope of assistance or sympathy from Southern Europe or South America would be gone. If the Nazis followed up with bombing attack on Vatican City, it would mean war with Spain and Italy for a certainty. That would be the second front the Russians so desperately need. Although trying to invade Italy by crossing the Alps or Spain by crossing the Pyrenees would be doomed to failure. Would Argentina, Brazil or Chile declare war? They might and certainly any hopes the Germans had of using them as a launchpad for attacks on the United States would disappear.*

It suddenly dawned on Conrad that news of the assassination attempt getting into general circulation could be very beneficial to the Allied cause. Before he could develop that ominous and intensely disturbing line of thought much further, the telephone rang. "Oh, right, yes, send him up please."

A few seconds later, a knock on the door announced the arrival of *Inspettore Generale* Cristoforo Romano. Conrad let him in and called room service for an expresso tray. It arrived almost immediately. Conrad served a pair of cups, secretly enjoying the experience of unrationed coffee. "How are thing going, *Inspettore Generale?*"

"Please, call me Cri. I have been in touch with my counterpart in Rome. They are getting a flood of information in from all parts of the city. Even from the lowest elements, and none of them are asking for rewards."

"I believe they are expecting their reward from a higher authority?" Conrad spoke gravely.

"Undoubtedly." Romano sounded amused. "Most of the information is useless, of course. It's imaginary or repeated fourth or fifth hand and distorted far beyond the original. Those newspapers haven't helped either. Some, though, is useful. The Rome *Polizia Locale* has already made several arrests and are handing the suspects over to us for interrogation."

"So I have heard." Romano hesitated, took a breath and then continued. "Is His Eminence, the Prefect for Extraordinary Ecclesiastical Affairs, recovering from the recent events?"

"What do you mean?" Conrad was slightly puzzled but very wary.

"I heard him speaking about the destruction of the Rafael fresco. I thought I heard him say 'I stood by Raffaello the day he completed the work. He thought it was his masterpiece.' He seemed . . . very distraught. I fear that the balance of his mind may have been disturbed."

"He was indeed. I believe the fresco was his favorite and he would spend hours contemplating its beauty. I can understand why. I do the same when I am here. He was weeping, and I think he was deeply shocked at the wanton destruction of such a work of art. I heard his words, although the noise and activity around us at the time made them very unclear. Personally, I thought he said 'I understood Raffaello said, when he completed the work, that he thought it was his masterpiece.' I thought it was an odd thing to say, and very poorly phrased, but I was deeply shocked as well and might have misheard. I think we all were, to be honest. It wasn't just the destruction. There were so many dead. It's the Swiss Guards for whom we should feel pity; even for trained soldiers it's a hard thing to kill a man for the first time."

"The attackers showed no such restraint." Romano sounded bitter. "They shot our men down without a second thought. It is no wonder that His Eminence was so disturbed. To see the effects of such brutality in the House of God and then the destruction of the common heritage of us all, it must shake the faith of us all."

"Do you not think that faith is the better for being shaken?" Conrad was very, very happy to divert the conversation away from Conti di Segni's injudicious remark towards religious sophistry. "After all, how can faith be strengthened if it is never challenged?"

"You are a member of the Society of Jesus, aren't you, Father? That sounds like something they would argue." Romano swallowed his coffee and looked hopefully at the pot. Conrad poured him another cup and did the same for himself, once again enjoying the fact that he could do so without having to worry about rationing. "That is a good point though. Trials and tribulations serve the vital role of strengthening our faith and spirit. They also show us where weakness may lie."

"And in this case, that weakness was the inadequacy of the Swiss Guard when faced with a professional force of commandos armed with real, military, weapons."

"That is what *Oberst* Herrmann says, yes. He is making a report that suggests the Guard should be enlarged and have a better inventory of weapons. He also is a deeply-shocked man. I do not think he has experienced the loss of men under his command before. There is, of course the *Guardia Nobile* and the *Guardia Palatina d'Onore*. The Noble Guard has only seventy part-time volunteers and their role almost entirely ceremonial. The Palatine Guard also consists of part-time volunteers, mostly shopkeepers and office clerks, but there are about five hundred of them."

"Which would just be five hundred targets against the men fought by the Swiss Guard. Those shopkeepers and office clerks must realize that yet already there are more volunteers lining up to offer their services and there is talk of quadrupling the strength of the Palatine Guard. How this will all end, I do not know."

CHAPTER FIVE

THE AFTERMATH

Mausoleum Crypt, Underneath Basilica of Saint Peter, Vatican City

"This is remarkable, quite remarkable." Doctor Sergio Alinari was probably the only happy person in the Holy See. "We found the remains while digging a foxhole for the Swiss Guard. The body of a crucified man!"

"That is remarkable." Conrad realized why he had been summoned down here again. His opinion as to the identity of the remains was about to be sought. Being down in the crypt pleased him; it meant he didn't have to look at the damage wrought in the Apostolic Palace vestibule. "We are sure that the remains are of a crucifixion victim?"

"Come and see." Alinari was effusive; either he had realized that he was now in charge of what could be the most important archeological dig of the century or was overcome by sheer relief that the attack had come and gone without his dig site being destroyed.

The bones had been exposed but not yet removed from the soil. Conrad studied them carefully. "Did the digging before the attack remove the feet?"

Alinari shook his head. "We thought of that. We have searched very carefully all around the body, but we couldn't find any foot bones. Not human ones anyway; some animal bones, but no human ones."

Conrad nodded and inspected the ends of the skeleton's legs. "The feet were removed with a semi-sharp object. See, we can see where the cutting took place, but also the impact effects. So, something semi-sharp like an axe or a sword."

He looked at the arms, then knelt down and looked again. "You were right; this is a crucifixion victim. See how the nails driven through the wrists have chipped and splintered the bones? I have seen this before; sadly

237

somebody being crucified is not a thing of the past. But, normally, the damage is spread over an area of bone as the weight of the victim's body dragged the wrists against the nails. There is no sign of that here. The damage to the bone is localized, as if no weight or stress was placed on the wounds. There is only one thing I can think of that would explain that. The victim was crucified upside down, so that the weight of the body was carried by the nails placed through the feet."

"Then this must be . . ." Alinari hardly dared speak the words.

Conrad was cautious. "That is going too far, too quickly. The feet were probably chopped off as a quick way of removing the dead victim from the cross. We would need to know how old these bones are and we should get a proper analysis of the wounds to see if these injuries really are what we think they are. But, subject to detailed analysis and careful evaluation of the evidence, we can say that there is a significant chance these are the mortal remains of Saint Peter."

Appartamento Pontificio, Top Floor, Apostolic Palace, Vatican City

"Where should we go from here?" Pope Pius XII was suffering agonies of guilt as the full implications of his participation in the assassination plot sank in.

"Holiness, the first thing we must do is to keep quiet. We have confused the issue by making sure our friends in various newspapers have circulated contradictory stories. The German Embassy must be aware by now that we know what really happened and who was involved. They must also be aware that we know the potential implications of us releasing that information."

Conti di Segni was still obviously shaken by the ferocity of the attack on the Apostolic Palace but there was more to his faltering composure than that. He hadn't needed Conrad to tell him that his injudicious words in the vestibule had endangered the secret existence of the long-lived. That was gnawing away at his peace of mind, despite Conrad's assurance that he had obfuscated the issue with the one man who had overheard them. Nevertheless, the near-indiscretion had caused him to default to say nothing. Conrad suspected that it would be a long time before he spoke again without very carefully considering his words.

"Conrad, you spend your time in the world, surrounded by the complexities of modern life. We live here in an artificial world isolated from those realities. What do you think?" The words were very friendly, but there was a lash of rebuke in them for Conti di Segni, whose role it was to ensure that the Vatican authorities were kept advised of those realities. *His Holiness is aware of how much of the responsibility for this situation lies with him, but also that the system in which he lives has failed him.* Conrad was nodding slowly, more to gain time than anything else.

"We must indeed step very carefully and weigh our words with care. It is not just the fate of our brothers and sisters under German occupation that we must consider, but the wider impact of what really happened here getting out. It would be convenient for the Allies and it would benefit their strategic position greatly." *And if anybody is capable of exploiting this situation, it is The Seer. He would extract every last drop of advantage from it without regard for scruples.* "That we know as much as we do about what happened is a great benefit for us. Sometimes the greatest virtue of knowledge is that it tells us what we should not know."

Conti di Segni nodded vigorously in agreement. "And, Conrad, we have you to thank for being in the position that we are. If it had not been for your skills, we would still be fumbling in the dark without a source of light to guide us. Is how you obtained the truth here how the Inquisition always operated?"

"In theory, yes. In practice, the problem with organizations like the Inquisition always was that they attracted the worst of people, ones who saw in them the chance to indulge their darkest desires. At its best, the Inquisition was a guiding light intended to rescue souls in peril. But the road to hell is paved with good intentions." Conti di Segni looked up sharply, aware that what Conrad had said about the Inquisition could be applied with equal force to the Orders Committee. *Or to the Pope's attempts to end the war that is bleeding the world white.*

There was a long silence while the three men contemplated Conrad's words. Eventually, His Holiness sighed deeply. "What is done is done; we can but learn from our errors. Now, I hear that the dig in the Basilica crypt has made a remarkable discovery. Should we keep quiet about this as well?"

Conti di Segni glanced at Conrad. "You have seen the remains, old friend. What do you think?"

Conrad recognized the olive branch for what it was and seized it with relief. "The remains are of a man who was crucified in the Roman style. He was probably crucified upside down, although the amputation of the feet makes confirming that difficult. I do not know how we would judge the age of the remains but, if we can confirm they come from the right time, then the probability we have discovered the remains of St. Peter becomes very high. I would recommend we consult with experts on dating these remains before we make the discovery public."

"Very wise advice." Conti di Segni emphatically approved of Conrad's words. "We should hasten slowly here."

His Holiness agreed with equal fervor. "Normally, such remains are dated by reference to artifacts found in the grave, but that is not the case here.

Indeed, such dating would be highly misleading since the soil in the crypt has accumulated over the centuries and the layers are mixed up. Until such time as the remains can be dated in isolation, I believe they should be placed in storage and treated with reverence and respect."

Pope Pius hesitated before continuing. "And there is all the legends about how the presence of St. Peter's bones here in the Vatican protect us from attack by the ungodly. I would say that the events of the last few days have lent weight to those legends."

"The bravery of the Swiss Guard, and the warning from Conrad here of course, have something to do with that as well, Your Holiness." Conti di Segni had a half-smile on his face. For the first time since the attack, the haunted look had been erased from his eyes.

"They did indeed and we have issued instructions that, subject to agreement with the Swiss authorities, the establishment of the Guard is to be increased from 130 to 500 men, organized as a single battalion. We have also issued orders that they be issued with the proper equipment for soldiers when not performing ceremonial duties. The *Gendarmeria* will also be reinforced."

The Pope looked very sad. "I fear that the times have caught up with us and the old ways are no longer appropriate."

Again, there was silence as the implications sank in. His Holiness looked at Conrad with a half-smile on his face. "I believe that the Swiss Guard who worked with you has rendered great service to the Holy See. Would you say that *Wachtmeister* Julian Hüber merits advancement? There will be many new vacancies for good and loyal men in the enlarged Pontifical Swiss Guard."

"I would say that he is a good man, as well as loyal and honest." Conrad was happy to help advance the career of a man who had become his friend. "Also, I suspect he may soon marry. Being raised in rank would make the start of his married life more secure."

The Pope smiled and was about to say something else when his secretary burst in.

"Holiness, I have urgent news from the Vatican radio station. They have just intercepted a news broadcast from Berlin. *SS-Obergruppenführer und General der Polizei* Reinhard Heydrich, *Stellvertretender Reichsprotektor* of Bohemia and Moravia has been assassinated while his car was passing through a small village called Lidice in Czechoslovakia. The assassins were killed by Heydrich's bodyguards but the *Obergruppenführer* died of his wounds soon after the attack."

Pope Pius XII, Conti di Segni and Conrad all exchanged horrified looks. "And so it begins."

Appartamento Pontificio, Top Floor, Apostolic Palace, Vatican City, Ten Days Later

"In conclusion, Your Holiness, Mr. Hull concludes his message by suggesting that if you are going to do such damned stupid things, don't do them in such damned stupid ways."

"I don't understand?" Igrat had caught the withering patrician contempt of an old-school American Episcopalian exhibited by Cordell Hull perfectly. Pius XII was not used to being spoken to in that way.

"Let me lay it out for you. Don't ask where this come from, but you can assume this has multiple sources and they all agree on the essentials." Igrat was speaking with somebody else's voice now and Conrad assumed her mimicry was its usual accurate self. Nevertheless, he wasn't quite sure who it was. "It appears that information on the attack that took place here was leaked to a Czech resistance group, one that was strongly Catholic in orientation. It also appears that, quite separately, the Canadians had inserted a sabotage team into Czechoslovakia to sabotage an essential military production facility there. The Canadians strongly deny this by the way, possibly because the operation was very badly organized. Several members of that team were also devout Catholics, French Canadian variety. That part of the group forgot who they were working for and the resistance group recruited them to help with the actual assassination. As a result, the idiots used Capsten Mark II submachine guns in the attack.

"On the morning of the attack, Heydrich was undertaking a tour of the same munitions facility that was the subject of the Canadian operation. As he was passing through Lidice, his route took him along a road that featured a very tight hairpin turn. The group of three assassins was waiting there because the curve would force the car to slow down. When Heydrich's vehicle reached the curve, one of the three assassins tried to open fire with his Capsten submachine gun, but it jammed. Heydrich ordered his driver to stop the car, then stood up and shot the assassin dead with his pistol.

"At that point, the second assassin sprayed Heydrich with submachine gun fire and the third threw a hand grenade into the car. Heydrich staggered out of the car, returned fire and killed a second assassin, and tried to chase the third but collapsed. The SS bodyguards chased the third assassin, who tried to take shelter in the Lidice church, where he was joined by several members of the Catholic resistance group. There was a gunfight, in which two of the SS guards were severely wounded and the surviving assassin plus four members of the resistance group were killed. Heydrich was rushed to hospital but was dead on arrival.

"After the attack, the town of Lidice was completely destroyed. 193 men were shot immediately. 184 women and 105 children were taken to Ravensbruck concentration camp and gassed. The village buildings were blown up and their ruins bulldozed and buried. Another 157 men were arrested and executed in a nearby village of Ležáky. The women went to Ravensbruck for gassing and that village was also destroyed." Igrat looked up and returned to her own voice. "I was asked to add, there's nothing secret about these massacres; the Germans are openly boasting of them. They have taken to calling the complete destruction of any village that houses resistance fighters Lidice Rules."

"Miss Shapiro, do you think . . . "

Igrat held up her hand. "No, I don't think, Holiness. I carry messages; some written, some in my head. What I bring to you is from the people who sent it. I will not make additions or add my own comments. Having delivered the material, I must take my leave. I do have another important visit to make. I'll be leaving for Washington on tomorrow's Constellation. If you have return messages, please let me have them before then."

Igrat bowed slightly to the group and left. Conrad watched her depart, then spoke very carefully. "This all sounds wrong to me. We are being played. The question is, by whom?"

Appartamento 6, 10 Via del Fontanile, Anagnino

Igrat hesitated before knocking on the door. Conrad had once told her that people who didn't want to be found, usually had a good reason for not wanting to be found. There could be many such reasons and a wise person found out which one applied to a particular case before doing anything drastic. She had taken the advice to heart and done some extensive research on Peter Apano before making this visit. As soon as she saw his picture she realized her suspicions had been correct; she knew him as Phaeton Phoebus Apollo.

The file she had obtained from the Pan-American offices in New York has been interesting. Pan-Am was desperately short of airline pilots and the chance of hiring a young, highly competent pilot whose childhood injuries disqualified him from military service had been too good to miss. Especially since he was single, had no family connections and didn't mind living abroad. So, they had made him senior pilot for the Rome operations hub. That left a mass of things unsaid and she needed to fill in the details. That was her excuse for coming here, anyway.

She took a deep breath and banged her knuckles on the door. It opened and she saw the flash of recognition in Apollo's eyes. She leaned against the doorpost in the traditional lady-for-hire stance. "Hi, Senior Pilot Apano. Buy a girl a drink?"

"Of all the gin joints in all the world, you had to walk into mine" Apano smiled wistfully while he misquoted Humphrey Bogart's line from *Cairo*. "It's 'Irene,' now, isn't it?"

Despite her pose, Igrat was watching him very carefully and, as usual, her heavy-lidded sleepy eyes missed nothing She saw the smile of welcome on his face but also the wariness in his expression. Apollo knew very well that she was a member of The Seer's innermost circle and privy to nearly everything that went on in Washington. "Irene Shapiro, yes. Or at least that was the name on the ticket when you flew me to Casablanca and on to the Azores a few days ago. The first class compartment was close enough to the cockpit to pick up a tingle. Now, are you going to invite me in?"

She slipped past him with all the skills of a lifetime spent sliding past people who wanted to stop her going somewhere. Apollo surrendered to the inevitable and seated her on the couch. She smiled her thanks. "Now, tell me all about how you got here? We lost track of you after *Kristallnacht*."

"Liar." Apollo's smile deepened into a genuine grin. "I know for a fact you pester Branwyn, and Loki, for news about me every time you visit Geneva."

He crossed to a small cabinet, wordlessly fixing drinks. The apartment was close enough to Ciampino for convenience, yet classy and stylish enough to fit the stature of a senior pilot and eminent, handsome bachelor. While built at the height of Mussolini's Fascist ambitions, the three-story building's once grim stone exterior now reflected the wealth and gaiety of what Italians were now calling The Economic Miracle or *la dolce vita*. The furnishings were the equally modern, yet sophisticated, products of the burgeoning Italian consumer goods industry. Yet, for all their splendor, none was more than a few years old.

Gone were all the artifacts, relics and treasures of a lifetime of lifetimes Igrat expected to find.

Apollo unobtrusively placed her glass beside her, before settling into a chair opposite, roguishly resting his legs over one arm in an insouciant pose before taking up his verbal foil to spar again.

"We have, in fact, met on at least three occasions recently." He ticked them off on his fingers as he spoke. "The first was in Falmouth. The second was in Paris, after the war. And, at the third, you gave me this."

As if by magic, a small, delicate, blown-glass Christmas tree ornament appeared in his right hand.

Igrat frowned. She honestly could not remember meeting Apollo since the destruction of his home during *Kristallnacht* in 1938. The mention of after the war had thrown her as well until she had reminded herself that, for people in Western Europe, the war had ended in 1940. Americans and Russians had a different perspective. There was also the small matter that men invariably gave her presents rather than the other way around.

"I haven't been to England or France for more than two years now, not since America got into the war. My father won't let me go into enemy-occupied territory. Even before the Occupation began, England was getting too close to being hostile territory for comfort. Vichy France wasn't that far behind. Now, they're both full of German troops and going there is out of the question. Geneva is as close to occupied territory as he'll let me go and he insists I have Henry and Achillea along for that. I don't take them along when I go to Yekaterinburg."

Igrat sipped her drink, trying to remember when she might have been close to Apollo before. The fact she might have been without realizing it worried her; she depended on her situational awareness for survival. "Falmouth? In Britain? That would have been after I came over the Atlantic on one of the Boeing flying boats. Were you flying it? They're all gone now, you know; the Army requisitioned the whole fleet. Anyway, you're right, I do pester Loki and Branwen for news about you, although neither of them will say anything."

Igrat was aware she was gabbling, buying time with her mouth while her brain processed the information she had just been given. There was one thing she needed to say though and it was the real reason why she had come. "Lillith and Naamah are worried sick over what happened to you. Gusoyn too. For a while they thought you'd been killed during *Kristallnacht* and they're still not certain you're alive. You should let them know that you're OK, even if you don't tell them anything else. Just leaving them hanging like this is cruel."

Apollo had bit hard on his lip to keep from laughing as Igrat babbled. A petty part of himself, one he was slightly ashamed of, enjoyed watching the usually suave and sure Igrat wrongfooted and foundering. Especially when she had intruded on his time, and his home, without consideration of what other plans he might have, and with whom he might have them.

A more astute part of him knew why she dissembled. Her claims of ignorance, and of knowledge denied, were a gambit; Igrat knew far more than she claimed. Even at his most spiteful and puckish, Loki knew better than to defy Apollo. Despite his short stature, slight build and boyish appearance, Apollo possessed all the fury, malice, caprice, cunning, ruthlessness and wrath that had become part of the legend of a vengeful god he was identified with. Loki might have been the inspiration for a trickster god, but youth and skill lost to old age and treachery every time. Nor did Apollo only speak unto Loki and Branwyn. He spoke to all the walkers, occasionally mixed in the same circles as the Seer, and sparred often with Richard Strachan about the times their swords and paymasters had crossed on the fields of Europe.

Apollo knew she was pushing him for his story in his own words; words, tones, infections, that she could, and would, flawlessly repeat to another. Just as he knew the questions she was dying to ask, and couldn't. Not yet. Just he knew neither questions nor answers were for her, or Naamah or Lillith.

Just as he wasn't sure if he was ready to answer them. Speaking to Igrat was speaking to Gusoyn, and that was something Apollo hadn't done in over a millennia. Something he wasn't sure he ever could do again. Something he desperately wanted to, and yet didn't. Or couldn't.

So Apollo sat, and let her dig herself in deeper, until her accusation of cruelty hit home. His eyes flashed, the green growing darker with anger. He fixed her with a stern, militant, almost menacing, captain's stare, one totally at odds with his relaxed posture and usual polite, shy, almost sad demeanor. Anger rising, Igrat's voice trailing off, Apollo left her in a now awkward, and almost dangerous silence. One minute turned to two, then three. Still he fixed her with an angry glare. The scars on the backs of his hands, formerly faint, now darkened as his grip on chair and glass tightened.

Finally, he decided to throw her a lifeline. Apollo grinned. The tension flooded out of the room. Igrat's worried expression rapidly turned to puzzlement. Then he laughed. Not the shy, uncertain laugh Igrat could vaguely remember from somewhere, but the deep, full-throated mirthful laugh she hadn't heard in centuries.

"I was living in Vienna in '38."

He laughed again. "And I meant Falmouth in Virginia, and it was seventy-nine years ago. You were spying for the Seer; I was with the Balloon Corps. Paris was after the War to End all Wars, or so we thought. You were spying for the Seer, again, and I was . . ." Apollo blushed. ". . . well, nevermind. And this . . ." he picked up the fragile glass ornament ". . . was from the last Christmas *you* had peace."

Igrat was still puzzled. Apollo laughed again. "Oh, God, I hate having to explain inside baseball. It's Corning. I don't know if you remembered, but all American Christmas ornaments were made over here in Europe, mostly in Germany or Czechoslovakia. Once this war started, you couldn't get them, so Corning converted a light bulb factory to ornaments, with the help of some of my money. I was a silent, silent partner." His eyes laughed.

He carefully lifted the top off the ornament and handed it to Igrat.

"Feel it. It's cardboard, not metal. Even in '41, scrap was too dear for that. We couldn't even put tinsel inside for a sparkle; had to make do with silver nitrate." She handed it back, and he deliberately reassembled the ornament.

"Anyway, we met at a party in New York. You were with Mike, and I believe Henry, Naamah, and the Seer and Lillith were circulating. No wonder you couldn't sense me; I'm not like Conrad. Anyway, you were chatting up a bomber pilot, and, in the end, you handed that to me."

Apollo's sad demeanor returned as he remembered. "Keep it. I have two . . ."

"I'm not here for my father." Igrat guessed what Apollo had been thinking. Personally, she rated his angry stare at six out of ten at best. She'd been given furious glares by experts, her father included in that number, and that had given her an expert education in such things. "He isn't involved in this. Not yet anyway and, frankly, he has much more important issues to worry about. Yes, he knows everything I do in my professional capacity, but that doesn't extend to things that are my personal affairs. Some things are my private business and this comes under that.

"I'm here on behalf of Lillith, Naamah and Gusoyn, although none of those three know it yet. They kept track of you even after the great family row. Only, they lost sight of you after *Kristallnacht* and thought you had been killed in Küstrin during that nightmare. I don't know why they thought you were there, but they couldn't find any trace of you coming out and assumed you were one of the victims. Nobody knew you were in Vienna. If they had, they'd have even more cause to believe you were dead. Vienna was a real pogrom, the worst of the worst. But, you know that, you were there.

"I thought you were dead until I picked up the flicker in that Constellation. Even then, I only knew it was one of us. I checked out the pilot list at Pan-American headquarters; it's just down the street from where I live. Then I saw your picture on your personnel file and knew. I'm not here to ask you to make peace or even come back to us, although I think you should. All I'm asking is that you contact those three; through cut-outs if you really don't want to see them. Just to let them know you're alive and safe. Before you answer, think about this. You chose to work for the one airline I travel on and the one route I use on a weekly basis. You know how we can sense each other. You really wanted me to find you, didn't you? In your heart, you know it's finally time to come back to us."

"I'm not a child. I'm not helpless. I don't need looking after." The hard edge was back. "I'm sorry; that was the absolute wrong thing to say, and you don't deserve it." He set his drink on a coaster at the side table and walked to the window. "Oh, God. You're going to repeat that back, word for word and tone for tone, unless I give you something better?"

Igrat didn't say anything, but her smug smile was its own answer. As she knew it would be.

He laughed playfully, showily checking his pockets. "Of course you are. At least I still have my wallet. And my pants. Don't look at me like that!"

He sighed dramatically, a sound effect offset by an impish grin. ". "Oh, all right, fine. Here's the deal; I'll give you a better quote, and a night of dinner and dancing on the arm of a glamorous Pan Am pilot. But I'm keeping my pants right where they belong, safe from your evil clutches. You can tell them for me, though, that they really do need a better class of spies, or to hire you to do their digging for them. Küstrin was two centuries ago; Prussia is so damn dreary and serious, I haven't lived in that hateful place for ages."

He saw her open her mouth and cut her off. "No, besiegers and armies of occupation do not count!"

"Well, they do if one is the besieged or occupied. Nell was in England earlier this year and says it's grim there. They've never been occupied before so they don't really know how to cope with informers and everybody is turning against each other. Of course, it's the innocent who really suffer. Was it that bad for you?"

He sensed he couldn't evade the question. "You've spent too much time around Conrad. But, yes, it was bad. Just not the way you think."

"Because you're . . ." Igrat didn't quite know how to phrase the reference to Apollo's sexual orientation. It was not something that the long-lived considered even remotely important. "Is that why they tried to kill you?"

Apollo faltered but quickly recovered. "No, no, no, not like that. Danger wise, I rate it a six out of ten, at best." He couldn't resist a smile. "They never laid a hand on me. But, yes, it was bad. I didn't know how they found my address; and never will. But, somehow, they did. Thousands of years of knowledge, and they just burned it in the alleyway. They didn't even dare torch it inside, might offend the gentile landlord. Can't have that!"

His voice was quiet, level, and hard. "I came 'round the corner, and there they were. Another load of books for the fire. Catholic books. Protestant books. Atheist books. I think they even put a copy of the Norse Sagas on the fire. Quite an ecumenical little blaze they had going in that dark little alley. A bunch of goose-stepping morons who should try reading books instead of burning them! If the clapped out misbegotten bastards even knew how to read. Just three drunken louts in an alleyway, having a lark. All they needed was some marshmallows.

"I remember the wave of hate and anger coming over me. I remember a few quick strikes in the dark, dead men at my feet." Apollo unconsciously flexed his hands, opening and closing them. "Achillea always says 'Never hit a man with a closed fist.' But it is, on occasion, hilarious. I remember laughing over them, an angry, taunting laugh; I'm sure I said something taunting, once they were safely dead. I remember more laughs from down the street, the happy sounds of shattered glass, axes and sledgehammers on ancient stone. I remember the acrid, hateful stink of burning. I remember breaking into a run, wanting to come tearing out of the alley. I remember wanting to hurt, to kill, to destroy, with my bare hands. I remember pounding footsteps behind me, then Loki grabbing me, or trying to.

"Then, just pain. Lots and lots of pain."

Apollo sheepishly rubbed the back of his head. "He *hit* me. Loki sure can throw a punch. But, in all fairness, I think I bit him first." He held up one hand, looking at a scar on the palm. "Then, I think I fell, badly.

"I woke up in Loki's villa. He has a nice one in Vienna, given to him by Maria Theresa, no less. It's nice. Sometime, after the war, you should let him take you there . . ." The words just trailed off. "Tell Loki I said he could tell you; he tells it better than I do. You'll get a laugh out of what he did with the bodies."

He'd wandered from the window to the chair, to the liquor cabinet and to the chair again. Somehow, the glass ended up back in his hand, and it was empty. "If something happened, you'd know. Yes, I have made arrangements in case of something happening. Yes, I know how to find you. But that's not why. You'd just know.

"I honestly didn't know you traveled Pan-Am, and I don't really have a file on you. I get a fuzz in the back of my head often enough now; even with the war, air travel is a small, small world, and we all are part of it. Only Conrad really stands out, unless I am paying attention; he just feels different. I think it's all the guilt. And I'm not ready to come in from the cold. I can't explain why. Not won't, but can't; because *I* don't know why, yet. Just that I'm not ready. Until then, whatever happens, don't worry. I am all right." Those words were for her, to share, or not, as she saw fit.

"Since you flew all the way to Rome solely on my account, I would be quite the cad if you did not thoroughly enjoy your respite from the wars, Ms. Shapiro. Now, does the lady have a preference on where we shall dine and dance, or will she trust me to show her *la dolce vita*?"

Interview Room, Corpo della Gendarmeria dello Stato della Città del Vaticano, Vatican City

SS-Standartenführer Stephan Bähr had diminished enormously since their first meeting. That was normal; being held in custody by men who made their contempt for him and everything he believed in obvious would diminish even the strongest of men. There was something else at play, though. Conrad recognized the signs and knew what it was. *This man has been removed from the poisonous environment to which he was accustomed and slowly its evil influence on him is ebbing. As it does so, he begins to see his former self with the eyes of a new man and, slowly, understanding of the malevolent sins he has committed eats away at his self-assurance.*

"Father, I welcome this chance to leave my cell, but truly there is nothing more I can tell you." Bähr looked hungrily at the coffee pot in one corner of the recreation room. Hüber knew the drill and carefully poured a cup of fresh expresso coffee for him. As he did so, he proudly displayed the single silver star that now adorned his shoulder. He was now *Leutnant* Hüber, the first junior officer of that rank for many, many years. Soon, a new company of 150 Swiss Guardsmen would be marching south, following the route of the original company that had marched to Rome in September 1506 under the command of Kaspar von Silenen. The mission of the new company would be the same as that of the badly mauled unit it was reinforcing: to protect the Pope and the security of the Holy See. Two more companies would be following them as they were raised in Switzerland.

Conrad waited politely until Bähr had finished his coffee and, incidentally, until the heavy shot of caffeine it contained worked its way into his bloodstream. "Stephan, may I call you that? I'm Conrad."

Bähr nodded. Conrad gave a little dip of the head before continuing. "I have some news for you from your homeland. *SS-Obergruppenführer und General der Polizei* Reinhard Heydrich has been murdered by bandits in Czechoslovakia. I assume he was your commander?"

There was a muddled explosion as Bähr almost snorted with laughter then managed to control himself. "Absolutely not. The SS reports to *Reichsführer Schutzstaffel* Heinrich Himmler, by way of military commanders appointed by him. You said it yourself; Heydrich was mostly a policeman. He had no longer had any authority over military units. Although, he has . . . he had . . . quite a distinguished war record. He was a fighter pilot, you know?"

"No, I didn't." Conrad found that bit of information only mildly interesting but he listened carefully. *The critical thing is to keep this man speaking. He must not get back into the habit of saying nothing.* "What did he fly, a Messerschmitt 109?"

"110. His idea of a holiday vacation was to go to the Russian Front and fly there. He flew 97 missions until he was grounded by order of the *Führer*. It is rumored the *Reichsführer SS* himself instigated that, fearing that Heydrich was becoming too popular and presented too much of a threat to his own position. That was ridiculous, of course; it was well-known to everybody else that Heydrich was almost slavishly loyal to the *Reichsführer SS.*"

"So your orders for the attack here came from Himmler? Did he plan the operation also?"

"The *Reichsführer SS* is a firm believer in the doctrine of mission commands. This means that orders were given as broad directives, with authority delegated downward to the appropriate level to carry them out in a timely and efficient manner, allowing officers leeway to act on their own initiative to obtain the desired results. So, no. We were told what needed to be done and left to make the plans ourselves."

"Thank you, Stephan, that is most interesting. One last question. As a professional soldier, what do you think of the Capsten?"

The grateful look in Bähr's eyes at Conrad's reference to him as a soldier was almost pitiful. "The Canadian machine pistol? A piece of rubbish. Very poor feed design and it jams all the time."

"You're fired one then?"

"Of course. The Russians received many such weapons as aid in 1942 and 1943 and we captured a lot of them. We tried some of them out, but the results were so poor we would not issue them. They were the wrong caliber anyway. I suppose they were all melted down for scrap. Even the Russians don't use them now."

Commonwealth Consulate, Vatican City

"It was nothing to do with us." Colonel Terrance Hodges was very emphatic on that point. "I know the fascists have been claiming it was our assault group that went rogue and assassinated the wretched man, but it wasn't. The truth is that we have no idea who was responsible."

"Do you have any covert operations inside Czechoslovakia?"

"I can't discuss that and, frankly, Father, I am slightly surprised that you think I would." Hodges looked indignant. Conrad hadn't expected an answer to his question and was thus not disappointed. Especially since Hodges' tone of voice and body language told him very clearly that the answer was no.

"My apologies, Colonel. No offense was intended, but I had to ask. Now, the assassins of Heydrich used Capsten submachine guns. Could you enlighten me on where they may have come from?"

Hodges thought about that. "I am told the killers used Capsten Mark II machine carbines. That's chambered for 9x19mm ammunition. The first troops in Kola were issued with those weapons; the ones we supplied to the Russians were the Mark III, chambered for 7.62x25mm Tokarev. Those early ones had a lot of problems, but we're getting them straightened out now.

"If they really were Mark IIs, somehow they got them from us. Probably captured on Kola, but that is a guess. There weren't that many Mark IIs made and we replaced in pretty quickly with the Mark IV. We've adopted the 7.62 Tokarev ourselves now and fixed the feed problems."

"So, the Mark IIs were either supplied by you to the Czech resistance . . . ."

"What Czech resistance?" Hodges sounded more than slightly derisive. "And, if there was one, how in the name of God . . . sorry, Father . . . how would we get the guns to them? They're in the middle of Europe. I doubt if even a B-29 can get that far in and we don't have anything like that. They must have been captured weapons. I honestly can't think of anything else they could be. Anyway, why would we drop Capstens? We've got captured Schmeissers that would have been far more appropriate."

"It feels like to me as if by using those guns, somebody was trying to link the killing of Heydrich directly to you. And they really over-egged the pudding in doing so."

"That sounds a reasonable assumption, Father. I must admit, one of my colleagues came to much the same conclusion by the same route. The only question that leaves is why?"

Appartamento Pontificio, Top Floor, Apostolic Palace, Vatican City

"The weapons allegedly used to kill Heydrich had to come from German sources, probably captured on Kola. The Canadians are adamant they did not supply Mark IIs to Russia and I believe them. If they were responsible for this, either directly or indirectly, they wouldn't have made it clear they were the only source for 9mm Capstens. So, we have a very unusual situation developing here." *In a long life filled with unusual situations*, Conrad thought, *this is probably the strangest.*

"Are we sure that the information about the attempt on my life didn't come from here?" His Holiness was bewildered. The knowledge of how far out of his depth he was gnawed away at him.

"Very sure. Quite independently, I had Segni di Conti and *Inspettore Generale* Cristoforo Romano check under conditions of strict secrecy. Neither knew the other was also checking and both came back with the same answer. Our security at this end is tight. As far as most people are concerned, there was an attempt to pillage the Apostolic Palace that went badly wrong. The fact we have three of the perpetrators under arrest remains secure, as does the identity of the attackers. If people know there was an attempt on your life, that the attack was a pre-planned assassination, then they must have known before the attack took place."

"You are saying that the attack on Heydrich was initiated from within Germany and was not related to the attack on me?"

"That is correct, Holiness. I was about to say that the guns used came from Germany, the information serving as a pretext came from Germany and thus we can conclude this was a German attack. Then, something else struck me. We really know very little about what happened in Lidice and we probably never will. All we have are the German statements and they have little credibility. Their reprisals for the attack, very conveniently, wiped out any eyewitnesses. I am quite certain that the same measures were taken with all the other potential sources of information on the attack. Including the actual killers, by the way. It is quite possible that the Capsten Mark II was named as the killing weapon, not because it would implicate the Canadians but because it fired the same round as the standard German Schmeisser."

"Why? Why go to all this trouble?"

"That is the key question we have to solve. Although I would turn the question on its head. Rather than asking who was responsible for the attack, instead I would ask why Heydrich was selected as the target?"

"Given his record since the outbreak of the war, I am surprised he wasn't attacked earlier." His Holiness looked deeply saddened. "At least 92 people were executed, and 4,000 and 5,000 people were arrested, within three days of his arrival in Prague. He shut down almost all public expressions of Czech culture. His attacks on Czech cultural and patriotic organizations, the military, and the intelligentsia resulted in the practical paralysis of Czech resistance. The Central Leadership of Home Resistance has been almost completely neutralized and only the communist resistance was able to function in a coordinated manner. The terror Heydrich masterminded also served to paralyze resistance in society, with public and widespread reprisals against any action resisting the German rule. The Czechs do not call Heydrich 'the Butcher of Prague' for nothing."

"So why was he killed? He was doing exactly what his superiors expected of him. In fact, I have no doubt that he was probably held in high regard by the leadership." Suddenly a great light switched on in Conrad's head as he remembered one of the messages Igrat had brought to the Holy See. "Do you remember what Miss Shapiro said on one of her visits here? *'The Seer says, looking at who knows about it and who doesn't, is a very good guide to who is really in power and who isn't. Goebbels knows, Goering does not; Heydrich knows, Himmler does not.'* The most important political development in Nazi Germany for years and Heydrich knows all about it, Himmler does not.

"Does that not tell us that Himmler is slipping out of favor in Germany and being replaced by Heydrich? Probably as a result of exactly the developments you just described. Heydrich was instrumental in fighting Czech resistance to the Nazi regime, and keeping up production quotas of Czech military equipment that is extremely important to the German war effort. That must have given him a wide base of support. He also seems to have gathered a lot of respect in the German armed forces, including the SS, by heading for the front lines every chance he got. In short, knowingly or not, he was edging Heinrich Himmler out of power. I wonder what Himmler would have thought of that?"

"Are you saying that Himmler had Heydrich killed because he saw him as a potential threat to his position?" His Holiness was incredulous.

"It has been done many times before. Including by some who sat in that very seat." Conrad gestured slightly at the Pope's chair.

His Holiness flushed slightly at the reminder. "How does that fit in with everything else?"

It was obvious to Conrad that he meant the attempt to assassinate him. "I would see it like this. The attempt to assassinate Hitler failed, and those in positions of power were briefed on what had happened. A man like Himmler always has his own network of informants, so he knew what had happened without being briefed. He also took one look at the list of who had been briefed and who had not and came to the same conclusion we did; the list shows us who is really in power and who is not. Whose star is rising and whose is falling. Himmler, who is by all accounts a good decision maker with a talent for selecting highly competent staff, and thus one of the most powerful men in the Third Reich, saw that he was now in the second category of both groups. He was steadily drifting away from power and his star was falling fast. So he decided to do something about it.

"Hitler's tirade when he found out about your Holiness's involvement in the assassination plot gave him his chance. He set the wheels in motion for the assassination attempt here, but also started a second operation to assassinate Heydrich. Again, all people in Himmler's position have expendable people they can use for attacks of that nature. They also have clean-up crews who can eradicate any witnesses. As soon as word of the attack here started to spread, he ordered the second attack to go ahead. I very much doubt if the Czech resistance, something that doesn't seem to be taken seriously, by the way, had anything to do with it. It's just as much a fabrication as our involvement in the Heydrich attack." Conrad was tempted to add '*and your involvement in the Hitler assassination has given that idea much credibility,*' but realized that putting the thought into words was superfluous.

"That sounds far-fetched." The Pope's voice showed that he too had realized the implications of his actions.

"Not really. If we run though the options, it is very logical. If the two assassinations are both successful, Himmler has got rid of a rival and struck a serious blow at the credibility, moral standing and authority of the Holy Church. If you had been killed but Heydrich escaped, he would have achieved the first result and turned Heydrich into a dedicated, vengeful enemy of the Church. If both attempts had failed, the results are the same. If you escaped but Heydrich was killed, what actually happened of course, then Himmler gets a more limited degree of damage to the Church, but he still gets rid of a rival and makes it look like we did it. No matter what happens, he advances his anti-Christian agenda, gets rid of a rival and restores his power."

Conrad sighed and shook his head. "Looked at objectively, it's brilliant. Julius II would have loved it."

"I will try and pretend I didn't hear that." His Holiness reflected on the very carefully hidden fact that there were at least two people in his immediate circle of advisors who had known both Pope Julius II and Pope Alexander VI and that both their sympathies lay with the latter. "Where do we go from here?"

"I do not know, Holiness. We now leave my sphere of expertise and enter that of Conti di Segni. You should consult with him on this."

"Very well; please remain, Conrad. You have rendered great service today, but we must ask more of you. When Conti di Segni arrives, please brief him on what has happened and why."

An hour later, Conti di Segni nodded slowly as Conrad finished his presentation. "I agree, Conrad, both with your conclusions and with His Holiness's appreciation of your efforts. Also, with your thoughts about Julius II; this is exactly what he did when he had Alexander VI poisoned. Removed a rival and used the scandal to discredit a movement opposed to him."

Across the desk, His Holiness looked as if he wanted to clap his hands over his ears and emit yodeling noises. "Please, friends, do you wish me to lose even more sleep? Now, how do we deal with this?"

Conti di Segni shook his head. "We can do damage control and limit the effects of the situation. We know the Nazis do not want to admit there was an attempt on Hitler's life. They will not mention that part of it. I now think that they are the other people spreading the story that the attack on the Vatican Museum was aimed at looting the place, not the assassination attempt it really was. That makes our alleged involvement in the killing of Heydrich even less forgivable. Now, the Germans know that we have some of their prisoners and can prove SS involvement in the attack here. Releasing that information would take the sting out of the charges being thrown around, but we can do better than that."

"Please go on." His Holiness sounded encouraged at last.

"If we released everything we know concerning the assassination attempt on Hitler, excluding, of course, Your Holiness's involvement in that, and the attack on us here, the effects in Germany's position would be catastrophic. Italy and Spain would immediately move into the Allied camp, either as friendly neutrals or, more likely, as combatants. The rest of the Catholic countries worldwide would follow them. Himmler would be blamed and our deductions concerning the assassination of Heydrich would also be believed. That would also have the merit of discrediting any information the Germans release about the Hitler attack. I would say that Himmler would find himself under arrest and facing a noose very quickly.

"So we approach him first and offer a deal. We keep quiet about his plans and involvement if the matter ends here, and if he drops the effort to persuade people that we are involved in the Heydrich assassination. We need to get the message to Himmler. Is Joey Ox around?"

"And we need to put a lot of guards around those prisoners." Conrad added.

Conrad's Room, Domus Sanctae Marthae, Vatican City

Conrad had risen just before 7 A.M. as usual. His first step was to turn on the radio. In this case, it was tuned to the BBC World Service, transmitted from Cairo. The somber voice of the newsreader immediately told him that something was badly wrong.

"Good morning. this is the Free British Broadcasting Company World Service. We now present the news at 8 A.M. and this is Freddie Grisewood reading it. Our news bulletin today starts with tragic news of a bomb attack here in the middle of Cairo.

"At 6 A.M. this morning, a massive explosion destroyed the main building occupied by General Headquarters, Middle East Command. More than three quarters of a ton of explosives were believed to have been carried in by a truck that parked directly in front of the headquarters building. The blast has completely destroyed the building, and the death toll is expected to reach several hundred.

"Amongst the dead is known to be General Archibald Percival Wavell, the hero of the North African War three years ago. At the time of his death, General Wavell was the officer in charge of Middle East Command and the de-facto ruler of Commonwealth territory in North and East Africa.

"Berlin Radio issued a statement a few minutes ago, claiming that the bomb attack on Middle East Command was carried out in retaliation for the assassination of *SS-Obergruppenführer und General der Polizei* Reinhard Heydrich last week. The German Government has claimed that, since a state of war exists between Germany and the Commonwealth of Nations, the attack was a legitimate act of war.

"Expressions of sympathy and condolences are pouring in from all over the Free World as news of the attacks spreads. We will be making additional reports on this tragedy as more information becomes available.

"Meanwhile, on the Russian Front, Allied troops have regained ground in a series of counter-attacks launched against fascist forces in the region of Archangel'sk . . ."

Conrad looked into the mirror and realized he had cut himself shaving. He then looked down and saw that his hands were shaking uncontrollably.

Conrad's Other Eye

"Conrad, I would like you to meet Joseph Mueller. He carries messages between the authorities here and the Orders Committee in Germany."

"Most people call me Joey Ox." The man stood up and held his hand out to Conrad. He took it, expecting and getting a bone-crushing handshake. Joey Ox was as large and strong a man as his nickname suggested. Conrad knew from Coni di Segni that he was a practicing lawyer but, on meeting the man, he decided that Joseph Mueller appeared to have a lot in common with the mafia leaders Conrad had known in New York. *Then again, quite a few lawyers in New York had a lot in common with mafia leaders. Including their business activities.*

"Conrad Lorenz. I have heard much, Joey, about your work on behalf of the Church. I can only hope that one day all Catholics will know how much they owe to the dangers you have endured on their behalf."

"You'll excuse me, Father, if I wish for some significant political changes in Europe before that is ever the case."

"You mean an end to the Nazi regime in Germany?" Conrad guessed that, despite his jovial expression, there was an intense depth of purpose buried within Joey Ox's character. To his surprise, Mueller shook his head.

"As a first step, yes. But the political changes I refer to must go far beyond that. This war is teaching us a lesson, paid for in blood and treasure, that Europe must change. This war must be the last war in Europe; this holocaust must never happen again. Europe must be united in a peaceful and democratic union, or the next war will be the ultimate last war for all of us. I very much fear that the events of the last month have taken us a step further away from that goal."

"It is those events we wish to bring to an end." Conti di Segni looked grim. "This chain of tit-for-tat assassinations must be brought to an end before it brings about even greater destruction. According to Radio Cairo, the death toll there has reached 184, including General Wavell. Since it is our unwise actions that have started the whole affair, it is now down to us to end it. Conrad, please explain to Joey what has transpired here and how we envisage bringing it to an end."

Conti di Segni's words had contained a stinging rebuke to Mueller, who bore much of the responsibility for not only involving Pope Pius XII but for writing down records of the negotiations and, far worse, allowing them to fall into hostile hands. Looking at Mueller, Conrad could see that simple statement of fact had struck home. *Why, in contravention of all good conspiratorial practice, did this man write everything down? I suspect it is because he is a lawyer and lawyers want everything in writing. Something to remember. If ever I am in this position, share nothing with a lawyer.*

That train of thought led Conrad to the aching realization that he was alone in the world and that there was not one person with whom he could discuss his fears, his problems and his feelings. Suddenly, his loneliness and desolation seemed to crash in on him. *Oh Lord, could there be just one person I could share my burdens and joys with? If it is your will, could I have just one friend?*

With that thought nagging at his mind, Conrad gave a careful account of everything that had happened since the attempted assassination of Adolf Hitler. How the documents that had linked Pius XII to the assassination plot had been discovered, how Hitler had gone into one of his rages and demanded that Pius be killed. How Himmler had used that rage-induced demand to plot the killing of Heydrich, who was supplanting him, and the simultaneous assassination of the Pope as part of the scheme to place the blame of the Heydrich killing on the Catholic Church.

He described the elaborate assassination plan, with its complex and convoluted deception scheme, and how that plan had come apart with the capture of three survivors from the assault team. How the whole plot had unraveled and Himmler's scheme had been exposed. Now, with the bombing of Middle East Command HQ, the situation had lurched still further towards disaster.

"So, the necessity is to see Himmler and explain to him that if these tit-for-tat assassinations continue, we will expose him and his schemes. Heydrich was a favorite of Hitler's and the *Führer* will recognize the truth when he hears it. Himmler will not survive. If, however, the assassination plans stop and the attempts to implicate the Church in them end, then we will hold our tongues and the real truth will remain a Church secret. Can we get that message to Himmler?"

Mueller thought about it carefully. "I can do that. This might surprise you but Himmler and I are, if not friends, at least honest enemies. In 1934, I was arrested by the Gestapo; arrested and charged with a treasonous conspiracy, an offense punishable by death. Heinrich Himmler himself directed my interrogation. As part of that, he asked me what advice I would give to anybody involved had our plans succeeded.

"I told him the truth; that I would urge anybody taking over the government to have him shot and asked him if he would not have done the same if our positions had been reversed. Himmler laughed. He said it was the first manly reply he had had to that question and that I was the sort of tough, two-fisted man-sprung-from-the-people whom the Nazis could respect as an opponent. Then, he let me go.

"We've had a sort of guarded friendship ever since. The simplest way for me to see him would be to go to his office."

"That's incredible." Conrad couldn't believe what he was hearing. He was also gravely suspicious of Mueller, unable to credit the loathed and dreaded Heinrich Himmler with any kind of decent feeling. *It seems incredible that a man so deeply and unrepentantly evil as Himmler could have a friend so opposed to everything he believes in.* That was when Conrad remembered his own anguished prayer just a few minutes earlier. *Perhaps even Heinrich Himmler needs a friend.*

"Nevertheless, it is true. My friend, Nazi Germany is the kind of place where incredible things happen all the time."

Conrad shook his head. "So, now we know why the Germans accused a Canadian commando group of being responsible for the killing of *SS-Obergruppenführer* Reinhard Heydrich. They were setting up this attack on the Cairo headquarters all the time. This is becoming the sort of complex, Byzantine plan that the highest circles of the German command seem to love."

Conti di Segni agreed although it was obvious that the thought grieved him deeply. "Does this mean that the Nazis will be renewing their attacks in the Mediterranean?"

Mueller laughed at that. "What with? The Russian Front is bleeding Germany white. The family in Germany that has lost but one of its sons counts itself fortunate. You know what typical jokes amongst German families are? '1944 is twice as bad as 1943, but don't worry; it is only half as bad as 1945'. 'Enjoy the war, because the peace will be terrible'.

"The Germans are barely hanging on to their front line in Russia and it is taking all their resources to do that. The only uncommitted asset they have is their fleet and that is in Norway. Trying to commit that to the Mediterranean would see it being sunk in the North Atlantic. No, you here in Southern Europe can continue to sit this out and wait."

"For what?" Conti di Segni was obviously pleased that Italy would not be sucked into the maelstrom.

Mueller thought about that. "The one thing all their leadership fears is what will happen when the Americans start bombing Germany itself. If that causes civilian morale to crack, they fear the German war effort could collapse. When the B-29s start their missions into Germany, that will be the decisive battle of the war and they know it."

Dumbarton Avenue, Georgetown, Washington, D.C.

Igrat glanced around the room, making sure everybody she needed was present and nobody else. That meant three people, Lillith, Naamah and

Gusoyn. Getting this meeting of a widely-dispersed group set up in the face of a very busy schedule for everybody had taken longer than she had expected. It was beginning to press in on her own desperately overcrowded schedule. She would be leaving for Rome again as soon as this meeting was over. Her schedule was that tight.

Nevertheless, it was essential that her messages be passed through only to those entitled to receive them. There was one obvious absence from the room; The Seer had not been invited, although Igrat guessed he already knew about this meeting and its subject matter. Nevertheless, he had chosen not to be here. Amongst other things, that told her he trusted her to handle this matter properly.

"Thank you for coming, everybody. I have some very important news for you. I am pleased to tell you that Phaeton Phoebus Apollo is alive and well. I spoke with him a few days ago."

"Thank the Gods." Lillith had her eyes closed in relief. "Where is he?"

"In Rome. He wasn't in Küstrin during Kristallnacht and he doesn't know why you thought he was. He was in Vienna, which is no better, of course, and was in process of taking on the entire SA with his bare fists when Loki took him in hand and got him out. The SA had burned his books and almost everything else he possessed."

Igrat closed her eyes and repeated the messages that Apollo had asked her to bring back. Even across the enormous number of years that had passed, his voice was still recognizable in the lilt and inflections of her own. One of Igrat's friends had once described her as a human dictaphone and she had taken the description as high praise.

The gift of her mimicry had an unexpected effect. Tears were trickling down Gusoyn's cheeks. The three women exchanged glances; Gusoyn had been alone ever since Apollo had stormed out of the family home so long ago. Every so often it got to be too much for him and he would go on a spree for a few days, ending up in a drunken stupor.

After a couple of near-disasters, Achillea had followed him at a discrete distance during those debauches, making sure he came to no permanent harm. Naamah gave a slight nod; she would give Achillea the heads-up that her services would be needed again soon.

Before anybody could say anything, Igrat held up a hand. "He's on his way back to us. He's made the decision, although even he doesn't realize it yet. It will take time and we must allow him to come back on his own. Don't go out there to persuade him. You'll only make him dig his heels in again."

"But I must know . . . I must speak with him. I must tell him . . . " Lillith's expression was a strange mixture of relief, guilt, self-righteousness and obstinacy. It made Igrat sigh quietly to herself.

"No, you mustn't." Igrat restrained herself nobly from telling Lillith she'd done enough damage the last time she had tried to explain herself to Apollo. The same obstinacy that had made her walk again after her feet had been burned had its downside.

Lillith would never admit defeat or that she might be wrong. That was forgivable, but the self-righteous tone of voice and condescending conceit in manner when she tried to explain herself set everybody's teeth on edge.

"He must make this decision in his own time and of his own accord. He's a man, Lillith; that's his right."

"But . . . I must . . ." Lillith spoke through pursed lips. Igrat didn't let her get any further.

"No, you mustn't. I'll say this again. Apollo is his own man and he's made a reasonably successful life for himself. If you want him back in the family, you are going to have to accept that."

"Would it help if I went?" Gusoyn also had a strange mixture of hope and fear in his voice.

Igrat shook her head. "At the moment, no. He needs to justify everything that has happened in his own head. That includes leaving you for all these years. Let him come to his own answers. He will; he wants to. He needs to. All we have to do is open the door and bring him back in when he's ready."

She glanced at her wristwatch. "Alright, I have to go to Geneva and then Rome. That damned fool pope has set an avalanche in motion and it's getting worse every moment."

"All of you, I'll say this again and I really do mean it. Leave Apollo alone. I'm talking to him now. Soon, he'll be home again."

Appartamento Pontificio, Top Floor, Apostolic Palace, Vatican City. One Week Later

Everybody present looked at each other and then at the news Igrat and Mueller had brought back from their respective visits. Eventually, His Holiness broke the silence. "Is there any good news?"

"Richard Austin Butler is dead. That counts for something." Igrat had picked the report up in Geneva after Loki had obtained it. "He was a repulsive man. The British Resistance blew him up with his escort while he was on a visit to the Midlands war industry. They killed Butler himself, the Cabinet Secretary, Sir Edward Bridges, and ten Blackshirts."

"The Free BBC in Ottawa have claimed the Resistance killed him in retaliation for the murder of General Wavell. According to the information we have from the Canadians, the travel plans were leaked to the Resistance by Sir

Edward. Apparently, the Gestapo were closing in on to him and this way he took Butler with him."

"A brave man." Mueller spoke sadly and seriously. "I have a return message from Heinrich Himmler. He notes with pleasure the assurances from the Pontificate that the Holy Church had nothing to do with the planned assassination of Adolf Hitler and believes that Gestapo investigations will reveal that documents suggesting otherwise were forgeries intended to delude the naïve into supporting a plot that they would not have otherwise countenanced.

"Therefore, criticism of the Church and investigations of innocent Catholics will cease. Of course, if the Church were to take any other actions or positions that might disprove the validity of the forgery theory . . ."

"In other words, they'll leave our people alone as long as we shut up and leave them alone." Conti di Segni sounded both pleased and saddened.

"Exactly. Not quite as Himmler phrased it, but that was his meaning."

In the background, Igrat started to say something, then stopped herself. In her eyes, Mueller had just committed a series of grievous errors. Firstly, and most grievously, he should have transmitted Himmler's words exactly and as accurately as possible. Secondly, he had interpreted his words instead of leaving the audience to interpret them. Thirdly, he had failed to distinguish between what he knew to be facts and what he had personally deduced from those facts. Finally, he had let his own personal opinions affect the messages he carried. If he had worked for her, she would now be firing him.

Conrad looked over to her and caught her eye. He knew exactly what she was thinking and agreed with her. Joseph Mueller had meant well, but his actions had set this whole grim affair rolling.

"What about these attacks?" Pope Pius XII was oblivious to the undercurrents in the room.

"Himmler points out that they are the result of various groups, *franc-tireurs*, partisans, resistance fighters, bandits, call them what you will, over which nobody has any real control.

"While the actions of those who plotted against Hitler have started the current spate of assassinations, now the decisions are being taken by unknown parties for their own reasons. He cannot promise that they will cease doing so any more than he can expect us to make the same commitment."

"In other words, the cycle of tit-for-tat assassinations will continue and we can do nothing about it. If we raise our voices, our people in occupied Europe will be made to suffer.

"This war will take yet another cycle downwards into barbarity. This business will get out of control. It is already getting out of control and we'll be lucky to live through it. The Nazis have won this one. They have found a way of taking the war to the territory of their enemies and we have enabled them." Conti di Segni was on the verge of breaking down.

His Holiness dropped his face into his hands, understanding that it was his own actions that had brought about the calamity. "This is my fault. All I wanted was a way to end this war before it destroys us all. Instead, I have made a nightmare into something so terrible no words exist to describe it."

Conti di Segni looked at him with compassion. "*Bonum intentiones, strata via ad infernum.*"

Conrad looked at Igrat and said softly. "Good intentions pave the road to hell."

Igrat nodded softly in agreement. "They always do. Listen to me, Conrad and the rest of you. This is me speaking now, so you can take what I say and put as much weight on it as you wish. This situation has gone to hell and there is nothing we can do about it. All we can do is to try and learn from the things that have happened.

"Conrad, no matter what you do now, this tit-for-tat exchange is going to continue. You can do whatever you want to bring justice here and you can protect the innocent all you want. It won't make any difference at all Nothing any good will come of what happens now. It may be bad, it may be worse but it won't be good.

"There's an old saying, 'this is beyond my pay grade.' Well, this one is beyond ours and we count for nothing now. We don't matter. There's nothing more you, I or anybody else here can do. What will be, will be."

EYE OF THE DESPOILER
Verviers, Belgium, 1947

CHAPTER ONE

STARVATION

*Refugee Compound, Displaced Persons Camp, Verviers, Belgium.
December 1947*

"**P**lease, Father, come quickly. My baby needs you." The voice called out from the snow-covered hovels beside the dirt track that led through the refugee camp. It was a weak voice, one that quavered with a mixture of misery, despair and anguish.

The air was thick and heavy with the acrid smell of burned wood from the fires that people kept to try and ward away the bitter cold. The fires were tiny things, a few twigs carefully gathered and hoarded as if they were life itself. That was not far from the truth; for these people, the tiny warmth from a few burning twigs and a modicum of shelter from the biting wind were all that stood between them and death.

"Careful, Father. Keep to the cleared paths." Commissioner Laurentin Morin had a more than urgent note of caution in his voice. The snow had been cleared to make paths through the camp and to each of the huts in it. It had also been cleared from the roofs and from around the walls. Everywhere else, it was more than waist-deep. It wasn't just this camp that was affected; the same conditions were hitting people across Europe and Great Britain.

This was the worst winter in European history and pretty much everybody blamed the American bombing of Germany for it. The meteorologists had a different explanation. They spoke of an anti-cyclone sitting over Scandinavia that prevented low-pressure depressions from crossing the Atlantic Ocean and bringing warm air with them.

They said that the same anti-cyclone was causing the strong easterly winds that had deluged Europe with snow. The key word in all of that was easterly. That meant the wind was coming from Germany and Germany was a radioactive

Conrad's Other Eye

wasteland. It wasn't just the cold that could make snow lethal, or so people believed. They used new words that spelled doom. Fall-out.

Conrad waved his arm in acknowledgment. Digging paths to buildings created the problem of where to put the snow. It was banked up around the cleared paths and every snowstorm made the piles higher. He dreaded to think what the situation would be like once winter really set in during January. A tall man, Conrad could see over the banks, but the margin was narrow. A few more storms and it would be gone. Then, the refugee camp would cease to be a compound and instead be a maze of secluded paths. That would make it an even more dangerous place.

The woman's shelter was built on a small rise that had kept it clear of the worst of the snow. She was standing outside it, waving frantically at Conrad with one arm while the other held her baby to her. "Father, please hurry. There is so little time left for my poor Josef."

Conrad looked at the baby that was resting still in his mother's arm. Suspiciously, ominously still. His eyes took in the mother as well. She was gaunt and haggard, her eyes deeply shadowed above cheekbones that seemed unnaturally prominent. *'A ruined beauty.'* Conrad remembered the description from one of Messalina's friends, a cartoonist whose works had a weirdness around them that Phillip Stuyvesant enjoyed. The baby she was cradling was absolutely still. Even in this biting cold, his skin was marked with the purple marks of decomposition. *How long has this baby been dead? Two weeks? More? It is hard to say, for the temperature has slowed decomposition.* He reached out and carefully placed his fingers on the child's neck. Conrad felt the hardness of frozen flesh and the sliminess of decomposing skin. That he could feel, but no sign of a pulse.

"There is still time." Conrad said gravely. *Of course there is time. There is always time. What kind of God would condemn an infant to eternal damnation because the right words were not said at the right time?* Conrad took a small box from one pocket of his coveralls. He carried it for exactly this purpose and had performed the service more often than he wished to remember. Inside was a small bottle of olive oil that had been blessed by the pope. Which pope was a question better not asked. He put a tiny dab on the forehead of the baby, spreading it into a small cross. *"Per istam sanctam unctionem et suam piissimam misericordiam adiuvet te Dominus gratia Spiritus Sancti."* He then put another tiny dab on the baby's hands. *"Dominus a peccato liberat te, qui praeter te sublevabit te."*

There was one last thing to do. Conrad took a fragment of wafer from the box and touched it to the baby's lips and followed it with a spot of wine from his finger. He finished the words of the viaticum and then carefully packed the supplies back in their case. When he had finished, he touched the baby's neck again, then a sorrowful look at the mother and quiet words. "He is with God now." There was a tiny spark of life in the mother's eyes, or, at least, the gaunt, vacant look was not quite so overpowering.

"Thank you." Her voice was lifeless. Conrad doubted how much contact she actually had with reality.

"We must get little Josef buried. What is your name?" He hoped that somehow, simple things could bring this woman back from wherever it was that her mind had retreated.

"Holzknecht. Elli Sophia Holzknecht."

"Elli, we must go to where the dead are buried. Can you show me where that is?"

She said nothing, but left her shelter and set off down the path through the snow. Once back on the main pathway, she picked up a little speed, walking more quickly. It was not a healthy walk. It had an obsessive quality about it, the movements jerky and stilted. It was as if her brain wasn't quite controlling her movements properly.

Ahead of them was a guarded section of the camp, fenced off with barbed wire. It was the burial area. Conrad did not want to speculate on why a burial area needed barbed wire and armed guards. Once inside, the small party headed for a freshly dug area. There was space for the tiny body. The woman carefully laid it down. Before she could do anything else, there was a sudden stillness. A silence enveloped the whole camp and seemed to have almost tangible form.

It was a few seconds before Conrad heard a strange throbbing drone. He searched the sky, seeing the watery sun peeking down. He also saw the strange silvery clouds that covered the sky. To Conrad's eyes, they looked almost like a bridal veil. He knew they were far stranger than that. They were something that had never been seen in the skies before; not in human memory, at least. The atomic attack on Germany had blast-pulverized dust and ash, then thrown them high into the sky. There they had stayed and shadowed the ground beneath. Oddly, the dust caused temperatures high up to actually increase, but those at ground level were down. Not by much, in the great scheme of things, but enough to give credence to those who blamed the Americans for the vicious winter.

Then he saw a tiny silver cross, trailing a thick stream of white. The B-36 was relatively high up by most standards, 25,000 feet or so. Yet, Conrad knew that this was much lower than the crews preferred to fly. They liked to cruise at 35,000 feet or higher, where the air was smooth and the cold helped cool the engines. To a B-36 crew, 25,000 feet was worryingly low. They were only flying at that altitude here because their presence was a political message. It was a warning of what would happen to any country that tried to start another war in Europe. Once they were over Germany, they would climb higher to complete the rest of their flight to Russia. Another warning there, an attack on America's only trusted ally would bring about a nuclear disaster for the attacker.

The silver bird crossed the sky, leaving a wide, white contrail behind it. Eventually, it vanished to the east. There was a tangible feeling of relief at its disappearance. Only then did Conrad fully understand the fear that had gripped the camp at the sight of the American bomber. In front of him, the burial area diggers were covering the tiny body of Josef Holzknecht with dirt. Conrad recited the prayers expected. When they were finished, he added a silent prayer of his own.

Merciful Lord, I beseech you to take the soul of Josef Holzknecht into your arms and carry him into Heaven, for surely he has served his time in Hell.

Administration Area, Verviers Displaced Persons Camp

"So, how is the food and aid situation at the moment?" This was why Conrad was here. He had been in Rome the day of The Big One, working with Conti di Segni to try and ameliorate the disaster that was taking place and also using the opportunity to update his records. It was a periodic function that prevented anybody looking into Conrad's background from finding things they shouldn't know. Despite his work, Conrad had no idea that the day would be so significant. He still remembered the stunned shock that had spread through Rome, as the fearful reality of what was happening north of the Alps had sunk in. Now he was here on behalf of the Orders Committee, to find out what the situation on the ground was really like and how the Church could best help.

"First few months, we thought everything would be fine." Commissioner Morin almost wept as he remembered those first optimistic days. The war had ended. The Germans had gone. For a few brief weeks, it had been a happy time. Then summer had turned to autumn. The temperature had started to drop and the crops had gone yellow in the fields. What had promised to be a fine harvest had withered in the ground.

"We thought we would be all right here. The Ami fighter-bombers never got this far in. We were too far to the east for the raids from the Atlantic, and too far south for those launched from the north. Our ports were operating perfectly as usual. Even when the crops died and we had to import food, we thought all would be well. We never expected this."

Conrad nodded slowly. He had travelled through the areas of France where the U.S. Navy fighter-bombers had cut their destructive swathe across the countryside. He hadn't seen a single bridge left standing. The roads and railways were tangled, shattered wrecks, all covered with the burned-out remains of trains and vehicles. People were slowly clearing the damage by hand, so that some form of trade and transport could be restored. It was an agonizingly slow process.

It was also extremely dangerous. Western France was littered with unexploded bombs. The toll they exacted from the clearance teams mounted daily. Only the week before, teams working in Cherbourg had brought up a Skyraider that had been shot down and crashed in the port entrance. The team had thought they had disarmed the mines the aircraft had been carrying, but they were wrong. They hadn't known the mines had pressure fuses in addition to their contact and acoustic fuses. The mines had exploded as the aircraft had broken clear of the water. Twenty men had been killed and nearly a hundred wounded.

It had almost been possible to work out the tactical radii of the various aircraft from where the destruction had come to an end. The Corsairs had struck deepest; they were capable fighters on their own and all they had to do if intercepted was to jettison their bombs. Of course, that was a problem for those underneath them. The Skyraiders carried the big punch, but they had to be escorted by Shooting Stars and that restricted them to shorter-range missions.

The result was ironic. The areas of France devastated in the First World War had been left virtually untouched in the Second. Belgium, the Netherlands and Denmark were almost untouched by war. Conrad had heard from Nell in England that the western and northern parts of the country had been wrecked by the carrier strikes, but East Anglia and the Kent/Sussex region was almost untouched. The dividing line had run right through the middle of London, which had been good news for the East Londoners and bad for those living in the West.

So, right up to September, things hadn't seemed too bad. The ports in the unbattered east were operational and enough food could be brought in to replace the lost harvest. Distributing it in the bomb-ruined west was a problem, but one that could be solved given manpower and the willpower to use it. The Commonwealth of Nations had sent aid to England, restoring the relationship that most wished had never been broken.

Aid for Western Europe had come from Spain, Portugal and Italy. Everybody had given thanks that the failure of the harvest hadn't spread south of the Alps or across the Pyrenees. Then, the first week in October 1947, the snows started. What had been a chill in the air in September became an unseasonable cold in October and a bitter freeze by November.

By early December, the more northerly ports were beginning to ice up. There were reports of ice floes in the Channel. There might be plenty of aid, made available by most of the rest of the world now, but getting it in and moving it to where it was needed had become major problems.

"We are running out of stores very quickly. The ships cannot unload and, when they do, the food just sits in the warehouses. The snow is blocking the railways and the roads here just as badly as the war damage is shutting things down in France. There are shovel gangs trying to dig their way through, but, as fast as they make progress, another snowstorm starts and their labors are for nothing."

Now, Commissioner Morin really was on the verge of weeping with despair. "A trickle is coming in, that is all. But, that is not the worst of it. We have no reserves, nothing put by for a rainy day. The Germans took it all. They had their seven years of fat by looting us of everything we had. They kept the best for themselves and distributed the rest as it suited them. Now, we are starting the seven years of lean and there is nothing left to feed us. What went to Germany is gone.

"And that is still not the worst of it. I said all the aid is piling up in the ports and the ships offshore? Well, it is being stolen and being sold on the black market. People in this camp can get more food ,but they must pay for it at exorbitant prices. You know the difference in this camp between a good woman and a bad one? A good woman sells her body to get food for her children; a bad woman sells her body to get food for herself. With rations being cut every week, the crisis gets worse."

"Are there more refugees coming in?" Conrad was overwhelmed by the horror of the situation that was growing in post-war Europe. He had assumed that the problem was basically one of getting aid to where it was needed, but the sheer extent of the disaster that was unfolding measured up to anything he had ever seen. Since that included the Thirty Years War, the yardstick was a nightmare to contemplate.

"That is the one merciful thing. No." Commissioner Morin was emphatic about that. "There were a few refugees from the bombing, the ones along the border, but the rest stayed where they were. They had to. Those who try to move, die."

That was another horrible thing. Conrad thought. *Even The Seer hadn't expected the radiation problem. Nobody had. It had been assumed that if anybody was close enough to Ground Zero to be killed by radiation, they would have died first from blast and fire. So, nobody had really thought about the threat of radiation.*

The Germans certainly hadn't. When the bombs had fallen and the cities burned, emergency services from all over Germany had rushed to the stricken areas to try and save those who were left. They hadn't known they were also rushing to their deaths. The fallout from the bombing had killed them as surely as the bombs themselves had killed their earlier victims.

Now, the ground was a patchwork mess of areas that varied from the uncontaminated to places so radioactive it was lethal just to step on them. A walk in the woods could kill quietly and silently. The victim would get no warning. No warning at all. "Nobody is coming over?"

"Nobody. Those who are outside, stay outside. Those inside cannot leave, for they dare not move out of the areas they are sheltering in. All we have here are those who were living in Belgium before the bombing. Mostly, they were in service camps or German bases, but we have a few who came over from Germany itself."

Morin was about to continue, but one of his assistants entered the office. "Commissioner, I am sorry to interrupt, but you asked to be told immediately if there was another one."

"And now, Father, you will see the final depths to which we have sunk. Come with me."

He led the way into a warehouse. A pallet of hessian sacks were being unloaded. There was a man in the warehouse with an instrument that clicked slowly. Conrad recognized it as a Geiger counter, designed to measure levels of radiation. He was standing off to one side with a look of disgust on his face. The workers who were unpacking the load had gathered around one sack in particular.

Conrad looked at the sack curiously. It seemed normal enough; a standard Hessian sack with a simplified, almost cartoon, elephant and the words, in clumsy English script, 'A gift from the King and People of Thailand' printed on it. Rice, food aid from the Far East. Conrad had heard that a quiet deal had been struck between Bangkok and Paris. The Thais would send a vast quantity of rice to France without charge, aid to prevent famine. In exchange, the French would accept the results of the 1941 war as a done deal and not create difficulties over them.

Conrad guessed that it had been a hard agreement for the French to swallow, but feeding their people came first. And it would stand to their eternal credit that the French had shared the food they had obtained by that agreement with Belgium and the Netherlands. He smelt the sack in question. The odor sickened him.

"Someone has urinated on the food? I cannot believe it." Conrad was appalled beyond anything he could imagine. *In the midst of a developing disaster, somebody deliberately fouled desperately-needed food?*

"As far as we can tell, only on the sacks sent here for the German refugees. Not the ones that go to the Belgians." Now, Morin had finally broken down and was weeping at the sight of the fouled sack. "What have we come to?"

"It was clean and safe." The man with the Geiger counter looked as if he was about to weep. "And then somebody did that."

"I . . . " Conrad didn't know what to say. "Have you any idea where this happened? Or who did it?"

"It must have happened after the sacks were allocated. Somebody saw that these sacks were coming here and urinated on this one. It has contaminated the ones above and below it, but the rest are still clean. At first, we tried to wash the rice as best we could, thinking there isn't enough food for us to throw any away. But the fouled rice went rotten and stank so fast, even washing did no good. I think the person who did this knew that. He must be a Frenchman."

Conrad heard the desperation in Morin's voice and knew that he was frantically trying to find some reason to believe that a fellow Belgian had not done this vile thing. But Conrad had devoted his life to defending the innocent and couldn't let the accusation pass. "I doubt it. The French are a great people; great in their vices as well as their virtues. A Frenchman might steal this rice and sell it, or use it to feed his family. He might even give it as aid to somebody else. But, a Frenchman would not do this. It is too petty; it is too small and mean a thing. A Frenchman would do something more . . . flamboyant. We must look elsewhere for this person."

Morin shrugged. "Perhaps we will know soon enough. I have made some inquiries over this and the thefts of food and medicine. There are always a few who have the courage to speak out and condemn those responsible. Soon, I will hear from them and they will point me in the right direction."

Evening, Lodging House, Rue Donkier, Verviers, Belgium

Dusk would soon be falling and, with it, all activity would cease until dawn. There was no electricity to power lights and no coal to make gas. *That isn't strictly true*, Conrad thought. *There is coal but nobody can move it around. Even if they could, the power stations and transmission lines have been destroyed.* Most of the power in Belgium had come from over the border in Germany, generated in the stations powered by brown coal or the great dams on the Rhine. Before the war, electrical power had been a major German foreign currency earner. Now, all of that was gone and there was nothing to replace it.

No available coal also meant no heat. The lodging house offered a bare minimum of warmth; better than the freezing temperatures outside, but not much. The family who lived here and their guests shuffled around in overcoats and slept beneath a mound of quilts. In the morning, there would be ice on the inside of the windows and the water in the overnight jugs would be frozen.

In reality, there was no division here between hosts and guests. There were only people huddled together for mutual survival. The rent the guests paid was food for the communal kitchen. Conrad was hungry. For a moment, he was tempted to try and find the black market, so he could use his comparative wealth to buy a little extra. That was when he reminded himself that the food on the black market was stolen. Every mouthful he bought would have been taken from people far more needy than he.

So, he went to bed early and hungry. That was when his stoic endurance of the privations he suffered brought their own reward. For, that night, Conrad didn't suffer from his usual nightmares of Medina del Campo. Instead, he dreamed of a plate of fried chicken.

Next Morning, Lodging House, Rue Donkier, Verviers, Belgium

Turnip stew was not Conrad's idea of a favorite breakfast. But, it was hot and it filled his stomach; mostly, anyway. The people gathered in the front room of the lodging house didn't complain about the food; they were all too aware that there were others far worse off than they. In fact, the group was eating quite well by local standards. The food might be monotonous and the quantities smaller than ideal, but the diet was actually quite good. The ladies who run this house know what they are doing. *Madame Margreet Neske is a staunch woman, the sort who keeps a family home running against all the odds and she is bringing her daughter Rosina up in the same image. One day, she will make some fortunate man a strong and capable wife. I wonder if Monsieur Neske realizes how lucky he is?* Then Conrad saw the pride in his eyes as his wife brought in the breakfast for their guests and knew that he did.

"I think it will snow again today." The words were said cautiously. Gerard van Can looked around as he said them and his voice dropped a level. It was easy to tell when somebody had spent the last few years living under German occupation. They spoke quietly and guarded every word, for nobody knew who might be listening to their words and noting them down. It might be a Gestapo informer or a malicious neighbor with a grudge. It said something about those years that people preferred to think it might be the Gestapo. They would note what was said accurately. While they were brutal and merciless, they were honest in their evil. But a neighbor with a grudge would twist innocent words into something that carried a death sentence.

Van Can was a linesman, one of the men trying to restore some lectrical power to the towns and villages. That meant re-routing the transmission lines so that the handful of generating stations in the Netherlands could send some power to Belgium. Just as the French were sharing the food they had obtained from the Far East, the Dutch were sharing what power they could generate.

"Will this make your work impossible?" Dorothea Heimans was equally cautious and also looked around before she spoke. Her words were more dangerous, for they could be interpreted as a criticism of the authorities. The time for such care had gone, but the habit remained fixed and would do so for many years.

Conrad knew that and knew the reason why. There were marks on trees and lampposts where those who had not been careful with their words had been hanged. The Germans had made their point very emphatically, using a fixed noose with no drop so their victims would thresh around for up to half an hour before they finally died. *It will be a long time before people forget that sight and speak freely again.*

Van Can was obviously thinking carefully about his answer; force of habit made him decide whether anything he said could be construed as criticism or defeatism. "The main problem is that the ground is frozen hard and that makes it very difficult to put new posts in. Stringing the wires is not difficult as long as we have the posts. So, we are doing the best we can with those we have."

"Does that mean we will have some power soon?" Rosina Neske asked the question diffidently, the combination of brutally-ingrained caution combining with the shyness of a young girl intruding into the conversation of adults. Conrad felt sorry for her; the war and this frozen aftermath meant that she would have missed her childhood almost completely.

"A little, perhaps." Van Can was still being very careful, now with the desire not to raise hopes in people who had already seen their dreams dashed by war. "But it will go to public services first, I think."

As if to illustrate that point, the telephone in the front hall of the house rang. It was one of the little oddities of the situation. The telephones were working since they needed little power and the lines remained up. Madame Neske excused herself and left to answer the call. The telephones might be working, but a call using the system was something that kept for emergencies.

"Could you use the telephone poles to string power lines?" Rosina was still diffident and shy about putting the idea forward.

"You know, we could." Van Can sounded surprised. "We hadn't thought of doing so, but we could do that. At least it would keep us going through the winter. I honestly don't know why we never thought of it because it is a very good idea, Rosina. I will speak of it to my manager."

Conrad knew why. *When people are hungry and cold and have lost all hope, they stop thinking of new ideas and concentrate on simply going from this moment to the next. They just give up and their minds seek refuge in the familiar.*

The call only took a couple of minutes. Madame Neske came back, a look of shock upon her face. "Father, there has been an emergency at the camp that demands your presence. Commissioner Morin has been brutally murdered."

Rue Donkier, Verviers, Belgium

Getting around was a real problem. The snows gave roads a thin but treacherous glaze of ice that made riding a bicycle or motorcycle desperately dangerous at best and impossible for most of the time. The same slippery conditions made walking any great distance tiring in the extreme, while falling and breaking bones was an ever-present danger. The older citizens had given up walking for that reason. The combination of age and poor diet had left their bones too brittle to take the risk.

Even horse-drawn carts had gone. The Germans had taken all the horses and sent them to the Russian Front. None had come back; they had all died there. *Europe's horseflesh will never recover*, Conrad thought. *Thousands of years of bloodstock and breeding wiped out. French Breton and Pecheron,*

Scottish Clydesdale and English Hackney, German Branderburgers and Hecks, all gone forever.

His thoughts were interrupted by the first flakes of snow falling on his nose. The sky had the leaden grayness that promised a much greater fall in the near future. That was when the police car pulled up. It was an ex-German Army *kubelwagen*, hastily repainted blue with what looked like building paint. *Politie* and *Gendarmerie* were painted clumsily on the side, the letters done by hand. The paint had run slightly on some of the letters, making it look as if the words were weeping. Given the reputation of the police in what had been occupied Europe, they might well do so.

Across the road, a local woman saw the *kubelwagen* and ostentatiously spat on the sidewalk. The driver of the *kubelwagen* was an old man with the extravagant moustache that marked him as a veteran *poilu*. He was far too old to have been a soldier in this war. Conrad guessed he had served in the First World War, or possibly even earlier, and was only in the police because the younger men had gone. His eyes were brimming with tears at the sight of the woman's actions. Conrad was not going to let this pass. He looked at the woman. Her eyes narrowed with defiance under his gentle, unforgiving gaze.

"And why do you condemn the mote that is in your brother's eye, but consider not the beam that is in your own?"

The woman's expression changed slightly; guilt joined the defiance in her eyes as his quiet words carried across the icy street. As Conrad knew all too well, those who were most ostentatious on the condemnation of others were also those had the most to hide. She shuffled away, taking care not to slip on the ice. As she turned the corner, her sneer of "collaborators" echoed down the *Rue Donkier*.

"She is right, Father, we are all collaborators. But what choice did we have? With the young men away, first in the Army and then taken as forced labor, somebody had to uphold the law." The old *poilu* was now crying openly. "Should we have let thieves, rapists and murderers run free because arresting them meant upholding German law and subjecting them to German justice? What were we to do?"

Conrad sighed to himself as he climbed into the *kubelwagen*. "The Lord said, 'Judge not, that ye be not judged' and, in doing so, caused no end of trouble. I will let you into a little secret, well known to those of us from the Society of Jesus, but one that is not so well understood to those whose study of scriptures is more superficial. The Lord sometimes didn't phrase things as well as he might have done. What he meant to say was that 'if you judge others, they will judge you by the same measure as you have used towards them. By accusing others of collaboration that woman is setting a process in motion by which others will examine her conduct and make their own charges. What is your name?"

"Étienne Bonnaire, Father. *Brigadier de police*."

In most other countries, the rank would have sounded impressive but Conrad knew that it equated to a police sergeant. "Etienne, what the Good Book teaches us is that we must first judge ourselves, and get our own lives in order, before we can take upon ourselves the duty of helping others do the same. Only the Good Lord will make final judgment upon us. Let me ask you something, Etienne. When you finally stand before Him and look into your own heart, knowing it is open before Him, will you be able to say that you did what you believed would help the people of your community endure the situation that had been forced upon them?"

Bonnaire settled himself behind the wheel, carefully positioning the truncheon hanging from his belt so it would not obstruct the controls. Then, he put the *kubelwagen* into gear and started to drive cautiously along the road. The snow was thickening. Gray-white flakes pattered on the fabric roof and formed half-frozen blobs on the windscreen. The vehicle slid slightly on the road. The rear-wheel drive tried to spin it around on the slick cobblestones, but Bonnaire managed to keep it under control. "These things are too light. They slide too easily."

Conrad knew that the remark was buying time while Bonnaire thought over the question that had been put to him. "Father, I do not know if what we did helped people or not. We all believed that, if we did not enforce the law, then it would be those least able to protect themselves who would suffer. And, if everything was in chaos, then the Germans would enforce their laws, their way, for their ends. And that would mean all would suffer greatly. So, I would say that, honestly, we did believe that our actions were intended to help our people. We may have collaborated in small things, but we did so to preserve the greater good. That is what we told ourselves, anyway."

"Do you think that woman in the street was trying to preserve any kind of good? Or that she stays awake nights, anguished over whether she is doing the right thing by making such accusations?"

Bonnaire shook his head and the contrast seemed to cheer him a little. Conrad decided to press his success a little further. "You know, another small secret for you to enjoy. I have always believed that when the final Day of Judgment comes, a lot of souls are going to be very surprised at the verdict that is passed on them.

"There will be as many of those who are weighed down by guilt, yet find that the sins they counted so grievous amount to little in the great scheme of things, as there will be those who took pride in their virtue without understanding that virtue without humanity is a sin all of its own."

Bonnaire snorted with laughter and nearly lost control of the *kubelwagen* on a patch of icy snow as a result. "You're a strange priest, Father. I would not be so impertinent as to speculate on how well you get along with your superiors, but I will say that you would have had a devoted following in the trenches."

Food Storage Warehouse, Verviers Displaced Persons Camp

Conrad looked down at the body spread-eagled on the ground, once more reminded that everybody was diminished by death. Commissioner Laurentin Morin was face down on the cement floor, his blood spreading around him in a semi-congealed pool. Conrad reached down and put his fingers to the man's neck, feeling for the pulse that he knew he would not find. As he straightened up, he caught sight of Mari Annick's horrified eyes fixed on the body.

"It could have been an accident, couldn't it? He was on top of the piles and slipped. He fell. It could have happened that way, couldn't it?" Her voice was desperate to find a way of denying the obvious.

Conrad shook his head, slowly and sadly. "He was struck with a heavy object. A steel or lead pipe, perhaps. There are no marks from him trying to defend himself. I think whoever killed him walked up and swung the weapon without any warning at all. The commissioner was struck before he had time to realize he was under attack. Then, his unconscious body was thrown from the top of the stack."

"How could you tell that, Father?" Bonnaire was looking at the body as well, his eyes pools of grief mixed with memories that he would rather forget.

"Look at his face. It is peaceful, composed. If he had fallen, he would have been in fear; if he knew he was being attacked, he would have been angered. His face shows neither. And look, there are two pools of blood. One is very dry, set hard. Over it is another, greater pool, but one that is not so dried. He was struck here, then taken up and thrown off so that he landed in the pool of his own blood. The killer thought it would be assumed he slipped and fell."

"Can you tell if he was struck from behind?" Bonnaire was beginning to realize that, as the only real representative of the law here, he would be in charge of the investigation. Coupled with that insight was the knowledge that he was hopelessly ill-equipped to undertake it. He desperately needed all the help he could get.

Conrad was about to give an opinion when he stopped and thought carefully. When he did speak, he did so very cautiously. "I was about to say that he was hit from the front, but it may not be so. The first rule of any case is never to make assumptions."

He looked at the body carefully, noting how it was sprawled on the floor. "I think the blow that killed him was this one here. The one on the left side of his head, above his ear. The depression in his skull is deep enough for it to be fatal."

"A man swinging an iron or lead pipe with his right hand could create such a wound. If he was standing in front of the commissioner." Bonnaire thought for a second. "But so could a man who was behind the commissioner and swung the pipe with his left hand. If he was taller, or was hiding on top of the sacks, the wounds would be identical."

"And the commissioner was not a tall man." Conrad looked again, this time with great care. "Nor need the blow that killed him have been so hard. After the shortage of food over the last few years, and the poor diet that has resulted, people's bones have been left brittle from loss of calcium. A heavy pipe could easily have inflicted this injury. The problem is that we have no idea how he fell. The position of his body might have told us much about the attack on him but, in moving him, the killer denied that evidence to us. That may well have been part of his plan, of course."

Bonnaire was looking at the area around the body, also with great care. Something caught his eye and he looked more closely. "Father, come and look at this. See how the spray of blood has stained this sack."

Conrad stepped over to where Bonnaire was standing and looked closely. It was indeed a spray of blood, fresh and very distinctive. It ended in a distinct smudge. "If we assume that the Commissioner was standing here, with his back to this pile of sacks, and the killer was on top of those sacks, hidden and laying in wait, then this would be the spray from the attack. Imagine the pipe sweeping down and striking the Commissioner over his left ear. He is knocked sideways and falls to the ground, the blood from his wound making the first puddle on the ground. But the pipe continues its arc. Now it is covered with his blood and that blood sprays of it to make this stain. See how the stain arcs downwards and is denser at the high end than at the low? Finally it ends in that smudge, where it hit the sacks."

Bonnaire looked at the stain carefully and nodded his head in agreement. His bottom lip was pushed out while he did so and that made his *poilu*'s moustache all the more prominent. "I think, in the absence of other evidence, we can say that the Commissioner was struck from behind by a killer hiding on top of these sacks. From that, we can also say that he was lured into a carefully-conceived trap."

"Very good, yes. If our working assumption is correct, then we are looking for somebody who is left handed. People are weakened by hunger, here more than most. I do not think that a murderer would take the chance of using his weak hand and sacrificing yet more of the power behind the blow. Madam Annick, are there records of who has access to this area and is left-handed?"

Mari Annick shook her head. "Of the men who work here, yes, there are records; but they do not state whether they are left-handed or not. Nor if they were working here yesterday. We do not have the resources to keep such information. We have a sign-in sheet by the door that the workers are supposed to use to record the time they arrive and the time they depart. That is all."

"Perhaps if we could see those sheets?" Conrad knew that the information on them would be of marginal value at most, but he had to follow up the possibility that it might be otherwise.

"What about women who work here?" Bonnaire sounded almost reluctant to ask. "A woman could swing a heavy pipe as well as a man."

"Surely you cannot think that a woman could do such a terrible thing?" Madam Annick sounded shocked at the very thought.

"In America, a husband killed by an angry wife wielding a cast-iron frying pan is common enough for it to be called a New York Divorce." Conrad had hoped to lighten the mood a fraction with the comment, but the awkward silence that followed his comment made him realize that it had been inappropriate. That was when he remembered the eerie stillness and silence as the B-36 had flown over the camp the day before. The almost-tangible fear that the overflight had caused came back to him. For the first time, he truly realized the psychological impact of the destruction that had ended the war. "But, our prime object now must be to find out why the Commissioner was killed. Once we can determine that, then it will help us find who committed this crime."

Commissioner Morin's Office, Verviers Displaced Persons Camp

Conrad had an unfamiliar feeling dominating his thoughts. Many years before, when he had been discussing his cases with his old friend Arthur Conan Doyle, he had taken issue with Conan Doyle's depiction of the police as bumbling incompetents. He had pointed out that police work was ruthlessly Darwinian, that the inept or slow of thought did not make it to the higher ranks. At most, they remained on their beats until the day they retired.

For all their faults, personal and professional, detectives were able men and depicting them otherwise was unjust. Also, police forces had resources and support that no outsider could match. Therefore, to depict a private detective as a man who could substitute for a whole police department was too great a stretch. Conrad prided himself on having influenced Conan Doyle in improving his depiction of the police in his later stories.

That made his current predicament all the more ironic. The feeling that so confused him was a sense of helplessness. He habitually worked with the police, not against or separate from them. Their abilities and capabilities were complementary to his own.

Now, for the first time in many, many years, all the assets they brought to the table were no longer accessible. He would have to start from basics and rely on what was available to him. At the moment, that was a desk, a set of cards and an aged police sergeant with little in the way of investigative expertise.

"Where do we start? Where can we start?" Étienne Bonnaire sounded demoralized, defeated. Sadly, Conrad guessed that he was one of those police officers who had risen as far as he would go and would never wear the plain clothes of a detective. Another way the dice were being loaded against him in this case.

"We start with basics. Why was Commissioner Morin killed?" Conrad took out the pack of index cards and looked around. There was no display board. *A flat piece of wall only. That will have to do.* "Although they can manifest themselves in many ways, there are only four basic motives for murder. Sex, money, revenge and to cover up another crime."

He wrote each motive on a card and looked around for a way to pin them up on the wall. There was no sticky tape, no obvious source of pins. Conrad looked around, glancing out of the window as he did so. The snow was falling steadily, coating the camp in a shroud of white. "Madam Annick, do you have any pins?"

"I regret, Father, we have none. A few paper clips, that is all."

Conrad acknowledged the reply, and looked around the room. The desk caught his eye. It was an old one, solidly built, and with a glass sheet covering the top. "Étienne, help me lift the glass off the desk. I think I know how we can start our investigation."

It was only a moment's work to lift the heavy glass off the desk. Conrad sighed with relief and started to spread his cards out. "You see, we now have four columns for our motives. Let us put cards for our suspects in each column. We surmise, based on the evidence to date, that the killer was either a right-handed person who struck the commissioner from the front, or a left-handed person who struck him from behind.

"We can also surmise that the commissioner was taken by surprise, since he made no effort to defend himself. So, if he was struck from the front, he must have known and trusted his killer. That does not apply to the person who struck him from behind. So, our suspects are a right-handed person, known and trusted, or a left-handed person. Already, Étienne, we have made our start."

"It does not take us very far."

"A first step rarely does. But, let us take a second step. Of our four motivations, which appears to offer most scope? In our conversation yesterday, the commissioner said that commercial sex was commonplace in the camp. Is there a motive in that I wonder?"

"The men in the camp greatly outnumber the women. Perhaps a woman thought she could better her position by becoming the commissioner's mistress and her existing partner did not want to lose her, with so little hope of finding another. Not willing to kill her, he instead killed his rival."

"A plausible theory of the case indeed. I will offer you another. The oldest in the world. The commissioner got a woman pregnant, but refused to marry her. And so, betrayed, she killed him." Conrad went to the office door. "Madam Annick, do your records show if any of the women in the camp are expecting a child?"

"No, Father, there are none. In the weeks after the bombing, most of the women with child lost their babies. There were very few who did not miscarry and the few babies born were weak and sickly. They died soon after birth. Since then, there have been no pregnancies." Mari Annick paused and added the rest tentatively, as if aware she was stepping outside a boundary. "I think that some women must have conceived, but they lost the child almost immediately, before they or anybody else was aware of their condition."

"Well, Étienne, your theory stands its first test; mine does not. So, let us use yours as our standard. Is money, more or less plausible than your existing theory of the crime?"

Bonnaire thought hard about that. "I would say less so. There is so little money here and there is so little for money to buy. I would think that most trade, such as it is, would be by barter. If the commissioner was attacked and robbed for any money he might have had, what would the criminal do with his gains?
"

Conrad considered the possibilities of the murder being associated with robbery. When he spoke, it was with infinite sadness. "Étienne, I have known men who were murdered for their shoes, or the hat that they wore. All murders are a tragedy, but sometimes it can be made even more so by a man's life being worth so little. If trade is by barter, he could easily have been killed for a watch or a ring. The only reason why we know he wasn't killed for the shoes or hat that he wore was that he was wearing them when he was found. Madam Annick, you have finished the list of everything that was on the commissioner's body. Is there anything that strikes you as missing from that list?"

The woman read the list carefully, moving her finger down from item to item. "The commissioner had a tie clip; not expensive, but one that was elegant and suited him well. It is not here. Of course, he may not have been wearing it."

Conrad carefully hid a knowing smile and nodded in appreciation for the information. "We will have to search the scene for that tie clip. And also his room. If we cannot find it, the possibility this was a murder motivated by theft will become stronger. As it is, with the poverty here, and the willingness of people to kill for the smallest gain, I think we must rank money as a slightly higher probability than sex. For the moment, at least. And now we have revenge. Étienne?"

The policeman once again took time to marshal his thoughts. "Father, this is a very hard one. There is so much that might create a demand for revenge here. Perhaps a man thought the commissioner denied him food that might have kept his wife alive? Or a woman thought the same about her lost child? Perhaps somebody thought that they had been denied something that was rightfully theirs? There may have been no logical cause; it could be that somehow, somebody came to believe that the commissioner was responsible for this situation. Perhaps this comes from the war and somebody blamed the commissioner for something that happened then. There are so many ways that revenge could account for this crime; it must be the most probable motivation. But, how we could investigate it and find the cause, I do not know."

Conrad nodded. "I agree. So, we have revenge, then money then sex. Now where can we place the last of the motives, to cover up another crime?"

"I think at the end, Father. The only crime here would be stealing food and, while that is a terrible thing to do, it would not motivate a man to kill. After all, it would be easy to hear the commissioner's footsteps as he approached and there are many places a thief could easily hide. To kill the commissioner for something he had on him, yes, that I can see. But not just to hide the theft of some rice or grain."

"I agree. Yesterday, the commissioner showed me how somebody had urinated on a sack of rice. Perhaps he caught such a person, and the shame of being caught committing such a vile act was too much. He killed the commissioner rather than be exposed. But, if that were true, the commissioner would have been facing his killer and on his guard. We would not see the type of injuries we know were inflicted. Unless we find evidence of something much more widespread and serious than we have found to date, then covering up a crime must come last."

Conrad placed the last card on the desk and looked at them. "And there we have it. Of our possible motives, revenge is the most likely. So, it is there that we must start. Who could have wanted revenge upon the commissioner so much that a killing was the only solution?"

CHAPTER TWO

INVESTIGATION

Commissioner Morin's Living Quarters, Verviers Displaced Persons Camp

A methodical search of the sparse quarters did not take long. Commissioner Morin had brought little in the way of personal possessions to the camp. That had probably been a wise decision; it would have been an unwise man to flaunt personal property in an environment where destitution was the norm. That search revealed a few photographs, certainly of his family, a limited selection of practical clothing and his razor and other personal effects. The commissioner seemed to have few interests or activities outside his work. That was, in Conrad's opinion, the first lucky break he had had in this case. Limited interests meant a limited pool of suspects. It was becoming likely that whatever it was that had brought about his death was a matter restricted to this camp.

One thing had become clear. The commissioner's tie clip was not in his room. Conrad ran over the previous day's meeting with Morin in his mind. He was reasonably certain that he had been wearing his tie clip during their tour of the camp. In fact, if Conrad's guess was right, Morin wore that clip every day. A careful search of the area where the body had been found had failed to find the missing clip. That suggested it had indeed been stolen. Why it had been taken, but the commissioner's watch left, was a puzzle.

There was another result that had emerged from the search of Morin's quarters. There was no indication of the commissioner ever having received any threats. There were a few letters from people complaining about problems or asking for help over disputes with other refugees, but the overwhelming tone was that of people approaching a sympathetic ear for aid. Each letter had received a prompt and courteous response. There was no indication that any of the authors of the original complaints had harbored a grudge over how their issues had been resolved.

"I see nothing here that can help us." Bonnaire seemed depressed again.

Conrad shook his head. "Slowly, we are eliminating the potential motives from this case. What helps us here is what we have not found. There is no indication of anybody being angry enough to threaten the commissioner, let alone carry out those threats. That suggests, if revenge is really our motive, then it must predate his arrival in this camp. Perhaps, when he arrived here, somebody already in the camp recognized him and an old grievance was reborn."

"This is possible." Bonnaire seemed reluctant to give up the idea. "But to locate such a grievance would take much effort. How can we trace the commissioner's history so that we can find such a person?"

All I need to do that is spend ten minutes with a friendly police officer and his station records. Messing around with cigar ash and so on has its place but records are the most important place to find the history of those involved. But now, there are no records that I can access. So now comes the next best thing, "We can start by asking Madam Annick."

Commissioner Morin's Office, Verviers Displaced Persons Camp

Conrad expected what the answer to his first question would be and got exactly what he had anticipated. "But, Father, Commissioner Morin had no enemies. Everybody loved and respected him."

"Madam Annick, forgive me, but that isn't true. Somebody was his enemy; someone whose animosity was deep enough to kill him. The cause for that enmity may not be rational or justifiable, but it must be there. Let me ask this a different way. Were there any great changes in the commissioner's activities over the last few weeks? Was he seeing somebody in particular . . ."

"No!" Annick's voice was high-pitched, sharp and decisive. It was also very defensive. Bonnaire and Conrad exchanged glances.

"Do you have a list of the commissioner's appointments and meetings for the last month or so?" Conrad's question was only partly to get an idea of what particular issues had interested Morin. He watched while Annick left the room to search through her files.

Bonnaire looked at her as she departed. Once she was gone, he spoke in a voice that was both low and thoughtful. "You know, she could be a possible suspect. Even though she is right-handed, she could have walked right up to the Commissioner and he would not have suspected a thing until the blow was struck."

Conrad thought carefully about that. *Viewed from one level, it is perfectly true; she might well be a good suspect. But, Étienne has shown more about himself than he realizes with the statement. He has not yet realized the most important thing about Mari Annick we have learned today.*

"Father, most of the meetings the commissioner had were with people in the camp. Mostly over routine issues; issuing rations and so on. Then there were meetings with agencies who were supplying aid, especially food. There have been more of those recently, especially with the French. It is the work of the Good Lord that, as our own supplies have dwindled, aid from outside is increasing."

"When I spoke with Commissioner Morin yesterday, he was concerned about food supplies for this camp being stolen and sold on the black market. Were any of those meetings concerned with that problem?"

Annick smiled sadly. "Almost all of them. Especially those with outside agencies. There is little point in delivering aid if it is being stolen and sold to those who already have food. There were long discussions about placing guards on the supply trucks and in the warehouses, and of monitoring movements more carefully. But, the problem is . . ."

"Who shall guard the guards?" Conrad finished the sentence off for her.

Annick smiled a little sadly, but with a hint of pride. "Not this time, no. The aid comes in trucks, once a week. The trucks are guarded by French paratroopers. I do not think they care much for us, but they take great pride in their unit. If the paras thought one of their number was taking bribes or selling food on the black market, they would take great exception to him. I would not care to be such a man when they did so."

"So, if food is not taken or sold from the trucks, it must come from the warehouses. Étienne, could you organize a very careful search of the area where we found the commissioner's body? We need to find that tie clip."

Bonnaire set off, obviously delighted to be entrusted with a task that was well within his capabilities. Conrad watched him depart. *Not the most imaginative or incisive of men, but one who will carry out a meticulous search.*

"That is what the commissioner thought. He said the theft must come from our warehouse." Suddenly, Madam Annick put her hand over her mouth. "Do you think he was checking the warehouse for thieves and one killed him?"

"I think that is a possibility we cannot rule out at this time." Conrad looked carefully at the secretary. "Madam Annick, while there are just two of us here, I must ask a delicate question. You were a close friend of the commissioner, were you not? And you gave him that tie clip?"

Annick flushed and looked at the floor. "The poor man, he was so lonely. He had left his wife in Spain to come here, but he would not let her join him. He said that to the west of the Pyrenees she was safe but, to the east, it was too dangerous for her. And, I am a widow. My husband was killed on the Russian Front, in 1944. Is it so wrong that two lonely people should comfort each other?"

"Not long ago, I told our policeman that when the Day of Judgment comes, as many people will be shocked by how the sins they had thought were grievous weighed little in the balance as those who thought themselves virtuous but were condemned. Judgment is always tempered with mercy, Madam Annick. You have committed a sin, certainly, but also the fact that you comforted a lonely and desperate man must count in the balance. You realize that your great sin was deceiving the commissioner's wife?"

Madam Annick nodded, tears forming in her eyes. Conrad's hands made the quick sign of the cross and he repeated the age-old formula. "Showing true repentence, you are absolved. Your penance is to help us find the man who killed Commissioner Morin and bring him to justice."

"Father, I must ask. How did you know?"

"When you took such pride in how well the tie-clip suited the commissioner. A man might take pride in the value of a gift, but only a loving woman would take pride in how well a man looked. The tie-pin was once your husband's?"

"It was."

At that point, Bonnaire returned, saddened and despondent. "I am sorry, Father. There is no trace of a tie clip in the area."

"So, we can conclude that the clip was stolen. Perhaps we have a crime of theft here after all."

Rue Donkier, Verviers, Belgium

Bonnaire dropped Conrad some way from his lodgings because *Rue Donkier* had been blocked by a column of snow-covered trucks. Conrad recognized them. They were British-built all-wheel drive AECs, almost certainly inherited from the German Army. The AEC had a reputation for being able to go anywhere, anytime. Today, in a snow-covered Belgium, that reputation was being tested.

Civilians from all over Verviers, mostly women, Conrad noted, were lined up in the falling snow to collect the food aid that was being delivered. The reason was apparent when he struggled through the accumulating snow to reach the trucks. Not only were sacks of rice being handed out, but there were portions of meat being distributed. Pig carcasses were hanging up in the trucks so that everybody could see what sort of animal the meat came from. That it needed doing at all was something Conrad found disturbing.

Ahead of him, Rosina Neske picked up a sack of rice from one truck and started to carry it back to her home. The sacks had the same cartoon elephant on them as the ones he had seen in the displaced person camp, but were in different sizes. Each woman would hand up her ration cards for the people in her household, and be given a sack sized for that number of persons.

The process of sharing out the pork was slightly different. The meat was distributed from a truck that had its bed carefully screened from view. Each woman presented her ration cards to the driver. He would count them and call out a number. The paratroopers distributing the pork would then take out the correctly-sized portion and give it to the recipient when she appeared at the back of the truck. Conrad realized that the system meant who got what portion of meat was completely random. As he watched, one lady received a leg cutlet with the bone in the center. She scuttled off with her prize.

The next person to arrive at the back of the truck was Madame Margreet Neske. Conrad saw her being given a six-person ration of pork ribs. He had expected her to be disappointed, but the delight on her face suggested to him he had much to learn about running a kitchen. Then he saw something that amazed him. Each time a person was given a portion of pork, the paras handed the recipient a packet of herbs and seasonings. It was a detail that made him smile; the small gift seemed incredibly French somehow.

That was when a question occurred to him. He went up to the officer who was watching the distribution with a keen eye. He was wrapped up in camouflaged cold-weather clothing except for an oddly-shaped cloth cap. It was camouflaged as well, but it seemed inadequate to face the ever-increasing snow. He cleared his throat and started to speak, but never got beyond the first sound.

"Get back in line and wait your turn." The young lieutenant didn't sound as angry as his words indicated, but the young voice had a lot of authority in it. Then he turned around to see Conrad. "I am sorry, Father, can I help you?"

"It is I who owe you an apology, Lieutenant, for interrupting such worthy efforts. Truly to be distributing food in such weather is work pleasing to God. Would you have time to answer a few questions about aid distribution? A man was murdered here yesterday and there is a possibility that irregularities in food distribution may be connected with the crime."

The lieutenant smiled. "I will answer your questions on one condition, Father. You see those trucks there? They are AECs. Despite being made by *les singes capitulard,* they are good trucks and I have good drivers. But, in this weather, accidents can take place all too easily. If you will bless my trucks and my men before we leave, I will tell you what I can. Let me make a guess. Your first question is who shall guard the guards? The answer, Father, is that we guard each other."

"So I had heard. The administration of the displaced persons camp speaks highly of the French paratroopers who guard their supplies. I am Conrad Lorentz, by the way. Now, is much food stolen from the convoys, Lieutenant?"

"Please, Father, my name is Guy Fabron. From the convoys, no. A few desperate people may try to grab something from a truck that is halted for some reason or is distributing supplies. We are always on our guard if a road is blocked by a fallen tree or something. Enough of my men are from the Resistance that they know all the tricks. But, the weather is on our side. It is too bad for any organized attacks. What we have to deal with are single people taking what they believe is a chance. They are not bad people, Father, just desperate ones with a family to feed. Usually, I just give them a lecture and send them away."

"So, if food is stolen, it is either before you get it or after you deliver it?"

"That is what I would think, yes. More likely to be before we get it than after it is delivered. I cannot imagine people giving up their food lightly."

"Do you have people trying to buy food or other supplies with jewelry or other valuables?"

Fabron laughed, slightly grimly. "Only every day, Father. The only thing that cuts down the number of people who try and do so is that the Germans stole so much of value. But, as always, even the smallest items of value can be exchanged for food. Especially gold. You would be surprised how many people love gold so much that they would sell food to get it. Particularly, if they stole that food in the first place. This convoy might be a target for such theft, if it were not well guarded. You see, the food here is aid we have received. Well, most of it. The rice and other staples are additional to the rations people are entitled to."

"I wondered at the meat being handed out. The portions seem very generous."

"And they will remain so for a while. And then there will be none. You see, Father, the farmers cannot feed their livestock. Rather than watch their animals starve to death, they are killing their breeding stock. These pigs, on this truck, would have been the parents of next year's herds. Now, with them gone, there will be none. This famine will not end with the winter, Father."

"So, somebody who steals food and accumulates valuables will be in a better position to survive, come spring?"

"That is exactly right. A much better position. Or, if he steals valuable items and hides them away for the future. You said a man here was killed. Was he also robbed?"

"He was. We think. A gold tie-clip."

"I will tell my men and if anybody offers us a gold tie clip, we will bring them here. But, if the thief is wise, he will keep it hidden for times will surely get worse before they get better. Now, Father. We have finished unloading here. Is there anything else you wish to know before I assemble my men?"

"How was Verviers selected for today's distribution?"

"There is a list of towns in this area, in random order. As extra food becomes available, we are sent to the next town on the list. It is the only fair way."

"So, anybody who can see that list can know where the food convoys will be going."

"That is correct." Fabron suddenly looked very hard at Conrad. "That is correct. And it is a problem I must draw to the attention of my commander."

The paratroopers were in line by their vehicles. Conrad dabbed a tiny spot of his water on the hood of each vehicle and then the forehead of each soldier, intoning the words of a blessing as he did so. The gratitude on the faces of the paratroopers sent a warm glow though Conrad's heart. It compensated for the biting cold and falling snow, comforting him as he made his way into his lodgings.

Dining Room, Neske House, Rue Donkier

In reality, the house was no warmer than it had been the day before; but it seemed that it was. Margreet Neske had cut the pork ribs she had been given into small sections and simmered them with the first portions of rice. The resulting risotto had been carefully seasoned. Madam Neske hadn't made the mistake of overdoing the herbs and spices. She obviously was aware that people had become accustomed to bland food and had adjusted the recipe accordingly. That would also, of course, make the little packet of herbs last longer.

By the time everybody had finished eating, there was an air of satisfaction at the dining table that had been absent for a long time. There was also a wistfulness from everybody's knowledge that today's bounty would not soon be repeated.

"Madam Neske, may I ask something?" Conrad was still a little confused about the rations. Margreet Neske smiled at him, pleased with the knowledge that she had important information to share. "I thought that would you would have been displeased at getting the ribs, when another woman got a leg-steak. Obviously there is something here that I do not understand."

Madam Neske's smile broadened. "Father, the meat on that leg steak will be tough and tasteless, no matter how long it is cooked for. But, our ribs, gently simmered, are soft and tender. Much more important though is the broth we cooked them in. In this bitter cold, it will keep almost indefinitely. The rib bones will give it a rich favor that will season our turnips when the pork itself is but a memory. We did very well out of the distribution, Father, and I will be sure to give thanks for that."

Conrad returned her smile, pleased that his question had made a good woman happy, even if only for a moment. "Thank you, Madam. There is so much about running a kitchen that I do not know."

"You are not alone in that, Father. The children have grown up with rationing and food shortages and the ways of running a kitchen are being lost. I am teaching Rosina what I can, but there is barely enough food to keep us alive, let alone for teaching the children how to cook."

"Father, there are terrible stories amongst us." Rosina spoke as diffidently as always. From her tone, Conrad knew that the us in question represented herself and the other children. "We have heard that some of the meat that is sold on the black market is human meat. It comes from people. Surely this cannot be true?"

"What a dreadful thing to ask the good Father. And at our dinner table too!" Madam Neske's anger was feigned, though; when she waved her ladle at her daughter, it was half-hearted. "Human meat indeed. It cannot be true. Can it, Father?"

Conrad thought long and hard before answering. It wasn't just the content of his answer that troubled him. It was that the rumors fitted too many of the things he had seen over the last two or three days. The guarded cemetery; the pig carcasses hung up for all to see. They all fitted a pattern that was horrible to contemplate, yet he knew was all too common for times of famine. And there had never, to his knowledge, been a famine as bad as this one promised to be.

When he did speak, it was slowly and with great care. "In all the great sieges on the Russian Front, Smolensk, Stalingrad, Petrograd, Moscow, Gorkiy, Archangel'sk, people suffered great privations. They were starving and many of them tried to make soup out of things like glue or motor oil to survive. All too many of them died from trying to eat things that were poisonous. It is rumored that some people in those great sieges succumbed to temptation and ate meat taken from the bodies of their neighbors. I do not know of a case that was ever proven." *Because I never asked*, Conrad thought, *although I know of events in the past where such things have happened.* "I do know that the taboo against consuming our own kind is very great and it takes much for people to go against it. I would be more worried about black market meat being poisoned or radioactive."

"Stay away from the black market, Rosina." Madam Neske shot a look of gratitude to Conrad for giving her the opportunity to turn a tactless question into a valuable lesson. "Listen to what the Father says. The people who sell things there are liars and thieves. Why should they tell you the truth when they say what it is they are selling?"

Eye of the Despoiler

Gerard van Can leaned forward. "When I was in Copenhagen a few weeks ago, there was much concern about the fisheries. The herring being brought back from coastal waters are contaminated. The fishermen have to go further and further out from the coast each voyage to find fish that are safe to eat. I think it is all too likely that condemned fish are being stolen and sold on the black market."

There was much nodding at that conclusion. Dorothea Heimans was the one who drew the obvious conclusion. Or at least was the one who voiced it. "But what shall we do for food when we cannot eat the fish?"

There was no answer to that question and the shadows of the impending famine seemed to darken. Everybody knew Europe was eating its breeding stock of animals and its seed-grain. It had to, just to survive this terrible winter. It seemed as if everything was conspiring to bring about a cataclysm in northern Europe.

"There is one piece of good news." Van Can was obviously trying hard to lighten the mood. "I spoke to our managers today and told them of Rosina's idea about using telephone poles for power lines. They were most enthused and the suggestion went up the chain of command with great speed. We have been told that we will get the necessary line orders tomorrow. It will greatly speed up repairing the power grid. Rosina, I regret to have to tell you that my manager claims it was his idea. He will get all the credit."

"And that, my girl, is your lesson for today in the way of the world." Rosina's father looked at her with a twinkle in his eye.

"As long as we get some power." Rosina spoke bravely, although in truth she was greatly disappointed that somebody else would get the credit for her insight. The applause that followed her comment compensated for that disappointment a little.

"Well spoken, young lady." Van Can gave her the accolade with fervor.

"Is there any prospect of this terrible winter ending?" Dorothea Heimans was still distraught at the news that another source of food was in danger.

"The winter will end, it always does." Conrad wasn't actually as sure of that as he might have been. *Nobody knows what started the ice ages or brought them to an end. If they are at an end. Could it be that a tiny fall in temperature and a few unfavorable weather patterns might do it? This world of cold, dark summers and bitter winters might be the new normality.* "But I heard from the French soldiers that even when summer comes, food will still be in very short supply, here at least."

"It has been whispered . . ." Rosina was speaking in a very tiny voice, obviously scared of what she was saying. ". . . that there are recruiters going around who want young women to work in Spain and Italy, where it is warmer. As maids and nurses."

The adults exchanged glances, knowing all too well what any such recruiters would really want young women for. Yet, they were reluctant to say so, to put a name on it. And also, behind all of that, was a nagging question. *Even though the women who took such offers would be exposing themselves to great risks and terrible exploitation, would they still not be better off than here? Was a shameful life not better than a lingering death from cold and starvation?*

Suddenly Conrad realized that this was another possible explanation for Commissioner Morin's death. *Had such recruiters come to the displaced persons camp and tried to lure the younger women away?* Morin might very well have stopped them and they had removed him from their path. To such men, killing an administrator who stood in their path would be of little consequence. That would put his murder into the category of covering up another crime.

"Rosina, this is very important. Have you heard of such men approaching women with the kind of offer you describe? It may well have a bearing on the death of Commissioner Morin."

Conrad watched as Rosina's eyes clouded with confusion and then suddenly lit up with understanding. *She knows what really lies behind those offers and she has asked herself the same questions as everybody else was thinking.*

"No, Father. Not directly. The story is always that somebody had a friend whose sister or cousin was made such an offer." She smiled very shyly. "When I heard the story, I amused myself by thinking how rude I would be to anybody who made such an offer to me. I do not think that Mama and Papa would approve of the language I would use."

"Don't be too sure of that." Rosina's father was quite firm. "You be as rude as you like and then tell us right away. We will go to *Brigadier de Police* Bonnaire and have them run out of town. Such people we do not need here."

There was general agreement at that, then the conversation drifted away to other subjects. Conrad felt himself growing sleepy despite the cold eating into him. *Or is it because of the cold?* He was not displeased when people made their way to their rooms so they could sleep. That was another fact that Conrad had forgotten; the bitter cold made people tired so they slept far more than normal. Now that the thought was back in his mind, he remembered that such extended sleep was something from which too many people never awoke.

As he lay in his bed under the mound of coverings, his mind kept running over everything he had learned during the day. *None of it fits together. Much of it is contradictory and the patterns change every time I add something new. I feel that I am seeing parts of two pictures all mixed up and I will have to sort out which picture is which before I can make sense of them.*

Commissioner Morin's Office, Verviers Displaced Persons Camp

Before they had left the previous evening, Conrad and Bonnaire had replaced the glass top on the commissioner's desk so that the cards underneath wouldn't be disturbed. On entering the office, Conrad had looked down at them again and was shocked to see that the order had been neatly reversed. Now, covering up a crime had moved to the most probable spot, followed by sex, money and revenge. For a moment, he wasn't sure whether he was going mad or if somebody had interfered with the cards. Then, he looked again and realized that he had simply read the line of cards backwards. He shook his head, telling himself that the cold was slowing his mind down.

That was when he looked at the cards again. Conrad suddenly realized that the order he had mistakenly observed actually made a great deal of sense. *Based on what I learned the day before, black market racketeering and even viler forms of depravity are widespread enough to be a prevalent motive for the commissioner's death. It really does belong to the most probable class. And, based on what Rosina had said, some link to a form of the sex industry is an outgrowth of that motive. It needs to go in second place. That leads inevitably to the third category, money.* Conrad had little doubt that the black marketers and human traffickers were doing well in their vile exploitation of the suffering around them. *And killing Morin out of revenge for interfering in their operations completes the package.*

Many might have found it odd that Conrad didn't actually believe in miracles. He thought it far more likely that God preferred to achieve his wishes by small nudges at opportune moments that by some drastic display of wonder. They caused less trouble that way. He did not, however, doubt that his mistake of just a few second before had been one of those divine nudges. Suddenly, what had been a confusing mass of conflicting motives and opportunities had distilled into a neat and all-encompassing theory of the crime. It also changed several essential elements of the way Conrad had been thinking about the case.

Any further musings on the workings of Divine Providence were cut off by a knock on the door. Lieutenant Guy Fabron was leaning against the doorframe, watching Conrad quizzically. "Good morning, Father. Investigating another murder, I see?"

Conrad looked at the paratrooper sharply. He hadn't missed the 'another'. Fabron was smiling at him, an easy, good-natured smile. "Still the death of Commissioner Morin. I am afraid the case is beginning to develop some ugly overtones."

"Like the case on the *Ile de France* back in '29?" Fabron hesitated slightly. "Forgive me, Father, but you are a bit younger than I had expected."

Conrad quickly made some calculations. *The case on the* Ile de France *was 18 years ago and my supposed age back then was in my early thirties. So, that makes me fifty or thereabouts. And, remember, this friendly young paratrooper is a lot sharper than he seems.* "I was in America for most of the war. The hardship here makes people seem so much older than they are."

Fabron nodded. "I spent the war in Dakar. You know, Senegal. Our parachute regiment was formed there. We were supposed to be part of the invasion of Aquitaine, but it never happened, of course. Instead of doing a combat jump into Sainte-Hélène, we arrived at Bayonne on American C-99s. My first thought on leaving the aircraft was how old everybody here looked. Anyway, I checked you out. Father, forgive me but here and today, we can make no assumptions. Fortunately, the Gestapo just loved files and the one on the *Ile de France* case had survived the occupation and was easy to find. So, Father, I found our regimental doctor and asked him to come down here with me. It seemed to me you probably need some specialized help."

This young man is sharp indeed. And it seems that the Seer's concerns are well founded. As news records and official files become more extensive and accessible, the risk they pose to us becomes greater. "You have no idea how right you are. We haven't even been able to perform an autopsy yet. One good thing about this constant cold; the body is still preserved and ready for your doctor."

"He may already be at work. The young lady outside was very helpful and offered to take him to where the body has been placed. She seemed . . . very fond . . . of the victim."

Dispensary, Verviers Displaced Persons Camp

"Anyway, Conrad, we were told we would be dropping at Sainte-Hélène on June 30th. Our other battalions were dropping at Carcans and Hourtin. They were the three main road junctions, you see. We would hold them while two French divisions landed along the Lacanau Beach. Only, the planners called the northern part of Lacanau Sword and the southern part Hammer. One name for each beach assigned to a division. Then, we'd have swept straight in to Bordeaux. The whole landing force north of the Gironde was to be French. Even the ships giving us fire support were French. But, of course, none of it ever happened. The B-36s did their work first."

"Do you think it would have worked, Guy? The invasion, I mean?" Sometime in the walk from Morin's office to the dispensary, the lieutenant of paratroopers and the Jesuit priest had become Guy and Conrad.

Fabron thought for a minute of two. "It would all depend on the first few hours. There is a 40-meter ridge between the beaches and Bordeaux. We were being dropped along that ridge. If we held it until we were relieved, then yes, we would have taken Bordeaux the first day. South of the Gironde, it was the same. If the American marines had taken that ridge after their paratroopers had dropped on it, then they would have taken Bayonne very quickly. They had to, of course; we needed that port. After the initial phase of the landings, the fight would have been much harder. I think few of us would have lived to see Paris liberated. The B-36s did their work well and saved us from that."

And it is well that the invasion was never more than a decoy and an insurance policy against the failure of Dropshot. I wonder if my young friend here suspects that his invasion was a giant hoax.

Conrad was suddenly aware that Fabron was looking at him with a mischievous grin on his face and realized that his brief silence had been misinterpreted. "So, Conrad, I mention the B-36 and you think of the Champs Elysee. Yes?"

"I know that many Americans regret it and think it was a bad mistake."

"So do many Frenchmen. But not all of us and that is an issue at the elections. De Gaulle decries the bombing and condemns those who planned it. Marshal Purneaux decries it also, but says that we brought it on ourselves by our worship of the past and neglect of the future. De Gaulle wishes to restore the France that was; Purneaux wants to build a new France whose future is all that it can be."

"How do you feel, Guy?"

"Conrad, I am a para. We go to battle by jumping out of aircraft, not riding horses. The para regiments will break solidly for Purneaux. But, whoever wins, we can be thankful for one thing. We are not *les singes capitulard.* We *fought.*"

"And there speaks a true para." A man in a stained white coat looked up as the two men entered the dispensary. "Father, I see you have met some of our gallant paras. I will tell you this. When the Devil comes to collect their souls, they will shoot at him. Of that, you can be certain. I am Renard Lémieux, the doctor condemned to care for this gang of cutthroats and brigands."

"What do you expect our army to do with a doctor who is also a barbarous Breton? Now, if you were a civilized Frenchman, they would have put you in a cavalry regiment where you could hear about how they won the Battle of Austerlitz. Every night and twice on Sundays." Fabron had his usual mischievous grin firmly in place.

"And is your beloved Marshal Purneaux not also a Breton?" Lémieux's counter was equally friendly.

Fabron laughed and made a quick gesture of concession. "That he is. Now, *Toubib,* what have you learned for Conrad here?"

"Well, we have a man in late middle age, malnourished and in poor overall health. He has multiple bruises and broken bones in his arm and both legs. All of those are consistent with the fall that killed him."

"Wait a minute." Conrad was shocked. "The fall killed him? What about the wound to the side of his head?"

Lémieux folded his lower lip between his teeth. "That wound. Yes, it would have killed him in time. There was bleeding under his skull that would have been fatal had it been left untreated. But, it hadn't killed him when he fell. In fact, a man in better health, and properly fed, might well have survived the fall, only to die of the blow to his head. But the victim's bones were weak and fractured easily with the fall. Some fragments pierced his heart; others cut open blood vessels. I looked at where the body was found; the amount of blood there shows he was alive when he fell."

"We thought that he was struck a blow on the head that killed him, then his body was taken up to a stack of sacks and thrown down to make it look like an accident." Conrad was deeply upset at having made such an elementary mistake. *The cold must be slowing my brain down. I should have realized there was too much blood in the second pool to have come from a dead man. God have mercy on me, that stupidity could have caused an innocent man to be accused.*

"The killer may have very well thought that." Lémieux pondered the matter for a few seconds. "The commissioner would have fallen immediately on receiving the blow and the killer may well have assumed he was dead. Do you know what the weapon used was?"

"I thought a lead or steel pipe."

"A very good guess, I think. Let us look closer." Lémieux bent over Morin's head and probed gently at the wound above his ear. "There is no debris in the wound that I can see. That would suggest a metal club. Oh, wait. I think I see something."

Lémieux probed gently at the wound with a pair of tweezers and came out with a fine black spike. "Now that might well be debris from the killer's weapon. A wooden splinter."

"But it could equally have come the floor or been pushed in the wound while the body was being moved." Fabron looked around with disgust. "This place needs to be swept properly."

"There are few women to sweep the floors and the men will not clean up properly." Madame Annick sounded offended that the cleaning standards of the rooms met with such disapproval, although Conrad guessed she was really trying to keep herself composed while the death of her lover was being discussed in such clinical terms.

"Madame, my apologies. I meant no disrespect." Fabron was genuinely appalled that his words had distressed a lady. "In the Army, we get used to making the men sweep their barracks every time they have nothing better to do.

We make it clear that the alternative is making them run around the parade ground until they die."

For the first time in days, or longer, Mari Annick giggled. "Lieutenant, you must teach me how to achieve such things."

"Only if you call me Guy, not Lieutenant. Otherwise I must assume I am not forgiven for my ill-chosen words."

Although Conrad's face never moved a muscle, inside he was also chuckling. *Dear Lord, the French never change.*

Annick's giggle turned to a real smile. "But of course you are forgiven, Guy. And you were right, the floor here is too dirty for a dispensary."

At that point something clicked in Conrad's mind. He looked at the floor again. It really was dirty and covered with debris. He could make out the footprints of the four people currently in the room but that was all. *So few people come here, in a dispensary for a displaced person's camp this large?*

"Madam Annick, how many people come here for treatment?"

"Almost none, Father. People are afraid of medicines now. They believe that the bombing has changed them so they no longer help the sick. Some even believe they know people who have died from medicines the Americans changed with their atomic bombs."

Conrad, Fabron and Lémieux stared at each other in sudden mutual comprehension. It was Lémieux who broke the brief spell. "Oh my God. Sorry, Father, but if this is true . . . Madam Annick, where do you keep the medicines?"

"In the cupboards. Commissioner Morin had the keys." Her face suddenly went white as she realized what the three men had understood just a few seconds earlier. "And the keys were not on him when the body was found."

The doors to the medicine cabinets were locked. Fabron shrugged and produced a wicked looking knife from his belt. He thrust it into the crack between the cabinet doors, twisted and stood back as the doors flew open.

"You see? Cutthroats and brigands." Lémieux's stage-whisper to Conrad carried around the dispensary,

There was a wide selection of bottles inside the cabinets, most of which showed no sign of having been touched for weeks. Fabron made short work of opening the other cabinets, revealing the same array of disused bottles. "Hey, *Toubib*, these are called medicines. I think they work better than your spells and incantations."

"I wouldn't be too sure of that." Lémieux took one of the bottles down. "This is supposed to be stomach powder. Doesn't look like any stomach powder I've ever seen."

"You mean, you've actually seen some stomach powder? Conrad, a prayer of thanks, please; our *Toubib* has actually seen a bottle of real medicine."

"If I hadn't before, I still wouldn't have." Lémieux had very cautiously stuck a fingertip into the contents of the bottle and even more cautiously touched his tongue to it.

His reaction had been immediate; he spat the tiny amount of powder out. Fabron had quickly handed him a water bottle and watched while the doctor thoroughly rinsed out his mouth. At first, Conrad had been alarmed, for the doctors spittle had been bright red; but he realized Fabron had parted with his precious red wine ration to help the doctor clean out his mouth.

"That stuff is mostly chalk dust." Lémieux was appalled at what he had found. "But there is something else in there as well. Something very bitter. Strychnine, perhaps."

Madam Annick clapped her hand over her mouth. "You mean our medicines have been poisoned?"

Lémieux thought carefully. "Perhaps not. A very, very dilute solution of strychnine causes vomiting. It may be that somebody stole the original contents of the bottle and replaced it with this . . . filth . . . thinking its effects would hide the change."

"That's horrible." Annick still had her hand over her mouth.

"It could be only the start. We must have every bottle in this dispensary checked." Fabron's good-natured bonhomie had vanished completely and he was suddenly a very professional army officer taking over a critical situation.

"Mari, do you have an inventory of what should be here? If so, get it quickly. I will need a telephone also. If you do not have one, there is a communications set in my jeep. I will go out and use that. My superiors must be told of this development immediately."

Fabron and Annick left, leaving Conrad and Lémieux to guard the dispensary. They looked at each other in shock, stunned by the way the case had suddenly exploded. Conrad broke the silence. "Doctor Lémieux, what is a *toubib*?"

Lémieux laughed, more from a nervous reaction than anything else. "Para slang for a doctor. It is a corruption of the North African Arabic word for doctor. It is, of course, quite insulting. What do you think is happening to the stolen medicines?"

"Being sold on the black market, of course. What I don't understand is why they stole real medicines and replaced them with fake. Why do they not simply sell the fake medicine?"

Conrad answered his own question almost immediately. "The black marketers go to an area and start to sell medicine, but everybody is suspicious of them. So they start by selling the real stuff and those who buy it report that it is indeed real. So people flock to them and they make a killing selling them the false medicines.

"By the time people realize that they have been duped, the black marketers are gone. This means that the whole racket is much greater than just the stolen bottles here."

"Much greater. There is no reason why this camp should be alone in its problem. I would bet a week's rations that all the displaced persons camps are suffering this way. The scale of this racketeering could be very large indeed. And, a black market operation of this size could not survive without the backing of corrupt officials."

Refugee Compound, Displaced Persons Camp, Verviers

"And so, Étienne, I think we must completely reconsider our theory of this crime." Conrad had been explaining the morning's developments to the policeman and, in doing so, had clarified them in his own mind. "If our fears about the medical supplies reaching this camp, and others like it, are correct, then we have to consider the possibility that we are dealing with a widespread black-marketeering conspiracy that may reach into the upper echelons of the government."

"Forgive me, Father, but I cannot agree with that. Such a widespread enterprise would need good communications and a strong central authority to control it. Otherwise, it would quickly collapse, as the various parts came into conflict. As a simple policeman, I can tell you that most crimes are solved when the criminals taking part fall out over the proceeds of their crimes. They fight and the losers inform on the winners. Here, it is quite impossible for such a conspiracy to be effective."

That worried Conrad, and he reminded himself that Bonnaire was a local policeman who had rarely, if ever, dealt with crimes more serious than poaching or the occasional burglary. *He is judging this issue within his own terms of reference and limited experience. If he had ever dealt with organized crime in America, he would know that criminal racketeering can prosper in the absence of central control. All that is needed is that fear should overcome greed.*

"That may well be true, but we do have at least one case of medicines that have been stolen and replaced by an imitation. An imitation that is potentially lethal. Now, let us find our first contact."

Mari Annick had prepared a list for Conrad, one that included all the people Commissioner Morin had met in the days before his death. The first name on that list was supposed to be living in one of the huts just off the path Conrad and Bonnaire were walking along.

"Herr Marius Dressler?"

The man was shoveling the newly-fallen snow away from the front of the hut. At the sound of Conrad's voice, he stopped working and rested on his spade. Moving even freshly fallen snow was exhausting work for a malnourished man. "I am Dressler."

"I am Conrad Lorenz and this is *Brigadier de Police* Bonnaire. We are investigating the death of Commissioner Morin and we know that you talked with him a few days before his death. May we ask what you discussed with him?"

"No." The reply was short and uncompromising.

Conrad blinked and tried again. "We are trying to find out what issues concerned the commissioner in the days before he was killed. Your help could be invaluable to us."

Dressler said nothing but started to resume his digging. Instead, Bonnaire put his foot firmly on the spade and held it down. "You misunderstand the good Father's courtesy. He asked you if you would answer our questions. I, on the other hand, as a *brigadier de police*, am telling you that you will answer our questions. If not here, then we will take you away to where we can speak at length."

The truculent expression on Dressler's face was replaced by raw fear. It was an ingrained response; everybody knew that the people who were taken away by the police never returned. "It was private business. That's all."

"There is no such thing as private business in a murder inquiry." Bonnaire was relentless. Conrad realized that, at last, he had found something that he could do in this investigation and a role he could play.

"I had heard that my daughter had arrived in another camp soon. I had asked the commissioner if he could confirm that she was safe and if one of us could move so we could be together."

Conrad frowned slightly. This was another piece of the picture that didn't fit. "Where did your daughter come from?"

"My family came from Dusseldorf. I thought I had lost them all in the bombing but suddenly I got the message that my daughter had escaped Germany and would be arriving in another camp soon."

"But the border with Germany is closed. Nobody comes out of there. It's too dangerous for anybody to move outside the areas they are already in." Conrad was bewildered by what he was hearing. It was contrary to everything he had been given to understand.

"The Amis move around in there, don't they? If they can, why can't other people?" Dressler sounded furious. "But I don't know anything about any of that. All I know is that my daughter survived the bombing and she said she would be coming out soon. She was supposed to be going to another camp, only she never showed up. So I went to see the commissioner about it. He said he couldn't help. Said the same thing you did; that the borders were closed and that nobody left Germany. That the hellburners had left the country too dangerous to move around in."

The next question was going to be very delicate and Conrad knew it. But it had to be asked. "When you heard that your daughter was coming out to join you, did the person who told you ask for any money? Or anything else?"

Dressler seemed to cave in suddenly. "They wanted money, to get my daughter out. They said they had to pay bribes to the guards on the border so she could cross. I gave them everything I had and promised them more. Anything they wanted."

"Who was it who came to tell you this? And asked for the money?" Bonnaire seemed exasperated at Dressler's foolishness. Conrad understood the emotion, even if he couldn't condone it. Bonnaire was either a bachelor or a widower and he had no children of his own. He couldn't comprehend the lengths a parent would go to if there was a small chance of recovering a lost child.

"I do not know. I hadn't seen them before. The one who spoke to me, he stood in the shadows most of the time. And his hat was pulled down over his eyes. I couldn't see his face properly; it was disguised somehow."

"And yet you still gave him everything you had?" There was derision in Bonnaire's voice. "Without proof?"

"Of course not!" Dressler was getting angry again. "The man, he had a ring, one that had once belonged to my wife. I recognized it instantly. He said that my daughter had saved my wife's jewelry and gave it to them to buy her way out. Only it wasn't enough. They needed more."

Bonnaire and Conrad exchanged glances. It was painfully obvious to them both that Dressler had been taken in by a well-constructed hoax. *Even if his daughter really is alive, which I very much doubt, she is not coming out of Germany. The confidence men who constructed this hoax have been very careful and probably have much practice in similar extortions. I even doubt if the ring he saw was really his wife's. Probably a generic ring, one that was simple enough to look like anything. That, and wishful feelings, would fool a man into seeing what was not there.*

"Herr Dressler, I must ask you to accompany me to the *gendarmerie*." Bonnaire suddenly spoke with crisp authority. "There are more questions I wish to ask you about this affair."

"Étienne, don't you think this is premature?"

301

"Father, you are a good man, and one worthy of much respect, but this case is quite clear to me now. Herr Dressler here heard from the criminals that they had got his daughter out and she was in another camp. He went to see Commissioner Morin and ask if he could be transferred to the same camp, or if she could be transferred here. The commissioner checked with the other camp and found the information was wrong. Herr Dressler did not believe him. You will note how he slipped up when we first talked and said that his daughter had got out, not was getting out. He assumed that Commissioner Morin was extorting more money from him. He had, after all, been the victim of one group of extortionists. Faced with another, he lost his temper and struck the commissioner, killing him. He is our man, Father, I am sure of it."

Bonnaire's impassioned speech came as a great relief to Conrad. The thing that had worried him above all others in this case was that there had been no innocent person he had to protect. Now, with the arrest of Herr Dressler, he had that innocent person. He was guilty of being rude and aggressive certainly. In the eyes of the French and Belgians, he was guilty of being German. But he was not guilty of the murder of Commissioner Morin. Conrad was sure of that. Even if he had not been, he knew that the case against Dressler was so weak that any court would throw it out on the spot. *Dear Lord, protect him. The case he faces is even weaker than that against George McManus, and I know who really killed the man he was accused of murdering. That case was thrown out by the judge before his lawyers even started their defense.*

Bonnaire had seized Dressler and was walking him towards the *kubelwagen*. "Étienne, you are taking him to be charged?"

"That would be premature, Father. No, I am taking him to our cells where, as the prime suspect, he will be questioned and expected to prove his innocence. Can I drop you back in Verviers on the way?"

Conrad had noted there was an American jeep outside the camp administrative building. One that had not been there a few minutes before. "No, Étienne, thank you, I have more to do here."

CHAPTER THREE

THE BLACK MARKET

Commissioner Morin's Office, Verviers Displaced Persons Camp

"Father, I'm glad I found you."

"And I you, Guy. I think I have discovered another angle to this case. Please, you go first."

"We have checked the medicines we took from here. They are all useless. Mostly a mixture of salt and chalk, with other things in there to give them a semblance of some effect. Our *toubib* was right, what was supposed to be stomach powder had a trace of strychnine in it. If somebody took too much, or too often, it could kill them. At some point in the distribution channels, the real medicine was stolen and replaced by the forgeries."

"Are we sure it was ever genuine?"

"We were able to trace the source of the supply. It came over the Atlantic as aid, from America. We even know the C-99 that brought it. Last night, we were able to telegram the company in America with the batch number and they told us what it was supposed to be. It was old, made in 1945 under a U.S. Army contract, but it had two years to go before it expired. It's just a mixture of kaolinite and pectin."

"And morphine." Conrad added, absently.

"They didn't say that." Fabron's comment was slightly sharper than before. "That explains a lot. We were wondering why anybody would steal clay and pectin but, if there's morphine in there . . . You wouldn't happen to know how much, would you?"

"Just a trace. It slows down the movement of the bowels and gives the other ingredients time to work." *Thank you Naamah for the occasional lesson in basic healing potions.* "But, given the situation here and in Germany, I think that medicines to reduce diarrhea and other stomach complaints would be worth much, with or without morphine."

"Perhaps. Although, I am inclined to look hard at that morphine. I wonder how hard it is to extract? Anyway, Conrad, you said you had some insight into this case as well?"

"I do indeed, Guy. I spoke with one of the people who met with Commissioner Morin before his death." Conrad quickly related the important details of his conversation with Dressler.

"And so our policeman has arrested Dressler and taken him to the station for questioning." Fabron looked quizzically upwards at a watery sun trying to pierce the silver veil of high-altitude clouds. "I agree, Conrad. The only thing Dressler is guilty of is multiple counts of being German."

"Is it possible that there is a racket built around getting refugees out of Germany?"

"Of course it's possible. Conrad, imagine you are living in one of the German refuges and you could get out. But, there is one chance in a hundred of being killed by the radiation. Would you take it?"

Conrad didn't even hesitate. "Of course."

"Now, suppose the odds were one in ten. Would you still take it?"

This time Conrad thought about it. "I suppose so. It depends how bad things in there really are."

"Oh, they're bad. Epidemics are running riot through the survivors. Typhoid, typhus, you name it. One in three?"

Conrad shook his head. "No, with those odds it's better to stay put. By the way, I think you've just told us where the stolen medicines are going."

"My superiors agree. Now, suppose you are in a refuge. Somebody says they know a way out and you don't know the odds. But, nobody you know has made it out. Will you take the chance?"

Conrad thought about that a long time. "I wouldn't. But somebody with the enthusiasm of youth might think they would be the ones to beat the odds. And, something else, Guy. The people running the racket won't want the people they get out to stay silent. They'll want word to get out so that others will know that it can be done."

"Go on." Fabron was curious as to where this was going.

"Imagine this. Dressler finds out that his daughter is escaping, but the smugglers want more money. He goes to Commissioner Morin to ask for help, perhaps, or simply to make arrangements for him to be with his daughter. But, the Commissioner is an honest man and an honorable one. He will not countenance a crime, let alone one that will risk spreading the epidemics you speak of into this area. So, he goes to the criminals and threatens to expose them. Do they kill him? Of course not. They laugh at him, shake him by the hand and thank him very much. Because his exposing them will prove to all the people who want to escape from Germany that a way exists, and is relatively safe. They are the last people who would kill Commissioner Morin."

"I do not think I have ever heard of being part of a criminal affair used as a defense before. Conrad, do you get the feeling this is turning into a most unusual case?"

"Guy, let me show you something. Could you help me move this glass to one side please?"

Once the glass was shifted and the cards on Morin's desk exposed, Conrad pointed to the top four. "Those are the primary motives for murder. Covering up another crime, money, sex and revenge, in that order. Now, let us write out additional cards for the crimes we have identified. They are the theft of food and its sale on the black market, the theft of medicines and their sale, smuggling refugees in from Germany, and extorting money from people by pretending to smuggle people in from Germany.

"Now, all of these fit very well into the first category. Only the last fits into the second and none fit well into the rest. But, we have already concluded that those responsible for the trafficking are most unlikely to kill the commissioner. That would eliminate them from this investigation, unless all other suspects have been eliminated from suspicion."

Fabron nodded in agreement. "There is also a very good possibility that the food and medicine black marketers are linked in with the human trafficking. It is a natural pattern of trade; food and drugs into the German refuges one way, bringing people back out the other. That kind of trade is very profitable, as long as it remains undisturbed. I do not think such people would kill somebody as prominent as the commissioner. It would create too much disturbance and interfere with their business. I can see them killing an amateur who tried to compete with them, but not a senior official."

"Guy, ever since this case started, I have had the impression that there are two quite different cases here, all mixed up with each other, and the great problem was telling which pieces belonged to which case. Now, I think we can see where the division lies. The murder of Commissioner Morin is not part of the black marketeering or the human trafficking, although I suspect there may be an indirect link to them.

"And there is another criminal activity going on here, Guy. I have heard that young girls are being approached, offered work as maids or nurses in Italy and Spain, well away from the wreckage that is northern Europe. The girls claim that they hear of such offers only at second or third hand, and that they have never personally been approached. But, they are well aware of what those offers really mean. I think the fact that, even knowing that, they consider accepting them is frightening them."

"I suspect that this trade is linked with human trafficking from Germany." Fabron was not surprised by the news. "In fact, I would think that the primary route would be from Germany outwards, and this would only be a stop along that route. Indeed, the women you spoke with may have heard echoes of refugees being moved through this region. This would explain why they have not been approached themselves. The women from Germany would never be missed. I doubt if any of them have relatives or friends over this side of the border."

"One did," said Conrad.

Truck Convoy, Rue de Grande Rechain, outside Bruyers, Belgium

> "J'aime l'oignon frît à l'huile,
> J'aime l'oignon quand il est bon,
> J'aime l'oignon frît à l'huile,
> J'aime l'oignon, j'aime l'oignon.
>
> Au pas camarade, au pas camarade,
> Au pas, au pas, au pas.
> Au pas camarade, au pas camarade,
> Au pas, au pas, au pas."

The singing from the trucks at the front and rear of the little convoy echoed off the snow-covered banks of the road and blended with the roar of the diesel engines that pushed the six-by-six trucks along the icy road. In the cab of the lead AEC truck, Lieutenant Fabron was singing enthusiastically with his men. He and Conrad were sitting in the cab, with four paratroopers in the back. Behind them were two cargo-carrying trucks, then a fourth AEC with six more men in it. In all, sixteen men. An appropriate escort for the cargo these trucks carried.

"You know, Conrad, you shouldn't be here. This could get very dangerous, very quickly." Fabron glanced at his friend without ceasing his musical tribute to the alleged virtues of fried onions.

"Which is what anybody watching us will think. That you would not bring a civilian, let alone a priest, on anything other than a routine supply run."

Fabron nodded in reluctant agreement. The plans for the delivery today had been carefully discussed with Major Jourdain Roul, who was in command of the parachute company in this area. Initially, Conrad's request to accompany the convoy had been rejected out of hand but Conrad's patient arguments had won the day. And so, when the delivery roster for the day had been posted, it had included the note that a civilian would be riding on the trucks. The note was right before the single word that announced the cargo. Penicillin.

Everybody knew about the American wonder drug, penicillin. How it could save even those suffering from the worst stages of pneumonia or laid low by blood poisoning from a wound. There were those who whispered that penicillin could even save those dying from radiation poisoning. Conrad knew that wasn't true. *There is only one thing that can help somebody dying from acute radiation poisoning. A cup of Naamah's special tea.*

That didn't change the reality of what penicillin could do, though. That reality made the white powder the most valuable substance in Europe. The black market would do anything to get its hands on a supply of penicillin and every gram of it was subject to rigorous safeguards. The supply of penicillin in these trucks represented the only source of the wonder drug in Belgium. Conrad believed that by the time the black marketeers had finished diluting it, the cargo would be worth more than a million dollars.

The black marketers would do almost anything to get their hands on a million dollar's worth of penicillin. Even take on French paras.

"I never knew the paras were so devoted to fried onions." Conrad was humming along to the song as it echoed around the convoy.

"Nobody ever understands what soldiers like to sing about." Fabron roared out the punchline of the song, *"mais pas pour la singes capitulard,"* with gusto. "When our regiment was formed, there was a competition to write a marching song for us. The first line of the winning entry was 'we jumped into battle for the honor and glory of France.' Within a day, my boys had re-written it as 'we jumped sixteen thousand meters without a parachute.' And so it has been sung ever since."

Conrad tilted his head back and roared with laughter, letting out all the tension that had been building up since the case had started. He carefully dabbed the tears from his eyes and looked over at Fabron. Suddenly, Conrad was aware of a very faint, very mild, tickling sensation in the back of his mind. He decided to take a small chance.

"How old are you, Guy?"

"Twenty-seven, Conrad."

There was something in the way he answered that aroused Conrad's inquisitorial interest. "I mean, how old are you, really?"

Fabron looked sideways at him and smiled wryly. "That will teach me to lie to a priest. I am twenty-four, Father. I was a year underage when I joined up. But I was big for my age and nobody questioned it. With France in its hour of need, there were those younger than I who stood up and wore the uniform. Some are with us today."

Conrad smiled softly and thought quietly to himself. *If my guess is right, Guy, you have a long life ahead of you. Provided your chosen profession doesn't get you killed.*

"*Merde.* Here we go." Fabron's words cut off Conrad's train of thought. Up ahead, a tree had fallen over and blocked the road. It was one part of a small patch of trees and looked as if the snow had brought it down. A ruined farmhouse was just off to the left, one that provided adequate cover for an ambush. "You stay here, Conrad. It doesn't look like it, but you're behind twelve millimeters of armor plate. I don't want to see you out of this cab."

There was authority in his voice that Conrad had no wish to challenge. Fabron brought his truck to a stop and got out. He wandered over to the tree and inspected it. "We will need everybody to move it. Dismount and come help us."

The two men in the cab of each truck got down. They joined Fabron by the tree. The eight guards in the first and last trucks got down as well. There were fifteen men around the tree, starting to heave it clear, when shots rang out.

There were eight men in all; four in the ruins of the old farmhouse, four in the group of trees. One man in each group had a rocket launcher; the rest had ex-German Stg-45 rifles. *Banana guns,* thought Conrad. *And all those weapons are trained on the men by the trees. This could be a massacre.*

"Hey, Paras. There's no need for anybody to get killed today. We just want what is in the trucks. Don't give us any cause to start shooting."

"You want what is in the trucks? All right. You can have it." Fabron shouted the reply at the top of his voice.

His last words were drowned out by the withering blast of machine gun fire that roared out from the two middle trucks. Both contained four MG-45 crews, two each side. The firepower they put out was enormous.

The ambushers were watching the paras around the fallen tree and had their backs to the trucks. Both men with rocket launchers, and at least half the riflemen, were cut down before they had a chance to understand what was happening. The rest realized they had been tricked. They threw down their rifles and raised their hands. The whole ambush and counter-ambush had taken barely more than a single second.

Conrad stayed put in his cab. Doctor Lémieux swung himself down from the back of the third truck. He made his way to the casualties from the first group of ambushers, sprawled on the ground. He looked briefly at each one, shook his head and went to the other group. He made the same quick inspection, with the same shake of the head. Five of the eight men who had tried to halt the truck convoy were dead. That was when Fabron waved Conrad over.

"Conrad, we have done our work, the *toubib* has done his, now you must do yours." Conrad sighed slightly and went over to the bodies of the men on the ground. He could see why Doctor Lémieux had been so cursory with his inspection. The bodies were mangled, almost beyond recognition. *People talk so much about banning inhumane weapons, as if any other such things existed. If they could see what simple rifle bullets can do to a human body, they would be less keen to make judgments.*

He reminded himself that it didn't even take rifle bullets to inflict grievous injury. Before coming to Europe, he had gone to visit Igrat at the home on Long Island she shared with Mike Collins. He had known how badly hurt she had been in Geneva a year earlier. She had greeted him at the door, seemingly recovered from her ordeal. Yet he had noticed that, tucked out of casual sight, was the wheelchair she still had to use because her injuries and illness made her tire so easily.

He walked down the line of shattered bodies, administering the appropriate benedictions to each of the five dead men. The other three were sitting on their heels, their hands on their heads. He could sense their fear. Not quite so much of death itself, but of not knowing whether they were going to die.

"Help us. Father. I beg you." One of the men muttered the words while he looked down at the ground.

"The best help I can give you is good advice. Answer questions truthfully and hide nothing. These are good men, honest and honorable." Conrad tried not to notice the paratroopers looking at each other with feigned puzzlement and mouthing 'who, us?'

"The father speaks the truth." Major Roul had dismounted from the back of his truck and was inspecting the scene. "Answer our questions honestly, do not deceive us and you will not suffer for it. Be honest with yourselves, as well as us. Are you so important in this gang that we should waste time and effort on you?"

"It's true." One of the men spoke up. "I tried to steal food from a truck like this before. The lieutenant there caught me and I thought he would kill me then. But he just gave me a lecture on my own stupidity and kicked me up the backside to help me on my way home. And we are of no importance to men like Harry Lime. We owe him nothing."

"Who is Harry Lime?" Fabron asked the question.

Conrad noticed that Major Roul stayed out of the way, although he watched the interrogation of the three survivors with keen attention.

"He is an American. We do not know his real name. He took the name Harry Lime from the radio show."

Conrad recognized the reference. The radio show was an NBC production about an adventurer in Cairo who moved in the shady area between normal society and the underworld of gangsters, spies and black marketeers. *He was a man who had his own code of honor and ethics and the shows usually ended with him doing the right thing because the need to do so conformed to that code. It could well be that he chose that name because it fits his self-image. If not of the man he is, but the man he would like to be.*

He caught Fabron's eye. The lieutenant gave him a quick nod. *He probably has heard the show on American Forces Network and has drawn the same conclusions I did.* Conrad spoke quietly to his friend. "Guy, I wonder how they were going to tell this Harry Lime that they had the penicillin he wanted?"

"Let us find out, shall we?" Fabron turned to one of the three survivors. "Once you had the penicillin, what were you to do? How would you tell Harry Lime you had succeeded?"

The man spoke readily, desperate to seize the chance of salvation that had been offered to him. "We were to take the penicillin to a small village, not far from here. Herve. There is a working telephone there. We were to call a number from there and tell Harry that we had the stuff. He would then tell us where to take it so he could meet us and give us our money."

Fabron went over and spoke quietly to Major Roul. There was much nodding of heads. Then Fabron returned. "Well, Father, we have a plan. If you are willing, you could be an important part of it."

9 Place le Comte, Herve, Belgium.

"Yes, we got the stuff, Harry, but it was a disaster. The paras fought back . . .

"Yes, we did it the way you said, but they still tried to fight. Somebody started shooting, and by the time it was over, five of our people were dead and a dozen paras . . .

"It was horrible, their bodies were scattered all over the road. We just got out of there. We got the stuff though . . .

"No, moving it is going to be bad. There are paras pouring into the area. Whole regiment of them, at least. They're searching everybody. One man made a joke; said he had an atomic bomb in his pocket. They made him strip naked and stand in the snow while they carefully searched every item of clothing he had. He'll get pneumonia for sure."

The man on the telephone listened for a couple of minutes. "*D'accord.*" He put the receiver down.

Then, he took a deep breath. "Harry Lime is going to come here to collect the penicillin. He says that you won't search him. We are to wait here for him."

Major Roul thought quickly. "We go with the plan we had settled on. Fabron, you take eight men and the father here to Soumaigne. We have a company headquarters there. Lime must go past it to get here. So, there we will be mourning our dead for him to see. Father, holding a fake mass for the dead will not conflict with your beliefs?"

Conrad shook his head. "It will not be a fake mass. We will have the five men who were killed in the ambush placed out for everybody to see and seven more stretchers, covered with bloodied blankets. I will hold the mass for those five men and them alone, but those seeing it will assume it is for twelve." *And, even if God does not accept my little deception, my soul could hardly be damned more than it is already.*

Roul nodded. "Good. The rest of us will wait here and pick up this "Harry Lime" when he appears.

Cantonment, Premier Compagnie, 2e Régiment de Chasseurs Parachutistes, Soumaigne, Belgium.

"Major Roul sounds like an experienced man. And not just military experience." Conrad was back in his seat in the lead truck. It was different now. The trucks each had four blanket-covered bodies in their cargo areas. Five of the bodies were real. Seven were just more blankets made to look like the torn-up bodies of men. All the blankets were liberally soaked with blood and each had one of the oddly-shaped, lizard-camouflaged caps on it.

"He is. He served with the *16e Regiment d'Infanterie Coloniale* in Indochina and then was transferred to the *5e Regiment Etranger d'Infanterie . . .*"

"The Foreign Legion!" Conrad spoke the hallowed name with awe. "I didn't know he was a legionnaire."

"He wasn't. He was transferred after the 16th RIC was broken in the fighting with the Thais. Then he was taken prisoner when the Indochina Army was defeated at Yang Dham Khung. The 5th REI has never been reformed; the Legion has no place for units that admit defeat while a man still stands. He was in a Thai prisoner of war camp for a few months, then was released when the peace agreement was signed. He, and the man who now commands our regiment, Colonel Belloc, made their way to Senegal to join with General de Gaulle. When the 2nd RCP was formed, General de Gaulle went to great lengths to pick out men who were experienced and had fought well. He also made a point of finding men who had tasted defeat and who had sworn never to do so again."

Fabron was about to say something more, but the little convoy had reached the command post. The play was about to start. There were paratroopers standing in the forecourt of the cantonment. They were bareheaded, despite the driving snow, with their submachine guns reversed. As each truck came to a halt, men stepped forward to take the covered bodies from the back. A lone trumpeter sounded "*Aux Mortes*".

In a measured slow-step, the stretchers were carried in to the barracks. Then the empty truck pulled out. Another pulled in and the process was repeated. Conrad was in the third truck to be unloaded. He dismounted from the cab, took out his Bible and started to intone the words. Nobody not part of the deception could know that the stretchers he was praying over were the only ones carrying genuine bodies in the procession.

As the bodies he accompanied were being taken in, one of the paras shifted his grip slightly. A blood-stained hand fell from the stretcher to dangle in the snow. A watchin para moved over, took the dangling hand and reverentially replaced it under the blanket that covered the stretcher. *It is a neat touch of theater, I have to give them that.* Once they were inside, he relaxed slightly.

"Guy, how did you get this organized so quickly?"

Fabron laughed. "We are paras, Conrad. We don't need to be told how to do things; we just need told what our commanders want and we do the rest. "

"Lieutenant, you may want to see this." One of the paras was calling from a window that overlooked the road.

Conrad and Fabron joined him. The para pointed at a car that had stopped just outside the gates of the cantonment. It was a Ford Fordor Deluxe staff car, painted light blue, with a SAC band on the front door. The driver might have sensed he was being watched, because he suddenly accelerated and left the scene.

"I think that is our man." Fabron sounded mostly convinced.

"I know it is." Conrad knew beyond any doubt that the charade had been successful. "Air Force staff cars are dark blue, not light blue, and they have a white star on the rear doors. And they never, ever carry the SAC band."

9 Place le Comte, Herve, Belgium.

The man calling himself Harry Lime recognized he had walked into a trap as soon as he entered the meeting place. His small, slightly bulging eyes widened with shock. His hand had dived into his overcoat pocket, with the unmistakable intention of drawing a pistol. He never got the chance. One of the paras, wearing a hastily-borrowed overcoat over his uniform, swung a tire iron taken from their truck. He swept Lime's legs out from under him.

Lime was on the floor. He tried to hold his battered kneecap with one hand while attempting to put up a pro-forma resistance to arrest with the other. Major

Roul quickly put an end to that. He stamped hard on the arm trying to reach a pistol.

"No, you don't, you bastard. You've killed enough people today. You'd better come up with some damned good reason why we don't just string you up *à la lanterne*, as the Parisians would say." Roul's face was contorted with hatred.

Lime's face was supercilious, almost contemptuous. "You won't string me up. You'll have to put me on trial first. And I never killed any of your men. They did." He gestured at the three surviving members of his robbery gang.

"Thank you." Roul snarled the words. "You heard him, Sergeant. Take them out the back and shoot them."

The three men were dragged to their feet and hustled out through the back door. Their desperate, anguished appeals were crudely ignored. The door banged shut behind them. A few seconds later, there was a shot. An agonized scream, and the rapidly-diminishing sound of a man sobbing in pain, follwed. Before the sound could fade away completely, there was another shot and more screams. Then a third shot and more screams. Profound silence followed.

Roul nodded with satisfaction. "Sounds like my sergeant gutshot them. At least he didn't waste ammunition. We'll take you to Soumaigne. The boys there can have at you for a while. My guess is, in an hour or so, you'll wish you'd been taken out to the alley. Get him into the truck, boys. No need to be gentle about it."

A few minutes later, Sergeant Mathis put his finger to his lips as the sound of the truck driving away echoed into the alley. The three prisoners sat in the snow. They were holding their groins and trying not to make audible groans. Each one had been solidly kicked in his genitals by a burly private. Mathis thought that their screams, following the shots he had fired into some convenient rubble, had made a very convincing mock execution.

"Just remember, you three, if you'd tried this on the Germans, they really would have killed you. And then they would have wiped this whole village out. But we're Frenchmen, not Germans. So we're going to let you go, this time. If we ever see any of you again, then, that day, we will not be playing games. Understand?"

The three men nodded. They started to limp away down the alleyway. Mathis nodded to one of the paras with him. There was a dull thud, as each man was helped on his way by a well-aimed kick to his rear end. Once they'd turned the corner and were gone, Mathis sighed. "Come on boys, time to get back to Soumaigne."

Conrad's Other Eye

Cantonment, Premier Compagnie, 2e Régiment de Chasseurs Parachutistes, Soumaigne, Belgium.

"Please, tell me what your real name is?" Conrad was sitting opposite the prisoner. He noted the split lip, black eye and bleeding nose with a certain degree of distaste. *But roughing this man up was necessary to maintain the fiction that he had planned a robbery in which a dozen paras had been killed.* Then he came to an abrupt mental stop. *And so it begins. The justification of the unjustifiable always started with 'well, this one time.'*

"Harry Lime." The voice was loaded with arrogance, on the surface at least. Hidden within that was a tremor. Belief that he was in the hands of people who were consumed with hate for him, and wanted nothing more than to kill him, was chipping away at his self-confidence.

Conrad sighed, just a touch theatrically. "No, you are not Harry Lime; no matter how much you would like to be. I can tell from your accent that you are an American. We have your fingerprints. We'll know who you are soon enough. And you are a deserter. The Marines look on deserters almost as direly as the paras here look on those who murdered their comrades. Frankly, unless you can help me find a reason why the paras should spare your life, I do not think you will live to dusk."

"I'm not a marine. Who says I am? And why do you think I'm a deserter?"

"Because military training changes a man's bearing in ways that are never lost. You were in the military once, and the only reason why an American would be here is if he deserted. So, help me out. Who are you and what unit did you belong to?"

"Richard Griffin." He deflated, now that his real name was known. "Staff Sergeant Richard Griffin, 75th Air Bridge Squadron. We flew C-99s to Russian during the war. Then after The Big One, we started an Air Bridge to France."

"Who was she, Richard?" Conrad leaned forward slightly, not enough to be threatening, enough to be seen as offering support.

"How did you know?"

"It's an old story, one every priest knows. You are well paid, well fed. You come from the winning side. A local woman sees you, and also sees a way out of the misery that surrounds her. She'll give her love to you, for a loaf of bread or a block of chocolate. It's too good to pass up, so you desert to be with her. But, without the Air Force, you have no bread and no chocolate. So you turn to crime to get the things you need to keep her. Now, you sit in a cell, waiting for a noose and she finds the next man who can look after her."

"That's not true. She isn't like that. She didn't sell herself to me and I didn't buy her. We met, it doesn't matter how, and we fell in love. I wouldn't exploit her. I told her we would wait until we were married. But the Air Force wouldn't let us get married, and that's why I deserted. We live in Brussels now, under one name, and I do what I have to under another, as Harry Lime. Richard Griffin doesn't exist anymore."

With the barrier down, Griffin started to speak. The whole story tumbled out in a stream that became a flood. Conrad quietly listened to him tell of how he had met the woman who was now his wife; how he had deserted in order to be with her. That had been in the happy days; after the end of the war but before the terrible cold had clamped down.

She was a schoolteacher, but her class had been hit by an outbreak of strep throat. That was a minor thing in the U.S.; here in Europe, with people weakened by starvation, seven years of German occupation and now the effects of the falling temperatures, strep throat was a killer. Griffin had taken a huge chance. He had gone back to his transport aircraft base and raided the sick bay for sulfa powder. He had stolen enough to treat the children in his wife's class and he thought that had been the end of it.

Only, it hadn't been that way. Strep throat wasn't in just one school or one town; it was an epidemic. Other teachers had noted how her class had mysteriously recovered from the sickness was sweeping through the region. They had wanted to know why, and how. Soon, Griffin had found himself stealing greater and greater quantities of medicines from the Air Bridge terminals.

When they ran low, he started stealing from other aid shipments. Still, demand exceeded supply, and he started to dilute the sulfa powder with extenders. The first experiments seemed to show the sulfa powder still worked, so he increased the dilution again and again. At first, the money had been a secondary thing. As the income from selling the diluted drugs rose, it became more and more of a factor.

By the time the winter had closed down for real, he was running a theft and smuggling ring that covered most of Belgium and Northern France. Even the established gangsters, the *Unione Corse* and the *Milieu* would not challenge his supremacy. They were family men and they didn't know when their children would suddenly need the magic of sulfa powder or penicillin.

That was when Griffin had discovered the conditions inside Germany. German refugee survivors would pay, could pay, much more than French and Belgians for the drugs. Now, with all of the products diluted almost to the point of worthlessness, Griffin had started smuggling the drugs over the border. He had told himself that the income from the Germans, paid in the jewelry and valuables they had left, would allow him to stop diluting the medicines he was supplying to his own people. Somehow, that never happened. Always he had needed more money to keep his businesses running, more money to look after his family, more money to do the things he had to do.

"You say you smuggled the medicines to Germany? How?" Conrad asked the question when Griffin paused to draw breath.

"Have you looked at a map, Father? Just 30 kilometers north of here is Aachen. Or the still-smoking ruins of what used to be Aachen. It's got a pretty-looking blue lake in the middle. A perfect circle, and it's death to go near it. But, the wind was from the northwest that day and the radiation plume stretches south and east. The people here should be thankful for that, because otherwise they'd be the ones dying of radiation. But, head towards Aachen from the north and west, stay clear of the city itself, and the refugee camps are easy to find. Just watch the C-66s landing. They're the aircraft that can land easily anywhere. Wherever they go, there are the refugees. We've got all the routes marked out. Just go straight from one marker to the next. For 30 kilometers, that's easy enough."

"And you brought the women out the same way?"

"Of course. Father, at first we told them we were recruiting them as maids and other domestic help for families in Italy and Spain. The women knew the truth, but wanted to go anyway. Soon, we just stopped pretending and told them what they would have to do. Then, we took them out and passed them along a chain of handlers until they reached their destination. Some of those women, they sent word back, thanking us for giving them the opportunity to escape."

What must Germany be like, for women to thank those who charged such a price for helping them escape? That set Conrad's mind working in directions that surprised him. "The chain of handlers? That must have taken a great deal or organization to set up?"

Griffin shook his head. "It was already there, Father, set up by the Resistance. It had been used to help Jews escape from Germany and later to help Navy pilots who had been shot down escape to Switzerland, Italy or Spain. We just used it for a different clientele, that's all. None of us are bad people, Father. Most of us fought in the Resistance against the Nazis. When the women we were taking out of Germany had children, we took them out as well and didn't charge any extra for it."

Conrad noticed how Griffin had identified himself with the French and Belgians with whom he lived. "So, you would bring the women out to a given point and hand them over to the next group, who would take them on another stage? So, I have to ask you, to whom did you hand over the women for transit in this area?"

"I don't know, Father, and that is the honest truth. We would take them to a handover point and leave them there. The guides from the next group would then pick them up and take them further. We do not know who they are and they do not know us."

Conrad had already guessed that would be the case. *In 1942, when I was leaving Europe ahead of Germany's war with America, a group of us took some Jewish refugees out, disguised as priests. They were all men. We had to leave women and children behind. Does that make us better or worse than these people today?* "If you didn't know who would take them on, how did you get paid?"

"Each refugee was told how much they needed for the trip. They were also told that the guides who would meet them at each stage would take their share of that payment. We told them how many stages there would be and how much each group of guides should be given." Griffin leaned back, his story told.

"Richard, did you have any dealings with Commissioner Morin, the administrator of the displaced persons camp at Verviers?"

"I did, at first. He bought some of our medicines. But, he said to me that he couldn't buy any more, there wasn't any money for them. Anyway, the people in the camp wouldn't take medicines any more. They said the atomic bombing had changed them. Foolish, of course."

"You know he was murdered?"

"So I heard. But it was nothing to do with us. He was a small customer who ran out of money. No more, no less. If anything, I was sorry to hear of his death since he might have come back to us if he'd got some more cash. And if people in the camp got over the idiotic superstitions they'd picked up."

"You'd better see these." Doctor Lémieux entered the room. He had with him a collection of photographs. "Griffin, you said you diluted the drugs you sold in Germany. What did you dilute them with?"

"Originally salt and chalk. But, when salt ran short, with whatever we could find. We dug up chalk and used that. We were careful, Doctor. We ground the chalk up very fine and washed it over and over again with water. Then we dried it carefully."

"You fools! You damned, incompetent, stupid fools!" Lémieux almost screamed in anger. "Don't you realize that just washing with water does no good at all? Just to sterilize dirt, you have to heat it to over one hundred and sixty five degrees and saturate it with bleach! Even that won't clean it completely. In fact, the water you used may have made things worse. Did you know what was in that chalk you dug up? More diseases than you have ever heard of!

"You go outside, take a spadeful of dirt. I guarantee there is anthrax in it. There's also the bacteria that cause meningitis, septicemia, encephalitis . . . The list goes on and on. Then there are the fungus spores and all the diseases they produce. None of them, do you hear me, you imbecile, none of them, are even mildly inconvenienced by washing the soil with dirty water! Look at these pictures! Just look at them!"

He threw them on the table. Conrad saw the ones on the top. People with the massive blackened ulcers of anthrax, limbs rotting while the patient still lived. The mildest ones were at the top. Conrad was thankful that he saw no more. Richard Griffin didn't have such luxuries. Doctor Lémieux stood over him and forced him to carefully inspect every single picture. By the time they reached the bottom of the stack, Griffon had vomited on the floor and was sobbing helplessly. All shreds of his carefully constructed image had gone. Conrad saw him as he really was. A poorly-educated man who did not know enough to know how little he knew, yet was trying to cope with a situation that demanded knowledge he had no chance of possessing.

"Father, we didn't know. I swear to you, we didn't know. We were proud of the fact we worked so hard to clean everything. We didn't know. Please, believe me, we didn't know."

Conrad sighed. This was a situation that he had come up against so many times that he had lost count. It was a commonly held belief that all the victims of the Inquisition had been innocent. Most of them had been, Conrad knew that. He also knew that there were some who had not been innocent, who had deserved the fate that had befallen them. *We even had a motto for it in the Inquisition:* Scimus autem diabolo et operibus ejus vultus habet. Immo, ut melius cognoscamus eos. *We know the Devil, his face and his works. Oh yes, we know them very well. And was it the Devil's joke that we had pronounced the words wrongly?* Conrad remembered the amusement on Achillea's face as she had patiently taught him the correct pronunciation.

"Richard, when the Devil comes to steal your soul, he doesn't do so as the hideous creature of evil that he is, stinking of sulfur and with glowing trident in hand. Instead, he comes to his victims as a gentle, kindly visitor. One who points out how much good can be done there by just a little compromise here; accepting just a little badness there, so that the greater good could be served here." *And have I not done just that with the beating you received?* "And indeed, in the short term, perhaps much good is done. Or seems to be. But already the path is downwards.

"The bad gets a little stronger every day. The goodness gained becomes less obvious and, soon enough, it is also contaminated with evil. By the time the poor victim sees the Devil for what he is, the good has gone and all that is left is the evil. The victim's soul is forfeit and all he can do is scream the words you have just said to me. 'I didn't know, we didn't mean this.' But is does no good for the damage is done. Tell me, when your request for permission to marry was refused, did you go to the chaplain or welfare officer and ask for help?"

"I don't need people's help and I don't want their charity." Griffin almost spat the words out.

"And that was the chink in your armor that the Devil was looking for. The sin of pride. There's a reason why pride is a deadly sin, you know. It's not because it is bad in itself, but because it is an open portal for much worse things. Richard, you started off with the best of intentions. You wanted to treat the woman who loved you properly. At first things, conspired against you, and the Devil pointed out the simple, easy solution. Your pride made you take it and the path has ended here.

"I will take one burden off your soul. When your men tried their robbery, they did not kill any of the paras who guarded the convoy. The paras killed most of them and let the others go. With a solid kick to the rear, I believe. I said it to them, and I will say it to you. They are good men, honest and honorable. But, your plan did cause the loss of five lives and, for that, you must give the law what it demands. I would urge you to see God's hand in that, for it means no more of this poison will find its way to helpless victims. If you wish to speak of this further, ask for me and I will be here to listen."

Outside the room, Fabron was waiting. "Father, where do we go from here?"

Conrad was filled with grief, for he was certain he had been in the presence of an innocent soul that had fallen foul of the Devil's snares. But, there was still the case of the murder of Commissioner Morin to solve and the innocence of Marius Dressler to prove. That thought gave Conrad an idea.

"Guy, I have a thought. When I was talking with Étienne Bonnaire, he hinted that the relations between the police and the resistance were quite a bit closer than the public believed. Griffin said that the pipeline for refugees used most of the structure set up in the war to save Jews and Navy pilots. I wonder if Bonnaire knows who was involved in that pipeline? I believed Griffin when he said that he and his people had no reason to kill the commissioner. But might those further down the line?"

Fabron nodded. "Let us find out. I'll drive us to the *gendarmerie* at Verviers."

Gendarmerie at Verviers

Fabron had put the canvas roof of the jeep up and the inside was comfortably warm. It made Conrad realize that he hadn't been really warm for weeks. "I didn't know that jeeps had heaters."

"They didn't, not at first. The first winter the U.S. Army spent in Russia, they learned a new definition of the word cold. So Ford developed a winterization kit, called the GPW. By 1945, most jeeps had been fitted with it. When we persuaded the Americans to let us keep these, we kept the ones that had the heaters and returned the ones that didn't."

"It sounds almost as if your leaders were expecting this." Conrad's investigative senses were aroused by the seeming coincidence of the French

Army keeping equipment that was suited to the frigid winter that had enveloped Europe. Suddenly, he realized that the deal with the Thais that had obtained so much food aid for a France threatened with starvation fell into the same category.

"I'm just a lieutenant of paratroops. I wouldn't know that. But, you may be right."

Conrad settled back in his seat, admiring the casual skill with which Fabron maneuvered the jeep along the icy road. "Last time I rode along here it was in a *kubelwagen*."

"Then you are lucky to be alive, Conrad. There is a good reason why we kept our jeeps instead of using those things. This jeep is four-wheel drive; the *kubelwagen* is only two. And, the jeep is heavier, so it pushes its tires through the snow and ice. The *kubelwagen* is far too light and underpowered. You are much better off in a jeep. Especially one with a heater." Fabron frowned for a second. "There was something about the conversation we had with Griffin that made me uneasy."

"About the women who sent word back to thank those who helped them escape from Germany?" The same thing had worried Conrad.

"I cannot imagine a woman thanking the men who made her live that kind of life, however bad the alternative. It just does not ring true to me."

"Nor to me." Conrad thought back over the thousands of confessions he had taken over the years. "I can imagine a woman being grateful to those who got her out of Germany, but she would express that gratitude by silence. By not incriminating them. Sending word back, thanking such people, it is a degrading story. It is something that a man who has a very low and contemptuous opinion of women would invent."

"And Griffin is not such a person. He sacrificed everything he had so he could treat the woman who loved him properly. He would not invent such a story."

"No, but he might well be tempted to believe such a story without questioning it too deeply. It would fit his own image of himself too well." Conrad looked out of the window of the jeep and saw the ominous black-blue clouds piling up along the horizon. "Guy, it looks as if we're in for . . ."

He didn't get any further. There was a loud bang and a whip-like crack. The jeep lurched and started to spin. Fabron spun the steering wheel in his hands. He turned into the skid. He managed to get the spin straightened before the jeep bounced off the snow banks that lined the road. The jeep ricocheted off the packed snow. It teetered on the edge of a roll. Fabron's hands were still deft and sure. Again, he turned into the danger, keeping the vehicle upright. Finally, he brought the jeep to a stop. He breathed out, deeply and very shakily. "And, if we'd been in a *kubelwagen*, we would both now be dead."

"What was that? Did somebody take a shot at us?"

Fabron shook his head. "Something much, much nastier, I think. Come with me, Conrad. Let me show you something."

He led the way out of the jeep and around to the front. There was a peculiar attachment welded to the front. It looked a little like a shepherd's crook, reinforced by two metal bars. "That is a Volga Hook. The Russians showed the Americans how to make it and fasten it to all their vehicles. You see, Conrad, sometimes the Germans, or those in their pay, would stretch thin wire across the road. Or sometimes the partisans would, only to see a jeep come down the road instead of a *kubelwagen*. Without a Volga Hook, the wire would slice the heads off those who rode inside. But, the vertical bar of the hook catches the wire and causes it to ride upwards. Then the angled piece at the top breaks it. The bang was the wire breaking; the crack the sound of the broken pieces of wire flailing through the air."

Conrad looked at the Volga Hook. The olive drab paint had been scraped off and the metal was bright and clean. "You are right, Guy. I can see where the upright caught the wire. I heard of a case like this in England, before the Armistice. The wife of a magistrate, a French woman, but one from Alsace and who had a German name, liked to ride in the woods. Somebody who thought she was German stretched a wire across the path she used and it killed her. Who would want to do that to us?"

"Somebody who does not want us to speak with *Brigadier de Police* Bonnaire I think. We had better move quickly. There is a storm coming, and not just one that comes from black clouds and snow."

Fabron backed the jeep up slightly. Then Conrad climbed on board and the pair set off down the road again. After a few hundred yards, Fabron flipped the headlights on. The blue-black clouds that had been on the horizon were now overhead and the daylight had been swallowed by them. It wasn't quite as dark as night, but it was getting close to that level. By the time they reached the *gendarmerie*, the first flurries of snow were falling fast. Fabron's face was grim as he parked the jeep so that its radiator grill was as close to the wall as he could get it. He explained why to Conrad as they were getting out. "That shelters the radiator from the wind. Stops it freezing solid."

Conrad only just heard the explanation. All his attention was fixed on the front door of the *gendarmerie*. It was open and was flapping back and forth in the wind. "Guy, I really don't like the look of that. Everybody I know here is careful to keep doors closed. Keeps the warmth in."

'I was thinking that as well. Conrad, I want you to go back behind the jeep and take cover there. "Fabron had his MP-40 submachine gun with him. He took a roll of thread out of his pocket and tied a loop around the extreme end of the barrel. He let a long length dangle down. Then he approached the door with great care.

Conrad watched him push the barrel of the MP-40 into the open door. Even in the gloomy light and increasing snow, Conrad saw the thread beginning to bend back as it caught on something.

"Conrad, the door has a booby trap. Keep down."

Fabron felt inside the door and carefully traced the wire to its source. It had been stretched across the doorframe from one side to the other so that it would trip anybody who tried to enter. One end was simply wrapped around a screw in the wood. The other was attached to a hand grenade in an old tin can. The pin had been pulled from the firing lever of the grenade. When someone tripped, the grenade would be pulled from the can, the lever would fly off and the grenade would explode. Fabron removed it carefully and checked it over. The set-up made the hand grenade too dangerous to keep around. "Conrad, I've got a live hand grenade to get rid of. Stay under cover."

Fabron threw it as far as he could, aiming for the thickest snowbanks. He dropped flat as he did so. The grenade went off very quickly. Metal fragments from its case fell to the ground around him. "We're clear. And Conrad, it is my guess you were praying hard just then. Thank you; it worked."

Conrad waved in acknowledgment. "Guy, first the wire across the road and then this grenade. So you get the feeling somebody doesn't want us to speak with Étienne Bonnaire as well?"

Fabron waggled his hand parallel to the ground, palm down. "I suspect that they may have taken more decisive steps in that direction. This place has a stillness about it that does not auger well."

Inside, the *gendarmerie* was complete chaos. The walls behind the desk were pockmarked with gunfire. Two streams seemed to cross where a shattered, blood-soaked chair lay on the floor. There were blood trails out towards the door. Conrad suspected they were on the ground outside as well, now covered by falling snow. The contents of cabinets and files had been torn from their shelves and thrown in a confused, random heap on the floor. There were other patches of blood around, and smaller patterns of spray on the walls. Conrad reached out and touched Fabron's arm. On the wall, near the entrance door, were three pockmarks. Smaller and shallower than the others, they were clearly the result of pistol shots.

"I would say that the attackers burst in firing automatic weapons at Bonnaire. He got off some shots from his revolver before they killed him. And then, they dragged the body away." Fabron's eyes were moist as he looked at the wrecked chair that marked the place where a gallant old man had made his last stand.

"I think it is more complex than that. The people who came here didn't just want to silence Bonnaire. They wanted something that was held in the records here. They burst in as you said, and Étienne shot one of them. I think the blood on the floor is from the man Étienne shot. They searched the place, but couldn't find what they were looking for. So they tried to beat the information out of him." Conrad shuddered at the memory of the pictures he had seen of Igrat after two men had tried to beat information out of her. Even now, almost two years later, she still hadn't fully recovered and she still had nightmares. "When they couldn't get what they needed they took him, and the man he had shot, away so they could continue interrogating him."

"In that case, we had better find him without any delay. Fabron opened the door leading to the rear of the *gendarmerie* and went in. A split second later, Conrad heard his voice, made pale by shock. *"Le Bonne Dieu!* Conrad, come quickly."

Conrad stepped through the door and stopped. The back of the *gendarmerie* was equipped as a small jail, with the traditional barred door on each cell. Inside the middle cell of three was hanging the body of Marius Dressler. His face was cruelly distorted by the agony of slow strangulation. Yet, Conrad saw there was more there than that. He had seldom seen such a look of abject horror on a man's face. Nor had he seen such all-enveloping fear. Even in the days when he had been a servant of the Inquisition, he had seen nothing like it.

Fabron was fumbling with the lock on the cell door. The keys had been hanging on the wall. Finding the right one took a second or so. Then, he was inside. Fabron hacked at the rope with the heavy-bladed knife that he'd used earlier. He and Conrad eased the man to the floor. It was more a matter of respect than anything else. Dressler was clearly and indisputably dead.

"What happened here, Father?" Fabron spoke quietly, but his voice quavered slightly. The tough, competent para was profoundly disturbed by what he had seen in the *gendarmerie*. Out of the corner of his eye, Conrad saw him finger the crucifix he wore around his neck and his lips move in prayer. "Is this suicide or murder?"

"We can be sure of one thing. The people who attacked this place knew his body was here. It may be he committed suicide and they left him here to make us think they hanged him as a warning; that we would get the same if we continued to make inquiries. Or, it may be he was alive, and they hanged him in his cell to try and make his murder look like suicide, and thus diminish inquiries. Or any permutation of those deeds and motives."

"I would believe that they murdered him, Conrad. Probably because he was a witness to their identities and to what happened here. I will tell you something else. There is so much evil in this place it chills my bones."

"I know, Guy, I feel it too. Something truly terrible has happened here. I can sense the Devil's hands here."

"Conrad, I must confess something to you. As a man to his priest. There is an old saying, that there are no atheists in foxholes. Well, it isn't true. I know a lot of men who were on the front lines and what they saw made them lose their faith. I kept mine, but it was a struggle to do so and I only won that struggle by the thinnest of margins. I know many, many men who have been in battle and who do not believe in God any more. But after what we saw, every one of us believes in the Devil."

Conrad nodded and reached into his pocket where he kept his small box of emergency supplies. He took a tiny drop of the blessed oil and touched it to Guy's forehead, spreading it out into the cross. As he did so, they both heard a growling scream from the front room. Fabron went back first, his MP-40 at the ready. Conrad was close behind him. They collided in the doorway to the front room. Fabron had stopped, relaxing slightly. "It's the door. It's just the door moving with the wind and snow. Conrad, the snow is getting worse. If we are going to leave here, we'd better do so now. Otherwise, the roads will be blocked again and we will have to stay here, possibly for days or longer. And, a door blowing in the wind or not, I would not wish to stay here longer than I have to."

"Nor I, Guy. But there are two things we must do before we leave. One is simple. *Dominus noster Jesus Christus te absolvat; et ego auctoritate ipsius te absolvo ab omni vinculo excommunicationis et interdicti in quantum possum et tu indiges. Deinde, ego te absolvo a peccatis tuis in nomine Patris, et Filii, et Spiritus Sancti.* Amen." Conrad's fingers made the sign of the cross. As he did so, the growling scream again echoed around the *gendarmerie.* "Let's get Dressler's body and get to Verviers as quickly as we can. This storm is getting worse by the minute."

It took only a minute to load Dressler's stiffened body into the back of the jeep. Even so, by the time they set off, there was a thick layer of snow on the road. On their way to the *gendarmerie*, Conrad and Fabron had been chatting about matters consequential and inconsequential. On the way back, Conrad kept silent. He could see that Fabron was holding his lower lip between his teeth and peering through the windscreen with intense concentration. Conrad was that rarity, a good passenger who knew when to keep quiet and that any advice he might offer was both unwelcome and even hazardous. After a while, he could feel the jeep sliding on the fresh snow. He realized something Fabron had known right from the start of this drive. *What we are doing is very, very dangerous. And yet, I would rather be out here in this blizzard than back there in the* gendarmerie.

By the time they got back to the *Rue Donkier* in Verviers, there was almost a full half-meter of snow banked up. Once again, Fabron parked the jeep so that its radiator was up against a solid wall. Then he grabbed a small sack from the back seat. "We can leave the body here; it will be safe enough in this storm. And it's too cold for it to decay."

CHAPTER FOUR

HUMAN TRAFFICKING

Lodging House, Rue Donkier, Verviers, Belgium

"Father, we were so worried about you. The storm is the worst one we have ever seen. Already, our thermometer is reading twenty degrees below and still it falls." Madame Neske peered through the gloom. "And who is your friend?"

"Don't you recognize him, mother? It's the nice para who gave us our pork." Rosina Neske smiled at Fabron and got a wink in exchange.

"May I ask shelter, Madame? The storm out there will not permit any movement for hours." Fabron's voice had its normal amused, mischievous character back. Clearly, the sight of an attractive teenage girl had driven away the overpowering stench of evil that had filled the *gendarmerie*.

"Of course, but . . ." Madame Neske wanted to say that they were short of food and the rations didn't provide for an extra person. But she didn't know how to say so without seeming very rude.

Fabron gave her his most beaming smile. "Madame, I have some fresh-baked bread from the regimental bakery. It is poor stuff, I fear, but our regimental cooks do the best they can. And, being paratroopers, they know they can always be thrown out of an aircraft if their best is not good enough. I also have some canned meat and vegetables, garlic, some of the strange yellow stuff the Americans fondly but mistakenly believe is cheese and a flask of red wine. It is rough red wine, the ration for soldiers, but palatable. A small glass each will, perhaps, hide the taste of the American cheese?"

The laugh that went up was that start of what became a convivial evening. Monsieur Neske pretended not to notice the attention his daughter was lavishing on the handsome para lieutenant. Madame Neske did make it clear she had seen the same attentions, but was quickly reassured by the scrupulous observation of the proprieties by both Rosina and Fabron. They flirted with each other, but were careful not to make that fact an embarrassment to the others. Outside, the snow grew steadily heavier. The cold began to seep into the living room. Eventually, the sociable evening started to fall victim to the increasing cold. Before the occupants of the house could go to their rooms, Fabron coughed gently.

"Good people, the temperature continues to drop and is now more than twenty-six degrees below zero. This is a killing cold, the kind of temperature our troops faced on the Volga Front. I recommend that we all stay in this one room tonight, to save warmth. I know this might seem immodest, but this is the worst storm I have ever seen, or heard of."

"The lieutenant is right." Conrad spoke quietly, but emphatically, for he understood just how dangerous the situation was. "In the old days, people would gather in communal halls during winter for just this reason. Indeed, such gatherings were a cause for festivities, since they reinforced the communal spirit. Faced with the need for warmth and shelter, people forgot their petty grievances and celebrated what they had. May I suggest we have one last sip of the lieutenant's red wine, to toast our little community here, and then settle down together in good fellowship?"

There was a smattering of approval and a clink of glasses as the group followed his suggestion. The women collected as much bedding as they could find and set up the room for sleeping. Margreet and Rosina Neske and Dorothea Heimans at one end, Gerard van Can, Monsieur Neske and Lieutenant Fabron at the other with Conrad discretely placed between the two groups.

While things were being readied, Fabron stood beside Conrad. "Conrad, there's something I have been meaning to ask. When you gave me the absolution, it sounded unlike the one I have heard before."

"It is an old one, Guy; one used by the Spanish Inquisition when in the face of great evil. It is rarely used these days, and only when the situation seems to warrant the strongest measures. Such was the atmosphere in the *gendarmerie*, I felt it was one of those situations."

"Ahh, I understand. I didn't expect the Spanish Inquisition."

Conrad smiled. "Guy, nobody expects the Spanish Inquisition."

Rue Donkier, Verviers, Belgium

The shovel gangs had started their work singing. By mid-day, they were too exhausted to continue. By the time the storm had slackened off, more than two and a half meters of snow had fallen, leaving Verviers with the frightening task of digging itself out. Everybody was out in the street, trying to clear paths through the thick layer of snow that had fallen during the night. The fittest and strongest were at the front, hacking a way through the snowfall. The weaker and less able followed behind, finishing off the work. A big problem was where to put the snow they were clearing. Previous snowfalls had left great banks on the sides of the roads. Putting more there was impossible. In the end, it had been decided to clear only one lane through the streets and put the snow on the other side. It was a poor solution, but nobody could think of anything better.

Conrad heard a cheer go up. The snow clearance gangs on the *Rue Donkier* broke through the snow wall and joined those trying to clear the *Chausee de Heusy*. There was an impromptu celebration going on, with the workers dancing around in glee. It was a small victory, perhaps. But, after the strength of the storm, it was a welcome one. More than that, it was an affirmation of Vervier's desire to survive. All over the town, other little celebrations were taking place as the cleared roads were joined up.

"Well done, Conrad! Everybody thought the Americans were mad when they sent us planeloads of snow shovels after the first few storms, but thank God they did."

Conrad turned round to see Fabron behind him. The para lieutenant looked unperturbed by the hard physical work he had been doing all morning. That told Conrad just how fit his friend was. "Guy, have we any news?"

"About the storm? It has passed for a while. We were lucky. The main center of the blizzard passed north of us. I understand *les singes capitulard* have been hit very badly; up to four meters of snow in some places. They have probably surrendered already."

The words might have sounded like a joke, but Conrad knew they were not. Lord Halifax's betrayal of his French allies had sunk too deeply into the French consciousness. "I have managed to get through to my regimental commander and report in. He told me there are small groups of our people calling in from all over the area. We do not think we have lost anybody, but we will all feel easier when everybody is in contact. In the meantime, my orders are to continue assisting you."

"That's good to hear. But, I was wondering if there was any news about Bonnaire or the attack on the *gendarmerie*?'

Fabron shook his head. "My report was the first thing anybody had heard of it. Digging our way through this mess, that is their only concern at the moment."

Conrad's mind was suddenly seized with a grim picture of what might be happening to Bonnaire. The storm was working in favor of the criminals, whoever they were, and allowing them to do their work undisturbed. Once again, he remembered the stench of evil in the *gendarmerie*.

"What is it, Guy, that people could have wanted so badly that they would have attacked a *gendarmerie* to seize it?"

"Something of great importance, obviously. To attack a *gendarmerie* is an attack upon the whole French state. If we weren't here, once the news reached Paris, we would be on our way. This area would swarm with troops until those responsible were found and brought to justice. We would have roadblocks on every street and lane; everybody would have to produce their identity cards every few paces. We would make life so inconvenient that even other criminals would turn on their own and help us find those responsible."

"I saw that, sometimes, in America. They call it The Big Heat."

Fabron laughed and looked around at the snow-filled streets, swarming with shovel-wielding men, women and children. "We could use the big heat here. But that avoids the question. What is it that Bonnaire had in his records that was so important that the criminals would risk such an operation?"

His further musing were cut off by a loud bang and a shattering of glass. One of the blue-painted *kubelwagens* used by the gendarmes had tried to turn the corner into the *Rue Donkier*. The driver had lost control of the little vehicle and it had skidded into an ornamental fountain. The old stone of the fountain and its statue were undamaged, but the *kubelwagen* was twisted and broken by the impact. A chorus of ironic cheers went up from the nearby crowd. The three gendarmes inside the vehicle had extracted themselves from the wreck with little difficulty. None seemed to be seriously hurt. They glowered at the crowd with all the sincerity of greatly offended dignity.

"You see, Conrad, I told you those things were death-traps." Fabron went over to speak with the gendarmes. He came back clutching a piece of paper. "We have a map of the roads that have been cleared. My regiment has four trucks equipped as snowplows and they have cleared the road from here to my regimental headquarters. I'd better put in an appearance, Conrad, or they may forget to pay me."

"That's probably a good idea, Guy. Being without your pay could be a problem. God will provide, but sometimes he appreciates it if we help him along a little."

Fabron stared at him and then burst out laughing. "You're a strange one, Conrad. Are you sure you've never been a paratrooper?"

Then, he stopped laughing and looked very thoughtful. "And, you are, of course, right. If the Good Lord provided for us without expecting us to help ourselves also, then we would grow lazy and believe it was our right to have all our needs satisfied. We would neither work for ourselves nor appreciate the gifts we were given. So, the Good Lord expects us to work hard for ourselves. And, if we do, then he rewards us by crowning our efforts with success.

"That's what has gone wrong, isn't it? Why we are here today, like this. We stopped trying. We thought that we could just sit back and everything would be all right. We let the Nazis grow without doing anything about it and so we were brought down. If we'd fought them harder, and earlier, then the Good Lord would have brought us success."

Conrad looked at him solemnly. "You're a strange one, Guy. Are you sure you've never been a priest?"

The two men laughed at the shared joke and set off back to the lodging house. By the time they got there, the women had cleared the snow off Fabron's jeep and even dried the seats with towels. Conrad presumed they had taken great care not to look at the body in the back. When Rosina Neske heard the jeep engine start, she came running out with a bag in her hand. "Guy! Guy! I made you a sandwich for your lunch."

Fabron looked slightly embarrassed; a sandwich was a princely gift that the giver could ill-afford. Rosina looked slightly embarrassed as well, a young girl having her first experience of being in love. Conrad was happy for her. *She has the good fortune in falling in love with a man who is good and honorable. As well as being a handsome, dashing paratrooper,* Conrad thought.

Fabron took the sandwich carefully and stored it in a pocket of his fatigues. "Thank you, Mademoiselle Rosina. I shall enjoy it on our drive back to our base. And, perhaps, if your mother is willing, I might call on you again?"

At that, Rosina Neske's nerve broke. She collapsed into giggles and fled indoors. As they drove off, Conrad saw her mother watching them leave. He swore she gave Fabron a friendly, knowing, smile.

Cantonment, Premier Compagnie, 2e Régiment de Chasseurs Parachutistes, Soumaigne, Belgium.

"The body is still frozen stiff." Doctor Lémieux had taken time off from the routine task of treating the injuries the paras had received in clearing the snow to look at the body of Marius Dressler. "I will know more once it has thawed. From a brief inspection, my verdict would be suicide. But, I must warn you that distinction between murder and suicide may be impossible by an examination of the body alone. Detailed investigation of the scene, reconstruction of the position of the suspended body, examination of the rope, the knots, the direction of the fibers on the rope may serve to separate a homicidal hanging from a suicide."

"Our *toubib* is trying to ensure he gets all the credit again." Fabron looked up at the ceiling in mock despair.

Lémieux looked at him with a certain level of asperity. "Getting all the credit around here is no great achievement. You *fripouille* wouldn't be paratroopers if your mothers hadn't dropped you on your heads too often. But, we do have some evidence to work from. You see, a suicidal hanging almost always leaves an inverted V bruise. This makes it easy to tell from ligature strangulation, which leaves a straight-line bruise. The cold has worked in our favor today. It has made the bruises much more apparent, and we can see we have the characteristic inverted V. So, he was not strangled with a ligature and then hanged to make it look like suicide. Also, hanging compresses the veins, but arterial blood flow continues, causing small bleeding sites on the lips, inside the mouth and on the eyelids. All of these things we can see here. So, we can be sure he did die by hanging.

"I can see no defensive wounds or bruising, so I would guess that he killed himself. If somebody had hanged him, there would have been a struggle. Also, his hands were not bound, yet he made no effort to save his life. It took him several minutes to die, in great distress, yet he did not attempt to take his weight off the noose around his neck. It is even possible for somebody to save their life that way. I know of it being done, once."

Conrad was nodding thoughtfully. The doctor's observations agreed with his own experience in such things. He agreed also with the conclusions. "We can suspect suicide then, even if the evidence is not good enough for a court?"

"I would think so." Lémieux nodded. He looked as if he wanted to say something else and then decided not to. "I will come back later, when the body has thawed, and then we will know much more."

After he had left, Fabron spoke quietly, "Conrad, the doctor knows hanging well. When you meet Madame Lémieux, you will perhaps notice that her voice is hoarse and she has a red mark around her neck, one that will never go away. The Germans hanged her in reprisal for his work in the resistance. She is the case he knows of a person who escaped the noose by her own efforts. Remember what we discussed this morning? She fought hard for her life that day, and now I understand that the Good Lord rewarded her efforts by restoring her to her husband."

Conrad thought about that for several minutes. He had become used to the banter that passed between Doctor Lémieux and the paratroopers. Casual insults were exchanged, and they poked fun at each other. It did not seem to fit the image of a man who had so nearly lost his wife. Yet, when he thought about it, it explained so much. "I think I would be honored to meet Madame Lémieux."

"She is an honorary member of the regiment." Fabron said, and then switched his attention to other things. "We still have not decided what it is that Bonnaire knew that made him so important a target, the criminals would be prepared to take on the whole French nation."

Conrad was still thinking about Madame Lémieux. Somehow, her story also seemed to bear on this case, yet he couldn't possibly see how. "When Madame Lémieux was hanged, the Germans must have left her to die alone?"

"In the woods, yes. She was one of ten who were taken there and left alone to hang slowly. Why the Germans chose to do that, we will probably never know. But, somehow, she got her hands free and pulled herself up enough to escape. Why do you ask?"

That was when the bits started to fall into place. Conrad had the eerie sensation of looking through a kaleidoscope and seeing the patterns form. "We need to speak to Griffin again."

Prison, Soumaigne, Belgium.

Griffin was far removed from the swaggering gangster who had been arrested the day before. He seemed to have physically deflated to match the collapse of his spirit. Imprisonment, and the certainty that he would face the gallows for what he had done, brought its inevitable toll. Fabron looked at him curiously as Conrad sat down at the desk in the interrogation room.

"Griffin, when we talked recently, you told us about how the women you helped escape from Germany were taken by stages to their destination. There is something I must know. When they were handed from one stage to the next, were they left alone between stages?"

Griffin nodded. "Of course. The whole object was to ensure that if one stage of the chain was compromised, they could not identify anybody else. So, they would be taken to a meeting point and left there. Sometime later, the next guide would come and collect them."

"And how many women at a time were left at that staging point?"

"One or two. Three at the most."

"And they were locked in so they could not leave?"

"Of course." Griffin shuffled his feet and looked down, his face flushed with embarrassment. That small detail, the fact that the women they were helping to escape had to be locked in, destroyed the artful edifice of self-deceit he had built around himself.

Conrad looked at him, and asked the next question very carefully. "Griffin, I am asking you this next question, not expecting confession in either the religious or legal sense, but in the hope of getting expert advice and guidance. Is it possible that somebody could go to where the women were waiting and tell them he was the guide sent to take them onwards? Could it be that such a man would be able to rob and murder those women and nobody would ever suspect it, because nobody knew were there?"

"NO! It couldn't happen!" Griffin's shout was agonized, a denial to himself more than anybody else. Reality once again asserted itself ". . . No, I am wrong. It could. Father, what you suggest could happen. We never thought of it. The people were the Resistance. We never believed they could do such a thing, but it could happen."

Then his face brightened with relief as he desperately sought self-justification. "But, we know it did not. Some of the women sent us notes, thanking us for helping them."

"Griffin, no woman I have ever known would do that. She might feel grateful. She might keep her silence. She might even feel that she had been treated kindly. But, she would never openly thank the men who had put her into the life she was now leading. That kind of submissiveness is the fantasy of a depraved mind. Those notes of gratitude were forgeries, intended to convince you and your associates that the women you were trafficking had indeed reached the destination you intended."

Griffin collapsed, sobbing, his face in his hands. Conrad's words, quiet and measured, had an impact that angrier or censorious speech would have lacked. "Everything. Everything we did went wrong. The medicines we smuggled spread disease, poisoned and killed. Now, the women we thought we had helped were murdered. What you said, Father. It makes too much sense. How did we not see it?"

"Because you didn't want to, Griffin. You saw yourselves the way you wanted to be. You saw yourself as Harry Lime, the outlaw with a code of chivalry that meant you were doing the right thing, even though you did so outside the rules of justice. And, you needed to believe that so much, you closed your eyes to everything that did not agree with that picture."

"Conrad?" Fabron was confused by the speed with which things were developing.

"Griffin here smuggled the women in from Germany. They were brought to a staging point where they would wait for the next stage of their journey. Two, perhaps three, young women; with enough gold or silver to pay the exorbitant fees charged by this gang. They were left somewhere, locked in and had to wait for their guide. Only, the man who turned up to take them onwards didn't do so. Instead, he stole their gold and killed them. Nobody knew they were there, so there was no search. The people who had left them there assumed they had been taken onwards by the next stage of the escape route. The people to whom they were to be delivered never knew they were coming.

"This was as near perfect a set of murders as one can imagine. Only one thing went wrong. This time, one of the women was the daughter of Marius Dressler. Somebody this side knew she was coming and was waiting for her. When she didn't arrive, he started to make inquiries. Probably he went to Commissioner Morin and told him the whole story. Commissioner Morin started to make inquiries also. Only, unlike Marius Dressler, he had the position and authority to get things moving. So, before he could do so, the man who murdered the women killed him also.

"Then, poor Étienne Bonnaire and I spoke to Dressler. He was very curt with us, perhaps because he was afraid we were imposters and trying to kill him also. By the time we had convinced him we were not, Étienne was convinced of his guilt and arrested him. Being taken to the *gendarmerie* left Dressler certain beyond doubt that Étienne was indeed a policeman. Dressler told him the whole story. Somehow, the murderer knew; perhaps he had seen Étienne take him in and decided to take no chances. "

"Wait a minute . . . Guy, we have been discussing how Étienne probably had a working knowledge of the Resistance around here. As soon as he heard the story from Dressler, he knew who was responsible and, if the murderers were watching, they knew he knew. Then, the *gendarmerie* was attacked. They took him away to find out who else he had told. That was the reason for the booby traps. They thought anybody who came must have been told the identity of the killer."

"And Dressler?"

"He killed himself when he realized his daughter had survived the bombing only to be murdered. In despair and grief."

Outside, there was a sudden surge of excitement as an aircraft flew low overhead. Conrad went outside and looked up. A ski-equipped biplane was circling, obviously looking for somewhere to land. The pilot selected a convenient stretch of cleared road and put the aircraft down neatly. As he did so, Conrad saw the roundels on the side, a blue circle with a white center and a red kangaroo in the middle. *Australian. A Dragon Rapide, I think. I heard the Australian liaison squadrons from Russian were still here. With the roads blocked or treacherous, they are the only means of getting around.*

The pilot let the Dragon Rapide slide to a halt and then turned off the engines. Conrad was surprised to see a small German Iron Cross painted under the cockpit, right next to the name "Matilda". The pilot climbed out and looked around. "Is Major Roul here? I'm George Brumby. I've got a cargo of replacement medicines here, and some paperwork for one of your officers."

Cantonment, Premier Compagnie, 2e Régiment de Chasseurs Parachutistes, Soumaigne, Belgium.

"And here we have the file on *Caporal* Étienne Bonnaire. He was conscripted into the Army in 1912 and would have been discharged just before the war, but he volunteered for continued service on the outbreak of war. Filled, no doubt, with the desire to regain Alsace and Lorraine for *La Patrie*." The words could have sounded sarcastic, but there was a depth of sadness in Fabron's voice that prevented that. "He served well throughout the war, was often mentioned in the dispatches, awarded the *Croix de Guerre* for 1914 to 1918 and the *Croix du combattant*. He had the campaign medals for the Marne and Verdun and the 1914-18 Commemorative Medal. We even have a picture of him in 1917."

Conrad looked at the picture of a young Étienne Bonnaire. His proud *poilu*'s moustache was clearly visible, despite the age and poor quality of the picture. He was holding his rifle at porte-arms, the bayonet hanging on his right hip. "And yet, despite his good service and his decorations, he finished the war as a corporal? Did something go wrong for him?"

Fabron shook his head. "It is more common than you might think. A good soldier, brave and dedicated. One who follows orders and knows how to execute the tasks to which he has been assigned. Does his duty willingly and cheerfully, whether it is attacking machine gun post or peeling potatoes. Yet he lacks the flair and ingenuity required for higher ranks. He is unimaginative, staid. He can follow orders as well as any, and better than most, yet he cannot give an order. Or, to be more accurate, he cannot decide which order to give. To promote him would be the ruin of a good soldier and not the creation of a good NCO.

"So, he remains at his lowly rank. Instead of promotions, his officers see that, if there is a leave pass around, he gets it. If there is a soft assignment for a few days, he gets it. When he left the Army in 1919, he joined the *Gendarmerie*. The dates tell us much here. He was discharged from the Army on June 30 1919 and was enrolled in the *Gendarmerie* on July 1st, 1919. We can be sure that his officers spoke for him and arranged everything so he would go straight from one position to the other.

"And his *Gendarmerie* file tells us much the same thing as his army file. A good policeman, well-liked by the community, decorated and commended for his achievements yet never promoted beyond the lowest of ranks. He was the sort of *gendarme* I think, who knew every child in his town by name."

Conrad sighed, remembering his first meeting with Bonnaire. "And with a career like that, with thirty years of honest, dedicated service to his country, a woman calls him a collaborator."

"I think there may be a reason for that." Fabron looked up, holding two files, one marked with the Cross of Lorraine, the other with the *Fraktur* print of the Gestapo. "In 1942, Étienne Bonnaire was still a *gendarme*, but he joined the Resistance. At that time, he was stationed at Charleville, southeast of here. He was part of a resistance cell that aided Jewish refugees to escape into Spain. Later on, they did the same for American pilots who were shot down over France.

"In December 1945, their cell was discovered by the Gestapo and all its members were arrested. Here, in the Gestapo file, we have their names. Étienne Bonnaire, Roger Deforest, Ferdinand Labelle, Christophe Thomas, Marcel Petiot, Arnaud Soucy and Dianne Villeneuve. The Gestapo record says that Deforest was the leader of the cell and notes that the arrests were made possible by the boastfulness and bragging of one of its members. I think, perhaps, that it is not a good idea to brag of one's membership of the resistance while still under German occupation."

"I don't understand?" Conrad couldn't see where this was going.

Fabron held up a hand. "Patience, my friend. Roger Deforest, Arnaud Soucy and Dianne Villeneuve were sentenced to death and hanged at the Gestapo prison at Nancy. Interesting, there is a note here from a Gestapo officer named Hartzleff that Villeneuve was to be hanged properly, with a two-meter drop so that her neck would break. I suppose that counts as kindliness on his part."

Another victim of Medina del Campo was a young woman. It was whispered that she had turned down a suitor and that denouncing her for witchcraft and heresy had been his revenge. Perhaps she was the cleverest of them all, for she had immediately made a very full and detailed confession and sincerely repented her sins. Her reward was around her neck, a rope. Of all the eight, she was the only one who would be strangled before the fires were set. Did Dianne Villeneuve buy an easy death with information or her favors? Or was this man Hartzleff possessed of a streak of decency that would not allow a young woman to suffer unnecessarily?

Fabron had noticed Conrad's eyes glaze over for a moment and paused. Then, he continued. "Bonnaire, Labelle, Thomas and Petiot were transferred to the prison at Verviers. We do not know what happened to Labelle, Thomas and Petiot because the records for the Verviers prison were held at Aachen. Now, they are ashes, of course. But, we do know that Bonnaire was released in June 1946. He went to the *gendarmerie* here and asked to resume his duties. The authorities, of course, checked his credentials, as much as they were able to in a time of war, and were pleased to be able to add him to the force."

"And that is the reason for the accusation of collaboration." Conrad knew now why the woman in the street had been so virulent in her condemnation. "She knew that four men had been sent to the prison at Verviers and that only one of them had been released. So, she had assumed that Bonnaire had bought his freedom with collaboration. Perhaps a relative of hers had been in the prison too and had not been so fortunate?"

"Or perhaps she knew that he had become a collaborator." Fabron sounded apologetic but his voice was still firm. "He had been in German hands for six months. Perhaps he just couldn't hold out any longer. Conrad, I know you like the man, but we have to ask the question. Why was he released?"

"One of the subversive things about evil is that it is arbitrary. This young woman is left to spend the last few minutes of her life choking at the end of a rope while that one gets a quick, clean death. Why did this Hartzleff chose Dianne Villeneuve for a broken neck? Perhaps because she smiled at him once? Or because she reminded him of his own daughter? Perhaps he just felt good humored that morning? What we do know is that if he was sitting here with us today, he would point to that note and say 'see, I am not such a bad person' and there are some who would believe him.

Conrad's Other Eye

"So it may also be with Bonnaire. Perhaps, somebody read the record we have here and came to a conclusion. This man is a follower, not a leader. He will do the legwork but never the planning. He is a tiny cog in the machine. Perhaps the man making the decision had also been in the trenches and decided to give a decorated fellow veteran a break. Perhaps, there was a more practical reason. They could release him and follow him to see if he led them to more resistance cells."

Conrad sighed. "Or he may have become a collaborator. It occurs to me that there is another possibility. We know that the group Bonnaire was associated with ran an escape route. We have decided he is an unimaginative man; would it not be natural for him to go back to the things that he knew? He returned to being a *gendarme*. Could he not also have returned to being a guide for escapees? That would confirm our suspicion that the attack on him was because he knew who the killer might be."

"There is a way we might find out who the other people in the smuggling ring were. The problem is that we will have to ask our friend Griffin for help."

Prison, Soumaigne, Belgium.

"Griffin? His wife is here to visit him." The janitor didn't need to check; Griffin's wife had gone in only a minute or two before.

"I had her sent here from Brussels. Our friendly Australian pilot picked her up and brought her down." Fabron explained to Conrad while they went in to the main body of the prison. "My superiors think that this case is that important."

That gave Conrad a thought. "Guy, could your superiors do me a great favor? I need to send a message to Washington. If we could get it to Paris and to the U.S. Embassy there, it would go straight through."

"We can send a message to our divisional headquarters, yes. And they will take it to the Embassy. Ahh, here we are, and Griffin's wife is waiting for him to be brought in. Now, that is a surprise."

Conrad saw immediately what Fabron had meant. He had expected Griffin's wife to be a hard-eyed, soul-less slattern; a woman who had made her way in the world using her body to exploit those around her. He had assumed that Griffin's image of her as anything else had been just another example of the way he had created a wall of self-deception to shield himself from what he did and what he had become.

Instead, the adjective he would use to describe Griffin's wife was mousy. She was at least ten years older than Griffin, plain and had obviously no great skill at presenting herself. Yet, there was an air of kindliness about her. Conrad was quite convinced that she was indeed the schoolteacher Griffin had described. She was also timid, and it was all too clear that she was overwhelmed by the unexpected change in her life. Finally, and this added to the pathos of the picture, she was obviously pregnant.

Conrad and Fabron patiently stood in the background while Griffin was brought in and sat at a table with his wife. After fifteen minutes had passed, they made their way in. Griffin's wife saw them first and her distress was obvious. "Please, *Messieurs*, could we have just a few minutes more?"

"We need to speak with your husband for a few minutes, Madame. After that, you may have as much time as you wish." Fabron kept his voice level and neutral, as befitting an officer.

After she had left, Conrad and Fabron took her place at the small table. Conrad opened the conversation. "Griffin, we need some more help from you. Nobody yet knows you have been arrested. That is one of the advantages of this terrible winter. Nobody knows anything about anything more than a few kilometers from them. We need to find the next stage in this alleged escape route. We have reason to believe that somebody involved with that next stage is responsible for the crimes that have taken place here."

"I have told you; I do not know. The whole system was set up so that no one group of people could bring down the others."

"But, you know where to leave the people you were smuggling, yes?" Conrad looked at Griffin and saw the sudden flash of insight dawn. "If you were to pass word that you were bringing out another woman and left her at the agreed place, then the people in the next stage could come for her and we could pick them up."

"You'd ask me to lure them into a trap?" Griffin was outraged, or at least putting on a good imitation of being outraged.

Fabron leaned forward a little. "Griifin, let me make this very clear to you. These people have murdered an unknown number of women. They have killed a commissioner. They have attacked a *gendarmerie* and, at the very least, kidnapped a *gendarme*. That means they have declared war on the government. You may have heard what happens when somebody does that. In America, it is called The Big Heat, I believe."

"I've heard of it." Griffin sounded grim.

"What you may not have heard is that when this situation occurs, the French Government is unforgiving towards those who perpetrated the crime, but rewards well those who help bring the guilty to justice. You are a thief and a smuggler. But even a thief and a smuggler, who had helped the authorities bring such criminals to justice, might find his slate wiped clean. Provided, of course, that he never again resumed his criminal activities."

"Griffin, there is more here at stake than just your own position. Your wife carries your child. If you are executed, who will look after them? You know how bad the winter is and that there is worse to come. A woman, on her own with a young baby? How could she survive without a man to protect her?"

Conrad got a sudden eerie sensation that Achillea was looking at him with an eyebrow raised.

"I promise you that, regardless of whether you help us or not, I will do my best to protect them. However, it was your pride and refusal to ask for help that led you to this place. You do not strike me as the sort of man who would leave his family to the mercy of others, nor the sort of man who would wish to die carrying such a debt. Will you let the sin of pride take you further down this path?"

Griffin shook his head slowly. "I'll help you. Ginny and our kid are about the only things in my life that I haven't screwed up . . . yet. We'll need to have a woman to act as a decoy, though. And, with respect to you both, I have seen few women priests and even fewer women paratroopers."

"He's right, Conrad, although I have heard the Russians had some women in their para units. And, of course, in their partisan units. But, we need to have a woman with us to act as a decoy."

"I think I know of a candidate." Conrad thought carefully. "A good candidate."

Commissioner Morin's Office, Verviers Displaced Persons Camp

"Madam Annick, we need help badly." Conrad quickly explained what had happened and how he believed all the pieces fitted together. "We need a woman to act the part of a refugee from Germany who is being trafficked to Spain or Italy."

"Will this help find the man who killed Laurentin?"

"I believe so. Mari, I am convinced that Commissioner Morin was killed because he was making inquiries into the trafficking of food, medicines and women in this area. I also believe we have a man of great evil involved here, one who does not fear even the most dire consequences for himself.

"It is likely that he has killed many of the women who were trafficked through this area. We have caught the person who is responsible for the thefts of food and medicines and he has agreed to help us set a trap."

"And he will benefit greatly from his cooperation." Mari Annick said the words with a flat intonation that gave no hint of her feelings. Yet, by that very lack, showed how deep those feelings were.

"Indeed. We are forgiving a lesser evil in exchange for dealing with a greater one." Conrad was suddenly and very unpleasantly aware that he had, just recently, given a lecture on how the Devil used that very argument to ensnare over-trusting souls. *Truly, there is a slippery slope to perdition and it is hideously easy to take that first step.*

"Very well, I will assist you. But, how do I know that this man will not simply take me away to another location and kill me there?"

"You'll have a platoon of paras around you, watching every exit." Fabron was reassuring. "And we will have searched the area thoroughly. There will be no place for this man to go."

"There is a problem." Griffin was looking at Mari Annick and shaking his head. "This lady will not do. She doesn't look like a refugee from Germany. She's wrong.

"The German refugees are beaten people, haunted by what happened to them. It shows in their eyes, in their bearing, in everything they do. They woke up that morning the lords of Europe. They had everything they wanted and none dare deny them even their most trivial demands. By noon, they were dying in the millions. By evening, they were paupers, refugees in their own country, with everything they had destroyed and burning.

"The suddenness with which they were cast down has left them empty, tormented, trapped in a living nightmare. This lady does not show any of that. Anybody who has seen real German refugees will know she is not one of them. I am sorry, Madame Annick, but you will not do. We must find somebody else."

Madame Annick looked at him and nodded. "You are the one who would know this. Lieutenant, Father, do you agree with him?"

Conrad and Fabron exchanged glances. "As you say, Mari, he is the one who knows. It appears we must find another candidate."

She nodded and stepped closer to Griffin. Suddenly her hand lashed out and connected with Griffin's cheek in a slap that had the echo of a pistol shot. "And that is for the people who died because you stole our medicines."

Then, she quietly left the room, leaving Griffin staring at the floor.

"Well, we could bring a woman in from Germany?" Fabron didn't sound convinced. The three men left the administrative offices and returned to Fabron's jeep. Halfway there, Conrad heard a familiar voice.

"Father, father." It was Elli Holzknecht. She still had the haunted, lost look in her eyes. But she was also the first person Conrad had met who looked better now than she had done a week, or more, earlier. "If you have time, could you hold a mass for the souls of the dead children here? There are so many of them."

"Of course." Conrad noticed that she was thinking outside her own little world now. "As soon . . . "

Conrad was about to say more. Griffin cut across him. "This one would be perfect if she would agree to help us."

"Perfect for what?" Elli Holzknecht sounded puzzled. Conrad quickly explained the situation, just as he had with Mari Annick.

"Of course I will help you, Father."

"You do understand there are some risks." Conrad knew Fabron was confident his paras could control the situation, but things could always go wrong.

"What have I to lose, Father? If all goes well, then nothing has changed for me. If it goes badly, then I will be with my little Josef again. So, what have I to lose?"

CHAPTER FIVE

PRICE OF JUSTICE

Cantonment, Premier Compagnie, 2e Régiment de Chasseurs Parachutistes, Soumaigne, Belgium.

"We have set the ambush up. Now all that remains is for the beast to enter the cage." Fabron was meticulously inspecting the ammunition he had been issued, making sure that the rounds were undented and the bullet was loaded true. Already, there was a small pile of 9mm rounds he had rejected for one reason or another. There was also a magazine that had damaged lips in the reject pile. Conrad had seen the ritual before, when Achillea was going out to fight somebody. The same meticulous attention to detail; the same scrupulous elimination of as many elements of chance as possible.

"What happened?" Conrad had only just arrived on the armory and was out of touch with the developments.

"Griffin took us to the place where the handover is scheduled. He has contacted some of his friends and told them that he was bringing a woman out of Germany for transfer to Spain. We have some people watching it already, in case the *voyous* turn up early to make sure the place is not under surveillance. Then Griffin will take Elli to the building and lock her in. She is a very brave woman, Conrad."

"I will pray for her. And for Genevieve Griffin. Doctor Lémieux is very concerned for her. He fears she may lose her baby."

Fabron grimaced. "The thought occurred to me as soon as I saw her condition. Conrad, there are few women who become pregnant and most lose their baby early in their term. The tiny handful who do not, deliver a sick and weakly child that dies soon after birth. Perhaps, if she is very lucky and her husband used his criminal earnings to get her the food and rest she needs, she may beat the odds."

"Doctor Lémieux said the same thing, only he was less hopeful." Conrad sighed. "You know Madame Holzknecht also lost her baby?"

Fabron was thrown for a second by the formal reference to the woman he knew as Elli. "So I gather. That was her little Josef, I assume?"

"It was. I do not think she will ever recover from the loss. Perhaps tonight may help her. Her selfless act, putting herself in extreme danger to make sure that the suffering caused by these people ends, is the result of her starting to look at the world again instead of hiding from it."

"She said one interesting thing, Conrad. I mentioned Marius Dressler in passing. She did not like him. Says he was a solitary man who shunned company. Apparently, he bought some sausages on the black market a week or so before he died. He ate them all himself, refusing to even consider sharing some of them with those around him."

"Unsocial of him. And very unusual. People usually pull together in times like this." Conrad shook his head. "When will we be leaving?"

"You're not coming, Conrad. You'll stay here until the shooting is done." Fabron's voice was fierce. "We have every reason to believe that the gangsters have banana guns and those things are killers. I don't want to have to worry about keeping you safe in the middle of a firefight. That truck convoy was one thing. You were behind armor and we knew what was about to happen. This is very different. It could end up as a wild scramble with automatic weapons in pitch darkness. Looking after you could get somebody killed."

Conrad was about to reply, but Fabron held up his hand. "Conrad, it the job of a priest to speak for those who cannot speak for themselves. Right? Well, it is the job of a soldier to fight for those who cannot fight for themselves. Tonight will be the time for soldiers. Yours will come later. Of that, I am certain."

Conrad knew that Fabron was right;he would get in the way and endanger the people he was with. There was only one thing he could do. "*Dominus noster Jesus Christus te absolvat; et ego auctoritate ipsius te absolvo ab omni vinculo excommunicationis et interdicti in quantum possum et tu indiges. Deinde, ego te absolvo a peccatis tuis in nomine Patris, et Filii, et Spiritus Sancti. Amen.*" Conrad's fingers made the sign of the cross. "May God look after you as you do his work this night."

Fabron kissed the crucifix he had around his neck. He went outside to join his men. They boarded the trucks that would move them to the scene of the ambush. Conrad heard the platoon of paratroopers move out. Then he took out his rosary and started to pray for the safety of the men who had just left.

He did not know how long he had been praying when the door behind him crashed open. A para private was in the doorway. His chest heaved with the effort he had made to get there without delay. "Father, come quickly. Your services are desperately needed and time is very short."

Rue Vieux Couvent, Bolland, Belgium.

Conrad was reasonably certain he would have been safer accompanying the para platoon that had set out earlier than riding this jeep. The para behind the wheel was hurling the vehicle down the ice-covered roads. He relied on the snow banks either side to keep them from ending up in the ditch. He had already bounced the jeep off the snow three times. Hanging on to his seat, Conrad felt a sudden, very urgent desire for a strong drink. Instead, he managed to moisten his mouth enough to speak. "What happened?"

"Don't know, Father. All I do know is that things went sour and there are casualties. Some very bad, and in need of your services. I was told to get you here without delay."

The jeep bounced off another snowbank. It swerved to a halt in front of a dilapidated building. Conrad recognized what it had once been, even if he didn't know this particular example. Once, when this whole area had been forest, the local landowner had built a small hunting lodge. Nothing elaborate, just somewhere he and his friends could get away for a few days and pretend to be huntsmen. Then, as the area had changed and the trees were cut down for farmland, the lodge had fallen into disuse. Now, there was only a small sliver of forest left. Just enough to hide the lodge from the narrow lane that ran past.

Conrad had already put some snow-shoes on. He ran towards the lodge. The paras were gathered around it. "Quick, Father, there may still be time."

He didn't know who had shouted, but it gave him all the impetus he needed. Inside the lodge, there were four people on the floor. Doctor Lémieux was working on one para who had taken a bullet through the shoulder. Just across from him, Elli Holzknecht was on the floor. A para jacket was folded under her head. Achillea's voice echoed to him across the years. *Here, there's no reason you should be uncomfortable.* Her breath was coming in quick, shallow pants, with long pauses between them. Conrad knew well what that meant. She was dying fast. He could see why. Her stomach and abdomen were chewed to pulp by bullet wounds.

He knelt beside her and saw the flash of recognition in her eyes. *"Per istam sanctam unctionem et suam piissimam misericordiam adiuvet te Dominus gratia Spiritus Sancti. Dominus a peccato liberat te, qui praeter te sublevabit te."*

There was one last thing to do. Conrad took a fragment of wafer from the box. He touched it to her lips and followed it with a spot of wine from his finger. She looked up at him. She tried to say something but the massive wounds had stilled her voice. Then, she died.

"She saved us all." One of the paras had tears trickling down his face. "When that bastard opened fire, she threw herself at him; threw her arms around his neck. Trapped his gun between her body and his. She hung on even when he was firing into her. That's how we got in. Most of us."

He glanced at another figure on the floor, one covered by a lizard-camoflage cape with the lizard cap placed on top. Conrad didn't need to look under the cape to know who it was. He lifted the cape anyway, hoping that his sure and certain knowledge would be wrong. It was not.

Guy Fabron looked up at him, his eyes glazed already from the cold, both of death and the snow. His expression was hard to gauge; a mixture of shock, surprise and anger. Conrad guessed the anger was not directed at the person who had shot him, but at the fact Fabron was dying without finishing the task he had in hand. There was something else there as well, an ironic element of peace. Suddenly, Conrad was very glad that he had given his friend absolution before he had set out this night.

Doctor Lémieux looked up, his eyes full of pain and pity. "Father, I'm sorry. I know he was your friend. He was first through the door, like any para officer, and that swine over there shot him. Madame Holzknecht saved him from the worst of the burst, but one bullet cut his aorta. There was nothing anybody could do. He bled out in seconds. Can you help me here please?"

Conrad tore his eyes away from the body of Guy Fabron. *Guy, you never knew it, but you had many, many lifetimes ahead of you. Yours is a loss that many people you never heard of will mourn. Phillip Stuyvesant will say that you were one in 6.8 million, but to him people are statistics. He is wrong. We are all individuals and our loss is incalculable.* Conrad hesitated for a second. *But, if you meet a cavalryman called Derya Shafrid on Fiddler's Green, tell him that after 2,000 years, his wife still loves him and honors him by bearing his name.* "What would you like me to do?"

"Help me with this man. We have to stop the wound bleeding. Just push hard here." Lémieux pointed at the para he was treating. The man had a blood-soaked shoulder and was pale. "I need to tie the bandage tight."

Conrad looked around again. Elli Holzknecht's body had been covered by a cape, and a para had placed his lizard cap on the body. He knew now what that meant; even in death, the paras looked after those they considered their own.

Then he saw the last figure on the floor. Even pinned down by four paras, Étienne Bonnaire was still struggling to get free. He was making weird, strange noises, ones that sounded as if a rabid beast had been caught in a trap. Conrad had heard those noises before, at the *gendarmerie*. Without thinking, he held up his crucifix to protect the man Doctor Lémieux was treating. As soon as he saw it, the strange, bestial noises from Bonnaire redoubled.

"What happened here?" Major Roul was standing in the doorway, surveying the scene.

"We saw him entering the building. He didn't seem to be armed, but we know now he had one of these under his coat." The para sergeant handed his officer an odd-looking weapon. It was similar to a banana gun, but had no shoulder stock and a very short barrel.

"*Sturmpistole*. StP-46." Roul saw Conrad looking up at him and explained. "Cut down StG-45 assault rifle. Germans made them for truck drivers and so on. Gestapo loved them as well. What happened then?"

"We heard the lady start to scream, so we closed in fast. The lieutenant kicked the door down, but got hit by a blast from that. Then, she grabbed him and that allowed the rest of us in." The sergeant's voice broke. "We tried, but the lieutenant was already dead."

"And he's the bastard who did it." Roul's voice had a deadly, icy cold to it. "Étienne Bonnaire, you are detained by the French military authorities on God knows, sorry Father, how many charges of murder."

Conrad stared at Bonnaire as he was hauled to his feet. He was still struggling and lashing out at the men around him. His efforts were thwarted with a singular lack of gentleness. That was when the final piece dropped into place.

"Major Roul, I do not know who this man is, but he is not Étienne Bonnaire."

Roul looked at him curiously. "Guy spoke well of you, so I assume you have a reason for saying that?"

"Something has been worrying me. It never registered until I saw the picture of Étienne Bonnaire from his army file. Even then, I have only just realized its significance. You see, when I first met this man, he was driving a *kubelwagen* and he had to position his baton properly, hanging over the side, to stop it obstructing him. It was on his left, you see." Roul was frowning, unable to see where the story was going. "A *gendarme* carries his pistol on his right hip, so it can be drawn with his right hand straight up. But, his baton is on his left hip, so it can be drawn across his body. That assumes the *gendarme* is right-handed, of course. And, this man is indeed right-handed. I saw that just now with his struggles."

"So?" There was a tinge of impatience in Roul's voice.

"The *gendarme*'s baton hangs in the same place as the *poilu*'s bayonet. It is the same belt, you see. But, in the picture of Corporal Étienne Bonnaire, the bayonet hung on his right hip. The real Étienne Bonnaire was left-handed."

"So, who the hell is he?" Conrad mentally forgave Roul for his anger. With one of his officers and a civilian dead, he was looking for anybody he could strike out at.

"We know that Étienne Bonnaire, Ferdinand Labelle, Christophe Thomas and Marcel Petiot were sent to the prison at Verviers. We know that one man and one man only was released. That man claimed to be Étienne Bonnaire, but we know now that he was not. So, this man must be Ferdinand Labelle, Christophe Thomas or Marcel Petiot. I think, perhaps, the files in Paris may help us narrow it down still further. Perhaps also, if we speak with the authorities in Charleville, they may have information that will help us."

Cantonment, Premier Compagnie, 2e Régiment de Chasseurs Parachutistes, Soumaigne, Belgium.

In fact, the information they needed was waiting for them in the regimental base. The Gestapo file on Étienne Bonnaire and his associates had given the ages of all those involved. Going by that information, he assumed that Roger Deforest, Arnaud Soucy and Dianne Villeneuve were the leaders of the cell. Deforest and Soucy had been in their mid-30s when they had been executed. Villeneuve had been 29. She had been listed as a nurse, the other two as industrial workers. Ferdinand Labelle and Christophe Thomas were listed as students, in their very early 20s. Obviously, neither of them could be the man now sitting in the cells.

"I think we can piece this together. We know Deforest was the leader of the group, and we can assume that Soucy and Villeneuve were his lieutenants. That's why the Germans hanged them first. They were the core of the cell and the heart of this resistance group. Labelle and Thomas did the legwork. Both fit young men, they escorted the escaping Jews and pilots from one hideout to the next. They probably shared the work between them, so that the connections would not be too obvious. Bonnaire was the inside man. He covered for them, buried any complaints that might point to them and warned them of any undue interest being shown in them."

"So, where does that leave Petiot?" Major Roul was nodding in agreement with Conrad's assessment.

"I don't think he was a member of the group at all. I think he boasted of being so, probably when he drank too much. Eventually, he did so in the wrong company and was arrested. He knew much of the resistance group though, probably because Bonnaire arrested him when he was in his cups and cautioned him against speaking so openly of those who were in the Resistance. I think Petiot started talking literally the moment he was arrested, and the first one he implicated was Bonnaire. That may be chance, may be spite on his part for the caution he received. Whatever it was, it deprived the group of the warning they would otherwise have received and they were all caught."

Conrad paused for a second. Guy Fabron and Elli Holzknecht were both laying side by side in the Soumaigne chapel, watched over by an honor guard of four paratroopers. The guard was relieved every four hours. Conrad made a point of being there to say a Mass for them and those they guarded.

"I think the Germans very quickly realized that Petiot was not a member of the group, even though he had been instrumental in betraying them. That was why they let him go. If we could get at the Verviers prison records, I am sure we would find that Bonnaire, Labelle and Thomas were executed about the time Petiot was released. The Germans may even have hoped that he would revert to type and find another resistance group to start boasting about. Probably, during their imprisonment, Petiot learned enough about Bonnaire to impersonate him. We can also assume that, when the refugee trafficking route was set up, somebody who knew a little about the resistance cell in Charleville saw his name and thought his knowledge of how the escape route worked would be invaluable. I think we need to know a lot more about Marcel Petiot."

"I will get it sent up from Paris as soon as possible. In the mean time, we can leave him to sweat in his cell for a little." Roul hesitated. "Father, I was sharp with you earlier. You have done much for us and my rudeness was unwarranted. Please forgive me."

Conrad waggled his hand, palm downwards. "There is no need to apologize. We were all in shock last night. I do not think any of us realized there was any chance of it turning out the way it did. Perhaps Guy did. He was checking his ammunition vary carefully before he left."

"All my boys do that. Something we learned in Indochina. But we do have something else to work from. We searched that old hunting lodge very carefully. Not much turned up, but we did find something. What appears to be an account book. It appears that Petiot was into black marketeering as well as robbery and murder. There are lists of good supplied to various intermediaries. Mostly sausages and other foods."

Conrad looked up, remembering the conversation he had had with Rosina Neske. A terrible suspicion was beginning to form in the back of his mind.

Prison, Soumaigne, Belgium.

Conrad stared at Marcel Petiot, noting the smug smile of satisfaction on the man's face. *He had been sitting alone in his cell for two days, doubtlessly imagining that the authorities would be hoping the solitary confinement would break his will. He also now thinks that the fact he has been brought here means he has won that round. He has yet to learn just how mistaken he is.*

For those two days, the French authorities had been scouring their archives, locating all the information they had on Petiot. The picture it had revealed was chilling. Marcel André Henri Félix Petiot had been born at

Conrad's Other Eye

Auxerre in 1897. He had been expelled from a series of schools and only escaped convictions for theft and vandalism because the local magistrate had been convinced he was insane.

The French army had agreed with him. Although Petiot had been conscripted in 1916, his military record had been bad, to the point where, despite the desperate shortage of manpower, he had been discharged due to "mental disequilibrium, neurasthenia, mental depression, melancholia, obsessions and phobias." The Army had suggested he be committed to an asylum but, incredibly, Petiot had somehow turned that into an opportunity. Aided by an accelerated education program for war veterans, he had completed medical school in a stunning eight months and served a two-year psychiatric internship at Evreux. He received his medical degree on 15 December 1921, from the *Faculté de Médeceine de Paris*.

He had moved back to Auxerre and set up in medical practice. He had been convicted of theft and frauds but, to Conrad's eye, there was something even more significant. People started dying around him. His first girlfriend, Louise Delaveau, had mysteriously disappeared. Others had suffered accidents or curious and terminal illnesses. It seemed almost as hazardous to be his friend as his enemy; Conrad quickly became convinced that anybody who learned anything about Petiot was in mortal peril.

By the mid-1930s, he had become mayor of the town of Villeneuve-sur-Vonne. The authorities had noted that the town appeared to have had an unusually high number of aliens registering to live there. Prosecutors investigated, finding that 138 alien registration applications and F2,890 in fees had been held at City Hall, never relayed to the proper authorities. Nor was there any trace of the aliens who had allegedly made those registrations. They had assumed the people in question had never existed, but Conrad had a much more sinister explanation now.

Petiot had served a few weeks in prison for fraud and, when released, had moved to Paris. There, he set up in practice under an assumed name. Although he had purported to be a general practitioner, subsequent inquiries had shown that he had served mostly as an abortionist and drug dealer. Once again, a surprising number of his patients had disappeared, after turning up as his offices with large sums of cash for their treatment.

Once France had surrendered in 1940, he began providing false medical certificates to Frenchmen drafted for slave labor. Petiot also apparently treated sick and wounded workers returned to France from Germany. Once again, many of them appeared to have vanished after approaching him for treatment. This had quickly grown into another one of his schemes, where he had been claiming to run a pipeline from occupied countries to Spain. The Gestapo had got wind of it fairly quickly and investigated the allegations. They quickly ran into a major problem. No matter how hard they tried, they couldn't find anybody who had been conveyed to freedom by the network. They had tried to infiltrate it, but the agents they sent in had simply vanished.

By the time they had an idea of what was really happening, Petiot had vanished. The Gestapo found a mass of human remains in the basement. They had been incinerated in a furnace, but the fragments left had convinced the Gestapo investigators that at least sixty people had been killed in that location alone.

Petiot had resumed his own identity in Charleville, and continued his activities there. He was aided by the almost complete collapse of civil organization in France. Simply the fact that the Gestapo was looking for somebody was enough to convince others that the quarry was an anti-German resistance worker. There, in Charleville, with the arrest of the resistance group, the trail had ended.

Dear God, just how many people have you killed? Conrad continued to stare at Petiot. *If I add these figures up right, the number must be more than three hundred.*

"You led everybody on a merry dance, didn't you, Doctor Petiot? You even fooled the Gestapo, and that is no mean achievement. I can truthfully say that in many years as an investigator, I have not met anybody quite like you."

Conrad watched carefully as a degree of vindictiveness crept into the smugness. "I certainly fooled you. You actually believed that somebody like me could be a slow-witted, unimaginative policeman. I managed to steer you away from every possible lead to what was really going on. You and your foolish little cards."

I wish he was wrong there. He did play his part to perfection. "You hoodwinked *Kriminalinspektor* Robert Jodkum, that's certain. He never had any idea of what you were really doing. All those refugees you robbed and murdered and he never even guessed what was happening right under his nose. A masterful plan."

"It was nothing. I had already worked out the basics of it before the war. I just applied the same technique to the new circumstances."

"Ahh yes, the missing aliens in Villeneuve-sur-Vonne. You killed them all, of course."

"Indeed. It was easy enough. There were so many people who wanted to settle in France for varying reasons. Mostly they were from Spain and wanted to escape the war there. I spread word that, for a fee, I would see they had proper papers to live in France. After I had been paid and made out the permit, I would tell them they had to be inoculated against disease. I'd give them the injection, it was poison, of course, and watch them die. Then I would take the rest of their belongings, dispose of the bodies and sell their property. The authorities were too stupid to put everything together."

"Just like you did in Paris and Charleville."

"Exactly. You are beginning to understand my genius at last. Paris, during the German occupation, was full of people who were desperate to escape to Spain or Italy. So, once again, I allowed word to circulate that Dr. Eugène would help them. They came, I inoculated them, they died. This time, the profits were great, for the refugees would bring all their valuables with them. The first six were a pair of pimps and four of their women. The prostitutes were Jewish and the pimps wanted to get them to safety in Spain. So, I poisoned all six of them. I knew both men. I'd done abortions for their women when necessary. They were stupid. If they'd left the women to their fate, they'd be alive today."

"One thing puzzled me about Paris." Conrad looked up his notes. "You may not be aware of this, but *Kriminalinspektor* Jodkum of the Gestapo survived the war. A little chastened, perhaps, since his wife was knocked off her feet by a Corsair when the Navy aircraft beat up the streets of Paris the day of The Big One.. He was, of course, sentenced to death for his actions, but he was reprieved so he could testify against you. I do not think you realize how important you are to the authorities. Anyway, he mentioned that there was a soundproof octagonal chamber, with wall-mounted shackles and a peephole centered in its door, in the basement of the Paris place. What was that all about?"

Petiot has visibly swollen with pride. "Poison was getting hard to get with the occupation. The Germans started to control such things, in case they were used against them. So, whenever I could, I started to strangle them. It was so much better than poisoning them. Especially the women. I could look into their eyes as they died. Sometimes, if I had time, I would strangle them until they passed out, then let them revive and do it again. Nobody knew what was happening. If it hadn't been for that stupid fire, I could have stayed there for years."

Conrad nodded sympathetically. *If it hadn't been for an accidental fire at his slaughterhouse, he would indeed have been able to continue his massacre. When the firefighters broke into the house on the* Rue le Sueur, *what they found made them vomit. The cause of the house fire had been a coal-fed stove burning full-blast, with a human arm dangling from its open door. Nearby, a heap of coal was mixed with human bones and fragments of several dismembered bodies. "Kriminalinspektor Jodkum thinks there may have been as many as sixty bodies there."*

"Sixty! There were so many even I lost count. Two hundred, certainly; could be three hundred. It doesn't matter though. What is important is that I'd seen the possibility of detection and arranged a quick escape route. I had all the loot ready to go and a new false identity prepared. As Henri Valéri, I travelled to Charleville with the story that the Gestapo had closed in on my escape route. There, people knew of my work with the Resistance, or so they thought, and they begged me to help them set up a new escape route. I did, of course, just like the old one."

Conrad frowned slightly. "The records show that you had a wife and child. What happened to them?"

"They were in the way. So I killed them, of course." Petiot showed signs of irritation at Conrad's obtuseness. "Everything went well at first. Deforest and his resistance group thought they were on the first stage of an escape route and it never occurred to them that they were the only stage. They were stupid, you see, as stupid as the police and Gestapo.

"Then, as the American Navy started its fighter-bomber raids, Deforest and Villeneuve wanted to use the escape route to get shot-down pilots out. That was a problem, because they were fit young men, too strong for me to kill by hand and too well-informed to fall for the inoculation trick. So, I put poison in their food."

"So, you even fooled the U.S. Navy." Conrad shook his head in feigned admiration. "Is there anybody you didn't make look like idiots?"

Petiot shook his head. "The Navy pilots were a problem because I found out the radio operator, Soucy, had told the Americans that they were coming out. They hadn't arrived, of course, and Deforest wanted to know why. But, I'd only killed about a dozen of them by then, so it was a small problem and easy to solve. I informed on the group and they were all arrested.

"We were all sent to prison but the Germans didn't bother much with me. They hanged Deforest, Sourcy and Villeneuve first, then Bonnaire, Labelle and Thomas a few months later. They let me go. I put on a good act for them, you see. The drunken loudmouth, who boasted a lot but never did anything. They'd identified me as Petiot, but they never linked me to the Paris operation. I could see the value of being a policeman, so I took Bonnaire's identity."

"And then you made the black marketeers look like morons as well."

"They were morons. They'd heard I was associated with the escape route and wanted me to set it up for them. So I did. Just like the others. I found the old hunting lodge as a waypoint and started again. I'd learned from the American pilots This time, I wrote some forged notes from the refugees who were supposed to have escaped. But, I couldn't get any poison, so I had to hang them all. I got the idea from the prison at Nancy. The Gestapo made us watch Deforest, Sourcy and Villeneuve being hanged. I was looking forward to watching that arrogant bitch Villeneuve choking on the end of a rope, but that bastard Hartzleff ruined it. He allowed her to wash and put on make-up and a new dress before breaking her neck."

The mystery of Hartzleff. Conrad shook his head to himself. *He allowed her to die with dignity. I wonder why.*

Petiot was still talking. Conrad realized he had missed a little of what he had said. "Then, when the winter started and food became short, I realized that I had all this meat I could sell. So, I turned it into sausages and sold them. Some of the black marketeers acted as middlemen. They didn't know where the sausages came from, of course. I think they believed they had come in by the same route as the refugees went out. Which they had, of course."

Conrad was stunned. In his long life, he had run across many vile criminals. But of them all, Doctor Marcel Petiot had to be the worst. *There is not the slightest sign of grief or repentance in him. Dear God, forgive me, for the first time in centuries, I wish I was still an inquisitor.* "And why did you kill Commissioner Morin?"

"Oh, you finally worked it out, did you?" Petiot was openly sneering at Conrad. "I didn't think you had it in you."

"I know you killed him. He looked on you as a policeman and an ally. He trusted you and you walked up to him and smashed in his head with your baton. Doctor Lémieux found a splinter of wood from your baton in the wound. The armorer has your baton and he is trying to fit the splinter to it. When he does, and he will, you can be sure of that, the case will be complete. Not that it needs to be. You can go to the guillotine right now for the killing of Lieutenant Fabron and Madame Holzknecht. So, I ask again, why did you kill Commissioner Morin?"

"It was that fool Griffin's fault. All the women he had brought over earlier had no relatives; they just vanished. Then, he brought over Martina Dressler. He didn't even have the sense to pass on the message that there was somebody waiting here for her. She was just left in the usual place. By the time I found out she was different from the rest, she was already dead.

"Dressler had gone to Morin, told him what was happening, asked for his help in locating his daughter. Morin called me in, asking me to investigate from the law enforcement side, but he said that he would be talking with the traffickers as well. He knew them from buying medicines for the camp. That I couldn't allow, of course. So, when a noise made him glance away, I killed him.

"I was going to find Dressler and kill him. But, instead, you led me straight to him. I arrested him and took him to the *gendarmerie*. I used the cells there to get rid of the refugees, so I put him in one and persuaded him to hang himself."

"You managed to talk him into killing himself?" The marvel in Conrad's voice would have convinced anybody who didn't know him well.

"It was easy. He was just a stupid German. You see, he had bought some black market sausages to celebrate his reunion with his daughter. Food in Germany is even more limited than the rations here and a plate full of sausages would have been a splendid way of celebrating her escape."

So that was why Dressler ate the sausages himself. He bought them to share with his daughter and, when he believed she was dead or had failed to escape, he ate them himself, pretending that his daughter was with him. A strange thing to do, perhaps, but who can tell what a parent who believed their child was dead, found them and then lost them again will do?

Petiot was still talking. "What he didn't know was his daughter was already dead and the sausages were made from her flesh. That's right, priest. He had eaten his own daughter's flesh. I told him that; showed him the entry in my book. Told him how his daughter had screamed as I carved the flesh from her body, how she had begged me to kill her. He was in the cell I had used to hang her and the noose was still there. As I told him what had happened, he broke down weeping and he hanged himself. Weak, pathetic apology for a man."

To Conrad's horror, as he watched Petiot describing the terrible end of Martina Dressler, the man's face started to change. It became redder and narrower. The eyes grew deeply shadowed and seemed to glow in the ill-lit interrogation room. His beard, full and overgrown, seemed to change into a narrow, pointed goatee.

Conrad blinked. The illusion was gone. Conrad still held up his crucifix and rosary. The words of the short exorcism rolled off his tongue. *"Sáncte Míchael Archángele, defénde nos in proélio, cóntra nequítiam et insídias diáboli ésto præsídium. Ímperet illi Déus, súpplices deprecámur: tuque, prínceps milítiæ cœléstis, Sátanam aliósque spíritus malígnos, qui ad perditiónem animárum pervagántur in múndo, divína virtúte, in inférnum detrúde. Ámen." And thank you Achillea for teaching me the proper pronunciation of the Latin. Even if you do use the language for some of the most luridly obscene curses I have ever heard.*

Petiot's reaction was immediate and violent. Once again, he reverted to the bestial, rabid snarling that Conrad had heard before. He hurled himself across the table, clawing for Conrad's eyes and throat. He never made it. Conrad felt himself being hurled to one side as two sergeants crashed into the room. They picked Petiot up by his throat and hurled him against the wall, hard enough to shake the solid stone walls of the prison. Then, one held him pinned by the throat. The other started with a barrage of punches to his stomach and abdomen. Petiot screamed. This time, an intelligent, human scream.

"Hey, Father, the lieutenant was your friend as well. You want to take a swing?"

"Good people, please. There is great danger here. I do not know if this man was truly possessed, but I read the rite of exorcism. And, if he was, the demon that held him is seeking another lair. All he needs is a moment's opening, a minor sin, and he will enter. So far, you were protecting me and your actions are pure. But now he is subdued. A further assault might be just the sin the Devil looks for."

They let Petiot go and he slumped to the floor. "Do you think he really was possessed, Father?"

Conrad thought carefully about that. "No, it is bitterly cold and we are all hungry. That impairs judgment. After hearing a story of such unrelenting evil, I could only think that he was possessed. My eyes saw what the mind told them to see. Petiot is evil beyond anything I have ever met, but I think he is man's evil."

They left the cell together and went their separate ways. But, as Conrad turned the corner, he heard one sergeant speaking to the other. "The Father may say he wasn't possessed but I know what I saw."

Major Roul's Office, Premier Compagnie, 2e Régiment de Chasseurs Parachutiste, Soumaigne, Belgium.

"Father, are you well?"

Conrad smiled weakly at the Major. "To my great relief, yes. That was . . . intense."

"You will be pleased to know that Petiot is to be tried by court martial for the murder of Lieutenant Fabron and Madame Holzknecht. A portable guillotine is already on its way here. This way, he gets the chop as quickly as possible. I will not sleep easily until I know, beyond all doubt, that monster is dead."

Chapel, Premier Compagnie, 2e Régiment de Chasseurs Parachutistes, Soumaigne, Belgium.

"So he shot up the *gendarmerie* himself? Major Roul was getting all his ducks in a row.

"He did. After he manipulated Dressler into hanging himself. I think he was preparing to disappear again and set up elsewhere under another name. But the snowstorm held him up. By the time it had passed, word was spreading that another refugee was being brought over. The killings had long since become the main interest for Petiot. He couldn't resist just one more, especially since he didn't know how long it would be before he could do so again. I think the *gendarmerie* was where he started to come apart. It was overdone. He overegged the pudding with those booby traps."

Roul nodded in agreement. "And in doing so, he made his worst mistake. Shooting up the *gendarmerie* is an attack on the French state itself, a crime that carries the death penalty. The last entry on his record will be that he was executed as a traitor and a collaborator who murdered a sick woman and a soldier who tried to help her. A sordid, dirty end to his career."

"And a fitting one." Conrad was all too familiar with the glamour of evil. He knew that, when the full details of Petiot's crimes came out, there would be those who would become obsessed by him. The postscript to his life would, as

Roul had said, be sordid and pathetic. It would discourage such misguided people.

"Father, I don't think you met my wife?" Doctor Lémieux had joined them. "Francine, this is the good Father who helped us bring Petiot to justice."

Conrad looked at Madame Lémieux. He saw the white scar around her neck. She caught his eye and touched it with a slight smile. "I do not try and hide it, Father. I look on it as a medal, like those awarded to our gallant paras. And a tribute to those who died that day."

Her voice was hoarse and broken. It reminded Conrad of another woman whose voice had suffered the same way from cruel ill-treatment. Julia Barco was long in her grave, overwhelmed by the harm done to her. He knew that Madame Lémieux would not end her own life the way Julia Barco had. But he still felt driven to try and aid her. That was why he had with him a box that had arrived from New York. "Madame, I took the liberty of telling an old friend of mine about the harm that had been done to you. She is a herbalist, one of the finest I have ever known,"

"A herbalist!" Doctor Lémieux struck a horrified pose. "I am betrayed!"

"Be quiet, *Toubib*." Roul looked at him severely. "The Father is an honorary member of the regiment. By the way, Father, we have a lizard cap for you. It is not Lieutenant Fabron's, I fear. That will be buried with him. But, it is a tribute to you from the regiment and our thanks for all you have done for us. Now, Toubib, for insulting our good Father, you will run around the parade ground until you die."

"Please, Major, may I intercede for our *toubib*." Conrad had his best supplicatory voice on, although he knew well that the exchanges were good-humored. "He knows not what he says."

Lémieux joined in the laughter. "Actually, herbalists are sometimes of great service, as long as they are indeed skilled and understand the limitations of their craft. Some of their treatments work well and we use many of them today, when other medicines are in short supply and adulterated. What did your friend recommend?"

"She knows of the damage to the throat and recommends a tea made with honey mixed with sage, thyme, hyssop and elderberry leaves. It must be hot, but not uncomfortably so, and you must gargle with it before swallowing. Be careful, for the hyssop is harmful in large quantities. Take but one cup per day."

Madame Lémieux smiled sadly. "You and your friend are kind to try and help, but such things are not available here. But thank you both for trying."

Conrad held out the box he was carrying. "My friends thought that would be the case. So, a mutual friend of ours made this package for you. It contains everything you will need. The herbs are dried, so they must be left to stand in hot water before you use them. When the box is nearly empty, let her know and she will send you more."

Conrad handed over the box, looking at Igrat's handwriting on the package. Igrat had learned to write when an adult and her handwriting still had a schoolgirlish quality about it.

He suddenly remembered the night in Washington when she had arrived back from Geneva. The C-69 Constellation had come straight through the traffic pattern for Washington National, the crew firing off the red flares that warned people on the ground that they had critically injured patients on board and nothing was to get in the way. The airport had broken the blackout and put on its runway lights to bring the aircraft in. On the ground, the Connie had been surrounded by emergency vehicles. Igrat had been rushed out on a stretcher. Conrad had wept when he saw the state she was in. All the way to Bethesda Hospital, he had held her hand and prayed for her.

Madame Lémieux was smiling at him. "You have very kind friends, Father. What is the lady's name, so I may thank her?"

"Igrat Shafrid. She was badly hurt herself, by much the same kind of men who harmed you. Now, she feels kinship for others who have suffered similar misfortunes at the hands of such people and desires to help them when she can."

"Thank you, Father." Madame Lémieux suddenly looked haunted by guilt. "It is a strange coincidence, but the place the Germans hanged me, it was the same patch of woods around the hunting lodge where Petiot trapped his victims. How did I survive when so many died there? There were ten of us hanged that day. I am the only one who lived. Why did I live, Father?"

Conrad knew that was a question that had no real answer. "Madame, the answer that by custom is given to those who suffer from survivor's guilt is that God's plans are mysterious and known only to Him. It is not for us to try to understand or question them. That is a theological way of saying damned if I know."

There was an eruption of laughter around him. A couple of paras gave him a mock salute. "Father, you must become our regimental chaplain. Truly, you are one of us."

Conrad smiled at the lieutenant who had made the invitation. He was actually tempted for a second, but shook his head. Then, he carried on. "But in your case, Madame Lémieux, I do know the answer. You see, when I heard your story, suddenly everything we had learned in this case fell into place. It was your story that allowed me to realize what was happening.

"I am sure that your life was saved so that, when the time was right, the news of women being left to die in those woods would reach us. Once, Guy and I spoke together about how God gives us the chance and it is up to us to work hard, so that we may make the best of the opportunity we have been offered.

That day, He gave you a chance by loosening the rope that pinned your hands. You accepted his charge by fighting hard for your life.

"When you saved your life, Madame, you showed that you were strong enough to bear the burden. You were chosen by God to stand testimony for all those who had died. Now, your charge is complete. Your duty is done and you may carry on with your life, knowing that, by surviving, you have rendered great service to both God and man."

Prison, Soumaigne, Belgium.

"Richard, I have both bad news for you and good. Firstly, it is my sad duty to tell you that early this morning, your wife lost her baby. She received the best available treatment, and the doctors fought hard to save the child, but their efforts were unsuccessful. You should know that your wife is as well as can be expected and will recover.

"As for you, the news there is good. In view of the assistance you provided, and the real benefits the medicines you stole did bring at first, the French authorities have decided not to press charges against you, yet. You will be deported to the United States and, if you ever return to French jurisdiction, you will be prosecuted.

"Normally, the American military authorities would arrest you for desertion, but fortune has favored you. You were responsible for the arrest of Marcel Petiot who, by the way, goes to the guillotine tomorrow at 0500. Based on the information we obtained from him, we were able to locate the way station he used in his escape route at Charleville. We found the remains of his victims and, in those sad relics, were the dog tags of eight Navy pilots he murdered. He claimed twelve but he was not, I fear, a truthful man.

"Anyway, you were scheduled to be arrested for desertion. But Admiral King, the Navy commander, heard that you were responsible for the arrest of the man who had murdered eight of his pilots.

"Admiral King is not known to be a kindly man, but he is one who believes in paying his debts. He called in some favors and your desertion is being administratively expunged from the record. As a result, you have been discharged from the Air Force. You and your wife may take up civilian life in America."

Conrad paused for a second. "Richard, you have been given a second chance at life, a privilege granted to few. You have a clean record and a woman who loves you. Remember what happened before, when you let pride overcome good sense. Never let it happen again."

Conrad's Other Eye

Courtyard, Prison, Soumaigne, Belgium.

At 0500, it was still dark and bitterly cold. The portable guillotine had arrived at 0330. It had been assembled and was ready to do its grim work an hour later. Summoned from his cell, Petiot refused the traditional glass of rum but accepted a cigarette.

The closing ritual was swiftly completed. Petiot signed the register. His hands were bound, his neck shaved, and the collar cut from his shirt. He approached the guillotine calmly. Conrad watched him carefully, noting that, despite the bitter cold and biting wind, he moved with ease, as though he were walking into his office for a routine appointment. The paras were not gentle when they strapped him to the guillotine's sliding table.

The blade dropped at 0505. Conrad watched his head tumble into the basket. In the seconds between the blade severing Petiot's neck and the death shadow stilling his face, he was smiling.

Lodging House, Rue Donkier, Verviers, Belgium

"It is, perhaps, a good thing that her first love should end on this note." Madame Margreet Neske looked up the stairs to the room where her daughter was weeping. Conrad had told her of the death of Guy Fabron and it had devastated her. Even the account of how bravely he had died was no consolation.

Conrad looked at Madame Neske, slightly confused. She saw his expression and explained. "Rosina will get over it quickly, for the young are strong and resilient. She will meet another man, I hope a good one, and marry him. But, all her life, she will look back on what her life with a dashing para officer could have been like and be warmed by the memory. She will turn him into a perfect knight in shining armor and that memory will honor him also."

Conrad nodded thoughtfully. Her words rang true. "Madame Neske, I must thank you for what you have done for me here. Your hospitality and care will always be a fond memory for me. I wish you the best of fortune and know that I will pray for you."

Outside, Conrad saw a semi-familiar figure. It took him a second to place her. Then, he recognized her as the woman whose condemnation of the man she had believed was *Brigadier de Police* Étienne Bonnaire had been so venomous. She recognized him as well and her eyes narrowed with a mixture of guilt and defiance.

"Madame, I owe you an apology." The woman's eyes narrowed further, with suspicion dominating her expression. Conrad continued in his soft, merciless voice, for he had an innocent to defend and a wrongfully-accused to exonerate, "The man you accused was indeed a collaborator, one of the vilest sort and that was the least of his crimes. But, you believed you were accusing Étienne Bonnaire and, in that, you were bearing false witness.

"The man you accused was not Étienne Bonnaire, but Marcel Petiot, who had stolen his identity. Étienne Bonnaire was a brave and much-decorated veteran of the trenches, a respected and admired policeman and, finally, a gallant member of the Resistance, who was executed for his acts against the occupying forces. Your accusation against him was a grievous injustice. I would urge you seek forgiveness for that sin, even as you know that Petiot was indeed a worthy recipient of your harshest accusations."

The woman looked confused by the mixture of apology and blame and scuttled away. Conrad shook his head softly, wondering if she would indeed seek absolution or whether she would simply justify her sins to herself. *Probably the latter*, he thought.

He swung his bag into the back seat of the jeep and then boarded the little vehicle. For a brief second, he thought he saw Guy Fabron sitting behind the wheel, but it was Major Roul. He'd offered to drive Conrad to Liege, the first step in the long road back to Rome.

"So, you're all finished here?" Roul sounded regretful at Conrad's impending departure. "Must you leave?"

"I must. I have a report to deliver to His Holiness, one that stressed how vital it is that Europe receives as much aid as possible. From all the information I have gathered, we can expect to see no end to this famine any time soon."

Conrad had a second report in his bag, one on Marcel Petiot. It would go to a secret collection in the Vatican, one which dealt with suspected cases of demonic possession. Those who kept that collection hoped that it would one day result in a better understanding of the affliction and how it could be prevented or cured.

Roul let the clutch in and started taking the jeep down the *Rue Donkiers*. Overhead, the sky was darkening. Another great snowstorm seemed inevitable. "I was reading the file on the Petiot case. Something struck me when I finished. Did you know that he never hanged anybody until after he set up operations at that hunting lodge?"

"He said he had been inspired to take up hanging by watching the German executions." Conrad thought for a second. "He really didn't say that much about how he killed his victims."

"I compared the Gestapo reports and our own, and it appears that the murders here were the only ones where he hanged his victims. Now, that set me thinking. I looked up the records for here and the other small villages in the area. I found something quite surprising.

"Those records go back a long way, centuries. And they show that there has always been a disproportionately high numbers of hangings in those woods. Some murders, some suicides, even some accidents. But, the records are full of people being hanged there. A couple of hundred years ago, when the woodlands were much more extensive than they are now, the whole area around that hunting lodge was called *La Forêt Maudite*. And the Germans called it *die Verfluchten Wald*."

"The Accursed Forest." Conrad thought that over. "I don't like the sound of that."

"And here's another one. The hunting lodge itself was built by one Écuyer Albert d'Oliver. He hanged himself after his wife left him. Wasn't the first, though."

"It wouldn't be the first time an area like that has acquired a bad reputation. Something, an idea, or belief or simply gossip, becomes established and it preys on people's minds. It is hard to know whether things happen because of something there ,or whether people with an aim in mind are drawn there because of the reputation. I will say that I would not like to walk there late at night, nor would I recommend anybody else to do so."

"Fortunately, they won't have to. I have ordered the hunting lodge to be blown up and the last sliver of forest cut down. The trees will be burned and the ruins of the lodge buried. I just hope that we have destroyed what was there and not set it free."

Conrad thought about that for a very long time.

POSTSCRIPT

It is not known how many people Marcel Petiot killed. In our world, he was executed in Paris on May 25th,1946 for the murder of 27 people, all positively identified. The Gestapo agent *Kriminalinspektor* Robert Jodkum was prepared to swear under oath that the body parts he and his investigators found came from at least sixty people, but nobody was listening to the Gestapo in 1946. There was a catch. Every month, a man in a horse cart removed four-dozen or more suitcases from the Paris slaughterhouse. Assuming the fleeing refugees had a suitcase each, it is quite possible that Petiot was killing sixty or more people a month. For two years. We just don't know, but it seems probable he was the most prolific serial killer in history. We also don't know how he killed most of his victims. The inoculation method was one Petiot confessed to. We also have some evidence that some of his victims, mostly women, were strangled. The Gestapo claim that some of the bones they found had marks on them consistent with meat being flayed from them.

EYE OF THE HUNTER
Bangkok, Thailand, 1992

Conrad's Other Eye

Eye of the Hunter

CHAPTER ONE

REINCARNATION

Pan American Sonic Clipper **Flying Eagle,** *Approaching Don Muang Airport, Thailand*

Experienced travelers always booked seats in the center section of the Boeing 3707. The supersonic airliner had inherited the habit of porpoising when taxying from its B-70 Valkyrie ancestor. The resulting up-and-down oscillation made the forward section uncomfortable while the aircraft was moving on the ground. The aft section was between the nacelles that held the eight J-93 jet engines. That made for noise and a low-frequency vibration that disturbed some passengers.

This allowed Conrad to deduce that Ann Bonney had booked his seat. Naamah would have put him in the nose and Nell in the tail. In either area, the four-hour flight from San Francisco to Bangkok wouldn't have been too bad, but it was better to be comfortable. Lillith would have condemned him to sixteen hours on a people-hauler just to save money.

"Ladies and gentlemen, we will be landing at Don Muang Airport, Bangkok, in five minutes. Please fold away your table and return your seats to the upright position. Please make sure that your immigration and arrivals documents are complete prior to disembarking from the aircraft." The stewardess looked around at her passengers. Conrad saw her nodding slightly as she checked for signs of concern. There were none. Her passengers were well fed and happy, even the ones in the front and rear.

Conrad looked out of the window, but the view of the ground was limited by the great delta wings. He did see that the wingtips had already elevated to the horizontal position. Only by looking right forward could he see a sliver of the luxuriant fertile green beneath him. He could also see the horizon. Its changing angle meant that the pilot had raised the nose of the aircraft for its final approach. By the time he looked back inside, both stewardesses in his section were seated and fastening their safety harnesses. One saw him looking at her and flashed a quick but mechanical smile. The 3707 was already bumping from low altitude turbulence as it slowed down and dropped towards the waiting runway. Then, there was the thump, a slight bounce and another thump as the Boeing touched down.

This was where the Boeing 3707 and its siblings differed from the DC-12 and the other people-haulers. When the large subsonic airliners came to a stop, groups of passengers would be allowed to go down to the lower deck. There they would open their luggage lockers and collect their baggage. Then they would leave from the cargo deck to enter the terminal. The much smaller fuselage of the supersonic airliners didn't allow them to use that system. Instead, their terminal was equipped with elephant's trunks that mated up with the forward and midships doors. While the passengers disembarked via the trunks, the pod containing their luggage would be detached from the fuselage and towed into the baggage reclaim area. There it would be opened so the passengers could collect their bags.

Conrad looked at his seat number and went to the assigned locker. His seat card was also a magnetic door key for his locker. A simple swipe opened the luggage cabinet. He took it out, knowing that it had been untouched since he had put it in the compartment five hours earlier. As he turned around to head for immigration, a patter of applause swept across the luggage reclaim area. The six stewardesses, in their light blue uniforms and pillar-box hats, had left the aircraft and were crossing the hall. They were walking in step. Conrad had to admit, they made an impressive sight, deserving the applause they had received.

Immigration was its usual pain, with long queues in front of the officials. Conrad was slightly uneasy at this point; he was travelling as a normal civilian, his passport giving his profession as a historian. There was a diplomatic spat going on between the Vatican and Thailand at the time, and he'd thought it would attract too much attention if a member of the Society of Jesus was to arrive. The whole purpose of this trip was for Conrad Lorentz to disappear and be replaced by a new identity. So he needed to keep a low profile for a few years and he'd never been to this part of the world before.

"*Khun* Conrad?" Conrad turned around. He saw a woman, apparently in her mid-thirties, standing behind him. She was wearing a dark green ankle-length skirt and a matching jacket that buttoned down the front. A sash ran from her left shoulder to right waist. As Conrad turned, she made a respectful wai. She held her hands together, as if in prayer, then lifted them up while her head dipped down. It was a standard Thai greeting, one that was graduated according to the relative status of the greeter and the greeted. In this case, the hand lift was small and the dip of the head was almost a formality. Her next words explained why. "Welcome to the Kingdom. I am Lani. Her Royal Highness sent me to meet you."

Conrad had read a tourist's introductory book on Thailand during the flight over and he knew the polite response. He made a wai himself, one deeper than Lani's, with a more pronounced lift of the hands. "Thank you, *Khun* Lani."

The official handling Conrad's queue had overheard the greeting, as he was supposed to, and had pressed an alert button. The supervisor of the immigration shift scuttled out of his office with a speed that was almost comical. He took one look at Lani's outfit, dived into a vacant booth and waved Conrad over. In a brief few seconds, his documents were stamped and filed, his passport stamped with a six-month visitor visa and he was through. Behind him, the booth closed and a relieved shift supervisor returned to his office. Dealing with VIPs was never anything other than a stressful event.

As Conrad had moved from the airliner through the elephant's trunk, the air had been cool and antiseptic. Since then, it had become slowly warmer and the spiced atmosphere of Thailand had become more noticeable. Still, when he stepped out through the doors of the terminal, the change hit him an almost physical blow. The heat, the exotic assortment of smells, the noise as people spoke in an incomprehensible language, the sound of traffic as taxis and busses arrived to pick up the passengers.

Conrad realized that, while he spoke seven European languages fluently, not one of them was of any great use here. There was an olive green limousine parked to one side of the doors with a uniformed chauffeur standing beside it. The man took Conrad's case, slid it into the trunk, and opened the back door for his passengers. Lani waved Conrad in first and slid in beside him. When she closed the door, the heat, strange cocktail of smells and the cacophony of noise were shut out. Oddly, Conrad missed them. They had a humanity that the sterile efficiency of the airport had lacked.

The limousine slipped out into the chaotic swirling mass of traffic and made for the on-ramp to an elevated highway. Conrad looked at the mass of traffic that surrounded them; everything from heavy trucks and busses to motor scooters dodging from gap to gap. He reflected that even Gusoyn would have trouble coping with this. Lani looked at him, a half-smile on her lips. "This is your first time here, Conrad?"

"Yes. It's . . . amazing."

"Don't worry about the traffic. It's a lot better than it used to be. We put this four-lane elevated highway in from the airport to the city center. Before then, all the airport traffic had to go through the city and everything just froze up. We're starting to build an elevated railway next. Trying to get a mass transport system in place before the city freezes up completely."

"How many people live here, *Khun* Lani?"

"Eight million in the city itself; twelve point six million including the surrounding province. By the way, Conrad, there's no need to keep using the

Conrad's Other Eye

polite prefix when we're in private. Anyway, we've both been around a long time."

Conrad looked slightly nervously at the driver. Lani caught the glance and laughed. "Oh, don't worry, Sun is one of us as well."

Sun took one hand off the steering wheel and gave Conrad a friendly wave. Then, he accelerated slightly, dodged sideways into a gap in the traffic and took an off-ramp. "I'll take us off here and go to the old part of the city the back way. Traffic is freezing up on the throughway."

What happened next was something Conrad found completely bewildering. The limousine took a complex route down a series of narrow streets, some little more than alleyways, before coming out into another wide road. Ahead of them was what appeared to be a large traffic island, with four white columns surrounding a central chamber. Lani pointed to it. "That's the Democracy Monument. You know what the four white columns represent?"

Conrad shook his head. "No?"

"The four basic principles of democracy. Fraud, corruption, nepotism and duplicity."

He looked at her with his mouth hanging open. "You're joking!"

"Of course not; we are a very realistic people." She broke off for a second as the car turned left on to another main road. "The building off to our left is the Bangkok Metropolitan Administration. If we follow this road along, it will take us to the Ministry of Defense. Beyond that, is the Royal Palace. His Most Gracious Majesty is away at the moment, so the Palace is open to the public. I will take you there if you wish."

The limousine turned into another narrow sideroad, this one so narrow the car could barely fit between the garbage cans on either side. It ended in a dirty, battered pair of green-painted wooden gates. Sun sounded the car's horn. The gates creaked open to reveal a carefully-concealed paradise. Lani smiled at Conrad. "Welcome to the Bang Phitsan Palace."

Reception Room, Bang Phitsan Palace, Bangkok, Thailand.

"I can't believe this place is tucked away in the middle of a city." The sun was going down and the harsh, glaring daylight had melted into a soft evening glow. Around them, Conrad could hear the cicadas chirping. Mosquitoes were being held at bay by the scented torches that surrounded the party. Conrad nibbled at a deep-fried shrimp that had been dipped in a chili-garlic sauce. Slowly, very slowly, he was getting used to the taste of real Thai food. His stunned, and slightly desperate, expression when he had tried the first shrimp had greatly amused the other members of the party. Beside him, one of the maids put some ice in his glass, a second poured some whisky over it and a third topped up the glass with a jet of soda water from an old-fashioned siphon bottle.

"There are more like this than you think. The modern city has engulfed the old Bangkok but, inside the city blocks, sheltered from the traffic and noise, are little islands of our old way of life. For us, they are the lungs that allow us to breathe." Suriyothai smiled gently at Conrad. "Eat, drink and be merry, Conrad, because tomorrow, you die."

Conrad nodded. In theory he was waiting here until the King returned and he could attend an audience, where the history of Siamese interactions with Spain in the 17th century could be discussed. In reality, he was going to have a heart attack during the night. He would be rushed to Phramongkutklao Hospital where, despite the efforts of the best doctors in the city, he would pass away. He would be cremated and his ashes scattered on the Chaophrya River.

At the same time, Conrad de Llorente, a cousin from the French side of the family, would take his place living here. Conrad could wash the silver dye from his hair, allow it to grow out as its normal black and make a few other superficial changes to his appearance. One of them was that he had acquired a yearning to grow a beard.

The record would show that Conrad had grown up in Thailand, the child of French expatriates from Indochina. In 1940, his parents had elected to stay in Thailand as refugees. He had gone to college in Thailand before leaving for a seminary. On hearing of his uncle's death, he had returned home to pay his respects. His uncle's reputation had inspired him to follow his example and devote his life to aiding the falsely-accused.

To Conrad, this proved two things. One was that the transfer of identities that was the trademark of life as a Daimones went like the smoothly-running machine that it was. The other was that the Princess Suriyothai Bhirombhakdi na Sukothai had a much tighter grip on the government in Bangkok that The Seer could ever hope to achieve in Washington.

"Of course, we'll have to find you a girlfriend." Lani sounded hesitant and thoughtful.

Conrad was flustered and thrown off his balance. "Uhhhh, I know I'm changing identities, but I'm still a priest."

"Not really." Suriyothai's expression gave no hint of how much she was enjoying herself. "Conrad Lorenz dies tonight. Conrad de Llorente won't appear for a couple of days. So, you're in limbo for a short time. Make the most of it. Lani and I will find you a nice girl. She'll be Daimones as well, so you'll have nothing to worry about."

"How about Tim?" Lani sounded very thoughtful. "Well-mannered girl, half-French, so she can help Conrad with his back story."

"But she's only a receptionist, no real position. Don't you think Jip would be better?" Suriyothai nodded thoughtfully. "She's got a lot of influence and knows the right people. I hear Jip is a skilled beautician as well, so she can help Conrad modify his appearance. Yes, I think Jip is the kind of girlfriend Conrad needs. And she's supposed to be quite something in bed."

"People, please." Conrad sounded almost anguished.

"Conrad, this is Thailand." Lillee Nakchatree looked up from the spit-roasted pig from which she was carving a portion of the ribs. "You have to have a girlfriend. The only excuse for not having one is that you prefer to have a boyfriend."

"But I can't . . ." Conrad nearly wailed the response. Then he thought he would try and escape by way of distraction. "How are we going to get the date of my ordination sorted out? Lotario dei Conti di Segni will need to know what you've fixed up, and the Vatican and Thailand aren't on speaking terms at the moment. How did that happen, by the way?"

"We were chasing after a human trafficking gang." Conrad looked at the speaker, slightly relieved that he had deflected the conversation. The man was in the uniform of a police colonel. "He was a devout Catholic, so we thought he would probably want to confess his sins now and then. So, we bugged the confessional in the local cathedral."

"Oh, my . . . dear Lord." Conrad shuddered slightly. He could see this conversation getting even more embarrassing than the previous one.

"Worked like a charm. We got the evidence we needed, so we pulled him in and used the tapes to send him away. Took the whole gang down, in fact. Then, we got an official letter from the Vatican telling us that the conversation between a priest and a penitent was confidential, privileged, and instructing us to let him go."

"Well, it is privileged." Conrad could see how this was going to go.

"Not here, it isn't. As long as the police get a warrant from the appropriate Ministry of the Interior official, we can bug where and when we please. Our law applies to everybody, regardless of their religion. And we don't like being told what to do. So, we sent back a message telling the Pope just that. He threatened us with an interdict. We threatened him with releasing the sordid details of what some of his priests get up to here. Everything went downhill from there."

Suriyothai was almost laughing. Conrad realized that compared with some of the issues she handled as The Ambassador, this was probably minor indeed. "Anyway, Conrad, back to important matters. Your girlfriend. You have to have one you know. You can't survive here without one."

Conrad was looking desperate. Lani took pity on him. "Conrad, a man's girlfriend is much more than just a bedmate. She is his . . . social secretary. If he wants to see somebody important and he makes a request for an interview, it is a potential embarrassment to everybody. If the person he wants to see can't, or doesn't, want to see him, the refusal causes offense and diminishes him. Instead, his girlfriend sees the girlfriend of the person he wants to see and the two women decide if the meeting is desirable and, if so, make the arrangements. That way, everything runs smoothly and nobody gets offended by a refusal or embarrassed by an unwanted request."

Despite the explanation, Conrad was still flushed with embarrassment. "But I can't, I . . ."

Lillee Nakchatree looked up sharply. She had the edge that she lived and worked in a town with a very large Catholic population. "Conrad, you've never gone with a woman, have you?"

He shook his head. "I went straight to a seminary when I was still a child. And, after I took my vows . . . well, I take them seriously. I know some do not, but that is between them and God."

Lani smiled gently at him. "Now, keeping promises is something we value greatly. But, I must tell you. Conrad, you are missing out. This is a very pleasant country in which to be a man."

Later that night, after he had gone to bed, Conrad reflected. Thailand might be a very pleasant country for a man, but it was very challenging for a celibate one.

Conrad's Suite, Bang Phitsan Palace, Bangkok, Thailand, Six Weeks Later

Jip stepped back a little and looked at her work critically. "We've made a good start, I think. Your beard needs to fill out a bit more, but that will come. Anyway, it's appropriate for your apparent age the way it is. Your skin tone is doing well also."

Conrad looked in the mirror she was holding and nodded appreciatively. Jip had styled his hair and, although it was still short, it looked elegant, as befitted a man in his early twenties. His Van Dyke beard gave him a fashionable appearance. Much more importantly, it made him look quite different from his previous self.

Jip had run him through a whole series of cosmetic treatments, including skin peels, exfoliations and some others that he'd never heard of. She had also set him up with a series of dietary supplements and put him on a strict diet. He'd lost a lot of weight as a result. The total effect was that he genuinely looked like a man in his mid-twenties. In six weeks, she had taken at least sixty years off his apparent age. Half of that had been simply undoing the means he'd adopted to look older, but it was still an impressive achievement.

"A good start?" Conrad was surprised. In his mind, Jip had achieved wonders already.

"Oh, don't be a baby. Women have this sort of thing done every week, not every half century. Do you realize how much trouble we go to so we can stay attractive?" Jip laughed, a musical tinkle that reminded Conrad of wind chimes in a gentle breeze. "No, I suppose you don't. Anyway, we've got where we want to go. Now we have to make sure that everything stays in place. For you, that means keeping on the diet I gave you. Quite apart from holding your weight down, it's much healthier for you. Even if they aren't Daimones, people would live quite a bit longer if they'd just eat properly."

"That's what Naamah says. Have you met her?"

Jip hesitated. Conrad had learned a bit about the way Thai children, especially girls, were brought up. One of the earliest lessons was if you can't say something nice about somebody, say nothing. "I've met her, yes. She taught me a lot about herbs and herbal treatments. They are very useful, because sometimes herbs have a balance of ingredients in them that we cannot easily replicate. But, I think she does not quite realize how fast the techniques we have available to us are advancing. There are many things we can do today that were impossible just ten years ago."

"Which is fortunate, the way things are closing in on us. Remember when all we had to do to start a new life was go to a village a few kilometers away?"

"That was before my time, Conrad. I'm only fifty."

That made Conrad think. One thing all the Daimones were aware of was that, no matter what their current status, the key people in their continued lives were not the top leaders like Loki, the Seer or Suriyothai. They were the army of county and town clerks who kept the records suitably modified and people like Jip who could make enough changes in people's appearance to allow them to start a new life. Then Conrad realized that Jip was looking at him critically as he inspected himself in a full-length mirror. "Conrad, hold yourself erect. You are slumping like an old man."

"Sorry, Jip. Old habits die hard. Is that better?"

"Much. Conrad, I took the liberty of arranging a meeting for you with Police Colonel Chaowit. You met him at your welcome party. His *mia noi* approached me, asking if he could consult with you over a case he has on his files."

"That's a good idea. I need to get back into the world." Conrad hesitated. "What's a *mia noi*?"

"*Mia noi* means minor wife. What you might call a girlfriend, but it is a bit more than that though. A *mia noi* is supported by her lover who pays for her apartment and living costs. You don't have a *mia noi*, so Colonel Chaowit's came to see me instead."

"Thank you, thank you. Everybody has been very kind, but I was getting so bored . . ." Conrad looked at Jip. He saw the self-satisfied smirk quickly cross her lips. *Why do I think that girl understands me much better than she is letting on?*

Colonel Chaowit's Office, Bangkok Metropolitan Administration Building, Thanon Sirothong, Bangkok

"What a beautiful view!" Conrad looked out of the window, over the sea of rooftops and the patches of green to where the ornate roofs of the Royal Palace glistened in the sun.

"Thank you, *Khun* Conrad. Please accept a little tea? And we have some snacks for while we talk."

"Thank you, *Khun* Colonel." *And there, I think, ends the diet Jip wanted me to live on.* "How may I be of assistance to you?"

Chaowit had a pile of files sitting on his desk. He took the top one and opened it, checking that the contents were what he wanted. "*Khun* Conrad, like any big city, Bangkok is divided up in police precincts. Sometimes, communications between them is good; sometimes it is not. Occasionally, things fall through the cracks. Where they do, it is the work of my department to put those things right. I report to the Central Investigation Bureau, who do the same thing, on a national scale. The problem we have is that some precinct captains do not like us investigating their affairs. So, that is another barrier to things working smoothly. There are times when a problem becomes well matured before we can intervene. I fear that we now face one of those situations. Let me start at the beginning.

"About eight weeks ago, a young man was found beaten in an alley behind a night club. He was badly hurt, although not dangerously so. The local police performed a cursory inspection and found that he was a homosexual. It was discovered that he had left the nightclub with a *farang*, a foreigner, about half an hour before he was found. The police really didn't investigate beyond that. Their presumption was that he had been picked up by a tourist, there had been a dispute and a fight.

"Conrad, despite what you might see in the cinema, the truth is that in such fights, the *farang* usually wins. Unless the Thai has been trained in the martial arts, and that is rarer than you might think. *Farangs* are simply bigger, heavier and stronger. In the half-world, such fights are common and neither participant wants to make them public. And so it was here. The victim spent a few days in hospital, a few more at his home and then went back to the half-world. The local police kept a closer eye on nightclubs for a few nights and that seemed to be the end of the matter. Another night in Bangkok, one of the prices we pay for our vibrant nightlife, as the tourist brochures like to put it. We assumed the tourist had left when his vacation ended and so the case was closed."

"Only, it's happened again." Conrad guessed that much and thought sadly that it hardly required any great insight to do so.

"A week later. The case was almost identical, a man who made his living in the half-world, found beaten in an alley. It happened in a different precinct and there was no connection made to the earlier case. The police made a slightly more thorough investigation, since the half-world has a much smaller presence in that area, so they were less . . . jaded. One of the ladies working the bar remembered the victim leaving the bar with a *farang*. Fortunately, she is a gifted artist and was able to draw a good picture of him. The local police made copies of the picture, showed it around the bars, but nobody recognized him. Once again, the victim spent a few days in hospital, a few more at his home and then went back to his life."

"Do you have pictures of the victims where they were found?"

"Of course. Here. First case . . . second case."

Conrad looked at the pictures carefully, then frowned and looked closer. "Your theory of the crime is that the victim was picked up at the bar, left with the attacker, there was a fight, over money, I would assume, and the victim lost?"

"That was the local police precinct theories of the crimes, yes. A sordid crime, but one we are quite familiar with. The patoot community . . ."

"I'm sorry, patoot?"

"My apologies. I forgot you do not speak Thai. Patoot is a humorous nickname for homosexuals. Anyway, that community seems to be more vulnerable to such incidents than the ladies of negotiable virtue. Probably because the ladies usually carry switchblades and the man who attacks them does not expect them to do so."

"I don't think the theory holds up, *Khun* Chaowit . . . "

"Please, call me Kwang. My friends all do."

"Thank you, Kwang. Look at these injuries. Especially the ones on the victim's back. They're long, straight lines. I'd say about two inches, say six centimeters, wide."

"Sixty-six millimeters. Could be an anti-tank rocket."

Conrad's jaw dropped for a split second, before he realized he was being teased. "Possibly, if the attacker was American. But, I think a baseball bat is more likely. Looking at the way this man is on the ground, I would say he was punched in the stomach, so he doubled over. Then he was beaten across the back with the bat until he went down. Then he was kicked a few times before the attacker left. Now, we look at the second victim. We see the same injuries, the marks on his back where he was beaten down with a bat and then those in his sides where he was kicked."

Conrad looked at the pictures again. *For a priest, I have an unholy knowledge of nightclubs and how they operate.* "This is a big problem. I know of no nightclub anywhere in the world who would allow a customer to walk in swinging a baseball bat. That means he acquired the bat between the time he and the victim left the nightclub and the time the attack started. Either he concealed the bat outside and led his victim to where it was hidden, or he had accomplices waiting and he led his victim into them. Either way, this wasn't a pick up gone wrong. This was a deliberate ambush."

"I agree." Chaowit returned to his files. "And we have several more. All similar, in different parts of the city, always on a Friday night. The pattern went unnoticed because each of the precincts thought it was an isolated attack, one which was just another dispute in the half-world."

Conrad was looking at the pictures. "I have a feeling this was a group of attackers. The bruising from the kicks are on both sides of the body. It's possible the poor man might have rolled over while he was being beaten, but I think it is much more plausible that there were two or more people, surrounding him and kicking him. These young men are very lucky to be alive. Normally, with mob attacks like that, the victim is killed or beaten so badly they never recover. These attackers cannot be very strong."

Conrad drew a deep breath. "My theory of the crime is this. There is a small group of young men who have started hunting homosexuals for some reason. They pick out a bar where their victims like to gather and one of their number goes inside to act as a decoy. He picks up a victim, or allows a victim to pick him up. They go out of the club, where the rest of the pack is waiting. They attack their victim, overwhelm him and escape. I am afraid, Kwang, that they are not tourists. This is a local problem."

"Why do you say that?"

"The duration of the attacks. You said there had been several more, always on a Friday. That means the attacks have been going on for weeks; eight or nine, at a guess. I doubt if many tourists stay here for that long, nor would they be in a pack like this." Conrad thought for a second. "Do you have a gang problem here?"

"Of course. We have the Chinese Tongs, both the traditional ones and the White Fists. Ever since the Imperial Empire collapsed, we have Japanese gangsters here. We have a Triad presence, of course. The Russian Mafiya has a growing presence and, for reasons we do not understand, they maintain good relations with the Triads. Especially the 14K. We also have our own organized gangs. They have slices of the half-world, drugs, prostitution and so on. But open violence almost never happens. We are like Cuba in some ways. The half-world makes so much money for those involved, it is cheaper for them to negotiate and make deals than fight. If one group starts to get too aggressive, the others combine against them until things revert to their normal, peaceful selves."

"I wasn't thinking of organized crime so much. I've been to Cuba and I know how it runs. If this was organized crime, you would wake up one morning and find the people responsible lying dead upon the police station steps with their confessions nailed to their chests. I meant youth gangs."

Chaowit thought carefully. The clock ticked in the background. Eventually, he spoke slowly. "The only groups I can think of would be the vocational schools. You see, Conrad, children here take tests at regular intervals and, at each stage, the best are separated away and sent to schools where their talents can be fully developed. By the time the children have reached sixteen or seventeen, all the children with potential have been located and sent to their proper schools. The ones that are left, ones without talent or initiative, go to vocational schools where they are taught the basic skills necessary for life.

"Their fate is to be the barely-skilled labor that does the lowest jobs. They tend to violence and the only discipline they know is in their own cliques. They would be the only candidates for this, but it does not fit their style."

"Could I see the picture the girl drew, please?"

Chaowit opened a file, took out the picture and handed it over. Conrad looked at it and his lips twitched. "The lady notes that he had an olive complexion and curled hair."

"Yes, she made a point of that. With some contempt, I must add." Chaowit saw that Conrad was slightly confused. "Here, a white skin is a sign of high status. It means that the person does not have to work out in the sun."

Conrad nodded. *So that's it. Thinking about it, I've never seen one of the women here out in the sun when she can possibly avoid it. And Jip always wears a wide-brimmed hat when she comes to see me.* "This is a very good picture. The young lady is indeed a talented artist. She has even caught something in his eyes, a . . . nastiness."

"I am glad you think so. Our forensic department was so impressed, they have offered her a job as a police artist. She declined politely, but has promised to reconsider when the income from her present profession begins to ebb." Chaowit laughed. "At the moment, I think she makes more in a week than a police corporal would do in a year. Anyway, here are the other victims, all but the last one."

Conrad looked at the pictures and shuffled through them. "I can almost place these in order for you. With each attack, the beating gets a little worse, the attackers a little more skillful when it comes to harming their victim. Kwang, one day, not so very far off, they will kill somebody."

"They nearly have. Conrad. Have you ever heard of Kanya Tamaraptri?" Conrad shook his head. "A professional entertainer, on the nightclub circuit. Sings under the name of Mailee. Not top rank, but has recorded a few songs that have sold well. Performed as a guest on television a few times. In short, a promising start to a showbusiness career. Only last night, Kanya Tamaraptri was a victim of an attack that could be part of this case."

Chaowit handed a picture over. Conrad took a look, then gasped slightly and looked again. The victim was laying on her back, the torn, blood-splattered rags of what had been an expensive evening dress over and around her. The beating she had received was of an entirely different order from that of the previous victims.

Looking at her, Conrad found himself praying for her recovery, but wondering if she ever could her health from such injuries. His mind quickly flashed back to the night in 1945, when the Constellation bringing Igrat back from Geneva had landed and he had seen her, nose broken, face and body covered with purple and scarlet bruises. Kanya Tamaraptri was in far worse condition and almost certainly did not have the aid of Daimones heritage to help her recover.

"How is this similar, Kwang? The beating is far worse than any of these other victims, it seems to have been carried out by a single person and the victim is a woman." He paused for a second. "This is brutal."

Chaowit smiled sadly at him. "Yes, Conrad, the beating is far worse and we also think there was only a single attacker. But, he used a baseball bat, which is rare here and that does link it to the other cases. But, you are wrong on one point. Kanya Tamaraptri is not a woman. Kanya Tamaraptri is what we call a *khatoi*, a man who chooses to live like a woman. Tourists often call them ladyboys, but that is considered to be very insulting. Extremely so. Some *khatoi* simply dress and behave as women; others have surgery to make their appearance more feminine. In the most extreme cases, they have gender reassignment surgery that, for all purposes except childbearing, turns them into women. In such cases, they are known to us as *sao prapade song*. This means woman of the second kind. Kanya had said that was her final goal."

"So everybody knew he was a man?" Conrad was having a little difficulty getting his mind around the casual acceptance of the gender issue. He couldn't help wondering what would have been his course of action if he'd been here during his days with the Inquisition.

"Of course." Chaowit hesitated slightly, "Conrad, we consider it polite to refer to such people by their chosen gender. So, in this case, you should say 'she.' She is not the only one; there are many such entertainers on the nightclub and popular music circuits. I must explain something to you. In this country, you could line up the entire population by order of status, from the highest to the lowest. His Most Gracious Majesty, of course, has the highest status and would be at the top of the line. The lowest, most depraved criminal you could imagine would be at the bottom. In that line there is a place, and one place only, for every person.

"Where that place is, depends on many things. Age, occupation, education, wealth, family, many things. And we are brought up with this and we know our place in that line without thinking about it. A farmer ranks higher than a lawyer; a soldier higher than a policeman. Now, normally entertainers rank low on the line, but the *khatoi* are different. You see, the Lord Buddha taught that extremes are to be avoided if possible and all things should be kept in balance. Male and female are extremes, but the *khatoi* have male and female in balance so they are closer to the Lord Buddha's ideal and they gain status from that."

"Let me guess. *Khun* Kanya loses status because she was an entertainer, but regains some by being successful and some more by being khatoi. And we're here because, being a more prominent person, the attack on her attracted more attention than a fight outside a nightclub."

"Exactly. The reports of the attack on her made the front pages of the newspapers and that made the local precincts realize that their cases were linked. Also, she has had some success and her fans immediately turned up at the local police stations, requesting an urgent investigation be made. And that's when we got called in. Our conclusions were the same as yours by the way, young gang, probably *farangs*, hunting *patoots*. That's why I asked for your help. *Farangs* have such strange ideas, we need help sometimes if we are to understand them."

CHAPTER TWO
DIFFERENT WORLDS

King Chulalongkorn Memorial Hospital, Thanom Rama IV, Bangkok

Chaowit's driver maneuvered the police cruiser into one of four parking spots reserved for police vehicles. After he'd opened the car door for his passengers, he went back to the driver's seat and settled into it. Chaowit spoke to him and gave him some money. In response, the man made a deep wai.

"I said we'd be here for an hour or so if he wanted to eat and get some tea." Chaowit explained. "Now, we have to find the intensive care unit."

That didn't take long; the way was well signposted in both Thai and English. A doctor was standing outside one room. He started to cross the hall towards Conrad and Chaowit when he saw the latter's uniform. There was the normal exchange of wais. Conrad noted that, for the first time, Chaowit's was deeper than the doctor's. *All right, so a doctor has a higher status than a police colonel.*

"Excuse me, you are here to investigate the attack on Kanya Tamaraptri?" The doctor glanced at his clipboard again. "I fear she is in no condition to speak with anybody. And will not be for a long time, if ever. She had two severely depressed fractures of the skull, a jaw with multiple breaks, and that's just the damage to her head. With the damage to her jaw, there is no doubt that her singing career is over. As to the skull fractures, there is undoubtedly brain damage. There is also a high risk of increased pressure on the brain, or a hemorrhage to the brain. Either of those could easily be fatal."

"She was beaten with a baseball bat?" Chaowit was holding the conversation in Thai and then quickly translating for Conrad. The doctor waited politely while he did so.

"She was. When we were cleaning out her wounds, we found splinters of wood. Our laboratory identified them as ash." The doctor's voice was suddenly

377

grim. "It is fortunate she was already intending to have gender reassignment surgery. The damage to her private parts is very severe."

"Could you ask how the blows were struck?" Conrad spoke in English. The doctor switched to the same language. The realization that all three men spoke a common language after all caused a ripple of amusement that slightly offset the tension in the emergency room.

"The first group hit her across the back, probably knocking her to the ground. The attacker was standing beside her for those and the blows are at right angles to the spine. We are checking for spinal damage now. Second group of blows were to her lower body, when she was on her back. They are parallel to the axis of her body and concentrated on her groin."

"The attacker stood over her and pounded her groin with the bat." Conrad shook his head. "Kwang, that wasn't part of the attack pattern we've seen before. That was deliberate torture."

Both the doctor and the police colonel nodded in agreement. The doctor resumed his briefing. "The last group of blows were to the head. We think they were intended to kill and we are still not certain that they have failed to do so. *Khun* Kanya was in emergency surgery for many hours and may be too weak to undergo another operation. If her condition deteriorates . . ."

"Excuse me, please." Another man had joined the group. He was young; his cheap suit, vividly-patterned shirt and gaudy tie screamed gangster. "Uncle Ho sent this for *Khun* Kanya's treatment."

He pushed an envelope into the doctor's hands and scurried away. The doctor looked at it. It was stuffed with cash. "That's the tenth envelope like this we've received since the newspapers hit the street. From all over the underworld. Thai, Chinese, Japanese, Koreans, you name it. If there's a gang, they've sent some money over."

Before Chawit could reply another man, also Chinese, had joined the group. This one was more like a businessman, in a tasteful gray suit with a stylish dress shirt and tie. He passed over another envelope. "The Neighborhood Association would like you to accept this for *Khun* Kanya's treatment."

"First one was from the Red Crickets Tong. The second from the Triads, probably the 14K. They both came for the same reason though. Shame." Chaowit explained to Conrad. "The gangs all run protection rackets and the nightclubs and massage parlors all pay to make sure this kind of thing doesn't happen.

"If it does, then the gangsters are deeply shamed in front of the whole community. Not just the gang who was paid off for this particular area, but all the gangs. They can only purge the shame by coming together, treating the victim with great generosity and exacting a terrible revenge upon the attacker.

If they get him, I fear his gender reassignment surgery will not be voluntary. Or quick."

"Then we had better make sure we find him first." Conrad had decidedly mixed feeling at this point. On one hand, he had found people who had to be protected. On the other hand, they were hardly innocents and a part of him almost felt that they deserved the fate the gangs had in mind for them.

Chaowit was saved from answering by a teenage girl who came up to him. She was wearing a school uniform that bore a distinct resemblance to a sailor's outfit, and her *wai* to the police colonel was deep. She spoke quickly to him. Chaowit replied gently. Then they exchanged *wais* again and the girl left. "She asked me to please find the person who did this to *Khun* Mailee. She said Mailee is her idol. I said we would do everything we could and had even brought in an expert from abroad to help."

"Kwang, I noticed that your *wai* to the doctor was deeper that his. I assume that means his status is higher than yours. You also said that a soldier has higher status than a policeman. So, what is the status of a soldier related to a doctor?"

"Soldier is higher, but it depends on rank. A doctor has about the same status as an Army major."

"But your *wai* to the girl was deeper than I expected?"

Chaowit laughed. "I am a policeman, a public servant. She is a member of the public. Her family's taxes pay my salary. That affects our relative status."

"Ahhh." Conrad thought for a second. "So, the depths of each *wai* is graduated in tiny fractions of a millimeter and everybody knows the rules by instinct."

"Now you're getting it." Chaowit turned to the doctor. "Could we see *Khun* Kanya please?"

"You will have to wear sterile clothes and a breathing mask. She has serious open wounds and infection is a terrible danger at this time." The doctor led the way to a changing room. Once his visitors had changed, he took them into the isolated recovery room. A bandaged-wrapped patient was on the bed; she was heavily intubated and the lower half of her body was covered by a tent. Two visitors, also in sterile suits, were sitting either side of the bed. They were holding the patient's hands and one of them was reading quietly from a book.

"We have evidence that people in comas can hear what goes on around them and familiar noises can help keep them tranquil at a time when they need tranquility most. Her friends are reading to her from *Khun Chang, Khun Phaen*. I am told it is her favorite book. Soon, two new friends of hers will come to take over the vigil and these two will go back to work."

"Are they ladies of the first or second kind?" Conrad asked, still trying to get things in order in his mind.

The doctor shrugged. "I don't know. Who cares anyway? All that matters is that they are performing an act of great merit."

Colonel Chaowit's Office, Bangkok Metropolitan Administration Building, Thanon Sirothong, Bangkok

"Another question about status. A lot of foreigners try and use the *wai*, to be polite. They must get the depth and so on very wrong, mustn't they? Doesn't that offend people?"

Chaowit shook his head, "We know that foreigners get it wrong. They always do. But, they are trying to be polite, so we keep smiling and understand that their hearts are good. Nobody takes offense because the *wai* is inappropriate. We are a very understanding people. Until we are pushed too far; then we become quite vicious. That is what I am afraid of now. At the moment, things are quiet. But, if it gets out that Mailee was attacked by a *farang*, then it is likely that some of her fans will seek revenge. Another reason why we must get this case wrapped up quickly."

And another reason why an innocent may get swept up in the investigation and accused because it is convenient. "Kwang, all the attacks took place on a Friday, is that right?"

"Yes . . . no. The attack on Kanya Tamaraptri was last night. That makes it Wednesday. Another discrepancy between this last attack and the ones that went before."

"Let us put that to one side for a moment. I wonder why the attacks take place on a Friday? I would have thought the entertainment night would be Saturday."

"This is Bangkok, Conrad. Every night is entertainment night. Even the factory workers will go out during the week for noodles at a roadside stand. We are a hedonistic people."

"I'll tell you what doesn't happen on a Saturday, Kwang. School. The schools run Monday to Friday. That makes Sunday night to Thursday night school nights and the students stay at home to do their homework. But, Friday night is their night off; they can do their homework any time over the weekend. Everything fits. The attackers are foreigners, they are young, and they use one or more baseball bats, probably stolen or borrowed from their gymnasium. We're dealing with a gang of students from one of the international schools here."

"Why not one of the local schools, or a vocational school?"

"The doctor said that they found fragments of ash wood in Kanya Tamaraptri's wounds. In America or Europe, baseball bats are made out of ash or hickory. Hickory bats are heavier and rarely used in schools. I have noticed out here, the local schools use bats made of bamboo. The sound is very distinctive. I think we will also find that ash baseball bats are expensive here. How many international schools are there in the city?"

"Fourteen, but two of them only handle children up to twelve."

Conrad nodded; that was a very practical number to investigate. "The young lady who drew the picture for us? Could she draw some more if we speak with witnesses? Then we can take the pictures to those schools and see if the staff recognize them."

The Orchid Nightclub, Nana Plaza, Bangkok

"It's terrible news about *Khun* Mailee. All the girls here are scared. Whoever did it must be mad." The girl who had drawn the picture in the casefile was almost in tears.

Conrad wasn't quite sure what to expect, but this wasn't it. The girl was wearing a white T-shirt and blue jeans, no makeup and her hair was pulled back in a ponytail. She'd made a deep *wai* when she had joined them. Now she was gently but firmly pumping her two visitors for information on the case. Chaowit coughed and tried to take back control of the conversation. "*Khun* Vanna, your picture was very helpful to our investigation. If we take you to the other clubs where people were attacked and get the witnesses to speak with you, could you make more pictures?"

"So you think this was a gang?" Vanna looked around. "I am supposed to be here between six and twelve every night. I do not want to lose my job here. This is a good club with nice customers."

A man behind the bar called out her name and waved her over. The two spoke for a few minutes, then Vanna returned smiling. "That is one of the owners of the bar. He says I can go and work with you for two days. There is a condition, Colonel. The police must make it well known that the club is helping you with finding the people who attacked *Khun* Mailee. That will bring great credit to us and people will come here to support the club."

Vanna paused. "I will not be earning money while I am helping you. I have to support my parents and their water buffalo is sick. I was going to send money for the animal doctor and I have my rent to pay."

Chaowit shook his head. "It is amazing how unhealthy water buffalo can be. As an informant, I can only pay you three thousand *baht* per day. We are just the police, not the Army."

The girl looked unhappy. Conrad leaned in slightly. "I can add a hundred U.S. dollars a day to that."

Vanna sighed. "I'm just a poor working girl who does not understand international finance. The exchange rate today is 38.143 *baht* to the dollar, but the latest American M3 figures and unemployment totals are not good and the trade balance remains a concern, so the dollar will fall in value. On the other hand, the *baht* is part of the Sovereign pool and that is gold-backed. The rice crop is excellent this year and the price of gold has risen, increasing the value of the Sovereign against the dollar. So currency movements are in your favor. Yes, I think we have a deal."

Shangarila Restaurant, Silom Road, Bangkok

"So, we have six members of the gang?" Conrad looked at the pictures again. The three had been working hard all evening, going from bar to bar, finding the witnesses and getting descriptions from them. Vanna produced the drawings using artwork supplies Conrad purchased for her. He'd been slightly puzzled by the storekeeper giving Vanna a small envelope after Conrad had paid for the supplies and was leaving. The same thing happened in one or two other places they had stopped.

Eventually, well into the evening and hungry, Conrad offered to buy dinner for the group. And so, they had ended up at the Shangarila restaurant. On the way, Vanna had stopped to change and pick up a friend of hers to make a foursome. Both women were now dressed in Bangkok copies of stylish Italian designer evening dresses and were busily making up duck skin pancake rolls for the two men. "And this one is the leader."

"Please tell me, how do you know that?" Vanna slid a made-up roll onto Conrad's plate. It was perfect. Somehow, she'd managed to work out just how Conrad would like it.

"It's a boy's gang. The leader has to go first or nobody will follow him. So, he would be the first. We have eight drawings, four of which are of the same two people. So, the first and seventh are of the gang leader; the second and eighth, probably his main lieutenant. Tomorrow, we have to circulate these to all the bars and clubs and tell people to be on the lookout. Thank you, Vanna, this roll is delicious."

Vanna's eyes sparkled with delight. She immediately got to work making him another. "Will I be working with you again tomorrow?"

"If it will not cause you problems, please." Chaowit was eating a duck skin roll made by Vanna's friend. "We will need to go to other bars and find out if the group, or members of it, have been seen there. Also, if there are any we have missed. If there are other members of the gang, we'd like you to draw them for us."

"My manager said two nights. So, tomorrow will be all right. *Khun* Conrad, I can stay with you tonight if you like. I give you special price because you help to find man who attacked *Khun* Mailee. Only eight thousand *baht*."

To everybody else's secret delight, Conrad flushed bright red. "Vanna, it's a very kind offer, but I can't accept."

"*Khun* Conrad is a priest as well as a very skilled investigator." Chaowit explained, perfectly straight-faced.

"Oh, that does not matter. I have had many clients who were priests. I know that because they were praying all the time we make love. All the time they keep saying 'Oh my God, Oh my God. OHH MY GOD.'" Vanna's expression was completely innocent.

"I'm sorry, Vanna, and please do not be offended, but I have taken vows, like your monks here." Conrad looked at Vanna and caught a glimpse of relief in her eyes. *For a woman like her, a night alone. when she can let her hair down and not play a part for a companion, must be a precious gift indeed.* "With a talent like yours, you should go to art school. Good commercial artists make a very comfortable living."

"I would so much like to go to art school." Vanna suddenly sounded very unhappy. "But my parents are very poor farmers from the recovered provinces and one year, when the crops failed, they had to sell me to an agent here. Now, I must work very hard and earn much money so I can repay that money, and all the interest they charge, to buy back my freedom. Only when I am free, and not owned by others, then can I think of going to art school."

"*Khun* Vanna, your father is a mechanic and your mother is a nurse. They are both Khmer, yes, but they are moderately well off and have always lived in Bangkok. You were born here. And you go to art school three days a week." Chaowit shook his head.

"Did you really think we would let you work on a police investigation without running a background check on you? *Khun* Conrad, there are some women who have been brought into the city from the north, or the recovered provinces, but they are few. The pimps know that country girls cannot compete with girls who have been brought up in the city. But all these girls have very sad stories they will tell anybody they think might give them money, in the belief it will help them."

"All right, I took a shot. So, sue me." Vanna was laughing. Conrad found it hard to think ill of her.

After the meal was over, Conrad paid the bill for the four and they left. Once again, as they did, the manager slipped Vanna a small envelope. Chaowit saw Conrad's curiosity and explained. "Her commission. She brought us here, so the management gave her a commission on the amount you spent. But, because she negotiated for you, you paid local prices, not tourist rate prices. So you still ended up better off. You know, Conrad, if you are going to live here for a while, you really do need a *mia noi*."

Conrad's Suite, Bang Phitsan Palace, Bangkok, Thailand.

"Good morning *Khun* Conrad." Jip's *wai* was deep and respectful. Conrad returned it and she nodded slightly. "Very good; you are learning quickly. I also hear that you have decided to sample our local delicacies after all."

Conrad shook his head. "The young lady is helping us with our inquiries and she just brought a friend along."

Jip looked surprised. "I was referring to your Peking duck in pancake rolls. What are you referring to?"

"Jip, that's cheating. But, the girl really is helping us with the case of Kanya Tamaraptri. She was drawing pictures of the suspects for us. We were working late, so I took us all to dinner. She collected a friend of hers, I suppose to keep her company." Conrad was aware he sounded unduly defensive. "And she got a commission on the check for dinner."

"She brought a friend because one woman eating with two men would be considered . . ." Jip hesitated, not quite certain of the correct word in English. "Inappropriate? Objectionable? Improper? Something like that. And of course she got a commission. Conrad, she has only a limited time as a top earner. She must use that time to earn every *satang* she can find. Anyway, you were working on *Khun* Mailee's case? The newspaper says she is in critical condition."

"She is, Jip. And that is something I don't understand. We have determined that the attackers are not strong, yet they did appalling damage to her jaw. It's broken in so many places; shattered, I think, would be the best word. The doctors say she will never sing again and it will be months before she can eat solid food. How can somebody, who is not strong, do so much harm?" Conrad was asking a rhetorical question and he was surprised to get an answer.

"Because *Khun* Mailee is *khatoi*, on her way to being a *sao prapade song*. One of the things she will have had done is to have her jaw and cheekbones shaved down to give her face a more feminine line. The operation does that, but it leaves the bones gravely weakened." Jip looked at Conrad, noting his surprise. "I know that, in your country, a beautician has taken a three-week course in how to slap makeup on, but here it is different. I studied for two years to qualify and some of that time was studying the bones of the face and skull and how they all work together. I know as much about that as any doctor. I have to, if I am to do my work well."

"I apologize for any offense, Jip. I didn't mean to imply your skills were doubtful. I have myself as an example that you are a true master of your art. Could you give me some more insights? Would the same apply to the skull?"

Jip smiled delightedly at being asked to help. "Conrad, there's no need to apologize to women here; if there are apologies to be made, we make them to our men. To answer your question, it could be. I would have to know what procedures have been carried out. There are operations that do affect the skull. For example, men have a boney ridge above their eyes that women do not. So there is an operation called bossing that removes that ridge. It seriously weakens the skull."

"So, the critical head wounds could be the result of her surgeries? Not any strength in the attacker?"

"Very much so. If *Khun* Mailee had been far advanced in her surgeries, her facial bones and skull could be very weak. Her attacker might not have realized how weak. That would not be a defense for him, would it?"

Conrad shook his head. "No. Not in any court I've ever heard of."

"Oh good. When you catch him, he will be executed. That is very good. Now, will you be going back on this case soon?"

"About midday. At the moment, *Khun* Chaowit is having warning posters with the pictures of the suspects distributed to all the bars and nighclubs." A thought them made Conrad frown slightly, "Jip, how easy is it to tell the difference between a woman of the first and second kind?"

Jip thought about that. "It depends. *Khatoi* are sometimes quite obvious, especially if they are new to the life. They see a picture of an actress, or somebody else they wish to imitate, and think that what works for their model will work for them. Then they find out it will not, and they need expert advice.

"I have some clients like that. If they take advice and practice hard, some *khatoi* are very hard to recognize. Until they take off their clothes, of course. But, *sao prapade song* can be almost impossible to detect. There are legends that some *farangs* have married them without realizing that they are of the second kind. With good surgeons and care, it is almost impossible to tell.

"One thing to watch for is height. *Sao prapade song* are taller than women of the first kind. Look at forearms and wrists also. Cultural thing; see if the lady is wearing a bra. Thai women always do, *sao prapade song*, not so much."

"So, it's quite possible that the attacker could have picked the victim up at a bar, thinking she was a she, and then attacked her when he found out his mistake?"

"Of course. Mistakes happen all the time." Jip giggled. "Another reason you should have a girlfriend. Women are much better at spotting *khatoi* and *sao prapade song* than men.

"Now, please, lean back in your seat. I want to work on your teeth. They are yellow and this was good when you needed to look older. Now, we must whiten to look younger. I have some whitening paste to use. Also, so sorry, but your breath smell. *Farangs* probably not notice, but we do. You should see a good dentist for proper cleaning."

International Laureate School, Thanom Rama IV, Bangkok

"How did the morning go, Kwang?"

"Very good. Vanna and I went to every bar and nightclub in areas where the attackers haven't hit before. Well, we tried to. There are so many. Vanna asked all her slinky sisters to pass word on. She will rejoin us this evening when she has finished her class. Now, we must hit all the international schools. Today is Friday and that means we will see another attack. I am sure of it."

"So am I. Is there any reason why we are starting at the International Laureate School?"

Choawit nodded, then looked suspiciously at a car that was following them. "Mip, the white Holden behind us. Get its plate number and radio it in. Usual check. I'm sorry, Conrad. The ILS? I was thinking about this and I thought we would leave predominantly American schools until last. This crime, it does not fit Americans somehow. Even though the use of a baseball bat suggests Americans, they are too . . . easy-going about people for this."

Conrad knew what the police colonel meant. "You're right, Kwang, some time ago, I worked with a homosexual detective in Los Angeles. He and his partner brought up two fine daughters and nobody thought there was anything odd about that. There were some good things that even came out of the Russian Front. In America, tolerance of different lifestyles was one of them."

"That is what I thought. Now, the International Laureate School caters mostly to people from South America. Their primary languages there are Spanish and Portuguese. I chose them to start because we have had some problems with pupils from this school. Mostly fights over girls and such things."

"That can't go down well here."

"Conrad, there is a saying in ours. 'Women and cats do what they want and men and dogs must learn to live with it.' Some people find that very hard to understand."

"So, the pupils here must be quite old if they're fighting over girls. By student standards, of course."

"This school specializes in teaching for the international laureate, a qualification for university. So, its pupils range from 15 up to 19. There are some younger students doing preparatory classes. I think it fits our profile very well."

A few minutes later, Conrad agreed. He reflected ruefully that, while his teeth might smell by local standards, this school had a stink of corruption about it that could be detected by anybody's standards. He was watching the school principal, Guilherme Sérgio D'cruze, while the principal checked through the pile of artist's impressions. He was shuffling through them quickly, taking only a superficial glance at each.

"I know none of these. They are not students here."

"Are you sure?" Chaowit asked mildly and politely. "Perhaps you could take a closer look?"

"It would not do any good. These people do not study here. Anyway, these pictures could be anybody."

"Señor D'cruze, if I may ask you a few more questions?" Conrad found himself admiring Chaowit's patience. There were places Conrad had visited where the principal's attitude would have got him thrown into a cell. As to what would have happened to him in Cuba during the good old days, Conrad could only imagine.

"I think not. I have been very patient with you and I am a busy man. When I agreed to see you, I did not expect to be questioned by the Spanish Inquisition."

"Nobody ever expects the Spanish Inquisition." Conrad rolled out his favorite phrase with relish. "But, I think you do not quite understand what is happening here. These people, in the pictures, were recognized by witnesses as the primary suspects in a series of assaults. Including the attack on the singer Mailee.

"Now, I know you recognized them and, therefore, they are students here. I am sure you are, in your mind, protecting them from youthful folly and also protecting the reputation of your school. What you do not realize, Señor, is that the people they attacked were under the protection of gangsters. Those gangsters are now looking for the attackers. Especially the attackers of Mailee. I would say they are, twenty-four hours, behind us?"

"I think twenty-four hours at the moment, Conrad. But they have more people, and more money, than us. And there are no restrictions on what they can do to the people they question." Chaowit looked deeply concerned. "They will catch up fast. We were followed by a car, owned by a man with known underworld connections, today."

"And there are restrictions on what you do to the people you question?" The principal's voice was jeering and derisive. "I have heard what happens in the back rooms of your police stations."

"Perhaps you ought to bear that in mind." Chaowit was still impeccably polite.

Conrad took up the line of questioning. "I know you recognized those students. You cannot hide the reflex in your eyes. I also understand your concern about your school's reputation. But, think about this. The gangsters are coming, and they will ask you the same questions we do now. Only they will do so in ways that have not been seen since medieval times. At best, they will beat the information out of you."

"Or put a bag over your head with a starving rat inside." Chaowit sounded helpfully informative, as if he were a bank manager discussing options on an investment account.

"And after you have told them what they want to know, they will pick up those students. Now, what will harm your school's reputation worse, Principal? Six or seven students arrested for assaulting people in night clubs or six or seven dismembered students, plus their equally dismembered principal, turning up in garbage bags scattered all over the city?"

"This is Thailand, Conrad. The gangsters will hold the school responsible. We would be lucky if it's just the students and the principal. They could easily set the school on fire. After locking everybody inside, of course." Chaowit shook his head sadly.

That casual mention of an *auto da fe* shook Conrad deeply and he had to swallow hard. Nevertheless, the conversation had achieved the desired results. The principal had gone white. "All right. All right. Those students are enrolled here."

"Where will they be now?" Conrad was getting a distinct feeling that time was running out. It was a Friday and the sun was setting.

"We use the sports ground over at Lumpini Park. Every Friday is baseball night there. The students go home when it is over."

"You know that these students are there?"

"Of course they are. They said so. We have an honor code here. A student shall not lie, cheat or steal."

Conrad stared at him with contempt. "You missed the five most important words. The honor code is a student shall not lie, cheat or steal *nor tolerate those who do*. Without those five words, it is meaningless."

Chaowit nodded. "I want the files on these students, right now. Immediately."

Baseball Ground, Lumpini Park, Bangkok

Jonathan Day had the air of an ex-soldier about him. He also had a kindly smile that made Conrad guess he was a good friend and advisor to the students who were wise enough to take him into their confidence. When he and Chaowit had arrived, Day had seen them walking across the park to where the International Laureate School students were doing their sports session. He had immediately walked over to meet the two investigators short of his students. His *wai* was clumsy and of the wrong depth, making Conrad guess that he hadn't been in the country very long. When Day spoke, his Irish accent was obvious.

"Now, gentlemen, how may I be helping you?"

"Principal D'cruze said you would be here with your students. We need to talk to these six. Could you bring them over here."

Day took the pictures, inspecting them a lot more closely than the school principal had done. "A talented artist you have here, that is for certain. I recognize all six of them, but they are not here."

"But they are part of your class?" Conrad was taking the lead in the interview, with Chaowit hanging back. This hinted to Day that the Thai police colonel didn't speak good English. The hope behind that was that Day would let something slip as a result.

"They are." Day hesitated. "Let me be telling you something about kids in a Physical Education class. There are four groups of them. The first are the kids that are good at sports and work hard at these classes. They almost teach themselves and I just keep an eye on them and coach them when needed. Then there are the ones who are no good at this, but do the best they can and work hard. Those ones, I coach a lot and try to find sports they are good at. Then there are the ones who are no good at sports and don't care. Time they spend here is wasted. If they want to sit on the grass and make a start on their homework, that is fine by me."

"And the fourth group?"

"The smallest group, they are, and the ones we can all do without. Games they are not interested in, and they try to spoil them for everybody. If one of the lads is making a home run, try and trip him up, they will, even if he is on their team. An easy catch comes their way and they will stand there and watch it land at their feet. All six of these are of that kind. Two, three months past, they stopped coming here and heartily glad I am of it. Troublemakers, all six of them."

"Did you report the fact that they weren't coming here?"

"To be sure, I did not. Principal D'cruze does not want to be knowing of problems, and no thanks would I get for bringing him any. And, if I did, those brats might come back and ruin things for the rest of the class."

"Are they starting fights?"

"In a manner of speaking. Like I say, they go out of their way to ruin whatever game they were supposed to be taking part in. That stirred the rest of the others up agin them. And those six, they were a might bit closer to each other than was normal for lads their age. Went everywhere together, they did. Had their own table at lunch, and woe betide any others who tried to join them. Of course, rumors started to spread and, I'll be honest with you, it was the sports teams here who were at the root of it. Boys here are just at the age when they are starting to get interested in girls, and soon the rumor was these six weren't. It spread around the whole school fast enough. That was just before they stopped coming to the sports afternoon here."

"Was there any truth in the stories?"

Day thought carefully and then shrugged. "Not that I know of. More that they liked to think everybody was against them and that held them together."

"Who is the leader of this group?"

Day thumbed through the sheets and picked out two. "These. This one is José Herrera Silva. He comes from Venezuela. In fact, all six of these lads do. The other one is Rodríguez Crespo. Silva is the top dog, no doubt about that, but Crespo is snapping at his heels. If I was Silva, I'd be watching my back. Crespo is a nasty piece of work. The other four, they're just followers. They hang out with Silva and Crespo because it makes them feel like somebody."

Conrad looked at the two pictures. Crespo was the one Vanna had drawn first and Silva was the one they had marked out as the probable leader. Day had confirmed that at least. "You've no idea where these boys are?"

Day shook his head. "That I have not. They're not here, that is for sure."

"One last question. Has any of your sporting equipment been stolen or otherwise gone missing?"

"To be sure. We lost three or four baseball bats a few weeks ago. We thought local lads had stolen them for their own games. Or to sell. We have good equipment, one thing we can thank Principal D'cruze for. He never stints on buying the best equipment. Good ash bats they were, worth a good few *baht* on the street market."

"And they disappeared about the time Silva and his clique stopped coming here Friday afternoons?"

That was, at last, when the anvil dropped on Day's head. "They are the ones that stole them? That singer in the newspapers, you think they carried out the attack on her?"

"That attack was one of a series that has been going on for the last two months. In each case, the victims were beaten with ash baseball bats." Chaowit joined in the conversation and Day finally realized he spoke fluent English. "The attacks started when Silva and his clique stopped coming here and the ash baseball bats were stolen. We have witnesses who identify members of that clique as having left bars with the victims. My colleague and advisor asked you where they are and you do not know. Now, I am telling you that your negligence in supervising these lads, as you call them, may be considered as a contributory factor to their crimes."

33 Soi 31 Thanon Surawong, Bangkok

"Excuse me, Colonel. Can we help you?" The woman standing in the doorway was being defensive. Some of it was the natural reaction to having a senior police officer suddenly descend on her house, but there was also another element there. Conrad recognized it as the fear of a suspicion being confirmed.

"Please forgive the intrusion, but you are Ava Arroyo Villaño, the mother of Ricardo Causera Villaño?" Chaowit spoke in English. This time the game was reversed, with Conrad keeping quiet and not revealing that he spoke fluent Spanish.

The woman clapped her hands to her mouth. "Oh no. He hasn't been in an accident, has he?"

"We do not think so, but it is essential that we contact him very quickly. There was a report of a rabid dog near the school and we are trying to find all the pupils in case any came into contact with it. The dog need not bite, you know. Touching its saliva might be enough. Is he here?"

"No, he's off at Lumpini Park, for the sports afternoon. Then he will be at the school dramatic society." The woman looked around, seeking the reassurance of her husband. "Nic, the colonel says Ricky may have been infected by a rabid dog."

The man who had appeared looked deeply suspicious. Chaowit looked at him carefully. "You are Nicasio Oliverio Puente Villaño? Father of Ricardo Causera Villaño? Do you know where your son is?"

"My wife told you. He's at the Lumpini Park Sports Ground."

"We've just come from there. He isn't attending the sports afternoon. He hasn't been there for weeks."

"Of course he has. Where else would he be?"

"That is what we are trying to find out. It is absolutely vital that we find him quickly."

"He said he was at the sports ground. My son doesn't tell lies." Ava Villaño now had a mulish determination on her face. Conrad sighed to himself, although his face was impassive. In his opinion, 'my child doesn't tell lies' was second only to 'everybody loved him' as the most idiotic remarks he heard during criminal investigations.

Conrad's Other Eye

"I told you something was going on." Nicasio Villaño rattled the remark off to his wife in very rapid Spanish, obviously in the belief that the words would not be understood.

"It's just a check for rabies infection." His wife replied equally quickly.

"Believe that and you will believe anything. A police colonel doesn't go around knocking on doors for a rabies scare. They'd send a boy scout to warn us. This is something very serious. Ricky is in real trouble. I knew those thugs he's been hanging out with would get him into trouble with the police." Despite the rapidity with which the couple spoke, Conrad had no trouble following the conversation. Spanish was, after all, his native language.

"Do you have any idea where he might be? This really is very important." Chaowit was continuing to speak with massive patience, but a perceptive observer might have noted the signs that the patience was wearing very thin.

"If he is not at the sports ground, I have no idea where he could be." The admission from Nicasio Villaño made him flush bright red.

"Well, if he comes home, please call us immediately. His life may very well be in danger."

As they left, Conrad heard the wife asking her husband "What does he mean, if Ricky comes home?"

Silpakorn University Campus, Bangkok

"Six for six." Conrad was deeply depressed by their visits to the suspects' parents. "Not one of them had any idea where their children were. Just what is happening to us?"

"Did the children go off the rails because their parents ignored them, or did the parents give up on them when they went out of control?" Chaowit was also depressed, although his reasons were different. This case was developing all the signs of becoming a fine political mess and he was already involved in one of those. He had a haunting presentiment that he might find himself being transferred to the police recruiting office in a small countryside village. *Where I would stay for a very, very long time. Sometimes, there are problems with being Daimones that outsiders never guessed at.*

"My experience is both, with one set of circumstances feeding the other. Our artistic friend here, I wonder if her parents know how she makes her living?"

"Of course they do." Chaowit was looking out for Vanna leaving class. "They don't admit it, even to themselves, but they know. And when she leaves the life to settle down, start a real career and get married, it will never, ever be mentioned.

"It isn't such a bad thing, you know. It takes a lot of money to send a child through university. But, without going to college, sons are good for working on a farm and for manual labor, but little else. But a daughter can make enough money in the half-world, even without a degree, to put herself and her brothers and sisters though college. Or, she can make a very advantageous marriage or become the *mia noi* of a rich and powerful man, thus linking her family to one of position. That means daughters here have great value and are regarded as a gift from the gods. I can think of a few countries where baby girls are killed at birth instead."

He was interrupted by a knock on the window. Conrad opened the door and Vanna slid into the back seat with a bright smile on her face. "Where are we going now?"

"Around all of the nightclubs we can reach. We'd like you to speak to the other girls, of both kinds, show them the pictures and tell them to be alert. Above all, if they see the suspects, call us straight away."

Vanna nodded. "Is there a reward?"

"Five thousand *baht* for information leading to the arrest of any of these six. So, if a girl phones in information leading to all six being pulled in, she'll get thirty thousand."

To Conrad's surprise, Vanna didn't seem impressed. "The Red Crickets are offering ten thousand sovereigns, in gold, for information on those who beat *Khun* Mailee. One of the ladies in my class, her brother is a Cricket, and she passed on the news of rewards."

"The Red Crickets are one of the Chinese Tongs, mostly based in Saigon." Chaowit explained to Conrad. "If old Uncle Ho is offering ten thousand, the other gangs will be doing the same. You know, Vanna, you could make a lot of money here. We'd be happy to confirm that you helped us find the attackers. If you want the police spreading word that you helped us, of course."

"Wonderful man! That would help me so much." She turned to Conrad. "I have four brothers and five sisters to put through college. This makes me very poor girl, but they will get good jobs and look after me when I am too old, sick and worn out to work anymore."

Vanna had adopted a pose of noble self-sacrifice. Chaowit looked at her and snorted. "You have one brother, one sister and you have more money in your bank account than I do. Let's get to work. We're running out of time and, if the pattern holds, another victim will be attacked tonight. Conrad, you bring Vanna up to date and don't let her talk you into giving her any more money."

The Crazy Horse Saloon, Soi Cowboy, Bangkok

The pattern was well established by now. They entered the club. Vanna peeled away to approach an older woman who was sitting in a corner. Vanna's *wai* had been deep and respectful and she had spoken very politely as she had explained why she was here. Then, she'd asked permission to go to the bar and speak with the others working there. Each time, the best girl had looked at Chaowit and Conrad, seen Chaowit's uniform and given a satisfied nod. Then, permission had been granted with a casual wave.

"She's the manager's best girl." Chaowit had explained. "She manages the girls, draws up work schedules, settles disputes and so on. She also represents the interests of the girls to the management and keeps relations harmonious. Vanna went to see her first so her actions wouldn't be misunderstood."

Conrad would watch while Vanna passed around pictures of the suspects and gave away smaller versions that could be kept behind the bar. At one bar, a pair of tourists pestered her; Conrad thought they sounded Australian. They made highly obscene and insulting suggestions to her, in the belief that she didn't speak English. Eventually, she turned to them and spoke in her perfect English. "I am sorry, I am not working here. I am with my friend, the police colonel." The two tourists had gone white and left the bar very hurriedly.

Now, Vanna was with the girls at this bar, huddled over the pictures while she described who they were, what they had done and how they operated. She stressed that only one of them would come in to act as bait, but the others would be waiting outside. Most importantly of all, she stressed to the girls working the bar the rewards that were being offered by both sides of the law for the identification and/or arrest of these six. The reaction of the other women was mild interest in the police rewards, but much greater appreciation of those being offered by the gangs. *I think that there is an interesting balance there for the girls,* Conrad thought. *The money from the gangs is better, but being smiled upon by the police is a long-term investment.* He knew that, all over the city, other groups of police officers were doing the same thing, setting up a web that would snare the six suspects. He just hoped it would be in time to prevent another attack.

That was when Chaowit tapped him on the arm. "We're too late. There's been another attack and this one is really bad. You were right, *Khun* Conrad; they were building up to killing somebody. We just found the body behind a nightclub in Nana Plaza. A *farang*, beaten to death with a baseball bat. And, this one isn't just a *farang*, he is an important businessman. As Her Royal Highness likes to say, everything has just dropped in the pot."

CHAPTER THREE

COLLISIONS

Paradise Nightclub, Nana Plaza, Bangkok

Bangkok's night life withstands most things. Fights, disagreements over money or customers, raucous behavior, the half-world goes on despite them all. Only, it had not withstood the sight in the alley behind the Paradise Nightclub. The club was at a literal stand-still while people stood around, trying to get a grasp on what had happened in their midst. Even the raucous music had been stilled. To Conrad's all-too-experienced eye, the scene had the same threatening eeriness of a deserted funfair late at night.

There were two maroon and yellow police cars blocking off the entrance to the alley. A trio of police motorcyclists had turned up; they were checking the identities of everybody present. It was makework until the investigation proper started, and everybody knew it, but they were too shocked to object. As Conrad followed Police Colonel Chaowit towards the crime scene, he saw copies of Vanna's drawings stuck to the windshields of the police cars and motorcycles. The hunt had been thorough and careful but it hadn't been enough.

Conrad and Chaowit ducked under the yellow tape. Conrad couldn't read the Thai script on it but guessed it had to say crime scene or the functional equivalent. As he did, he glanced back. Vanna was sitting patiently in the police car. Chaowit had told her to stay there and she would, for as long as she wanted to.

"Back here, sir." One of the junior police officers led Chaowit into the alley. It was filthy, covered with garbage and stank of human urine. This was something Conrad had noticed before. If the alleyway belonged to somebody, it would be kept scrupulously clean; one that was common property quickly deteriorated into a squalid garbage dump.

There was a figure curled up in one corner, twisted against a sidewall and soaked in a pool of blood, already black with flies. Three police officers were standing around the body, keeping people away.

As Chaowit approached, a woman stepped out of the shadows. She made a very deep *wai* to Chaowit and spoke to him, a note of pleading in her voice. Conrad saw him shake his head sadly. The woman seemed likely to start crying. As she stepped back into the club, Conrad saw her in the light from inside the building. She looked older, more tired, than Vanna. She was much more heavily made-up and her clothing, a skinny tank top and a pair of short shorts, was more openly provocative that anything he had seen Vanna wearing.

Chaowit saw Conrad looking at the woman. "That's the next step down for our artist friend. Vanna works in a high-class cocktail club at the moment. In three or four years, if she doesn't get out, she'll be working in a bar like this. Then a cheaper bar, and then one cheaper still. Eventually, she'll be calling to potential clients from a back alley and hoping that they don't see her too clearly."

"Was that woman a witness?"

Chaowit shook his head. "No. She asked if she and the other girls could take the body inside, wash it and lay it out properly. She said his wife shouldn't see her husband like this. I told her we had to wait for the forensic people to process the scene, but the body would be taken to the hospital where it would be prepared properly before his wife was allowed to see it."

"That was a kind thought." Conrad paused for a second. "Will Vanna really end up like this?"

Once again, Chaowit shook his head. "Not that one. She's smart. She's already planning for the day her place gets taken by somebody younger and fresher. She saves every *satang* she can and is getting a good education while she can pay for it. The girls who start the slide down are the ones who live large on their earnings and don't save. They are young women who suddenly come into possession of large sums of money and do not know how to control their finances. Mostly, they lose a lot of their earnings gambling and, as they slide down, start drinking or taking drugs. But, Vanna? When I said she had more money in her bank account than I do, I wasn't joking."

Conrad looked down at the body on the ground. He was a westerner, given his appearance, possibly European or American. His beaten and blood-splattered body made anything more precise difficult. The cause of death was not difficult to see; the man's head was crushed along one side. The side of his skull was so pushed in by the blows that his face had been severely distorted. That made Conrad frown. "You said this man was an important businessman?"

"He was indeed. His name is Tomáš Lubomír Valentin Klímek, a senior management officer in the Skoda Engineering Company. He was their local representative here, a resident for some years in this country. His position has become very important recently. Skoda are one of the companies shortlisted for the contract to build the new elevated light railway system. He had many good friends in our government and knew everybody of importance. It is fortunate we already know who did this terrible thing. There will be much pressure from those high up to convict those responsible."

Conrad felt his stomach lurch at those words. He liked Chaowit, and knew him to be a capable officer, but all too often pressure from above to arrest the most obvious suspect was too intense to be ignored. "He was a homosexual?"

"No. The Skoda Engineering International Group have their head office on *Thanom Sukhumvit*, a few meters from here. *Khun* Tomáš would come to this bar regularly for an after-work drink. He was popular with the girls who work here; not because he used their services, but because he was polite to them and treated them with respect. They saw him almost as a father figure and would ask his advice if they had problems. They are all very upset at what has happened to him. Right now, they are making a collection so they can offer a reward to the person who catches the killer of their friend."

Conrad looked at the body again. The man hadn't been wearing a jacket, but that wasn't surprising. Few people in Thailand did. What did surprise him was that there was no wallet in the man's pocket. Most men carried their wallets in the front pockets, where having them stolen by a pick-pocket was slightly less probable. "No wallet, Kwang. That's a new factor. None of the other victims have been robbed."

"He might have dropped it when he was attacked. Or somebody might have seen it and picked it up before the crime was reported. What interests me is that there is so little blood here. With a murder so violent, I would have expected to see blood sprayed on the wall or scattered from the bat."

"I do not believe the victim was killed here." The speaker was a woman who had arrived with a forensic team. Conrad looked at her curiously. Her hair was dyed in multiple colors and set in a jagged, spiked style quite unlike anything he had seen during his stay in the country. She was wearing a black T-shirt and black jeans. To Conrad, she looked like one of the more recalcitrant teenagers in a large American city. His guess was that she was in her mid-thirties, although her face looked older. "The way the body is slumped against the wall is not natural. He was thrown there. He did not collapse there."

"This is Khunying Pornthip." Chaowit explained. "She is organizing our first real forensic evidence laboratory. Her experts have sometimes found remarkable evidence."

Conrad made his *wai*, deepening it when Chaowit caught his eye and made a gesture hinting more respect was needed. "I am pleased to meet you, Khunying Pornthip. I agree with your assessment. The awkward posture and the absence of blood splatter all indicate the victim was killed elsewhere and dumped here. I would look for tracks where he was dragged, but this alley is such a mess, finding them will be hard."

The strange-looking woman glanced around and nodded. "We will have to do a centimeter-by-centimeter search of this alley. I have heavy protective gloves for your men in our truck."

"In case of needles?" Conrad looked at the piles of garbage that surrounded them.

Pornthip shook her head. "In case there is a krait or cobra in there. And this is a bad area for taking photographs. You are a forensic expert?"

"Conrad de Llorente, a criminal investigator and consultant. We have an artist, a very good one, in the car. I am sure she would be pleased to make drawings of the scene for you."

"The police have an official artist as part of the investigations? Wonders will never cease." Pornthip looked at Vanna who was trotting over in response to Chaowit's wave. "Ahhh, I see. Colonel Chaowit, is there a theory of this crime yet?"

"Yes, Khunying. I believe it is the latest manifestation of a series of attacks in recent weeks. *Khun* Conrad predicted that the attackers would soon kill and tonight he was proved right. Fortunately, we have identified the gang and will be arresting them as soon as they are found."

33 Soi 31 Thanon Surawong, Bangkok

Ricardo Causera Villaño saw with relief that he was nearly home. The house rented by his parents was just a few meters away and, once he reached it, he would feel safe. A split second later, any hopes he may have had of sanctuary were dashed. The spotlight on a police car illuminated him. Around him, the Thai passers-by dispersed quickly. They knew when something was about to get very unpleasant.

"Ricardo Causera Villaño, you are under arrest for assault and attempted murder." The loudspeaker on the car blared the words out in Thai, Spanish and English. The message was actually on a tape Colonel Chaowit had made for the police cars he had left staking out the parents of the students accused of carrying out the beatings. The Thai message was Colonel Chaowit himself; the English and Spanish words had been recorded by Conrad. It was a little bit of forethought that impressed Conrad.

At this point, Villaño made a whole clutch of mistakes in quick succession. Any Thai citizen stopped by the police like this would have stood still and cooperated. The Thai police are generally genial souls; their basic operating principle was that, if people didn't cause them problems, they wouldn't cause those people any. On the other hand, if suspects made a police officer's life difficult, those suspects would quickly find out how inventive the police could be when it came to finding ways to make life awkward. So it was extremely foolish of Villaño to try and escape.

His decision was even more wrong-headed because he had nowhere to run to. He was on the street, surrounded by people who had pulled back just far enough to take them out of danger from any stray shots that might be fired, but close enough to have a good view of an incident that had much promise of livening up an otherwise dull evening. Those spectators formed a solid wall. The only way out was through the two police officers closing in on him.

Then Villaño made another bad mistake. He and his friends were used to using their size and strength to push local people out of their way. So, instinctively, when facing two Thai policemen in his way, he tried to do the same to them. The result was predictable to anybody who had ever watched a Muay Thai wrestling match. Villaño ended up on the sidewalk, winded by the impact with the cement. A patter of applause went around the spectators, who appreciated the free display of applied martial arts. In the local sports stadium, they would have had to buy tickets to watch.

At that point, Villaño completed his litany of errors. Despite being on the concrete, he tried to kick out at the nearest officer. The police corporal responded with a kick of his own that landed squarely in Villaño's genitals. The scream of anguish caused another light patter of applause from the spectators, who didn't like to see their local officers disrespected. Villaño was hauled to his feet and handcuffed.

"You have the right to make a full confession. If you do not wish to make a full confession, we will beat the crap out of you until you change your mind. You have the right to have a lawyer write your confession for you. If you cannot afford a lawyer, boy, are you screwed. Do you understand the rights I have just read to you?" The police corporal turned to the other officer. "Did I get that right? It sounded like what they say on American television shows."

At that point, the corporal realized that his official cap had come off during the brief struggle. But, all was not lost. A young boy picked it up, dusted it off and now returned it the corporal. There was a solemn exchange of *wais*. The child ran off, secure in the knowledge that he possessed a story that would make his schoolfriends seriously jealous.

And so, the arrest of Ricardo Causera Villaño was completed. The local spectators dispersed and went on with their business. At the Villaño home, Nicasio Villaño received a telephone call that told him his son was now in police custody on serious charges. He and his wife exchanged long, distressed looks, thinking that their worst fears realized.

They were wrong. Outside their home, two gangsters in a stolen car had also been watching. Only the intervention of the police had stopped them from picking the student up. Had that happened, Ricardo Villaño would never have been seen again.

At least, not undismembered.

Colonel Chaowit's Office, Bangkok Metropolitan Administration Building, Thanon Sirothong, Bangkok

"We have them in custody. And only just in time. The Red Crickets and the Mafiya were closing in at the same time we were. Bolt cutters at the ready." Colonel Chaowit was beginning to sense that he was getting on top of the situation at last and the possibility of spending decades in the back end of nowhere was slowly receding.

"Is there any news from the hospital?" Conrad was also feeling slightly better about the situation. The students were out of the reach of local gangsters; for a while, anyway. Though there were still a lot of aspects of this case that were worrying him.

"About Kanya Tamaraptri? She is still in critical condition and in a coma. The latest medical report is that she is a little stronger, and more stable, but she could still go into a downward spiral and die, almost at any time. She needs operations, but can't have them yet. The surgeons are still trying to decide what to do about her jaw." Chaowit sounded very sad. "We'd better start interviewing these idiots and find out what has been going on here."

He led the way out of his office and down to the holding area in the basement of the building. Normally, the students would have been detained at the precinct station, but this case was already becoming unusually complicated. In one office, hastily arranged as an interrogation room, José Herrera Silva was sitting handcuffed to a desk. It had already been agreed that Conrad would take the lead in the interrogation. His fluency in Spanish made that almost inevitable.

"José Herrera Silva, I must advise you that you are being interviewed in connection with the murder of Tomáš Lubomír Valentin Klímek, the attempted murder of Kanya Tamaraptri and eight cases of assault with deadly weapons. I must advise you that the first offense carries a penalty of death or imprisonment from fifteen years to twenty years.

"The second charge, although your victim is still alive, is exacerbated by the employment of torture and acts of depraved cruelty. It is also punishable by death or imprisonment from fifteen years to twenty years. The eight assault charges each carry a maximum sentence of three years. The colonel advises me that the sentences will run consecutively, meaning you are looking at sixty-four years in prison. However, with two capital charges facing you, exacerbated by an accusation of torture, you will certainly be sentenced to death by machinegun fire."

Silva went white with shock. He started swallowing desperately. "What the hell are you talking about? We never killed anybody or tortured anybody. I've never heard of anybody called Klímek or Tamaraptri."

"You may not have known their names; that, I'll grant you. But you may recognize them, or what is left of them." Conrad took the pictures of the latest victim from the file he had brought in. He laid them in front of Silva. "That is, or was, Tomáš Lubomír Valentin Klímek. He's the man you killed tonight. Then, earlier this week, you beat Kanya Tamaraptri and left her for dead."

Conrad put another picture in front of Silva. His color changed from white to green. Conrad could see he was desperately trying not to be sick. "Bad isn't it? I wonder how you can sleep nights. This is what she looked like before you and your gang of thugs did that to her."

The final picture Conrad put in front of him was a publicity shot of Kanya Tamaraptri as the singer Mailee. It was enough; Silva vomited all over the floor. "We never did that. We never hurt a woman. I'd never allow it. You've got to believe me, we would never do that."

"I wish I could believe you, José, but I cannot. You see, we have evidence linking the murder tonight with the torture and attempted murder of Kanya Tamaraptri earlier this week and the assaults on men around night clubs and bars over the last two weeks." At that point, on cue, a police corporal came in with a file. She handed it to Conrad. He read the English summary with interest. He then thanked the corporal. They exchanged *wais* before she left the room.

"And this does it, José. This report is from the Police Forensic Laboratory and is signed by Khunying Pornthip herself. She states that the wood fragments found in the wounds inflicted on Kanya Tamaraptri are from the same weapons that were used to kill Tomáš Lubomír Valentin Klímek. Since we have already linked the attack on Kanya Tamaraptri to the other eight cases of assault, we have therefore established a positive link between all ten attacks.

"Do you know what is happening now? Police cruisers are visiting the victims of those previous eight assaults. We are requesting that they come here to identify their attackers. The police have already picked up the other five members of your gang. When those victims identify their attackers as members of your gang. That will be the end of the matter. Forensic evidence links them all together; eyewitness accounts link you to the package of crimes. I honestly cannot think of a court in this world that would not convict you all."

"But we didn't do either of these things." Silva's voice was agonized as the realization of what was happening to him sunk in. Then his face brightened with relief. "But I can prove I didn't do this one."

He pointed to the picture of Kanya Tamaraptri. "I was somewhere else on Wednesday. I was with my girlfriend, Pakpao. She'll tell you I was with her."

"The police will talk to her, but it won't do you much good. Even if you were away for that particular attack, you are still part of the conspiracy and are equally guilty of its results. Anyway, your own words have just convicted you. You gave me an alibi for Wednesday, but I never told you which day the attack took place on. I just said that it had taken place earlier this week."

Conrad frowned, then got his emotions back under control. "This was a loathsome attack. The deliberate torture of *Khun* Kanya is unforgiveable. All she wanted was to be a singer and live as an elegant woman. You and your friends took all that away from her. Even if she lives, the injuries you inflicted on her have destroyed her life completely."

Silva was stunned. "You mean she was . . . he was one of them? A *maricón*?"

Conrad looked at him curiously. "José, there are those who think that some crimes are justified by the identity of the victim. There are others who think the identity of the victim makes some crimes particularly heinous. I do not believe in either proposition. We are all God's creatures, equal in his eyes. An offense against any one of us is an insult to Him. I think perhaps you ought to look to your soul in the time you have left."

Director-General's Office, Bangkok Metropolitan Administration Building, Thanon Sirothong, Bangkok

"There have been arrests in the cases of Tomáš Lubomír Valentin Klímek and Kanya Tamaraptri." Director-General of the Thailand National Police Department Pratin Santiprapop was not an unreasonable or unfair man. In fact, he was known for his enlightened approach to law enforcement and his firm belief that the laws of the land should be applied without fear or favor. However, he was also aware that his police force operated in a political environment. The effective performance of their duties had to allow for that. In his eyes, a good part of his workload was balancing those two principles, so his officers were left free to do the best job they could. With a prominent foreign businessman dead and a popular entertainer in critical condition, the political ramifications of this case were piling up deep and fast.

"We have made arrests, yes." Chaowit spoke carefully. The situation was very delicate and he knew it. "We have found a youth gang, with six members. They are all Venezuelans, between the ages of sixteen and seventeen. *Khun* Conrad de Llorente has been serving as my consultant on this matter and he has been interrogating these youths. His command of Spanish has proved invaluable in this respect. Conrad?"

"With your permission, Director-General, over the last two months, there have been a series of attacks on members of the homosexual community. We have tied these attacks to members of the gang arrested tonight. We have eyewitness accounts that link them firmly to those attacks. We have forensic evidence that also connects those attacks to the attacks on Kanya Tamaraptri and to Tomáš Lubomír Valentin Klímek. The evidence linking those last two attacks is quite strong but linking them to the earlier attacks is weaker."

"The forensic evidence is solid." Pornthip was very firm. Conrad thought she was being dogmatically so. "We have linked the bats used in the last two attacks by comparing the wood and varnish fragments found in the wounds. The wounds inflicted by them are similar in appearance, although not in severity to the earlier victims."

Conrad looked at her curiously. He understood now why she looked so much older than she was. She had survived three separate bouts of cancer and the battles had left their mark. Chaowit had added she had also been bitten by a king cobra and, after several days of intense pain and great suffering, the cobra had died. Conrad could understand why that legend could spread about her. She had very little in common with the other Thai women he had met.

"I have spoken with all six suspects in depth. All of them deny the last two attacks, although four of them have admitted to the first eight."

"I suppose the fact that the first eight could carry only a large fine or a nominal prison sentence, while the last two carry a death sentence, might have something to do with that?" The Director-General was a little droll, but Conrad had to admit that he had a point.

"The four who have admitted their attacks are the followers in the group. The other two are the leaders. It seems this whole thing started when the six began to hang out together. There is nothing mysterious about that. They were the only Venezuelans in their age group and they formed a mutually supportive social group.

"Unfortunately, it appears that one of the things they shared was a complete inability to do well at any sporting event. This attracted the ridicule of those who were good at sports and they were isolated by the hostility. They retaliated by drawing in closer to their peer group and being more exclusive of outsiders. At some point, the sporting groups started to spread rumors that they were homosexuals. It is my experience that South American youths take those accusations a lot more seriously than Americans or others. In Americanese, to that particular group, such accusations are 'fightin' talk.'

"That's where things went bad. Right up to this point, there was nothing here that was particularly unusual. We had two opposing cliques, neither of whom had any time for the other. The school staff was not really interested in the situation. Even the games master, who seems a decent sort, was only interested in the students who were interested in sports. If they weren't, he did not bother with them.

"Anyway, the accusations from the sportsmen cut deep. For some unknown reason, these six kids decided that they would prove their masculinity by luring some homosexual youths into a trap and beating them up. Why they thought that, I do not know. The people spreading the stories about them would not know of the attacks they had carried out. It doesn't make sense, but little of this kind of situation in schools does to outsiders. And so, we have our first eight attacks. By that time, Silva, the leader of the group had found a much more convincing response to his enemies. He got himself a girlfriend.

"Under normal circumstances, the school situation would have faded away at that point, as the various groups found other interests, primarily female ones. The Venezuelan group would either drift apart, or evolve into a normal group of adult friends. Only, the series of attacks meant the situation wasn't normal. Originally, the attacks weren't really meant to hurt people. Or, rather, the attackers didn't understand that the sort of attacks they were committing could hurt people.

"Silva claims that he stopped anybody from hitting their victims on the head and made sure everybody was wearing tennis shoes, not the kind of boots that could inflict crushing injuries. Even so, the attacks were getting steadily worse. What they did also was create an atmosphere of pressure, one that deterred people from drifting away. Then, he drifted away himself, preferring to spend time with his new girlfriend.

"That left a leadership void, one which Rodríguez Crespo was quick to exploit. Only, by attracting, and winning, a girlfriend, Silva had raised the bar. Crespo had to show himself equal to the leader he was challenging and that meant he had to do the same."

At that point, Conrad hesitated because he was moving from the area he knew to be correct to one where he was hypothesizing. "I think though, there was something else. I talked with Crespo and gained a clear picture of him. This is my opinion only, but I think, when he lured the victims from the bars, he found himself feeling things he did not wish to admit even to himself. I think he began to realize that the things the sports groups had been calling him might be true. That made him desperate to find a girl of his own. He went to a bar, on his own, without involving the others, and picked up a woman. How he came to pick up Kanya Tamaraptri I do not know, but he did, without realizing she was a man."

"I can explain that." Chaowit was fascinated by the way Conrad had put together the background to the case. "Kanya Tamaraptri, as the singer Mailee, would sing at nightclubs but as part of her contract with them, was expected to socialize with the club patrons after her act. She was probably flattered by the attentions paid to her by Crespo and may not have realized he did not know she was a man."

Conrad nodded in agreement. "It is important we remember that we are dealing with a young, inexperienced teenager here. Not an older man, with knowledge of the world. I think you are right, *Khun* Colonel, Crespo did not know she was a man and she did not know that he did not know.

"When he suddenly found out, possibly by groping her and finding something he didn't expect, he went berserk. Where he got the bat from, I do not know. Perhaps it was one the gang had hidden there for their next attack. Already doubting his own sexuality, the discovery that he was with another man, and may well have already kissed her, drove him over the edge.

"She wasn't expecting the attack and was probably beaten to the ground before she guessed she was in danger. Then, Crespo concentrated his attack on her groin. In his own mind, he was probably trying to destroy the evidence of the discovery he had made about himself. I have learned that Kanya Tamaraptri's bones, especially in her head and face, were especially weak and fragile."

There was a grim silence in the room as those present in the room were forced to imagine what Kanya Tamaraptri had suffered during the minutes she was being beaten. In one corner, the police stenographer taking minutes of the meeting had tears trickling down her cheeks. Although she was supposed to be recording the proceedings without taking part in them, she said something in Thai. Chaowit translated it for Conrad. "Police Corporal Dao said that it was terrible *Khun* Mailee should have been so viciously attacked over a dispute she had nothing to do with."

Conrad sighed in agreement. "That is the true evil of intolerance. Those it hurts most are frequently innocent bystanders, whose only offense was being in the wrong place at the wrong time." *And, Dear Lord, I should know that well, for the blood of so many such innocents is on my hands and they are so stained they will never be clean.*

"This raises a critical issue." Director-General Pratin had found Conrad's picture of what had happened convincing and, like Corporal Dao, he was deeply saddened by the suffering of a person who was nothing more than an innocent bystander in a situation she could not have known existed. "Those four. The ones you describe as the followers. If they had no knowledge of, or involvement in, the attack committed by Crespo, then there are grounds for leniency for them. But, if they knew of, or aided in, the attack in any way, no matter how slight, then they are as guilty as he is. And that would mean they could face the death sentence.

"*Khun* Conrad, when questioning those four further, you must find out if they did know what Crespo did. Even if it was as little as listening to him brag about his attack. At the same time, you must not hint to them how important it is that they deny any such knowledge. As for Silva, it is arguable that his involvement in the gang had ended due to his new girlfriend. Again, that is a matter of great importance for him. If it can be maintained, then he also would not be considered complicit in the attacks on Kanya Tamaraptri and to Tomáš Lubomír Valentin Klímek. Again., we must ask you to find the truth there.

"One last thing, *Khun* Conrad. Your account does not explain the attack on Tomáš Lubomír Valentin Klímek. How is this connected to the situation you have described?"

"This is the problem we face. The truth is that it does not. All our suspects, with the exception of Silva, who, he claims, was with his girlfriend, claim they were in a half-built office block that was suspended when the builders ran out of funds. They all deny any connection with the attack."

"The forensic evidence is solid." Pornthip repeated her earlier assertion. "The same weapons were used. The injuries are identical. The method of attack appears identical. The killing of Tomáš Lubomír Valentin Klímek is a part of the same sequence of attacks."

Before Conrad could reply, a police corporal came in and spoke quietly to Colonel Chaowit. He excused himself ad left. A couple of minutes later, he returned with a grim expression on his face. "Please excuse me, but I have just received information that makes a great difference to this case. I have received a message from the King Chulalongkorn Memorial Hospital. Kanya Tamaraptri died a few minutes ago. According to the doctor, she suffered an endogenous fatty embolism, whatever that may be, and died on the operating table."

"Bone marrow, probably from her shattered jaw, got into her blood stream and blocked blood vessels in her brain or lungs. I'd have to see the pathology reports to determine exactly what happened. But, I have no doubt she died of the injuries received during the attack on her." Pornthip looked around and saw everybody present, Conrad included, nodding.

"This changes everything." Director-General Pratin took a deep breath and made his decision. "We will charge all six suspects with ten counts of assault and two counts of murder, one of which is aggravated by torture. The Metropolitan Police Department will seek the death penalty for all six."

Conrad's Suite, Bang Phitsan Palace, Bangkok, Thailand.

"Well, this is my last visit, *Khun* Conrad. You have been a very good client and I am proud to have assisted you."

Jip spoke politely while she was running a final check on Conrad's appearance. *It's a strange thing*, Conrad thought. *She hasn't just made me look younger. She has made me feel younger as well.*

"I don't know how to thank you, Jip. You've worked marvels. I don't just look younger, I feel younger."

Jip smiled at him and handed him a bulging envelope. "It has been my honor. Your account."

Conrad looked at the contents of the envelope. It was a complete inventory of the supplies she had used and a statement of the time she had spent on him. He was amused to note that he had even been charged for consultancy on the Mailee case. Then, at the end, was a discount she had given him because he had helped solve that case. The percentage of the discount seemed a little strange. A quick glance showed him the discount amounted to the same sum as the consultancy fee. That made him smile.

"My accountant insisted on the consultancy fee." Jip explained.

"Well, we have to keep the accountants happy, don't we?" Conrad was surprised by the final amount he owed Jip. While it was a large sum, it was much less than he expected. He fished out his case and counted out the money she had asked for, adding a substantial tip in the process.

Jip's eyebrows almost met her hairline. "You're not going to try and bargain me downwards?"

"Of course not; your services were worth every pe . . . every *satang* you asked for."

"Ohh." Jip seemed slightly embarrassed. Conrad realized she had, in her eyes at least, padded the amount due, in the expectation of being negotiated downwards. "That is very kind of you. Thank you so much *Khun* Conrad. Could I ask another kindness? I have some of my business cards here. If, perhaps, you could recommend me to others of our kind who need these services?"

"I would be delighted to." Conrad took the stack of business cards, noting that they had been printed in English. "I fear that Naamah's treatments are no longer adequate for the degree of scrutiny we all face."

Jip nodded in agreement. "And now, if we are all done, Her Royal Highness wishes to speak with you."

Reception Room, Bang Phitsan Palace, Bangkok, Thailand.

"Jip has done good work. We will have to use her again." Her Royal Highness, the Princess Suriyothai nodded in satisfaction. She was a little disappointed that Conrad and Jip hadn't ended up in bed together; she would have liked to have had something on him, but she had long ago realized that she couldn't have everything she wanted. Not immediately, anyway. "Now, what is happening on the Klímek case?"

Conrad hesitated slightly. He was used to hearing it described as the Mailee case, reflecting the priorities of the local law enforcement personnel. He had had a feeling the Klímek case was being pushed into the background by the prominence of the deceased singer. "Highness, I have thought this over, in great detail. The alibi of the erstwhile gang leader holds up. His girlfriend, who is a lady of negotiable virtue by the way, confirmed his story. Police Colonel Chaowit believes, and I agree with him, that her profession makes her confirmation of his alibi more credible. If she was with him for love, she would lie to protect him without a moment's hesitation. But, since she was a hired companion, she would rather stay on good terms with the police by telling the truth."

Suriyothai snorted delicately. "Firstly, there is no need for the Highness thing when we are in private and, by that, I mean when only Daimones are present. Now the logic about the girl I can understand. So, the case against Silva for the two murders is weak?"

"It is. It could be argued that he had ceased to have contact with the group prior to the two fatal assaults, and therefore he was not part of any conspiracy. Colonel Chaowit hopes that this line of logic will encourage him to be more forthcoming with the other crimes. As to the alibis of the other five, their claim to have been in a hideout they had established seems to be true. At least, the stories from the four followers are consistent. Whether Crespo was there, we do not yet know. He says he was. The others have not confirmed that."

Conrad hesitated, then continued. "I believe them when they say they had nothing to do with this latest attack. I believe the forensic evidence and the statements of the suspects can only be reconciled one way. That some other people killed Klímek and they did so in a way that would throw the blame on the person or persons responsible for the attack on Kanya Tamaraptri."

Suriyothai nodded. "That would be convenient from many points of view. I will speak with Director-General Pratin and suggest that the background to the killing of Klímek needs further investigation. He is a good and fair man, and he probably already thinks that. I will just be encouraging him to do something he already wants to do. But the killer of Kanya Tamaraptri will be punished to the fullest extent of the law. We will not tolerate these kinds of attack in our country."

"May I ask what is happening in the dispute with the Vatican? Perhaps I could speak with Lotario dei Conti di Segni and aid in its resolution?"

Suriyothai chuckled. "No need for that. It's all working out. We're exchanging insulting notes and statements of position at the moment. In fact, the teletypes we're both just sending are just photocopies of the ones we had sent earlier. However, soon the Pope will make a speech in which he will remind his people that, in order to qualify for absolution for sins admitted at confession, the penitent must show both repentance and a desire to make restitution.

"In the case of the act confessed being a crime against the laws of the host country, repentance and restitution can only be demonstrated by the penitent surrendering to the police. In the absence of him doing so, the confession is void.

"A few days later, the Interior Minister here will make a speech to the Association of Jurists in which he will remind them that placing listening devices requires both the authority of a judge, ensuring that the laws are being obeyed, and the permission of an Interior Ministry official, who decides whether the matter is important enough to warrant the use of such equipment. The minister will remind his officials that their decision must include proper and full consideration of cultural beliefs. That's a compromise we can all live with."

Conrad was impressed. "That's clever."

"Not really. This kind of thing goes on all the time. Now, go find who killed Klímek."

17 Petchaburi Road, Bangkok, Thailand.

"So far, what we can see confirms the story. This is where the gang spent their time. The break in the fence is where they described it. We can see, from the bottles left around, that they drank beer and smoked cigarettes. They probably swore a lot as well." Conrad looked around. "You know, these battles have been tossed to one side and left here. Now, with the windows not installed and this place facing the street, it must get dusty and dirty in here pretty fast. We should be able to tell how long those bottles have been here."

"We are ahead of you." Pornthip had a smug expression on her face. "That is why we are photographing every bottle in its location and then bagging them as evidence. We should be able to divide them into groups by the number of weeks they have been here. Then, we can check each bottle for fingerprints and establish a record of who was there and when. That's evidence, *Khun* Chaowit, facts not opinions or beliefs. Evidence."

"It may be that neither Silva nor Crespo drank beer here." Chaowit sounded doubtful.

"Not in a group like this. If they had beers here, they all drank them. This is a street gang, albeit a small one. It has a group identity all of its own, that supersedes their individual identities. What one does, they all do." Conrad looked around the half-built room again. It seemed to have a menacing yet slightly desperate air about it.

"A group identity. That would run against the statements of the four and suggest Silva and Crespo were here."

Chaowit's remark made Pornthip look sharply at him. "We don't need to guess or theorize. We have evidence. We follow the evidence."

Conrad thought about that. "There's something we can do while your people complete their analysis of this place. Let's just assume that somebody other than these kids killed Klímek."

"There's no evidence for that."

"Let us just make the assumption, subject to further evidence becoming available." Conrad's patience was invincible. "Then, we are faced with the question of who? And, related to that, is why? There are only four basic motives for murder. Sex, money, revenge and to cover up another crime. Do we have any indication that his killing was revenge? And if so, for what?"

Chaowit shook his head. "Revenge killings tend to be carefully thought out and planned. Not just crushing somebody's skull and leaving them in a back alley. Revenge killings are common here, but they do not fall into this pattern. As for sex, this is Bangkok. Of your four, I would say that money is by far the most likely. After all, the victim's wallet was stolen."

"Perhaps that the amount of money in question was much greater than he carried on his person. You say he worked for Skoda?"

"He did. They are one of the four companies bidding on the Bangkok Mass Transit Railway. A contract worth eight billion sovereigns."

"I would say eight billion sovereigns is a motive for murder, wouldn't you?"

Transportation Secretary's Office, Bangkok Metropolitan Administration Building, Thanon Sirothong, Bangkok

"Eight billion sovereigns, yes. But that is only the first phase. Additional options for future work include extensions of the system out to both airports, across the river and covering the dormitory communities outside the city. The total project value, if all those options are exercised, will be in excess of 20 billion sovereigns.

"To put this into perspective, the first phase will involve constructing 103 kilometers of elevated railways, increasing to 375 kilometers if all the options are exercised. Just getting the project started will mean an investment of 1.3 billion sovereigns." Khunying Siri Santabutra sounded very proud of the mass transit project she was describing.

"And you have four bids for this contract?"

"We do. Two of them offer three-rail light railway systems. They are the British Carillion Group and a U.S. consortium consisting of Kaiser, Brown and Root and Grumman. The other two bidders are offering monorail systems. They are the Skoda Engineering Company from the Czech Republic and

Construcciones y Technologie de Ferrocarriles from Spain. All are good, solid bids from companies of unimpeachable integrity."

"Have you reached any conclusions on who should get the contract?"

Khunying Siri Santabutra bit her lip slightly. "We have decided to drop the three-rail solutions and go with the maglev monorails. The technology risk is greater, and the cost will be a bit higher, but the advantages are great. Most importantly, the magnetic levitation system proposed is quieter than either the three-rail or tires and beam systems. For a crowded city like ours, cutting down noise is a major advantage. Further into the future, we could use the same technology to join our cities and even establish rail links with our allies. A Maglev monorail could have a top speed of 580 to 700 kilometers per hour. The world would have a rival to the Rotodynes at last."

Khunying Siri stopped herself with a flush of embarrassment. "I am so sorry. I am so enthusiastic about this new system that I forget that to others it may just be a means of getting from one point to another. But, look at these pictures from the companies."

She produced images of the proposed monorail trains. Both Chaowit and Conrad sucked in their breath. The design of the sleek carriages was breathtaking and was supplemented by a paint scheme that could only be described as inspired. Conrad spoke for both of them. "These are incredible."

Siri looked delighted. "They are the offerings from the Spanish CTF company. Our analysis is that CTF offer the better train design, but Skoda are proposing the better system when it comes to traffic handling and administration. Also, their propulsion technology is just a tiny amount better. The obvious thing would be for the two companies to form a consortium and this is the approach we are urging upon them."

"Are the companies receptive to this?"

"Skoda is. Their local representative was Tomáš Klímek, the poor man found murdered. He knew everybody of importance on this project and understood why his company should form a consortium with CTF. He convinced his management that a consortium was the right way to go, mainly because this project could be so large that Skoda would not have the capacity to handle it. CTF were less convinced. Their local representatives were far less enthusiastic, not least because they knew that Tomáš was so well-established here that they would undoubtedly be demoted to his subordinates or even replaced completely."

Siri's eyes hardened. "Tomáš was a good man. One week, he even took time to help my children with their homework. If I was looking for his killer, I would start with those who stood to lose their jobs when the consortium was formed."

Conrad's Other Eye

Headquarters, Triple Alliance Division of CTF, Soi 31, Thanom Sukhumvit, Bangkok

"You know, if we had started off investigating this murder as an isolated event, rather than as part of a larger pattern, we would have been here yesterday."

Conrad agreed. "It happens too often. The investigators start off with a presumption and they follow it to the detriment of everything that does not fit that picture. In our case, though, we had no reason to believe that the case would lead us here until we made our first arrests."

"Gentlemen, the head of our South East Asian Operation, Señor Dimas Rafa Lázaro Machado, is ready to see you. Floor Fifteen." The Spanish receptionist waved the two visitors towards the elevator in the back of the reception area. Police Colonel Chaowit frowned slightly at that. Nevertheless, he led the way into the elevator and pressed the button for the fifteenth floor.

Conrad was slightly surprised they were met at the fifteenth floor by another receptionist. Again European and, to his experienced eye, almost certainly Spanish. He spoke, however, in English. "Police Colonel Chaowit and Conrad de Llorente to see Señor Machado, about the BMTR Project."

"Ah yes, *señors. Señor* Machado will see you . . . "

"Now." Chaowit's voice was firm. Conrad heard a note of anger in it, one that was almost always absent from his companion's voice. The abruptness flustered the secretary and she showed them immediately to the appropriate office.

Despite an unpromising start, Machado was both friendly and co-operative. He had arranged small snacks and tea for his visitors. After some small talk over the differences between running a business in Bangkok and Barcelona, the interview swung to the real point at issue.

"So, *Señor* Machado, we understand that CTF is one of the two finalists for the BMTR contract?" Once again, Conrad was carrying the load as the main interviewer, with Chaowit allowing the interviewee to believe that he did not speak good English.

"Officially, that is the position, yes. In reality, we have won the competition and we only await the right signatures on the contracts. Our rivals at Skoda are trying to persuade us to accept them as part of a consortium rather than lose out completely. But, to be completely honest with you, we see little to be gained by their participation. Their technology is rather dated and their design skills are, shall we say, inappropriate to this particular client.

"They have also tried using political influence from their contacts in the government to force the Bangkok Metropolitan Authority to enforce a consortium, but we believe their approaches have been firmly rejected. But, may I ask, why the Police are concerned with this contract?"

"The head of the Skoda operations here, Tomáš Klímek, has murdered. Surely you must have read about it in the newspapers. He was your opposite number in the Skoda group."

"Ahh, yes. Tomáš Klímek. I have met him many times, of course, since my arrival here. I found him to be a tiresome person, in the habit of frequenting places of dubious entertainment and associating with people of low character. When I read about his death, it did not surprise me. When one associates with the sort of people he did, it is all too easy to be sucked into their world and meet a sad end."

"So, you have no insights you can offer us as to suspects in his death?"

Machado shook his head. "From a business point of view, no. I know what you are thinking. The BMTR contract is a massive one, probably the largest civil engineering project of its type currently up for tender anywhere in the world. With the conventional three-rail solution being dropped from consideration, it was only us and Skoda left in contention.

"The death of Klimek would have been a crippling blow to Skoda, had they been in a leading position, But they were not. The contract is ours. To be honest, if I had been found dead in a back alley, you could be expected to suspect that Klimek had used some of his underworld contacts to redeem his company's position but there was no reason for us to kill him. No, *Señor* de Llorente, I think you will find his death had much to do with the company he kept."

Conrad nodded thoughtfully. "I am inclined to agree with you. The underworld has a hypnotic fascination for those who see it from outside and that can lead even the most innocent person astray. All they need to is to be in the wrong place at the wrong time and hear the wrong words spoken and their life is forfeit. *Señor* Machado, you have such an acute grasp of society in this city. You must have been here for many years?"

Machado shook his head. "You are very kind to say so, but I have only been here for four months. Of course, now we have won this contract, I will be staying here until it is completed. My family have already come out to join me. We have an apartment in one of the new condominium complexes on Rajdamri Road. I think we will be one of the first customers for the new railway."

"You mean the new complex being built at 185 Rajdamri. I have seen it advertized in the Bangkok Post. It looks a beautiful place to live. You are very fortunate."

"My wife was reluctant to move here at first. But, when she saw the kind of place we could be living in, she changed her mind. She is still concerned about our sons though."

"A good school can make a great difference there. Have you thought about a school for your sons yet?"

"We have been recommended to try the International Laureate School. But . . . . " Machado looked pointedly at his wristwatch.

Conra took the hint. "Thank you for your time and patience, *Señor* Machado. Your information has been most illuminating."

Forensic Science Institute, Thanon Changwattana, Nonthaburi, Thailand

"That is a lot of beer." Conrad looked at the array of more than two hundred beer bottles. "How long did it take you to get them all sorted out?"

"Not very long. We shone a laser through each bottle and measured the intensity of the light at the other side. The more light was absorbed, the dirtier the bottle. The dirtier the bottle, the longer it had been there. We had a few outliers that were either very dirty indeed or had been there longer than our period of interest, but the majority of them are from our time period. They evenly divided up into rough groups. Our report has the transmissivity for each individual bottle and the groups they were divided into. We then dusted each bottle for fingerprints. Some had the prints of only one of your suspects; some, several of them. But, every one of the bottles, other than the outliers, had the fingerprints of at least some of your suspects."

"How about Crespo and Silva?" Chaowit asked the question reluctantly, as if he was afraid of the answer.

"I'll come to them." Khunying Pornthip referred to her clip-board. "There are twelve groups of bottles, corresponding to the twelve Fridays that we believe the suspects used the room as their drinking club. All twelve groups of bottles contain exemplars of fingerprints from the following suspects. Ricardo Villaño, Geraldo Araya, Cirino Ramirez and Clemente Solos."

"The four followers." Conrad couldn't help cutting in on the presentation. Then he flushed slightly and apologized.

"Exactly. Now, we found the fingerprints of José Herrera Silva on exemplars from nine sets of bottles but not three. Those three sets are the latest ones. It is therefore our conclusion that the evidence does not contradict his statement that he was with his girlfriend on the last three nights the group used to meet. It also corroborates the evidence from the first four that he had drifted away from the group and no longer attended their Friday evening parties.

"In the case of Rodríguez Crespo, we found exemplars of his fingerprints on eleven of the twelve groups of bottles but not on the latest. Therefore, we can assume that he did not attend the meeting on the Friday, the evening when

Tomáš Lubomír Valentin Klímek was killed. That corroborates the statements of Villaño, Araya, Ramirez and Solos."

"So, it appears that we can establish a conspiracy for the assaults on the eight youths attacked prior to the two killings. The group met at their drinking den, then went out and attacked their victims. All six of them have admitted to that and we have eyewitness evidence to corroborate them. I would say that is case-closed would you not, *Khun* Conrad?" Chaowit sounded pleased at the results as indeed he was.

"Please remember that the evidence," Pornthip's voice put emphasis on the last word, "is that each of them had drunk three or four bottles of beer each before they committed the crimes. That means they were clinically drunk."

"An important point in our law," Chaowit explained to Conrad. "We recognize that somebody who is drunk will do things that they would not normally consider. So, that is grounds for leniency, provided other circumstances permit it."

"I must point out that we still have no evidence to link Silva and Crespo to either of the two killings." Pornthip was dogged in her demand that forensic evidence had to be presented. "What we have is that the weapons used in the two killings were the same as those used in the eight assaults. That links the crimes but not the criminals."

"We think Silva has been exonerated from the killings. He will have to face charges for the beatings, but all the evidence we have," Chaowit had put emphasis on the word all, "is that he was not involved in either killing. In fact, we are coming to the conclusion that the killing of Klímek was not linked to the killing of Mailee and the assaults at all. We have a different suspect in mind for that case."

Chaowit went on to describe their visit to the CTF offices. Pornthip listened intently and sucked in her breath slightly at word of how the receptionist had behaved. When she heard of where Machado was planning to live, her reaction was much more pronounced. "185? Do you know how much those apartments cost? They start at 32.2 million *baht*. Even a *farang* cannot afford that."

"Such apartments would be purchased by a company for the use of their staff." Conrad explained, "A head of a consortium responsible for a major project would merit such an apartment. He would have to entertain important people there and it would represent the honor and importance of his company. But only the head of that consortium; those lower down the corporate tree would have much less impressive accommodation. It is clear that the BMA wanted Klímek as the head of a Skoda-CTF consortium, so Machado would not have qualified for one of those apartments."

"And he remarked it was only the availability of that luxurious apartment that reconciled his wife to bringing her family here. That is a powerful personal motive for murder. He must have known that the BMA would insist on a consortium."

"Get me some evidence." Pornthip was dogmatic on that. "And, *Khun* Chaowit, let me have the names of the lawyers representing our existing suspects. I will send them a copy of my report."

"I don't think that will be necessary."

"I do. The defense must have access to all the evidence in advance, not have it sprung on them in front of the judges. I will not have an innocent person convicted on my watch."

Conrad and Pornthip's eyes met. For the first time, there was complete mutual understanding between them.

CHAPTER FOUR

CONNECTIONS

Colonel Chaowit's Office, Bangkok Metropolitan Administration Building, Thanon Sirothong, Bangkok

"The real problem we have is that we cannot clearly link the two killings with the eight assaults. That's the weakest point in the whole case." Conrad nursed a glass of Armagnac brandy. The truth was, he missed his favorite glass of pale sherry, but it was one of the minor details he had to change. Pale sherry was Conrad Lorentz's favorite drink; Conrad de Llorente preferred brandy. Of such small details was a change in identity made solid. "Kwang, the truth is that, if we hadn't come into this case the way we had, we would see this as a string of eight assaults and two separate murders that might have some connection with the assaults but might not."

"Khunying Pornthip is supervising a search of the homes of all six suspects right now. They are confiscating clothing so they can check them for bloodstains, searching for baseball bats that show signs of damage and anything else that may be related to the case. She is at the home of the Crespo family herself. That is a great compliment to you, Conrad. There are very, very few people whose opinions she listens to. To me, the big question is how much Silva is involved in the attack on Kanya Tamaraptri. You trapped him into admitting he knew of the attack and that is enough to have him charged with it."

That made Conrad's stomach lurch. "The problem, Kwang, is that traps like that can misfire. He may have said Wednesday by accident. He may have been repeating something he saw in the newspapers. He may have seen the news, and suspected Crespo's involvement, without consciously realizing it. The fact that he came out with an alibi for the right day, without being told it, puts him on the spot, it is true; but it stops short of convicting him. Really, it is Silva and Crespo who are at the heart of this thing. The others won't do anything except sit in their den and drink without one or both of those two leading it.

"That brings us to another real problem. The attack on Tomáš Klímek. Neither of those two have a motive for it. In fact, he doesn't fit the pattern of attacks at all. Klímek was not homosexual. He was not a member of the half-world. He was a foreigner. Most importantly, he was attacked by somebody with considerable physical strength and he was robbed. None of that fits Silva and Crespo."

"My officers have interviewed Klímek's neighbors. He was well respected in the community, which more or less confirms what we learned from the girls working in the bar. He treated people with respect and was always quick to make amends for any offense his foreign behavior might have caused. The general opinion was that he had a good heart. That's an important thing for us. The fact is, Conrad, we only have one good suspect for his killing and it isn't Silva, Crespo or their followers."

"And that thought leads us to another. There are enough similarities between the attack on Klímek to make it reasonable for us to assume that it was Silva's gang taking their assaults to a deadlier level. Looked at another way, it could be argued that the Klímek killing was deliberately carried out in the way it was as an effort to direct our attention to Silva and his followers. In Americanese, somebody tried to frame them. And, as you say, we have a good suspect for that."

"That sounds probable, although, as Khunying Pornthip would say, we have no evidence to support that theory." Chaowit refilled his glass from a bottle of Chivas Regal. "Wait a minute, we didn't know ourselves that all these things were connected until the day before Klímek was killed. To frame that group, somebody would have had to know that we were closing in on Silva's gang for the eight assaults and the attack on Kanya Tamaraptri. And we didn't get to that point until the morning of the attack on Klímek."

"Exactly." Conrad thought very carefully. "Who knew who we were closing in on? The people we interviewed?"

Chaowit shook his head. "They were only aware of their specific cases. They didn't know they were linked to others or who was involved. The gangsters?"

It was Conrad's turn to shake his head. "They were following us and still doing so when we made the arrests. They didn't know we had linked all these cases."

"They would have done, after they'd picked up a few of Silva's people." Chaowit spoke drily. "It is amazing what people will talk about when they are having bits of their anatomy removed with bolt cutters."

Conrad coughed and crossed his legs. "And that leaves just three people. Vanna, who was with us all the time, School Principal, Guilherme Sérgio D'cruze, to whom we laid the whole thing out, and Gymnasium Instructor

Jonathan Day. You say you have already carried out a background check on Vanna?"

"We did. There is nothing special about her; she's typical of a high-class lady of negotiable virtue. Discrete and, in her way, honest. As you will have noticed, if she can talk you into giving her extra money, she will, but she won't steal it. I'll get background checks run on D'cruze and Day now."

"We'll have to talk to Vanna, though. She might have given information to some of her coworkers when telling them about her adventures of the day."

Chaowit drew in his breath sharply. "You can ask that question. I won't. As you are a *farang*, she might forgive you, because you don't know any better."

The Orchid Nightclub, Nana Plaza, Bangkok

The cocktail bar was almost deserted, except for the bored-looking ladies sitting around the bar. Conrad looked across the room and saw Vanna sitting in one corner with a sketchpad on her knees. He waved to her and set off across the room to join her. Chaowit plowed along behind him. When they reached her, she looked up, smiling. Conrad had been in Thailand long enough to know that the smile was meaningless. "Vanna, we need your help again. And we need to ask a few questions."

"In the car, Conrad, not here." Chaowit's voice had a note of warning in it.

"You'll have to bar-fine me out." Vanna was genuinely apologetic. "But business is very bad after the killing over the road, so that will not be a problem. You need to see the manager."

"Bar-fine?" Conrad hadn't heard that term before.

"My main role here is to persuade the customers to buy me drinks at the bar. Especially expensive cocktails. If they order champagne cocktails for us both, his will have champagne in it, mine won't. The lady-drinks are always served without any spirits in them but, even if they weren't, mine would be. I don't drink alcohol, you see. So the profit margin on my lady-drink is very high indeed. If I leave for the evening with a customer, that customer must compensate the bar for the drinks people would have bought me. It's called the bar-fine and the manager decides how much that should be. Busy night, it's a lot. Empty night like this, not much at all."

"And you get a percentage of the bar-fine?"

Vanna smiled brightly. "Of course."

Conrad walked over to the manager, who was sitting in one corner. "Excuse me, we would like to bar-fine Vanna out for the whole evening."

The man looked around and noted Chaowit sitting with her. "Police business? Has she done something wrong?"

"No, quite the reverse. She has been very helpful in investigate the killing of *Khun* Mailee and the foreigner. Very helpful indeed. We need more assistance from her."

"All right. Bar-fine, one thousand *baht*." Conrad gave him two 500 *baht* notes and the manager took them carefully. He made a note in a pad before putting them in the box. Conrad noted that the banknotes were treated respectfully. They had the King's portrait on them, after all. Then the manager caught Vanna's eye and gave her a thumb's up sign. She nodded and started to gather her handbag, pad and pencils.

"What are we up to?" Vanna sounded relieved that an otherwise boring evening had suddenly become interesting. She slipped into the back seat of the police car alongside Conrad.

"We're down to two suspects for the murder of Klímek and we'll be seeing them this evening. We'll need you to make your pictures of the two though. People find them easier to recognize than photographs. First, though, Vanna, there is something I must ask you."

"What is that?" Vanna was obviously curious.

"Please, do not be offended by this question, but have you discussed the investigation you took part in with anybody?"

The smile vanished from Vanna's face. The skin around her eyes tightened. Conrad could see she was furious. Her stare made him feel cold, in a way that he hadn't experienced since he'd been in Belgium more than forty years earlier. The seconds creaked by and she relaxed slightly. "You are a *farang*, so you do not understand. I will explain this to you. I will not, ever, discuss anything my clients say to me, or do with me, with anybody else. Never. Your question is so insulting that, if you were not a *farang*, I would find it very hard to forgive you."

Conrad put every possible sign of contrition into his voice. "I am deeply sorry, Vanna, but I had to ask. You see, there are three people who know what happened in the days you were with us, and one of them is the killer of Klímek. You are one of those three and if, I had not asked you, the omission would greatly endanger our case against the killer. When the judge asked whether we had questioned you, and we said no, he could argue we had brought our case without exploring all other options and that would raise reasonable doubt.

"Now that I have asked the question, we are clear to investigate the other two suspects. Despite that, Colonel Chaowit did not want me to ask, because he sees you as a valued member of our little team here and did not want to offend you."

Vanna nodded, curtly, but her anger was obviously ebbing. Conrad reached into a pocket and produced a flat box. "Thank you for understanding, Vanna. To show how much I regret having been rude to you, please accept this."

She opened the box to see a gold necklace with a pendant shaped like a miniature pair of handcuffs dangling from the front. She gasped and took it out, running the chain through her fingers. "Wonderful man! This is 23 carat gold, the best. And the pendant celebrates our work together. Thank you so much. I will treasure this always."

Chaowit let out his breath slowly. "So that's why we stopped at the jewelry store. Conrad, I underestimated you. Let us go and see Principal D'cruze."

Principal's Office, International Laureate School, Thanom Rama IV, Bangkok

"It is late. I should be leaving for home." Principal D'cruze had the appearance of a man who was being greatly imposed upon. In his eyes, he was.

"Tomáš Klímek will never go home again. His wife will have to face life without her husband, and his children will grow up without the guidance and support of their father. In comparison with the loss they have all suffered, the loss of a few minutes of your time weighs but little in the balance." Conrad spoke quietly and gently, but the steel in his voice was utterly unmistakable.

"You have arrested six of our students for this. What more do you want?"

"The students we arrested were guilty of eight assaults on young men in this city. One of them is being charged with the brutal and depraved murder of Kanya Tamaraptri. Whether his guilt extends to the other five has not yet been determined. However, we are developing grave reservations over whether that group can be connected to the murder of Tomáš Klímek. The only link between them is that a bat from the same set was used. We need to know more about those bats." Conrad stared at D'cruze. His gaze was unblinking. In one corner of the room was a gentle, intermittent hiss as Vanna's pencil skidded over her pad.

"Baseball bats! You want me to give you information on baseball bats?" D'cruze sounded incredulous. "How can you expect me to remember little things like that?"

"They are murder weapons, not baseball bats. And we have reason to believe that you do remember them." Conrad was bluffing, but only just.

D'cruze went over to a filing cabinet and opened a drawer marked Sports Department. He fished around in it for a couple of minutes and pulled out an order form. "Ahh, yes. Now my memory is refreshed. We bought a consignment of fifty baseball bats from an importer. We got an excellent price on them, because they had been procured for a school in Singapore that had been unable to take delivery. American-style ash baseball bats, juvenile size. The importer wanted to get rid of them, so he made us an offer. They were too expensive for the stores here, you see."

"So there are no other bats like that in the city?" Conrad had the excited feeling he always associated with having found a key piece of evidence.

"None, as far as I know. They were a special import that went bad."

"And how many of those bats are now missing?"

"I will find out." D'cruze picked up the telephone and pressed the page button. "Mister Day, will you please come to my office."

There was a tense silence while those present awaited the arrival of Jonathan Day. Conrad reflected that it had been quite an evening for tense silences. He caught Vanna's eye and she smiled at him. He knew that didn't mean much, but he did notice that she was now wearing the necklace he had given her. That made him feel absurdly pleased with himself.

Then, he felt something else; a faint flickering in the back of his mind. It was a feeling he had not felt from a stranger for more than forty years. He looked at Vanna again. He saw, in the background shadows, a man in a French paratrooper's uniform; a friendly man with a wide, amiable smile. Then he started and came awake as Chaowit touched his knee.

"Conrad, you went to sleep for a moment there."

"I'm sorry. It's been a long day, hasn't it?" Conrad glanced at Vanna. Yes, she is wearing the necklace I gave her. Why does that please me so much? *And, Heaven be praised, I can sense that flicker from her. It's very, very faint; her full transition is a decade away, at least, but the first symptom is there.*

He was saved from saying anything else by Day arriving. "Yes, Principal D'cruze?"

"The fifty baseball bats we bought? They are still here?"

"They are, most of them. Five appear to have been stolen at some time."

"Take these people down to the games room. Show them those baseball bats. If they want to take them away, give the wretched things to them."

"But, we will need them, some of them anyway, for the games afternoon tomorrow."

D'cruze was obviously exasperated. "You are the games instructor. Find something else for the students to do. Make them run around the park or play football. Anything. Just see that I am not bothered with this mess again."

While ill-tempered exchange had been going on, Conrad had been watching Vanna. One thing had struck him with great force. When she saw Day for the first time, her eyes had widened.

Forensic Science Institute, Thanon Changwattana, Nonthaburi, Thailand

"Would it be impolite to ask if you recognized Jonathan Day?" Conrad had spent most of the car ride working out how to phrase that question.

Vanna smiled at him, understanding the effort he had made not to cause offense and how he had tried to phrase the question properly. The truth was she also regretted being angry with him earlier. *He is a* farang *and he is trying his best.* "That is very polite, *Khun* Conrad. And I did recognize him, although he is not one of my clients. He is a butterfly."

"Pardon?" Conrad was bewildered by the idiom.

"A *farang* comes here, perhaps on vacation. They do one of two things when they go to a bar for a girl. Some of them pick a girl they like, and come back for her perhaps two or three times a week, for as long as they are here. They want to think they have a girlfriend, you see. So we give them girlfriend experience. We call them regulars, because they come back. Others will take a different girl every time they come to the bar and never the same one twice. We call them butterflies, because they flutter around. All the ladies prefer regulars to butterflies."

"And so Day comes to your club?"

"Not just to ours; every bar in Nana Plaza. Three or four times a week. He must be a very rich man. Most ladies charge butterflies much more than regulars. Much, much greater risk of calamity, you see."

"She means catching venereal disease." Chaowit explained.

"I know." Conrad smiled at some memories of long ago. "How do you think Calamity Jane got her nickname?"

Khunying Pornthip's Office, Forensic Science Institute, Thanon Changwattana, Nonthaburi, Thailand

Vanna was looking at a skull that was on a shelf by Khunying Pornthip's desk. There were files underneath it, but it was the skull itself that seemed to be fascinating her. She was still staring at it when Pornthip came in, a broad smile on her face. For the second time in the evening, Vanna's eyes opened wide and she blurted out. "Doctor Death!"

Conrad's Other Eye

Chaowit was about to rebuke her for the lack of proper respect, but Pornthip made an ironic little bow to the woman instead. "That is what the press call me. It is a compliment, although it may not sound like it, because I speak for the dead when nobody else will do so."

Conrad met her eyes and again. The two understood each other perfectly. There was a slightly belated exchange of *wais*. Vanna's was very deep and was accompanied by a sideways movement of her hips as she dipped to an almost kneeling position. That made Conrad realize the status Pornthip held and he made a mental note to ask Chaowit about it. Courtesies having been completed, they all settled down. Vanna was in the background; Conrad could hear the now-familiar faint hiss of her pencil as she started sketching. He couldn't help wondering what she was drawing.

"I have very good news. How about you?" Pornthip was her usual direct and uncompromising self.

"I think we are getting a handle on this right now." Chaowit looked satisfied. "We have learned much today and have gained an insight into what has happened. We are now quite convinced that the killing of Tomáš Klímek had nothing to do with the Venezuelan kids at all. They were, in fact, the victims of a clumsy frame-up."

"This is confirmed by the evidence we have collected." Pornthip opened the file she had brought in. "We checked the clothes and shoes of all the suspects for blood stains. We used a chemical called luminol, which showed there were traces on all of them. However, on Villaño, Araya, Ramirez and Solos, the traces were slight and old. They had degraded with time and the luminol results were faint. However, the results on a pair of tennis shoes we took from Crespo's home were very strong, suggesting the amount of blood was large and its deposition on the shoes was recent."

"No disrespect, Khunying Pornthip, but I understand luminol also gives a positive reaction with urine and fecal matter. From what I have seen of the kind of alleyways behind these clubs, simply walking down one could contaminate one's shoes heavily enough to give a strongly positive result." Conrad felt uneasy about the evidence that was being brought forward. It reminded him too strongly of the experts who had given evidence before the Inquisition. The belief in their expertise implicitly crushed doubts as to their accuracy.

"Very good, *Khun* Conrad; you are exactly right." Pornthip beamed at him. "Luminol used on its own can give very misleading results. It is, at best, an indicator. But, the results on Crespo's tennis shoes were so strong that we took scrapings from the pattern on the soles of those shoes. The pattern was very deep and the flexing of the soles had caused cracks. Although he had washed his shoes, there was still a considerable amount of material lodged in the tread pattern and the cracks. There was urine there, certainly, but we also found a lot of caked blood; most of it fairly fresh. We were able to confirm that the blood types matched those of Kanya Tamaraptri. The quantity of blood is such that one might theorize he stepped in a pool of her blood while beating her, but that would be speculation without evidence to support it."

"But, can we prove that blood is hers?" Chaowit found himself being sucked into the prove it mentality that pervaded the Forensic Science Institute.

Pornthip looked saddened, mixed with carefully-concealed delight at Chaowit's comment. "No, we cannot. All we can say is that it is of the same type and that gives a probability of a match. One day, not too far in the future I think, if we get a blood sample we will be able to link it back to a specific person. Sir Alec Jeffreys at the University of Belfast in Ireland has devised a technique for determining the DNA profile from blood and tissue samples. His team is using it there to identify bodies found in mass graves dating from the German occupation.

"We will have that facility here one day. In the meantime, we have another chance. Kanya Tamaraptri was a woman of the second kind. Her medical records show she was taking synthetic female hormones in order to feminize her appearance. We have enough blood in our samples to analyze them for that hormone. If we find it, that combined with the blood groups should secure the match."

"There were no comparable traces on the shoes of the others? Including those of Silva?" Conrad had seen immediately that this evidence was likely to prove critical.

"None at all. Just the slight traces I mentioned earlier. If they are blood, then the amounts are so small they could not possibly have come from somebody as gravely injured as Kanya Tamaraptri. If one of the gang had stood in her blood, it is probable that others would have done so as well."

"Colonel Chaowit," Conrad was speaking formally for the audience. "I do not see how a conspiracy charge could be sustained here. Crespo has not admitted to telling the others about his attack on Kanya Tamaraptri and they claim that he never did so."

"I agree." Chaowit looked relieved. "The charges have served their purpose. Announcing that suspects had been arrested and charged in the murder of *Khun* Mailee took the tension out of the situation and allowed hearts to become less heated. If we had not charged them, we may well have had riots as her fans took their loss out on innocent *farangs*. That is something that we could not afford.

"Also, of course, sitting there in jail cells waiting a murder trial has been a . . . teachable moment . . . for them. Now, we can send Crespo for trial on charges of her murder and announce that the others are being charged with assault."

"Excuse me, Khunying Pornthip," Vanna spoke from the corner she had been sitting in. "May I ask why is the skull of that woman in your office?"

"You recognized it as a woman then? Very good." Pornthip smiled at Vanna. "Her skeleton was found in a cesspit. We have made no progress at all with her death. I keep her skull there to remind me of the hideous injustice that was done to her. She was not just murdered. Her body was desecrated in the most abominable way imaginable. But we do not even know who she was or how she was killed. The chemicals in the cesspit had destroyed all her soft tissues, leaving just the bones."

"Khunying, please excuse my presumption, but would this help?" Vanna held up a picture of a woman's head. It showed her with her head slightly tilted, looking over the artist's left shoulder, and it was that position which allowed Conrad to realize the source of the image. The pose of the drawing was identical to Vanna's view of the skull.

To both Conrad and Chaowit's secret delight, Pornthip seemed completely thrown for the first time since the case had started. "How did you draw that?"

Vanna smiled, pleased to be the center of attention again. "In art class, they teach us how the skin and flesh cover the bones. In the forehead, for example, the skin is very thin but it is much thicker around the jaws and cheeks. I assumed she was Thai, because news of a missing *farang* would have been a sensation and would still be in the news today. So, that gave us the shape of the nose and eyes. The date on the file said the case was about three years ago, so I used the hairstyle that was fashionable for mature women then."

Pornthip opened the file under the skull and took out another sketch. It was the standard police identikit-style drawing. It had none of the detail or life that Vanna's picture featured. "This is what our police artist came up with. It was quite useless, of course. Yours is recognizable as a person. May I keep this?"

Flattered by the praise, Vanna nodded. Pornthip pressed a button on her telephone and a secretary came in. "Take this picture down to records and compare it with photographs of women whose disappearances are still unsolved. Concentrate on those in their forties and well-off."

"Well done, Vanna." Conrad thought that appreciation would be well placed, not least because he still wasn't certain that he'd been forgiven for the offensive question he'd asked earlier.

"Well done indeed." Pornthip seemed oblivious to the sub-text of his comment. "She is your *mia noi*, Khun Conrad?"

"Err, no." Conrad went bright red with embarrassment.

"Not for want of me trying." Vanna's comment was dry, but had a droll note under it.

"Vanna was an eyewitness and, when we found she was so skilled, we hired her to help us."

"I see. I'm setting up a forensic art department here. Only, the staff are barely capable of producing the identikit pictures I showed you. They are scientists, trying to be artists. I need an artist. Would you like to join us Vanna? I can offer you GS-4 ranking. That makes you equivalent to a police lieutenant. You'll go up the scale quickly as the department grows."

"So sorry, Khunying, but I make much more than that now. I do have family responsibilities."

"Here we go again." Chaowit looked up at the ceiling.

Pornthip ignored his comment. "You do now, but in a year's time? Remember when you first worked at a cocktail lounge? You would sit at the bar for only a minute or two before you were bar-fined out. Now, you might sit for an hour, or more. Your bar-fine is much less. In a year or two, you will have moved down from a cocktail lounge to a go-go bar. There, you will be earning much less. Still, your income will go down every month. But here, your income will rise and the importance of your job will increase. Long-term, the position I offer will be much better for you and for your family. And remember, I may speak for the dead. You put a face on them."

Vanna suddenly looked serious. "I must think on this. Very carefully. May I speak with you in a day or so?"

Pornthip nodded. Before she could reply, her telephone rang. She answered it and held out the receiver. "Your background checks on Guilherme Sérgio D'cruze and Jonathan Day."

Chaowit listened to the caller. He grunted slightly in acknowledgment of the information he was being given, taking notes. Eventually, he thanked the person on the other end of the line and put the receiver down. "Well, D'cruze comes up clean. He is actually well respected as a good teacher and a better administrator. Our research people think the unfortunate impression he gave us was simply unfamiliarity with our customs. He is financially sound and apparently happily married. He doesn't appear to have a *mia noi*, which is a problem for him, of course."

"His wife probably wouldn't allow it." Conrad didn't want to imagine what a European wife would say about a *mia noi* suddenly appearing on the scene.

"There are two sets of *farang* wives in Bangkok." Vanna spoke up from the corner of the office. She'd snorted delicately when the idea of D'cruze not having a *mia noi* had been mentioned. "The ones that know who their husband's

427

mia noi is, and the ones who do not. If your report says that this person does not, then those who prepared it did not look hard enough."

"She's right." Pornthip was smiling broadly. She guessed that Vanna was already hooked on working in law enforcement.

Chaowit agreed as well. He made a private note to rebuke the person responsible for the omission. "It is Day who is interesting. He has been in this country for seven years, but has no Thai friends of any note and spends most of his time inside the *farang* community. He is very deep in debt. His bank accounts are heavily overdrawn and he has been red-flagged as a poor credit risk. There are orders issued against him for non-payment of debts. Based on what Vanna has told us, it would seem he is spending most of his money on women in the bars."

"I would think that is not unusual." Conrad has seen this situation all too often. "A person is in a foreign country and fails to make the break into the society that surrounds him. He becomes lonely and bitter, seeking the sort of companionship that can be purchased. With that as his only lifeline, he becomes addicted to it, and it is as complete a ruination as any drug addiction. As he slides downwards, his dwindling resources make it even less likely he will break out of the trap."

"Especially here." Vanna spoke again. "If a *farang* woman wants to ruin a man's judgment she says, 'oh you are so strong.' When we want to do that, we say, 'oh you are so rich.' Wealth means high status. Strength means somebody is of such low status they cannot afford to hire somebody to work hard for them. Or they do the hard work for those who pay them."

"Like bashing somebody's head in." Conrad was putting pieces together. "A person who needs money very badly will do many, many things to get it. Surely, if he was this short of money and the banks would not allow him to borrow any more from them, he might go to loan sharks? Vanna, you have such things here?"

She nodded, her eyes calculating. "Of course. An illegal loan shark will charge fifteen or twenty percent per week. And may the Lord Buddha have mercy on you if you do not pay them. I know one or two of the ladies who lost their money gambling and borrowed so they had money to live on. When they couldn't pay, the loan shark did awful things to them. That is why I do not drink or gamble."

"I told you she was clever." Chaowit made the comment to Conrad, but it brought a delighted smile from Vanna.

The telephone rang. Pornthip answered it. She listened for a minute or so, thanked the person who had called and hung up. "Well, that did not take long. The clerk in records recognized your drawing, Vanna, and went straight to the right file. The victim was Doctor Phassaporn, the wife of Doctor Wisut

Boonkasemsanti. She disappeared about three months before the body was found. Doctor Wisut always was the prime suspect. The police couldn't even prove she was dead. Vanna, you have made yourself much merit today."

"Indeed." Chaowit was impressed. "Vanna, carry on like this and you'll be the next Director-General of the Thailand National Police Department."

A few minutes later, Conrad and Chaowit were waiting to depart on the next stage of the investigation. Conrad had pointed out that the loan sharks who had Day in their grasp probably worked out of the bars he had frequented. If they pulled them in for investigation, they could find out just how badly he was indebted to the criminal elements. One of them might even have hired him to do the killing in exchange for cancelling his debts.

"Kwang, there is something else. I think Vanna is one of us. Or will be."

"Are you sure?" Chaowit was seriously surprised.

"Not quite, but I think so. Kwang, forty years ago I met a man, a good and honorable man, who was destined to become one of us also. He died before he ever knew about his heritage. I would not like to see that happen to her."

Chaowit smiled at him. "I think I can fix that."

Reception Room, Bang Phitsan Palace, Bangkok, Thailand.

When Suriyothai entered the room, both Conrad and Chaowit made their *wais* deep and respectful. Beside them, there was a delicate thud as Vanna hit the floor. Conrad saw that she was almost on her knees, her head bowed down and her hands raised high. For the first time, it suddenly dawned on Conrad how privileged were the circles in which he had been moving. Suriyothai was very close to the top of the status line; Vanna was very far down it. He caught Suryothai's eye; she nodded slightly. His feeling had been right.

"Stand up, girl. I don't like people groveling in the dirt. Nor, by the way, does His Most Gracious Majesty." Suriyothai's face was stern and uncompromising. She gazed at Vanna while the young woman stood up. "Now, Khunying Pornthip believes you have great talent as a forensic artist and she wishes you to join the Forensic Science Institute. She offered you the rank of GS-4. I have spoken to her and she has told me of your work tonight. I have instructed her to employ you at the level of GS-5.

"Also, His Most Gracious Majesty has established a fund to pay allowances to especially talented people so that they will be able to serve the people of this country. You will be given one of these allowances to add to your pay. It will make your salary equivalent to GS-6. You will, of course, cease your present profession immediately."

Vanna almost hit the floor again. "How could I thank His Majesty for such generosity?"

"By using all your skills and talents to serve the people of this country. That is all His Most Gracious Majesty asks of you and He does nothing less himself. Now, Lani will take you outside where you can tell Khunying Pornthip that you will be joining her. You'd better call your cocktail bar as well and tell them you won't be working there anymore."

As soon as Vanna and Lani had left, Suriyothai dropped the severe and authoritative attitude and smiled impishly at Chaowit. "I told you I'd fix it."

"What just happened?" Conrad was confused.

"I steamrollered Vanna and used her allowance to put her in a position where she couldn't say no without insulting people it is better not to insult." Suriyothai was obviously amused by the events. "Soon, she will start to be instructed in what she needs to know when transition starts. Although she won't know it yet, of course. Also, as a recipient of the King's Stipend, she will be protected from any harm that might otherwise befall her. Now, Conrad, I need your help. This business with the Papacy is getting complex again."

"I thought that had been solved?"

"So did I, but it appears messages got scrambled somehow. I would like you to assist me in finding out exactly what they're promising us. I think the messages were translated in ways that reflected what the translator wanted them to say rather than what they actually said. Could you please tell me what they are really saying?"

CHAPTER FIVE

COMPLICATIONS

Conference Room, Bangkok Metropolitan Administration Building, Thanon Sirothong, Bangkok

"Conrad, what you are about to see is a part of our justice system you may find strange or even disturbing. Under our law, if a criminal and victim can come to an agreement over the former compensating the latter for the offense, then the matter is dropped. The eight victims of the assaults have come to meet with the families of Villaño, Araya, Ramirez and Solos to try and negotiate a settlement."

Conrad was horrified, although he tried to hide it. "Doesn't that mean somebody who is rich could buy their way out of a criminal conviction?"

"Conrad, anybody who is rich can buy their way out of a conviction. They can bribe the judges, or the witnesses, or the prosecutors, or all of the above. This way, at least, the money goes to the people who were harmed by the crime. Now, I must go and sit with the representatives of the police. You may not, since you are not formally a member of the force. Instead, you will sit with the witnesses to the proceedings. I have arranged for an interpreter for you."

Conrad joined a small group of people sitting at one end of the room. One was an Army officer, another in the orange robes of a Buddhist monk. They all exchanged polite *wais*, Conrad noting that the monk received the deepest and did the same himself. Then a group of eight young men, the victims of the initial series of attacks, filed in. They sat down one side of a long conference table with a man who was obviously their lawyer.

Then, Villaño, Araya, Ramirez and Solos filed in and sat down the other side of the table with older men, obviously their fathers, and another lawyer. Conrad noted the two lawyers exchanged nods and glances. He guessed the two had already agreed upon a settlement. Finally, Chaowit and a pair of police officers came in. They sat at the head of the table. Chaowit made a brief introduction and the proceedings started.

The lawyer representing the victims stood up and started to speak. He described the injuries inflicted on his clients, how they had to be treated in hospital at great expense and had lost income from the days in which they had been unable to work. Thus, in addition to their physical injuries, they and their families had suffered economic harm. They had also suffered from the shock of being attacked and the long-term distress that resulted from being the victims of the assault.

Halfway through the presentation, Conrad had a strange sensation. Right from the start of the case, he had felt himself isolated from it by his inability to speak Thai. It had literally been centuries since he had been in an environment where he was incapable of understanding the words spoken around him. It had started that way with the presentation on behalf of the victims. Then he had suddenly found himself understanding what the speaker was saying. The individual words were still unknown to him, but he could follow the gist of the presentation in outline. Instead of being both a lifeline and an isolating wall, the translation was filling in the gaps in his understanding. Conrad felt a huge swell of relief pass through him.

The victim's lawyer sat down. Colonel Chaowit stood up. He described how the police had first linked the attacks, then started to investigate them as a serial offense. He produced the pictures Vanna had drawn of the suspects. He described how a police artist had interviewed the victims and the witnesses at the bars. Those interviews had produced the likenesses of the suspects who had lured the victims from the bars. He then went on to describe the arrests, interrogations and the location of the drinking den, together with the evidence that had been found there. Finally, he revealed the confessions made by the four. At the end of the presentation, a round of applause went around the room. Nicasio Villaño had initially not joined in until his lawyer elbowed him sharply in the ribs.

"A good job." The Army colonel whispered the compliment to Conrad. Although it was in Thai, Conrad found he understood the sentiment perfectly, even though the actual words eluded him.

The lawyer for the suspects then stood up. He described Villaño, Araya, Ramirez and Solos as youngsters who had allowed drink, the natural overaggression of youth and the malign influence of bad peers to overcome their good sense. Now, they realized the consequences of what they had done and how nearly they had come to being charged with much more serious offenses. Their families wished to compensate their victims for the harm they had done and thus restore their good name in the eyes of the community.

Colonel Chaowit looked around, "Does anybody else have anything to add?"

There was a silence. Eventually the lawyer for Villaño, Araya, Ramirez and Solos looked at the victims. "Would compensation of 15,000 *baht* from each family be adequate?"

The defendents lawyer looked regretful. "My clients have large medical bills and were off work for many days. Perhaps 25,000 *baht* from each family would be more appropriate?"

"We should not waste the time of our police and the witnesses by going through the formality of bargaining. Why do we not go straight to a compromise? 20,000 *baht* from each family?"

The lawyer representing the victims made a show of consulting with his clients. Then, he stood up. "My clients have agreed that they are satisfied."

That led to a murmur of agreement all around. The fathers of Villaño, Araya, Ramirez and Solos stood up and went over to where the victims were sitting. Each then placed a packet of twenty one-thousand *baht* notes in front of each of the victims. They exchanged *wais* with the victims and then returned to their seats.

Colonel Chaowit then rose to his feet again. "Since the victims of the crimes are satisfied, there is no need to press the matter any further. The case against the accused is concluded. They may leave without further proceedings."

The sigh of relief that went around the families of the four youths was palpable. They gathered up their materials and left. Conrad did some quick mathematics; they'd paid each of the eight victims 20,000 *baht*, for a total of 160,000 *baht*. That meant their son's misdeeds had cost each family roughly $4,000. *They may have bought their way out of a criminal trial, but doing so didn't come cheaply.*

There was a brief interval while José Herrera Silva and his family entered. With him was a Thai woman in her late teens. She was dressed in a carefully-tailored, form-fitting purple shirt and an elegant gray pantsuit. With the sort of expertise acquired by his stay in the city, Conrad guessed her clothes were locally made copies of Italian designs. He also guessed that the workmanship and materials were at least as good as the originals, and probably better. One could buy cheap, poorly made copies in Bangkok, but one could also find well-made imitations. As he watched the family take its seats, he saw Silva's mother staring at the woman with anger and dislike. Silva's father was staring at her as well, but with intense curiosity. *The mother is looking at the woman who will take her son away from her. The father is looking at the woman who may soon be joining their family. No matter what the country, some things never change.*

The meeting followed the same course as the first session, with statements from the victims, the police and the lawyer for Silva's family. The only difference was that the police stressed that Silva was the ringleader of the attacks and bore primary responsibility for them. When Chaowit had asked if anybody had anything to add, José Herrera Silva had stood up and went over to stand in front of the first of his victims. He spoke in Thai, haltingly and without great confidence. Conrad guessed that his girlfriend had patiently taught him what to say and how. Again, Conrad found himself understanding what was said, without actually understanding the individual words.

"Please accept my most sincere apologies for the harm my actions have caused you. I encouraged the attacks on you, so the harm they caused is my responsibility and nobody else's. The blame should fall upon me alone. I will do everything I can to make amends for my actions and pray that peace and tranquility may be restored to your life."

He started to move down the line of victims, making a deep *wai* to each and repeating the same speech. Half way through, he faltered and glanced at his girlfriend. She gave him an encouraging smile. That seemed to strengthen him to finish his apology. When he finished speaking to the last victim, he made another *wai* and returned to his seat. Then, his girlfriend stood up and also made a deep *wai* to the victims. Again, Conrad understood what she was saying and the translation he got only filled in the gaps.

"I am so sorry for what my friend did to you. He is an idiot and he made a very bad mistake. But he has a good heart despite his youth and only needs proper guidance from civilized people to mature into a good person." She looked affectionately at Silva. Conrad wondered if he knew she had just called him an uncivilized idiot. "We all did things when we were young that were foolish and cruel. Please show him warmth from your hearts so that he may learn kindness, tranquility and good judgment from your example."

There was a murmur of respect from the occupants of the room. Then the Silva's lawyer stood and offered the eight victims 40,000 *baht* each in compensation. Once again, the lawyer for the victims made a show of consulting with them. This time, his surprise at the instructions he received was obvious. *He and the other lawyer agreed to offer 40,000, demand 60,000 and settle on 50,000,* Conrad thought.

The lawyer cleared his throat. "I have been advised by my clients that their hearts have been softened by the sincerity of the apology offered and by the plea they have heard. 40,000 *baht* will satisfy them."

That caused a ripple around the room. Silva's father took the eight packages of money from his briefcase, removed ten thousand *baht* notes from each package and gave out the rest. Then Chaowit took charge once again. "Since the victims of the crimes are satisfied, there is no need to press the matter any further. The case against the accused is concluded and he may leave without further proceedings. The family of the sixth member of the gang has refused to discuss compensation, so this meeting is now closed. In his case, the law will take its course. Each of you who have received compensation is now in possession of large amounts of cash and this endangers your security. A police corporal will escort you to a local bank so you may pay your compensation in safely. Please note that a donation box for the police widows and orphans fund is on your left as you leave."

Conrad watched the meeting break up. Silva's father was trying to thank his son's girlfriend for her efforts on his behalf. She, on the other hand, was looking pointedly at the 80,000 *baht* that was left on the table. Behind her, Silva's lawyer lifted eight fingers in the air. The father finally got the message. He counted out 8,000 *baht* and gave it to her. She made a *wai*, took the money and stowed it in her handbag. Then she and Silva left the room holding hands. Silva's father followed them, looking at his son's girlfriend with a mixture of affection and amusement. Silva's mother had an expression that would curdle milk at 100 paces.

Conrad looked at the Army colonel sitting beside him and noted the Saint-Cyr ring he was wearing. It was time to try out his French. "*Khun* Colonel, I see that some things never change."

"Ahh yes, the traditional relationship between mother and daughter-in-law." As Conrad had expected, the colonel's French was fluent. "When my father brought my mother to meet his parents for the first time, Mother was carrying a Mauser rifle. Father said it was the first time he'd ever seen his mother keep quiet about something."

"Your mother was in the Army?" It was the only reason Conrad could think of for a woman carrying one of the old Mausers.

"Retired as a lieutenant general." The Colonel seemed very proud. "She is a senator now. Senator Sirisoon Chandrapa na Ayuthya, representing the recovered province of Kampong Cham. I'm Colonel Suchart by the way."

"Conrad de Llorente. I've been helping Police Colonel Chaowit with this case. You attended Saint-Cyr?"

"Exchange course. We're back to being friends with the French again, after the unpleasantness of 1940. There's not as much choice in foreign military academies as you might think, though. Saint-Cyr is about the best, although Sandhurst is coming up fast, especially after the Falklands business a few years back. All West Point teaches these days is how to duck when SAC drops a nuke. What do you think of Bangkok?"

The question had Conrad slightly flustered. "This seems to be an incredibly tolerant city."

"That's one way of putting it. I suppose the police would tell you that. They have their perspective and we have ours. Are you involved in the case of that *khatoi* singer who was killed?"

Conrad nodded. "We originally thought that the attack was linked to this gang. It is, distantly. The gang member who refused to discuss compensation here? He's the prime suspect."

Colonel Suchart looked thoughtful. "Did you know that the *khatoi* community is responsible for a disproportionate number of attacks on people? Also, they tend to be light-fingered. A lot of the medical people here think it is a result of the combination of the drugs they take to feminize their appearance. Impairs their judgment, makes them volatile. Like women at the wrong time of the month, only more so. The person they are with does something the *khatoi* sees as disrespectful, or they get caught stealing something, and they attack their companion. Sometimes, other *khatoi* will see one of theirs in a fight and come to her aid."

"The police never mentioned that." Conrad was worried by what he had just heard and, more importantly, why he hadn't heard it sooner.

"They wouldn't. Look, the *khatoi* community is a major part of the night life in this city and Bangkok's budget is supported by that night life. You know the new monorail that's coming? Well, it's supported by the taxes paid by tourists, mostly the ones here for our nightlife. No tourists, no taxes and the city doesn't get a monorail. So, the police keep quiet about things that might scare tourists away. In the Army, we take a broader view. My mother says that the invasion of foreign tourists has done more damage to this country than the French and Japanese combined."

"*Khun* Conrad, I see you have met with *Khun* Colonel Suchart." Chaowit and Suchart exchanged *wais*, Conrad noting that Chaowit's was much deeper than Suchart's. *Obviously an army colonel has a lot more status than a police colonel.* "*Khun* Colonel, thank you for honoring us by acting as a witness. Conrad, the proceedings here are completed, very satisfactorily. With your permission, *Khun* Colonel, we must get back to work."

Vanna's Office, Forensic Science Institute, Thanon Changwattana, Nonthaburi, Thailand

"*Khun* Vanna, your new office is beautiful." Conrad looked around. The office wasn't large, but it was well lit and had a pleasant view of the park opposite. A filing cabinet had just been moved in and was positioned next to a light-table. It was well on its way to becoming a well-equipped studio for a professional artist. He had thought carefully about what to say at this meeting. He remembered what Chaowit had said. 'When she leaves the life to settle down and start a real career, it will never, ever be mentioned.' So, Conrad had phrased what he had to ask very carefully. "Will you be continuing with your art classes?"

Vanna almost beamed with excitement. "Oh yes, and the Institute will pay my tuition fees. And, I will be going to take classes on anatomy."

"That's great, Vanna. I got you a small present for you. Most police officers keep a scrapbook of the cases they worked on, with the convicted criminals being led away. So, I got you a photograph album and put the photographs of the meeting this morning in it for you. Now you have a record of your first case."

"Wonderful man! That is so kind." Vanna looked at the pair of pictures and put a finger lightly on Silva's girlfriend. "I know this girl well; she is Pakpao Duong. Khmer, like me. Why was she there? She is not in trouble, is she?"

Conrad shook his head. "She is Silva's girlfriend and she made a very favorable impression. Colonel Chaowit said she works in a bar."

"You mean as a bar hostess? No, not at all. He is most wrong. Pakpao is a coyote."

Conrad sighed. "Please, Vanna, what is a coyote?"

Vanna chuckled. Conrad saw that the outfit she was wearing was almost identical to Pakpao's. The shirt was white rather than purple, and the suit was navy blue, but the styles were almost identical. Conrad saw that his guess had been right. The workmanship was excellent and both shirt and suit were silk.

"*Khun* Conrad, a coyote is a professional dancer, one with formal dance training. coyotes are independent agents hired by a club for their ability to dance well. coyote are not go-go girls, who dance to advertize their availability. The coyote's only duty is to dance energetically and enthusiastically. Although they dress provocatively, coyote dancers do not make an intimate show of themselves. Mostly they are not something *farang* tourists see. The *farangs* want girls they can hire.

"Coyotes entertain in clubs that are for Thai people only and they are strictly unavailable. The rule is you may look, but not touch. The status of a coyote is much higher than a bar hostess. Even an inexperienced coyote dancer can make 60,000 *baht* a month, while the most sought-after dancers can make ten times that. The problem is that coyote dancing is very strenuous and the dancers must be very fit. It is for the young only. Mostly, they are teenagers and have retired by the time they are twenty. But, by then, they have paid for their university courses and are set up with enough savings for a comfortable life."

"Which raises an interesting question. I wonder how Silva met her and became her boyfriend? Still, we can deal with that later." In truth, Conrad was perturbed by this further discovery. Then he thought carefully over what he had been told before. Chaowit had said that Pakpao had worked in a bar, and Conrad had assumed that meant she was a lady of negotiable virtue. *I wrongly assumed that simply based on my own prejudices. How often have I done that here? Time*

Conrad's Other Eye

to get back to the main issue. "Vanna, do the ladies who work in bars and night-clubs carry weapons?"

Vanna smiled at him and her hand dropped into her bag. A second later, there was a *schnick* noise; one Conrad found very familiar from the time he had spent with Igrat. Conrad looked down and saw the shine of a four-inch steel blade in Vanna's hand. She raised an eyebrow. "A switchblade. Illegal, in fact, but every lady I know carries one."

"Would Kanya Tamaraptri have carried a switchblade?"

"Of course." Then Vanna frowned. "I wonder why she didn't use it to protect herself?"

Cloud 47 Club, Soi Patpong I, Bangkok, Thailand

"I have seen this person around the bars sometimes. He is a butterfly. But I do not hold any paper on him." Arthit Wattanapanit looked at Vanna's drawing of Jonathan Day again. "No, I am quite sure. This person does not owe me any money."

Conrad looked at him curiously. This was the sixth bar he and his party had visited, and the sixth time they had sat down with a loan shark, shown him the picture and asked about any business he might have had with Day. In the previous five cases, the answer had been an emphatic none. Yet Conrad's growing understanding of what was being said around him was ringing alarm bells. There was something about the answer they were being given that was different.

He took a glance around the bar. He noticed something else, something not quite related to this investigation. As he began to understand more of his surroundings, he was beginning to look on the foreigners in a different light. It was as if a sheet of frosted glass was separating them from him. He realized he was beginning to see the *farangs* as the local people saw them. The sight was not a complimentary one.

"You say you do not hold any debts from this man and that he does not owe you any money. But, you have not told us whether he has owed you money in the past, or what happened to those debts." Conrad noted that both Chaowit and Vanna were staring at him with wide-open eyes.

Arthit looked distinctly uneasy. Chaowit swallowed and coughed. "I would be interested in an answer to that question."

Arthit added a slight shade of greenish gray to his face. "Yes, he borrowed money from me. A large sum, by usual standards. At first, he kept making the payments, capital and interest. Then he started paying the interest only and then he started missing interest payments. The missing payments are added to the capital, of course. Soon, the sum he owed was worrying me and I was going to discuss it with him."

"With the aid of chili peppers?" Vanna's voice was neutral.

"Possibly." Arthit hesitated and was looking extremely evasive. "But it never got to that. Another *farang* bought his debts from me."

"Describe him to me." Vanna sat next to him and took out her pad. "First, his face. Was it a long face or a round face?"

Half an hour later, she held up the final picture. "Excuse me, please, but do you recognize this person?"

Conrad and Chaowit exchanged glances. They did, but they weren't going to say who it was in front of Arthit Wattanapanit. They nodded to Vanna, but said nothing.

She also nodded, then got up to speak with the manager's best girl and then with the other women sitting at the bar. When she got back, she spoke directly to Arthit. "Thank you for helping us. Now, please help us some more by not calling any of your friends to warn them. You should know that there are eight ladies working here tonight. Every one of them knows what you do to ladies who cannot repay their loans. Should you try to leave before midnight or contact anybody, they will let The Auspicious Society know that you have been skimming from the money you collect for their local house. They may do other things as well, I do not know; but I do know you will meet the Black Dragon Slayer. But, if they do take action first, it is because they will be assisting the police. Do you understand what I mean?"

Arthit swallowed and nodded. Chaowit whispered to Conrad, "I think you have just seen the steel under the orchid. She will make an excellent asset for the police department."

Conrad, Chaowit and Vanna gathered their things and set off for the next bar on their list. By midnight, they had visited fifteen bars and found four more loan sharks who had loaned Day money and then sold the debts to a foreigner. They also found one loan shark who hadn't loaned Day any money, but had quickly invented some debts and then sold them to said foreigner. In Chaowit's police car, the three compared Vanna's pictures. There was no doubt that they all were of the same man and that man was easily recognizable. Conrad was the one to say it. "Dimas Rafa Lázaro Machado."

Home of Tomáš Klímek, Thanon Sukhumvit, Bangkok

A maid answered the door and ushered Conrad into the reception room of the house. It was small, set well back on a medium-sized plot of land. "Sir, you are?"

Conrad's Other Eye

"Conrad de Llorente. An advisor working with the police on the murder of Tomáš Klímek. I have news for *Madame* Klímek."

"Excuse please. *Madame* has visitors. I will speak." The maid disappeared and then returned a moment later. "Come please."

Conrad took in the meeting at a glance. *Madame* Klímek was sitting on a couch, a Thai woman beside her, holding her hand. Two late middle-aged men were sitting on another couch, facing the women. Conrad switched languages to Swiss. Really, he was speaking in German, which was still the commercial language of Eastern Europe, although the dialect now taught was that of Switzerland and the language itself was called Swiss. "Madame Klímek, I am Conrad de Llorente, a consultant for the police. Please accept my deepest sympathy for your loss."

"Thank you, sir. This is my husband's friend Ploie, and these gentlemen are Bronislav Karel Cerny, the President of Skoda Engineering and Ferdinand Slováček, Company Secretary of Skoda."

Conrad shook hands with the two men and then made a *wai* to the Thai woman. She replied, trying to smile at him, but he could sense the waves of despair and misery sweeping her. That was when a revelation hit him. *This woman lives in an apartment paid for by Tomáš Klímek and she receives an allowance from him. Yet, in European eyes, she has no official status at all. With her patron dead, she faces homelessness and destitution. Truly when a murderer commits his crimes, the ripples of harm go on to affect so many other people. This woman is as much an innocent victim as any other and surely she deserves protection as well? And does that not mean that catching the guilty, especially those who are on a trajectory to hurt, main and kill more people, is also protecting the innocent?* That question raised issues that made Conrad severely uncomfortable.

"Is there any news in the case, sir?" Cerny sounded deeply concerned.

"I am pleased to say there is. That is why I came here today. I am pleased to tell you that two people are being arrested by the Thai police at this moment. One is the man who killed your husband, *Madame*; the other is the man who we believe hired the killer. I cannot disclose more than that at this time, but we have assembled a strong case."

"You said we?" Slováček sounded curious.

"I have been an advisor on the case. I am an investigator but also, a priest."

"Catholic? That must be . . . interesting for you, given the present situation. Could you tell us what the motive for the killing was? Was it related to the work Tomáš did for us?"

"I can answer the second question, yes. His death was the direct result of his activities on behalf of your company."

440

"Double indemnity!" Slováček was triumphant. Everybody else was confused, so he hastened to explain. "All our employees have life insurance provided by the company. For an employee as senior as Tomáš, the benefit is 350,000 sovereigns. But, if his death occurred as a result of his official duties, then the benefit payable is doubled. Jana, I thought you might need money immediately, so I discussed your case with our insurance carrier. Skoda Engineering is paying you your standard death benefit immediately and our carrier will reimburse us for this. Here is your check. When you get back home, our carrier will pay the balance to you."

He handed the check for 350,000 sovereigns over. Jana Klímek looked at it, knowing that it was the final confirmation that her husband really was dead. Ploei was looking at the paper as well. Conrad knew that, to her, it was confirmation of a world-ending disaster. *Madame* Klímek intercepted her look, understood, and took her hand, squeezing it gently. "Ploie, Tomáš always asked me to make sure you were cared for if anything happened to him. We will share this money."

Slováček was curious. "That is very generous, Jana. But, may I ask who this lady is?"

"She is . . . was . . . my husband's friend. He was her patron and she helped him with his work. Made appointments for him, introduced him to the right people . . ."

"Wait a minute." Slováček cut across her. He looked at Ploie with well-simulated anger, "You helped Tomáš with his work? You were his assistant in fact. Why did you not say so? With the death of Tomáš, we will have to bring a new executive over here to head the consortium with CTF. We have been worried about how he would pick up all the strings that Tomáš's death had cut. And now we find that you know them all and can help out new man get off to a good start. You really should have told us earlier. Now, please tell me you will continue to work for us as our new executive's assistant."

Conrad looked at Slováček with respect. In his experience, there were two kinds of company secretary; those who could point to a company regulation that forbade somebody from having something they wanted and those who would hunt through the books until they found a rule that would allow them to give somebody something they needed. Slováček was obviously one of the latter.

Ploie's face was one great beaming smile. She was nodding her head frantically, while also starting to cry with relief. That was when Conrad realized the importance of the compensation hearing he had attended the day before. For many people, facing ruin as the result of a crime, sending the perpetrator to prison meant little. Financial compensation could be the key to salvaging their lives.

Cerny and Slováček, stood up. "Please forgive us, Jana, but we must go. Ploie, come to our offices tomorrow and we will introduce you to our new executive for this area. Now, we must go to CTF and tell *Señor* Machado the bad news."

"I don't think he will be there, gentlemen." Conrad was working hard to keep from smiling. "He has already had some very bad news this morning."

"Ahhh." Cerny understood immediately. "In which case, we will take our time. Perhaps we will go and see some tourist sights first."

On the couch, Ploie had broken down and was sobbing with relief. Jana Klímek was hugging her. Conrad cleared his throat.

"Excuse me, but I must be going as well," he hesitated and then continued, "*Madame* Klímek, you have done a very kind and gracious thing today. One that God will surely find pleasing."

She smiled slightly, probably for the first time since her husband had been killed. "You know, when I found my husband had a *mia noi* tucked away, I wanted to kill her, then him. I hated her; all I wanted was to claw her face until my fingernails scraped on her bones. Then, I knew I was going to meet her. I was going to try my best to drive her away. Only, as we talked, I found myself liking her. We became friends. Is that so strange?"

Conrad smiled at the picture. His growing understanding of the society around him allowed him to picture what had happened. "I think that God always smiles upon replacing hate with friendship."

The Ambassador's Personal Office, Bang Phitsan Palace, Bangkok, Thailand.

Conrad couldn't help but wonder how old Suriyothai's desk really was. The wood was obviously teak, but it had darkened and hardened with age to the point where he believed it was pretty much impervious to gunfire. There was a line he remembered from one of the Washington Circle; 'we only properly grasp what we are when we see a wall we helped build broken down by age.' *Had Suroyothai sat at this desk when it was fresh and new?*

"Your Highness, I have examined the exchange of messages between the Vatican and the Foreign Ministry in detail. Your suspicions were right. The translators at the Ministry did a very poor job of catching the nuances of the messages coming in. Their translations are not, technically, inaccurate but they are not really complete. They miss the subtle details of wording and phrasing. Also, they are shaded to accommodate the Foreign Ministry's positions."

Suroyothai was curious. "How do you know? You don't read Thai."

"No, but the originals were sent in Italian and I translated them into English. I speak Italian fluently. Then, I had the Thai translation of the Italian translated into English and I compared the two. When one does that, the deficiencies in the translation become much more obvious. A bit like looking through a magnifying glass. Of course, being Catholic, I understood what the original text was really saying."

"So, if the original translation is perfect, the English translation of the Thai should be the same as the English translation of the Italian. Clever. I must remember that trick. So, what is the Vatican really saying?"

"The problem is that really there is a complete failure of each to understand what the other is saying. The two governments have been talking past each other, each addressing the issue in terms that reflect its own concerns. Since those concerns were not identical, the exchanges did not relate to each other very much. To the Vatican, the important issue was that their religious customs should be respected; to you, that your laws should be respected."

"I know that." Suriyothai was slightly impatient. To her, this minor quarrel was taking up all too much of her time. Even for a Daimones, a day still only had twenty-four hours.

"My apologies, but I felt I had to explain what happened so that no blame would be attached to officials who were doing their best. What they did not understand was that their translation of the Pope's words, that 'that in order to qualify for absolution for sins admitted at confession, the penitent must show both repentance and a desire to make restitution. In the case of the act confessed being a crime against the laws of the host country, repentance and restitution can only be demonstrated by the penitent surrendering to the police. In the absence of him doing so, the confession is void,' is completely counter to Catholic doctrine.

"The key word used is actually 'contrition' not 'restitution.' Restitution means to make things right with the victims; contrition means to make things right with God. Your translators missed that distinction completely.

"This misunderstanding changes the meaning of all the rest. Absolution cannot be granted if the penitent does not display repentance and contrition. In other words, the whole thing is about the penitent's relationship with God, not man. The restitution owed to the human side of the situation does not figure in the equation.

"What the statement says is that a priest may suggest that genuine contrition could be demonstrated by the penitent surrendering to the authorities, but he cannot make that a condition. Also, the statement points out that repeating sins, which presumably includes offenses against the laws of the host country, should throw doubts upon the sincerity of both the expressed repentance and the acts of contrition. That is a very long way from saying that the confession is void if the penitent does not turn himself in. After all, the confession is nothing to do with the laws of man."

"So, they used sophistry to deceive us." Suriyothai's gaze was as steady and unblinking, and as merciless, as a snake's.

"Not consciously, no." Conrad spoke hurriedly, trying to complete his explanation before he made matters worse. "They certainly did not realize that you would fail to make that distinction. It took me some hours of study before I realized what they had done. They are so used to that distinction, that they made it without thinking. The real heart of the issue is not your police bugging a confessional per se.

"By our beliefs, your police are subject to immediate and automatic excommunication for doing so. But the Vatican officials believe that is their problem. They are concerned the threat that a confession may be bugged will deter people from making confessions, and thus interfere with their relationship with God. The purpose of absolution is to forgive sin, not to punish transgressors. They are concerned only with the spiritual side of this; you are concerned only with the secular. As a result, you've been talking past each other."

Suriyothai looked thoughtful for a moment. "I can see that. So, how do I make this problem go away?"

"Do nothing immediately. Look, your Highness, this is nothing new. It has been going on since the invention of the microphone. Indeed, in some form, it's been going on from the earliest days of the Church. A suitable person hidden in the shadows is conceptually no different from a bug. The Church will make pious noises, but there really isn't much we can do to stop the practice. I can't see priests sweeping confessionals for bugs.

"In fact, they don't really have to. There is no reason confession has to take place in a confessional. It is merely a convenient private place where the penitent does not have to be face to face with the priest, if he finds that easier. It is not unknown, for instance, for it to take place right in the middle of a very large church with nobody nearby. Much harder to bug that. Or the confession could be held outside, in an open space. Just issue a statement welcoming the Papal clarification and say nothing about the secular side of this. Or about the places your electronics may find themselves in."

"In other words, we keep quiet about what we get up to. I can live with that." Suriyothai sighed and for a moment she looked tired. "You know, I can solve an international crisis that threatens the lives of millions in a few minutes. Yet this stupid little row over a mistranslated word has taken three weeks of my time. Why is that?"

Conrad couldn't resist the answer. "Because, Your Highness, sometimes the Good Lord works in mysterious ways."

CHAPTER SIX

CONFLICTS

Hollywood Planet Club, Thanom Rajdamari, Bangkok

"Pakpao? She'll be doing her first routine on the hour." The club manager looked curiously at Conrad. "Your friend knows this is not a *farang* club?"

Vanna reached into her bag and brought out her badge. It was so new, it still had traces of the plastic wrapping on it. The manager wasn't expecting to see it and didn't notice that it was a Forensic Science Institute badge. "We both know. We think Pakpao can help us with an investigation. We'll only take a few minutes of her time."

"Of course, *Khun* Vanna, I will get her for you now." The manager made a *wai* to Vanna, something that he had notably not done before, and left.

A minute or so later, Pakpao appeared. She had already changed for her dance and was wearing a black-cropped top with black short-shorts. Convincing himself that a close look was needed to gather evidence for the case, Conrad took that close look. To his surprise, Vanna had been correct; despite the apparently revealing nature of the outfit, Pakpao was actually dressed quite decently. She was wearing a bra under the top and, although the short-shorts appeared skintight, there was no hint of camel toes.

Vanna caught his look and smirked. "She's taken, Conrad. I, on the other hand, am not."

Conrad gave a weak grin. He was saved from answering by Pakpao seeing Vanna and coming over. "*Sawadee kha, Khun* Vanna. I will come to talk in a minute. The police want to talk to me about something first."

"*Sawasdee kha, Khun* Pak. We are the police. Didn't you know I've got a new job now?" Vanna produced her badge and showed it to the other girl.

Pakpao looked at it and her eyes went wide. "No, I didn't know. What are you doing with the police?"

"I'm a forensic artist. I am helping Conrad here with the *farang* who was killed a few nights back."

Pakpao looked at Conrad and caught her breath. When she spoke, she had switched to English. "I recognize you! You were at the settlement hearing this morning. There is no problem, is there? I thought everything was settled."

"It is, there are just a few details I wish to make clear. For my own education, really. How did you come to meet José Herrera Silva?"

"He came here one night, on his own. I do not think he knew this was a Thai club and picked it by chance. He sat at the bar, drinking beer, but he was on his own. He looked so lonely, I felt sorry for him. Nobody would talk to him, you see? He didn't belong here. So, when I had finished my routine, I went and sat with him. This caused a stir. The dancers here are supposed to sit with customers and help them spend money on drinks, but no more than that.

"People were watching him to see what he would do and help me if he became unruly. But, he behaved very well. I found he spoke Spanish and it was a chance to practice mine. Only, I speak some European Spanish while he spoke South American Spanish. We laughed together while we compared them. Then I had to dance again. When I came back, he asked me if I would like to eat. I told him I was not allowed to go outside with bar patrons but there was a good restaurant in the club we could go to. We went there. One of the other coyotes here, a friend of mine, joined us.

"I was half expecting to spend my meal pushing away his hands. *Farangs* think coyotes are available, but we are not. But, he behaved very correctly and politely. Just like a civilized person. When it was time to pay the bill, my friend was going to pay for herself; but José would not let her and paid for all three of us. He even asked if I would mind if he came to watch me dance again. That was very polite of him, and I told him what my schedule would be for the rest of the week. He kept his promise and came more nights to see me. Our meals together became a regular thing. One thing led to another and . . ." Pakpao shrugged. "I was his first."

Vanna frowned slightly. "Was there any problem with you going with a *farang*?"

Pakpao shook her head. "At first, yes. But José tried so hard to behave like a civilized person, soon everybody's heart softened towards him. And I received respect for teaching him to behave properly. So, it all worked out in the end. Except with his mother, of course. At least she isn't Thai."

Both girls started laughing. Vanna dabbed her eyes and explained to Conrad. "When a man's fiancé is invited to dinner by his mother for the first time, she would be well-advised to bring her own food-taster and wear body armor."

"Of course, the mother has good reason to be alarmed." Pakpao responded. "Thai women make wonderful girlfriends but terrible wives."

"This is true. But we are Khmer, and we make wonderful wives and girlfriends."

"Unlike the Vietnamese, who make terrible girlfriends and worse wives." Both women erupted into peels of laughter again.

Once they had stopped laughing, Conrad got to the area he had wanted to resolve. "Pakpao, please do not take offense at my next question, and, if it is rude, please just put it down to me being an uncivilized idiot. In the original police report, it just said that you worked in a bar and some assumptions were made that should not have been. You confirmed José's alibi but, it was assumed that you would tell the police the truth because you were a paid companion and it was in your interest to do so. But, that is obviously wrong and unjust to you. Now, I must ask, did you and José do anything else the night Kanya Tamaraptri was killed?"

The merriment faded from Pakpao's eyes and her expression became noncommittal. "Why would you want to know?"

"Because there is a grave danger that, if the police put the information together the way I did, José may be the subject of a grave injustice."

"He's a good man, Pak. You can trust him." Vanna's comment pleased Conrad and he suddenly realized how important it was to him that she should look on him with favor.

"Very well. I told the police the truth. I was with José that night. But, we were not in my apartment all evening. You see, José had confessed to me what he and his friends had done. I had been very angry with him and told him that if he ever did anything like that again, I would leave him and never speak to him again. But, that evening, he told me that one of his friends, Rodríguez Crespo, would be going out to look for a girl of his own. He had a terrible fear that it would end badly, so we went out together to look for him. We never found him but, when we got back, we heard about the attack on Mailee. Somehow, we knew it was Crespo without being told."

That was what I was afraid of. Conrad thought carefully. *It is enough knowledge to put Silva, and possibly even Pakpao, into jail on a conspiracy charge. Neither of them deserve that.* "Pakpao, did anybody you know see you or recognize you when you were out with José that night?"

She shook her head. "I wasn't dressed like this. I was just wearing normal street clothes. Top and jeans. The streets are full of women dressed like that with *farangs*. But coyotes don't go with *farangs* so, even if somebody who knew me saw us, he would have assumed I was not the coyote Pakpao, just somebody else who looked a little like her. And, all *farangs* look the same, so José wouldn't be recognized."

Conrad relaxed slightly. "*Khun* Pakpao, please allow me to give you some advice. If the police prosecution of Rodríguez Crespo does not go well, they may look for others to charge. The two of you could easily be victims of such an accusation. So, do not admit what you have just told us to anybody else. Stick to the original statement that you two were together. Don't overdo it or try to add extra details. Just say, you and José were together and let people draw their own conclusion."

Pakpao's eyes widened. Conrad could see that the possibility had never occurred to her. Then, she whitened as she realized how easily she could have mentioned the real events of the evening to somebody and then found the story return to harm her. "Thank you, *Khun* Conrad, you are indeed a good man. Vanna, are you his *mia noi* yet?"

She shook her head sadly. "I keep trying, but he is very hard-headed."

"Well, hurry up before another girl snatches him away from under your hand. Now, are you two going to watch me dance?"

To Vanna's surprise, Conrad nodded. "It would be discourteous to leave before watching you dance when you took the time to answer our questions. Do you want a drink, Vanna? We can sit at the bar and watch."

"Orange soda for me, please. If I was working here, I would have ordered a mimosa. I'd still get orange soda, but you'd pay for champagne."

Conrad nodded. "One orange soda and one Armagnac brandy please."

The bartender lifted up a bottle of Armagnac Tenareze Hors D'Age and Conrad nodded appreciatively. Then, savoring the excellent brandy, he watched Pakpao dancing. He'd been expecting a standard bump and grind, but the dance was far more complex than that. Soon, he started spotting traditional Thai dance motifs woven into the performance and started to appreciate the difference between the skilled, professional performance he was seeing and the pale imitations in the clubs he'd visited earlier. That left just one question he had to ask to complete this aspect of the case.

"Vanna, how does she get her bottom to shake like that?"

Forensic Science Institute, Thanon Changwattana, Nonthaburi, Thailand

"There is a brief medical examination of prisoners before they are sent to jail." Khunying Pornthip sniffed disdainfully. "And when I say brief, I really mean cursory, to the point of being negligent. Essentially, the doctor just counts the bruises, so the prison authorities know how many times the prisoner got beaten once inside."

Conrad had suspected that much. "Nevertheless, those cursory records might tell us what we need to know. Were you able to get the records for Rodríguez Crespo?"

"Of course." Pornthip opened up the file and ran her eyes quickly down it. "Minor bruises to the abdomen. The warders probably gave him a punch of two as a warning. Aahhhh, this might explain why they went easy on him. Doctor noted a six-centimeter gash on his ribs, left hand side. Level with the lowest rib. They were probably afraid a good tuning up would open the wound and cause a serious problem. The warders didn't really want to hurt him. Just to remind him they could. If they had to."

"The sort of wound that could be caused by a sharp knife? A switchblade, for example?"

"Exactly that sort of wound. Given the position and angle of the cut, somebody right-handed lashed out with a knife but the blow was knocked to one side and inflicted only a superficial cut."

"And Kanya Tamaraptri was right-handed?"

"Yes." Pornthip looked up sharply, "I'm beginning to see where you are coming from in this."

"Khunying, we have assumed right form that start that Crespo picked up the victim, thinking she was a woman. And, when he found out she was a man, tortured and killed her in an unprovoked attack. One that could very well get him a death sentence."

"One that almost certainly will. Go on."

"Suppose it didn't go quite like that. Suppose, Crespo picked her up, took her outside and then found she was a man? Instead of attacking her, he insulted her; probably in foul terms and certainly very impolitely. He shouted abuse at her. I have been told that the *khatoi* are volatile and easy to anger. Also, that Kanya Tamaraptri almost certainly carried a switchblade. Suppose, angered by his insults and humiliated by his accusations, she drew her knife and lashed out at him with it? Having spent so much money and time achieving a feminine appearance, she was probably enraged by the fact he saw through it. No, that doesn't work. She thought he knew she was a man. She probably thought he'd lured her into a trap and was going to attack her. She thought she was defending herself; he thought he was doing so."

"This happens often, but it is rare for things to get this violent. If the man picks up a *khatoi* by accident, they usually end up apologizing to each other and that ends the matter. Nobody pulls knives. Or guns."

"But these are not normal times. There had been a string of attacks on homosexuals around bars. Kanya Tamaraptri must have been afraid that she was next and knew that her surgeries had left her vulnerable to a beating. So, she drew her knife and lashed out.

"Crespo panicked, deflected the first blow and fought back. He knew he was bleeding, didn't know how badly he was hurt. Fear, panic, adrenalin, all added up and he went berserk. He knocked her down, but then found he was enjoying the sense of power that winning the fight gave him. He pounded her groin, probably her screams added to the thrill of the moment. Then, he realized what he was doing and killed her."

"There's no proof for any of that. And how did he get the baseball bat?"

"Perhaps it had been hidden there in anticipation of another ambush and he grabbed it. He may have come there deliberately so that, if he was being lured into an ambush, he would have a weapon to fight back with. You know that is another possibility. I have heard that the *khatoi* are known to steal from their . . . friends. Perhaps Kanya Tamaraptri tried to rob him and the incident proceeded from there. We have no proof as you say, except the fact he was cut with a knife. But there is no proof for the original theory either. If anything that knife cut points to the latter two theories."

"It does. At the very least, doubt over the sequence of events will take the death penalty off the table. You do realize, whatever actually happened in that alley, Rodríguez Crespo is a very sick young man. I do not think you will be popular with the police when this comes to trial."

Thonglor Police Station, Thanom Sukhumvit, Bangkok, Thailand

"And what food has Mr. Day been offered?" Consul Gearalt Ó Fearghail had a list of questions on a clipboard.

"He was offered the same food as is served to my officers in our canteen. When he was arrested yesterday morning, he was given pad thai goong, that is noodles with chicken for lunch. In the evening, sticky rice with pork and mixed vegetables. This morning, breakfast was kao tom, which is boiled rice soup with egg. It is basic food, and variety is limited, but quite good. The wives of my officers cook for the canteen. Lunch will be pad thai goong again. Would you like to try it?"

Ó Fearghail nodded and a bowl was brought to him. He ate some and nodded appreciatively. "It's very good."

"Police Corporal Noradom's wife made it according to her family recipe. They come from the Isaan, where the food is milder than here. More suited to *farangs*."

"Very good. You're a lucky man, Corporal Noradom." In the background, a police corporal swelled visibly with pride. "Mr. Day complains that he is not given proper food, but I see no justification for that complaint. If he wishes to eat European food, he should arrange to be arrested in a European city. The consulate has found him a lawyer who will defend him. We have also arranged for a doctor to attend him, should the need arise. With all of that arranged, everything is in order, I think?"

Police Captain Supphavit nodded in agreement. "Captain Diaz, does your national have any issues?"

A Spanish Army officer looked up. "I must explain that I am only here because the regular official who handles such things is on leave. As military attaché, I happen to be underemployed at this time and am filling in for him. There is no other significance to my presence here. My national has no complaints and, indeed, mentioned the professionalism of your men with respect and appreciation."

In the background, Conrad and Chaowit exchanged glances. Machado was obviously maneuvering to place himself clear of suspicion and throw the whole case at Day. It was an obvious ploy, but that would not prevent it from being an effective one. Supphavit obviously thought the same, although he said nothing.

"Captain Supphavit, I am Police Colonel Chaowit of the Central Investigation Bureau. This is Conrad de Llorente, a consultant who has been helping us with investigations into recent events. We have come to provide any assistance your station may need. This remains your arrest, of course; one that was carried out in an exemplary manner."

"I understand CIB have been handling this case from the beginning." Supphavit spoke a little stiffly, realizing his time in the spotlight was ending. "It is my station who will be pleased to assist you. We have an interrogation room in the rear of the station building. Please feel free to make use of all our facilities here."

"Thank you, Captain. Now, Conrad, who should we start with?"

It took Conrad only a moment to decide. "Day. Definitely Day."

Interrogation Room, Thonglor Police Station, Thanom Sukhumvit, Bangkok

"I am Attorney Noppadom, representing Mister Jonathan Day." The lawyer was bald and had a round face behind a set of circular, rimless glasses that gave him a friendly, inoffensive look. He made a respectful *wai* to Chaowit and then stretched out his hand to Conrad. Conrad took it and felt a strange sense of relief at the familiar gesture of shaking hands. Then, he caught a slight smile on the lawyer's face. He realized the handshake had been carefully calculated to influence him on behalf of his client. Conrad made a mental note. *Don't be deceived by appearances. This lawyer is much cleverer and more devious than he appears.*

Chaowit had produced the files that included the evidence gathered from the investigations to date. He handed them over to Noppadom who started to flip through the contents. The lawyer looked up after the first few sheets. "Your records of the investigation appear to be exemplary. May I ask how my client first became a person of interest?"

"We found that he was deep in debt and that he frequented the bar where the victim would stop for a drink on the way home. We took a police artist to meet with him and another person of interest and she drew a picture of him. When we showed that to loansharks, they recognized him as somebody who was defaulting on debts, but they also told us that those debts had been purchased by a European, subsequently identified as Machado. Machado has a very, very strong motive for wanting the victim dead."

"A drawing by a police artist? I have seen such pictures. With all due respect, Police Colonel, they are hardly works of art. They could be anybody. Sometimes, the face they show is barely human. It could even be of a lawyer."

A chuckle went around the room. Chaowit reached into the file and got out Vanna's drawing of Jonathan Day. "We were most fortunate that our artist is a very talented young lady. This was the picture we used."

Noppadom looked at the picture and his eyebrows lifted almost comically. "My apologies to your artist. She is indeed skilled. I will stipulate that the identification is properly made. Perhaps we should get started with the interview?"

When Day was brought in, Conrad was struck by the change in his appearance. The confident gymnasium teacher had evaporated during the day and night he had spent in the police station cells. His eyes were deeply shadowed and his skin was sallow. The major change, though, was less tangible. The man's self-assurance had vanished and his expression as he entered the interrogation room was one of apprehension. Yet, Conrad caught something else. There was a strange sense of relief about Day; as if he was glad this whole business was finally ending.

Even so, when he was seated at the interrogation table, his first reaction was to bluster. "Why have I been brought here?"

Chaowit was unfazed. "To answer the charge of murdering Tomáš Lubomír Valentin Klímek."

"Who told you that I did that?"

Chaowit nodded slightly at Conrad, who took over the questioning. "Actually, Mr. Day, you did. You see, the first time we talked, you told us four baseball bats had gone missing. We told you the details of the assault cases we were investigating. Then, Mr. Klímek was killed in a way that seemed similar enough to those assault cases to make it apparent that an attempt had been made to disguise the killing as one of those assaults. To do that, somebody had to know the details that we had found in our investigation. That narrowed it down to three people. Then, in our second discussion, we again asked you how many baseball bats had been taken and you answered five. Of the three suspects who knew the required details, we had already eliminated two and you were the third. And you had just told us that another baseball bat had gone missing. We have the trifecta, Mister Day. Means: the baseball bat. Motive: paying off your debts. Opportunity: waiting outside the bar until Klímek walked past you and then crushing his head with your bat. Something, by the way, that needed much more strength than any of the youths who committed the assaults had."

For the next hour, Day tried to talk his way out of the net that was closing in around him. Conrad remained his normal polite and courteous self. Every question he asked drove another nail into the coffin Day could see being built around him. In the end, he fell silent and just stared down at the table surface.

Chaowit looked at him, knowing that he had the killer of Tomáš Klímek trapped. "Day, there is something you should know about Thai justice; a quirk of our own. In most countries, when somebody kills another person for money, this is viewed as being especially reprehensible and carries a greater penalty. We do not quite see it like that. I can explain this best by referring you to a man called Boonpart. He was of the criminal kind from his childhood. He stole from other children and when he grew up, he became a burglar and a sneak thief. We caught him and sent him to prison. Let me read to you what his police file says. 'On release from prison, Boonpart reformed his character and became a hired assassin.'

"You see, when a man steals, he does so for himself. But, when he is hired to kill, in a sense he does so for an element of the community. So, to be hired to kill somebody is, to us, a less reprehensible motive for murder than killing somebody to rob them or killing them because the murderer enjoys the act of taking a life. Also, we know that most hired assassins are people like yourself, who found themselves trapped in a situation with no easy way out."

Noppadom was listening and nodding in agreement. "You really want the man who hired my client, but you need his evidence that Machado did hire him to make the case solid. How about a settlement in which my client pleads guilty, gives a full statement of the case and presents it in evidence against Machado. For that cooperation, I think a sentence of ten years would be appropriate?"

"I'm not . . . " The lawyer cut Day off with a hand gesture.

Chaowit stepped in again. "The normal prison term for murder is fifteen to twenty years, so ten years is generous. But, I think, the judges will be guided by our recommendation to accept it. However, if you do not confirm that you were hired to carry out this killing, obviously you did so to rob the victim and that carries a death penalty. You know how we execute people here? By automatic firing squad. You will be taken into a courtyard and secured to a stake. Soldiers will come in and set up six Robow submachine guns in a special rack. They will aim each of the guns at your heart and load them each with a magazine of thirty 9x25mm Browning rounds. The soldiers will leave and a thin paper screen will be placed between you and the machine guns. Finally, the executioner comes in, pulls a lever and empties all six guns into your heart."

Conrad's eyes widened as he did the mathematics. "Kwang, that's a hundred and eighty rounds!"

Chaowit smiled. "Not quite. We are a very traditional people. And, in accordance with tradition, one of the rounds is a blank."

"Even so, the damage to the body must be appalling!"

"Usually we send in prisoners to collect what's left with those pointed sticks park attendants use to pick up litter. I'm told there is a good deal of competition for the detail, since the prison gives each prisoner a glass of brandy and two bottles of beer afterwards."

Day swallowed. "I'll be needing a pad and a pen. I'll tell you everything you need."

Conrad watched Day beginning to write. Then a thought occurred to him and it led directly to his next suggestion. "Attorney Noppadom, if you have no urgent appointments, might I suggest you stay in the police station for a while? I have a feeling your services might be needed by *Señor* Machado."

Noppadom shook his head. "*Señor* Machado will have a lawyer provided by his company. One from a large company, with great resources at its disposal. At best, I would be a very minor figure there. Frankly, I prefer to be the only fish in my own small pond."

Conrad didn't say anything; he looked at the long statement that Day was writing. He could swear that the nib of Day's pen was smoking, so furiously was the man pouring out what had happened to him. *Day isn't a killer, or even a particularly bad man. Careless, perhaps. Of narrow interests and of limited perspective, certainly. Unable to integrate into, or even co-exist with, a society that had radically different values from his own. He allowed himself to be drawn into an existence that lacked meaning or future and gave up on any effort to improve his position. Then, trapped on his own and without personal resources to draw upon, he found himself locked into a situation where the only apparent way out was a loathsome and reprehensible act. And then, having taken that way out, he has been unable to forgive himself.*

That was when Conrad had another of the eerie phenomena he had experienced in the nightclub when he and Vanna had been meeting with the loan-sharks. Watching Day write out his confession, and pour out his soul into the bargain, Conrad saw him as if a sheet of frosted glass was separating them. He saw Day as the local residents of the city saw him; a man who refused to take the opportunities offered to him and instead wallowed in his own self-pity. That was when the picture changed. It blurred. For a brief second, Conrad saw himself sitting at that table, writing out his confessions, too wrapped up in his own guilt to understand the opportunities that were all around him. The force of the image came close to physically knocking the breath out of him.

"Ahh, I see what you mean." Noppadom's eyes suddenly lit up. "When *Señor* Machado's employers read that confession of what he did in their name, they will disavow him. They will say he was mad, insane, out of control. That he acted on his own without any form of authority, which is certainly true, by the way, and they will wash their hands of him. He'll be on his own. No expensive corporate lawyer for him. Another client! Billable hours! Excellent!"

Conrad looked back at Day. The strange illusion had faded away. All he saw was the shrunken figure of a European who had fallen foul of circumstances in a strange land and was now paying the consequences. Yet, for all that, Conrad still felt a strange light-headedness. Suddenly, he realized what the sensation represented. *It is as if a great weight has been lifted from me.* He looked at Attorney Noppodom and smiled. "Do I get a commission?"

Beside them, Chaowit coughed slightly. "I see you are learning our ways quickly. Of course you get a commission."

Conference Room, Thonglor Police Station, Thanom Sukhumvit, Bangkok

"I would like to introduce *Señor* Nicolao Geraldo Timoteo Gutiérrez, President of *Construcciones y Technologie de Ferrocarriles* and *Señor* Ceferino Martín Fabricio Vela, Chief Executive Officer of *Construcciones y Technologie de Ferrocarriles.*" Police Captain Supphavit rolled the Spanish words and titles out with a degree of relish. "I have just finished briefing them on the case against *Señor* Dimas Rafa Lázaro Machado."

"Thank you, Captain." There was the usual elaborate exchange of greetings. Business cards were handed out before everybody settled down again. Chaowit drew a deep breath. "In the last few minutes, we have received a full confession from the assassin hired by Señor Machado. It completes our case against him. We have witnesses, forensic evidence and financial data. We have affidavits from the loan sharks that he purchased the assassin's paper from; they give the amount and dates of those purchases. We have his bank account data that shows cash was withdrawn from his account in amounts and on dates that correspond to those purchases. The truth is, he didn't cover his tracks very well at all."

"And what was his motive for this alleged crime?" President Gutiérrez sounded deeply concerned. *And he has every reason to be so*, Conrad thought, *this crime could cost his company billions of sovereigns. The shareholders will not be happy.*

"He opposed the formation of a consortium between Skoda Engineering and *Construcciones y Technologie de Ferrocarriles* to handle the Bangkok Mass Transit Railway. He believed that the established position of Tomáš Klímek would make him the choice to be the local head of that consortium and that he, Machado, would be relegated to an inferior position. As part of that, he believed that the position he would occupy in the consortium would not entitle him to one of the luxury condominium apartments on Rajdamri Road. His wife would only agree to come out to join him here if they could live in one of those apartments. So, he had Tomáš Klímek killed."

"Pointless and stupid." Vela's voice was harsh and ugly. Conrad guessed that he and President Gutiérrez put on a good-cop/bad-cop act together. "The agreement to form a consortium has already been negotiated and signed. We advised the Bangkok Metropolitan Authority of this yesterday. Neither Machado nor Klímek were senior enough to head such a large and important operation, nor did they have the experience needed. We, and Skoda, have agreed on the man who would be the head of that operation and we just need the consent of the BMA before making the announcement. Klímek would have been its deputy, it is true, but Machado would not have been involved. We were intending to bring him back to Madrid. He had that poor man killed for nothing."

"I think it is obvious that *Construcciones y Technologie de Ferrocarriles* had nothing to do with this crime. Our agreements, which make the act so pointless, were in place before the crime was committed. Martín, make sure the police have copies of those documents. Machado acted on his own and pursuant to his own interests. We wash our hands of him."

President Gutiérrez paused. When he resumed, his voice was sad. "Nevertheless, a family has been deprived of its father and a wife of her husband by the acts of one of our employees. Colonel, I understand that here, a Thai company would pay compensation to the family of the victim as an apology to the community?"

"That is correct, yes. It would be considered a sign of good faith, of respect for the community, and of making merit for the company. Not as an admission of any degree of guilt."

"Then we shall do the same." Vela's voice was decisive. "Colonel, when you have a few minutes, perhaps you could advise me on a suitable amount to offer. And to whom."

Interrogation Room, Thonglor Police Station, Thanom Sukhumvit, Bangkok

"This is an outrage. No jury will listen to such a feeble case!" Machado was doing a very good imitation of outraged innocence. But, to Conrad's practiced ear, it was an imitation.

"You will not be going before a jury." Attorney Noppadom spoke quietly and patiently. "You will be going before a panel of three judges. They will reach their judgment based on the law and nothing but the law. I have a degree in law from the Harvard Law School and I can assure you, they are less likely to come to an incorrect verdict based on confusion or emotion than a jury would be."

A further dissertation on the merits of a panel of judges over a jury was forestalled by a knock on the door. On receiving an invitation to do so, Vela opened it at Machado. An hour or so earlier, he had told Machado that the company would not be assisting him in his defense and he would have to make his own arrangements. Now he spoke to Machado again. "Machado, President Gutiérrez and I have been discussing your case and we have decided that we did not make your situation adequately clear. You are fired. Thank you, Colonel. My apologies for the interruption."

Vela left. His footsteps could be heard echoing down the corridor. Noppadom sighed. "I am going to have to ask you for funds in anticipation of your legal expenses."

Machado looked furious. "I don't even need a lawyer. There's no case against me."

"The case is very strong." Conrad took over at this point, speaking in Spanish. "We have eyewitness statements. We have corroboration for those statements. You bought Day's debts? Why?"

"Because I felt sorry for the man. He was deep in debt and I wanted to help him."

"But we have his confession; in which, he tells us that you made it clear that you now held his debts and that you had explicitly told him to kill Tomáš Klímek to clear those debts."

"He's lying. I never said that."

"You may challenge him in court. But, I warn you that your behavior to date has not been such as to promote a picture of a man who would spend large sums of money to help out a stranger. I would refer you to your comments on Tomáš Klímek when we first met. They were hardly complimentary to a man who is regarded by everybody else we met as a kindly and decent man. You said that he associated with people of low character. Yet those very people, who have barely enough money for their daily necessities, gave up some of what little they had to offer a reward for the capture of the man who killed their friend. Their characters may be low, *Señor* Machado, but what does that make yours?"

"Make a confession and we will take the death sentence off the table." Chaowit sounded severe. Remembering the behavior of the staff at the CTF offices accounted for that. "Confess and we'll ask for 25 years. Otherwise, the firing squad."

"Please, don't describe it again." Noppodom was alarmed. "I've just had lunch. *Señor* Machado, this deal is a good one. Take it."

"Because if I'm executed, you won't get paid?" Machado snarled the words. In doing so, his true character slipped out.

"I would collect my fees from your family. You see, *Señor* Machado, the difference between a lawyer and a lady of negotiable virtue is that the lady stops screwing her client when he is dead."

"I didn't think I'd hear a lawyer joke here." Conrad was laughing and shaking his head.

"In Harvard, I loved lawyer jokes; but I had to hide it because the other students hated them. That's the trouble with lawyer jokes. Lawyers don't think they are funny and most non-lawyers don't think they are jokes."

The sight of Conrad, Chaowit and Noppadom laughing together finally drove home to Machado how completely isolated he was. He was, in the profoundest of all possible terms, on his own. And so, while the others laughed, he started to write out his confession.

Bangkok Criminal Court, Ratchadaphisek Road, Chatuchak, Bangkok

It took Conrad only a few minutes to realize that, by refusing to come to a settlement agreement with the victims of the first series of assaults, the defense team representing Rodríguez Crespo had made a catastrophic strategic error. The case against Crespo included eight charges of assault against those victims, in addition to the charge of aggravated murder of Kanya Tamaraptri. Those eight assault victims were all presenting evidence against Crespo. But, because they had accepted compensation from the other five members of the Venezuelan gang and declared themselves satisfied, they never mentioned the other five in their evidence. After all, that side of the matter was closed.

So, it looked as if Rodríguez Crespo had alone been responsible for a series of attacks against members of the homosexual community. Attacks that had escalated in viciousness, until they had culminated with the brutal death of Kanya Tamaraptri.

The prosecution placed great emphasis on that brutality. They showed pictures of her body and the injuries that had been inflicted on her. They described the excruciating pain she had endured, before blows to the head had mercifully left her unconscious. The reaction in the audience had been unmistakable. Conrad had picked up the sudden alertness from the Thai Army guards in the courtroom. The prosecution wanted this trial to go by the book. The defendant being lynched in the courtroom by outraged spectators didn't fall into that category.

Conrad had noticed something else. There were five judges on the bench, not three. There had been three judges when Day and Machado had made their appearances. In accordance with the agreements made, Day had been sentenced to ten years and Machado to twenty-five. Speaking for Day, Attorney Noppadom had requested that Day's sentence be served in the Recovered Provinces, so he could make amends for his crime by aiding in the development work there. That request had been granted, with the comment that the schools in the Recovered Provinces could profitably use his experience in education and physical training. Machado had been sent to the north, where he would be working in the mountains and jungle on the road-building program.

But, now there were five judges and that meant the prosecution had been deadly serious when they had demanded the death penalty.

With the parade of assault victims completed, Crespo was now firmly characterized as a vicious, sadistic bigot. The case moved to the murder of Kanya Tamaraptri. The doctors who had treated her had described her injuries. They explained how those injuries had led directly to her death. Conrad had watched with interest as Vanna had been called to the stand to show how her drawings had led to the detection of Crespo. Again, the other members of the gang were never mentioned.

Conrad was struck by how much she had changed since she had left her previous life and joined the Forensic Science Institute. It wasn't just her appearance that had altered. Her behavior and attitude were different as well. She was respectable. He had also seen something else. By now, he realized that the tailored shirt and pantsuit she wore were the standard dress for Thai businesswomen. Today, in court, her shirt was yellow. Yellow was the King's color. By wearing it, she was hinting at her position. Just to drive it home, in introducing her, the prosecution had mentioned that she received the King's Stipend as a person whose talents were considered of special value to the people.

She had been replaced on the stand by Khunying Pornthip. She steadily increased the pile of damning evidence against Crespo. Pornthip showed how the splinters of wood in the wounds of the victims had come from the same baseball bats, an unusual type of bat for the country and one whose availability was very severely limited. She had spoken of the blood found on Crespo's tennis shoes. The combination of blood identifiers and the presence of synthetic female hormone had confirmed the blood came from Kanya Tamaraptri. Now, she ended by describing the evidence she had gathered when Crespo had been arrested.

"Khunying Pornthip, in examining the medical records of my client after his arrest, did you notice any reference to wounds that might be considered unusual?" Crespo's defense attorney had realized how badly the case was going and was desperate. This was about the only throw he had left.

"In addition to the usual minor injuries, he had an incised wound on his lower left thorax. Shallow, but about six centimeters long."

"Could this have been a knife wound?"

"The evidence suggests that would be the most likely explanation. The wound was clean and sharply defined. That would eliminate almost everything but a knife."

"So, it is possible that my client was attacked with a knife prior to the rest of this incident?"

"There is no evidence to support or refute that suggestion."

"So, it is possible that my client was defending himself before the situation escalated out of control?"

"There is no evidence to support or refute that suggestion."

"Do we, in fact, know what happened in the minutes before the actions that led to the death of Kanya Tamaraptri?'

Khunying Pornthip shook her head. "No, we do not. And we probably never will, unless a witness comes forward."

Conrad saw Police Colonel Chaowit wince slightly at that. But the moment passed and the rest of the case was presented. One thing that struck Conrad was how much quicker the proceedings were than those he was used to. Both prosecution and defense knew that they scored points by not laboring the obvious or contesting the uncontestable.

Eventually, the five judges rose. They left the courtroom to consider their decision. They were gone for almost an hour. From the people around him, Conrad gathered that was unusually long time. People in the courtroom were pointedly looking at their watches and obviously discussing what it might mean. When they finally did return, the hush that fell on the room was profound.

The central judge cleared his throat and started to read the verdicts. "In the eight cases of common assault, the defendant Rodríguez Crespo is found guilty and is sentenced to six months imprisonment on each charge; the sentences to be served consecutively. In the case of the murder of Kanya Tamaraptri, the defendant Rodríguez Crespo is found guilty and aggravating circumstances apply. In view of the deliberate attempt by the accused to maximize the pain and suffering endured by the victim, we sentence him to death by firing squad."

The court erupted into cheers and the judge banged his gavel furiously. "If that happens again, I will clear this courtroom. To continue. There is some doubt raised as to the circumstances that preceded the murder of Kanya Tamaraptri and there is a possibility that the murder may have started as an act of self-defense. While this does not excuse her brutal death, we have concluded that the element of doubt means the death sentence should be suspended and a prison sentence of thirty years substituted. This will be served consecutively with the other terms imposed. If Rodríguez Crespo's behavior in prison is such that the possibility of an element of self-defense is eliminated, the death sentence will be reinstituted."

The silence in the courtroom was profoundly menacing. At the prosecution desk, Chaowit turned around and looked furiously at Conrad.

Reception Area, Bang Phitsan Palace, Bangkok, Thailand.

"You damned fool. Do you know what you have done?" Chaowit was quite exceptionally angry. His voice ricocheted off the walls.

Conrad decided it was probably not a good time to explore the religious and moral significance of being damned or not. In any case, since his epiphany at the Thonglor Police Station, he was reevaluating his own stand on the matter. "I simply made sure you didn't execute somebody who might not warrant it."

"Might not warrant it? Have you met that psychotic sadist? Crespo is a sociopath, who is well on the way to turning it from being a mental condition into a career choice. He's a serial killer waiting to happen. And now you've put him in jail, at an impressionable age, with some of the most vicious, hardened, criminals in the country. In the whole damned Triple Alliance in fact! You're arranged for him to have a post-graduate course in applied murder. Even if he does his whole sentence, he'll be out by his mid-forties. Well done, Conrad! You've haven't just unleashed a mass-murderer into society. You've made sure he is really well-trained for his new role in life."

"We can't execute people for what they might do. And you were going to execute him."

"No, we weren't. We were going to sentence him to death. Big difference. He wasn't going to be executed, unless somebody fouled up the paperwork. In a year or so, we'd have had a request from the Venezuelan Government to release him to their custody. By that time, Kanya Tamaraptri's fans would have found a new idol and she'd have been forgotten. So, we'd let Venezuela have Crespo and he's their problem. More importantly, our streets would be quiet and our tranquility undisturbed.

"Do we get that now? Oh no, you've put paid to that. Mailee's fans are out there looking for revenge on the first *farang* they can find. We've got every police officer in the city called in from leave and as many battalions of military police as we can get our hands on keeping the peace.

"So far, we've had one attack. Group of *khatoi* cornered a tourist couple. Man pushed his wife into a corner and kept her safe, but got knifed for his trouble. He's in the emergency ward being stitched up, she's having hysterics and a *khatoi* is going to jail because you had to interfere. Do you want to explain why to them?"

"Perhaps I should." Conrad was definitely annoyed.

"You're impossible! Do you ever think about the consequences of what you do?"

Chaowit was about to continue when the door opened. Suriyothai entered the room. "Boys, boys, keep it down. This may be an administration center, but it's also my home. And I'm getting complaints from my neighbors in Klongtoi."

Conrad could see Chaowit was stopped by that. He visualized a map of the city. Klongtoi was about the furthest point one could get from the Bang Phitsan and still be in Bangkok.

Suriyothai looked at them curiously. "What's all the row about anyway?"

"Conrad interfered with the prosecution of the idiot who killed Kanya Tamaraptri and we've had to get extra police out in the city to keep order."

"He suppressed or altered evidence?" Suriyothai's voice was neutral.

"No. He pointed out the significance of some evidence to the defense when they'd missed it."

"Hmm. What's your side of this, Conrad?"

"I didn't want to see somebody executed when there was evidence available that would justify giving them a prison sentence instead."

"So you'd rather see the city in turmoil? Anyway, living on death row for a year or so might have been the shock that little bastard needed to kick him into line!" Chaowit was still livid, but he was trying to keep his voice down.

"So, Kwang, you're talking about public order and, Conrad, you're talking about justice. The problem is that really there is a complete failure of each of you to understand what the other is saying. You are talking past each other, each addressing the issue in terms that reflect your own concerns. Since those concerns were not identical, the exchanges did not relate to each other very much."

Conrad caught the trace of a smirk on Suriyothai's face. He suddenly realized her words were eerily familiar. Her next comments confirmed that. "I don't think either of you realize that the other would fail to make that distinction. It took me only a few seconds of study before I realized what you were doing.

The trouble is, you are so used to your particular way of things that you do it without reflection."

Suriyothai left, leaving both Conrad and Chaowit dumbstruck. Eventually, they both burst out laughing. Chaowit wiped his eyes and swallowed. "I think we've been told off. I'm sorry Conrad. It's just after seeing what he did to that singer, I wanted to see him get sentenced to death even if I knew it was never going to happen."

"And I'm sorry I messed up your prosecution. I should have told you what I'd worked out. Anyway, let's go and have a drink to calm our nerves."

Private Area, Bang Phitsan Palace, Bangkok, Thailand.

"I don't often get women asking me to make them look older." Conrad recognized Jip's voice and guessed she had another Daimones in to benefit from her expertise.

"I've got to look in my fifties. A very well-preserved fifties, of course." There was no mistaking that husky contralto. Conrad realized Igrat was in town. He hastened over and knocked on the door.

"Come in." It was Igrat speaking. "Oh, hello, Conrad. I hear you're causing trouble again."

"No more than usual. Good morning, Jip. Be careful of this one; she has a taste for other people's husbands."

Jip looked at the two and tried to stop herself from grinning. "The way you two talk, you have to be married. No, wait. Of course. Conrad, Igrat here is your *mia noi,* isn't she."

Igrat looked appalled. "Ewwww. Gods preserve me. No, Conrad and I are just old friends. Conrad, I took you up on your advice; Jip's helping me age a bit. You were right, she is very good."

"We don't need to do that much, *Khun* Igrat. We can change your eyeshadow a little and the lipstick line around your mouth. And we can change your hairstyle to a less flattering one. I have some dye you can comb into the roots of your hair so it will look as if you're going gray, but dyeing your hair." Jip stood back a little and frowned. Then she looked at Igrat, her head slightly to one side and growing concern in her eyes. "Did you know you've got a lazy eye?"

"No, what's that?"

"Your left eye. The eyelid is beginning to droop. The usual reason is that, for some reason, the brain has stopped using the information from that eye and you rely on your right eye. I'm no doctor, but, the way I understand it, although your left eye is capable of seeing perfectly well, the fact your brain won't use it means your left eye is essentially blind. The result is that your left eyelid is beginning to droop down. It's hardly noticeable now; on you it's actually a little erotic. But, unless we do something, it's going to get steadily worse. Have you had trouble with your eyes?"

Igrat winced slightly with the memory. "I got badly beaten a good few years back. Two men got a lot of pleasure out of hitting me in the face. The doctors back then said they'd damaged my left eye. Bleeding into the retina, or something. Whatever it was, my vision in that eye was all blurry until it healed."

Looking at her, Conrad saw her skin pale. Beads of sweat appear along her hairline. She caught the expression on his face and smiled weakly. "All the bad things that have been done to me over the years, and what happened in Geneva is still the one that gives me nightmares. How strange is that?"

Jip was still frowning and her concern was obvious. "I don't think it did heal. I think your brain, getting blurry information from one eye and good from the other, stopped using the blurred data." Jip grunted and took out a flashlight and shone it into Igrat's left eye. "Well, the eye isn't blind. The pupil reacts to light. Now, let's see how much vision you have."

Jip's fingers moved and she grunted again. "Well, as far as I can see, you're effectively blind on your left-hand side. You don't react to movement until my finger moves into the arc of your right eye. I've noticed that you move your head when one somebody talks to you, so you see them with your right eye.

"Very well, this is where I stop. I'm a beautician, not a doctor. I'm trained to hand things over to people who know what they are doing when I see a problem. You're going to need to see an expert opthamologist. We've got good ones here. If your eye is damaged, you'll need surgery to fix it. Either way, we'll need to retrain your brain to use your left eye again. The usual way to do that is put a patch over your right eye and that forces your brain to use the data from the left. Excuse me for a few minutes. I'll make some calls and get an appointment for you."

Jip left. Igrat arched an eyebrow at Conrad. "Well, that's scary. Looks like I owe you one, Conrad. How's it going for you here? Seriously?"

"I found another one of us, a woman named Vanna, and she's being brought into the fold. We caught her really early so no problems. But, Igrat, I think I had a revelation here."

"Let me guess? Girls are wonderful. Well, this is the right country to learn that."

"No, something you said years ago. You told me that our gift isn't a curse the way I thought it was. It was a gift and it was up to us to use it well or badly. Well, the girl I mentioned? She's an artist and one of her friends is a dancer and I watched them talking together. Like any other pair of young women. And I thought, in sixty years time, the dancer will be old and looking back on her life while Vanna will still look much the same as she does now and still be looking forward to hers. Something like that can't be a curse, can it?

"And I realized something else. I always thought I was irrevocably damned for the things I did in the Inquisition; that I could try and redeem myself, but the effort was futile because my sins were too great. But being here, seeing things from a different perspective, things that took me away from myself, I realized I was falling victim to heresy.

"All one needs to gain forgiveness is to ask for it. To repent for our sins. To ask God for forgiveness. I showed both repentance and contrition, but I lacked the faith to realize that I had been forgiven. I blamed myself for being unable to gain absolution, when it was my own blindness that kept me from it. I've got two sets of debts I must pay. One to God for the sins I committed in His name and one to man for the crimes I committed against them. But, all I needed to settle the first set was the faith to ask and the devotion to understand that I'd been granted forgiveness. I still owe my debts to man, but I can concentrate on paying those debts now.

"Iggie, in a way, we've both been blind and never knew it. We both got so used to seeing only what our minds allowed us to see, that we didn't realize we were misleading ourselves. God has steered me to the work He wants me to do and I've been doing it. It's just I was too wrapped up in my own guilt to understand that doing so was pleasing to Him. You told me that years ago and I was far too self-absorbed to understand what you were saying. So thank you, Igrat. Very late, and seriously overdue, but thank you."

"So you think you are saved now?"

"No, but I know I'm on the right path now. All I have to do is stay on it. Now, let me pray for you so you'll get your sight back too."

"That's kind of you, Conrad. By the way, how many innocents did you save this time around?"

"Five young kids who were stupid and nearly got charged with a murder they didn't commit and a man whose foolishness got him trapped into a situation he couldn't escape. But, I think, this time around, the innocent I rescued was me."

THE END

But Conrad Will Return

Conrad's Other Eye

www.ingramcontent.com/pod-product-compliance
Lightning Source LLC
Chambersburg PA
CBHW020248030726
47499CB00001B/102